GW01606021

Bunter at St. Jim's

by Frank Richards

Probably the most 'weird and wonderful' collection published by the Greyfriars Press to date. A mixed volume of Magnets and Gems, culled from a period when the 'Companion Papers' — as they were called — worked in close alliance under the inspired, if sometimes eccentric, editorship of John Nix Pentelow.

By clever inter-relationships the two schools of Greyfriars and St. Jim's were made to operate in harness: thus it was hoped that readers of the Magnet would feel it incumbent upon them to buy the Gem also, and vice versa.

Altogether, a most stimulating and exciting period in the history of the Magnet and the Gem.

Serious historians of Hamiltonia will find this volume irresistible. Even the most casual reader will find it fascinating.

The titles of individual stories contained in this volume include: *Wally Bunter's Luck, Billy Bunter's Wheeze, Wally of the Remove, Dog with a Bad Name, Billy Bunter at St. Jim's, Bunter of the New House, Spoof, In Search of a Study, The Two Bunter's On the Warpath, The Haunted School, Bunter — and Bunter, Return of the Native.*

Magnet issues Nos. 569 to 572 and 585
Gem issues Nos. 571 to 574 and 576, 578, 579 and 585

THIRTEEN ISSUES IN ONE VOLUME! A BAKER'S DOZEN!

BUNTER at St. JIM'S

Conamur·Tenues·

BUNTER at St. JIM'S

by

FRANK RICHARDS
and
MARTIN CLIFFORD

HOWARD BAKER
LONDON

Bunter at St. Jim's

Frank Richards: (The Magnet, 1919)
Martin Clifford (The Gem, 1919)

Originally published in single issues.

Hardcover edition, 1978

ISBN: 0 7030 0151 5

Greyfriars Press Books are published by
Howard Baker Press Ltd.,
27a Arterberry Road, London, SW20, England.
Printed in Great Britain by
Per Fas Printers Ltd., of Croydon, Surrey.

BUNTER — and BUNTER!

An introduction to the first Magnet/Gem 'twinning' series

by Eric Fayne

(Editor of Collectors Digest)

This was one of the several occasions when Charles Hamilton employed the "doubles" theme and, though on the face of it the whole thing was incredible, it was handled so well that it provided splendid entertainment for the reader.

It was also the first instance of what has been called "twin series" – in which the plot was played out at both Greyfriars and St. Jim's, with *The Magnet* and *The Gem* being synchronised.

Of necessity, the foundation for the series was laid at Greyfriars, and three stories were written in preparation in *The Magnet* before *The Gem* joined in. Taken as a whole, the series occupied 18 weeks in *The Magnet* and 15 in *The Gem.*

It is my opinion that *The Gem* had the better part of the arrangement, and the reason for this was that Billy Bunter went to St. Jim's.

Nowhere in the entire range of Hamiltonia is the importance of Billy Bunter as a valuable Hamilton asset more obvious than here.

So St. Jim's gained Billy Bunter – temporarily – and, in *The Gem,* we had a number of outstanding stories in the series. Billy, taking advantage of the old-world courtesy of Gussy, was hilarious.

Then, in what was possibly the best story in the series in either paper, Billy and Wally had to "change back" for one afternoon while Mr. Penman, Wally's benefactor, visited St. Jim's, so we had, in a shorter but not less effective form, the joy of seeing Bunter surprising the natives at St. Jim's.

Billy Bunter, of course, was a ventriloquist and in a couple of wonderful *Gems* he turned St. Jim's into a haunted school. It was a formula of inevitable success for any but those who had a lofty aversion to the extravagance of such stories. And it is invaluable as showing the worth of Billy Bunter to his creator.

Between 1919 and the present time, this intriguing "twin series" was only partially reprinted once – in the Popular of the mid-nineteen-twenties. Plenty of readers have never met it before, and for them this volume will provide many hours of joyous entertainment.

For those who knew it all long ago, to read it again will be like meeting a much-loved friend after many years.

It would, of course, be impossible to reprint so immense a series in one book, but in the Howard Baker volume now in your hands you have the cream of the tales, carefully selected and presented in a worthy setting. The story starts and ends at Greyfriars, as it always did and, for so long as they are pertinent to the main plot, it follows the adventures of Wally Bunter, impersonating uncomfortably, at Greyfriars, his wily cousin Billy.

But the major part of the volume is given over to following the amazing experience of Billy Bunter in his new school at St. Jim's, related with all the whimsical humour and skill of the master school story writer . . .

The Magnet

No. 569. Vol. XIII. 1½d. January 4th, 1919.

WALLY BUNTER'S LUCK!

BUNTER BAULKED!

4-1-19

WALLY BUNTER'S LUCK!

By FRANK RICHARDS.

A Magnificent New Long Complete Tale of Harry Wharton & Co. at Greyfriars School.

THE FIRST CHAPTER.
An Awkward Position!

"IT'S dashed awkward!"

Billy Bunter was reading a letter in the junior Common-room at Greyfriars,. and he shook his head over it as he made that remark.

"Dashed awkward!" he repeated "I say, you fellows, what would you advise a fellow to do?"

Bunter addressed that question to Harry Wharton & Co., who were chatting round the fireplace.

The Co. were discussing the St. Jim's footer match, which was coming off on Wednesday, and was just then the one matter of supreme importance to the Greyfriars Remove.

Bunter's question passed unheeded.

"Hazeldene in goal!" Harry Wharton was saying. "He put up a good game to-day, and he will be all right. You and Mark Linley at back, Johnny."

Johnny Bull nodded.

That selection seemed to him eminently satisfactory. In fact, he did not see how it could be improved upon.

"Then Tom Brown, Toddy, and you, Bob——"

"First-rate!" said Bob Cherry heartily. "You're a skipper in a thousand, Wharton."

"I say, you fellows——"

"Inky at outside-right——" went on Harry Wharton.

Hurree Jamset Ram Singh, the dusky member of the Co., nodded with a beaming smile, which showed all his gleaming teeth.

"The outside-rightfulness will be terrific," he remarked.

"Nugent inside-right——"

"Hear, hear!" said Frank Nugent. "I must say, Harry, old scout, you're showing a lot of judgment in selecting this team."

"I was thinking of Redwing——"

"Then it's lucky you thought again, old man. Don't do any more thinking on the subject!" implored Nugent.

"I say, you fellows——" bawled Bunter.

"Little me at centre," continued the captain of the Remove. "Then Squiff and Smithy."

"Good!" said the Co., in chorus.

"I'd like to put Redwing in, but we can't very well play twelve men."

"Ha, ha! No!"

"And there's Bunter left out, too," remarked Bob Cherry. "I've no doubt Bunter would offer to play centre-forward, if you asked him. Wouldn't you, William?"

Bunter sniffed.

"I wouldn't mind, and if you really wanted to beat St. Jim's you couldn't do better," he answered. "I know there's too much jealousy about, though, for me to have a chance in the St. Jim's match."

"Too much something about, certainly," grinned Bob. "I call it common-sense, my fat tulip."

"The weather looks like being decent," Wharton remarked. "We can get some more practice together to-morrow. We shall have to pull up our socks to beat St. Jim's."

"I say, you fellows——"

"Hallo, hallo, hallo! Bunter's still talking!" exclaimed Bob Cherry. "Have they wound you up, Bunty?"

"What would you advise a chap to do?" asked Bunter, having succeeded at last in gaining the attention of the Co.

"That depends," said Bob. "What's the row? Have you been punting on races again? If so, I'd advise you to chuck it."

"Oh, really, Cherry! I've got a letter here——"

"Is it your postal-order at last?" queried Bob. "Don't tell us too suddenly, if it is. Break it gently."

"It's from my cousin Wally!" hooted Bunter.

"Oh!"

The Co. looked interested. They thought a good deal more of Bunter's cousin Wally than of William George Bunter himself. True, Wally Bunter was exactly like Billy Bunter to look at; but that, as Bob Cherry had charitably pointed out, was his misfortune, not his fault.

"I told you the chap had written to me that he was coming here to pay me a visit," said Bunter, blinking at the Co. through his glasses. "Well, he's fixed the date for to-morrow."

"We'll be glad to see him," said Harry Wharton. "He's always welcome."

"Is he still at the office in Canterbury?" asked Frank Nugent.

Bunter shook his head.

"No; he seems to have left. He's coming down from London. As it's such a jolly long way he's asked me if he can put up here for the night. I'm to let him know."

"That's easy enough. Mr Quelch will agree at once, if you ask him," said Wharton. "No difficulty about that."

"The fact is, I suggested it to him," said Bunter. "In his other letter he spoke of staying the night at Friardale, at some inn. I answered that that would be a reflection on Greyfriars hospitality, and they would stick him for ten shillings at least."

"Very thoughtful of you," said Harry Wharton, in some surprise. William George Bunter was not generally thoughtful for others.

"It will save him ten bob, if he puts up here," argued Bunter. "Under the circs, he couldn't very well refuse to lend me the ten bob, could he?"

"Wha-a-at?"

"I don't see how he could refuse. Do you, Wharton?"

"You blessed worm!" was Wharton's reply.

"If you're going to be personal, Wharton——"

"Br-r-r-r!"

"But it's dashed awkward!" said Bunter, frowning. "You see, that will land him here over Wednesday, when the St. Jim's match comes off. He's rather keen on seeing that; he's gone on footer, you know."

"Well, he can see it while he's here. We'll all be glad to have him around," said Bob Cherry. "He looks like you, Bunter, but otherwise he's quite a decent fellow."

"The otherwisefulness is terrific, my esteemed Bunter."

"Oh, don't gas!" growled Bunter. "I say, it's jolly awkward for me. Of course, I'm kind to Wally. I'm not the fellow to turn my back on a poor relation——"

"In fact, you're the fellow to borrow ten bob of him!" remarked Johnny Bull.

"Ahem! You fellows can't say that I'm snobbish," continued Bunter, blinking at the Co. "I've had Wally here, and introduced him to the fellows, though he's only a kid quill-driver in an office. 'Tain't all lavender for a Greyfriars chap to have a relation polishing a stool in an office, but I've made it a point to be kind to Wally."

"Give us a rest, old chap!"

"But there's a limit," said Bunter. "You fellows see, of course, that there's a limit. A chap can't introduce his poor relations to everybody. Now, can he? The St. Jim's chaps will be here on Wednesday. I'm very friendly with Tom Merry——"

"Does he know?" asked Bob.

"Ha, ha, ha!"

"And I am quite thick with Gussy—the fellow you call D'Arcy. I always call him Gussy, because I'm such——"

"Such a pushing bounder?"

"No!" roared Bunter. "Because I'm such a pal of his. I've got a lot in common with Arthur Augustus, my old pal at St. Jim's. Being a highly-connected fellow myself, I naturally get on with members of the nobility."

"Ha, ha, ha!"

"Blessed if I see anything to cackle at! I think you're unfeeling, when I'm in this dashed awkward position. As I said, I'm kind to Wally—very kind; we have always patronised that branch of the family. But I simply can't introduce a poor relation to a fellow like D'Arcy. It would let me down. Now, wouldn't it?"

"Could anything let you down lower than you are already?" asked Johnny Bull, with a snort.

"Oh, really, Bull——"

"My dear porpoise, you needn't be alarmed," said Bob. "If D'Arcy sees your cousin, it will give you a leg-up in his esteem. It will show him that all the Bunters are not rank outsiders and pushing cads."

"You cheeky ass!" roared Bunter.

"Besides, you've introduced your poor relations, as you call him, to us," said Harry Wharton, laughing. "It hasn't hurt us, and it's not likely to hurt the St. Jim's fellows."

"That's different."

"How is it different?" demanded Bob Cherry warmly.

"My old pal Gussy is rather particular, you see. He isn't at all a common fellow, like——"

"Like whom?"

"Like—like some fellows," said Bunter hastily. "It's dashed awkward for me, having a poor relation here when Gussy is present. I don't see how I can let him come. Do you, Wharton?"

"You silly chump——"

"Eh?"

"You needn't worry about D'Arcy. The last time he was here he spent half his time dodging you to keep away from your rotten familarity. All you've got to do is to keep your distance."

"Look here——"

"As for Wally—if your cousin Wally is here, I shall show him to the St. Jim's chaps myself, because he's a decent fellow they'd like to meet," said Wharton. "And as for you, if I catch you bothering D'Arcy with your friendliness, I'll boot you off the scene so quick it will take your breath away! Savvy?"

Billy Bunter fixed a glare on the captain of the Remove that almost cracked his spectacles. The Co.'s liking for Wally—so different from their estimation of William George—was exasperating to Bunter in any case; but this was really too much.

"You—you—you——" spluttered Bunter. "I—I've a jolly good mind to give you a thumping good licking, Wharton!"

"Ha, ha, ha!"

"Don't!" implored the captain of the Remove. "Have mercy! Spare me!"

He backed hastily away from Bunter, with a look of great alarm.

That was quite enough for Bunter.

He pushed back his cuffs at once, and came on with a truculent air. Harry Wharton backed away and away, the Owl of the Remove following him up valiantly.

"Yah! You funk! Stop!" howled Bunter. "I'm jolly well going to lick you!"

Wharton stopped suddenly, and Bunter rolled fairly into his arms. Those arms closed round him like a vice, and Bunter gave a sudden gasp, like air escapng from old bellows.

"Groooooch!"

"Ha, ha, ha!"

"Burst him!" roared Bob Cherry.

"Ha, ha, ha!"

"Yarooh! Ooooooch! Leggo! Yow-ow!"

"But you're going to lick me?" said Wharton.

"Nunno! I—I'll let you off! Yaroooh! Leggo!"

"Certainly!"

Wharton let go so suddenly that Billy Bunter sat down on the floor with a sudden bump.

"Yoooop!"

"That all right?" asked Harry.

"Yarooh! Beast! Ooooop!"

"Some people are never satisfied," remarked Bob Cherry. And the Co. strolled out of the Common-room, leaving Billy Bunter still sitting on the floor, gasping for breath, and not in the least inclined to proceed further with licking the captain of the Remove.

THE SECOND CHAPTER.
Hospitality Required!

Harry Wharton & Co. were rather interested in the forthcoming visit of Walter Bunter, and the next day they condescended to inquire of Billy Bunter when he was expecting his cousin.

Wally Bunter had been at Greyfriars twice or thrice, and the Co. liked him. He had proved himself a good sportsman, and was a good player of games, in spite of a rotundity of figure that rivalled Billy's.

As Billy's chief object in receiving him seemed to be to borrow ten shillings of him, the Co. thought of looking after Wally a little during his visit, and making him welcome to Greyfriars.

It was pretty certain that William George would not over-exert himself for the sake of the visitor. In fact, the Co. rather wondered why Wally took the trouble to visit William George at all. He was not the kind of fellow to pay court to a better-off relation for what it was worth to him, and certainly Billy in himself was not a fascinating personality.

But it seemed, according to a letter Wally had written some time before, that he had had good luck of some kind, which he wanted to tell his cousin about. He had good news, and perhaps he thought Billy Bunter would be glad to hear it, and would help him to rejoice in it. If his good luck was in the form of cash, it was certain that Billy would help him spend it, at least.

"When's Wally coming?" asked Bob Cherry, tapping Bunter on a fat shoulder, as the Remove came out of their Form-room on Tuesday.

Bunter blinked at him. He never could understand why his poor relation was held in so much higher estimation than his worthy self, and it always had an irritating effect upon him.

But the Co.'s liking for Wally, though he could not understand it, was useful in its way; and Bunter always had an eye to the main chance. The Famous Five being incomprehensibly interested in Wally, Bunter of Greyfriars intended to make the most of it. If his cousin was sought after, it was his business to be stand-offish, and keep his cousin to himself, unless the Co. were extremely civil.

"Eh?" said Bunter carelessly. "Wally? Oh, some time, you know!"

"Before tea?" asked Bob.

"I shouldn't wonder," said Bunter, still more distantly.

Bob stared at him. He was far from understanding that the Owl of the Remove considered this was a favourable moment for displaying stand-offishness.

"Well," said Bob, "I suppose if he comes before tea he will want some tea."

"Probably."

"If you'd care to bring him to Study No. 1 we'll be glad to see him," said Harry Wharton.

"Really, Wharton, I'm not going to allow you to bag my visitor in that way!" said Bunter loftily.

"What?"

"I shall take Wally to my own study."

"Oh, all right!" said Harry. "As you're generally hard up I thought there might be some difficulty. I don't want to bag your visitor, you crass ass! I was only thinking that it wouldn't look hospitable to stick him in Hall for tea, as he knows we generally feed in our studies. Do as you like!"

"I say, you fellows——"

The Co. went out into the quadrangle without heeding Bunter further.

Billy Bunter looked rather dismayed. Stand-offishness was not, after all, quite in place just then, he realised. He had missed a chance of planting himself on Study No. 1 for tea.

He rolled away to his own quarters, No. 7, where he found Peter Todd. Peter had settled down there to work at mathematics, and he waved an impatient hand at Bunter without looking up.

"I say, Peter——"

"Scat!"

"My cousin's coming to tea——"

"Bother your cousin, and you, too! Dry up!"

"I want to have a bit of a decent spread for him," urged Bunter.

"I'm not stopping you."

"I happen to be stony," explained Bunter.

"Br-r-r-r!"

"I suppose you're going to stand something decent for once?"

Peter looked up with a glare.

"Can't you see I'm wrestling with maths?" he roared. "Shut up! I'm going down to Hall to tea. Money's tight! Scat!"

"Oh, really, Peter——"

Peter Todd clutched at the inkpot, and Bunter jumped out of the study. He looked for his other study-mate, Tom Dutton, and found him in the Remove passage. Tom Dutton was deaf, not wholly a misfortune in a study-mate of Bunter's. The fat junior gave him a poke in the ribs.

"I say, Dutton——"

"Eh?"

"My cousin's coming to tea."

"Is he?" said Dutton, with interest. "Jolly plucky of him, I must say, considering the submarines, and all that."

"Wha--a-at?" stuttered Bunter.

"When was he at sea?" asked Dutton.

"Oh, my hat! Not sea—tea!" roared Bunter. "Tea—tea in the study!"

"What utter rot! He may get wet at sea, but I don't see at all how he could be muddy. You're talking rot, Bunter!"

"Oh, dear! My cousin Wally's coming to tea!" shrieked Bunter. "I want to stand him something decent. See?"

"Yes, I see. I know it must be recent, as he was in an office at Canterbury when I last heard of him. What about it?"

"Will you stand something decent for tea?" raved Bunter.

"No fear! I'm going to be an engineer!" said Dutton. "Of course, I may go to sea as an engineer. Not for years, though. What's put it into your head that I'm going to sea, Bunter?"

Billy Bunter gasped.

He put his mouth close to Tom Dutton's ear, and bawled:

"Cousin—Wally—coming—tea! Will you stand something?"

Dutton jerked his head back.

"I wish you wouldn't breathe over me like a blessed walrus, Bunter! You needn't shout, either; I'm not deaf! I can hear you all right when you don't mumble. If your cousin's coming to tea, I'm sorry I sha'n't see him; I'm going to tea with Ogilvy and Russell."

And Tom Dutton walked off, leaving Bunter gasping with his vocal exertions, and several other fellows in the passage chuckling.

It was evident that there was nothing doing in Study No. 7, so far as tea was concerned, and Bunter wished he had not been so stand-offish with the Co. It was rather humiliating for Wally's rich relation to have to take him to tea in Hall, considering how extremely frugal tea in Hall was just then. The Owl of the Remove decided to look for the Famous Five, and put his stand-offishness in his pocket for the present.

The Famous Five, however, had no time for Billy Bunter just then. The early dusk was falling, and the Remove fellows were making the most of what light remained for footer practice. Billy Bunter arrived on Little Side, and bawled to Wharton, who appeared to be as deaf as Tom Dutton just then. It was not till the light failed, and the players came off, that Bunter found an opportunity.

Then he joined the chums of the Remove as they threw on their coats and walked back to the House.

"I say, you fellows, my cousin Wally will be here soon," said Bunter.

"Well?"

"As you seem rather keen to have him to tea in Study No. 1——"

"Not at all, ass!"

"Well, I don't mind bringing him, Wharton——"

"Sending him, do you mean?" asked Nugent.

"I mean bringing him!" howled Bunter. "You're jolly well not going to have my cousin without me!"

"Oh, buzz off!"

"I—I mean, I'd be glad to bring him, you fellows," said Bunter, almost pleadingly. "There's no tea in my study, and he's bound to be hungry after a long journey, and—and I'm stony, owing to a disappointement over a postal-order, and—and——"

"Well, bring him, and cut it short," said Wharton.

"You'll have something decent, I suppose?" said Bunter.

"What do you say to a high tea?" asked Bob Cherry.

"First-rate!"

"Right-ho, then! There's some sardines in my study that are a bit wangy, so I'll bring them along and make it a high tea—a very high tea!"

"You—you silly ass!" said Bunter. "Look here, if you're not going to give my cousin something decent I sha'n't bring him."

"Don't, then!" said Wharton cheerfully. "We'll try to survive it."

"I—I mean, I—I'll bring him, of course, as you're so pressing. Anyway, he'd be rather late for tea in Hall. I say, he will be jolly tired after a long journey, and I'm thinking of hiring the hack to bring him here. Think that's a good idea, Wharton?"

"Quite!"

"The man charges three-and-six now."

"Oh!"

"I suppose you could lend me three-and-six till my postal-order comes?" said Bunter.

"To save you walking from the station!" exclaimed Johnny Bull.

"To save Wally walking, after a tremendous long journey," said Bunter. "Besides, if you're going to wait tea for him, you'll have to wait a jolly long time if he walks from the station."

Harry Wharton slid his hand into his pocket.

"There's half-a-crown," he said. "The man will do it for that, without any surplus for you, you fat spoofer!"

"Oh, really, Wharton——"

"Oh, scat!"

Billy Bunter took the half-crown, and "scatted." He rolled away at once to the gates, calculating that he had time to call in at Uncle Clegg's, in the village, and expend the half-crown on tuck before he went to the station to meet Wally. It seemed very probable that if the Co. waited tea till the guest arrived they would have to wait while Wally walked from the station, after all.

THE THIRD CHAPTER.
The Price of Punting!

"MASTER BUNTER!"

Billy Bunter was close on the village, in the thickening dusk, when a man stopped in his path, and the fat junior halted.

Bunter's round eyes grew rounder behind his big glasses as he recognised the man before him.

It was Mr. Jerry Hawke, the billiard-sharper, who was usually to be found at the Cross Keys public-house.

Bunter breathed hard as he eyed that dingy and unsavoury gentleman, who evidently had business with him.

"Good-evening, Master Bunter!" said

Mr. Hawke genially, removing the strong-smelling, black cigar from his mouth.

"G-g-g-g-good-evening!" stammered Bunter.

"I been expectin' a call from you, sir."

"H-h-h-have you?"

"I have!" said Mr. Hawke, with emphasis. "You owe me a little bill, Master Bunter."

"D-d-d-do I?"

"I suppose that you are aweer, Master Bunter, that the 'orse you backed last week didn't win?"

"D-d-didn't he?"

"He did not, Master Bunter."

"Oh!"

"Convenient to you to settle up now, sir?"

"Oh, crumbs!"

"Only a matter of ten quid!" said Mr. Hawke. "A werry small sum to a rich young gent like you, Master Bunter, I dessay."

Billy Bunter groaned aloud. His essay as an amateur blackguard had been a dismal failure; and his dead certs were coming home to roost, as it were. He had hoped to win Mr. Hawke's money; he had none of his own to lose. It had looked like quite a paying speculation to Bunter at the time. But there was an hour of reckoning.

"I—I say," he gasped, "I—I can't settle at present, Mr. Hawke! Not at—at all convenient just now. I—I want you to wait a little."

"Till when?"

"Next year——"

"Wot?"

"I—I mean next term," stuttered Bunter.

"You mean to-morrer, I dessay?" said Mr. Hawke genially.

"I—I've been disappointed about—about a remittance," said Bunter.

"I'm sorry to 'ear that, sir," said Mr. Hawke, in significant tones. "Werry sorry, because I've got to 'ave my money."

"Oh, dear!"

"Not that I'm a 'ard man. 'And over 'arf the amount, and I'll let the rest stand over for a week. That's fair an' liberal."

"I—I can't! Look here, Mr. Hawke," said Bunter desperately. "Gambling debts can't be collected from minors. I'm a minor. You can't ask me for the money. You know it ain't legal!"

Mr. Hawke frowned.

"You put it on that footin'?" he said. "Well, I ain't going to county-court you, that's a cert, Master Bunter."

"You can't, you know, as I'm under age," said Bunter, with more confidence.

"'Course I can't! I shall simply call on your 'eadmaster and ask 'im wot's to be done. I'm goin' that way now," added Mr. Hawke carelessly. "So I may as well drop in."

He made a movement forward, and Bunter caught at his sleeve in blank terror.

"You—you—you're not going to see Dr. Locke?" he howled.

"Why not?"

"I—I—I should be—be flogged!" howled Bunter. "Expelled, very likely!"

"That ain't my business."

"Dr. Locke wouldn't believe you, either!" gasped Bunter.

Mr. Hawke grinned.

"Gammon!" he said. "I've got a bit of writing to show him, Master Bunter. You don't squirm out of it like that. Good-hevening to you!"

Mr. Hawke walked on.

Billy Bunter stood frozen with terror for some moments. Then he raced desperately after the sharper.

"Stop!" he gasped.

"Don't ketch 'old of my sleeve, Master Bunter. I ain't got nothing to say to you," said Mr. Hawke. "You ain't honourable, Master Bunter."

"I—I—I say, I'm going to pay you, you know," stuttered Bunter. "I—I am really! I—I've got a half-crown now——"

"A 'arf-crown!" said Mr. Hawke, with utter contempt. "Wot's that?"

"It's all I've got!" groaned Bunter.

The sharper's shifty eyes scanned him, and he could easily see that the unhappy Owl was speaking the truth. Bunter was too terrified to do anything else.

"Well, it's precious little," said Mr. Hawke. "But I ain't a 'ard man. 'And it over!"

Harry Wharton's half-crown disappeared into Mr. Hawke's waistcoat-pocket.

"And now wot's goin' to be done?" said Jerry Hawke. "I ain't the man to serve a young gent an ill turn if I can 'elp it. 'Ow much can you 'and over to-morrow, if I wait till then?"

"I—I can't——"

"Wot!" growled Mr. Hawke, with a terrifying growl.

"Ten shillings!" spluttered Bunter.

"Make it a pound, and I'm your man."

"I—I can't!" Bunter groaned. "I—I've got to get it out of my cousin, and I'm not sure he will lend it to me, anyway. Oh dear!"

"Better make sure of it," said Mr. Hawke. "I'll take the ten, though I'm a fool to do it. Let me 'ave the ten to-morrow, and I'll wait till Saturday for the rest. That's generous; but I always was a good-natured cove."

"I—I say——"

"That's all. Good-night, Master Bunter!"

"You—you—you're not going to Greyfriars?" gasped Bunter.

"Not till Saturday; and not then if you do the square thing."

"Oh dear!"

Mr. Jerry Hawke walked on, and disappeared into the shadows, grinning over his cigar. Bunter was not a very rich prize for the unscrupulous sharper, but he was at least an easy victim, and it was pretty clear that, though his financial resources might be small, Mr. Hawke would have complete command of them, such as they were.

Bunter was gasping as he rolled on to Friardale in a state of utter dismay. He did not call in at Uncle Clegg's. There was nothing to call in for now. He rolled on dismally to the station, where he was in time to meet his cousin Wally coming out.

THE FOURTH CHAPTER.
Bunter Is Not Pleased!

"MY heye!"

The old porter at Friardale made that remark as he blinked at the two youths who met at the station entrance.

The likeness between the two Bunters was astonishing.

Separately, anyone would have taken them for one another; and even when they were together it needed a close scrutiny to discover which was which.

The chief difference was that Bunter of Greyfriars wore glasses, and Wally Bunter did not.

They were clad differently, too—Bunter in Etons, and Wally in tweeds.

But, apart from those superficial differences, they were the same fellow to look at; and Wally in Bunter's clothes and glasses would have been taken for Billy by Billy's own father.

On close examination it could be seen,

however, that Wally, fat as he was, was not quite so podgy as Billy, and was certainly in much better condition, and more alert and active. He walked with a springy step in spite of the weight he had to carry, instead of rolling tubbily like William George.

As he was not short-sighted, he saw Billy long before Billy saw him, and he greeted Bunter with a slap on the shoulder that made him splutter.

"Yah! You beast! Hallo, is that you, Wally?"

"Little me, old top!" answered Wally cheerily.

"Don't punch me, you ass!"

"That was a friendly, cousinly greeting, old bird!" answered Wally reproachfully.

"Well, don't do it!" snapped Billy.

Bunter's temper had not been improved by the meeting with Mr. Hawke and the loss of the half-crown.

Wally only smiled, however. He knew William George too well to expect Chesterfieldian manners from him.

"How are you going on, Billy?" he inquired.

"Rotten!"

"Too bad! Feel the rations?" asked Wally sympathetically.

"Awful!"

"Well, they do hit a fellow hard!" agreed Wally. "Still, it's beaten the Huns."

"Blow the Huns!"

"Blow 'em as hard as you like! They've had it in the neck, anyhow, and that serves 'em right for shoving us on rations. Hallo, my son John, what interests you?" asked Wally, looking at the porter, who was blinking at the two in great surprise.

The porter trundled off with a trolly without answering, but he looked back twice or thrice at the two cousins who resembled one another so amazingly.

More than one or two glances were cast at the two juniors as they left the station together, Wally carrying a bag in his hand.

"Good boy to meet me at the station!" said Wally. "I suppose you're rolling in money, Billy?"

"No."

"Then it's my treat."

"Eh?"

"There used to be a tuckshop in this street. I don't know what you've got for tea at Greyfriars, but I could do with a snack. Could you, Billy?"

"Could I!" said Billy, with deep feeling.

"Come on, then!"

Billy Bunter led the way to Uncle Clegg's with great alacrity. The effect of his meeting with Mr. Hawke was wearing off now. Bunter was not a fellow to meet troubles half-way; indeed, he generally put them off till the last possible moment, and then contrived somehow to land them on somebody else. At the present moment his thoughts were all given to the tuck in Mr. Clegg's little shop.

He blinked at his cousin, however, several times with surprised inquiry. Wally had never been over-blessed with money, and what money he had he had to work for, and was consequently very careful with it. It seemed as if Wally was better off than heretofore.

"You've had good luck, you told me in your letter, Wally," Bunter remarked.

"Yes, my pippin!"

"I suppose your pater hasn't come into a fortune?" said Billy Bunter, not quite pleased at the idea.

He had always looked on Wally as a poor relation, and it was not gratifying to think of him as being on an equal footing.

"Not exactly," said Wally

"You've had some luck on the Turf?" asked Bunter eagerly.

"Ha, ha! No. Mug's game!"

"Well, I've had some jolly bad luck that way," said Bunter. "I've been going in for punting lately, and I've got left."

"Serve you right, old chap! You ought to have had more sense."

"Look here——"

"Here we are again!" said Wally. And he walked into Uncle Clegg's shop, and Billy forgot everything but eatables.

Uncle Clegg gave Billy Bunter a rather suspicious look, perhaps suspecting that the fat junior had come to try once more to obtain a little tick. Then he stared at Wally, and put on his spectacles, and stared at the two of them.

"My heye!" said Uncle Clegg, just like the porter at the station.

Bunter grunted. He was not at all flattered by the resemblance between himself and his poor relation, and he considered that people exaggerated that resemblance. As a matter of fact, Wally held exactly the same view. He had been roused to wrath on more than one occasion by being mistaken for his cousin Billy.

Uncle Clegg became more civil and obliging, however, when he saw a red ten-shilling note in Wally Bunter's fat hand.

"Go it, Billy!" said Wally invitingly. "Anything that isn't rationed, you know. Must play the game."

Snort from Bunter. He was not so very keen on playing the game, so far as the rations were concerned. But there were various agreeable and indigestible articles in Mr. Clegg's stock upon which the eagle eye of the Food Controller had not yet fallen, and upon these the two cousins began a gorgeous feast. At ten shillings Wally called a halt. But it was evident that he was in unusual funds to be able to expend such a sum upon a snack.

Billy Bunter had travelled through two-thirds of the good things, and he was prepared to continue till further orders; but Wally paid up and left the shop, and William George had to follow him.

"I feel better now," Bunter remarked. "We've got to walk, Wally."

"I don't mind walking."

"The fellows will be waiting tea for us," remarked Billy, as they started for Greyfriars. "Never mind; let 'em wait."

"Oh!" said Wally, rather dismayed. "I wouldn't have stopped if you'd told me that. We ought to have gone straight on."

"Rot! It's all right. Let 'em wait."

"Your study-mates?" asked Wally.

"No; Wharton and that lot in Study No. 1. I've promised to bring you with me," explained Billy. "They wanted me, of course. I'm a good deal sought after at Greyfriars. But I told 'em I couldn't come unless I brought you."

Wally knitted his brows a little.

"Those chaps were friendly enough when I was at the school last time," he said. "I'd like to see them again. But I don't want to be planted on them for tea, Billy. I suppose there's tea going in Hall?"

Bunter bawls! (*See Chapter 2.*)

"Too late for that now."

"Well, I don't want any tea. I've had enough, if you come to that."

"I haven't! Look here, Wally, I've promised my friends to bring you."

"Oh! If they really want me——"

"Naturally they want a relation of mine. It's a case of love me, love my dog!" explained Bunter.

Wally seemed about to say something, but he refrained, and they walked on in silence for some time. But Billy's curiosity was aroused, and he soon started questioning his cousin.

"You've got a lot more tin than you used to have, Wally."

"Yes, rather!"

"What's happened?"

"A jolly stroke of luck!" said Wally, with great satisfaction. "I'm not in the office any longer."

"Sacked?"

"No; getting on in the world," grinned Wally.

"Well, I'm glad to hear it!" said Billy

Bunter. "It was a bit rotten for me, having a relation working in an office!"

"Oh, was it?" said Wally.

"Of course it was! I should have thought you understood that!"

"Oh!"

Another silence. Wally Bunter did not seem to be enjoying his cousin's society, somehow.

"But what are you going to do now, if you've left the office?" asked Billy Bunter. "Looking for a job?"

"No."

"What's the game, then?"

"I'm going to school."

Bunter jumped.

"You've been to school," he answered.

"Yes; but I only went to a small school, and had to leave early and work," said Wally. "I didn't have your luck. I'm no older than you."

"But it's jolly queer for you to go to school again!" said Bunter, puzzled. "What sort of a school?"

"Public school."

"Wha-a-at?"

"Surprises you—what?" asked Wally cheerily. "I thought it would surprise you, old chap, and I knew you'd be pleased."

Billy Bunter did not look pleased, somehow.

"Gammon!" he grunted.

"Honest Injun!" answered Wally.

"What school are you going to, then?" asked Bunter. "Eton or Harrow?" he added sarcastically.

"Better!" answered Wally coolly. "I'm going to St. Jim's!"

"Gammon!"

"Honour bright, old fellow! I told you I'd had good luck."

Wally's fat face was beaming, and he evidently expected his cousin Billy to rejoice in his good luck. But his cousin Billy did not look joyful. He was frowning.

Wally had so long been a poor relation, loftily patronised by the egregious Owl, that the news was very disconcerting. Evidently there would be no room in the future for patronage. That circumstance was not gratifying to William George Bunter.

"Congratulate me, old chap!" beamed Wally.

Grunt!

Wally's bright face fell as he looked at his cousin, and Billy's feelings on the subject dawned upon him.

"I—I say, Billy, you're glad, ain't you?" he said reproachfully. "It's a big stroke of luck for me! I thought you'd be no end pleased."

"I don't see it!" answered Bunter stiffly. "If you want my candid opinion, I think it's like your cheek!"

"What?"

"Your people ain't well enough off to send you to a public school!" said Bunter, with growing indignation. "I call it dashed cheek! Why, you'll be putting on airs of equality with me next!"

"Wha-a-at?"

"I believe in people remaining in their own stations," said the Owl scornfully. "Cheek, that's it—pure cheek! That's my opinion!"

Wally halted.

"I'm sorry you look at it like that, Billy," he said quietly. "I thought you'd be pleased. I've never thought for a moment that you'd take it like this! I—I'd have liked to come to Greyfriars, but——"

"Well, of all the nerve!" exclaimed Bunter, quite exasperated. "You at Greyfriars! I never heard of such cheek! What could I say to the fellows, I'd like to know? I think it's pretty good for you to come to Greyfriars as a visitor! But to think of being a Greyfriars chap—well, I must say, Wally, that I'm surprised at you!"

"Well, I can't come, so you needn't worry," said Wally, very quietly. "It's settled that I go to St. Jim's. I'm sorry you take it like this, Billy!"

"I don't know how you expected me to take it, I'm sure!" said Bunter, with a sniff.

"Well, perhaps I might have expected it, but I didn't! I'm sorry! I—I don't think I'll come any farther, Billy, if you don't mind."

"Eh? You're stopping at Greyfriars for the night. I've asked Mr. Quelch."

"I think it would be better for me to get home, on the whole."

"What utter rot!" exclaimed Bunter, in astonishment. He did not seem aware that he had uttered anything calculated to wound his cousin's feelings. "The fellows are expecting you."

"You can make my excuses, then. I don't suppose they'll miss me much."

"No reason why they should, that I can see," answered Bunter.

"I agree with you," said Wally, in a low voice. "I'll be off, then."

"There's no train back to-night. I suppose you know that?"

"Oh!"

Wally paused.

"Come along, and don't play the goat!" said Bunter. "The gates will be locked pretty soon."

"I intended to stay the night at the Friardale Arms if you hadn't asked me to put up at Greyfriars," said Wally. "I'll go there, anyway."

"Look here——"

"Good-bye, Billy!"

With that Wally swung round, and walked away quickly towards the village. Billy Bunter blinked after him in great surprise and annoyance.

"Wally!" he called out.

Walter Bunter did not answer, and in a few minutes he disappeared into the shadows. Bunter stood nonplussed for a minute or two. Then, with a grunt of disdain, he rolled on to Greyfriars, where he arrived just in time to escape being locked out by Gosling.

THE FIFTH CHAPTER.
Harry Wharton Takes a Hand!

"HALLO, hallo, hallo! Where's Wally?"

The Famous Five were waiting in the big doorway for Bunter to come in. They were surprised to see him roll in alone, without his cousin.

Impelled by considerations of hospitality and politeness, the chums of the Remove were waiting tea in Study No. 1.

After footer practice in keen weather their appetites were naturally good; and waiting tea was not a pleasant process. And tea that evening was unusually good, in honour of the guest. There was no fatted calf to kill; but the chums had done their best to supply a good spread for the visitor.

"Hasn't Wally come?" asked Wharton.

"Oh, he's come!" grunted Bunter.

"Where is he, then?"

"He's staying in Friardale, after all."

"Well, you fat duffer!" exclaimed Johnny Bull indignantly. "Here we've been waiting tea, all of us as hungry as hunters, and your blessed cousin isn't coming, after all!"

"'Tain't my fault!" growled Bunter. "He got his back up over something—blessed if I know what—and just marched off. I'm ready for tea."

"You needn't tell us that!" growled Nugent.

"I say, you fellows, if it's ready we may as well set to," said Bunter. "I'm pretty sharp set."

"Never mind tea just now," said Wharton quietly. "You asked Mr. Quelch for permission for Wally to stay here to-night. Why hasn't he come?"

"He preferred not to, I suppose."

"Does that mean that you've been springing some of your snobby caddishness on the chap?" growled Johnny Bull.

Bunter blinked at him.

"Oh, really, Bull! I suppose it's my own business how I treat my own relations?" he said.

"Well, I suppose it is!" said Johnny. "That's so! All the same, you're a fat worm, and your cousin is worth fifty of you!"

"Fifty thousand!" grunted Bob Cherry.

"The fifty-thousandfulness is terrific!" remarked Hurree Jamset Ram Singh. "If the esteemed Wally is not coming, I see no reason for endurefully bearing the excellent society of the disgusting Bunter!"

"Hear, hear!" from Nugent.

Billy Bunter glowered at the Famous Five. Apparently tea in No. 1 for Billy depended upon his bringing Wally with him. On his own, William George was not persona grata.

"Wally wouldn't have turned back like that for nothing," said Wharton, his brows knitted. "Bunter must have done something. It's a reflection on our hospitality for the chap to stay at Friardale. Isn't he coming along to-morrow, Bunter?"

"I suppose not. What does it matter?"

"Then he won't see the St. Jim's match."

"What the dickens does it matter whether he does or not?" snapped Bunter. "Let's go and have tea. I've only had a snack, and I'm hungry."

"Have you quarrelled with Wally?" asked Wharton, really concerned about a visitor who was so hapless as to depend on the hospitality of Billy Bunter.

Bunter sniffed.

"I should hardly be likely to demean myself by quarrelling with a poor relation, Wharton! I simply told him what I thought of his cheek."

"His cheek?" repeated Wharton.

"I call it cheek!" said Bunter warmly. "That chap going to a public school! As I told him, he'll be putting on airs of equality with me next!"

"Is Wally going to a public school?" asked Harry, in astonishment.

"So he says! I don't wonder you're surprised at his nerve—a poor relation who works in an office!" sneered Bunter.

"You fat Hun!" growled Wharton. "Why shouldn't he go to a public school, if he has the chance, as much as anybody else? He would do it more credit than his cousin Billy, anyhow!"

"Look here——"

"So that's the good luck he spoke of in his letter?" said Bob. "And I suppose he expected you to congratulate him?"

"I dare say he did!" sniffed Bunter.

"Instead of which you worked off some caddish snobbishness on him!" exclaimed Johnny Bull angrily. "Nice idea you've given him of Greyfriars manners, you toad!"

"Oh, really, Bull——"

"By Jove! I'd like him to come to Greyfriars!" exclaimed Nugent. "What school is he going to, Bunter?"

"St. Jim's."

"My hat! And the St. Jim's crowd will be here to-morrow for the footer match!" exclaimed Wharton. "It's a chance for Wally to meet them and make their acquaintace before he goes to their school."

"Look here, Wharton. I'm not keen

on introducing my poor relations to my friends at St. Jim's—especially D'Arcy!"

"Oh, dry up, you fat ass! Look here, Wally's got to come," said Wharton. "He's got to come if only to let him see that we're not all snobby toads here. He may think that we look at it the same as you do."

"He wouldn't think we look at anything like Bunter if he's got any sense!" growled Johnny Bull.

"Well, he doesn't know us well enough to be sure of that. In justice to ourselves we've got to have him here, and show him that Bunter's the only sneaking cad in the Remove!" argued Wharton.

"You—you—you——" spluttered Bunter in great wrath.

"But we can't fetch him," said Nugent. "Gates are closed now. We can see him to-morrow, though."

"No need to see him!" howled Bunter. "He's not coming; and I don't want him, for one."

"Have you borrowed his ten bob already?" snorted Johnny Bull.

Billy Bunter started. He had forgotten the ten shillings he had intended to extract from his cousin; and at the same moment he remembered Mr. Hawke and his demands.

"Oh!" he ejaculated. "On second thoughts, I—I'd rather he came! Of course, a chap wants to be hospitable. Besides, there's a bed rigged up in the Remove dorm for him. But I tell you what, Wharton," added Bunter, struck by a bright thought, "I can tell you how to arrange it nicely."

"Well?" snapped Wharton.

"You lend me that ten bob——"

"What?"

"And you can bike down to-morrow and see Wally, and get it from him. It will come to the same thing, won't it?"

"My hat!"

"That will save trouble for all parties," said Bunter, blinking at the astonished juniors. "I think that's satisfactory. What do you think, Wharton?"

"What do I think?" gasped Wharton. "I think you're a measly worm, and I think I'll jolly well kick you along the passage!"

"Yaroooh!"

Bunter just eluded the boot of the indignant captain of the Remove.

"We've got to get Wally here," said Harry, more quietly. "The poor chap must be feeling wounded over the way that fat beast has treated him. He may be thinking Bunter's a fair specimen of the lot of us. I'll ask Wingate for a pass out of gates, and we'll go down to Friardale and see him, and simply make him come."

"Good egg!" said Johnny Bull. "But will Wingate——"

"I think so, the way I shall put it," said Harry. "Wait for me here, while I put it to old Wingate."

Harry Wharton hurried away to the Sixth Form passage, where he found George Wingate in his study. The captain of Greyfriars was talking footer with Gwynne of the Sixth. He looked round as Harry appeared in the doorway.

"Well?" he said laconically.

"Can I have a pass for two down to Friardale, Wingate?" asked the junior meekly. "It's rather important."

"Generally is important, isn't it?" grinned Wingate. "I'm afraid you'll have to explain the importance first."

"Bunter's cousin is there," explained Harry. "Mr. Quelch has given permission for him to stay the night here, but he's put up at the Friardale Arms owing to Bunter having been an ill-bred little beast. We—we want to be hospitable."

"Oh!" said the captain of Greyfriars.

"You see, we don't want a chap to think we're all tarred with Bunter's brush," explained Wharton. "It's for the honour of Greyfriars, you know."

Wingate laughed.

"You say Mr. Quelch has given permission for him to stay the night?"

"Yes; there's a bed for him in our dorm."

"You can go, then."

Wingate scribbled a pass for two, and Wharton thanked him and left the study with great satisfaction. He rejoined his chums in the doorway, flourishing the pass.

"Two!" he said. "I thought it better not to ask for five—more likely to get a pass for two, you know. Who's coming with me "

"I say, you fellows——"

"Scat!"

"But I say," persisted Bunter, keeping a wary eye on the captain of the Remove. "I'm ready for tea——"

"There's no tea for you, you Owl! Go and eat coke!"

"I—I say, you know!" said the dismayed Owl. "I'll come to Friardale with you, if you like, Wharton——"

"I don't like! You come, Franky?"

"Right you are," said Nugent.

"And you fellows see that that fat slug doesn't crawl into the study and scoff the grub while we're gone," added Wharton.

"You bet!"

Wharton and Nugent started at once, and Bob Cherry, Johnny, and Inky went to Study No. 1, where, on three or four occasions during the next half hour, they hurled things at a fat face that looked in at the doorway with a hungry look.

THE SIXTH CHAPTER.

All Serene!

WALLY BUNTER was not looking happy as he strolled slowly along the old High Street of Friardale. He was killing time; the evening yet was early, and he did not want to take up his quarters at the inn yet. There was little to be seen in the quiet village street, and Wally sauntered the length of it, and sauntered back again with a thoughtful and clouded face.

He had come down to Friardale in great spirits, fully expecting that his cousin Billy would rejoice in his good luck, and being eager, naturally, to tell Billy all about it, and receive his congratulations.

Even the fact that Billy had never allowed him to forget that he was a poor relation made it seem likely that the Owl would be glad to see him on a more prosperous footing. The petty jealousy of the miserable Owl had given him a painful shock; and, worse than that, it had rubbed the gilt off his golden anticipations.

If Billy Bunter looked at the matter in such a way, probably other Greyfriars fellows would do the same; and the St. Jim's fellows might be tarred with the same brush. Was he going to be looked on as a pushing outsider, as the Owl evidently considered him? Wally was sensitive—a quality that Billy did not share with him in the least; their resemblance, in fact, was only skin-deep. His happy anticipations of his new life seemed to crumble away within him, and his cheery spirits were gone.

Just then, indeed, he was almost wishing that good fortune had not come his way, and that he was still on the office stool in Canterbury.

A sudden clap on his shoulder made him jump.

He turned quickly, to see Harry Wharton and Frank Nugent smiling at him in the dusky street.

"Couldn't mistake you!" said Wharton, holding out his hand. "We were coming to the inn for you, when we spotted you, old scout."

Wally coloured.

"Give us your fist, old chap!"

Wally mechanically gave the captain of the Remove his hand. Nugent bagged it next, and shook heartily.

"You—you were coming to see me?" stammered Wally.

"Exactly! No need to go to the inn now, though—you haven't engaged your room yet, have you?"

"N-n-no!"

"Then come on!"

"Eh? Where?"

"Greyfriars, of course!"

"I—I'm not going to Greyfriars!" stammered Wally, his colour deepening. "I—I—you see——"

"Exactly! Come on!"

"But—but I told you I wasn't coming to Greyfriars!"

"Yes, I know; but we told you that you are!" chuckled Nugent. "This way, my son! We've waited tea for you. Better call it supper now."

"But—but—but——"

"My dear man, we're hungry," said Nugent. "Get a move on!"

"I—I——"

"Take his other arm, Franky!"

"What-ho!"

Wally, like a fellow in a dream, found both his arms taken, and he was walked away down the street by Wharton and Nugent. He was so astonished that he went without resistance, and they walked him out into the lane. There Wally demurred.

"But—but I'm not coming!" he stammered. "I—I don't want to see Billy, as—as it happens——"

"There we sympathise with you," said Wharton. "We don't want to see him, either, but we have to see him every day. You can put up with him for once."

Wally laughed.

"But—but you don't understand!" he said.

"We do—perfectly. I don't want to run down your cousin, old top. You'll admit yourself that he's rather a pig, but he can't help it," said Harry. "But, you see, we've been expecting you in our study, and we've killed the fatted calf—at least, the fatted haddock—and we're not letting you off. You're staying at Greyfriars to-night."

"But——"

"Billy is dying to see you!"

"Is he?" exclaimed Wally, in amazement.

"Yes; he forgot to borrow anything of you, it seems."

Wally laughed again. His good spirits were returning. Indeed, it would have been difficult for even a misanthrope to feel down under the kindly influence of the Greyfriars fellows' hearty cordiality.

"Besides, we're not going to let him come to tea unless you come," added Frank Nugent. "So, you see, you must come, for Billy's sake."

"But—I say——"

"Billy's told us your good news, too," added Wharton. "Congratulations, old chap! I wish you were going to Greyfriars instead of St. Jim's, though."

"Do you really?" stammered Wally.

"Yes, rather!" said Nugent, with emphasis. "I say, couldn't you work it with your people to send Billy to St. Jim's instead? Then you could come to Greyfriars instead of Billy. The whole school would pass a vote of thanks."

Wally chuckled.

"I jolly well wish I could!" he said. "Of course, I'd rather come to Greyfriars. I don't know anybody at St. Jim's. You—you fellows would really like me to come?"

"Of course!"

"It's jolly decent of you. Billy said—ahem!—— After all, what does it matter what Billy said?"

"Nothing at all!" said Wharton. "Billy has an unfortunate habit of talking out of the back of his neck. But you'll meet some St. Jim's fellows to-morrow, my son—Tom Merry and his crowd will be over here for a footer match. We can introduce you to eleven of the best."

"I—I say, you're awfully good!" stammered Wally.

"What rot!"

"I—I suppose I was an ass to take any notice of Billy's rot," said Wally Bunter happily. "I—I was feeling a bit down, the way he put it——"

"Well, I don't want to call you names, old scout, but I must say you were an ass if you took any notice of Billy's gas. It would have been wiser to kick him. He would have understood that."

Wally Bunter chuckled, and his fat face was very bright as the cheery juniors marched him on to Greyfriars. They arrived at the school, and Wally came in with his companions, a smile on his face, to receive a cordial greeting from the

Remove fellows who happened to be about; and a still more cordial greeting from Bob Cherry and Johnny Bull and the nabob when he was taken up to Study No. 1.

There was no doubt lingering in his mind now. His good fortune was a matter of congratulation in Study No. 1; evidently they did not take the same views of the egregious Owl of the Remove.

Tea—or, rather, supper—was ready; and Wally's face was merry and bright as he sat down at the table with the chums of the Remove. Another fat face blinked in at the doorway, with eyes wary for a flying cushion.

"I say, you fellows——"

"Hallo, hallo, hallo! Hand me the tongs, Inky!"

"I—I say, you fellows, I've come, you know. Here we are again, Wally, old kid!" said Bunter hastily. "S-s-so jolly glad to see you at Greyfriars! So good of you to come, old chap!"

"My hat!" was all Wally could say.

"I suppose I'm going to have tea with my guest, you fellows?" said Bunter, with dignity.

Bob Cherry relinquished the tongs.

It was a very cheery tea in Study No. 1; and Billy Bunter made it a point to be very civil to his cousin—in fact, quite affectionate. For it was borne in upon his podgy mind that at the first sign of the cloven hoof he would depart from Study No. 1 on his neck; and with a powerful motive like that for good behaviour William George Bunter succeeded in the difficult task of behaving himself.

THE SEVENTH CHAPTER.
Wally's Luck!

WALTER BUNTER'S plump face beamed over the festive board. The good fellowship in Study No. 1 made him very happy. And the Co. were so genuinely interested in his good fortune that Wally was soon relating to them the particulars he had intended to relate to his cousin Billy. Billy certainly heard them now; but he heeded not; his thoughts were upon the feed.

"I jolly well wish I were coming to Greyfriars instead of St. Jim's," Wally said. "I'd have liked to suggest it, only it would have seemed ungrateful. Of course, I'm glad to go to St. Jim's—I shall like it no end. But I feel quite at home here, you know, as you fellows have treated me so awfully decently. I'd give a good bit to play in your eleven, Wharton."

"You would play in it if you were a Greyfriars chap," said Wharton. "I jolly well wish you were!"

"Couldn't it be fixed?" asked Bob Cherry. "Are your people specially set on sending you to St. Jim's?"

"You might tactfully mention to them that Greyfriars is really it," remarked Johnny Bull.

"Assure them that the itfulness is terrific, my esteemed Wally!" suggested the Nabob of Bhanipur.

Wally smiled.

"It isn't exactly my people," he said. "My people can't afford to send me to an expensive school. It's Mr. Penman."

Billy Bunter looked up.

"That's your governor at Canterbury, isn't it?" he asked. "I believe you call him your governor."

"My employer, anyway," said Wally; "and a jolly good sort. He's an old St. Jim's man, and he thinks no end of his old school."

"Your employer is sending you to his old school?" said Bob, rather puzzled by that curious information.

"That's it! I've been distinguishing myself," grinned Wally. "There was a burglary at the office. I was staying late, getting through some work with the chief clerk—we were in the back office, and the rest of the place all in the dark, and the rotters thought it was empty and shut up for the night. They opened the door of the back office, and you should have seen them jump when they saw us there at the desks. They'd got in without our hearing a sound."

"My hat! A bit exciting!" said Bob Cherry, with keen interest. "What did you do?"

"It wasn't what I did—it was what they did. There were two of them—hulking fellows. They were simply flabbergasted at the sight of us—and so were we. They ran at us, and the chief clerk got a rap on the head, and was stunned. I dodged."

Sniff from Billy Bunter.

"Pity I wasn't there!" he remarked. "I'd have knocked them down, Wally!"

"You would—I don't think!" said Wally. "You'd have squirmed up the chimney, or under the table, and howled for mercy."

"Look here——"

"Shut up, Bunter! Go on, Wally, old gun; this is jolly interesting!" said Bob Cherry.

"Well, I dodged, and they dodged after me," said Wally. "It was nip and tuck. I nipped and they tucked, you know. I got a rap on the shoulder from a club that was meant for my napper. But I dodged into old Penman's private office, slammed the door, and turned the key."

Wally paused, to dispose of a cup of coffee.

The juniors listened with keen interest when he resumed. It was odd to think of the fat, good-humoured Wally in such perilous straits.

"I was thinking of the governor's telephone, of course," he went on. "I fairly jumped at it when I'd locked the door. They heard me, through the door, giving a number, and, of course, they guessed I was ringing up the police. They started on the lock, and got it busted just as I got through to the inspector at the station."

"Phew!"

"Well, I heard them coming on behind me as I stood at the 'phone, and you can bet the Kaiser's whiskers that I wanted to drop the receiver and hop it," said Wally. "I expected every second to feel a crash on the head. But I wasn't going to let them rob the office; there were thousands of quids in Bonds and things in the safe. I just jawed at the inspector, and told him what was happening. Penman's office, burglars—help. That was all I got out, when I got it on the napper."

Wally ran his fingers through his hair, and made a grimace

"It was a cosh!" he added. "Like a blessed earthquake!"

"My hat!"

"And what next?" asked Bob breathlessly.

"Next, I was waking up in bed," grinned Wally. "You see, I'd got a terrific cosh on the crumpet, and I was stunned. The police found me there. The burglars had bolted, knowing I'd got through to the station, without waiting to do more than bag some petty cash. They hadn't time to tackle the safe. I had a bump on my head as big as an egg, and an ache that would have made a hippopotamus feel ill. And old Penman was almost weeping with sympathy and gratitude. He said it was no end plucky of me to stick at the telephone and get help, with those rascals just behind me. And so it was," added Wally. "I must have been a bit excited at the time; it made me shiver afterwards to think of it. In fact, I don't like thinking of it now; it's creepy. I was jolly proud of myself, you can bet! As swanky as Billy here, almost!"

"Oh, really, Wally——"

"Ha, ha, ha!"

"And the long and the short of it was that old Penman told me I'd saved him six thousand pounds, as well as heaps of trouble," said Wally; "and he was bursting to do something for me. Blessed if I don't think he'd have made me a junior partner if I'd been fifteen years older! He thought it out for some days, and then sprang it on me what he meant to do. He's marked out a big job for me in the firm later on when I'm older; and as a preparation for that job he's sending me to his old school. It will be a good berth, and it needs a tip-top man—a chap about my size——"

"Ha, ha!"

"Especially a man with a public school education," said Wally. "Well, being an old St. Jim's man, naturally he settled on St. Jim's, and decided to send me there. He arranged it with my father, who was no end pleased, of course. I'd have liked to suggest Greyfriars, but it would have seemed rather like looking a gift-horse in the mouth, wouldn't it?"

"Well, it would, a bit," assented Wharton

"Not that Mr. Penman would have cared either way, of course, but it would have been ungracious, I thought. So I accepted his offer, and, of course, I'm jolly glad to go to St. Jim's. And I've got a holiday till I go—next week," said Wally. "So you can bet I am feeling very chippy!"

"Congratulations, old fellow!" said Wharton heartily.

"The congratulatefulness is terrific!"

"You'll see Greyfriars sometimes, anyway," remarked Nugent. "With your form, you'll get into Tom Merry's team and play in the matches."

"I hope so," said Wally. "Perhaps I'll be with them next time they come over to play you. Of—of course, I don't know how they'll take to an office chap."

Wharton smiled.

"We've met a lot of St. Jim's chaps," he said. "There's no Billy Bunter among them, so far as I know."

"Oh, really, Wharton——"

"You'll meet a lot of them to-morrow—eleven of the best," went on Wharton. "You'll like them, I'm sure."

Billy Bunter blinked up, and blinked down again. Bob Cherry had an eye on him, and Bunter's intended remark, whatever it was, remained unuttered.

But Walter Bunter was not observing his egregious cousin. He was too happy to worry about William George just then.

"I'll be jolly glad to see them!" said Wally. "Now, I suppose you chaps have your—what d'ye call it?—to do——"

"Prep!" said Wharton, with a smile.

"That's it! Don't let me hinder you."

"I'll find you a book," said Wharton, as he rose from the table. Prep was indispensable, and could not be put off even for an honoured guest.

"I'll sit here and watch you, if you don't mind," said Wally. "I've been mugging up with a tutor the last two or three weeks, to get ready for St. Jim's; and I'd like to see you chaps at work, to get into the way of it, if it won't worry you."

"Not at all!"

And Walter Bunter sat and watched, with keen observation, while Wharton and Nugent did their prep in Study No. 1; the other fellows going to their own quarters.

After prep Wally went downstairs with Wharton to pay his respects to Mr. Quelch—rather late, as a matter of fact; but the Remove-master received him very kindly.

When the Remove went to their dormitory Wally Bunter went with them, and he was already feeling as if he were one of them.

A good many fellows in the Remove greeted him in a friendly way; and, in fact, Wally received so much kindness in the Remove that Billy Bunter could only blink on in astonishment and disgust.

Here was his poor relation received on all hands with friendly cordiality, while he—Billy—received more kicks than halfpence, so to speak, in his own Form. It was really very astonishing—to Billy Bunter!

THE EIGHTH CHAPTER.

Tom Merry's Recruit!

HARRY WHARTON & Co. were thinking chiefly of the St. Jim's match the following morning. Even in the Form-room, at lessons, that important matter did not quite leave their minds. With Mr. Quelch's permission, Walter Bunter sat at a desk in the Form-room during morning lessons. He was keen to pick up all he could of the school's manners and customs in preparation for his new life at St. Jim's; and Harry Wharton & Co. were ready to help him in every way possible. Wally did not join in the Form work, but he sat with eyes and ears open; and it was evident that as a pupil he would have done the Form more credit than his cousin Billy.

Billy Bunter glanced at him once or twice, and grunted. He couldn't understand a fellow sitting out lessons when he could have been slacking about if he had chosen. But that was another point in which the cousins were dissimilar; Wally was anything but a slacker.

Indeed, taken all in all, his resemblance to Billy Bunter was really a libel on him, as Peter Todd remarked.

But that resemblance was so extraordinary that, but for his clothes and Billy's glasses, it would scarcely have been possible to distinguish one from the other, and it attracted attention and surprised glances everywhere.

After morning lessons Billy Bunter joined his cousin at once; though Walter did not really seem eager for his company. He submitted to it, however, with fat cheerfulness.

"I say, Wally"—Bunter was very civil—"I really congratulate you, old chap!"

"Thanks!" said Wally.

"It's a rise in life for you, ain't it?"

"Exactly!"

"Of course, you'd better not put on any airs," added Billy warningly.

"Thanks for the tip; I won't!"

"Keep your place, you know," added Billy.

"Anything else?" asked Walter, showing signs of restiveness.

"I suppose if you're going to St. Jim's you're going to have an allowance," said Billy, blinking at him. "You couldn't be there without any money."

"Yes."

"So you're in funds now, I suppose?"

"Pretty fair."

"Lend me ten bob, will you?"

Wally paused.

"The fact is, Billy, I'm in funds, but I haven't any tin to waste," he said. "I've got to be careful not to put my people to any expense while I'm at school."

"If you're going to be mean, Wally, I—— Besides, I only mean it as a loan," explained Bunter. "I'm expecting a postal-order this afternoon. I'll settle up before you leave Greyfriars."

"Oh!"

"Look here, Wally, you were going to pay to put up at the inn at Friardale!" exclaimed Bunter warmly. "I've saved you that, haven't I?"

Walter looked at him, and silently took out a little leather purse, and extracted therefrom a ten-shilling note, upon which Billy's fat fingers closed greedily.

Marching orders for Bunter! (*See Chapter 9.*)

"You've got some currency notes there," said Bunter. "Come to think of it, you may as well make this a quid, Wally."

"Sorry!"

"I mean, then I'll hand you the whole of my postal-order when it comes this afternoon," explained the Owl.

"Oh, bother!" said Wally.

"The fact is, I've got to pay a debt with this ten," said Bunter. "Now, look here, Wally——"

"Hallo, hallo, hallo!" Bob Cherry joined them. "We're going to punt a footer about before tiffin, Wally. Like to come along?"

"Yes, rather!"

"I say, Wally, look here—— Beast!"

Walter Bunter walked away with Bob Cherry, probably very pleased to be rid of his Greyfriars cousin. Billy Bunter grunted discontentedly. He dared not omit to send that ten shillings to Mr. Hawke to keep him quiet, and so he had to remain as stony as before, which he considered very hard lines.

The Owl of the Remove frowned very

majestically at Wally when they met at dinner. He wished to impress his lofty displeasure on his poor relation.

But Walter did not even notice that he was displeased. He was thoroughly enjoying his visit to Greyfriars; the hospitality he did not receive from Billy was more than made up in other quarters, and, naturally, he was not thinking very much about William George.

After dinner the St. Jim's match was the one topic.

Tom Merry & Co. were expected early. Owing to war conditions, it was not possible to have a brake to meet them at the station, as on former occasions; but several of the fellows were going down to Friardale to meet them, and walk to the school with them.

Billy Bunter, who was very keen to meet his "old pal" Arthur Augustus D'Arcy, decided that he was going to be one of the party, and when the Famous Five started from the school gates Billy Bunter rolled after them. Wally Bunter was with the chums of the Remove, Wharton thinking this a good opportunity for making him known to his future schoolfellows; but Billy was not desired, though Billy was quite indifferent to that. But in Wally's presence the chums did not feel disposed to shift the Owl as they would have done otherwise, so Billy Bunter rolled along to Friardale with them.

They were at the station before the train was due, and were waiting on the platform when it came in at last.

An eyeglass gleaming from the window of a first-class carriage revealed the presence of Arthur Augustus D'Arcy, the ornament of the Fourth Form at St. Jim's, and Billy Bunter waved a fat hand in greeting. Apparently Arthur Augustus did not observe him, however, for he did not wave back.

The train stopped, and the passengers alighted, the St. Jim's crowd among them.

Harry Wharton glanced over them, and was surprised to see only ten of the St. Jim's fellows—Tom Merry, Lowther, Blake, D'Arcy, Figgins, Kerr, Wynn, Noble, Talbot, and Levison. Tom Merry's handsome face was a little clouded, though he smiled as he greeted the Greyfriars fellows.

"All here?" asked Wharton, as he shook hands with the St. Jim's junior captain.

"Man lost en route," answered Tom Merry. "Of all the asses, I think Man——"

"Yaas, wathah!" chimed in Arthur Augustus D'Arcy, before Tom could finish. "You will admit, Tom Mewwy, that I weminded you that Mannahs was wathah an ass, and suggested your playin' Dig instead."

"Fathead!" remarked Lowther.

"Weally, Lowthah——"

"Manners and Roylance were with us," Tom Merry explained. "Roylance was a reserve. They got out at Lexham, and the train started without them. They had the time wrong, the silly duffers. So instead of bringing along an extra man we've come a man short."

"Too bad!" said Wharton. "When's the next train?"

Tom Merry made a grimace.

"It's a case of war trains. Next from Lexham to Courtfield is two hours.

"Oh, my hat!"

"We've got to play a man short or ask you to lend us a man," said Tom Merry. "It's annoying, of course!"

"Yaas, wathah! If you had played Dig instead of Mannahs, I am suah Dig would not have got left behind at Lexham."

"Well, I must say I agree with Gussy there," remarked Blake. "Still, it can't be helped now."

"We'll lend you a man with pleasure," said Wharton. "Lots to spare. Any chap not in our eleven will be delighted to play for you."

"I say, you fellows, I'll be only too pleased!" chimed in Billy Bunter. "Rely on me, Tom Merry!"

"Bai Jove!"

"How do you do, Gussy, old chap?" said Bunter affectionately. "You remember me—what?"

"I believe I have seen you befoah, deah boy," answered Arthur Augustus, as distantly as politeness allowed.

"I haven't given you a look-in at St. Jim's for a long time, Gussy," said Bunter affably. "But I'll make it a point to do so soon. You can rely on that."

"Bai Jove!"

"This way, you fellows!" said Wharton, with a glare at Bunter. "By the way, here's a chap who's coming to your show this term. He's staying at Greyfriars to-day."

"Gweat Scott!" murmured Arthur Augustus, as Wally Bunter was presented.

The swell of St. Jim's turned his eyeglass alternately upon the two Bunters in great interest.

Bob Cherry grinned.

"Can't you tell t'other from which?" he asked.

"Bai Jove! They are weally vewy much alike," remarked D'Arcy. "Welations, I pwesume?"

"Cousins," said Bob. "Very like to look at—not otherwise. Walter Bunter is one of the best!"

Tom Merry shook hands with Wally Bunter, politely expressing pleasure that he was going to be a St. Jim's fellow. But the St. Jim's skipper walked with Wharton when they started for Greyfriars.

Tom Merry was evidently a little worried at having arrived a man short at Greyfriars for a match which was one of the most important in the junior list of fixtures. It was impossible to put off the match till Manners could arrive, as that would not have left sufficient light to finish the game. And though there would be no lack of willing recruits to be found at Greyfriars, naturally that kind of makeshift was not pleasing to the St. Jim's skipper.

Wharton was thoughtful, too.

"I've got a suggestion to make, if you like, Merry," he remarked. "About your missing man, I mean."

"Go ahead!" said Tom. "Have you some extra-special good man you don't want yourself?"

Wharton laughed.

"No; but that chap Bunter——"

"My dear man, you're not offering me Billy Bunter!" exclaimed the Shell fellow of St. Jim's.

"Ha, ha! No! Wally Bunter, I mean!"

"They look much of a muchness."

"They look it, but they're not. Wally Bunter is a topping player," said Harry. "If he were a Greyfriars chap I should have him in my eleven."

"By Jove! Would you?" asked Tom, glancing round with surprise and interest at Wally Bunter.

"Yes, really! He looks heavy, but he's got speed that would surprise you. He's played while visiting Greyfriars before, you know. He plays half or forward, and either of them jolly well. As he's going to your school next week, you might like him better than a Greyfriars man in your team; and, seriously, he's as good a man as I could offer you."

Tom Merry looked at Wally Bunter again.

So far as appearances went, Wally did not look like a topping footballer; he was too much like William George for that. But Tom was aware that Harry Wharton was a good judge of a player's form, and he had seen Wally play. And undoubtedly it was better to play a prospective St. Jim's fellow in his team, if he could bag one, than a player borrowed from the enemy.

Tom Merry thought it over as they walked to Greyfriars, with several glances at Walter Bunter en route.

Wally observed his glances, and wondered why the St. Jim's fellow looked at him so often; but he understood when they reached Greyfriars. There Tom Merry came up to him.

"Wharton says you're a good man in the front line," he said. "We're a man short, and if you'd care to play for us, we'd be obliged. What do you say?"

"By gum!" ejaculated Wally.

His eyes danced.

"You feel up to the game?" asked Tom.

"You bet! I'll play with no end of pleasure. I shall have to borrow some clobber," said Wally. "Count me in! I'm your man!"

"Right you are, then!"

Tom Merry rejoined his comrades.

"Bunter's playing for us——" he began.

"Gweat Scott!"

"Gone potty?" asked Figgins pleasantly. "What's the good of that barrel?"

"He's fat—awfully fat!" remarked Fatty Wynn. A remark that made his companions grin. Fatty Wynn was not a sylph himself.

"I mean the other Bunter—the chap who's coming to St. Jim's," said Tom Merry, laughing. "Wharton says he's a good man."

"Well, I wespect Wharton's judgment," remarked D'Arcy. "But I must weally wemark that I considah him offside this time."

"I must say he doesn't look much of a ripper," said Tom. "But Wharton wouldn't plant a dud on us. As he's going to be a St. Jim's chap, I'd rather have him in the team than any other fellow."

"Yaas, but——"

"So he's playing," said Tom. "Now, we'd better get ready."

The St. Jim's fellows got ready, but there were a good many doubts as to how the new recruit would turn out. As Jack Blake remarked, if Wally Bunter was a topping footballer, it was another proof that appearances were deceptive—very deceptive indeed.

THE NINTH CHAPTER.
Wally's Chance!

"BILLY, old chap!" exclaimed Wally Bunter breathlessly, catching his cousin by the shoulder.

"Yaroooh!"

"Billy——"

"What the thump are you grabbing at a chap for?" demanded Billy Bunter wrathfully. "You made me jump!"

"Sorry, but——"

"I may as well tell you plainly, Wally, that we don't want any of your office manners here!" said Bunter crushingly.

"Will you lend me——"

"No!"

"Lend me——"

"Certainly not. I'm surprised at your asking me, Wally, when you refused to lend me a quid only to-day. I——"

"Clobber!" yelled Wally.

"Eh?"

"I want some footer clobber, and

yours are the only ones at Greyfriars that would fit me!" gasped Wally.

Bunter sniffed.

"Mine wouldn't fit you," he answered. "You're fat, Wally!"

"Why, you ass——"

"I can't have a podgy chap like you bursting my clobber!" said Bunter, shaking his head.

Walter Bunter glared at him in almost speechless wrath. It was true that he was fat—fatter than he acknowledged to himself—but his cousin Billy could give him points in circumference. Bunter's clobber was certainly not likely to be too tight on Wally.

"Besides, what do you want footer clobber for?" said Bunter peevishly. "You're not playing. It's a match to-day, not practice."

"Merry's asked me to play for St. Jim's."

"Oh, don't be funny!"

"It's a fact, you ass!"

"Rot!" said Bunter emphatically. "You're making a mistake. I offered my services to Tom Merry, and he's mistaken you for me. That's what it is. It's me he wants, of course!"

"You—you—— Will you lend me your clobber?" gasped Wally.

"Certainly not! I shall want it myself if I'm playing for Tom Merry," answered the Owl.

"But you're not!" shrieked Wally. "I am!"

"Don't be an ass, Wally!"

Billy Bunter rolled away in search of Tom Merry, leaving Wally staring. He poked the St. Jim's skipper in the ribs, when he found him, in the objectionable way he had.

"I say, Merry, old fellow——"

"Hallo! Ready?" asked Tom, supposing that it was Wally.

"Yes. You want me?"

"I told you so, didn't I?" answered Tom.

"You spoke to my cousin by mistake," explained Bunter. "He's rather like me in some ways—not really much if you look at him closely. I'll get changed, then."

"Hold on!" exclaimed Tom Merry, noticing the fat junior's glasses, and remembering that Wally Bunter did not wear glasses. "Are you Billy or Wally?"

"Billy, of course!"

"Well, it's Wally I want."

"Oh, really, Merry——"

"Oh, here you are, fatty!" exclaimed Harry Wharton, hurrying up. "We want your footer clobber, Bunter. Wally's playing this afternoon."

"Don't interrupt me, Wharton, please! I'm speaking to Merry. Let's have this clear, Merry," said the Owl, with crushing dignity. "Do you, or do you not, want me to play for your team?"

"Not!" said Tom, not at all pleased by Bunter's manner, and not disposed to waste many words on the egregious fat junior.

"Oh, very well!" said Bunter loftily.

And he walked away. Wharton ran after him, and caught him by the shoulder.

"Get out your clobber for Wally, Bunter——"

"I decline to do anything of the sort, Wharton!"

"What?"

"I've been treated with gross incivility," said Bunter. "I've offered my services, and they've been refused. I wash my hands of the whole matter. I decline absolutely to have anything to do with it."

"You silly ass!" roared Wharton.

"That's enough!"

Billy Bunter turned on his heel, and was stalking away loftily, when he was suddenly spun back by a grasp on his fat ear. He halted, with a yell.

"Yooop! Leggo!"

"Your clobber's wanted, you fat owl!" said Wharton. "Wally would burst anything else at Greyfriars. Don't be a pig, Bunter. You hardly ever use the things yourself; and, anyway, they're wanted."

"Leggo!"

"Will you lend Wally your clobber, you fat rotter?" exclaimed Wharton angrily.

"No, I won't!"

"You—you worm!" said the captain of the Remove. "Well, if you won't lend them to him, I will!"

He started for the School House, calling to Walter Bunter to follow. Billy Bunter dashed after him in great wrath.

"Wharton, let my clobber alone! I tell you—— Yah!"

Ogilvy and Russell were coming along, and they chipped in. They took Bunter by his fat arms.

"Come for a walk, old gun!" said Ogilvy.

"Yah! I won't!"

"I think you will!" grinned the Scottish junior.

And Bunter did. With Ogilvy and Russell holding his arms he had no choice.

Meanwhile, Harry Wharton hurried the recruit indoors, and Billy Bunter's footer garb was routed out, and Wally changed into it. Bunter's consent had been asked, and, as it was not given, it had to be taken for granted. Certainly Wally couldn't play footer in a lounge jacket and trousers, and equally certain there was nothing but Bunter's things at Greyfriars that would be anything like a fit for him.

Plump as he was, Wally looked very fit in footer garb. Bunter's things, of course, were in the Greyfriars colours—blue and white—St. Jim's being red and white. But Wally's figure was a little too distinguished for him to be mistaken on the field.

He followed Wharton back to Little Side, and joined the footballers. Potter of the Fifth, who was referee, glanced at him.

"Bunter playing?" he ejaculated.

"Bunter's cousin," explained Wharton, with a smile.

"Oh, I see! This is an entertainment, I suppose?" remarked Potter.

"Wait and see!" said Harry.

Tom Merry looked Wally over critically. When the teams lined up Wally was put in the front line, at outside-right, Talbot falling back to the half-back line, where he was a good man—as he was anywhere. Wally being accustomed to forward play, the St. Jim's skipper wisely put him where he was likeliest to do his best, though perhaps he had some lingering doubts.

The whistle had gone when Billy Bunter arrived on the ground, Ogilvy having refused to let him escape till he heard the whistle. The Owl of the Remove blinked in great wrath at his cousin in the St. Jim's ranks.

"Cheek!" he gasped. "Cheek!"

"Hallo! What's biting you?" asked Skinner, who was lounging by the ropes with Snoop.

"He's got my clobber on!" snorted Bunter. "I refused to allow it, you know!"

"Well, you always were a pig!" was Skinner's comment.

"I offered my services——"

"Ha, ha, ha!" roared Skinner.

"Blessed if I see anything to cackle at! I offered my services——"

"Oh, don't be so funny, Bunty!"

"Br-r-r-r!"

"Hallo, there they go!" said Bolsover major. "St. Jim's are getting through! Why, that fat barrel rolls along like thunder! How the thump does he carry all that weight with him?"

"Yes, he is fat, isn't he?" said the Owl disparagingly.

"I should say so; jolly nearly as fat as you, Bunter!"

"Oh, really, Bolsover——"

"Jolly nearly as fat, but not nearly such a clumsy ass!" continued Bolsover major. "He knows how to play footer."

Billy Bunter snorted.

He did not feel inclined to watch the match and the exploits of his cousin Wally; and he rolled away, remembering that he had not yet sent the ten-shilling note to Mr. Hawke. He rolled away with the intention of sending it at once; but he passed the school shop en route.

There he paused.

The previous day Jerry Hawke had terrified him, but Bunter's mind never retained an impression for long. Out of sight was out of mind with William George Bunter. Mr. Hawke was not there, and the tuckshop was. After a struggle in his mind Billy Bunter resolved to risk it with Jerry Hawke, and he rolled into Mrs. Mimble's shop.

There he made a persistent raid on unrationed things, seated on a stool at the counter, and enjoying himself, recklessly putting off all consideration of the consequences, as he usually did.

The ten-shilling note was deposited in Mrs. Mimble's till, and ten shillings' worth of indigestible things were deposited inside Willam George Bunter, and he was looking very shiny and sticky when he rolled off the stool and waddled out of the tuckshop. It was, perhaps, fortunate for Bunter that Mrs. Mimble's goods were sold at war-prices, otherwise he would have consumed a quantity that might have had serious results for his overtaxed internal organs. As it was, he was feeling rather uncomfortable when he departed.

He heard, without heeding, a roar from the football-ground.

"Goal!"

"Bravo, Bunter!"

The Owl of the Remove rolled away, his inner Bunter satisfied for once; but, now that the money was gone, he was thinking of Mr. Jerry Hawke again. What would the sharper do? he wondered. It was not a happy afternoon for Bunter.

THE TENTH CHAPTER.

Bravo, Bunter!

"GOAL!"

There was as much surprise as appreciation in the shout that rang round Little Side.

It was the first goal in the match, and it had fallen to Walter Bunter for St. Jim's.

Hazeldene, in goal, had grinned when the fat forward bore down on him; but he ceased to grin when he missed the ball by inches and it found a lodgement in the net.

"Goal!"

"Well kicked, porpoise!"

"Bravo, Bunter!"

"Bai Jove!" ejaculated Arthur Augustus D'Arcy. "That was weally a wippin' goal, deah boy. Was it a fluke?"

Wally looked at him.

"No," he said. "It wasn't a fluke."

"Then I congwatulate you, deah boy," said Arthur Augustus cordially. "It was weally wippin'. I could not have beaten that myself."

"Couldn't even have come near it!" remarked Figgins.

"Weally, Figgay——"

"Good man!" said Tom Merry, clapping Wally on the shoulder. "That was first-rate! You'll be playing a lot of footer at St. Jim's, kid, if you keep on like this."

Wally smiled with satisfaction. All Tom Merry's doubts were gone now; he had a good man in the team, and he knew it. Wally was worth his weight in gold, and Tom no longer regretted the mishap which had landed Manners at Lexham for the afternoon. For it was pretty plain that Wally Bunter was a better man in the forward line than Manners. And as Wally was, at all events, going to be a St. Jim's fellow in a short time, he had a right to play for the school. It was ever so much more satisfactory for that goal to have been taken by a St. Jim's fellow than by a recruit lent by Greyfriars.

The footballers lined up again, the Greyfriars players eyeing Wally a good deal. He was plainly a man to be marked. Wharton, in suggesting him to fill the vacancy in Tom Merry's team, had only been thinking of doing his best for the visiting skipper and for the game generally. It had not occurred to him that he was, in point of fact, putting a rod in pickle for the Remove. But it was very clear now that the Remove champions would have to look out for Wally.

As for Wally, he was enjoying himself thoroughly, and playing the game of his life.

The game went on, the next goal falling to Harry Wharton, which made the score level just on half-time.

Both teams were glad when the whistle went; the first half had been gruelling, and they were glad of a rest. Temple of the Fourth strolled on to the field while the footballers were resting.

"You chaps are catching a train back, I suppose?" he remarked to Tom Merry.

"Yes, naturally," answered Tom, surprised by the question.

Temple grinned.

"Then I'm afraid you'll get left!" he said.

"How do you mean?"

"I've just been to the station; no trains running since three o'clock," said Temple. "There's a railway strike on. No more trains to-day."

"Phew!"

"Bai Jove! That is wathah awkward!" remarked Arthur Augustus D'Arcy. "If that is cowwect, we are wathah stwanded."

"Correct enough," said Temple. "You were lucky to get here; yours was the last train through. Don't worry; we can put you up at Greyfriars."

The St. Jim's fellows looked rather serious, however. They were many long miles from home, and there was no means of return excepting the railway.

"Weally, I do not appwove of these stwikes," remarked Arthur Augustus D'Arcy thoughtfully. "The mattah becomes sewious when it lands a footah team fah fwom home like this."

"All serene!" said Wharton cheerily. "You can send a wire to St. Jim's, and we can put you up easily enough. We'll whack you out among the junior dorms. I'll speak to Mr. Quelch about it after the match."

"You'll get out of morning lessons tomorrow," remarked Bob Cherry, with a grin.

"Bai Jove! That is vewy twue. Aftah all, I dare say the stwikahs have their gwievances, you know."

"Ha, ha, ha!"

"Hallo, hallo, hallo! There goes the hooter!"

The footballers lined up again, dismissing from their minds for the present the problem of the homeward journey.

That was a matter that could be considered afterwards, for the present the play was the thing.

The game was very fast in the second half. There were narrow escapes on both sides, but no goals came along for some time; on either side the defence was sound.

Fatty Wynn, in the St. Jim's goal, was very hard to beat; and though Hazeldene in the Remove fortress was not so good a man as the St. Jim's goalie, there was a very powerful defence in Johnny Bull and Mark Linley at back.

The goal, when it came, came to Squiff for Greyfriars, and there was a loud cheer from the crowd round the ropes.

"Two to one!" shouted Bolsover major. "Our game!"

But Bolsover major was counting the chickens a little too early for Greyfriars, for within five minutes the ball was in the home net, put there by Arthur Augustus D'Arcy, who, with all his elegant manners and customs, was evidently a valuable man in the front line.

Blake slapped him on the back with a slap that made the swell of St. Jim's yell.

"Good man, Gussy!" said Blake heartily. "I'm jolly glad now that I didn't leave you chained up at home!"

"Gwoogh! You uttah ass!" gasped Arthur Augustus.

"Two all!" said Bolsover major, with an air of great wisdom. "Anybody's game."

"What a prophet you are, old scout!" said Ogilvy. "You'll get it right on the nail in the long run, if you keep on."

"Ten minutes to go!" said Russell. "There they go again! I say, that fat chap is as fresh as paint! How does he do it? He must weigh a ton, at least!"

"Not much like his cousin Billy, the way he moves!" grinned Wibley.

"Bravo, Bunter!"

Wally was going strong, but he was robbed of the ball, and Vernon-Smith bore it away towards the enemy's goal. But Lowther neatly tipped it away from the Bounder's foot and centred to Tom Merry, who rushed it on. Tom's run up the field left his comrades behind, and he looked like getting through, but he was well tackled in time. He gave a hasty glance, and found a fat figure ready to take a pass, and let Wally have it.

A Greyfriars forward was shouldered away, and Wally fairly wound round a half with the ball at his feet. He rushed for goal, and Hazeldene, between the posts, was all eyes and hands.

Whiz!

The ball came in before Johnny Bull or Mark Linley had a chance at the enterprising recruit of St. Jim's.

Out it came, fisted by Hazel, only to meet a plump head and to bound back into the net like a pip from an orange.

The next instant Wally was staggering away from Johnny Bull, but a roar was rising round the field.

"Goal!"

"Good man! Goal!"

Hazel had had no chance; before he knew the ball was coming back it was in the net.

He blinked at it.

"Goal!" gasped Tom Merry.

"Yaas, wathah! Huwwah!"

"Well done, fatty!"

Wally Bunter sat up breathlessly. Johnny Bull, with a grin, gave him a hand to his feet.

"Not hurt, old scout?" asked Johnny genially.

"Ow! No!" gasped Wally.

"Goal!"

"Two minutes to go, deah boys!" remarked Arthur Augustus D'Arcy to his comrades. "I wathah think this is our game—what?"

"I rather think so, Gustavus!" grinned Blake.

And Hurree Jamset Ram Singh, who heard the remark, murmured that the ratherfulness was terrific.

"Three to two!" said Bolsover major, in his role of expert commentator and prophet. "Their game!"

And Bolsover major was right at last.

It was Tom Merry & Co.'s game; the last few minutes of play being without result.

Both teams were very nearly done when the final whistle went; it had been a hard and gruelling game. Wally Bunter looked as fresh as anyone, however. It was evident that he was as fit as he was fat.

"Awfully obliged to you, Wharton, for giving us that man!" said Tom Merry, laughing. "You've done us a good turn."

Harry Wharton smiled rather ruefully.

"Yaas, wathah!" chuckled Arthur Augustus D'Arcy. "It was a wod in pickle for yourself, deah boy. Buntah, old gun, I congwatulate you; you have done a gweat deal towards winnin' this game."

"Thanks!" said Wally.

"And you'll be playing for St. Jim's when you get there," said Tom Merry heartily. "I shall look you up as soon as you arrive, you can rely on that. You're a good man! Shoulder-high, you fellows!"

"Yaas, wathah!"

"Oh—I say——" gasped Wally.

But in spite of his modest expostulations the new recruit was swung up on the shoulders of the footballers—not a very easy task, as they soon found—and marched shoulder-high off the field.

Billy Bunter arrived on the scene in time to witness that triumphal march of his cousin.

He blinked at the scene in astonishment.

"What the thump is that game, Skinner?" he asked.

"Fathead! He's won the match for St. Jim's!" said Skinner.

"Oh, crumbs!"

"Give him a cheer!" grinned Skinner. "He's helped to take Wharton's lot down a peg."

And the charitable Skinner cheered.

Billy Bunter swelled visibly. Wally having distinguished himself, Billy was not slow to spread himself, as it were, in the reflected glory of his cousin.

"Well, I expected as much!" he said calmly. "We're all tremendous footballers, we Bunters, you know—we're a footballing family——"

"Ha, ha, ha!"

Bunter sniffed at Skinner, and rolled away to join the footballers.

"I say, you fellows——"

"Hallo, hallo, hallo! It's a pity Tom Merry didn't play you instead of your cousin," said Bob Cherry. "It would have made a better figure for us in our footer record if he had!"

"Oh, really, Cherry! I'm not at all surprised—Wally's nearly as good a footballer as I am," said Bunter. "Not quite, of course——"

"Ha, ha, ha!"

Wally Bunter found that he was quite as popular with the Co. after helping to inflict a defeat upon the Remove team; and he was popular, too, with the St. Jim's footballers. They knew a good man when they saw one; and Wally undoubtedly was one of the best.

After changing there was inquiry as to the accuracy of the information Cecil Temple had brought; and it turned out to be correct. It was rather a peculiar position for the St. Jim's team. They had come to Greyfriars to play an afternoon's match, and they found themselves stranded there—for the night, at least.

The Head was informed of the circumstances, and he at once extended the hospitality of Greyfriars to the stranded footballers. It was arranged for them to be whacked out among the junior dormitories—though the Head did not express it in those terms; and a telegram was despatched to St. Jim's in explanation.

There was quite a crowd in the junior Common-room that night, and all the St. Jim's fellows were made very comfortable—excepting, perhaps, Arthur Augustus D'Arcy, who was kept very busy in dodging his old pal Bunter.

Even Billy Bunter realised at last that, somehow or another, the fascination of his society was lost upon the noble Gussy; though he could not understand it.

And it was very irritating to him to observe that Gussy was, on the other hand, quite friendly and cordial to Wally—his poor relation!—a mere nobody, whose only importance was the fact that he was Bunter's cousin—at least, from the Owl's point of view. And the Remove fellows were equally cordial to him.

It was surprising, and it was irritating.

"Pushing bounder!" said Bunter, to himself, in great disdain. "Blessed pushing bounder! I jolly well wish he was staying at Greyfriars instead of me! Even Toddy's civil to him, and he's never civil to me! Even Mauly takes notice of him, and he walks away when I speak to him! Blessed if I can understand it—a beastly, pushing, poor relation! Simply a nobody! If they like him so much, I jolly well wish they could have him, and I could go to St. Jim's instead!"

Bunter gave a fat sigh at the thought of that.

"How jolly nice it would be!" he murmured. "I'd like to go no end. I should be along with my pal Gussy, and—and I shouldn't see that awful beast Hawke again, and—and—— Some fellows have all the luck! I—I wish——"

Bunter paused, and his little round eyes gleamed behind his spectacles. A strange idea—a startling idea—had come into his fat brain—an idea so startling and so attractive that it made him jump.

"My hat! If it could be worked——"

"Hallo, hallo, hallo! What are you mumbling about?" asked Bob Cherry genially.

"Rats!" said Bunter.

He rolled away without explaining what he had been mumbling about. But that strange and startling idea was still in his mind, and the more he thought over it the more he liked it: and consequences were to follow. But what that idea was, and what came of it, is another story.

(Don't miss "BILLY BUNTER'S GREAT WHEEZE!"—next Monday's grand complete story of Harry Wharton & Co., by Frank Richards.)

THE GREYFRIARS GALLERY.

No. 100.—PHILIPPA and PHILIP DERWENT.

LADIES first, you know. Perhaps Flip matters rather more to the stories than Flap, but that is only because they are primarily boys' stories, and naturally the girls cannot play such big parts in them as the boys.

To the many readers who have made a favourite of Flip, I fancy Flap is equally dear. They are very much alike, the twins. Flap has a good deal of Flip's pluck, and he has a good deal of her kindness. Possibly she has more common-sense than her brother. Certainly she is less inclined to be cocksure. But they are very much alike. Flap would make a better boy than Flip would make a girl; but, when you come to think of it, that would be true of many nice girls. It is not, as a rule, the really nice boy whom one could even imagine as a girl.

When this series was started the twins were unknown to readers of the MAGNET and the "Gem." As a matter of fact, people who only read this paper probably don't know very much about them even now. But I know that most MAGNET readers are keen on the "Gem" also, and followed the "Twins from Tasmania" during the twelve months in which it ran its course in that paper. And in several stories here the two have appeared—Flip, in fact, has played quite a big part in the last two.

"The Twins from Tasmania" began with the coming of Flap to Cliff House and of Flip to Highcliffe. On the journey they met with Johnny Goggs, who seems to have achieved immense popularity with some of the nuts of Highcliffe, and with some of the Greyfriars fellows. Cocky was with them. Cocky ought to have been in the picture which is inset. I don't know why the artist left him out, but I suppose it was really my fault for not saying that he was to be put in. And it was through Cocky that Flip quarrelled and fought with Gadsby, a quarrel out of which most of the story sprang. For while Ponsonby, attracted by the bright eyes of Flap, became in a sort Flip's friend, Gadsby was always at heart his bitter enemy.

The accidents of that day caused Flip to throw in his lot, more or less, with the nuts, though he was never really one of them in spirit. In an ordinary way he would naturally have taken his place among the supporters of Frank Courtenay. He was never up against Courtenay, however, and his frank, genial nature made the fellows who detested Pon & Co. like him. His close friendship with Merton and Tunstall, too, prevented his having so much to do with the Ponsonby clique, for those two never stood very close to Pon.

I am not going to tell the whole of the story over again—the great Greyfriars v. Highcliffe fight on the seashore, the falling-out with Hazeldene, the kidnapping of Cocky, the pursuit of Flap by Pon, the fight between Pon and Merton, the departure for a time of Merton, threatened with blindness, and Tunstall, both feeling very sore with Flip; the shady devices of Gadsby and Vavasour to keep him at odds with them, the plot of the nuts to make Flip one of them in deed as well as in name, the baser plot of Gadsby to get him into heavy trouble, his bolt, his meeting with Hazeldene, who had run away from Greyfriars at the same time, their wanderings together; the coming of Goggs to Highcliffe, and his discovery of Gadsby's plot, the end of the wanderings at St. Jim's; the pleading with the Head of Highcliffe that Flip should not be sacked, and his return after all in something very like triumph. If you remember these things you have the main outlines of the story, and that is all that is needed.

I must refer, however, to the strong bond of sympathy between the twins, which made Flap know when Flip was in danger or trouble. This is no wild invention, as a few of my readers were disposed to fancy. There have been many such instances, proven beyond all doubt. I don't pretend to explain the bond; physiology and psychology both come into that, and we have no use here for too much of those sciences.

Flip Derwent is not presented to you as a perfect character. Compare him with Frank Courtenay or Harry Wharton, and you will easily see defects in him. And, of course, neither Courtenay nor Wharton is absolute perfection; if he were, he would be less interesting.

There is more recklessness, less balance in Flip than in those two. He has a better conceit of himself, with smaller reason for it. But he is as straight and honourable as they, and every bit as plucky.

It may occur to some thoughtful readers that Flip at the end of "The Twins from Tasmania" is rather a different fellow from Flip at the beginning of the story. So he is. But it would be strange if he were not.

For he has been through the testing-fires, and has come out of them purged of much dross. Never before in his life had he had to face anything like the varied troubles of those journeyings of his with Hazeldene. He had shown before they had began that he knew how to forgive an injury, for Hazel had plotted against him, had been an enemy without cause. But to forgive something done by a fellow you see only once in a way is one thing; to go on putting it behind you, to treat that fellow with unfailing patience and kindness, to set your strength to buttress his weakness, never to let the past rankle in you, this is another, a far bigger thing. There is some of the true stuff of greatness in him who can do it.

Perhaps Flap has changed a little also. She has had no such troubles of her own as Flip has had. But are not his troubles always hers? And there may have been something else to make her feel a trifle older. Boy and girl love affairs do not, as a rule, mean much. But the feeling between Philippa Derwent and that queer, plain, eminently capable genius, Johnny Goggs, is at once something less and something more than a love affair. It is not that, because he has never made love to her; it is more than that because he knows, and she knows, that there is no one else in the world that counts for him as she does, because there is nothing he would not do for her or for anyone dear to her.

Flip and Flap are Australians. That does not matter a great deal. Australians are very like Britons—with a difference. I could tell you quite a lot about the lovely island they come from, had I but space. In ever so many ways Tasmania is one of the best spots on the earth. But there is not space.

No doubt we shall hear much more of these two in the future. Perhaps there may be a Cliff House or another Highcliffe serial before long.

Extracts from "THE GREYFRIARS HERALD" and "TOM MERRY'S WEEKLY."

TOWSER'S GUILT!

By ROBERT ARTHUR DIGBY.

I.

"HOW absolutely wippin'!" exclaimed D'Arcy, in a delighted voice, as he unfolded a superb handkerchief of Chinese silk.

"Where on earth did you get that awful-looking thing?" I asked, with a grin. But it's no use trying to pull Gussy's leg; he is always so dead serious about everything.

"It's weal Chinese silk, and it's come stwaight fwom China!" Gussy replied, with some heat.

"What's it for?" Blake broke in. "Surely you're not going to use that thing for a hanky?"

"It's weally an ornament—an etcetewa," Arthur Augustus explained. "Just to give one a finishin' touch to the coat, don'tcher-know! My uncle, who is twavellin' in China, has sent it along."

"Oh, put it away! It'll make Towser bilious," said Herries irritably. "It's a pity your uncle couldn't find something a trifle less girlish to send you! You're bad enough already, goodness knows!"

"Weally, Hewwies, I considah you are most wude! You haven't looked at my pwesent pwopahly, or you would appweciate its beauty!"

And D'Arcy folded up letter and handkerchief, and withdrew his noble person in stately ire from the room.

"Silly ass!" growled Herries, as Arthur Augustus departed.

"But Gussy's a very decent old ass, all the same," said Blake; "and if it suits him to look like a patchwork quilt we shall have to make the best of it!"

It can't be denied that Gussy's dress is a bit extreme at times, and some of his colour schemes rather get on our nerves. At the same time, we are all very fond of Gussy, and we go to quite a lot of trouble in trying to curb his tendency to brilliant colouring—trouble which Arthur Augustus doesn't always appreciate.

"Has anybody seen Gussy?" Blake asked the next day, as we were about to set off for a sharp walk into Rylcombe to get some special tuck for tea.

"He can't make up his mind which tie to wear, or his socks don't match his waistcoat, or some such rot!" said Herries sarcastically.

"Weally, Hewwies, deah boy, you do me an injustice!" exclaimed D'Arcy, coming into the study at that moment. "I have been looking for that handkahchief which my uncle sent me. Have any of you seen it about? I am afwaid I must have dwopped it somewhere."

"I shouldn't give it to you if I did find it!" Herries remarked bluntly. "I'm not at all keen on going about with a fellow dressed up like a Christmas rabbit!"

"You are extwemely wude, Hewwies, and I would wathah not come with you to Wylcombe!"

"Oh, come along, and don't be a fathead!" said Blake, catching hold of his arm. "We sha'n't get back by tea-time. We'll all help you to look for your hanky when we get back."

Towser followed us out of the study.

"Going to bring him, too?" I asked.

"Well, why not? He isn't hurting you, is he?" snapped Herries.

"I don't care whether you bring him or not. I was only thinking that the roads are rather dangerous for a dog now that the evenings are so dark," I replied.

However, when we got to the gate, Herries altered his mind about taking Towser.

"Go back, old man!" he said, patting Towser's head and turning him into the gate. "We'll soon be back, and I'll bring you a special cake for tea."

Towser gave a low growl of disgust, but trotted obediently into the quad.

Shortly after Blake & Co. had left Study No. 6 Wally D'Arcy knocked at the door, and, getting no reply, turned the handle and went in, his miscellaneous hound Pongo trotting at his heels.

"It's a good thing for you, my son, that Towser isn't here," he remarked to the dog.

He struck a match, and borrowed the sugar for which he had come in search, leaving an I O U pinned on to the bag. Lady Eastwood had included them half a pound each in their Christmas parcel.

"Got the sugar? Good egg!" exclaimed Levison minor, when Wally returned from his expedition to the Fourth Form passage. "Hallo! Where's Pongo?" he added.

"I thought he was with me," said Wally, looking round. "Don't bother about him. He'll be all right."

Before tea was over the dog's feet were heard pattering along the passage.

"What have you been up to?" D'Arcy minor exclaimed, as Pongo slunk in, and, with a furtive look at his master, crept under the desk.

Of course, Pongo hadn't any more right in the Third Form-room than Towser had in the Fourth studies, and if Mr. Selby had seen him there would have been ructions.

"Nothing particularly good, I should imagine, by his guilty look," laughed Frank Levison.

II.

"HALLO! Who's been in here and left the door open?" Blake exclaimed. "Here's Towser back, too!"

"It looks like your minor, Gussy," Herries commented, as he opened the cupboard door and saw Wally's I O U pinned to the sugar-bag.

"The young wuffian!" said Arthur Augustus. "I shall be weally cwoss with him if he takes my sugah again. "Bai Jove! What's that bwute got undah the table?"

"Who are you calling a brute?" Herries inquired angrily. "Just you be civil to Towsy!"

"Look what he has got, you uttah ass!" said D'Arcy frenziedly.

"Why, it's your hanky!" Jack Blake said, stooping down to pick it up from where it was lying beside the bulldog.

And then the whole horrible truth burst upon us. The handkerchief had been torn into shreds, and the scrap which Blake held up for us to see was chewed and damp and worthless.

For a moment we thought Gussy would hurl himself upon Towser; and the dog growled ominously as Arthur Augustus glared at him through his monocle.

"The bwute ought to be kept in his pwopah place!" said Gussy angrily.

"Brrrrr! Keep cool!" returned Herries. "How do you know that Towser did it? And what does a rotten old rag like that matter, anyway?"

"You can get another at the Sixpenny-ha'penny Bazaar!" said Blake, with a laugh.

"Or a 'Peace' flag would be just as effective," I suggested, "or a nice new school duster—one of the pink ones!"

"Ha, ha, ha!"

"You uttah wottahs! I don't believe you are even sowwy!"

"Never mind, old bean!" Blake said, with a grin. "These little things are sent to try us."

"Thank you, Blake! But I pwefer to be without your condolences!" Arthur Augustus returned, with dignity.

"I warn you, Hewwies," he continued. "If I catch that bwute of yours touchin' anythin' else of mine I shall give him a feahful thwashin'!"

"Hard luck on Towser!" laughed Herries. "Be careful that he doesn't hurt your 'twousahs'."

"I wefuse to talk to any of you! I am vewy disappointed in my fwiends!"

"Oh, buck up, Gussy!" said Blake cheerfully. "Come and help me to get tea."

"I do not wish for any tea, thank you, Blake!" D'Arcy replied icily. "I shall do my pwepawation in Julian's studay."

"Brrrr! Don't be a fathead!" Herries called after him.

But Arthur Augustus had already entered Study No. 5, and closed the door gently but firmly behind him.

In spite of what Herries said about there being no evidence, circumstances looked very black against Towser.

"Julian, deah boy!"

The occupants of No. 5 were quite aware of the presence of their noble visitor, but they had not yet bothered to notice him officially.

"Buzz off, Gussy! We're busy now!" said Julian, without turning round.

"Kewwuish, deah boy, I would like to do my pwepawation in this study."

"Would you?" Julian broke in. "Then the answer is in the negative. Anyway, why are we given this honour?"

"Julian, I am afwaid you are twyin' to be wude!" said Gussy sorrowfully.

"I'm not trying to be rude; I'm trying to get the tea, if you must know! Why don't you go and have yours?" said Julian, a trifle impatiently.

"I would wathah not go into Studay No. 6. They have been tewwibly wude to me. Pewwaps they did not mean to hurt my feelin's, but I would pwefer to stay here," D'Arcy explained.

"Oh, let 'im stay!" Hammond urged. "There's plenty to eat, and there are all those eggs the mater sent me. 'E may as well——"

"Weally! Pway don't twouble about tea for me, Hammond," Gussy interrupted. "I weally only want to do my pwepawation in this studay."

"Dry up, you silly old duffer!" said Kerruish. "Of course you'll have some tea, and afterwards we'll see if we can do anything to mend the rift in the lute."

"Who's been rude to you, Gussy?" Hammond asked, when tea had been cleared away, and the four chums had hospitably made room for their visitor.

"I would wathah not discuss the mattah," said D'Arcy solemnly. "I am tewwibly disappointed in my fwiends, but it is wathah bad form to discuss their failin's when they are not pwesent, don't you think?"

And from this somewhat quixotic standpoint Gussy would not budge.

A little while later Julian made an opportunity of visiting the chums in No. 6.

"What have you done to Gussy?" he asked. "It must be something pretty bad, I should fancy, as he refuses to discuss the matter with anyone."

"It's nothing at all," said Blake. "The fact of the matter is that when we came back from Rylcombe Gussy found that new atrocity he calls a handkerchief, torn to ribbons, lying on the floor beside Towser."

"Had Towser been chewing it, then?" Julian asked.

"Well, that's the point," said Herries. "Judged by circumstantial evidence, the case looks dead against him. But on the other hand, Towser isn't a destructive dog at all, but——"

"Oh, isn't he?" interrupted Blake.

"Ha, ha, ha!" we laughed feelingly. "We had all suffered.

"Shut up, you fatheads! As I was saying, for one thing, he wouldn't do it; and, besides, nobody actually saw him do it."

"Another funny thing about it is that we can only find a part of the hanky," said Blake. "We have never noticed that Towser

Printed and published weekly by the Proprietors at The Fleetway House, Farringdon Street, London, E.C. 4, England. Subscription, 8s. 10d. per annum. Agents for Australasia: Gordon & Gotch, Melbourne, Sydney, Adelaide, Brisbane, and Wellington, N.Z. South Africa: The Central News Agency, Ltd., Cape Town and Johannesburg. Saturday, January 4th, 1919.

had a taste for Chinese silk. But if he didn't eat it, where is it?"

"There is more in this than meets the eye," said Herries, with firm conviction. "And I don't believe old Towser had anything at all to do with it. Did you, old man?"—giving the dog's big, fierce-looking head an affectionate pat.

Towser plainly understood what was going on, and gave a little, whimpering, short growl, which Herries immediately interpreted as "No."

"There you are! What did I say?" he demanded. "He said 'No' as plainly as I could."

We laughed. Herries is rather apt to romance a bit where Towser is concerned; but certainly there was no positive proof that his bulldog was the culprit.

"Why don't you make it up with poor old Gussy?" Julian suggested. "He's in our study now doing his prep, and looking as miserable as his noble countenance and his monocle will allow him to look."

"We're quite willing to be friendly, but he isn't having any," I explained. "He has refused to come in here, so what are we to do?"

"If the mountain won't come to Mahomet, Mahomet must go to the mountain," Julian remarked. "You come into No. 5 with me, Blake, and try and persuade old Gustavus to come back here."

Blake went willingly enough, but Gussy wouldn't listen to him.

"I appweciate your kind thought in comin', Blake," he said. "I am not angwy, but I am vewy sowwy and disappointed, and pwefer to wemain here. I weally feel that I cannot talk to Hewwies as one gentleman should talk to anothah, and I would theahfoah wathah not come."

"Right-ho, old bean!" Blake said cheerily. "Only don't say we didn't ask you."

Arthur Augustus returned to Study No. 6 the next day, but the situation was very strained. He was, of course, studiously polite—it wouldn't have been D'Arcy if he had been otherwise—but apart from an occasional "Yes" or "No" he sat quietly by himself, and went about his business as though there had been nobody else in the room.

We had just started tea on the following evening when, with a terrific bang at the door, Baggy Trimble burst in upon us, his fat face shining with excitement.

"I say, you fellows, you've got kippers! I say, I've something very important to tell you!"

"Brrrr! Get out! We don't want any second-hand news here," said Herries, seizing Baggy by the shoulders to throw him out.

"D'Arcy," he yelled, "it's about your handkerchief! Lemme go, Herries!"

"Pewwaps we had bettah heah what Twimble has to say, Hewwies," Arthur Augustus said sedately.

"Lemme go! I won't say anything until Herries let's me go! Lemme go, can't you!"

Herries jerked him violently round.

"Now, let's have it! If your precious news is worth it, we'll give you the odd kipper and some tea; and if it isn't, you'll be jolly well bumped!"

"Just give me a cup of tea first, Herries!" Baggy gasped. "I've run all the way, and I can't talk until I've had some tea!"

"Oh, give the bounder some tea, for goodness' sake, and let's hear what he's got to say!" Herries said irritably.

After this slight refreshment Baggy got away with his story.

He had been passing when Taggles was cleaning out Pongo's kennel, and right at the back Taggles had found a piece of silk.

"I wonder where the tike got this?" Taggles had remarked.

Baggy had asked for and obtained the scrap of silk, and he now triumphantly exhibited it in our study.

"Gweat Scott!" D'Arcy gasped. "It's the west of my Chinese handkerchief! Are you suah it was found in Pongo's kennel, Twimble?"

"Certain!" said Baggy, vastly pleased with the sensation he had caused. "I was standing there when Taggles found it."

Jack Blake turned to me with a solemn face.

"Would you mind fetching Wally D'Arcy, Dig, old man?" he said.

When I came back with Wally in tow, Baggy was happily engaged in finishing off the kipper and generally clearing up things. As we had only just started tea, it was an opportunity in a thousand for Baggy.

"Wally," said D'Arcy major, in his most impressive tones, "Twimble has found the wemaindah of my Chinese handkahchief! Do you know anything about it?"

Wally looked at him in a perplexed sort of way.

"No! I don't know anything about it. I should have told you if I had known," he said.

"The fact of the matter is," explained Blake, "Baggy saw Taggles find this bit of Gussy's hanky in Pongo's kennel."

"Was Pongo with you when you came to borrow that sugar yesterday afternoon?" I asked, with a sudden inspiration.

Wally considered a minute.

"Y-e-s," he said slowly. "I remember now, he did come in with me, but when I got back I couldn't find the little beggar."

"Well, it's prefectly clear to me what happened," said Herries, anxious to clear Towser from blame. "Pongo evidently nosed around here, and found Gussy's handkerchief; spent a happy five minutes with it, and then, being disturbed or hearing Towser coming, bolted with it to his kennel—in his hurry leaving half of it under the table, where we found it."

Herries described what actually had happened, and when young D'Arcy remembered Pongo's guilty air he was convinced that his dog was the culprit.

"Herries, I'm awfully sorry old Towser was blamed!" he said impulsively. "I'd clean forgotten that Pongo came in here with me."

"That's all right!" Herries said shortly. "Keep an eye on the beggar, and see that he doesn't get into any more mischief."

"I'm sowwy I so misjudged my fwiends," Gussy said contritely; "and I'm vewy sowwy I annoyed Hewwies about Towser. Pway forgive me!" Arthur Augustus ended appealingly.

"There's nothing to forgive," Blake laughed. "After all, we pulled your leg about the hanky, and even now we can't restore that."

"Oh, wats to the hanky!" Gustavus replied. "I pwopose we have some tea now!"

THE END.

THE KINDNESS OF THE OWL.

By HARRY WHARTON.

I.

"CHEESE-CAKES!" muttered Billy Bunter. "Real cheese-cakes! Oh my!"

The porpoise stood with his fat face pressed against a pastrycook's window in Courtfield. He blinked longingly at the cheese-cakes. They looked very near to being the old original pre-war kind. The cheese-cakes seemed to taunt the hungry Owl.

He was roused by the sound of voices. Next door—it was a divided shop—was a plain, unadorned coal office, with samples of Wallsend and kitchen cobbles on exhibition.

A lady's high-pitched treble came from within:

"I call it a shame, Mr. Smeaks! I ordered the coal a month ago, and I must have it!"

"Very sorry, Mrs. Tompkins, but I have had difficulties at the wharf. I'll try and let you have some by the middle of the week."

Mrs. Tompkins gave a squeak, and Bunter turned his head, to see a lady in a black dress, with a fur coat which was far too small for her ample dimensions. She carried a string bag, which bulged with many purchases, including a paper bag which had burst, revealing buns. Bunter's eyes gleamed at the sight.

"Middle of next week!" she cried indignantly. "I can't wait! I'd give ten shillings for a sack of coals now! I've got Mr. Partlett coming to supper to-night, and he hates to have things cold!"

The coal-office man smiled in an exasperating way, and rubbed his hands.

"I am exceedingly distressed, madam," he said. "But it's the transport difficulty. We can't do anything without transport."

Mrs. Tompkins gave a snort, and made outspoken remarks about the Coal Controller. She was as red as a peony, and so agitated that as she bundled out of the shop she pretty nearly knocked down Billy Bunter.

"Get out of my way, little boy!" she said.

Bunter stared at her as if she were something in a museum.

"I——" he began. "I——" His ideas were shaping themselves slowly. Their pivot was the ten shillings which he had heard Mrs. Tompkins offer for a sack of coal. Bunter could do quite nicely with that half-quid.

"You said you wanted some coal."

"But you can't get any coal!" cried the lady. "You haven't any transport!"

"Oh, yes, I have!" said the Owl eagerly. "I've got lots—no end!"

He had no very clear notion what transport was; but a chap must risk something.

Mrs. Tompkins beamed upon him.

"If you can bring me a sack of coals from Messrs. Wells & Smith—I have paid for two tons, but a sack would do to go on with—you can have this, my little man," she said, extracting a crisp Bradbury from her purse. "And you shall stay to tea, too—a real good tea!"

Bunter's hand closed on the cash. The ample female smiled on him affably, and waddled off down the street. To Bunter she seemed a walking gold-mine.

Mrs. Tompkins turned the corner, and Bunter at once turned into the confectioner's shop to change his note, thinking a little of coal and a great deal of the banquet which awaited him if he could carry out the job for which he had already taken payment.

"I'd soon get the old coal if——" He had got thus far in his meditations as he sat perched on a high stool by the well-filled counter when a cart drew up at the door.

It was a small cart, behind a brown, unclipped pony, and the man who was driving it seemed to be a seller of wood logs for firing purposes. It was not much of a cart, but still, it was a cart, and it would carry a sack of coal and a butter-tub at a pinch.

It has been said that it is wiser to be born lucky than rich. Bunter crammed the rest of the cheese-cakes he had bought—if he had bought them—into his pockets, and descended from his stool in perspiring haste.

The personage who was vending Yule logs had left the cart and crossed the road to transact business of an important nature in a building with swing doors and a nice glass front, which displayed brewers' advertisements somewhat prominently.

Bunter gained the pavement. The pony looked as if he had ceased to take any special interest in life. The street was empty.

"If I just borrowed the cart and got the poor old lady her coals it wouldn't do any harm to anybody," said Bunter to Bunter. "A chap ought to do a kindness when he can!"

The porpoise clambered into the vehicle and grabbed the reins. It moved off. Bunter had been standing in the cart. He suddenly sat down. The pony stalked solemnly down the street, with Bunter tugging at the reins.

Now, what followed is not as clear as it might be; but one thing is pretty certain. Bunter asked his way to the coal-wharf, and by some means managed to wangle the handing over of a couple of sacks of coal. He had the address of Mrs. Tompkins all right, and he fancied he could get the load where it was wanted.

He was thinking so hard as he sat on the coal and let the pony go its own pace that he did not hear us shout to him.

We were Bob Cherry, Peter Todd, and myself.

"It is my one and only Bunter," said Peter Todd, as we pursued the cart. "Whither away, porpoise? This isn't the Lord Mayor's Show, you know."

"Laburnum Villa—two sacks," replied Bunter, taking a cheese-cake out of his right-hand pocket and cramming it into his mouth. "Go away!"

"Come out of that cart, you fat chump!" shouted Bob Cherry, seizing the Owl's arm. "You've stolen that cart, I know!"

"Also the coal!" said Peter Todd.

"Lemme go!" yelled Bunter, struggling in vain to keep his seat on the sack.

He rolled off into the bottom of the cart. The pony looked round to see what had happened, then stopped dead, apparently out of real kindness.

"I haven't stolen anything!" roared Bunter, as he rolled in the coal-dust. "Oh, really, Bob Cherry! Lemme gerrup!"

"You fat chump!" shouted Bob Cherry, climbing into the cart.

"I'm not!" shrieked Bunter. He tried to recover his footing, but slipped down once more, his head on one of the sacks. The cart had given a lurch owing to a side-step by the noble animal between the shafts. "I got the coal for a lady, and——"

"Stop, thief!" came from somewhere far behind.

"Bunter stole the cart!" cried Bob Cherry. "Look!"

He pointed to a man running down the street towards them, and yelling things as he ran.

"He isn't so fat as Bunter," said Toddy. "But Bunter can't come up to him in running or in language—and Bunter hadn't better try, either!"

"I only borrowed the cart, you fellows!" whimpered Bunter.

That explanation might have been good enough for some confiding people, but it did not appear likely it would satisfy the man who was racing after the cart, and getting even more picturesque in his language as he ran.

Bunter was desperate. A crowd had collected and a policeman loomed up like a thunder-cloud before it gets quite black.

Bunter scrambled up, his face as black as a sweep's, and grabbed at the reins. The pony backed all of a heap against the cart, and then shot forward.

Bunter was shot out of the cart, clutching wildly at everything as he went. He landed on the pony's back, and there he clung, his fat little legs embracing the quadruped and his hands grasping the harness.

"You young thieves!" screamed the fat man, as he came alongside.

"Oh, hang that yarn!" hooted Bob.

But Bob found it was no time for argument. He shook off the hand which had grabbed his collar, and tumbled into the cart, which was moving now as if it had been hitched on to a brisk locomotive.

The pony had fairly woke up. Enough to make it, with Bunter sticking to its back as if he had grown there.

Peter Todd and I jumped for safety, for there was a nasty look about the wood-merchant, and the crowd annoyed us.

"Help!" wailed Bunter, as the pony broke into a trot.

How could we help him? The cart was swaying from side to side; the stout chap with the purple face was dropping behind, and making up for lost way in language; and the crowd cheered and howled.

And if it had not been that Bunter was really making his way to Laburnum Villa, there would have been lots more trouble.

Just as Peter Todd caught sight of an excited lady standing on the footpath waving an umbrella at us there was a mighty crack, and the cart stopped dead—that is to say, the hind part did. It could not have been a really strong cart, for the front of it went along with Bunter and the pony, and the rest, with the coal, stayed with us.

The lady with the gamp proved to be Mrs. Tompkins.

She rushed up, and began to be really enthusiastic about the brave boy who had brought her coal. She seemed to take Peter Todd for Bunter at first, and was going to kiss him, but Toddy dodged. Then she told the policeman to put away his notebook, for it was quite all right. She was looking at the sacks as she said this.

The fat man, who seemed to own the cart—now a sectional affair—softened a lot when he saw a pound note or two.

Somehow, the pony soon got weary of Bunter's company. We sought poor Bunty, and found him groaning in a ditch, vowing he would never do any more kind actions. But the tea Mrs. Tompkins invited us all to pulled him round and bucked him up, and William was himself again!

He threw out hints that he really deserved a big reward for what he had done. But somehow, Mrs. Tompkins seemed disposed to transfer the credit to Toddy. I think she fell in love with Toddy's nose. It may have reminded her of Mr. Partlett's.

Anyway, I am jolly sure Partlett's supper wasn't any better than our tea. Mrs. T. may have her faults, but she isn't stingy!

THE END.

PLAYING THE MAN.

A Tale of the Cavaliers.

By DICK BROOKE.

Out of the house that was full of the foe young Gilbert stole into the night.
Was he too young to serve the cause? They had held him too young to fight.
But his chance had come now, and he clutched at his chance; and out of the house took flight.

The Cropears were there, in every room, with their psalms and their nasal twang.
They had raided the cellars, their horses' hoofs on the flags of the great hall rang.
They had captured Sir Hugh, and they vowed that by all the laws of war he must hang!

'Twas the foul red guilt of another they placed on the head of the good Sir Hugh.
Guilt there was none in that generous soul, to his God and his King most true,
As Captain Jonadab Smite-with-the-Sword, his old enemy, knew.

So out of the house young Gilbert stole, with naked steel in his hand,
With his young heart hot, but his young head cool—no braver lad in the land—
To ride for his father's life, to bring to the rescue Guy Vernon's command!

Full ten miles, and the roughest of miles, lay between them and him,
Darksome woods and brooding heaths, and a river full to the brim.
What did he reck? His purpose was set, and he and his grey could swim.

Into the gloom of the stable-yard he passed, with ready sword.
"Who goes there?" snuffled the Roundhead guard. Quick came the answering word:
"A foe!" In amazement stood the man; he could scarce believe what he heard.

Too astonished to shout, but not to fight, his blade and young Gilbert's clashed;
And Hezekiah Full-of-Grace, with a thrust through the heart, down crashed.
Young Gilbert had fleshed his maiden sword. Into the stable he dashed.

He saddled and bridled the gallant grey. His hands were steady and deft.
Softly he rode him out of the yard, and swung his head to the left,
Lest any might follow at once. To the right lay his path, through Clavering Cleft.

"Who goes there?" Again the challenge rang, and again he answered "A foe!"
And a bulky form took his point in the gloom as he leaned from his saddle-bow;
And another Roundhead lay dying there, for Gilbert's swift arm too slow.

He turned the head of Grey Gaunt to the right. For the Clavering Cleft he made.
Peril was there, as well he knew, but no peril could make him afraid.
For his father's life on the issue hung, and how should he be dismayed?

Two horsemen there in the Clavering Cleft, where the banks ran close and steep.
Grey Gaunt's hoofs padded the springy turf as he neared them; then a leap,
And rider and steed were between the two as they started like men from sleep.

The chase was hot over Ravening Moor; but Grey Gaunt travelled light.
And now the noise of pursuing hoofs died away through the darkling night.
And anon a ribbon of silver he saw as one moment the moon shone bright.

No spur the good grey needed; he plunged right over the brink.
To the boy's very armpits the water rose, ice-cold. It was swim or sink
For the gallant rider and gallant horse, with scarcely time to think.

A heave and a struggle—the grey's hoofs slipped on the bank—but strong was the hand
Of the boyish rider. He leapt from the saddle; he dragged Grey Gaunt to land.
Then for one moment, with heaving flanks, the good steed he let stand.

Up again in the saddle, and on he rode through the woods so dark,
And at long last to Somerton town, where Guy Vernon's troopers stark
Lifted him down, and patted his back, and brought wine for the brave young spark.

Welcome enough the wine and the praise to the lad; but well they knew—
Young Gilbert and gay Guy Vernon—there was yet to free Sir Hugh.
"Boot and saddle!" And into their ranks the war-worn troopers drew.

Hell for leather, through wood, o'er waste, they rode for Alliston Hall!
And young Gilbert rode by Guy Vernon's side at the head of the troopers tall,
To his father's rescue—to play the part of a man—like a man to fall!

The pity of it? Nay; that night was worth years of a common life!
True, he might have lived on to love some fair maid, to cherish a darling wife,
And rear brave sons of his own. But he passed in the heat of that stern, swift strife.

Passed with his boy's high heart aglow, not cold with age and dim.
They had thought the lad too young to fight. Never dream that death seemed grim.
He had played the man—he had saved his sire—what mattered death to him?

The Editor's Chat.

For Next Monday:

"BILLY BUNTER'S GREAT WHEEZE!"

By Frank Richards.

What is Billy Bunter's great wheeze?

I am not going to tell you that here. You must wait until next week—unless you are clever enough to guess something from various slight indications given in this week's fine yarn.

This series is, I do believe, the very finest Mr. Richards has ever written, and I am sure that it is going to be extraordinarily popular.

We have had the contrast between Billy and Wally Bunter before—the cousins so alike in face and figure, so unlike in their ways and their characters. But now we are going to have it in a new way, with——

Shush!

I came very near to letting it out then!

HURRAH!

I have good news for you this week—the very best of news!

THE "PENNY POPULAR" IS COMING OUT AGAIN SOON!

Very soon, indeed! The first number of the new series will be dated January 25th, and will, of course, be on sale before that day.

The price for the present will be three-halfpence, for we are not yet clear of war conditions, you know. But I don't think that will make much difference to any of you. The increase of price has not hurt any of the Companion Papers; they are too firmly established in the affections of their readers for that.

What a wail of despair there was when the "Penny Pop," as most of you call it—as we call it here—was closed down! Some letters almost threatening in tone were received. Some readers could not see at all why it should be the "Penny Pop" that was sacrificed that other papers might go on. But that was a matter of which they were naturally not the best judges

And what a shout of joy there will be when it is known that the "Penny Pop" is coming out again, with all the features which made it so popular—the Greyfriars yarn, the St. Jim's one, and that of Rookwood! For it is still to be the "All School Story Paper" that readers have shown so conclusively is the paper they really want.

Other attractions, too—very special ones! But about them you will learn more next week.

NOTICES.

Football Matches Wanted by—

BETHNAL GREEN—16½—play at Victoria Park.—A. Lawson, 21, Cranbrook Street, Green Street, Bethnal Green, E.

WALTHAMSTOW AND LEYTON CADETS—16-18.—L.-Cpl. Roberts, Drill Hall, Church Hill, Walthamstow, Essex.

YOUR EDITOR.

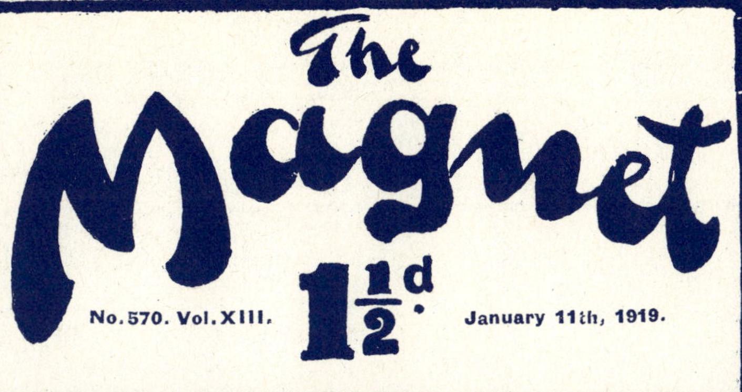

BILLY BUNTER'S WHEEZE!

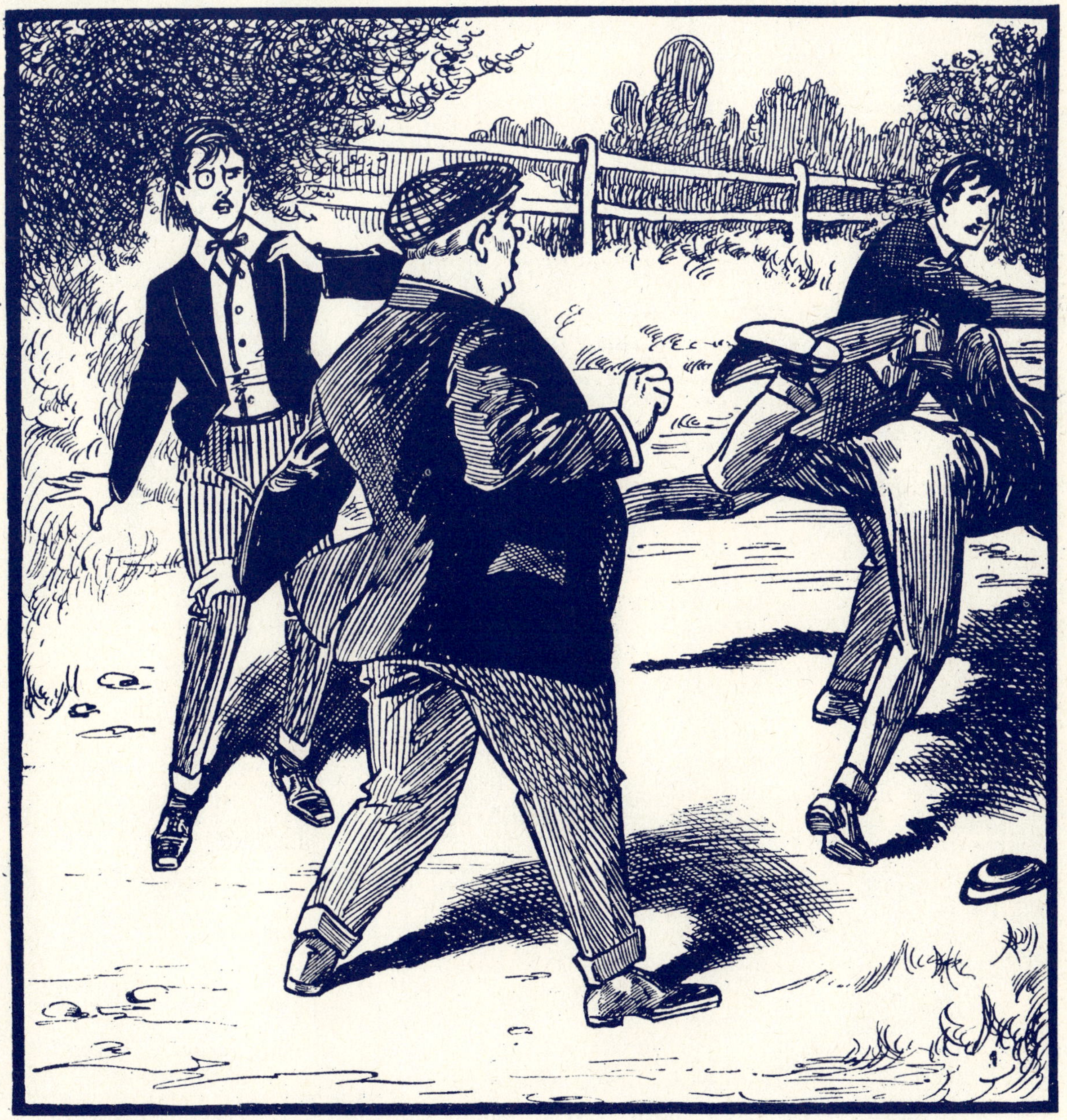

BILLY BUNTER'S DOUBLE DOES THE DEED!

Billy Bunter's Wheeze

A Magnificent Story of Greyfriars School.

THE FIRST CHAPTER.
Guests at Greyfriars.

"BED-TIME, kids!"

Wingate of the Sixth looked into the junior Common-room at Greyfriars with a good-humoured smile upon his face.

The Common-room was unusually full that evening.

Harry Wharton & Co., of the Remove, were chatting round the fire with a group of juniors who did not belong to Greyfriars.

They were Tom Merry & Co., of St. Jim's, who had arrived at Greyfriars that afternoon for a footer-match, and were stranded there by a railway strike, which prevented their return to St. Jim's.

Arthur Augustus D'Arcy, of St. Jim's, glanced at the clock.

"Bai Jove! Half-past nine!" he said. "Weally, the evenin' has wun away!"

"Yes, hasn't it, old chap?" said Billy Bunter, who was hovering near the swell of St. Jim's with a persistently agreeable grin on his fat face.

Arthur Augustus repressed a wince. "Old chap" from Billy Bunter appeared to have an unpleasant effect upon his noble nerves.

"Get a move on!" said Wingate.

"I say, Wingate——" began Bob Cherry.

"Well?"

"Couldn't you make it ten to-night?" suggested Bob. "Special occasion, you know—distinguished guests, and——"

"I'll make it a hundred lines if you don't move!" answered the prefect.

"Oh, in that case I'll make a move!" said Bob cheerily. "Come on, you fellows! Four of you are coming into the Remove dorm. Are you going to toss up for it?"

Billy Bunter slipped a fat arm through D'Arcy's.

"Come along with me, old boy!' he said.

"Bai Jove!"

"This way, Bunter!" said Bob Cherry, observing the suppressed discomfort of the swell of St. Jim's; and he playfully took the Owl of the Remove by the collar. "I'm waiting for you."

"Yah! Leggo!"

"Come on, my fat tulip!"

Bob Cherry marched Bunter off, and the fat junior had to relinquish D'Arcy's arm, much to the satisfaction of Arthur Augustus.

Billy Bunter and Bob were the first to arrive in the dormitory, and Bunter arrived there in a state of breathless indignation.

The rest of the Remove followed, with four of the St. Jim's juniors—Tom Merry, Blake D'Arcy, and Lowther The other guests were accommodated in other junior dormitories, where extra beds had been made up.

Billy Bunter, having escaped from Bob Cherry, approached Arthur Augustus with a beaming smile as that elegant youth was taking his boots off.

"Jolly cold, ain't it?" said Bunter affably.

"Yaas; it is wathah cold, deah boy."

"Like a hot-water bottle?"

"You are vewy kind, Buntah."

"Not at all, old fellow! I'll cut off and get a hot-water bottle, if you'd like one."

"Pway don't bothah, Buntah."

"No bother at all!" answered Bunter, blinking genially at Arthur Augustus through his big spectacles. "I know you'd like one, and I insist! I'll be back in a jiffy."

"You can't get a hot-water bottle, you owl!" said Johnny Bull, as the fat junior rolled to the door.

"Weally, Buntah, I wish you would not twuoble——"

"Leave it to me!" answered Bunter.

And he rolled out of the dormitory.

"You chaps are jolly lucky to have hot-water bottles on cold nights!" said Tom Merry.

"We don't!" said Harry Wharton. "I'm blest if I know where Bunter expects to bag one! Loder generally has one, but he's in the Sixth."

"Oh, my hat!" murmured Nugent.

It occurred to him that Billy Bunter, in his keen desire to make himself agreeable to the son of a lord, intended to raid Loder's hot-water bottle, and if Loder of the Sixth caught him raiding it the results were likely to be quite unnerving.

"The esteemed Bunter will get it neckfully if he is caught!" murmured Hurree Jamset Ram Singh. "He is after the excellent and disgusting Loder's bottle, my esteemed chums."

"Serve him right!" grunted Johnny Bull.

Before the juniors had turned in there was a hurried step in the passage, and Billy Bunter bolted breathlessly into the dormitory with a big hot-water bottle clutched in his hand.

"Here you are, Gussy!" he gasped.

"Bai Jove! I weally do not want it, Buntah."

"Nonsense, old chap! I insist!"

"But weally——"

"Here you are! I'll shove it in your bed."

Arthur Augustus D'Arcy could make no further demur; the laws of politeness forbade any further resistance to Bunter's officious attentions. The hot-water bottle was placed in his bed.

Billy Bunter, having disposed of it, blinked rather nervously at the doorway. It was pretty plain where he had bagged the hot-water bottle for his dear pal Gussy; and it was also pretty plain that he was thinking of the possible consequences.

Billy Bunter listened, with almost painful intentness, as he got into his pyjamas, expecting to hear the tread of Loder of the Sixth in the passage. He had found Loder's room empty when he raided the bottle, but he did not know whether he had been seen scuttling away from the Sixth Form quarters with it.

He gave a jump as a heavy tread was heard from the direction of the stairs.

Bob Cherry grinned at him.

"Look out, Bunter!"

"I—I say, you fellows——" stuttered Bunter. "If—if Loder comes here——"

"He's coming!" grinned Nugent.

"You stand by a chap, you know!" gasped Bunter. "Don't let Loder show off his beastly bullying when—when we've got guests, you know! Oh, dear!"

The heavy tread sounded in the passage. It was not Wingate returning to put the light out. The juniors knew Loder's tread. It was the bully of the Sixth, on the track of his hot-water bottle.

"You young ass, Billy!" murmured Wally Bunter, who had the next bed to his cousin Billy. "You're in for it now!"

Bunter blinked at his cousin Wally.

"I—I say, Wally," he muttered. "G-g-g-go out into the passage and—and see if that's Loder, will you?"

Wally chuckled.

"So that Loder can take me for you, and give me what he's coming to give you?" he asked.

"Oh, really, Wally——"

"Scat!" said Wally.

"Look here, you beast!" muttered Bunter. "You're my guest here, ain't you? It was jolly kind of me to ask you here, wasn't it? 'Tain't every public school chap who would ask a poor relation here, I can tell you! You just go into the passage and—and see if that's Loder."

Wally Bunter did not move from his bed.

Wally, though otherwise very different from his cousin Billy, was his exact double in appearance, excepting that he did not wear glasses; and so he did not need telling why Bunter wanted him to face the irate prefect.

Wally Bunter was a good-natured and obliging fellow, but he did not consider it one of a guest's duties to take a thrashing intended for his host.

So he did not move.

"Wally, you rotter!" said Bunter in a fierce whisper. "Look here, I won't ask you here again! I'll——"

Bunter broke off. Loder's heavy and hurried tread was just outside the door now; and Bunter bolted under his bed, and squirmed there, palpitating. A moment after he had disappeared from sight Gerald Loder strode into the dormitory, with a black brow and a gleaming eye.

THE SECOND CHAPTER.
Mistaken Identity!

HARRY WHARTON & CO. grinned as the prefect strode in.

It was pretty clear that Gerald Loder had missed his hot-water bottle, and was looking for it—and the fellow who had bagged it.

Bunter was quite out of sight under the bed, shivering there in a state of terror, and probably wishing that he had not been quite so attentive to D'Arcy of St. Jim's.

Loder glared round the dormitory.

The fact that there were guests present did not make any difference to the bully of the Sixth. He was not renowned for his good manners.

"Bunter!" he roared.

"Hallo, hallo, hallo! Looking for somebody, Loder?" asked Bob Cherry.

"That young villain Bunter!" roared Loder. "He's taken the hot-water bottle out of my bed!"

"Bai Jove!" murmured Arthur Augustus.

"I saw him streak off with it!" roared Loder. "Don't tell me he hasn't got it! I saw him, though the blind owl didn't see me! Oh, here you are!"

Billy Bunter was invisible; but Wally Bunter was sitting up in bed, with a grin on his fat face. Loder strode directly towards him. Wally Bunter gave a howl as the Sixth-Former's heavy grasp descended on him.

"Yarooh! Leggo! Wharrer at!"

"I'll show you what I'm at!" shouted Loder, dragging the fat youth bodily out of bed, and landing him with a bump on the floor. "Where's my hot-water bottle, you fat young rascal?"

"Yarooh!"

Spank, spank, spank!

Loder was evidently under the impression that it was Billy Bunter he was handling; a natural mistake under the circumstances.

It was an unfortunate mistake for Walter Bunter, however.

He roared and wriggled as the heavy slaps smote his pyjamas. Loder seemed to think he was in training as a carpet-beater.

Smack, smack, smack!

"Yaroop! Help! Oh, crikey! Yah!" roared Wally.

"Loder," shouted Harry Wharton, "let him alone! That's not Bunter!"

Loder did not reply; he went on spanking.

But the chums of the Remove were not likely to see a guest handled like that without interfering. Loder was a prefect, certainly; but the laws of hospitality came before everything else. The Famous Five rushed to the rescue, and Squiff and Todd and Tom Brown and several other fellows rushed with them. Loder was grasped on all sides, and dragged away from his victim.

"Let go!" roared Loder, in wrath and indignation. "You young sweeps! How dare you touch a prefect!"

"Yow-ow-ow-woop!" came from the unhappy Wally.

Under his bed Billy Bunter lay very low. His chief hope was that Loder would not discover that he had made a mistake.

The bully of the Sixth struggled furiously in the grasp of the juniors.

Tom Merry and his comrades looked on with wide-open eyes. This was an exciting interlude that the St. Jim's fellows had not expected while they were guests under the roof of Greyfriars.

"Let go!" yelled Loder.

"I tell you that's not Bunter!" shouted Wharton, dragging Loder back by the hair. "It's his cousin!"

"Let go!"

"Ow-ow-ow-ow-wow!" came from Wally.

"By Jove!" murmured Arthur Augustus D'Arcy, screwing his eyeglass into his eye, and surveying the scene with great interest. "This is vewy excitin'! Go it, deah boys! Mop him up, bai Jove!"

There was a hurried step in the doorway, and George Wingate came in. The captain of Greyfriars had been returning to the dormitory to put the lights out when he heard the uproar, and hastened his steps.

"Stop that row!" shouted Wingate, as he strode in. "You young sweeps! My hat! Loder, stop this at once!"

The juniors released Loder, who staggered to his feet, breathless, and crimson with rage.

"What on earth does this mean, Loder?" demanded Wingate.

"I—I—I——" Loder spluttered with rage. "I—I—— The young villains! Bunter's taken my hot-water bottle—yow!—and I came here for it—groogh!—and they set on me—ow-ow-ow!"

"Bunter"—Wingate stared at the gasping Wally—"if you've taken Loder's hot-water bottle——"

"Yow! I haven't!" gasped Wally.

"I saw him!" roared Loder. "I saw him, and followed him here!"

"That settles it!" said Wingate, frowning. "Bunter——"

"I haven't been out of the dormitory!" howled Wally. "Yow-ow-ow!"

Loder made a stride towards him, but Wingate stopped him.

"Hold on!" he exclaimed. "There's two of those fat bounders. Blessed if I know t'other from which. Which are you, you young sweep?"

"Ow! I'm Wally! Nice way to treat a guest, this is, isn't it?" hooted Billy Bunter's unfortunate cousin.

"Then where's Billy?"

No answer came from under Bunter's bed. William George Bunter was lying very low indeed.

"Oh!" ejaculated Loder, taken aback.

He remembered now that he had seen Bunter's cousin about the school during the day.

"Where's Bunter?" demanded Wingate. "He was in the dorm when I was here ten minutes ago!"

"Hiding somewhere!" said Loder savagely.

"Under a bed, very likely," said Wingate.

"Ow!"

That gasp of terror was almost at the feet of the Greyfriars captain. He stooped and looked under Bunter's bed.

"Here he is! Come out, Bunter!"

"Yow-ow! I'm not here——"

"What?"

"Ha, ha, ha!"

"Come out, you fat rascal!" roared Loder.

He plunged an angry hand under the bed to grasp Bunter and yank him out. The Owl of the Remove, too scared to be clear as to what he was doing, kicked out, and his fat foot came in violent contact with Loder's nose. A terrific roar came from Loder as he sat down suddenly, clasping his nose in anguish.

"Ha, ha, ha!" yelled the Remove.

"Oh, cwikey!" ejaculated Arthur Augustus. "How vewy funnay! Ha, ha!"

"I—I—I'll slaughter him!" spluttered Loder.

He made another furious grasp under the bed, and this time captured Bunter's fat ankle. The Owl of the Remove came rolling out, squirming and roaring.

"Yarooh! Help! Murder Fire!"

"Shut up!" snapped Wingate, in great exasperation.

"It wasn't me! Yarooooh!"

Spank, spank!

Loder's heavy hand descended, and Bunter yelled. Wingate caught the bully of the Sixth by the shoulder, and jerked him away.

"That's enough!" he said curtly.

"Look here, Wingate——"

"Leave this to me. Bunter, have you taken Loder's hot-water bottle from his room?"

"Yaroooh!"

"Answer me!"

"Yoooop!"

"Bunter!" Wingate jerked the fat junior to his feet. "Hold your tongue, you fat idiot, and answer me!"

"Yow-wow! How can I answer you if I hold my tongue? Yoop!"

"Where is Loder's hot-water bottle?"

"Yow-ow! How should I know?"

"Did you take it?"

"Certainly not! I—I never knew Loder had a hot-water bottle. I didn't know he was so soft."

"What?" shouted Loder.

"Better look in his bed," said Wingate.

Loder savagely looked in Bunter's bed, and then in Wally Bunter's bed, but the hot-water bottle did not come to light. Arthur Augustus' feet were resting on it at that moment, but he did not feel called upon to make a remark.

"It doesn't seem to be here," said Wingate. "Are you sure you saw him take it, Loder?"

"Yes, I am. I saw him scud off with it under his arm."

"Bunter——"

"Loder's mistaken, Wingate!" howled Bunter. "I didn't—I never—I wasn't! I haven't even seen his hot-water bottle!"

"Bai Jove!" murmured Arthur Augustus D'Arcy, almost overcome as he listened to that statement.

"Are you telling the truth, Bunter?" exclaimed Wingate, in perplexity.

"Oh, really, Wingate! Ask any fellow here. They'll tell you how truthful I am. I don't believe I could tell a lie if I tried. I don't know how!"

"Ha, ha, ha!"

"I say, you fellows, you can tell Wingate that I haven't been out of the dorm," continued Bunter, blinking at the Removites.

There was a unanimous silence. The Remove fellows were not likely to join the Owl in a lying competition.

"Ask Wharton, Wingate!" continued Bunter. "Ask D'Arcy! Ask anybody! Just as if I'd touch Loder's hot-water bottle!"

"I saw you with it!" raved Loder.

"You couldn't have! Perhaps you'd been drinking, and saw double!" suggested Bunter cheerily.

"Wha-a-at?" stuttered Loder.

"You couldn't have seen me, or I should have seen you," said Bunter, as a clincher. "There wasn't anybody at all in the Sixth Form passage."

"Ha, ha, ha!" yelled the juniors.

"Then you have been in the Sixth-Form passage?" exclaimed Wingate.

"No, I haven't! Not at all!"

"But you just said——"

"I—I was only making a remark, Wingate," stuttered Bunter. "No harm in making a remark, I suppose?"

"Ha, ha, ha!"

"I saw him from the door of Carne's study as he scuttled off," said Loder. "He's admitted it now."

"I haven't!" yelled Bunter. "I didn't notice that Carne's door was open——"

"What?"

"I—I mean——"

"Never mind what you mean," said Wingate, taking the fat junior by the ear. "You'd better produce that bottle at once. Otherwise, I shall ask Loder to spank you till it's found."

"Oh, dear!"

Arthur Augustus D'Arcy looked inquiringly at Bunter. He felt that it was time for the bone of contention to be produced. But Billy Bunter was watching Loder in great apprehension, and he did not look at the swell of St. Jim's.

"Keep off!" howled Bunter, dodging round Wingate as Loder made a stride towards him. "I tell you I haven't seen it! Some other fellow may have taken it—it may be in some other fellow's bed—D'Arcy's, for instance——"

"Oh, bai Jove!" gasped Arthur Augustus.

He groped in the bed and produced the hot-water bottle, and held it out.

"Is this your pwopahty, Lodah?" he asked politely.

Loder grabbed it.

"I twust you will excuse Buntah," said Arthur Augustus, with dignity. "He was kind enough to——"

"I'll excuse him! I'll—I'll——"

"Keep off!" roared Bunter, dodging again. "'Twasn't my fault if D'Arcy bagged your hot-water bottle, was it? I'm surprised at him—not at all the thing a guest ought to do! Cheek, I call it! 'Twasn't my fault, was it?"

"Oh, cwumbs!"

"You fat villain! I saw you——"

"You must have mistaken D'Arcy for me!" wailed Bunter. "He had it, you see."

Even Loder grinned at the idea of mistaking the slim and elegant Gussy for Bunter.

"Well, you've got your bottle, Loder," said Wingate. "That's enough. Bunter, you are a lying young rascal! You will take two hundred lines."

"I—I say, Wingate, you can see that it was D'Arcy——"

"Shut up!" snapped Wingate.

He followed Loder from the dormitory, turning off the light, and Bunter was left to scramble into bed in the dark. Then there was a regular chorus from the other beds.

"Bunter, you worm——"

"Bunter, you cad——"

"Bunter, you Hun——"

"I say, you fellows, you might be a bit sympathetic! gasped Bunter. "This is what comes of being hospitable; I'm really the only hospitable chap here. I say, Gussy, old chap——"

Grim silence from Gussy!

"D'Arcy, old fellow——"

No answer.

"Are you asleep, Gussy?"

Apparently Gussy was, for he did not speak; and Billy Bunter gave it up at last.

THE THIRD CHAPTER.
Wally Finds a Pal!

HARRY WHARTON & CO. were down early in the morning, and they punted a footer about before breakfast with the St. Jim's fellows. Tom Merry & Co. breakfasted in the old dining-room with the Greyfriars fellows; and after that they had to be left to their own devices, when the Greyfriars fellows went into the Form-rooms.

The stranded footballers were at liberty to join the Greyfriars fellows at classes if they liked; but Tom Merry & Co. preferred to pay a visit to the footer-ground, where they probably found more enjoyment than in the Form-rooms. How long the railway strike would land them upon Greyfriars the St. Jim's fellows did not know; but, in these circumstances, they did not at all object to a long stay.

Arthur Augustus D'Arcy did not join the footballers, however. He walked down to the village later in the morning to inquire at the station for news of trains. The strike was still on, but he heard from the stationmaster that trains were expected to begin running again that afternoon, as the trouble on the line promised to be brief.

Arthur Augustus was sauntering back to Greyfriars, timing himself to arrive for dinner, when there was a whir of bicycles on the road ahead of him.

He glanced at them, and recognised Ponsonby and Gadsby, of Highcliffe School, whom he had seen before, and remembered very well.

He stepped aside to allow the two Highcliffians to pass.

Ponsonby and Gadsby had recognised him at the same time, and they exchanged a glance and a grin.

"That's D'Arcy of St. Jim's," muttered Ponsonby. "What's he doin' in this part of the world?"

"Must be stayin' at Greyfriars," said Gadsby. "Slang him as we go by, Pon."

Pon grinned.

"Better than that—run him down!" he answered.

"Ha, ha!"

The nuts of Highcliffe remembered D'Arcy, and not with friendly feelings. Arthur Augustus was surprised to see that the bikes swerved, and still headed for him, though he had drawn to the side of the road. He drew closer to the hedge, and the bikes swerved a little farther.

"Bai Jove! Mind where you are comin'!" shouted D'Arcy. "You will wun me down!"

The two bikes came rushing on, and it dawned upon Arthur Augustus that the Highcliffians intended to run him down.

He jumped out into the road again, the bikes close on him now. They swerved out to catch him, and he made another jump, like a kangaroo, and just escaped. Pon's hand knocked off his cap as they rushed by.

"You uttah wottahs!" shouted Arthur Augustus, in great wrath. "If I could ovahtake you I would give you a feahful thwashin'!"

Ponsonby and Gadsby jumped off their machines.

Being two to one, the nuts of Highcliffe felt that a ragging was likely to be quite safe and very amusing; and they were greatly entertained at the idea of ragging a Greyfriars guest. It would be something off their old score against Harry Wharton & Co..

"Stick him in the dashed ditch!" muttered Ponsonby. "There isn't much water, but there's lots of mud. It will be nice for his bags."

Gadsby chuckled.

Arthur Augustus had fielded his cap, and was putting it on, when the two Highcliffians came up, evidently with hostile intentions.

The St. Jim's junior disdained to give ground. The noble Gussy was not wont to count his foes. He put up his hands at once as Ponsonby and Gadsby came on.

"You wottahs!" he exclaimed. "I shall be vewy pleased to give you a feahful thwashin'!"

"Nail him!" exclaimed Ponsonby.

Arthur Augustus had to give ground, but he put up a gallant fight. But the odds were too much, and in a few minutes the swell of St. Jim's was struggling on the ground in the grasp of the Highcliffians.

"Gwoogh!" he gasped. "Welease me, you wottahs!"

"Shove him into the ditch!" gasped Ponsonby breathlessly.

Pon's nose was streaming red, and he was in a savage temper by this time.

"Oh, deah!" gasped Arthur Augustus, in horror, as he was yanked towards the muddy ditch. "Oh, cwikey! You uttah wascals! Oh, cwumbs!"

He struggled furiously as he approached the ditch; but the two young rascals dragged him on.

Arthur Augustus was on the verge of the ditch, when a fat figure came rolling through a gap in the hedge. It was Wally Bunter. Wally did not waste time on words; he rushed on the scene at once.

Ponsonby glanced round quickly at the sound of footsteps.

"Only that fool Bunter!" he said carelessly. "Shove him in!"

If it had been Billy Bunter the Highcliffe nuts would have had nothing to fear, and they supposed it was Billy. But they quickly found out their mistake. Wally charged them behind, and Pon and Gaddy found themselves grasped simultaneously by their collars and dragged back.

Crack!

There followed a loud concussion, and louder yells, as the Highcliffians' heads came together.

"Ow!"

"Ooooop!"

Pon and Gadsby went spinning into the road, where they sat down. Wally, with a fat grin, gave Arthur Augustus a hand up.

"Just in time, old scout!" he grinned.

"Gwoogh! Thank you, deah boy!" gasped Arthur Augustus. "They were goin' to put me in the mud, the howwid wottahs! Gwooogh!"

"Come on, and lick 'em!" said Wally.

"Yaas, wathah!"

Wally and Arthur Augustus rushed to the attack; but Ponsonby and Gadsby were already fleeing for their bikes. They were not looking for a conflict on equal terms.

They reached the machines, dragged them into the road, and threw themselves desperately into the saddles. Just in time they ground at the pedals, and shot away out of reach.

"Stop, you wottahs!" roared Arthur Augustus wrathfully. "I am goin' to thwash you! Come back, you howwid funks!"

But the nuts of Highcliffe disappeared at top speed round the nearest corner. Wally Bunter burst into a laugh.

"Bai Jove! What wotten funks!" said D'Arcy. "Buntah, deah boy, I am vewy much obliged to you!"

"Not at all," said Wally.

"You are—are——" Arthur Augustus screwed in his eyeglass, and surveyed Wally doubtfully. "I—I pwesume that you are Walter, not Billy——"

Wally chuckled.

"That's it!" he said. "Blessed if I know why people think I'm so much like Billy!"

"You are wathah like, you know."

"But he's fat!" said Wally.

"Oh!"

Arthur Augustus really did not know what to say to that. Possibly in point of circumference Billy Bunter had the advantage—if it was an advantage—of his cousin; but the difference was not really perceptible to the naked eye. Apparently Wally was satisfied that there was a considerable difference.

"There's a difference between being plump and being fat," he added.

"Yaas; I—I suppose there is," assented D'Arcy. "Yaas, now I come to think of it, I am suah there is."

"Let me dust you down," said Wally. "You're a bit dusty."

"Thank you vewy much!"

Arthur Augustus was dusted down, and the two juniors started for Greyfriars together. They chatted on the way in a very friendly manner. The day before Wally had played for Tom Merry's team in the footer-match, the Saints being a man short; and he had kicked the winning goal for the visitors, which had given them a very good opinion of him. Arthur Augustus had already found that Billy Bunter's odious familiarity was quite absent from Wally, and he liked

Bunter's cousin, though his feelings towards Billy Bunter were not exactly pally.

"I am jollay glad that you are comin' to St. Jim's, deah boy," Arthur Augustus remarked, as they walked on to the school. "Wharton told me yestahday that you were goin' to do so."

"That's right!" said Wally.

"I am suah we shall be fwiends there," said Arthur Augustus. "Pew-waps you will be in the Fourth. That's my Form. What Form are you in now, deah boy?"

Wally coloured.

"I—I'm not at school now," he said.

"Oh! I supposed that you were changin' your school," said Arthur Augustus. "Been havin' a long holiday—what?"

Wally Bunter paused before replying.

"I've been at work," he said. "I was in an office at Canterbury, and it's a stroke of good luck my being sent to a public school."

"Bai Jove! You w'ite figahs in ledgahs and things?" asked Arthur Augustus, with great admiration.

"Something like that!" grinned Wally.

"That's jollay clevah! I suppose you can add up long columns of figahs and make them come wight?"

"Well, rather; I had to."

"You wequiah plentay of bwains for that," said Arthur Augustus. "I am wathah a bwainy chap; but I often find that if you add up figahs fwom the top it comes to a diffewent wesult fwom addin' them up fwom the bottom. I suppose it depends a lot on how you do it."

"Well, yes, it does, a little," grinned Wally.

"I suppose school will seem wathah slow to you, aftah bein' at work," remarked Arthur Augustus. "Still, it will come easy."

"I'm jolly glad of the chance!"

Wally was smiling cheerfully now. Apparently it did not matter to Arthur Augustus whether he had worked in an office or not, and Wally felt rather relieved. Gussy's views were evidently quite different from Billy Bunter's.

Gussy was so cordial, in fact, that Wally told him the whole story, on the way to Greyfriars, Arthur Augustus listening with keen interest to his description of the burglary at Mr. Penman's office, when Wally had won the gratitude of his "governor" by saving the contents of the safe from the thieves.

"Bai Jove! That was awf'ly pluckay of you," commented Arthur Augustus. "I shall tell the fellows about that at St. Jim's. That governah of yours must be a wegulah old sport, to send you to St. Jim's as a weward. But, of course, if he's an old St. Jim's man, he would be a sport!" added Arthur Augustus innocently.

By the time they reached Greyfriars Arthur Augustus D'Arcy and Walter Bunter were friends; and it was settled that they were to see a great deal of each other when Wally arrived at St. Jim's. They came in to dinner together; and Billy Bunter blinked at them in pained surprise. The fact that his "poor relation" was taken up in this chummy way, while he, William George, was kept at arm's length, caused the Owl of the Remove to feel an astonishment he was never likely to recover from.

THE FOURTH CHAPTER.
An Interesting Experiment!

"WALLY!"

"Hallo?"

"I'm going to do you a favour!" said Billy Bunter impressively.

Wally looked sceptical, but he nodded. Billy Bunter had run him down in the quad after dinner, finding him in conversation with Tom Merry and Monty Lowther of St. Jim's. The two St. Jim's fellows had strolled away. It was really remarkable how fellows strolled away when Billy Bunter came along.

But Wally, being in some sense Billy's guest, could not stroll away, and he submitted with his usual fat cheerfulness to the infliction of Bunter's company.

"I've been thinking about you, Wally," went on Bunter.

"My hat! Have you?"

"Yes. It will be a bit of a change for you, being at a public school, won't it? You'll find it rather strange at first."

"I dare say."

"It will do you good to pick up some of the manners and customs in advance, won't it?"

"Yes," said Wally, astonished by this unusual thoughtfulness on his fat cousin's part. "Wharton and Nugent let me go through their prep with them last evening, like good chaps. I was glad of it. But——"

"I'm going to do more than that."

"Wha-a-at?"

Wally stared.

"You see, by that means you'll get an afternoon's work, just like what you will get at St. Jim's, and it will be no end of use of you," said Bunter. "I don't mind missing the lessons—for your sake, Wally."

"But—but——"

"We've only got to change clobber, and there you are," said Bunter. "Of course, you'll have to be careful not to burst my clobber; you're so jolly fat."

"Your clobber will hang loose round me," grunted Wally.

"Don't be a silly ass, Wally! Talk sense, old chap! You can squeeze into my Etons."

"I could swim in them."

"Look here——"

"But suppose I did," said Wally. "I couldn't go into the Form-room in your place. Mr. Quelch would know."

"He wouldn't! Every chap in the Remove would take you for me," said Bunter confidently. "You can try it on one of the fellows first, if you like."

"What about the specs?"

A bump for Bully Bolsover! (*See Chapter* 6.)

"Go ahead!" said the mystified Wally. "Not much time to heap your benefits on me, Billy, as I'm going this afternoon."

"No hurry," said Bunter. "You needn't go till this evening, if you come to that."

"What do you want me to do?"

Bunter blinked at him loftily.

"I don't want you to do anything, Wally, but accept the big favour I'm going to do you out of sheer kindness."

"Pile in!" said Wally laconically.

"You're a good bit like me," said Bunter suddenly.

"People seem to think so," grunted Wally. "I'm blessed if I see so much of it myself!"

"Well, we're alike," said Bunter. "My minor, Sammy, tried to borrow a bob of me this morning, thinking it was you, as I'd taken my specs off."

"Ha, ha! I'll bet he didn't get it!"

"Never mind that! What I'm coming to is this—that your resemblance to me enables me to do you a big service. I'm going to let you go into the Form-room to afternoon lessons in my place to-day," said Bunter impressively.

"I can lend you a pair."

Wally snorted.

"I can't see through your specs, you duffer! My eyes ain't wangy—I—I mean, I'm not short-sighted."

"You can stick them low on your nose and look over them," said Bunter. "I do, sometimes. That's easy enough."

"But—but——"

"Now, look here, Wally, you're not going to refuse when I'm taking all this trouble, and giving up the lessons I'm entitled to, just to do you a big favour!" exclaimed Bunter warmly.

Wally Bunter grunted. He knew exactly how much William George was doing for him. The fact that Wally, with a change of attire, was his double, had suggested to the Owl a method of slacking instead of working that afternoon. With Wally receiving Mr. Quelch's valuable instructions that afternoon, instead of himself, Bunter was looking forward to a lazy afternoon.

But Wally did not care to refuse. Inhospitable as Billy was, he was Wally's host; and it was through visiting Billy that Wally had made the acquaintance of Harry Wharton & Co., whom he liked so much. There was no doubt that Billy's relationship had been useful to him; and, though there was no call for gratitude, Wally felt that it was up to him to do whatever he could.

Moreover, the idea of the impersonation rather appealed to him as being in the nature of a lark. He was curious to see whether it could be carried through successfully.

And although Bunter's real object was to cut lessons for the afternoon, it was true that the experience in the Form-room might be useful to Wally as an insight into his future life as a schoolboy at St. Jim's.

Billy Bunter blinked at him anxiously as Wally thought it out.

"Is it a go?" he asked, at last.

"I'll do it if you like," said Wally, making up his mind.

"Don't put it like that!" snapped Bunter. "I'm doing you a favour, out of sheer kindness of heart."

"Oh, all right!"

"Then we'll get off to the dorm and change," said the Owl, with great satisfaction.

And the cousins retreated to the Remove dormitory, where they changed clothes, and Wally's little fat nose was adorned with a pair of Bunter's glasses—which he put on low down enough not to impair his sight.

He looked in a glass, and started as he saw his reflection.

He was Billy Bunter to the life.

And Bunter, in Wally's tweed trousers and lounge-jacket, and with his glasses off, was Wally to the finger-tips.

"Well, my hat!" said Wally. "I am a bit like you, Billy, and no mistake! It's the clothes chiefly."

"And the specs," said Bunter, who was no more flattered than Wally was by the resemblance. "You look a lot better now, Wally. It's my glasses that give me my distinguished look."

"Oh, crikey!"

"You'll pass for me anywhere, now," said Bunter. "Mind, it's not only to do you a good turn this afternoon that I've suggested this. I've got another idea in my mind, too, that I'll tell you presently—a really corking idea! When you speak, try to use an aristocratic accent, will you?"

"Eh? Why?"

"Otherwise the fellows will spot that it's you, and not me," explained Bunter.

"Oh, crumbs!"

"I'd better keep my glasses off now, as you don't wear 'em," said Bunter thoughtfully. "I hope I sha'n't run into anybody. Here, mind—there's somebody coming!"

The dormitory door opened, and Sammy Bunter of the Second Form came in. He blinked at the two cousins, and came towards Billy, bestowing a sniff upon Wally—evidence enough that he was taken in by the change of clothes.

The genuine Wally rolled out of the dormitory with a fat chuckle, leaving Bunter minor to interview his major under the belief that he was interviewing his cousin Wally.

"I say, Wally, old chap!" said Sammy Bunter, addressing William George, who grinned. "I've been looking for you all day nearly. What was my brother up to? Has he been borrowing money of you?"

The Owl frowned.

"Look here, Sammy——"

"He borrows money of everybody," said Sammy. "Regular sponger, you know."

Bunter major opened his lips for a wrathful reply, but closed them again, remembering that he was Wally now.

"Keep clear of him, old chap," continued the unconscious Sammy. "I say, could you lend me half-a-crown, Wally?"

"No!" snapped Bunter.

"Do!" urged Sammy. "I'll send it to you at St. Jim's next week, honour bright! I'll get it out of young Sylvester—I mean, I'm expecting a remittance from home, and I'll settle up as safe as houses."

"Rats!"

The Owl of the Remove rolled out of the room, and Bunter minor blinked after him in great wrath.

"Yah! Office cad!" he hooted.

Billy Bunter only chuckled as Sammy hurled that Parthian shot after him. As he was not Wally he did not mind. Sammy followed him into the passage.

"Fat rotter!" he hooted along the passage.

"He, he, he!"

The Owl of the Remove went downstairs, heedless of his wrathful minor. He was feeling extremely satisfied. His own brother took him for Wally, in Wally's clothes, and had evidently taken Wally for him; and that was proof enough that the change of identity would be a success. And it was not only of the afternoon that Bunter was thinking; he had a scheme in his fertile brain which would have astonished Wally if he had known of it.

THE FIFTH CHAPTER.
Quite a Success!

"HALLO, hallo, hallo! Here you are!"

Bob Cherry greeted Billy Bunter as he came out into the quadrangle in Wally's tweed clothes.

For a moment Bunter was astonished by Bob's cordial manner. Then he remembered that Bob, of course, was taking him for Wally. He grinned.

"Hallo?" he replied.

"Don't you want to see the St. Jim's chaps before they go?" said Bob. "They'll be off in a few minutes now."

"Oh, really——"

"Come on, Wally!" called out Harry Wharton. "D'Arcy's been asking for you; he wants to say good-bye."

"I—I didn't know they were going!" stammered Bunter.

"The stationmaster's telephoned that there's a train," explained Wharton. "The strike petered out this morning—good luck to it! They're going home by a train at two-thirty, so they've got to get off."

Tom Merry & Co., with their bags, were already making for the gates. As it was close on time for afternoon lessons, the chums of the Remove could not see them off at the station.

But a crowd of fellows went down to the gates with the St. Jim's footballers.

Wally Bunter, hearing that the St. Jim's fellows were departing, hurried along to see them off, momentarily forgetting that he was Billy for the nonce.

He was surprised to see his cousin Billy shaking hands with Arthur Augustus D'Arcy in the friendliest possible way; and then he remembered.

"Oh, blow!" he murmured, in dismay.

Having taken on Billy's identity, he could not very well step forward and explain; but he could have kicked himself as he looked on.

Arthur Augustus, under the impression that he was speaking to Wally, was very cordial to Billy Bunter. He had not the remotest suspicion that the fat youth in tweeds was not the fellow he had walked and talked with that morning in Friardale Lane.

"I shall nevah forget the good turn you did me this mornin', deah boy," said Arthur Augustus. "My clobbah would have been wuined if those feahful boundahs had dwopped me in the ditch, you know!"

"Oh! Ah! Yes——"

"You tackled them like a Twojan, or, wathah, like a Bwiton," said Arthur Augustus. "I twust I shall see you at St. Jim's befoah vewy long, old fellow."

"Yes—I—ah——"

"Next week, isn't it?"

"Yes!" gasped Bunter.

"Good! I shall be expectin' you. We are goin' to be gweat fwiends at St. Jim's."

"Certainly!" said Bunter, beaming. "I——"

"Come on, Gussy!" roared Jack Blake. "Do you want to lose the train, and wait for another railway strike?"

"I am sayin' good-bye to Buntah, Blake."

"Well, buck up!"

"Weally, Blake——"

"Come on!" said Tom Merry, laughing. "You'll be seeing Wally Bunter at St. Jim's next week, you know."

"I say, you fellows——"

"Well, good-bye, old fellow!" said Arthur Augustus, shaking Bunter's hand. "I shall be lookin' forward to seein' you. I shall nevah forget how you saved my clobbah fwom sewious injahwy."

Tom Merry caught Arthur Augustus by the arm and dragged him off. The train had to be caught; it was not at all certain that there would be another that day. Tom Merry & Co. marched off up the road, and Arthur Augustus turned to wave his hand to the fat youth in the gateway—still in the belief that it was Wally.

Billy Bunter was grinning with glee.

He turned to go in, and bumped into Hurree Jamset Ram Singh, who uttered an exclamation.

"Yow! Gerrout of the way, Wharton!" snapped Bunter.

"I am not the esteemed Wharton, my excellent Wally," said the astonished nabob. "What is the matterfulness?"

Bunter remembered again.

"Oh—ah—yes—sorry!" he said.

Without his glasses Bunter was a lost soul, except at very close range; but he could not venture to put them on under the circumstances. Wally was glaring at him over his second pair of specs, but Bunter did not see him. Avoiding another collision, he rolled on into the quadrangle.

Wally joined him there.

"You fat spoofer!" muttered Wally.

The Owl of the Remove blinked at him.

"Is that you, Wally? I say, it's rotten without my specs! I shall have to keep out of gates this afternoon, so that I can put them on," he said. "He, he, he! Did you see Gussy saying good-bye to me?"

"He took you for me!" grunted Wally.

"Oh, it's all right! We're great pals!" said Bunter coolly. "He was only taking notice of you out of kindness, Wally. My pal Gussy is rather soft-hearted. You naturally couldn't expect him to feel friendly towards you, as he does towards me—a nobody like you!"

Grunt from Wally.

"In fact, it happened quite luckily, didn't it?" grinned Bunter.

"Not that I see. I wanted to say good-bye to D'Arcy," said Wally, with a clouded brow. "I never thought of your spoofing him, or I wouldn't have changed clothes with you."

"No need for you to say good-bye to him," said Bunter calmly. "He's been civil to you; but, my dear chap, you mustn't think too much of that. You're nobody, you know—in fact, I mentioned to D'Arcy yesterday that you were my poor relation. I felt bound to mention that."

Grunt!

"I shall get on no end with Gussy!" remarked Bunter.

"Seeing him again?" asked Wally.

Bunter chuckled.

"He, he! I think so! He, he, he! I haven't told you my great idea yet! He, he, he!"

"Hallo, hallo, hallo! There's the bell!" exclaimed Bob Cherry. And he came along and playfuly took Wally by the ear, in the belief that it was Billy's fat ear. "Come on, my fat tulip!"

"Eh? What?" ejaculated Wally.

"Lessons, my son!"

Billy Bunter chuckled as his cousin was led away.

The Remove fellows went to their Form-room, and Wally went with them. He took his place—or, rather, Bunter's place—in the Remove-room, and quaked a little when Mr. Quelch came in. But the Remove-master did not take any special note of him. It was clear that he supposed the fat youth in Etons to be Billy Bunter. In a few minutes Wally was feeling quite reassured.

Harry Wharton called to the fat junior as he was going in.

"Like to come in, Wally? You can sit in the Form-room, if you like, and enjoy the lessons, you know."

Bunter grinned.

"No fear!" he answered.

"Oh! You did yesterday," said Wharton. "I thought——"

"I—I mean, I'm going for a walk," said Bunter hastily.

"All serene."

The captain of the Remove followed the rest into the Form-room, and Bunter made for the gates.

Once outside the gates of the school he clapped a pair of glasses on his nose in great relief. It was a comfort to be able to see clearly again. He rolled down the lane in a mood of great satisfaction, jingling several coins in his pocket.

The coins belonged to Wally, and had remained in the pocket when clothes were changed; but perhaps Bunter took it for granted that the money was lent along with the clothes; or perhaps he considered that findings were keepings. At all events, he was heading for Uncle Clegg's, in Friardale, to expend those coins to the last penny—which he duly did.

It was fortunate that Wally had not left his purse in his pocket, or assuredly his currency notes would have followed the small silver.

Billy Bunter was feeling very fat and contented as he rolled out of Uncle Clegg's little shop and sauntered down the lane. He did not want to get back to Greyfriars till after lessons, and he strolled through the fields thinking out the great scheme that was working in his fat brain—the tremendous scheme that had flashed into his mind the previous night, and almost dazzled him with the prospect it unfolded.

That scheme, so far, had not been imparted to a soul; but the more Bunter thought over it, whatever it was, the better he was pleased with it.

But the grin of satisfaction faded away from his fat face at the sight of a shifty-eyed man, with a bowler-hat on the side of his head, who was coming along the footpath towards him. Bunter halted, and blinked round as if in search of a way of escape, and the shifty gentleman hastened to intercept him. And Billy Bunter, with a groan, resigned himself to his fate.

THE SIXTH CHAPTER.
A Startling Suggestion!

BILLY BUNTER blinked at Mr. Jerry Hawke, and the sharper stared grimly at Billy Bunter.

"G-g-g-good - afternoon, Mr. Hawke! stammered the Owl.

"Arternoon!" said Mr. Hawke grimly.

"N-n-nice weather, isn't it? Fuf-fuf-for the time of year, I mean."

"Never mind the weather!" answered Mr. Hawke. "You owe me money, Master Bunter, and I ain't received the ten bob on account what you promised me yesterday. I'm a man what pays when he loses, and I expects to be treated according."

"D-d-didn't you get my letter?" stuttered Bunter.

"I did not."

"It—it must have been lost in the post, then," said Bunter feebly. "War-time, you know."

"I didn't get no letter because you didn't send no letter," said Mr. Hawke. "Now, I ask you, Master Bunter, did you put money on a 'orse, or did you not?"

"Yes," gasped Bunter.

"Did you give me a bit of writing, or didn't you?"

"Ow! Yes," groaned the unhappy Owl, who knew that only too well.

"Did your 'orse win, or did he lose?" further demanded Mr. Hawke.

"He lost!" mumbled Bunter.

"Do you owe me the rhino, or don't you?"

"Ow! Yes! Oh dear!"

"That bein' as stated," said Mr. Hawke, "I'll drop in and see your 'eadmaster about it, as you don't seem inclined to settle."

"I—I say—— Oh dear! Oh, lor'!" gasped Bunter. "I—I say, I'm expecting a postal-order, Mr. Hawke."

Sniff!

"I was led to believe," said Mr. Hawke, "that you 'ad money. Otherwise, I wouldn't 'ave trusted you. It's always been my weakness that I've got a trusting dispersition. But I cuts up rusty when it's took advantage of, you mark my words!" added the sharper threateningly.

"I—I'm not rich, you know," groaned Bunter. "In—in fact, I'm short of money. But—but I'm going to pay up, Mr. Hawke, honest Injun! You wait till next week——"

"And then I can wait till the next arter, I s'pose?" suggested Mr. Hawke sarcastically.

"Nunno! Next week for certain—say Friday!" said Bunter eagerly. "If I don't settle on Friday, do anything you like."

Mr. Hawke scanned him closely. It was pretty clear that there was nothing to be got out of Bunter at that moment, and Jerry Hawke could see it. And he was not eager to carry out his threat, which would have placed it out of his power to get anything out of Bunter himself.

"I'll trust you once more!" said Mr. Hawke generously. "I'm too trusting a cove; but it's my natur', and I can't 'elp it! I'll give you another chance, Master Bunter. Friday next week, and if you don't square then I'm sorry for yer—very sorry for yer!" added Mr. Hawke, with a scowl.

"Rely on me!" stammered Bunter.

"I will!" said Mr. Hawke significantly; and he pursued his way without another look at the dismayed Owl of the Remove.

Billy Bunter trotted off towards Greyfriars, palpitating. It really seemed as if he was never to hear the end of his unfortunate flutter on the geegees; but really, he could not expect to hear the end of it until he had settled his debt. Certainly he would have taken the sharper's money if he had won—not that he had had the remotest chance of winning anything from Mr. Hawke, if he had only known it. The fact remained that he owed Jerry Hawke money, and that he could not pay a tenth part of it; and the sharper's threats filled him with dismay and apprehension.

He arrived at Greyfriars as the fellows were coming out after lessons.

Bob Cherry clapped him on the shoulder.

"Hallo, hallo, hallo! You taken to glasses, Wally?" he asked.

Bunter started.

"Eh? No! Yes—oh—ah!" he replied lucidly.

He grabbed off his glasses, which he had forgotten, being so used to them on his nose.

"Your cousin's been getting on unusually well in the Form-room this afternoon," said Bob.

"My—my cousin!" stammered Bunter.

"Yes; Billy's the biggest dunce in the Remove, you know," said Bob.

"Oh, really, Cherry—I—I mean—— Oh——"

"But he quite surprised Quelchy this afternoon—and us, too," said Bob. "He must have been mugging up, or else he's a dark horse, and he's been taking us in. He surprised us."

"The surprisefulness was terrific," concurred Hurree Singh. "The esteemed Bunter was not a dunce for oncefully."

"Oh, rats!" said the Owl; and he rolled away.

Bob Cherry stared after him.

"Hallo, hallo, hallo! Wally seems to be picking up his cousin Billy's manners," he remarked.

Billy Bunter went in to look for Wally, feeling anxious to change back into his own proper person. The part he was playing was beginning to worry him. He found Wally in the Form-room passage, with several Remove fellows. Bolsover major had stopped the supposed Billy there, being in a humorous mood.

"Hold on, Bunter," he said, "I'm going to show you that wrestling trick. Catch hold!"

Wally stopped, grinning.

"I'm your man!" he said.

Bolsover major grasped him, and Wally returned his grasp. Skinner and Snoop and Stott looked on with grinning faces. The bully of the Remove intended to bump the fat junior hard on the floor, that being Bolsover's idea of a joke. Wally was quite aware of it; but, as he was not really Billy, as Bolsover supposed, he was not quite so easy to handle.

"Ready?" grinned Bolsover major.

"Quite!"

"You see—I collar you like that—I twist you like that——"

"Ha, ha, ha!" came from Skinner & Co.

"And I sit you down like that—— Yaroooo!" roared Bolsover, in surprise. For it was Bolsover major who sat down.

He bumped on the floor with a heavy bump, astonished and breathless; and Skinner & Co. roared. This was funnier than Bolsover major had intended.

Wally turned away, chuckling, and saw his cousin.

Billy Bunter caught him by the arm and hurried him away, while Bolsover major was still sitting and gasping.

"Come up to the dorm!" whispered Billy.

"Want to change back?"

"Yes."

"Right you are!"

The two Bunters hurried to the

Remove dormitory, where they proceeded to change clothes once more. Wally Bunter relinquished Billy's Etons with a sigh.

"How did you like it in the Form-room?" asked the Owl.

"First-rate."

"No accounting for tastes," grunted Bunter. "I don't like it."

"Old Quelch isn't a bad sort," said Wally. "He took me for you, of course. He seemed rather surprised to find that I wasn't a dunce."

"Why, you cheeky ass!" exclaimed the Owl indignantly.

"You're a lucky bargee, Billy! I wish I could stay here," said Wally. "Of course, the St. Jim's fellows are all right; but—but I do wish I could stay at Greyfriars! I feel at home here."

"Like your cheek!" grunted Bunter.

"Oh!"

"But you really think you'd like to stay at Greyfriars instead of going to

St. Jim's?" asked Bunter, blinking at his cousin with a curious expression.

"Yes, rather!"

"I'd rather go to St. Jim's!" said Bunter.

"Would you, really?" asked Wally.

"Yes, I would! I'm not understood here," said Bunter loftily. "I'm not appreciated at my just value."

"Oh!"

"At St. Jim's it would be different. My old pal D'Arcy, for instance——"

"Oh!"

"I should chum with him there. Tom Merry and the rest, too—they'd understand me; they'd know how to treat a fellow according to his real worth."

"Oh!"

"Really, Wally, can't you say anything but 'Oh!'?" exclaimed Bunter irritably.

Wally did not answer; really, he did not quite know what to say in answer to Billy Bunter's remarks. So much conceit and so much obtuseness together were a little too much for Wally.

"Suppose it could be worked, Wally?" asked Bunter, as he finished his tie.

"Eh? What?"

"For you to stay here, I mean, and me to go to St. Jim's?"

"It couldn't."

"But suppose it could?"

"I'd like it no end. But it's impossible," said Wally. "I jolly well wish it was possible. But—but I couldn't ask Mr. Penman to send me here instead of to St. Jim's; that's his old school, and he might be hurt—and—and it would seem like looking a gift horse in the mouth. I suppose you could ask your father to change your school, if you liked."

"What rot! My father would jaw me if I asked him such a thing; besides, the term's fees are paid."

"Well, then——"

"I've got an idea, Wally!" said Bunter, sinking his voice.

"Well?" said Wally, again.

"We've tried it on to-day—in my clobber and with my specs you've been taken for me. Even old Quelch didn't spot you, and he's got eyes like gimlets. And D'Arcy took me for you, didn't he?"

"Well?"

"Well, then," Bunter breathed the words in a whisper, "why shouldn't I go to St. Jim's as you, and you stay here as me?"

It was out at last!

Wally jumped.

"You—you—you go to St. Jim's?" he stuttered.

"Yes."

"As—as me?"

"Yes."

"And I"—Wally looked dazed—"I stay here—as you——"

"Exactly!"

"But I'm not you, am I?" stuttered Wally. "And you're not me, are you?"

"Oh, you're dense! I mean, play the game like we did this afternoon. I'll use your name, and you can use mine—our initials are the same, anyway. And I can go to St. Jim's, and you can stay here. Nobody would know."

"Great Scott!"

"We could change back any time we liked, if it didn't work," said Bunter, his eyes gleaming behind his spectacles. "But it would work all right. I should get on at St. Jim's no end. You want to be here—you've said so. Easy as falling off a form. What do you think, Wally?"

Wally recovered his breath.

"Think?" he repeated. "I think you've got a screw loose, old scout! I think you'd better see a doctor!"

And Wally left the dormitory.

William George Bunter stared after him in angry surprise.

"Beast!" said Bunter.

THE SEVENTH CHAPTER.
In Doubt!

HARRY WHARTON & CO. were looking for Wally Bunter, and they met him as he came downstairs from the dormitory.

Bob Cherry tapped him on the shoulder.

"Walter, my plump infant——"

"Hallo!" said Wally.

"Study No. 1 have the honour to request your company at tea!" said Bob Cherry, with great solemnity. "There will be haddocks."

"Cooked by our own fair hands!" said Frank Nugent.

"Come along, kid!" said Harry Wharton. "That is, unless you're booked already."

"Not at all!" said Wally. "I'll come with pleasure! I shall have to clear off pretty soon after."

"Not staying longer?" asked Johnny Bull, as they proceeded to Study No. 1.

"Well, my visit's up," said Wally. "I really shouldn't have planted myself on Billy so long, but—but I like being here, and I own up."

"What a pity you can't stay and come into the Remove!" said Bob. "We'd change your cousin Billy for you with pleasure."

"The pleasure would be terrific!" remarked Hurree Singh.

Wally started a little.

That was, in point of fact, the very thing Billy Bunter had been proposing in the dormitory; the chums of the Remove were unconsciously backing up Bunter's extraordinary suggestion.

"Honest Injun?" asked Wally, his fat face becoming serious. "Would your fellows really like me here better than Billy, supposing—supposing I could come, and Billy buzzed off, say, to St. Jim's?"

"Honest Injun!" said Wharton, with a smile.

"Yes, rather!"

Wally looked very thoughtful as he came into Study No. 1 with the Famous Five. Somehow or other, those cheery juniors had a way of making him feel quite at home; quite as if he was a Greyfriars fellow like themselves. True, he liked the St. Jim's juniors, from what he had seen of them; but he did not really know them as he knew the Co.

St. Jim's was a new and strange place to him; he would find himself in totally new and unaccustomed surroundings there, and the change would be great, after his previous life. But he had grown accustomed to Greyfriars already.

Even Mr. Quelch, the somewhat severe master of the Remove, had impressed Wally favourably. He liked Greyfriars, he liked all the fellows, and he would have given almost anything to stay on as a member of that cheery community. But it was impossible to tell his benefactor so; it seemed too much like picking and choosing, and, in fact, looking a gift horse in the mouth—especially as Mr. Penman was a St. Jim's man himself.

It was impossible, and yet—yet it was not impossible, if Billy Bunter's amazing idea was carried out.

After all, suppose it was carried out? Wally found himself supposing that already.

There was no harm in it, certainly. It was not a question of depriving anybody of anything; it was an exchange. He would not be passing under a name that was not his own, for his name was Bunter. Even his initials were the same as Billy's.

Billy wanted to go to St. Jim's, for some reasons that Wally knew, and for some reasons that Wally did not know. And Wally wanted very, very much to be at Greyfriars.

Where was the harm?

That the exchange was possible was proved by what had happened that afternoon. In Billy's clothes and glasses he had taken his place in the Remove Form-room and no one had been the wiser. Mr. Quelch had been surprised to find the supposed Owl a little less of a dunce than usual; that was all.

The supposed Owl's unusual aptitude had, in fact, attracted some attention to him; but no one had dreamed for a moment that he was not Billy.

The exchange was easy enough. It would please both parties; and there was no harm in it. Suppose—suppose——

"Hallo, hallo, hallo! Are you falling asleep, old scout?"

Wally started out of a brown study, to find Bob Cherry regarding him with surprise.

"Eh?" he ejaculated confusedly. "D-d-did you speak?"

"Twice!" grinned Bob.

"I—I was thinking." Wally crimsoned. In his deep thought he had quite forgotten where he was. "Sorry! Go ahead!"

"I only said you'd have been surprised to see your cousin Billy in class this afternoon," said Bob, with a smile.

"My—my cousin Billy?"

"Yes; he was so bright he fairly dazzled us!"

"D-d-did he?"

It was on the tip of Wally's tongue to explain, but he refrained. Bob's remark showed how far he was from dreaming of the spoof of that afternoon.

Billy Bunter's spectacles gleamed in at the door. It seemed that he had scented the haddocks.

"I say, you fellows——"

"What a nose for a bloodhound!" said Bob Cherry admiringly. "Where were you when you scented them, Bunty?"

"Oh, really, Cherry! I came to offer to cook them for you!" said Bunter. "If there's one thing I can cook it's haddocks!"

Frank Nugent turned a crimson face from the fire.

"Trot in!" he said. "You're welcome to the job."

"I'm your man, old chap!" said Bunter affably; and he trotted in. Under Billy Bunter's masterly hand the haddocks were done to a turn, and a cheery party sat down to tea.

"Lots of time to catch the seven train, Wally," said Bunter, as he saw his cousin glance at the clock. "I'm coming to the station with you. I've got a pass out to see you off."

"Oh!" said Wally.

He could guess why Bunter was taking that trouble—it was to renew the scheme he had proposed in the dormitory, and urge its acceptance. Wally did not quite know whether to feel pleased or troubled. The scheme appealed to him very keenly; and yet——

"I want a talk with you before you go, you know," said Bunter. "We'll have a chat on the way to the station."

That was a hint to the Co. not to offer their company.

"Sure there's a train?" asked Bob Cherry.

"Oh, yes! That blessed strike petered out, and the trains are running all right," said Bunter. "Wally will have to change at Lantham, that's all. I've asked all about it, and found it all out for him."

"You're growing quite thoughtful in your old age!" said Bob in surprise.

Bunter grinned.

"You're on holiday till you go to St. Jim's, Wally?" Harry Wharton asked.

"Yes; except for mugging with my tutor."

"If you're free next Wednesday, and could come along here, we could give you some footer," said Harry. "We're playing a match on Wednesday, and, if you'd care for it, I'd put you in our team."

"Would you really?" ejaculated Wally.

"Certainly!"

"I'm going to St. Jim's on Monday, though," said Wally, his face falling. "It's all fixed."

"Too bad! Never mind, we shall have to wait till we come over to St. Jim's to play the return match," said Harry. "I expect we shall find you in Tom Merry's eleven."

"I—I hope so. I—I say, I should like to play for you on Wednesday," said Wally wistfully. "I—I wish it could be fixed."

"Perhaps it could be fixed!" grinned Billy Bunter.

"How?" asked Wharton at once.

"Ahem!" Bunter was not prepared to answer that question, only Wally understanding the inner meaning of his remark. "I—I mean——"

"Well, what do you mean?"

"I—I mean, I'll play for you, if you like!" said Bunter brightly. "I'm a better footballer than Wally, you know."

"Ass!"

Wally looked at his watch when tea was over, and rose to his feet.

"I shall have to buzz to get that train," he said. "I say, thank you fellows no end! You've given me a splendid time here! If you're coming with me, Billy——"

"I haven't finished the cake."

"I dare say Wingate would give us a pass to see you to the station, old scout," said Wharton.

Bunter jumped up.

"I'm seeing Wally to the station!" he said. "I've got some things to say to him—something rather important—family matters, in fact. Come on, Wally! I can put this cake in my pocket."

And he did.

"We'll come down to the gates," said Harry.

And the Famous Five and the two Bunters left Study No. 1 together.

Is Bunter ill? (*See Chapter* **10.**)

THE EIGHTH CHAPTER.
Quite Settled!

"BUNTER!"

It was Wingate's voice, as the juniors came downstairs. Billy Bunter blinked at the captain of Greyfriars.

"Yes, Wingate?"

"You haven't brought in your lines."

"I—I——"

"Don't be later than seven with them," said Wingate, frowning.

"I—I say, Wingate, I—I'm just going to see my cousin off at the station."

"Oh, in that case you can leave them till to-morrow!" said Wingate, with a good-natured nod to Wally. "Cut off!"

Billy Bunter took a bag from under the hall-stand as he went out with the juniors. Wally was carrying his bag; but what Billy wanted with one was a mystery.

He gave no explanation, but trotted down to the gates through the winter dusk bag in hand.

At the gates Wally said good-bye to his Greyfriars friends. He shook hands all round with the Famous Five, and with two or three other juniors who came down to see him off, and started up the dusky road to the village with Billy Bunter.

"I say, you fellows——"

"Hallo, hallo, hallo!"

"Come on!" muttered Wally.

"Hold on a minute! I say, you fellows, I've got something to say to you!" said Bunter, keeping at a safe distance while he said it. "I've had it in my mind for a long time, and I feel that I'd better get it out, now—under the circs. You're a swanking ass, Wharton!"

"What?"

"Bob Cherry, you're a fatheaded chump!"

"Wha-a-at?"

"You're a namby-pamby, baby-faced idiot, Nugent!"

"I—I—I——" Nugent stuttered.

"You're a clumsy, cheeky, bad-mannered hippopotamus, Johnny Bull!"

"Am I?" roared Johnny Bull.

"You're a cheeky nigger, Inky!"

The Famous Five simply glared at Bunter, and Wally stared at him blankly. If that was Bunter's candid opinion of the Famous Five, it was not a flattering one. And he seemed to enjoy telling them.

"Are you potty?" exclaimed Wharton, in utter amazement. "Do you want to be scragged, you fat chump?"

"Yah! I've a jolly good mind to lick you before I go!"

"He's potty!" said Peter Todd, in blank amazement.

"You're a rotten, skinny, mean, bony bounder, Peter Todd!" continued the Owl of the Remove.

"Oh, my hat! Anything else?" asked Vernon-Smith, who had joined the juniors at the gates.

"Yes. You, Smithy, you're a purse-proud, swanky, no-class son of a dashed company promoter!" said Bunter.

With that Billy Bunter scudded up the the road, followed by the amazed Wally, and just in time to escape a rush from Vernon-Smith.

There was a chorus of amazement in the gateway. That sudden outbreak from Billy Bunter astonished the Removites.

"Why, I—I—I'll skin him when he comes back!" gasped Bob Cherry. "The cheeky ass!"

"I'll skin him now!" exclaimed the Bounder.

But Wharton caught him by the arm.

"Not while Wally's here, Smithy," he said. "You can interview the fat idiot when he comes in."

The Bounder growled, but he assented. The chums could only conclude that Billy Bunter had depended upon Wally's presence to protect him, in stating his candid opinion of them; naturally, they did not want Wally's latest recollection of Greyfriars to be a ragging bestowed on his cousin. But their wrath was great; and they waited for Bunter to come back from the station, with intentions that were perfectly Hunnish.

Billy Bunter chuckled a fat chuckle as he rolled away down the misty lane with the astonished Wally.

"Rather a surprise for those bounders—what?" he chortled.

"I think you must be potty!" said Wally. "You can't expect fellows to be talked to like that. You'll get licked when you go in!"

Bunter chortled again, apparently not alarmed by the prospect.

"I've been wanting to tell them what I think of them for a long time," he said. "This was a chance too good to be lost."

"Blessed if I see it!"

They walked on in silence for a time, only an occasional fat chuckle escaping from Billy Bunter. The Owl of the Remove was not hurrying himself, and Wally hinted at last that it was getting near seven.

"That's all right," said the Owl cheerfully. "Your train doesn't go till seven-forty, old top!"

Wally stared at him.

"Twenty to eight!" he exclaimed.

"That's it!"

"Then, what have you marched me off like this for?" demanded Wally warmly. "I don't want to hang about at the station for three-quarters of an hour."

"You won't; that's all right. We needed time, you see."

"Time for what?"

"Time to change clobber, of course."

"Wha-a-at?"

"There's an old barn near the road, a bit farther on," said Bunter. "Nobody goes there after dark. We can change there all right. I've got a candle in my pocket."

"But——"

"This way, Wally!"

"But we're not going to change!" roared Wally.

"We must, you ass, if you're going back to Greyfriars as me!" said Bunter peevishly.

"But we're—— I—— You—— I'm not!"

"I hope you're not going to begin arguing now, Wally," said Bunter, with asperity. "After I've arranged it all for your benefit, I should think even you might show a little gratitude!"

"Gug-gug-gratitude!"

"Yes," said Bunter warmly. "Gratitude! I'm not thinking of myself at all—I never do——"

"Oh, my hat!"

"I've planned the whole thing for your benefit, because you want to stay at Greyfriars. I'm taking all the risk. You've seen that you can do it all right at Greyfriars, and I've got to chance it at St. Jim's," said Bunter. "Of course, a fellow of my resource and—and ability will do it easily enough. Still, I'm taking all the risk, such as it is. I really hope, Wally, that you're not going to begin raising difficulties at the last moment."

Wally could only gasp.

In spite of his refusal, Billy Bunter had evidently taken the thing for granted. That was the explanation of his startling defiance hurled at the Co.; he was not expecting to return to Greyfriars that night. That was why he had brought a bag with him. It contained the few valuables he possessed. Evidently the Owl had laid his plans carefully.

Wally, feeling quite dazed, followed Bunter into the barn, hardly knowing what to say or do. Bunter lighted the candle.

"Ready?" he said.

THE NINTH CHAPTER.
The Exchange!

Billy Bunter took off his coat. His cousin Wally mechanically followed his example. But he paused, with the coat half off.

"Billy——" he began

"Better not jaw now; I've got to catch the seven-forty," said Bunter.

"You—you've got to kuh-kuh-catch the——"

"Of course, as I'm you now!"

"Oh, crumbs!"

Wally seemed at a loss for breath. He finished taking off his coat, his mind was in a whirl. Bunter had taken the affair into his hands, and, between Billy's persistence on the one hand, and his own keen desire to become a Greyfriars fellow on the other, Wally was wavering.

"Why, it's ripping for you!" went on Bunter indignantly. "You'll be playing footer for the Remove on Wednesday, too."

"Yes, there's that!" said Wally, brightening.

"You're friendly with all the fellows—blessed if I can see how or why, but there it is——"

"Yes, there it is," said Wally, with a smile.

"And you'd be like a fish out of water at St. Jim's," said Bunter. "I shall be all right there."

"I suppose you would, but——"

"Ain't I taking all the risk?"

"I suppose so; but——"

"For goodness' sake, Wally, don't keep on butting like a billy-goat!" exclaimed Bunter irritably. "Anybody would think that I wasn't doing all this for your sake!"

"If you are, I'm grateful," said Wally.

"If!" exclaimed the Owl of the Remove indignantly. "I like that! I'm giving up Greyfriars for your sake, ain't I? Of course, I shall be with my pal D'Arcy. He's rich and soft——"

"What?"

"I—I mean, he's greatly attached to me. And, of course, I shall get out of Hawke's way——"

"What? Who's Hawke?"

Bunter stammered. He had not meant to let that out.

"D-d-did I say Hawke?" he mumbled. "I—I meant——"

"Well, what did you mean?" asked Wally, with a touch of suspicion.

"Nothing! I really meant to say we've got no time to lose. You're not getting your things off. Don't keep me waiting in the cold."

"But——"

"If you want me to catch cold, Wally, you'd better say so! If I get influenza, I'll jolly well give it to you. I warn you!"

"Look here, Billy——"

"You're like a sheep's head, Wally; nearly all jaw! Blessed if I ever knew such a fellow for chinwag! Do what you've agreed to do, and dry up!"

"I haven't agreed!" roared Wally.

"Are you going to begin all that over again?" exclaimed Bunter, in great exasperation. "Of all the annoying fatheads——"

"It's impossible!" exclaimed Wally. "I'd like it no end; but—— Look here! How can you pretend to be me——"

"Easy enough. Nobody knows me at St. Jim's, excepting the fellows I've seen—and they took me for you this afternoon, didn't they?"

"Yes; but——"

"Butting again!" snorted Bunter.

"But—— I was going back to my new tutor's in London!" gasped Wally. "I'm staying with him in his house till Monday, and he's taking me to St. Jim's. I've told you so. You asked me——"

"Of course I asked you, fathead; as I had to know what I've got to do. I'm going to your tutor's; you've given me the address and the name, and that's enough."

"But—but he's expecting me——"

"He will get me, and he won't know it; but if he did, he ought to be jolly glad," grunted Bunter.

"You—you're going to spoof Mr. Slimson——"

"Do you think I can't?"

"I—I suppose you can. But——"

"For goodness' sake, Wally, get your clobber off, and let me get them on!" said Bunter. "I'm waiting and shivering!"

"You—you really want me to, Billy?" asked Wally, wavering again.

The thought of Greyfriars, and the fellows he knew there, attracted him strongly. St. Jim's was distant and strange, but—— After all, why should he not do as Bunter wanted?

"Of course I do. Mind, it's for your sake—entirely for your sake," said Bunter. "It's simply my generosity, that's all."

"I'm not having it on that footing," said Wally resolutely. "If you're doing it for my sake, Billy, I call it off. I won't have it!"

"Is that what you call gratitude?" sneered Bunter.

"I mean what I say," answered Wally steadily. "The fact is, I can't help thinking you've got some motive for this, Billy; some motive I can't understand, and that you haven't told me."

"That's suspicious, Wally! It's low to be suspicious."

"Well, that's what I think; and I'll tell you what I'll do," said Wally, making up his mind at last. "If you tell me plainly that you really want me to do this, and that it will be a service to you, I'll do it. Not otherwise."

Bunter blinked at him angrily. He would have preferred greatly to carry through the scheme on the footing of a tremendous favour to Wally. But his cousin was evidently determined; and Bunter's principal object, after all, was to carry through the scheme on whatever footing. The thought of the impending interview with Jerry Hawke checked the angry reply on his lips.

Jerry Hawke was to be left for Wally to deal with; and Bunter charitably hoped that Wally would be able to manage him somehow.

"Well, I do want you to do it," he said ungraciously, at last. "I'm keen on going to St. Jim's, and—and there's other reasons, too. I'm fed up with Greyfriars. I—I ask you to do it, Wally, as—as a favour."

"Well, if you put it like that——" said Wally, hesitating.

"I do!" snapped Bunter

"It's a go!" said Wally, at last.

"We'll try it. If it turns out too difficult, we can meet somewhere and change. Try it for a month, and see how it works."

"Make it a month, if you like," said Bunter, who never thought half so much as a month ahead of the passing moment. "Mind, you don't give it away without my permission; and I'll undertake the same."

"Done!"

Wally peeled off his clothes at a great rate after the decision was come to. He still had some lingering doubts in his mind; but he was feeling elated. He was going to be a Greyfriars fellow, for a time at least; and that was the darling dream of his life; a happy dream he had often thought over, before the chance had come his way of going to a public school at all.

He put on Bunter's Etons, and his coat over them; and the Owl rapidly dressed himself in Wally's outfit.

"I'll give you my extra pair of specs, Wally. You can have plain glass put in them at the optician's to-morrow, and then they won't bother your eyes. You'll have to wear them, or you'll get spotted."

"What about you?" asked Wally. "You can't wear specs at St. Jim's, as Tom Merry and the rest have seen me without them."

"I shall manage somehow. Weakening of sight, or some yarn like that," said Bunter, with a grin. "Leave that to me. Now. I'll take your bag. Shove your things into mine. Better leave the pyjamas, as they might be recognised. You'll find pyjamas in my box in the dorm. By the way, I shall want some money for my railway-ticket."

"All right!"

"Better give me something over; in fact, give me the lot," said Bunter brightly. "Fellows would notice if you had any money. I was stony to-day, you know, and you've got to keep up appearances—as me."

"I'll keep up appearances without giving you all my money," grunted Wally.

"Don't be unreasonable, old chap!" urged Bunter. "Besides, you can have my postal-order when it comes."

"When!" grunted Wally

"You'll get my allowance, anyway," said Bunter warmly.

"Well, you'll get mine; and mine's bigger than yours."

"Just like you to think of a trifle like that!" snorted Bunter. "Well, if you're only going to give me this quid, I may as well be off. I think you're mean!"

The two Bunters left the barn, after blowing out the candle. They came back into the road.

There Wally hesitated once more. But Billy Bunter did not hesitate.

"Good-bye, kid!" he said briskly, and started off for Friardale.

Wally, with a thoughtful brow, took the road back to Greyfriars. He could hardly decide whether he had done a very foolish thing or not; but he knew that he was glad that he was going back to Greyfriars. But his heart was beating as he came up to the gates of the school and rang.

THE TENTH CHAPTER.

A Surprise for the Co.!

"HALLO, hallo, hallo! Here he is!"

"Bunter, you cheeky worm, what——"

"Collar him!"

"You terrific cheeky rotter!"

Wally Bunter jumped. He was entering the School House, in a strange and uncertain mood, but unsuspicious of danger. He had passed Gosling at the gate successfully; he knew that he would pass successfully in the School House. There was no doubt that in Billy's clothes and Billy's glasses he would be taken for Billy. But a feeling of sudden alarm came over him as the Famous Five and Peter Todd and Vernon-Smith closed in on him inside the House. Evidently the Removites had been waiting for him.

They grasped his arms and his neck—after a hurried look round to ascertain that no masters were nigh—and marched him into the Common-room before the new Bunter quite realised what was happening.

There they surrounded him, with wrathful and indignant looks.

"Now, you cheeky fat worm!" exclaimed Wharton. "What have you got to say for yourself?"

"Eh?" stammered Wally.

"What do you mean by it?" demanded Nugent.

Wally looked as he felt, utterly dismayed. He could only conclude that his imposture was already detected, and that it was a sudden and early end to his stay at Greyfriars as a Greyfriars fellow. He stared at the juniors, over Billy's spectacles, blankly.

"Swanking ass, am I?" continued Wharton wrathfully.

"Namby-pamby, am I?" hooted Nugent.

"And I'm a fatheaded chump—what?" roared Bob Cherry.

"And a bony bounder—that's me!" said Peter Todd.

"Oh!" gasped Wally.

He understood now.

He was taken for Billy, after all; and the indignant juniors were calling him to account for Billy's parting words. He had forgotten that; but he realised now that, as Billy Bunter, he would have all Billy's sins to answer for—and they were many!

His alarm evaporated as he realised the truth, and he grinned. He wondered what the juniors would have thought if they had known that they were talking to him, and not to Billy. But they had not the remotest suspicion of it; indeed, Wally himself, looking in the glass, would almost have fancied that it was Billy's reflection he saw.

"Blessed if he isn't laughing at us now!" exclaimed Bob Cherry. "What do you mean by it, you fat gnome?"

"I—I—I——"

"I suppose you know you're going to be licked?" demanded Johnny Bull.

"I—I——"

"You don't think you can slang us, before a visitor, too, without being walloped?" asked Bob Cherry.

"Ha, ha! I—I mean—I—I——"

"What was it you called my father?" asked Vernon-Smith, who was a good deal angrier than the other juniors. The Bounder keenly resented any aspersion upon his father.

"I—I didn't call him anything!" gasped Wally.

"What? You said——"

"I didn't! I—I mean——"

"What's the good of telling whoppers, when we all heard you?" exclaimed Wharton. "You picked out a moment when you knew we shouldn't want to thrash you before a visitor who was your relation, and insulted us all. If you were anything but a fat, funky frog, I'd make you put the gloves on!"

"Oh dear! I——"

"Kick him round the Common-room!" said Vernon-Smith.

"Good! Bunter, you know you've asked for it! Will you have the gloves on, or be kicked round the Common-room?" asked Bob Cherry.

"I—I—I——" stammered Wally in dismay.

"You can pick your man," grinned Bob. "You said you'd a jolly good mind to lick Wharton. Lick him now!"

"I—I didn't!"

"What?"

"I—I mean—— It was Bi—— I—I mean—— Ahem!"

"Lick me!" said Frank Nugent. "I'm namby-pamby, you know, so you ought to find it easy. Try!"

"You—you see——" stammered the unhappy Wally.

"Kick him round, and have done with him!" said the Bounder.

"Good egg!"

Wally stared at the juniors in great dismay. He had not had time to think out every aspect of his new character at Greyfriars, but he realised now what had not been at all clear to him earlier.

As Wally he had left on friendly terms with the Co., almost chummy terms. But as Billy he was the Owl of the Remove, the greedy, cheeky, assuming, selfish Owl in their eyes. He had Bunter's character to live down. It was likely to take some time.

He was jerked into the middle of the room, and Vernon-Smith drew back his boot for the first kick. Wally jumped away so energetically that Bob Cherry's grasp was thrown off quite easily, much to Bob's surprise.

Smithy kicked, and there was a roar from Bob. Wally was out of the way of the coming boot, but Bob Cherry's leg was in the way, and he got the kick.

"Yaroooh!"

"Oh, my hat!" ejaculated Smithy.

Bob Cherry hopped on one leg, with anguish in his face.

"Ow-wow-wow! You silly ass! Yow-ow! Wharrer kicking me for? Ow!"

"I was kicking Bunter——"

"Ow-wow-wooop! You kicked me!"

"Why didn't you hold him? If you shove yourself in the way——"

"I didn't! He shoved me—ow-ow!—you silly chump!" Bob clasped one leg, and hopped on the other. "Yah! You fathead! Ow!"

"Never mind——" began Peter Todd.

"But I do mind!" roared Bob. "I'm hurt!"

"The hurtfulness must be great, for the roarfulness is terrific!" remarked Hurree Singh.

"Yow-ow-ow!"

"Bunter, you fat villain! Collar him!"

Wally Bunter made a rush for the door, and the juniors made a rush after him, Bob hopping. Billy Bunter would have been collared half-way to the door, but Wally was a good deal more active. He reached the doorway, and darted into the passage.

"After him!"

"Chase him!"

There was a whoop as the juniors rushed down the corridor in pursuit. Wally dashed on, and rounded a corner, and almost ran into Mr. Quelch, who was sedately walking to his study from the library. The fat youth halted just in time.

Mr. Quelch turned a severe glance upon him.

"Really, Bunter, you should not race about the passages. You nearly collided with me!" he exclaimed. "Why, what—what——"

With a terrific whoop the crowd of juniors came tearing round the corner.

"Here he is!"

"Nail him!"

"Look out!" gasped Wally, in warning.

"Boys!" thundered Mr. Quelch.

"Oh!"

Harry Wharton & Co. halted suddenly as they grasped Wally. They released him again as quickly as if they had found him red-hot as they saw the Form-master.

Mr. Quelch regarded them with a thunderous frown.

"Wharton, what does this mean? Is this what you call a rag, with Bunter as the victim?" he exclaimed sternly.

"Oh! Ah-ah-ahem!" stuttered Wharton.

"Bunter, if you have been ill-used by——"

"Not at all, sir!" said the fat junior. "Only a lark, sir. It was my fault, really!"

The juniors gasped.

Such an opportunity of landing the Co. in hot water would not have been lost by the Owl of the Remove. But Wally's reply disarmed the gathering wrath of the Form-master.

"Oh, very well!" said Mr. Quelch. "I certainly supposed, Bunter, from your hurried flight, that this was what boys, I believe, call a rag."

"Oh, sir!"

"But you must not rush about the passages in that way!" said Mr. Quelch. "Kindly do not let it occur again."

And Mr. Quelch walked away.

Harry Wharton & Co. looked at Wally Bunter, who looked at them. They did not know what to make of it. For once Bunter had played the game.

"Well, my only hat!" said Bob Cherry at last. "What's the matter with him? I thought it was a licking all round."

"Bunter's growing decent!" said Peter Todd, in wonder. "I thought he was going to howl out to Quelchy, and get us all licked."

"Same here!" said Wharton, in wonder.

"The samefulness is terrific!"

"Oh, draw it mild!" exclaimed Wally warmly. "I suppose you know I'm not a sneak?"

"What? We know that you jolly well are a sneak!" exclaimed Johnny Bull.

"Why, you cheeky rotter——"

"Eh?"

"I—I—I mean——" stammered Wally, remembering again that he was Billy. "I—I mean—— Ahem!"

"I think we'll let him off the ragging he asked for," said Harry Wharton. "You can take that as a tip, Bunter, that it pays better to be decent."

The Famous Five and Vernon-Smith went their way, feeling that Bunter had earned his pardon. Peter Todd tapped the fat junior on the shoulder.

"You're improving, Bunter," he said.

"Think so?" grinned Wally.

"You are. You're not such a fat sneak as you've seemed. Come along and do your prep."

"P-p-prep!"

"Yes, ass! You haven't done your prep, have you?"

"Nunno!"

"Then come and get on with it; you're late already."

"I—I—I'm coming."

Wally realised that he was Peter's study-mate now, and was expected to do Billy Bunter's prep in Study No. 7. He followed Peter Todd up the staircase in some trepidation, wondering what luck he would have with Bunter's prep.

THE ELEVENTH CHAPTER.
An Improvement in Bunter!

"I GUESS I've been looking for you."

It was Fisher T. Fish who addressed Bunter the Second as he came along the Remove passage with Peter Todd.

Wally paused, and Peter went on to the study. Wally knew Fishy. It was fortunate for him, under the circumstances, that he had learned to know all the Remove at least by name and sight.

"Hallo, Fishy!" he said cheerily.

Fishy looked at him.

"Anything up with you?" he asked.

"Eh? No. Why?"

"You look cleaner than usual," said Fishy. "Your voice seems a bit different—not so much like the gurgle of a fat frog. Are you ill?"

"Oh, rats!" answered Wally.

"Waal, I've been looking for you," resumed Fisher T. Fish, "about that quarter."

"That what?" exclaimed Wally, in surprise.

"I guess I mean that shilling."

"What shilling?"

"Oh, come off!" exclaimed Fisher T. Fish impatiently. "I guess you savvy what shilling, you fat scallawag! Don't you try any gum-game; it cuts no ice with me, and don't you forget it! I lent you a shilling!"

"You didn't!"

"What!" roared Fishy. "I didn't lend you a quarter?"

"No, you didn't!"

"Why, you—you—you mugwump!" gasped Fisher T. Fish, in fury. "I've been tracking you down for over a week for that shilling, and now you say I didn't lend it to you! You scallawag! You jay! You hobo! You—you—you fat——"

"A week!" repeated Wally. "Oh, I—I see! You lent it to—to—ahem! I—I see."

"I lent it to you!" roared Fisher T. Fish. "Skinner saw me! He's a witness! Snoop was there, too! Skinner! I say, Skinner! Didn't I lend Bunter a shilling in your study——"

"You did!" grinned Skinner. "You thought he was getting remittances from home, and you lent him a bob. Serve you right to lose it!"

"I calculate I'm not losing that shilling, sir! I guess Bunter is going to pony up! Haven't I asked him for it every day? Haven't I——"

"Here you are!" said Wally.

He extended a shilling to the enraged Fish.

It was a dismaying prospect, that of being called to account for Billy Bunter's debts; but Fisher T. Fish's claim, at all events, was not overwhelming. Wally had no objection to settling his cousin's debts to the extent of twelve pence.

Fisher T. Fish grabbed the shilling.

"I guess it ought to be eighteenpence, after waiting all this time!" he said. "I've lost the use of that shilling for a fortnight. And only this morning you told me you were stony, you fat jay!"

"I didn't—I mean——"

"You did!" snorted Fisher T. Fish. "I guess it'll be a dog's age before you see a loan from me again, you owl!"

And Fisher T. Fish bit the shilling to make sure that it was a good one, and slipped it into his pocket and made off. He had never really expected to see that shilling again; and probably his expectations would have proved well founded if he had had to deal with Billy, instead of Billy's cousin.

"Well, my word!" said Skinner. "Here's Bunter settling his debts! This ought to be put in the papers, by gum!"

Wally went on to Study No. 7, where he found Peter Todd and Tom Dutton at prep. Peter wagged a warning finger at him.

"You've got none too much time, fatty," he said. "You'll get scalped by Quelchy in the morning if you haven't got your construe ready."

"I—I say, what are we preparing?" stammered Wally.

Peter stared.

"You know as well as I do. You can't have forgotten!"

"Nunno! Of—of course not! Let's see what you're doing, will you?" asked Wally nervously.

"You can if you like. Don't ask me to do your work for you, you slacker! And I advise you to let your crib alone. I believe Quelchy is beginning to smell a rat."

"My—my crib!" murmured Wally.

"Yes. Why don't you do your work like any other fellow, and try to learn something?"

"I—I mean to," said Wally. "I—I say, suppose you help me this evening, Toddy. I'll be awfuly obliged. And—and I'll promise never to use a crib again, if you like."

"Well, I suppose that's a sign of grace," said Peter. "I'll help you, if you like. We can work together; but mind, I shall hold you to it. If I catch you using a crib I'll skin you!"

"Done!" said Wally.

Wally got through prep successfully, with Peter's kind assistance—though Peter had not the remotest idea whom he was really helping.

"Is your sight improving, Bunter?" asked Todd suddenly, when prep was finished.

"My—my sight?"

"Yes; you're not using your glasses at all."

"Oh dear!" Wally pushed his glasses further up his nose. Then, as the lenses came before his eyes, he blinked, and pushed them down again. As his sight was normal he could not see through strong glasses. "Oh dear! I—I think I want a change of glasses, Peter."

"Then you'd better see to it at once; it's dangerous to monkey with the eyes," said Peter. "And mind you go to a good man—not some advertising quack. Go to the school optician at Courtfield to-morrow."

"I—I will, Toddy."

"I'll lend you the tin, if you want any," added Peter generously.

"That's all right, old chap; I've got some tin."

"What?" ejaculated Peter.

"I've got some tin!" answered Wally. "Nothing surprising in my having some tin, is there?"

"Something jolly surprising in your refusing a loan," answered Peter. "Your usual game is to bag all you can get your paws on, whether you want it or not."

"Oh!"

"You seem to be improving since your cousin was here," said Peter. "You couldn't do better than take him for a model, Bunter. If you were half as decent as he is, you'd do."

"My—my cousin?"

"Yes; your cousin Wally."

"Oh! I—I see! I—I'll try to do as you say, Peter."

"Do!" said Toddy. "If you succeed, it may save you a lot of lickings. It may save me the trouble of keeping a stump in the study for you, too."

"Oh!" murmured Wally.

He was learning more about his cousin Billy than he had known before.

Prep being finished, Billy Bunter's double made his way down to the Common-room. Successful as he had been so far, it was with some trepidation that he entered the lighted, crowded room. It seemed to him that some eye, among so many, must detect that he was Wally, and not Billy. But no one took an especial note of him. It was clear that he was regarded as the Owl of the Remove, and no one else.

It was a relief, but it was not wholly pleasing. Harry Wharton & Co. were talking football, and Wally joined the group. He was not quite used to being Billy yet, and it gave him a little shock not to receive the friendly looks he had grown accustomed to in his own person.

"Let Bunter give his opinion," said Bob Cherry, alluding to some matter under discussion. "Bunter knows all about footer."

"The knowfulness is terrific," grinned Hurree Singh. "Let us ask Bunter."

"Go ahead!" said Wally. "What's the argument?"

"Bob thinks that Hazel ought to have saved the last St. Jim's goal yesterday," said Wharton, with a smile. "The one your cousin Wally kicked for St. Jim's—or, rather, headed. What's the verdict, umpire?"

"He ought to have saved it," said Wally at once. "That fat chap who keeps goal for St. Jim's would have saved it. Still, it was a jolly good goal!"

"Why, Bunter isn't such an ass, after all!" exclaimed Bob. "He agrees with me."

"Ha, ha, ha!"

Hazel, who was in the group, sniffed. "I suppose you could have saved that goal, Bunter?" he said sarcastically.

"I think so," said Wally. "I should have expected the man to head it in, from his position; but you didn't."

"Rot!" said Hazel, and he walked away.

Harry Wharton glanced very curiously at the fat junior. As a matter of fact, the opinion he had delivered was sound, and, as a rule, Bunter's opinions on footer were absurd.

"My hat!" said Nugent. "We shall have Bunter playing footer some day!"

"You'll have me playing to-morrow, and every day," answered Wally. "And if Wharton wants me in the match on Wednesday——"

"Ha, ha, ha!" roared the Co.

"Oh, don't be too funny, Bunter!" implored Wharton.

"Why, you asked me—— I—I mean—you—you asked—ahem! I mean, I'm asking you——"

"You can ask, old scout!" said Wharton, laughing. "I'll play you when I want to make the other side a present of a match. That's a go!"

"Oh!" said Wally.

Wingate looked into the room.

"Bed-time!"

Wally Bunter went up to the dormitory with the Remove. There he turned into Billy Bunter's bed, in Billy Bunter's ample pyjamas. He laid his head on Billy Bunter's pillow, wondering where Billy was at that moment, and what he was doing.

It was some time before he slept. He lay thinking over his new and queer position. But, on the whole, he was conscious that he was very satisfied.

So far all was well, and the morrow could be dealt with when the morrow came. Billy had left difficulties for him—more than he was at present aware of—but he did not allow that to worry him.

When he closed his eyes he slept like a top, and dreamed that he was kicking goals galore for Greyfriars, amid cheers from the Remove, and there was a fat smile on his face as he slumbered.

(Don't miss "WALLY OF THE REMOVE!"—next Monday's Grand Complete Story of Harry Wharton & Co., by FRANK RICHARDS.)

THE GREYFRIARS GALLERY.

No. 101. JOHNNY GOGGS.

I AM not clear that Goggs has any real claim to a place in the Greyfriars Gallery at all. Those who only read the MAGNET know him as a Franklingham fellow in "The Fourth Form at Franklingham," for it was in the "Gem" that his visit to St. Jim's and his brief sojourn at Highcliffe were recounted.

But other Highcliffe celebrities have been given places in the Greyfriars Gallery, and I have had many requests for the inclusion of Goggs. Moreover, it is likely that before long MAGNET readers will have a chance of getting to know him quite well.

There can be no mistake about his immense popularity. Yet he has characteristics which have helped to make other well-drawn figures in the stories less popular than they should be on their merits. Thus—Goggs has a habit of speech only less pedantic than that of Herbert Skimpole. But while it is rare to find a reader who properly appreciates the excellent Skimmy, while most of those who mention him pour contempt on his long windedness, yet scarcely anyone objects to the manner of speech affected by Goggs. Johnny is essentially as obliging, and seems essentially as simple, as Alonzo Todd. Here the comparison is less close, for Goggs is not really simple at all; with all his straightforwardness, he is subtle in some ways. But he shares the willingness of Alonzo, and has a hundred times that good fellow's popularity.

I can explain it, I think. Goggs is efficient, and youth worships at the shrine of him who can—not him who only tries. It takes more knowledge of the world, wider sympathy, to perceive the greatness of a fine failure. Success is not everything it matters far more that one should have done one's best than that one should succeed. But it is at least nothing against a man—or a boy—that he should succeed; and it is success that shows—that seems to prove the doing of one's best.

There is another reason for the popularity of Goggs. His ability was more or less an open secret to the reader from the first. The reader knew that Johnny was not the fool he looked. And to see one person after another being taken in by his seeming simplicity was delightful. Like Bunter's greed, and Bunter's search for someone to cash a mythical P.O., and Bunter's lying his boot lace outside doors, like Mauly's laziness, like Lowther's jokes, like Glyn's inventions, like Fishy's commercial enterprises, like Cardew's whims, Grundy's conviction that he is IT, Coker's blundering, Squiff's japing, Wibley's impersonations, it was not a matter to be told of once and then left alone—it can occur again and again without boring.

They took Johnny for a very soft article at Franklingham at first. But that was not for long. His chums, Blount, Trickett, and Waters—otherwise Bags, Tricks, and Wagtail

—found out earliest how capable and shrewd he was; others discovered it later. The goggles helped, of course; they will help again. For to keep Goggs' bright blue eyes—which really have no need for glasses at all—from being seen is to go half-way towards creating the deception of his extreme softness. He is not a beauty, and he cultivates a look of simplicity. But when one meets his eyes the show is rather given away.

He can do lots of things. He is a ventriloquist as able as Bunter; he is an expert at ju-jitsu; he is a sprinter out of the common, and a first-rate distance runner as well; he can play cricket and footer as few fellows of his age can, so well, indeed, that he can more than hold his own among seniors. He can do other things as well, no doubt—dance, play hockey, tennis, golf—though we do not happen to have come upon him doing them as yet. He can make a speech—that is beyond all question—he is always making them! He has read a good deal and thought a good deal, and no doubt could write. He can talk with grown-ups like a grown-up; but there is no fag keener than he on a jape.

That he has pluck and tenacity there can be no doubt. He is a very loyal and unselfish friend—none better in time of trouble. There is in him a depth of feeling that is possibly unusual in a fellow of his age; his devotion to Flip Derwent's sister Philippa is more like the love of a strong man than the passing fancy which some boys take for love. It will last—one feels certain of that.

It was really for the girl's sake, rather than that of her brother, that Goggs came to Highcliffe and set himself to solve the mystery of the conspiracy which had resulted in Flip's making a bolt from the school. Through it all it was of her he thought most. Goggs does not often let his temper get out of hand; but when he thrashed Cecil Ponsonby there was something like sheer ferocity in him. For Pon had been guilty of the unpardonable sin in the eyes of Johnny Goggs; he had persecuted and insulted Philippa Derwent. So Goggs fairly let himself go for once. It is almost, if not quite, the only fight of his recorded. But he boxes as well as he does other things; and we may yet hear of more of his battles.

It is not necessary to tell here the story of "The Fourth Form at Franklingham"—of how Goggs surprised the school in many ways, and won high honour at the House sports, and defeated the rascally plot of Cardenden against his kinsman and enemy, the skipper of Franklingham. Nor does one need to tell at any length of "Johnny Goggs at St. Jim's," the short serial which appeared in the "Greyfriars Herald and Tom Merry's Weekly" section of the "Gem" eighteen months or so ago. But there was one point in the latter story which should be mentioned. The St. Jim's fellows generally could not make out how it was that Goggs quite took to Grundy, pulling his leg playfully, it is true, but obviously liking him and not despising him. I think it was because Goggs saw more deeply into Grundy than most people do. Of course, George Alfred is an ass; but what a straight, plucky, generous, indomitable, dear old ass he is! Of course, he is mostly wrong, while thinking himself always right. But does he deserve no credit for the way he sticks to it? I fancy that from behind those big specs Goggs saw Grundy with clearer eyes than most people see him.

But don't make the mistake of thinking of Goggs as too deadly serious, because he can fall in love man fashion, and talk like a Member of Parliament, and play the detective, and show insight into human nature, and prove himself good at everything he takes up. There is in him a perpetual fountain of fun, as Franklingham knows—masters as well as boys—and he does not relish a jape the less because he can see it through without once grinning. Do you remember the myth of his dear grandmother, which so long took in the Franklingham juniors, and his favourite apologetic phrase: "My silly mistake—I'm always making them"? Do you recall his dealings with Jarker and the bobby and the cook, and the mirth he made at St. Jim's by his schemes? They talk of him still in School House and New House alike.

Perhaps St. Jim's will renew acquaintance with him before long. For there is quite a chance that he, with his chums, Bags, Tricks, and Wagtail, may come to Rylcombe Grammar School.

Extracts from "THE GREYFRIARS HERALD" and "TOM MERRY'S WEEKLY."

DUPING THE DUFFER!

By FRANK NUGENT.

I.

"WHEW!" exclaimed Bob Cherry, as he kicked open the door of Squiff's study in the Remove passage. "What an unearthly whiff!"

"It smells like a glue factory in midsummer!" said Harry Wharton. "I say, Squiff, you duffer, what's the game?"

Sampson Quincey Iffley Field, generally called Squiff for brevity and comfort, looked up with a rather red and by no means stainless countenance, and greeted us with a grin.

"I'm mixing chemicals," he said.

We stared at Squiff in surprise.

"You're whatting?"

"Mixing chemicals," said Squiff, stirring an evil-smelling, nasty-looking concoction in a jam-jar. "That's my home-made developer."

"But what the dickens for?" inquired Bob Cherry. "Do you mean to say you're going to swallow that merry-looking muck just to develop your muscles?"

Squiff burst into a roar of laughter, and wiped his face. This had the effect of making it rather more dirty and gruesome than ever.

"No, you ass!" he said. "That's a photographic developer. You see, I've taken up photography."

We whistled.

"And it's a jolly interesting game, too," said Squiff enthusiastically. "A bit expensive now the war's made the prices high and the chemmies scarce, but——"

"But, you silly idiot," we roared, "you've got no time for photography this afternoon!"

"Why not?" inquired Squiff.

"You've got to come down to footer."

Squiff made a gesture of impatience.

"Oh, that can slide for this afternoon!" he said. "I'm busy—otherwise engaged, dear boys!"

That was about the limit of cool cheek, we thought. Here were we, with a stiff match with Highcliffe looming ahead, not very far distant, and Squiff calmly informing us that footer-practice could slide!

We all glared at Squiff, intending that conglomeration of stares to be impressive and awe-inspiring; but Squiff's awful-smelling chemicals got up our noses, and made us cough and sneeze, and the effect was somewhat spoilt in consequence.

"Look here, Squiff, don't be a mad-brained idiot!" exclaimed Harry Wharton. "You can't chuck footer practice!"

"Oh, but I can!" replied Squiff. "See here, you chaps, I must get this developer mixed and my dark slides oiled ready for to-morrow. You know, I am taking a photograph of the First Eleven to-morrow, and I can't disappoint old Wingate. Just you leave me alone for half an hour or so, and I'll come down to the ground as soon as ever I can."

Well, if Squiff put it like that, what could we do? We gave in, with very bad grace, however, and left the study, promising him all manner of dire punishments if he didn't buck up and come down to footer quick.

Left to himself, Squiff went on with the mixing of his developer. The study was just about full of fumes when a tap sounded at the door, and Skinner poked his head in.

Skinner blinked at Squiff and coughed.

"Groogh!" spluttered Skinner. "What the thunder are you up to, Squiff?"

"Oh, get out!" said Squiff.

Skinner did not get out—he got in, but was careful not to shut the door.

Squiff glared at Skinner far from hospitably.

"Don't worry me, Skinner!" he said. "I'm busy!"

"What's that stuff in the jam-jar?" inquired Skinner calmly. "A new explosive?"

"No!" snapped Squiff. "It's my developer."

Skinner whistled in surprise, and, looking round the study, his eye caught Squiff's camera lying on the sideboard.

"Gee!" he exclaimed. "That's a dandy little camera you've got, Squiff! So you've taken up photography—eh?"

"Yes," said Squiff gruffly.

"But what are you doing for a dark-room?" asked Skinner. "I suppose you don't do it in this study?"

"No," replied Squiff, stirring industriously away at his home-made developer. "I go into the vaults under the old tower after dark."

"Hum! Not a bad idea!" said Skinner.

He picked up a bottle, and, pulling out the cork, sniffed. He jumped back with a yell as he did so, and almost dropped the bottle.

"Groooogn!" he gasped. "What the merry thunder is that horrid muck?"

Squiff grinned.

"Serves you right for butting in!" he said. "Can't you see I'm busy, Skinner? I want to get down to footer as quick as I can, so why don't you get out?"

"Oh, steady, Squiff!" said Skinner. "I'm rather interested in photography, you know. Let's help you mix your developer."

"No, thanks!" said Squiff shortly. "Clear out, Skinner!"

Skinner sauntered to the door, and then paused. He picked up another bottle, and looked at it curiously. Squiff was too busy stirring the weird mixture in the jam-jar to notice the curious gleam that came into Skinner's eye.

Skinner opened the bottle, and, getting nearer the table, leaned over Squiff.

"Look here, Squiff," he said. "I know that formula, and you ain't mixing it right. You want a drop more of this."

He tilted the bottle he held in his hand, and a stream of red liquid came out and went into the jam-jar. There was a sizzling noise in the jam-jar, and a cloud of dense, brown fumes arose.

Squiff caught the fumes full in the face, and staggered back.

"Yarooogh!" roared Squiff. "You maniac, Skinner! What the——"

"Ha, ha, ha!" roared Skinner.

"You—you—you've ruined my developer, you——" howled Squiff.

"Never mind! Chuck footer for this afternoon and make some more!" grinned Skinner. "So-long, Squiff!"

He bolted for the door, but Squiff was too quick for him. He grabbed Skinner by the scruff of his neck just as that humorous youth was about to disappear through the door.

Squiff swung Skinner back into the study, and eyed him grimly. The jam-jar was still sizzling, and the study was full of the dense, choking fumes.

"Not so fast, Skinner!" said Squiff. "Now, you rotter, what did you do that for?"

"I—I—I——" stuttered Skinner, struggling desperately. "Lemme go!"

"I'll let you go soon enough!" said Squiff. "You cad! You did that purposely! Take that!"

He landed out at Skinner, and Skinner took a hefty one on the nose. He staggered against the table, and shot the sizzling contents of the jam-jar out upon the table and the study carpet. Squiff gave a bellow of wrath as he saw the ruinous mess on his carpet.

"You rotter!" he roared. "I—I'll half-kill you for that!"

And, setting his teeth grimly, Squiff went for Skinner hammer and tongs.

Skinner stood not the ghost of a chance against Squiff, and, moreover, Squiff was now justly enraged. He smote Skinner hip and thigh, and not until he was quite exhausted with hitting him did he hurl him from the study.

"There, you cad!" panted Squiff, as he kicked Skinner out of the doorway. "That'll teach you not to act the rotter—for a time, at any rate!"

"Ow-ow-ow-ow-ow!" wailed Skinner.

He staggered to his feet and limped away as the door of Squiff's study slammed upon him.

Skinner was not feeling happy.

Snoop and Stott, his two cronies, met him on the landing, and gazed at Skinner in surprise.

"Been scrapping with a steam-roller, Skinner?" inquired Stott.

"Crikey, but you do look awful!" said Snoop, not very sympathetically, however.

"That cad Squiff's been walloping me!" groaned Skinner. "I had a lot of chemical fumes down my throat and in my eyes, so that hindered my fighting. But I'll get even with him!"

"Hard cheese, old man!" said Stott, winking slyly at Snoop. "I should get my own back on him, if I were you!"

"Trust me!" said Skinner bitterly. "I'll make the rotter sit up—see if I don't!"

And he limped away towards the bathroom to bathe his wounds, whilst his chums grinned hugely at each other and went their way rejoicing. Although they were pals of Skinner's, they were not exactly overflowing with sympathy for him.

II.

BENEATH the shade of the old elms in the cloisters a figure was strolling in solitude and quiet.

It was Alonzo Todd, generally known as the Duffer of Greyfriars, and Alonzo was deeply engrossed in the pages of "A Treatise on Bacteria."

This treatise was Uncle Benjamin's latest present, and Alonzo, having rescued it from the wastepaper-basket and the study grate on many an occasion when his Cousin Peter had consigned it there, Alonzo was still endeavouring to glean knowledge and wisdom therefrom in his spare moments.

The cloisters was Alonzo's favourite spot for quietude and meditation, and, when he got the chance, he always carted his "Treatise on Bacteria" there, and spent a few quiet moments deeply absorbed its pages.

He had got to about the middle of Chapter Ninety-Five, when something on the ground attracted his notice, and he stopped in his walk.

"Dear me!" murmured Alonzo

A piece of folded paper lay in his path, and to it was tied a hard dog-biscuit.

Alonzo Todd blinked at this strange sign.

"Dear me!" murmured Alonzo Todd again, bending down and peering at the paper and the dog-biscuit. "How curious!"

He stooped and picked it up. The paper was folded in quarters, and to the string that was tied round it was attached an extremely ancient and formidable looking dog-biscuit.

"I—I wonder what it is?" murmured the Duffer, blinking at the paper uncertainly. "I—I suppose I had better open it."

Alonzo undid the string, and opened out the paper. His eyes opened wider and wider as he read, and he dropped the "Treatise on Bacteria" in his astonishment. For this is what he read:

"HELP! I AM A PRISONER IN THE VAULTS. I AM BEING TORTURED AND FED ON DOG-BISCUITS! I AM IN HOURLY PERIL OF MY LIFE! FOR HEAVEN'S SAKE RESCUE ME! DO NOT ENTER THE VAULTS IN DAYLIGHT, BUT NINE O'CLOCK AT NIGHT IS THE ONLY TIME TO RESCUE ME. TO WHOMSOEVER MAY FIND THIS PAPER, I BESEECH YOUR HELP!"

"G-g-ood heavens!" gasped Alonzo Todd, as he read this startling epistle.

The "Treatise on Bacteria" remained un-

Printed and published weekly by the Proprietors at The Fleetway House, Farringdon Street, London, E.C. 4, England. Subscription, 8s. 10d. per annum. Agents for Australasia: Gordon & Gotch, Melbourne, Sydney, Adelaide, Brisbane, and Wellington, N.Z. South Africa: The Central News Agency, Ltd., Cape Town and Johannesburg. Saturday, January 11th, 1919.

noticed upon the gravel, whilst the Duffer of Greyfriars gazed in horror at the paper in his hand, the ancient dog-biscuit dangling upon the string in the air.

Whilst Alonzo was still in the throes of astonishment and horror a figure emerged from the shadows of the cloisters and approached him.

Harold Skinner grinned as he saw Alonzo Todd contemplating the paper and the dog-biscuit.

"Hallo, Alonzo!" he exclaimed suddenly. "What have you got there?"

Alonzo gave a jump, and blinked at Skinner with startled eyes.

"My dear Skinner——"

Skinner gazed at the dog-biscuit in pretended astonishment.

"My word!" he exclaimed. "Surely you're not making up for the rations by chewing dog-biscuits, Lonzy?"

"No, my dear Skinner," responded Alonzo, still blinking. "I—I discovered this whilst walking beneath these cloisters. Really, Skinner, this is most extraordinary!"

"Let me have a look at it," said Skinner. And he took the paper from Alonzo.

He gave a low whistle when he finished reading it.

"Crumbs!" he ejaculated. "What a go, Alonzo!"

Alonzo blinked at the dog-biscuit distressfully.

"And to think that the poor man is being fed upon these horrible things!" murmured he. "Dud-dear me, Skinner!"

"Dear us!" said Skinner, seeming to have some difficulty in keeping back a laugh.

"Do you really think we ought to——"

"We must rescue the poor man!" said Skinner decisively.

"Bub-but——" said Alonzo, in a very distressed and anxious tone of voice. "Don't you think we had better acquaint Dr. Locke with the matter, my dear Skinner?"

Skinner shook his head.

"No, Alonzo," he said. "You see what it says, he is in hourly peril of his life. If we go yarning about the school the poor man's captor may get to know of it. We don't know who is responsible for keeping the man prisoner. It may be Herr Gans, for all we know!"

"G-good gracious!" gasped Alonzo. "Dud-do you really think it is as serious as all that, Skinner?"

"Certainly I do!" replied Skinner. "We shall have to keep this a dead secret, Lonzy, else all may be lost. You and I will make an effort to rescue the prisoner to-night, at nine."

Alonzo Todd gasped.

"It's up to you, Lonzy," urged Skinner. "You found the paper, you know, and, therefore, the man's appeal is to you. It is a matter of life or death, Alonzo!"

Alonzo Todd picked up the "Treatise on Bacteria."

"Very well, my dear Skinner!" he said. "I must certainly do all within my power to effect a rescue of this unfortunate individual."

"That's it!" said Skinner. "We must act quickly, Alonzo, else all may be in vain! If we don't get into the vaults to-night, the man may be dead to-morrow!"

"G-good heavens!" gasped Alonzo.

"I'll see you here at nine to-night, then, Lonzy," said Skinner. "You'll be ready, won't you?"

"Yes," said Alonzo.

"I'll bring along a light," said Skinner. "It'll be pitch-dark down there, and we must see where we are going."

"D-do you think it will be safe, Skinner?" asked Alonzo, blinking at him in uncertainty.

"Well, I tell you what, Alonzo," said Skinner. "To make sure of it, I'll get Bolsover major and Stott and Snoop and one or two others——"

"Oh, thank you, Skinner!" said Alonzo. "I should be so pleased!"

"And, mind," said Skinner warningly, "not a word to anyone else! Don't let your cousin Peter know, else he might tell all the others, and the cat would be let out of the bag, and the poor man might be murdered in consequence! We'll do it on our own, Alonzo."

"Very well, my dear Skinner," said Alonzo Todd. "I shall not say anything to the others.

"Good man, Lonzy!" said Skinner heartily. "We'll do somebody a good turn to-night, at any rate!"

And, comforted by that parting thought, the Duffer of Greyfriars went his way, the treatise tucked under his arm and the dog-biscuit in his pocket.

As for Harold Skinner, as soon as Alonzo Todd was out of sight he whistled, and a moment later he was joined by Stott and Snoop. They were grinning hugely.

"Ha, ha, ha!" howled Stott. "It worked like a charm, Skinner!"

"The Duffer took the bait like winking!" grinned Skinner. "So Alonzo is going exploring the vaults to-night—with a light!"

"Ha, ha, ha!"

"And old Squiff will be there, developing his photographs, and Lonzy and his giddy light will muck the whole lot up! Ha, ha, ha!"

"He, he, he!" cackled Snoop.

And, chuckling in high glee, the three young rascals made their way into the tuckshop. Alonzo Todd was standing outside, meditatively examining the dog-biscuit, and Skinner & Co. kicked up their heels in ecstasies of merriment.

III.

"JUST off to the vaults to develop my photos of the First Eleven," said Squiff, tucking his camera under his arm.

"Do you think they'll come out all right, Squiff?" inquired Bob Cherry

"Top-hole, I should think," said Squiff. "I reckon I'll have some record negatives when the plates are developed."

"Well," said Bob Cherry, "I think I'll come along and see the show. Shall us, Harry?"

"Let's!" replied Harry Wharton.

"Well, you can come if you like," said Squiff. "But there'll be a row if you muck up the business, I can tell you!"

"Oh, that's all right!" said Bob Cherry. "Lead on, Macduff!"

And the Famous Five trooped away across the quadrangle, and entered the vaults by the stone in the old tower.

All was pitch-black and eerie down in the ancient arches, and we could not repress a shudder as we looked around us.

Squiff soon had his dishes filled, ready for developing his plates, also the slides prepared and the ruby lamp lighted. Then we blew out our bicycle-lamps, and watched Squiff in the mystic red light as he started his photographic operations.

Meanwhile, in the old tower above, four stealthy figures met.

Alonzo Todd, true to his trust, was there, though looking far from heroic. Skinner and Snoop and Stott came up, bearing with them a huge old oil-lamp.

"Hallo, here you are, Alonzo!" said Skinner. "You see, old chap, here are four of us. so it will be all safe!"

"Y-y-yes, my dear Skinner," said the Duffer, eyeing the large lamp that Skinner held out to him.

"Take that, Lonzy," said Skinner. "We'll let you through the trap, and then, if it's all clear, we'll come along afterwards."

"I—I—I——" murmured Alonzo, blinking at the lighted lamp and the strange darkness of the old tower.

"Come along, Alonzo!" said Skinner. "Remember there's a poor man down in those vaults being fed on dog-biscuits, and tortured, and in hourly peril of his life!"

"Y-ye-es," stuttered Alonzo.

"Buck up, Lonzy!" said Stott, patting him reassuringly on the back. "We're here to look after you you know."

"It's up to you, Alonzo!" said Skinner, pushing him forward.

Alonzo went. Grasping the lighted lamp, which, despite its age, shed out a truly magnificent glare of light, Alonzo allowed himself to be shoved into the old tower, and down through the trapdoor into the vaults.

The poor Duffer's teeth were chattering as he stood alone in the cold darkness, but Skinner and Stott and Snoop looked down at him from above, and whispered him encouragement.

"Carry on, Alonzo!" called Skinner softly. "We're coming!"

Alonzo walked very gingerly into the depths of the vaults, the lamp lighting up the old place very brilliantly. Skinner had seen to that.

Meanwhile, Squiff had got his dark slides open, and was busy developing the first plate. We waited patiently as he rocked the developing-dish to and fro, and gathered round eagerly to examine the negative in the red light.

"My word!" said Bob Cherry. "They look like niggers!"

"Ass!" snapped Squiff. "That's a rattling good negative! Now—— Mum-mum-my hat!"

He dropped the negative upon the stone flags as a figure walked into view round one of the arches. A glare of light was shed over the group round the developing-table, and we all blinked at each other in the unwelcome illumination.

"Hallo, hallo, hallo!" exclaimed Bob Cherry. "What the merry dickens——"

Squiff seemed on the verge of apoplexy, and he choked queerly in his throat.

"I—I—I——" stuttered Squiff.

"What the deuce is the game?" gasped Harry Wharton. "Who is——"

"Ha, ha, ha!" yelled Johnny Bull. "It's Alonzo!"

"Alonzo!"

The Duffer of Greyfriars approached and surveyed us in horror in the glare of his lamp.

"My dear fellows——"

We stood there and gaped at Alonzo, the wind utterly taken out of our sails, so to speak, for the moment. As for Alonzo, he set down his lamp and wagged his forefinger at us.

"Wharton, Nugent, Cherry, Field!" said Alonzo Todd, in tones of horror and consternation. "I am extremely sorry to have found you here on such terrible work. Little did I dream, when I entered this place, that I should find my own schoolfellows—boys of my own Form—carrying on such abominable practices as you are!"

We gasped and gasped again, unable to utter words.

"It grieves me deeply," went on the Duffer, blinking at us sorrowfully. "It fills me with sorrow that I should be the one to have discovered you at your nefarious practices. Wharton, I am astounded! My Uncle Benjamin would be shocked—nay, disgusted!"

"Mum-my word!" gasped Bob Cherry.

Alonzo Todd looked at us in deep distress.

"I trust you are truly sorry for your wicked ways, my dear fellows," he said. "I must ask you to deliver into my safe keeping the unhappy person who is the victim of your crime. I——"

"You—you—you howling ass!" shrieked Squiff, thrusting his clenched fist underneath the Duffer's nose. "You thundering booby! You've messed up all my photographs! You've ruined my plates! You've mucked up all my work! You—you—— Oh, lemme get at you!"

He darted at Alonzo Todd, who had stood as one thunderstruck. Squiff's fist crashed upon the hapless Duffer's nose, and the water ran from Alonzo's eyes in streams.

"Ow!" ejaculated Alonzo, staggering back.

"I'll wring your neck, you thumping booby!" screeched Squiff. "I——"

But Alonzo had scented danger. He saw that Squiff was excited, and unreasonable in his wrath. That thump on his nose had hurt, and Alonzo, duffer though he might be, was not so green as to overlook the decided probability that there would be plenty more —and in greater variety—to follow.

With a startled blink at us, and a glare of terror at Squiff, Alonzo Todd skipped back, gave one yell of anguish, and fled into the darkness of the vaults.

With a bellow of fury Squiff dashed off in pursuit, and the footsteps of the hurrying pair re-echoed to the tune of their voices among the old stone arches.

We surveyed each other in amazement. It had all happened so swiftly and surprisingly that we were absolutely thunderstruck. Whilst we were still silently wondering the sound of other voices assailed our ears.

"Ha, ha, ha!" howled the voice of Skinner. "The Duffer's done it! Old Squiff's chasing him around the vaults! Hark at 'em!"

"Ha, ha, ha!" chortled Snoop and Stott.

"Quick, chaps!" chuckled Skinner. "We'll just have time to wreck old Squiff's photographic traps while he's walloping old Alonzo. Kim on!"

Their footsteps were heard approaching.

"Quiet!" muttered Harry Wharton. "We'll catch the cad on the hop! Get into hiding behind the arches, quick!"

We darted into the shadow of the arches just as Skinner & Co. arrived. They grinned hugely as they saw Squiff's photographic stuff lying unattended on the stones.

"Good!" chuckled Skinner. "Now we'll get a bit of our own back on Squiff—eh, what?"

"Oh, rather!" cackled Stott.

"Oh, will you?" cried Harry Wharton, stepping from the shadow of the arches. "Collar the cads, you chaps!"

Upon the word we sprang out, and soon had Skinner and his two sweet pals helpless on the cold, hard stones.

Skinner & Co. glared up at us in terror.

"W-what the——" gasped Skinner.

"Got you, my beauties!" said Harry

Wharton. "So you're at the bottom of this game—eh, Skinner?"

"Yes, Wharton, it was Skinner!" howled Snoop. "It wasn't me! Lemme go!"

Harry Wharton looked at him scornfully.

Skinner ground his teeth.

"Well, you've got us, Wharton," groaned Skinner. "What're you going to do with us?"

"Wait till Squiff comes back, and we'll ask him," retorted Harry Wharton.

Just then there came a howl from the darkness, and a wild figure dashed up. It was Alonzo Todd, looking like a scared rabbit, and hot on his track came Squiff. He grabbed the fleeing Duffer, and bore him to the ground just on top of Skinner & Co.

"Yarooogh!" roared Skinner, as Alonzo's boot caught him a beauty in the eye.

"Wow-ow-ow! Ow-ow!" wailed Snoop, as Squiff flopped down heavily on his face.

A roaring, kicking mass of humanity struggled together on the floor. Squiff and Alonzo Todd were on top, and evidently Skinner & Co. were getting the worst of it, to judge by the howls that arose.

"Here, steady on, Squiff!" gasped Harry Wharton, laughing. "I say, you fellows, call the idiot off before he does poor old Alonzo in!"

Almost sobbing with laughter, we rescued Alonzo Todd from his enemy.

Squiff glared at us, and panted and struggled to get at Alonzo again.

"Whoa, there, Squiffy!" said Bob Cherry. "Give it a breeze, old man!"

"Lemme get at him!" roared Squiff. "I'll —I'll——"

"Protect me, I beseech you, Wharton!" wailed Alonzo, blinking through one eye very pitifully at us.

The poor old Duffer looked a sorry spectacle indeed. His prominent proboscis was red and assuming a startling size. One eye was black and closed up, his nose was bleeding, and his hair looked as if a lawn-mower had been over it. Squiff himself was not much better.

"Half-time, Squiff!" said Harry Wharton. "It's all a mistake, I think you'll find. That ass Alonzo has been the victim of one of Skinner's rotten hoaxes. Here, Snoop, tell us what you've been up to, or we'll scrag you alive!"

Then Snoop let it all out. He told the story of how they had planted the bogus letter and the dog-biscuit on Alonzo, and got him to enter the vaults with a light. Squiff almost exploded as he heard.

"I'll slaughter that cad Skinner!" roared Squiff. "Wharton, you ass, lemme go!"

Well, Skinner deserved it, so we let Squiff go. And he did so—some! In five minutes it was impossible to see Skinner for Squiff.

As for Snoop and Stott, we subjected them to a severe bumping on the hard paving-stones of the vaults, and then kicked them out, howling, into the quadrangle.

Then we rescued what was left of Skinner from Squiff, and we left the vaults for the night. Poor old Alonzo was a case to be pitied and condoled. We bathed his wounds for him, and then stood him as good as spread as rations and restrictions would allow, in Study No. 1.

"Never mind, Alonzo!" said Bob Cherry, as he stuffed some more pineapple into the Duffer's mouth. "We'll take the will for the deed, and your action showed a good spirit, anyway Alonzo, old man, you're a giddy hero!"

And, accordingly, we toasted Alonzo Todd a hero, and accorded him three hefty cheers.

THE END.

OUR COMIC COLUMN.

By Monty Lowther.

It seems that our airmen's extensive raids exasperated the Germans. They certainly disaspirated the Hun rest-camps, and turned them into 'Un-rest camps.

Germany's efforts to win the war were said to be untiring. Ours were evidently Hun-tiring.

Why would a railway strike be more serious than a coal-miners' strike?

Because the latter at most would only be a "miner" strike, while the railway-men would have more sub-porters.

Why would it be difficult to steam a Dreadnought down the Styx?

Because the ship could never get "coaled!"

The Hun made war because war made the Hun.

What I'd like to know is, what the Hun maid wore? Someone said the "close" of a rotten Empire.

The mountain sighed! The cavern yawned! The torrent roared! The wind shrieked! But none could make the moon beam!

Shopkeepers are fond of queues. There have been sugar, potato, fish, whisky, and tea queues. There is one kind of queue that we shall never get, that's a "thank you." At least, not from Rylcombe tradesmen.

We may get better butter. But a better thing would be to have a better butter supply. I walked into a grocer's in Wayland, and "the girl behind the counter stood, whence all butter (but her) had fled." Re-marg-able!

What's the difference between a battleship and Percy M------?

One's the former, the other's the informer.

What is the difference between a Zeppelin commander and B. T------?

One studies raids; the other raids studies.

NOTICES.

Football Matches, Etc., Wanted by—

PARK WANDERERS—14-16—also players.—C. H. c/o Room 58, 83, Pall Mall, S.W. 1.

IVY ATHLETIC CLUB—17 and over.—F. Wickes, 78, Vestry Road, Camberwell, S.E. 5.

BRONDESBURY ATHLETIC—15-16—2 miles—away only.—Martin B. Assan, 60, Brondesbury Road, Kilburn, N.W. 6.

VICTORIA ATHLETIC—16½-17½—7 miles.—Percy Marns, 43, Joseph Street, Burdett Road, E. 3. Also five players, any position bar goal. Colours, green and white.

CHRIST CHURCH, OXFORD MISSION F.C.—players wanted, age about 16.—W. Haynes, 1, Faraday Road, North Kensington, W. 10.

AIRLESS ATHLETIC—16½—away only; any reasonable distance.—Wm. Rowley, 102, Landcroft Road, East Dulwich, S.E. 22.

NORTH ROAD OLD BOYS—14-15—5 miles—medium—all dates.—E. Hudson, 7, Alexandra Avenue, Southall, Middlesex.

WINDSOR ATHLETIC—16-17½—any date—5 miles—also wanted goalkeeper.—E. Robb, 122, Queen's Road, Everton, Liverpool.

GRANVILLE—16—home or away; end of year and beginning of next.—L. F. Turner, 52, Lea Bridge Road, Clapton, N.E.

OTTERSPOOL—15½—4 miles radius of Aigburth Vale.—A. Jones, 37, Milner Road, Aigburth, Liverpool.

WOODLAND ROVERS—any dates—also two backs.—T. Bond, 221, Union Square, Union Road, Borough, S.E. 1.

57TH S. L. JUNIOR B.P. SCOUTS—13, weak—3 miles Kennington Gate.—H. Smith, 53, St. Paul's Road, Kennington, S.E. 17.

POLLARDS UNITED—newly formed—16½—any dates.—C. A. Turner, 89, Clacton Road, Walthamstow, E.

CUSTOM HOUSE ROVERS—16½—3 miles.—J. Lang, 312, Victoria Dock Road, Custom House, E. 16.

Thos. Kelly, 56, Casebourne Road, Belle Vue, West Hartlepool, wants to hear from lads willing to join a team.

RICHMOND JUNIORS—15½.—H. C. Maddock, 105, Whitefield Road, Everton, Liverpool.

LODGE ROAD Y.M.C.A.—11, friendly—all dates.—Reginald Lane, 6/361, Lodge Road, Hockley, Birmingham.

VICTORIA UNITED—players wanted; right-back, left-half, and goalkeeper.—L. Rich, 70, Victoria Avenue, East Ham, E. 6.

ALEXANDRA JUNIORS—14-14½; strength, medium—5 miles.—E. Hudson, 17, Alexandra Avenue, Southall, Middlesex.

ALBION—16.—A. Godbold, 166, Percy Road, Canning Town, London, E. 16.

L. Marks, 13, Edwards Road, Burdett Road, Mile End, E. 3, wants place in football team—age 18—three miles.

Boy—15—wants to join team 5 miles radius of Southfields if possible.—C. K. Watts, 128, Havelock Road, South Wimbledon, S.W. 19. Postage paid for.

The Editor's Chat.

For Next Monday:

"WALLY OF THE REMOVE!"

By Frank Richards.

Wally Bunter has let himself in for a good deal more than he bargained for!

His cousin Billy has rather rushed him, of course Wally's desire to stay at Greyfriars, among the fellows he likes, the fellows who like him, is a very natural one. But—oh, it's a big, big BUT!

Wally at Greyfriars will be Billy! That's the big, big BUT!

He succeeds to Billy's tarnished character, to Billy's debts and troubles, to Billy's reputation as being the biggest duffer at games that Greyfriars ever had.

It is some load to stagger under—what?

You will be interested to learn how Wally, who is a fine, resolute, straightforward fellow, meets his troubles. In fact, I think you will find this series of stories as enthralling as anything we have ever published in the MAGNET.

And, while Wally Bunter is at Greyfriars, we have—

"BILLY BUNTER AT ST. JIM'S!"

If you miss next week's "Gem" you will be missing one of the biggest treats ever offered you.

Perhaps it takes more to make me laugh than it does most of you—I don't know. There are things in the stories which seem to you very funny indeed, and don't strike me as quite so funny. But I have been fairly roaring, cackling, chortling over the yarns about Bunter at St. Jim's. They would tickle anybody with any sense of humour at all.

Bunter and Gussy—Bunter and Figgins & Co.—Bunter and Tom Merry & Co.—Bunter and Baggy Trimble—they are all coming.

Charlie Chaplin? Poof! He isn't in it!

Bunter leaves him gasping in the rear.

NEXT WEEK'S "GEM" CANNOT BE DONE WITHOUT—YOU WON'T BE HAPPY UNLESS YOU GET IT

JANUARY 24th.

I want every reader of the MAGNET to make a special note of the above date, for on this day the "PENNY POPULAR" will make its reappearance. I know, from the numerous letters which I have received from time to time, that the suspension of the "Penny Pop" came as a great blow to all my readers. You will have to wait but a very little time now before you will have the unbounded pleasure of visiting your newsagent's and asking for the "Penny Popular."

You will, I feel sure, be anxious to learn what stories will appear in the paper on January 24th. Firstly, there will be a splendid, long complete tale of Harry Wharton & Co., entitled "BILLY BUNTER'S POSTAL-ORDER!" Then there will be a grand tale of Tom Merry & Co., entitled "D'ARCY'S DELUSION!" And the number will be completed by a story dealing with Jimmy Silver's arrival at Rookwood, and entitled "THE RIVALS OF ROOKWOOD!"

There is another special attraction in this splendid issue, and that is

A MAGNIFICENT PLATE

of Billy Bunter, which will be given entirely free of charge. This plate will not be like the ordinary run of plates, but—— Well, you have only to wait until next Monday to see what this plate will be like. A reproduction appears on the front page of next Monday's MAGNET.

In view of the fact that newsagents are still only ordering those copies of papers for which they have a certain sale, you would be well advised to order your copy of the "Penny Popular" in advance. Tell all your chums about this great news, and pass on my hint to

ORDER IN ADVANCE.

YOUR EDITOR.

The Magnet

No. 571. Vol. XIII. $1\frac{1}{2}$d. January 18th, 1919.

GRAND STORY INSIDE Of Harry Wharton & Co.

Wally of the Remove

Mr. HAWKE.

THE FIRST CHAPTER.
The Other Bunter!

"GOOD!"

Wally Bunter uttered that ejaculation in tones of the most heartfelt satisfaction.

He was first down from the Remove dormitory that morning.

He stood in the open doorway of the School House, looking out into the green old quad, bright and fresh in the morning sunlight.

It was a pleasant sight, and Wally Bunter was enjoying it.

He enjoyed it all the more because to come to Greyfriars had been a day-dream of his which he had never hoped to realise.

And now, here he was, a Greyfriars fellow—W. G. Bunter of the Remove!

It really seemed too good to be true.

In a sense it wasn't true, for Wally had been destined for St. Jim's, and he had only fixed himself at Greyfriars by changing places—and names—with his cousin Billy Bunter. But that was a secret between the two Bunters, and no one else at Greyfriars had a suspicion of it.

That the two Bunters were exactly alike the Remove fellows knew; but that Billy had gone off in Wally's place, and Wally had stayed in Billy's place, would have astonished them very much if they had known it.

Wally had had his doubts overnight. He had been uneasy, though he had yielded to Billy's persuasions and his own strong desire. But in the fresh, sunny morning he had no doubts. There was no real harm in the cousins' change of places. It suited them, and it interfered with nobody else. And Wally felt that he was going to enjoy himself at Greyfriars, and he charitably hoped that Billy was doing the same at St. Jim's.

His fat face was wreathed in smiles as he looked out into the quadrangle. The old trees, leafless now, the grey old stones, the red tiles of the porter's lodge, the playing-fields in the distance—all had a charm for his eyes.

"Good!" he repeated. "Jolly good! Ripping! I'm going to have a tiptop time here! Good!"

"Hallo, hallo, hallo!"

It was Bob Cherry's powerful voice behind him, and Bob Cherry's terrific clap that descended on his fat shoulder and made him jump.

Wally Bunter spun round.

The Famous Five had come down, fresh and cheery, for a run before breakfast. And their looks showed how surprised they were that Bunter had come down first. As a rule, Billy Bunter snatched the latest possible moment in bed.

Hurree Jamset Ram Singh had quite a concerned expression on his dusky face.

"My esteemed Bunter," he murmured, "I hopefully trust that you are not ill-full?"

"Ill!" repeated the fat junior. "No fear! Fit as a fiddle!"

"Then why this thusness?" asked Bob Cherry.

"Eh?"

"Why did you get up before I came to roll you out of bed?" demanded Bob.

"Oh!"

"What do you mean by being down first instead of last?" asked Harry Wharton.

"Must be ill!" said Frank Nugent gravely. "This is a case for the sanatorium."

"Oh, come off!" said Wally Bunter. "Don't be funny, you know. You won't catch me slacking in bed on a ripping morning like this!"

"Wha-a-t?"

"Well, my hat!" exclaimed Bob Cherry. "You fat bounder, do you ever do anything but slack?"

"My esteemed fat Bunter, the slackfulness is generally terrific!" remarked the Nabob of Bhanipur.

Wally gave a grunt.

He had realised already that he had Billy Bunter's reputation to live down, and it looked like being an uphill task.

"The fact is, you fellows——" he began.

"Halt!" exclaimed Bob, holding up his hand.

"Eh? What do you mean?"

"Ring off, my fat tulip! We know what the fact is," chuckled Bob. "We know you're expecting a postal-order by the first post in the morning, and we know you want a fellow to cash it in advance, and we know that it won't come——"

"Ha, ha, ha!"

"Give us a rest, old scout!" implored Johnny Bull. "Give the postal-order a rest! It's worn nearly threadbare by this time, you know. Put on a new record."

"Look here——"

"Chuck it!"

"I tell you——" roared the fat junior wrathfully.

"We know—we know——" interrupted Bob. "We know it all! Haven't we heard it before?"

"Many a time and oft!" grinned Nugent.

"We know it's from one of your titled relations, Bunty," said Harry Wharton, laughing. "We know it hasn't come owing to the delay caused by the war. We know all about it. We've got it by heart."

"You silly chumps!" shouted Wally. "I wasn't going to say I was expecting a postal-order."

"What?"

"You're not expecting a postal-order?" shouted Bob Cherry.

"No!"

"You don't want it cashed in advance?"

"No!"

"Great Julius Cæsar! Fan me, somebody!"

Bob Cherry staggered back, apparently overcome. He leaned on the door, and looked quite faint.

"Fetch me a whisky-and-soda!" he moaned.

"Ha, ha, ha!"

"You silly ass!" roared Bunter. "I tell you——"

"Don't tell me anything more!" gasped Bob. "It will affect my heart if I hear anything more like that!"

"Break it gently, old chap!" said Nugent.

"Hallo, what's the row?" asked Peter Todd, coming along to the door with Squiff and Vernon-Smith and Tom Redwing.

"Only Bob Cherry playing the goat!" growled Wally Bunter.

"Bunter's not expecting a postal-order!" gasped Bob. "He doesn't want to raise a loan on it in advance!"

"Gammon!"

"Spoof!"

"Draw it mild!"

"Fact!" said Wharton. "Some ass said the age of miracles was past! But that——"

"It isn't!" grinned Nugent.

"It's come back, anyway," chuckled Johnny Bull. "Sing it over again to us, Bunty! You're not expecting a postal-order?"

"No!" howled the fat junior.

"From one of your titled relations, you——"

"I haven't got any titled relations."

"What?"

The whole group of juniors howled in chorus. This was a clincher!

"You—you—you haven't got any titled relations?" said Wharton dazedly.

"No, you ass! Why should you suppose I had?"

"I didn't supose you had, old top; but you always said you had."

"I didn't!"

"Wha-a-at?"

"I—I—I mean——" stammered Wally Bunter, remembering that he had Billy's sins to answer for. "I—I—I mean——"

"The poor chap is wandering in his mind," said Peter Todd seriously. "He was very strange in his manner last evening. I had a tin of sardines in the study. It's still there."

"And Bunter knew?"

"He knew!"

"And it's still there?"

"It's still there."

"Poor old Bunter!" said Bob Cherry feelingly. "Off his poor old rocker! We had better tell Quelchy this, and get him to call in the doctor."

"Look here, you thumping asses——" exclaimed the fat junior, in great exasperation.

"Be calm, dear boy!" said Bob. "Calm yourself! Don't get excited. It's bad for a chap in your state of mind."

"You silly ass——"

"Shush! Shush!! Remember, you are off your rocker, old son!" urged Bob.

"If you want me to punch your nose, Bob Cherry——"

"Oh, my hat! Do!" grinned Bob.

"Well, I will!"

A fat fist came up like lightning. Bob Cherry, laughing, made a careless parry, but to his surprise his hand was knocked aside, and the fat fist was planted on his nose.

Bump!

Bob Cherry sat down in the doorway.

THE SECOND CHAPTER.
Bunter Causes Surprise;

"YAROOOH!"

That was Bob's remark as he sat down.

He sat and blinked at Bunter in astonishment.

Harry Wharton & Co. stared at the fat junior as if he had mesmerised them. Bunter, the Owl of the Remove, had knocked Bob Cherry down, and Bob Cherry was the champion fighting-man of the Lower School; the fellow who could lick Bolsover major and anybody in the Fourth, and who was treated with some consideration even by Shell and Fifth Form fellows!

They stared at Bunter and they stared at Bob, and they looked at one another. Nugent rubbed his eyes as if to make sure that he was awake.

"Ow!" said Bob. "Wow! Oh! Ah!"

He dabbed his nose dazedly as he sat. He was more surprised than hurt, but he was rather hurt, too. The fat fist had had unexpected driving-power behind it.

Bunter's expression changed at once, however. He stooped over Bob to give him a hand up.

"Sorry!" he exclaimed. "I didn't mean to hit hard. I hope I haven't hurt you, old fellow!"

Bob blinked at him. Bunter caught hold of him and helped him up, Bob being still in quite a dazed state.

"Am I dreaming?" he asked. "Did I only fancy I heard the rising-bell, and got up?"

"You shouldn't rag a fellow so," said Bunter apologetically. "I was excited. I'm sorry I punched your nose!"

"It isn't a dream!" said Bob, dabbing his nose with his handkerchief, which came away red. "That fat worm has really punched my nose! I suppose you know I'm going to slaughter you, Bunter?"

Bunter backed away.

That was quite like the old Bunter, if his previous proceedings were not. But it was not a case of funk.

"I've said I'm sorry," he answered. "After all, you asked me to punch your nose, you know. I'm not going to fight you."

"Fight me!" exclaimed Bob. "You! Why, you fat idiot, if I hit you you'd burst!"

"The burstfulness would be terrific!" grinned Hurree Singh.

"Oh, rats!" answered Bunter.

Bob Cherry dabbed his nose again, and eyed Bunter doubtfully. He had, in a way, asked for it, and certainly it was no use to think of fighting Billy Bunter.

"Easy does it, Bob!" said Harry Wharton, taking his chum's arm. "Come out for a run before brekker."

"That fat worm——"

"Never mind the fat worm; let him wriggle off," said Nugent. And he took Bob's other arm.

Bob was rushed out into the quadrangle, and the other juniors followed. Bunter looked after them, with a rather wistful expression on his fat face.

As Wally Bunter, he had been friendly with the Co. on his visit to Greyfriars. But as Billy Bunter, he was—Billy Bunter! He wondered whether he would ever be on a chummy footing with the fellows whom he liked and respected.

A tap on the arm interrupted his meditations. He glanced round, to see Sammy Bunter of the Second Form—Billy's minor.

Sammy eyed him curiously.

"Where's your specs?" he asked.

"My—my specs?"

"Yes. Lost them?"

"Nunno! I—I've got them in his pocket," stammered Bunter. And he jerked out the pair of glasses Billy had left him and jammed them on his nose, well below his eyes, however.

"What's the matter with you?" asked Sammy.

"Mum-mum-matter?"

"Yes. You can't see without your specs, can you? What's the good of putting them there?"

"I—I—— The fact is, these glasses don't suit me," stammered the fat junior. "I'm going to get a change."

Sammy blinked at him. He was conscious of some subtle difference in Bunter major, though the latter looked just the same as usual.

"How much did Wally shell out?" he asked, changing the subject.

"Eh?"

"You went to the station with him," said the fat fag. "I suppose you didn't take that trouble for nothing. What did you stick him for?"

Bunter major grinned. He was learning more and more about the cheery manners and customs of the other Bunter.

"Nothing!" he answered.

"Oh, come off it!" said Sammy incredulously. "I'd back you to screw a loan out of anybody, and you had Wally here a couple of days on a visit. You must have stuck him for something. How much?"

"Oh, rats!"

"Well, lend me a bob, Billy, till my allowance comes," said Sammy discontentedly.

"All right!"

Bunter major handed over the coin cheerfully enough, and Sammy pocketed it in great surprise. It was the easiest shilling he had ever extracted from his major.

"You ain't so jolly mean as usual!" he remarked.

"Thanks!"

"You can make it half-a-crown if you like!" said Sammy, with the idea of striking the iron while it was hot.

"Bow-wow!" was the reply to that. And Bunter of the Remove strolled out into the quad, leaving Sammy blinking after him curiously through his big glasses.

Two or three of the Fourth were punting a footer about in the quad as Bunter major came along.

"Hallo, here's Falstaff!" remarked Temple of the Fourth. "Watch me!"

Dabney and Fry and Scott stopped to watch him, grinning. Temple placed the ball carefully, intending to land it on Bunter's plump face as he came by, fully expecting that the short-sighted Owl of the Remove would not see the footer till it landed on his fat little nose.

But he had to deal with an unexpected Bunter that morning.

The fat junior was within a dozen feet when Temple kicked, and the footer flew with a whiz for his fat countenance.

Bunter promptly dodged the shot, and as the footer flew by he stopped it with his hand, and it dropped.

His eyes gleamed at Cecil Reginald Temple over his glasses.

As Temple, surprised, stared at him, Bunter major dribbled the ball a pace or two towards him, and kicked back.

The footer flew like a bullet, and before Temple knew what was happening there was a crash on his nose.

Temple staggered back.

"Ha, ha, ha!" roared Fry of the Fourth, as the footer landed on Temple's astounded face. "Good shot!"

Temple, taken utterly by surprise, staggered back two or three paces, and sat down with a bump. Such deftness on the part of the clumsy Owl of the Remove was astounding.

Cecil Reginald's face was streaming with mud, for the footer had been through a number of puddles. He sat and blinked and coughed and snorted, while his comrades roared.

"Goal!" chuckled Scott.

"Oh, rather!" roared Dabney. "Good shot, Bunter!"

Bunter major grinned.

"Try again, old top!" he called out.

"Groooooogh!"

"Ha, ha, ha!"

"Why, you—you—you cheeky fag," howled Temple, scrambling up. "I'll squash you! I'll burst you! I—I—I'll—I'll——"

"Oh, draw it mild!" exclaimed Bunter. "You were punting at me, you know!"

"Tit for tat, old sport!" chuckled Fry.

But Cecil Reginald Temple was not in a reasonable mood. To land a muddy footer on a Remove fag's face was one thing; to have it landed on his own aristocratic countenance was quite another. He rushed at the Owl of the Remove, breathing wrath and vengeance.

He expected Bunter to flee before the storm; but Bunter did not flee. He waited for Cecil Reginald to come up with perfect coolness.

"Hook it, you young ass!" called out Scott of the Fourth good-naturedly.

"Bow-wow!" was the reply.

Temple rushed on, and his grasp fell upon the fat Removite.

Bunter ought to have been bumped down in the quad with a terrific bump.

But he wasn't. Two fat hands grasped Temple; and, to Cecil Reginald's amazement, his legs somehow swept from under him, and he sat down without knowing how he got there.

Bump!

"Oh!"

"My hat!" gasped Fry. "Oh, Christopher Columbus! Oh, Temple! Ha, ha, ha!"

"Yaroooh!"

Bunter walked away, with a fat smile. Temple, quite out of breath, sat and gasped till his grinning comrades picked him up. He was picked up in a dazed state.

"B-B-Bunter!" he stuttered. "B-Bunter! You saw that!"

"We saw it, old top!" grinned Fry.

"I—I—I'll smash him——"

"Better get a wash before brekker!" chuckled Dabney. "Only three minutes; and if Capper sees your chivvy like that he——"

Cecil Reginald Temple controlled his wrath, and ran in for a wash. He wanted one badly. Bunter sauntered in the quadrangle till breakfast, and a good many glances were turned upon him there. Bunter was surprising his schoolfellows that morning.

THE THIRD CHAPTER.
A Surprising Meeting!

DURING the new few days nearly everybody in the Remove was interested in Bunter of that Form.

They couldn't understand it.

Peter Todd and Tom Dutton, his study-mates in No. 7, were the most surprised and interested of all.

It was extraordinary to find Bunter not taking the lion's share at tea, and still more extraordinary to find him "standing his whack" in providing the supplies.

During these days nobody was put to the trouble of chasing him out of a study with a cricket-stump or a fire-shovel; Bunter seemed to have dropped completely his habit of raiding other fellows' rations.

He even turned up to footer practice.

Still more amazing, he showed proficiency at the game, and the fellows who saw him could only marvel.

Mr. Quelch, the Remove-master, often looked at him with keen interest in the Form-room.

From being the dunce of the Form, Bunter had become one of Mr. Quelch's brightest pupils.

Mr. Quelch was a conscientious gentleman, and laboured hard with backward boys; and Billy Bunter had been the kind of pupil to turn any master's hair grey. But now the Remove-master's task was considerably lightened, so far as Bunter was concerned. True, he showed a curious ignorance of some of the customs of the Remove, and his mind appeared a blank on some minor points; but in general knowledge he was quite surprising. Even his handwriting and spelling had marvellously improved.

All the Remove simple stared when Bunter stood up to construe; they simply couldn't get used to it. It was Billy Bunter who had become famous for rendering "Arma virumque cano" into "The armed man to the dog." But now his construe compared quite favourably with anybody's but Wharton's or Tom Redwing's or Mark Linley's.

"He's reforming!" Peter Todd told the Famous Five. "It was bound to come in the long run. That is what comes of my keeping a cricket-stump in the study specially for Bunter! This is my reward at last—though I admit I expected to use up two or three stumps before it came to this!"

It really looked as if the Owl of the Remove was reforming.

Certainly, Billy Bunter had reformed before; and at that time he had assumed a lofty self-righteousness that made his Form-fellows wish that he would "chuck it." This time there was no trace of self-righteousness.

But Billy Bunter was a little too well known for his reform to be swallowed whole, so to speak. Most of the fellows decided that he was playing some very deep game, and they wondered what it was.

He had given up raising loans in the Remove. He never mentioned his celebrated postal-order; and no reference to his titled relations dropped from his fat lips.

He did not expend all his pocket-money in the tuckshop, though he was a good customer there. That was one point in which he had not changed—his appetite was as good as ever. But he seemed to have learned that it was not the thing to go up and down the Remove passage like a lion seeking what he might devour.

On Saturday afternoon Harry Wharton & Co. were going over to Cliff House to tea with Marjorie & Co.; and when they went round to the bike-shed for their machines they found Bunter there. He was in his shirt-sleeves, seated among what looked like the wreckage of a bike, very oily and dusty. The Famous Five regarded him with surprise.

"Hallo, hallo, hallo! Mending your bike at last?" exclaimed Bob Cherry.

"Looks like it, doesn't it?"

"Well, it's time you did!" remarked Bob. "You've got a long row to hoe. You've left it long enough!"

"Better late than never."

"The betterfulness is terrific!" remarked Hurree Jamset Ram Singh.

"I say, this jigger was in an awful state!" remarked Bunter.

"It was!" said Harry Wharton, laughing. "Why don't you keep your bike in order, like any other fellow, Bunter?"

"I'm going to, in future."

"Well, as you're growing so jolly industrious, I'll lend you a hand," said Bob Cherry. "We needn't start just yet, you fellows!"

"Right-ho!" said Johnny Bull. "Let's all help! Bunter ought to be encouraged, when he begins doing things for himself instead of worrying other chaps to do them for him."

"Well, you can help if you like!" said Bunter. "I'm up to my ears in it, and no mistake!"

The Famous Five took off their jackets, rolled up their sleeves, and piled in. Punctures galore had to be mended, the pedals had to be straightened out, the chain repaired, and several other things, as well as a staggering amount of cleaning to be done. But many hands made light work, and in half an hour Bunter's bike was looking quite a handsome jigger.

Then the bike-repairers had to clean themselves.

"We shall have to scorch a bit now, or we shall be late," Frank Nugent remarked, as he wheeled out his machine.

"You fellows going for a spin?" asked Bunter.

"Yes; to Cliff House."

"Oh! Like a fellow to come?"

"Rats!" said Bob Cherry.

Bunter blinked at him over his glasses. The fat junior had already been to the optician's in Courtfield for new glasses, and he had plain glass now in the spectacles, which did not trouble his sight so much. But he had a habit of sticking the glasses on his fat little nose well below the level of his eyes.

"Do you call that civil, Bob Cherry?" he asked.

Bob laughed.

"My dear porpoise, we can't plant you on Marjorie & Co., and you know it!" he said. "They can't stand you. It's your own fault."

"Oh, really, you know——"

"Come on!" said Harry Wharton. And the chums of the Remove wheeled their machines away to the gates.

Wally Bunter's expression was very thoughtful as he moved out more slowly with his bike. He knew Marjorie & Co., of Cliff House—as Wally. But he was playing Billy Bunter now, and Billy Bunter was not persona grata at Cliff House, or anywhere else, for that matter. The task of living down Billy Bunter's reputation was bigger than Wally had imagined.

Nobody was anxious for Bunter's company. He wheeled his machine out by himself, and pedalled away towards Friardale. In the road he came upon Fisher T. Fish, also on a bike, and Fishy grinned at him.

"Race you up the hill, Bunter!" he called out.

Bunter glanced at him.

"Get ahead!" said Fish. "If I catch you, I'm going to roll you off that bike, I guess! See?"

He pedalled towards Bunter, who grinned, and rode on. There was a rise in the lane towards Friardale, and Fisher T. Fish anticipated with great amusement that Bunter would crack up hopelessly. But the fat junior rode up the rise with perfect ease.

He glanced back and grinned at Fishy, who was labouring breathlessly behind.

"Get a move on!" he called. "Do you call this a race, Fishy?"

"I swow!" gasped Fish. "I guess I don't care for bike-racing; it's a mug's game! Go and chop chips!"

And Fisher T. Fish gave it up.

Wally Bunter grinned, and pedalled on cheerfully. He came over the rise, and free-wheeled down the other slope towards the village.

As he sailed down the lane a man, leaning on a fence by the roadside, stepped out, and raised his hand as a sign to stop.

The fat junior looked at him. He was a squat-looking man, with a bowler-hat on one side of his head, and a black cigar in the corner of his mouth.

He had a very horsy appearance, and the general look of a man who kept late hours, and did not wash or brush very carefully in the morning.

"Stop!" he called out.

Bunter slackened a little.

"Want anything?" he asked, without stopping.

"Yes, you young rascal!"

"Wha-a-at?" ejaculated Wally, in astonishment.

"Get off that bicycle!" said the horsy man authoritatively.

Bunter simply blinked at him. He concluded that the stranger was under the influence of liquor; there was no other way of accounting for his extraordinary behaviour.

The fat junior did not stop.

"Will you stop?" shouted the horsy-looking man angrily.

"No, I won't!"

"Mind, I ain't standing any more nonsense from you, Master Bunter!"

"Oh, you know my name, do you?" said Wally, pedalling on, while the horsy man strode along to keep pace.

The man stared at him.

"Know your name!" he repeated. "Of course I know your name, as well as you know mine!"

"I'm afraid I don't!" said Bunter. "What's your name?"

"Eh?"

"You look as if it might be Bill Sikes!" said Wally cheerily. "Is that it?"

"You cheeky young 'ound!" roared the horsy gentleman. "I'll 'ave you off that bike fast enough!"

He closed in on Wally, who swerved away at once, and eluded him. As the man lurched forward the fat junior released one hand, and reached out and knocked the bowler-hat off the greasy head. Then he drove hard at his pedals, and rode on, chuckling.

Fifty yards farther on he looked back. The horsy man was standing in the road, the dusty hat gripped in one hand, and the other clenched and waving threateningly in the air.

"Squiffy or potty!" murmured Wally Bunter. "Can't be a man who knows Billy, I suppose—even Billy would draw the line at an acquaintance like that!"

And he rode on cheerily into Friardale.

THE FOURTH CHAPTER.
A Highcliffe Rag!

UNCLE CLEGG came out of his dusty little parlour as the shop-bell tinkled. He grunted as he saw his customer.

Uncle Clegg was not glad to see him. Billy Bunter's visits to the village tuckshop were, as often as not, for the purpose of seeking to obtain tick, or to induce Uncle Clegg to sell rationed goods without coupons. Hence the expressive grunt of Mr. Clegg.

Wally Bunter, quite unaware of Mr. Clegg's thoughts, rapped out an order cheerily.

Uncle Clegg gave him a grim look, and made no motion whatever to carry out his instructions.

"Well?" said Wally, in surprise. "Haven't you got any ginger-pop?"

"I 'ave!" said Uncle Clegg stolidly.

"And tarts?"

"I 'ave!"

"Well, why don't you hand them over, then?" demanded Wally.

"Which you knows puffickly well, Master Bunter, that I makes it a rule to see your money first!" said Mr. Clegg. "You don't need telling that at this time o' day!"

"Oh, my hat!" ejaculated Wally.

He understood then; and he clinked a half-crown on the counter. Then Mr. Clegg, with another grunt, proceeded to serve him.

Wally Bunter sat on a high stool at the counter and piled in. He had his cousin's gift of enjoying a snack at any time of the day. Uncle Clegg's tarts were war tarts—decidedly war—but the fat junior seemed to enjoy them, and he beamed genially upon the crusty old gentleman behind the counter.

He had almost finished when three rather elegant youths came into the village tuckshop.

Wally did not look at them, but he recognised two of them, with the tail of his eye, as it were.

Those two were Ponsonby and Gadsby of Highcliffe School, whom he had seen before. The third was Monson, also of the Fourth Form at Highcliffe.

Wally's previous encounter with Ponsonby had been a hostile one, while he was visiting Billy Bunter at Greyfriars. But now he was in Billy's Etons and Billy's glasses, and Ponsonby & Co., who knew Billy well, were not likely to know that he was the fellow who had once mopped them up.

Wally Bunter was not anxious for a row with three fellows at once, and he knew the Highcliffian standard of fair play, so he finished his ginger-beer very sedately, affecting not to see the newcomers.

Ponsonby looked at him, with a sneering grin.

"Hallo, here's Fat Jack of the Bonehouse!" he remarked.

"Falstaff minor!" grinned Monson.

"Major, I should say!" said Gadsby brightly. "Bigger than Falstaff, anyhow, sideways!"

"Ha, ha, ha!"

Wally Bunter did not heed. It was manifest that the nuts of Highcliffe took him for Billy Bunter, and were bent on a little ragging. Billy Bunter was generally a safe subject to rag.

"Your treat, Bunter!" said Ponsonby, winking at his chums.

"Good egg!" exclaimed Monson. "You hear, fatty? You're standing the ginger-pop all round!"

Wally shook his head.

"Wrong!" he remarked. "I'm not!"

"Have him off that stool!" murmured Gadsby. "Don't waste time on the fat rotter!"

Ponsonby nodded.

"It was a relation of his punched us the other day," he said. "A cousin, or something—some office cad! We'll take it out of this fat beast!"

"Young gentlemen——" murmured Uncle Clegg anxiously.

He was very civil to the wealthy nuts of Highcliffe; but he did not want a shindy in his little shop.

Ponsonby & Co. did not heed him. They intended to have a little rag with the supposed Owl of the Remove, who looked a fat and helpless victim.

Gadsby hooked his feet into the high stool upon which Bunter sat, to jerk it over and land the Owl on the floor, to begin with. Wally Bunter spun off the stool as it flew, and threw his arms round Gaddy's neck.

They went to the floor together, the playful Gadsby underneath, and the still more playful Wally on top. And the yell of anguish that Gadsby gave rang quite a distance down the street.

"Yahooooop!"

"Oh, my heye!" gasped Uncle Clegg.

Gadsby wriggled feebly under Bunter's terrific weight. He was pinned down and helpless. Ponsonby and Monson seemed at a loss for the moment. The activity with which the fat junior had turned the tables on Gadsby took them by surprise.

"Help me, you silly chumps!" howled the unhappy Gaddy. "Yaroooh! He's a squook-squook-squashing me! Ow! Help! Draggimoff!"

"Smash the fat rotter!" said Ponsonby between his teeth. And he sprang towards Bunter.

With an agility that was really remarkable, considering the weight he carried, Wally Bunter leaped up.

He dodged the rush of Ponsonby and Monson, and they nearly stumbled over the helpless Gaddy. Wally backed to the counter, where he had spotted a soda-siphon—being a good deal sharper-sighted than the Owl, whom the Highcliffe nuts supposed him to be.

"Keep off, you rotters," he exclaimed "or—— There you are, then!"

Sizzz! Squish!

"Groooooooch!" spluttered Ponsonby, as he caught the stream full in the face, and went staggering.

Monson jumped away.

"Stoppit!" he howled. "Don't turn it on me—d-d-don't—— Yooooch!"

He caught it with his left ear as he dodged.

There was still a little soda left, and Wally cheerfully gave it to Gadsby as he staggered up. Gadsby collected it mostly in his hair and neck, and his remarks were sulphurous.

"Master Bunter"—Uncle Clegg was howling with wrath—"you'll pay for that there soda! You 'ear me? My larst siphon! You'll pay for it!"

"Certainly, old top!" said Wally cheerfully, throwing a ten-shilling note on the counter. "Change, my dear old infant!"

He kept a sharp eye on Ponsonby & Co. They were wiping soda from their faces, and almost weeping with rage. Wally Bunter picked up his change and walked to the door. As he reached it the three juniors from Highcliffe made in the doorway.

His fat fists were up, and his eyes gleamed at them over his glasses.

"Come on, old beans!" he grinned.

They came on together with a rush, and Ponsonby, the leader, reeled back from a powerful drive on the chin. Gadsby and Monson sprang back as Pon a rush, and Wally spun round instantly went down. To see Bunter of Greyfriars deliver a drive like that took their breath away, and they did not want to sample it for themselves. Ponsonby sat on the floor, stuttering.

"Ta-ta, my infants!" said Wally; and he walked out, leaving the Highcliffians staring and gasping.

He jumped on his machine and pedalled away. That was only prudent, for less than a minute later Ponsonby came dashing out with a barrel-stave in his hand. But Wally was turning out of the village street into the lane, and he pedalled away cheerily, leaving Pon brandishing the stave, and Gadsby and Monson their fists—in vain!

Biff! "Groogh!" (*See Chapter* 2.)

THE FIFTH CHAPTER.

Called Over the Coals!

"HALLO, hallo, hallo! Trouble for somebody!" murmured Bob Cherry softly.

It was Monday afternoon in the Remove Form-room.

The Remove had taken their places as usual; but Mr. Quelch—not as usual—was a couple of minutes late.

When he rustled in the Remove fellows noted at once the thunderous cloud on his brow, and they all made up their minds at once to be very careful indeed that afternoon. When Mr. Quelch looked like that he was not to be trifled with.

"Bunter!"

Mr. Quelch rapped out the name like a bullet.

Wally Bunter rose to his feet, wondering what was the matter. So far as he was aware, he had done nothing to incur his Form-master's wrath.

"Bunter! Come here!"

Bunter came there

Mr. Quelch held up a letter in his hand, and Wally blinked at it. All eyes in the Remove were fixed upon them.

"Bunter!" Mr. Quelch's voice was like the growl of thunder. "This letter has arrived for you!"

"Yes, sir," said the fat junior in wonder.

"You are doubtless aware, Bunter, that a general supervision is exercised over the correspondence of junior boys here," rumbled Mr. Quelch. "Although it is not often interfered with, there are occasions when it is necessary. In the present instance it appears to be very necessary indeed."

Wally started, and his heart sank.

He could only see the outside of the letter in Mr. Quelch's hand, and he concluded at once that it was from Billy at St. Jim's, giving the whole scheme away.

"Oh, sir!" he gasped.

"This letter came by post to-day!" rapped out Mr. Quelch. "It is addressed to you, Bunter!"

"F-f-from my cousin, sir?" stammered Wally.

"Your cousin? Certainly not!"

"Oh!" Wally gasped with relief. "Then, sir——"

"It is from a man of the name of Hawke!" thundered Mr. Quelch.

There was a slight buzz in the Remove. A good many fellows there knew the name of Jerry Hawke, the billiard-sharper, and knew the shiftless, rascally man by sight. Some of them—such as Skinner and Snoop—knew him better than that.

But Wally Bunter's fat face expressed only blank surprise. He knew nothing whatever about Jerry Hawke.

Billy Bunter could have enlightened him, certainly; but Billy Bunter had very carefully refrained from doing so before his departure from Greyfriars.

"You know that name, I presume?" rapped Mr. Quelch.

"No, sir!"

"What?"

"No, sir!" repeated Wally cheerfully.

"Oh, my hat!" murmured Bob Cherry under his breath.

"Of all the terrific fabricators!" murmured Johnny Bull. "How can he stand there and look Quelchy in the face and say it? It beats me!"

"The beatfulness is terrific!"

"Silence in class!" snapped Mr. Quelch, his gimlet eye roving over the Remove for a moment. And there was a silence that could almost be felt. "Bunter! You say you do not know this name?"

"I do not, sir!"

"The man has written to you."

"Has he really, sir?"

"I will read this letter aloud, Bunter, and then I will ask you again whether you know anything of this man."

"Yes, sir."

There was a breathless hush as the Form-master read the letter out. It ran:

"'Dear Master Bunter,—You wouldn't stop and speak to a man on Saturday, so I'm writing. I got to 'ave my money! Unless you 'op along to-morrow with it look out for trouble, that's all.—JERRY HAWKE.'"

Having read out the letter, Mr. Quelch fixed his eyes upon the fat Removite.

"Well, Bunter?" he rumbled.

But Wally only looked astounded.

It did not occur to him for the moment that the letter was addressed to Billy Bunter, and that he was getting this as a sort of legacy from William George. Billy Bunter had given him no hint of his disastrous sporting speculations with Mr. Hawke.

That the Owl was mixed up in such an affair, and that that had been one of his reasons for wanting to get away from Greyfriars, Wally was naturally slow to suspect.

"Bunter! Do you still deny that you know this man?" exclaimed Mr. Quelch.

"Certainly, sir!"

"Did you speak to him on Saturday?"

"A man tried to stop me in the lane and speak to me, sir, as I was going down to Friardale," said Wally, recollecting. "A beery, horsy-looking rotter. I knocked his hat off and biked on."

"You had not known him previously?"

"No, sir."

"You did not owe him money?"

"Nothing of the kind!"

"Why should this man Hawke write to you, Bunter, if you do not know him? And how comes it that he demands payment if you do not owe him money?"

Wally shook his head.

"I can't explain that, sir," he answered. "I should think the man was mad, or drunk! He looked like a boozer——"

"A—a what?"

"A—a man who drinks, sir."

"Bless my soul!" said Mr. Quelch, evidently perplexed. He crumpled the letter in his hand and stared at Wally Bunter.

He was at a loss.

That peculiar letter having been intercepted, the Remove-master had naturally supposed that Bunter was caught out, and he was prepared to pour the vials of his wrath upon the fat junior's head. Knowing Bunter, too, he had expected clumsy denials. But Wally's denials were not clumsy; they were frank and straightforward, and the junior looked as if he were telling the truth, and nothing but the truth—as indeed he was.

"This is very extraordinary, Bunter," said Mr. Quelch at last. "I am bound to accept your word against that of a man of such character. But it is very extraordinary indeed."

Wally was silent. He also thought it extraordinary.

"I shall destroy this letter, Bunter," continued Mr. Quelch. "It is possible that the whole incident is due to some drunken freak, or is an attempt to extort money. If anything further is heard from this man, I shall communicate with the police. In case of any communication from him reaching you, I command you to bring it to me at once!"

"Certainly, sir!"

"You may go to your place, Bunter."

Wally went to his place.

He was puzzled, and a little worried; and he was aware that his Form-master was still suspicious. He passed Harry Wharton as he returned to his desk, and was startled by the glance the captain of the Remove gave him. Harry did not expect Bunter to own up to the Remove-master; but the barefaced falsehoods—as he supposed—that he had listened to disgusted him, and his look showed his feeling plainly enough.

Wally started, and paused. But he could not speak to Wharton then, and he went on to his place. A little later, when lessons were in progress, Skinner leaned over and whispered to him:

"Well done, Bunty! You beat the Kaiser at his own game, and no mistake!"

"What do you mean?" growled Wally.

"How such a liar came to be born outside Berlin beats me!" went on Skinner admiringly. "How do you do it?"

"You cheeky rotter!" muttered Wally angrily.

Skinner closed one eye at him.

Wally Bunter sat with a flushed face. There was a sort of atmosphere of scorn and contempt about him that he felt keenly enough, without understanding why it was so. He had told his Form-master the truth; but to the fellows who knew of Bunter's essays as a sporting punter, naturally, he appeared to be a liar of the first magnitude. Skinner admired his nerve; but nobody else had any admiration for such an Ananias.

That was not a happy afternoon for Billy Bunter's double.

THE SIXTH CHAPTER.
The Sins of Another!

"YOU awful rotter!"

That was Bob Cherry's remark in the quad after lessons. He addressed Bunter.

Wally blinked at him over his glasses.

"What are you calling me names for?" he demanded.

"You take the cake!" said Bob in utter disgust. "How can you do it?"

"What have I done?"

"Told rotten lies as fast as you could pour them out!" said Bob scornfully. "Blessed if I understand how they didn't stick in your neck! You always were a beastly fibber; but this is really over the limit!"

Wally's eyes gleamed.

"I punched your nose the other day, Bob Cherry!" he said. "Do you want me to punch it again?"

"Oh, dry up, and don't talk like a silly ass!" growled Bob. "I've a jolly good mind to mop up the quad with you for lying to Quelchy as you did! You make me sick!"

"I haven't lied to Quelchy!"

"What? Didn't we all hear you?" demanded Johnny Bull. "Are you going to tell us that we dreamed it?"

"Bunter," said Harry Wharton quietly, "don't play the goat! You'd better be thinking how to get out of your scrape. Lying won't be of much use in the long run!"

"The liefulness is terrific, but the uselessness is also great!" remarked Hurree Singh.

"Why not own up to Quelchy, Bunter?" asked Frank Nugent. "It'll have to come, if that man kicks up a shindy—and it looks as if he will. Better take the bull by the horns!"

"Own up!" repeated Wally. "Are you potty? What am I to own up to?"

"Your bizney with Hawke, of course!"

"I haven't any business with him. I've never seen the man till the day before yesterday."

"Oh, if you're going to stick to that, no good us saying anything!" said Frank. And he walked away with the rest of the Co.

Wally Bunter stared at them angrily.

He had hoped to be on the friendliest terms with the Famous Five when he came to Greyfriars; but he was certainly not getting on in that direction.

"What the thump does it all mean?" muttered the fat junior. "What are they all driving at? It beats me!"

He rolled away across the quadrangle, and stopped to speak to Ogilvy and Russell, who were chatting near the gates.

"Buzz off!" said Ogilvy curtly. "No liars wanted!"

Wally's eyes blazed.

"You cheeky cad!" he shouted. "What do you mean?"

"Sit him down!" said Russell.

"You silly chumps, what—— Oh!"

The two juniors took him by the shoulders and sat him down hard, and walked away, leaving him there.

"Oh, my hat!" gasped Wally.

He jumped up in a fury, and started in pursuit; but he paused. He did not want to fight Ogilvy or Russell, both of whom he liked. There was a misunderstanding somewhere which he could not yet grasp

With a rather glum face Wally tramped out of gates in a glum mood. He was not desirous of coming into contact with any more of the Remove just then. He wanted to think out the strange affair.

"Hallo, my pippin! 'Ere you are!"

Wally stopped, his eyes ablaze, as Jerry Hawke came into view, not a hundred yards from the school gates. The man had been hanging about in sight of the school.

He grinned at the angry junior.

"I reckoned my letter would do the trick!" remarked Mr. Hawke. "Bit risky for a young gent getting letters at the school from me—what? But you would 'ave it! You own fault, Master Bunter!"

"So you're Jerry Hawke, are you?" said Wally, setting his teeth.

"You know my name well enough, you young rascal!"

"You wrote to me to-day?"

"I reckon that's why you came 'ere!" sneered the sharper. "If you 'ad not come out I'd 'ave wrote again, and if that wasn't enough I'd 'ave come up to the school, you bet! Square up, can't you?"

"You make out that I owe you money?"

"I make out that you owe me ten quid, and I make out that you're going to step up and settle!" grinned Mr. Hawke.

"I don't know you!" said Wally. "I don't know you, and don't want to! But you're not going to write to me, Mr. Jerry Hawke, and hang around the school to speak to me!"

"You'd like me to go to the 'Ead, p'r'aps?"

"You can go to the Head, or you can go to Jericho; but you're not going to bother me!" said Wally.

He took the glasses from his fat nose, slipped them into his pocket, and pushed back his cuffs.

Those warlike preparations surprised Mr. Hawke, and he stepped back a pace or two, staring at the fat junior.

"Wot's this 'ere game?" he demanded.

"I'm going to lick you!" said Wally determinedly. "I think I can do it! You're too full of smoke and whisky to be much good, you ruffian! Put up your hands!"

"Well, blow me tight!" exclaimed the astonished Mr. Hawke, and he burst into a roar of laughter. "Haw, haw, haw!"

His laughter was cut suddenly short by a smart rap on his red, inflamed nose, which made it redder, and made Mr. Hawke utter a sudden howl.

"That's to begin!" said Wally. "Now, come on!"

"My heye! I'll—I'll——"

The sharper backed away, almost dazed, as the fat junior attacked him.

Jerry Hawke was head and shoulders taller than Bunter, and certainly he ought to have been a good match for any two fellows in the Lower Fourth Form at Greyfriars.

But he wasn't! Wally had judged accurately the effects of smoke and whisky upon the unhealthy, unfit lounger. Mr. Hawke was in no condition for a scrap even with a boy, and he backed away from Wally's attack, which was fast and furious.

Billy Bunter, certainly, he could have disposed of with ease; but Wally was quite another proposition.

Rap, rap, rap! came the fat fists on his beery face, and Jerry Hawke yelled and dodged. But as the fat junior followed him up he put up his hands and fought.

There was a shout of surprise on the road, and Vernon-Smith and Tom Redwing of the Remove came running up. Wally did not heed them; he was giving all his attention to Jerry Hawke.

Crash!

A fat fist landed on Mr. Hawke's stubbly, flabby chin, and the sharper went fairly over, landing on his back. There was a splash as his shoulders squashed into a puddle.

"My hat!" yelled Vernon-Smith. "Bunter! Oh, crumbs!"

"Well hit!" grinned Redwing.

Wally glanced round at them. The Bounder eyed him in great astonishment. Bunter of the Remove had never shown up as a fighting-man before.

"The rotter was pestering me," said Wally. "I had to stop him somehow!"

"Ye gods!" murmured the Bounder.

Jerry Hawke sat up, muddy and breathless, feeling his stubbly chin as if to make sure that it was still there.

"Groogh! Hoooh! Yoooop!" were Mr. Hawke's first remarks. "Ow! Yow! Wow! I'll make you pay for this, you young 'ound! Ow-ow!"

Wally gave him a scornful look.

"Keep clear of me, and let me alone!" he answered. "That's all I want."

"Yes, I'll keep clear of you, I don't think!" gasped Mr. Hawke. "I'll come up to the school, you young rascal! I'll show you up afore all Greyfriars, I will! I'll 'ave my money, or I'll see you kicked out, on my davy! Ow-ow-ow!"

"Oh, rats!"

"I've got a bit of writing to show!" howled Jerry Hawke. "You know that! Forgotten that, p'r'aps, Master Bunter!"

"You've got no writing of mine," said Wally. "I've certainly never written to you, or to any cad of your sort!"

"You wait till I come up and see the 'Ead!" gasped Jerry Hawke. "You wait till then, young feller-me-lad!"

He picked himself up painfully, and limped away towards Friardale.

The Bounder whistled.

"Serve the brute jolly well right, Bunter!" he remarked. "But what the thump are you going to do now?"

"Eh? I'm going in to tea," answered Wally.

"I mean, when that fellow comes up to see the Head."

"Why should he?"

"Why!" exclaimed Redwing, in amazement. "Can't you see he's full of malice now you've punched him instead of paying him?"

"I don't owe him anything!"

"Oh!" said Tom.

"What's the good of piffle like that, Bunter?" asked the Bounder. "You know you owe him money, and that he's got your paper to prove it!"

"I—I don't, I tell you! What do you mean? What makes you think so?" exclaimed Wally, in great exasperation.

"You fat idiot, I think so because you told me so!"

"I told you?"

"Yes; when you tried to squeeze ten pounds out of me to pay him," said the Bounder, with a grin.

Wally stared at him.

"Ten pounds!" he repeated.

"Yes."

"Oh, my hat!"

"Remember now?" asked the Bounder sarcastically.

Wally Bunter did not reply.

He understood at last!

He understood, only too well, why Billy Bunter had been so feverishly anxious to change places with him, and go to St. Jim's in his stead!

Wally had let him have his way—and he had had his own desire—to become a Greyfriars fellow! And it had landed him in—this!

"Oh, my hat!" he repeated dazedly.

He went back to the school gates, and Redwing and the Bounder stared after him, puzzled.

"Blessed if I catch on!" said Smithy. "He knows it well enough—he hasn't lost his memory, I suppose? He was a silly ass to pitch into Hawke under the circs! The man will come up to Greyfriars now."

"That may mean the sack for Bunter," said Tom Redwing, very gravely.

"Well, as he's so well known to be a born idiot, he may get off with a flogging," said Vernon-Smith. "Dashed if I know what he expected! One thing's jolly certain—Jerry Hawke will give him all the trouble he can, after being knocked about! And where did Bunter get all that pluck from—and the strength, too? It beats me!"

"It's a corker!" agreed Redwing.

And all the Remove fellows, when they heard the news, agreed that it was a corker. And there was considerable speculation as to what the Owl of the Remove would do when Mr. Jerry Hawke came up to Greyfriars, with the "bit of writing" in his possession, to see the Head!

THE SEVENTH CHAPTER.

A Visitor for Billy Bunter!

PETER TODD eyed his fat study-mate with a peculiar look. Wally Bunter was unusually silent, and he seemed worried. Peter understood well enough what he was worried about. Apparently it had dawned upon Bunter at last that Jerry Hawke was going to cut up rusty, and that it was a serious matter.

Bunter ate his meal in glum silence, apparently not observing the peculiar looks of Peter Todd.

"What are you going to do, Bunter?" asked Peter at last.

Bunter started, and looked up.

"Eh? What?" he asked.

"About Jerry Hawke?"

"Hang Jerry Hawke!" exclaimed the fat junior irritably.

"But you can't hang him, old bean!" said Peter Todd. "And he's bound to turn up here, after what I've heard from Smithy. It was bound to come sooner or later, anyhow, as you couldn't pay him. What are you going to do?"

"Blessed if I know!" said Bunter.

"It's not much good saying, 'I told you so!'" remarked Peter ruminatingly. "But, as a matter of fact, Bunter, I did tell you so!"

"Did you?"

"Why, you know I did!" exclaimed Peter warmly. "When you started your silly-fool scheme of punting, as you called it, didn't I jaw you?"

"P-p-punting!"

"Playing the goat is the right name for it!" growled Peter. "Didn't I stump you for laying bets on a footer-match? What could I do more than that?"

"No, you didn't——"

"What?"

"I—I—I mean—— Oh, blow!" exclaimed Wally. "Never mind all that! The worry is, what am I going to do if that man comes along with a bit of writing, as the beast calls it?"

"You must have been potty to give him any in your fist!" said Peter. "Even you ought to have had more sense than that!"

"I didn't!"

"You didn't!" howled Peter. "But you told me you had!"

"Well, I didn't!" said Wally desperately. "He thinks he's got a bit of writing in my hand; but, as a matter of fact, he hasn't!"

"He's got something," said Peter quietly. "He thinks he's got your written acknowledgment of a debt, Bunter."

"I can see that now."

"Well, then, what is it that he's got, if it's not that?"

"Something else," said Bunter. "It's a fact that he's got nothing at all written by me."

He could not add that what Mr. Hawke held was a "bit of writing" in the hand of Billy Bunter!

There were unlooked-for difficulties in the role Wally Bunter was playing at Greyfriars!

Peter Todd eyed him very curiously.

"Well, in that case, you needn't be afraid of his coming to see the Head," he remarked.

"I'm not afraid. But——"

"But what?"

"Oh, nothing!"

Wally relapsed into silence. He was cudgelling his brains for a way out of this unexpected scrape.

What was he to say if Mr. Hawke persisted in his intention of betraying him to the Head, as was certain to happen? He could deny that the "bit of writing" was his; certainly it was not his, though Jerry Hawke believed that it was. But it was in Billy Bunter's hand, which was very like his own.

In Billy Bunter's name and place, could he deny Billy Bunter's handwriting?

It was an extraordinary position; and his chief feeling was a desire to be within hitting distance of Billy Bunter's nose for planting this on him.

No wonder the Owl of the Remove had been keen to change places with him; no wonder the fat, cunning young rascal had been eager to get off to St. Jim's, and leave Wally to face this outcome of his punting.

Wally had fallen unsuspiciously into the trap, and now how was he to get out of it?

"Do you want any advice from me?" asked Peter Todd at last, surprised at Bunter's silence. It was the Owl's usual game to land his troubles on somebody else's shoulders; or at least to seek to do so.

"Oh, yes, if you've got any offer!" said Wally. "Go ahead!"

"Why not go to the Head and make a clean breast of the whole bizney? You may get off with a flogging then."

Wally grinned involuntarily. The "whole bizney" had more in it than even Toddy, keen as he was, suspected.

"Well, what are you grinning at, like a Cheshire cat?" demanded Peter.

"Ahem! Nothing!"

"It's the best thing you can do," said Todd. "Dr. Locke may let you off lightly, knowing you to be a born fool!"

"Thanks!"

The study door opened, and Bolsover major put his head in, with a very startled expression on his face.

"Bunter here? You're landed now, Bunter!"

Wally looked round.

"What the thump is it now?" he snapped.

"There's a man at the gates asking after you," said Bolsover major grimly. "A man named Hawke."

"Oh, my hat!"

"Gosling doesn't want to let him in, but I fancy he's coming in all the same. He's after you, Bunter."

"Oh, dear!" groaned Bunter

"Cut off and hide in the box-room," grinned Bolsover major.

"Fathead!"

"Are you going down to see him, Bunty?" asked Peter Todd, looking a little scared himself. He was really concerned for his fat study-mate.

"What's the good?" said Bunter. "Besides, I haven't finished the jam."

"The jam?" said Bolsover major. "You're thinking of jam now, you fat idiot, when you're just going to be called before the Head, and very likely kicked neck and crop out of the school!"

"All the more reason why I should finish the jam while I've got a chance," remarked Wally philosophically.

"Bunter!" exclaimed Peter Todd. "What are you going to do?"

"I'm going to have another cup of tea."

And Wally took up the teapot.

"Oh, my hat!" exclaimed Peter Todd. And he rushed out of the study, to consult with Harry Wharton & Co. as to what was to be done. Bolsover major stared at Bunter, and then followed him. In Study No. 7 Wally went on with his tea.

Tom Dutton stared at him across the table. Tom was deaf, and had not heard a word that was said.

"Anything up?" he asked.

"Yes, rather! I'm in a scrape," answered Wally.

"Jape? Who's japing?" asked Dutton.

"Not jape! Scrape!" shouted Wally. "I'm booked for a thundering row, that's all."

"In Hall, do you mean?"

"Oh, dear!"

"Awful nerve to start a jape in Hall," said Dutton, shaking his head. "Likely to get the prefects down on them. Who are they?"

"Mercy!" said Wally.

"Eh?"

"Help!"

"Well, I can't hear them yelp," said Tom Dutton. "But I'm sorry for them if Wingate or Gwynne catches them japing in Hall, I must say."

And Tom Dutton went down to see who was japing in Hall; while Wally Bunter grinned, and went on with his tea as cheerfully as he could.

THE EIGHTH CHAPTER.

Mr. Hawke Drops In—And Out!

"The game's up now!"

"The upfulness is terrific!"

"What on earth's going to be done?"

"Bunter!" said Johnny Bull. "Bunter's going to be done, and done brown! And it jolly well serves him right!"

And Johnny Bull followed that opinion with an emphatic grunt. Johnny disapproved of Billy Bunter more than ever since the Owl of the Remove had displayed his remarkable gifts as a punter.

Perhaps Johnny forgot sometimes to temper justice with mercy. The other members of the Co. were feeling concerned and alarmed for the hapless Bunter.

The dusk of evening was thick in the old quadrangle. From the direction of the gates, which Gosling had been about to lock, came the sound of voices in dispute. The old porter was barring the entrance of a horsy-looking man with a cigar in his mouth and a bowler-hat on the side of his head. Gosling was quite shocked at the attempt of Mr. Jerry Hawke to introduce his disreputable person within the precincts of Greyfriars School.

"Wot I says is this 'ere!" came Gosling's voice. "You ain't coming in 'ere! Sich ain't allowed!"

"You let a man in!" roared Mr. Hawke's bull voice. "Ain't I told you a dozen times that I got business with the 'Ead?"

"You can tell me till you're black in the face, my man, and then I won't believe you," said Gosling with lofty scorn. "The 'Ead don't 'ave business with a low-down card-sharper, and that's what you are, my man, and that's the blooming long and the blooming short of it! Houtside!"

"Which I tell you——"

"Houtside!"

"Good old Gossy!" murmured Harry Wharton. "Suppose—suppose we go and lend him a hand and pitch the rotter into the road?"

"Good egg!" said Nugent.

"He'll only come back," said Peter Todd, with a shake of the head. "Still, it might do him good. Let's!"

The juniors moved on towards the gate, in which direction several other fellows were moving. Most of the fellows were indoors, but those who were in the quad had been attracted, like the Famous Five, by Mr. Hawke's truculent voice at the gate.

"Will you let a man pass?" roared Mr. Hawke.

"No, I won't! Wot I says is this 'ere——"

"Then take that, you old fool!"

"Oh, crikey! Yoooop!"

Gosling had been standing erect, with a lofty hand pointing out to the road; but as Mr. Hawke's angry fist jabbed at his nose Gosling's position became suddenly horizontal instead of perpendicular.

Over him Mr. Hawke came stepping, while Gosling blinked up, wondering if it was an earthquake or a belated air-raid.

"Hallo, hallo, hallo! You're not wanted here!" sang out Bob Cherry. "Collar the cad!"

There was a rush.

Mr. Hawke, grasped by unexpected hands, was rushed back through the gateway, to an accompaniment of fiendish yells from Gosling, who was rather severely trampled over in the process.

Bump!

"Whoop!"

Jerry Hawke was strewn in the road outside. He rolled in the dust, yelling.

"Shut the gate!" panted Wharton.

Clang!

Goslings staggered to his feet.

"Where is he? Call the police! I'll 'ave him prosecuted! Wot I says is this 'ere—— Yow-ow-ow-wow!"

"Lock the gates, Gossy!" said Bob Cherry, giving the porter a dig in the ribs. "Get a move on, old bird!"

"Yooop! Wharrer shoving a man for?" roared Gosling. "I'll report yer!"

"Lock the gates, or he'll be in again, and we'll leave you to him!" said Wharton.

The key turned in the big lock.

Jerry Hawke scrambled up in the road. His red, beery face glimmered outside the bars of the gate, inflamed with rage.

He shook a knuckly fist at the grinning juniors inside.

"I'll smash yer!" he roared. "I'll out yer! I'll 'ave the law on yer! I'll spiflicate yer! Ow-ow! I'll limb yer!"

"Nice man!" murmured Bob Cherry. "I hope a prefect won't come along and hear him."

Hawke shook savagely at the gates. He was too furious now to care what he did.

"Lemme in!" he yelled. "You 'ear me? I come 'ere to see your 'eadmaster! I come 'ere to see Master Bunter, who 'ave borrowed money of me to back a 'orse! Let me in! I ain't going!"

"Turn the hose on him, Gosling!" called Peter Todd.

"You wait jest a minute, my beauty!" said Gosling. "I'll give you sich a wash as you've never 'ad in your natural!"

There was a sudden disappearance of Jerry Hawke from the gate. Apparently he dreaded a wash. Doubtless he was not used to such things.

"Gone, thank goodness!" said Peter Todd, with a deep breath of relief. "Let's hope he'll keep away."

"Look out! Here's Wingate!"

The juniors melted into the mist as Wingate of the Sixth came striding up.

"What the dickens is this thumping row, Gosling?" exclaimed the captain of Greyfriars.

"A bloomin' 'ooligan kicking up a row," said Gosling. "Intoxicated, I s'pose. Arsking to see the 'Ead. A 'orrid character the worse for drink, sir."

"That's jolly queer," said Wingate. "Has he gone?"

"Oh, yes; he's gone, sir," said Gosling. "I was going hout to deal with 'im stringent, and he thought he'd better take hisself off!"

Wingate looked out through the bars, but nobody was to be seen in the road, and the prefect walked away to the School House very much puzzled.

A group of juniors in the mist under the old elms were very glad to see him disappear.

"All serene so far," said Nugent. "But is the man really gone?"

"Well, he knows that he can't come in now," said Harry Wharton. "Gosling isn't likely to let in such a coughdrop to see the Head. The Head would be rather surprised by a visit from Jerry Hawke."

The juniors chuckled at the idea of that sportive character stepping into the Head's study to interview the white-haired, scholarly old gentleman who governed Greyfriars.

Certainly the Head would have been very much surprised by a visit from the ornament of the Cross Keys bar-room and billiard-room.

"May as well go in," remarked Johnny Bull. "I haven't had my tea yet, and it's late."

Harry Wharton hesitated.

"I'd rather make sure that that Hun has really cleared off," he said. "He had been drinking, I believe, and he was in earnest. Being chucked out can't have improved his temper, either."

"Ha, ha! No."

"Bunter's landed himself in an awful scrape," went on the captain of the Remove. "Goodness knows what's going to happen to him——"

"Not our business," remarked Johnny Bull, with a grunt. "Bunter had his eyes open, I suppose, when he made bets with that blackguard."

"Ye-es, but——"

"But it's up to the virtuous to be kind to the wicked," said Bob Cherry, with great gravity. "The virtuous—that's us—ought to look after the wicked—that's Bunter——"

"Ha, ha, ha!"

"The virtuefulness of our esteemed selves is terrific, my worthy chums, and the temperfulness of the wind to the shorn lamb is also a wheezy good idea!" remarked Hurree Singh

"Hallo, hallo, hallo! What's that?"

"Oh, my hat!"

"That" was the sound of a bump a short distance from the juniors, and close to the school wall. It was evidently made by someone dropping within, after climbing over the wall from the road. And the bump was followed by a well-known beery voice:

"Ow! Blow it! Blow my buttons! Ow!"

Jerry Hawke was inside the walls of Greyfriars, after all!

THE NINTH CHAPTER.
In Defence of Bunter!

HARRY WHARTON & CO. ran quickly to the spot.

Mr. Jerry Hawke had just picked himself up, after dropping inside and rolling over.

He put himself into a defensive attitude as the juniors loomed up in the mist.

"'Ands off!" he exclaimed. "I come 'ere quiet and peaceful to see the 'Ead. 'Ands off!"

"You've no right in here!" said Wharton.

"Ain't a man a right to call on a hold gent when he's got business with 'im?" demanded Mr. Hawke in an injured tone. "Master Bunter owes me money—a matter of ten quid. I got his 'andwriting to prove it."

He blinked at them sourly in the mist. The juniors were round him, barring his further progress, but they were puzzled what to do.

The gates were locked now, and Gosling had gone back to his lodge. Jerry Hawke could not be run out. Neither could he be lifted over the wall and dropped outside—not, at all events, without a hullabaloo that would have brought half Greyfriars on the scene.

How to deal with him was a perplexity. But the Co. were anxious to keep the chopper from coming down on the reckless Owl of the Remove. How was it to be done?

"P'r'aps you'll let a man pass now?" sneered Jerry Hawke. "Don't you lay a 'and on me. I'll soon 'ave your 'eadmaster hout if you do. I dessay I could be 'eard from 'ere."

The juniors were afraid that the ruffian had been heard already. If a master or a prefect came on the spot it was all over with their lingering hope of shielding Bunter.

"Look here," said Wharton at last, "what do you want here? What have you come for?"

"I've come to collect a debt, my lad." said Jerry Hawke evilly. "A matter of ten quid from Master Billy Bunter of

Did he fall, or was he pushed? (*See Chapter 1.*)

this 'ere school. and if he don't pay on the nail I'm goin' to tell 'is 'eadmaster what I thinks of young gents what don't pay their just debts."

"You know you can't collect gambling debts from a schoolboy," said Peter Todd.

"This 'ere ain't a gambling debt," said Jerry Hawke coolly. "It's money lent to Master Bunter, fair and square."

"I don't believe it!"

"I've got his fist to prove it!"

"You lent Bunter money? exclaimed Wharton. "Money to gamble with?"

"The young gent may 'ave 'ad a fancy for backing a 'orse," said Jerry Hawke. "That ain't my business. He's written out a paper acknowledging a debt to me of ten quids."

"I think I understand," said Wharton contemptuously. "Bunter let most of it out to us at the time. You took his bet on a race on condition that he signed a paper admitting owing you the money in case the horse lost. You knew it had no chance of winning, of course."

"S'pose it had won, wouldn't Master Bunter have asked me for my money?" sneered Jerry Hawke. "And took it, too, for that matter!"

"You wouldn't have squared," said Johnny Bull.

Mr. Hawke raised his head loftily.

"Ask any gentleman what has done business with me whether Jerry Hawke pays on the nail or not!" he said, with a great deal of dignity. "There's young gents at this 'ere school know me for a feller of my word. I could name 'em if I liked. If I'd lost I'd have paid, honest. 'Course I would!"

"What you would have done isn't evidence, as the thing was impossible," remarked Peter Todd. "You only booked Bunter's bet because you knew the horse he selected couldn't win; and you'll get into trouble with the law for making bets with a schoolboy in a public place."

"Good old Toddy!" said Bob Cherry. "You've got him there. What he did was illegal."

"Who's talking about making bets?" said Jerry Hawke. "I ain't made bets with nobody, and I stands to that. I lent Master Bunter ten pounds, like a good-natured cove."

"That's not true."

"I've got it in his bit of writing!" grinned the sharper. "That there paper don't mention nothing about a 'orse."

Wharton bit his lip. He could guess easily enough that the sharper had fooled Billy Bunter at his own sweet will, and that there was nothing in the written paper to prove that Jerry Hawke had done anything worse than lend money to a schoolboy. He had lent no money, but Bunter had signed the paper, as he would have signed anything in his stupidity for the sake of getting his bet booked.

"And now, if you'll 'ave the goodness to let a cove pass, I'll trot along to the 'Ouse!" said Mr. Hawke sarcastically.

"Bunter can't pay you, and you know it," said Wharton. "You'll only get him in a row with the Head."

"P'r'aps the Head will pay up rather than 'ave a row," suggested Mr. Hawke. "I'm going to try. I know that Master Bunter 'andled me to-day, and that I ain't letting him off, not if I know it!"

Wharton looked helplessly at his chums.

It really looked as if the Owl of the Remove was in for it beyond help.

"Suppose we call Bunter here?" suggested Nugent.

"I'm coming up to the 'Ouse," said Jerry Hawke doggedly. "Master Bunter 'ad the chance of seeing me out of doors, and he pitched into me instead. Now I ain't giving him any more chances."

"Look here, you're not going to the House!" exclaimed Wharton savagely.

"Who's going to stop me?"

"We are!"

"We'll soon see about that!" said Mr. Hawke, and he shoved himself forward to break through the ring of juniors.

"Collar him!" muttered Wharton.

Jerry Hawke was collared fast enough. He struggled in the grasp of six pairs of hands. Against the six he had no chance, so far as fighting went; but, at the same time, his mouth was opened to yell, and he yelled with all the strength of his lungs:

"'Elp! 'Elp! I'm being assaulted! 'Elp! Yaroooh! 'Ands off! 'Elp!"

The bull-voice rang across the quadrangle as the sharper struggled in the grasp of the Famous Five and Peter Todd.

"Quieten the brute somehow!" gasped Bob Cherry. "We shall have all the school here!"

"'Elp! 'Elp! 'Elp!" roared Mr. Hawke vociferously.

There were voices and footsteps in the misty quadrangle already. From the distance Vernon-Smith's voice was heard:

"Hallo! What's the row there?"

"'Elp! 'Elp!"

"Great Scott!" The Bounder ran up through the mist. "What the thump —— You fellows committing a murder? Oh, my hat! Jerry Hawke!"

"'Elp!"

"Quelchy's just come out!" gasped the Bounder. "Look out!"

"'Elp!" roared Mr. Hawke. "'Elp!"

"Drag the brute along!" gasped Wharton. "Quelchy mustn't see him! Get him along to the wood-shed."

"Right-ho!"

"'Elp! 'Elp! Groooooogh!" wound up Mr. Hawke, as a handkerchief was stuffed into his mouth at last.

His voice died away in gurglings. The juniors were getting quite desperate now; they could hear Mr. Quelch's voice from the direction of the House.

"What is it? Who is calling? What is the matter?"

Fortunately, the mist from the sea hid the scene from the Remove-master, who was peering about him as he came along.

"Shush!" whispered Wharton. "Get him away, quick!"

"Gug-gug-gug!" came from Jerry Hawke.

"Quiet, you rotter!" muttered Bob Cherry fiercely, and he drove the stuffed handkerchief deeper into Mr. Hawke's mouth with his knuckles. Then Mr. Hawke was silent, though his feelings were deep.

The juniors lifted the sharper bodily, and rushed him away under the trees, and vanished into the mist about half a minute before Mr. Quelch arrived on the spot.

"Bless my soul!" exclaimed the Remove-master. "What is it? Here is a—a—a cap, and—and a hat—a bowler hat! Bless my soul! Someone has been here."

Mr. Quelch blinked round him in utter amazement, with Jerry Hawke's greasy bowler-hat in his hand. But though it was clear that someone had been there, that someone was gone; and the Remove-master peered about him in vain.

THE TENTH CHAPTER.

The Disappearance of Jerry Hawke!

HARRY WHARTON & CO. stumbled into the wood-shed in the dark, and there was a heavy bump. Bob Cherry had caught his foot in something in the gloom, and he stumbled over and went down, and Jerry Hawke went with him, gurgling. Two or three of the juniors rolled over the unfortunate Mr. Hawke.

"Oh, my hat! Gerroff!"

"Keep your boot out of my eye, idiot!" came in sulphurous tones from Johnny Bull. "What thumping idiot is that?"

"Oh, crumbs!"

"Get a light!" gasped Nugent.

"Fathead! It'll be seen!"

"Ow! Oh! Gerroff!"

The juniors sorted themselves out in the darkness. On the floor Mr. Hawke lay wriggling, making strenuous efforts to expel the handkerchief from his mouth. But some of the juniors still had hold of him, and he could not use his hands; and the gag had been well driven in. Jerry Hawke could only gurgle.

"Oh, dear!" gasped Bob Cherry. "What a life! Keep that beast safe!"

"We've got him!"

"I'm sitting on his tummy!" said Johnny Bull. "He's all right!"

"Ha, ha, ha!"

"Shush! Let's see if Quelchy has spotted us!"

Harry Wharton looked cautiously out of the wood-shed.

There was little to be seen in the mist, which was thickening with the advance of evening. A confused sound of voices could be heard in the distance, and that was all.

"Nobody's coming!" said Harry. "Keep that brute quiet! We can get him out by the back gate later if Quelchy doesn't spot him here."

"He'll come back!" said the Bounder.

"Bless him!" growled Bob.

"Perhaps we could make it worth his while not to come back," suggested Vernon-Smith. "We've got him by the short hairs now. Suppose we cut his hair and shave his eyebrows, and make him a regular guy. That will be a lesson to him to keep clear of Greyfriars after this."

There was a chuckle from the juniors, and a horrified wriggle from the unhappy Mr. Hawke.

"Not a bad idea!" said Peter Todd. "But——"

"The butfulness is terrific!" murmured the Nabob of Bhanipur.

"Hallo, hallo, hallo!" muttered Bob Cherry. "I can hear footsteps, you fellows! Somebody's coming this way!"

"Shut the door!" breathed Peter Todd.

Wharton silently closed the wood-shed door. But outside there was the gleam of a lantern and the sound of footsteps.

They were approaching the wood-shed.

Naturally, Mr. Quelch had not let the matter drop after discovering a disreputable bowler-hat within the precincts of Greyfriars. It was proof positive that some intruder was within the walls, and the matter had to be investigated. The Remove-master had called out some of the Sixth to help him search for the intruder.

Wingate, Gwynne, and Loder had come along, one of them with a bike-lantern. The Remove-master and the three prefects searched right and left for the missing owner of the hat.

"The man, whoever he is, must be still here," said Mr. Quelch. "He would not, presumably, depart without his hat. I certainly think that I heard the sounds of a struggle and someone calling for help—someone who did not pronounce the aspirate."

"We'll find him if he's here, sir," said Wingate. "There was a rough character trying to get in at the gates a while ago, and Gosling had some trouble with him. It may be the same man."

"Bless my soul!" said Mr. Quelch. "It is very extraordinary! The man must certainly be found, if he is here!"

"Hallo, here's something!" exclaimed Loder.

He picked up a cap.

"Some junior has been here," said Mr. Quelch, glancing at the cap. "And, bless my soul! What is this?"

"This" was a greasy necktie, yellow in colour, with red spots—a very striking necktie, which certainly had never been worn by anyone belonging to Greyfriars. Mr. Quelch blinked at it. Jerry Hawke's necktie had come off in the struggle, and remained on the ground half-way to the wood-shed.

"Extraordinary!" exclaimed the Form-master in amazement. "The man has, apparently, dropped his necktie as well as his hat! Evidently he is still within the precincts of the school."

"Hiding among some of the out-buildings, most likely, sir!" said Gwynne. "We'll soon rout him out."

"Try the wood-shed!" said Wingate.

And the party moved on.

Footsteps and voices and the glimmer of the lantern approached the wood-shed, to the utter dismay of the juniors hidden there with their prize.

"They're coming here, right enough!" muttered Wharton. "What—what the thump are we going to do with that brute?"

"Hide him!" said Bob.

"How? Where?"

"Under the logs!"

"Oh, my hat!"

Mr. Hawke gurgled in protest. But the juniors did not mind Mr. Hawke's objections. It was necessary to keep the ruffian out of sight, and there was only one way.

In the wood-shed were great stacks of logs cut from the wood belonging to the school, to eke out the winter supply of coal. Jerry Hawke was rolled to the wall, and the juniors, with hot haste, began piling the logs round him. Bob Cherry hunted out a rope and wound it round Mr. Hawke and his legs and arms, and knotted it with a terrific number of knots. By the time he had finished Mr. Hawke was a great deal like an Egyptian mummy, swathed in rope instead of bandages.

While Bob was thus engaged the others were piling logs round the sharper, and as soon as the roping was completed they piled logs on top of him as well.

Jerry Hawke disappeared from sight. The last that was seen of him was his face, with his jaws working frantically in a furious effort to chew away the gag.

Nugent had been striking matches to afford light. Now the last match went out, and left the juniors in darkness. Wharton muttered a warning as a gleam came through the little window from the lantern outside. Mr. Quelch and the prefects were very close at hand now.

The Remove-master's voice could be heard.

"I—I say, they're coming in right enough!" muttered the Bounder. "How are we going to account for being here—in the dark, too?"

"Goodness knows!" grunted Johnny Bull.

"Rehearsal!" said Wharton quickly. "We've rehearsed in the wood-shed before. Get on with Mark Antony's oration, Bob!"

There was a chuckle in the dark.

As it was still barely possible that the searchers would not enter the wood-shed the juniors did not care to show a light; and Bob listened for a hand on the door as a signal to begin Mark Antony's celebrated oration.

It was a flimsy camouflage, perhaps, but it was the best the juniors could think of in the peculiar circumstances. They were not aware that Jerry Hawke's hat and necktie had been found; and the sharper was quite out of sight under the logs.

The Removites listened breathlessly. The sharp, incisive tones of the Remove-master came to their ears more audibly.

"Pray search this shed, Wingate. It is very probable that the man has concealed himself there, as he is plainly trying to keep out of sight."

"Certainly, sir!"

That settled it! There was no further doubt that the wood-shed would be entered; and before Wingate could touch the door, Bob Cherry's powerful tones boomed out:

"'Friends, Romans, countrymen, lend me your ears;
I come to bury Cæsar, not to praise him.
The evil that men do lives after them;
The good is oft interred with their bones;
So let it be with Cæsar! The noble Brutus——'"

"Great Scott!" It was Wingate's voice. "There's somebody there—that's some fag."

He threw the door open, and the lantern streamed light into the wood-shed, full upon the group of Removites.

Heedless of the astonished stares of the Sixth-Formers, Bob Cherry boomed on with his declamation:

"'. . . . The noble Brutus
Hath told you, Cæsar was ambitious;
If it were so, it was a grievous fault;
And grievously hath Cæsar answered it.'"

"Shut up, you young ass!" exclaimed Wingate.

Bob Cherry gave a dramatic start.

"Hallo, hallo, hallo! That you, Wingate?"

And the "rehearsal" ceased, as Mr. Quelch strode into the wood-shed with the prefects at his heels.

THE ELEVENTH CHAPTER.
All Up!

MR. QUELCH stared grimly at the heroes of the Remove, who regarded him with respectful attention.

"Wharton! Cherry! You are here!"

"Yes, sir."

"What are you doing here?"

"I was reciting Shakespeare, sir," said Bob Cherry meekly. "We often use the wood-shed for rehearsals, sir."

Which was strictly true.

"You came here to rehearse Shakespeare?" exclaimed Mr. Quelch.

This was rather a poser, as the juniors had certainly not come there with the intention of rehearsing Shakespeare. But Hurree Jamset Singh came to the rescue.

"The quietfulness of the esteemed wood-shed is favourable for the excellent rehearsal, honoured sahib," he explained. "There is less danger of the unruly interruption by jokeful bounders."

"There is no harm in your using the shed for rehearsals," said Mr. Quelch. "No harm at all."

"Thank you, sir!"

"But surely you were not rehearsing in the dark?"

"We don't need light for spouting Shakespeare, sir," said Wharton. "After what you've told us, sir, about—about saving candles——"

"Quite so, Wharton. I am glad to see that you have learned the lesson of economy," said the Remove-master. "I am sorry to interrupt your rehearsal!"

"Not at all, sir," murmured Wharton.

"Can we go on now, sir?" asked the Bounder meekly.

"One moment, please! There is some unknown person within the walls of the school," said Mr. Quelch. "He appears to have been engaged in a struggle, of which I heard the sounds, and was calling for help. Have you boys seen anything of him?"

"What was he like, sir?"

"I really do not know. I have not seen him. I have found his hat and his necktie."

"Oh!"

"Where is your cap, Cherry?" asked Wingate grimly.

"Mum - mum - my cap?" stammered Bob.

"Yes. Is this it?"

"Eh? Oh! Ah! Yes."

Bob mechanically took his cap. His face was the hue of a beetroot. He guessed that his cap had been found with the hat or the necktie.

"It's pretty clear, sir, that these juniors know something about the matter," said the Greyfriars captain.

Mr. Quelch's brow became very grim. The fact that Bob Cherry's cap had been picked up along with the unknown person's necktie was pretty clear evidence of that, and the Remove-master did not need telling much more.

"Cherry——" he began.

He was interrupted at that point by what looked like a miniature earthquake.

A huge pile of logs close to the wall of the shed became endued with sudden volition.

Of their own accord, apparently, they rocked and rolled, and there was a crash as a dozen or more of them tumbled over.

Mr. Quelch jumped.

"What—what—what——" he stuttered, blinking at the logs, which had so oddly come to sudden life.

The earthquake continued. Logs rocked and rolled, and all eyes in the wood-shed were fixed upon them. From under the rolling pile came a weird and mysterious sound.

"Mmmmmmmmmmm!"

"Good heavens!" exclaimed Mr. Quelch. "What—what is it? Some animal appears to be under the logs! Bless my soul!"

Wingate grinned.

"I fancy the man's hidden there, and these young rascals know it!" he said.

"Investigate at once, Wingate!" exclaimed the Remove-master, with a terrific glance at the dismayed juniors.

The prefects proceeded to investigate at once.

Harry Wharton & Co. stood rooted to the floor with dismay. Wingate and Gwynne and Loder threw aside the logs rapidly, and a peculiar figure came to light—a beery-looking man, swathed in knotted rope, with a handkerchief stuffed into his capacious mouth.

"By Jove!" yelled Wingate. "Look!"

Jerry Hawke was dragged out into the light.

"It's Hawke!" exclaimed Loder.

"Jerry Hawke!" murmured Wingate. "Oh, by Jove!"

"The—the man is bound and—and gagged!" stuttered Mr. Quelch. "What can this mean? Release him, Wingate—pray release him at once!"

Wingate opened his pocket-knife, and cut the ropes, while Gwynne jerked the half-gnawed handkerchief from Jerry Hawke's mouth.

Harry Wharton & Co. stood quite silent. The game was up with a vengeance. They had not succeeded in saving Bunter; and it looked as if they had landed themselves into the soup.

Jerry Hawke sat up, gasping. His first remark was:

"Groooooooch!"

Mr. Quelch fixed a glittering eye upon him.

"Who are you?" he thundered.

"Grooooogh!"

"Who is this man, Wharton?"

"I—I think he's named Hawke, sir," murmured Wharton.

"Did you tie him up in this manner?"

"Ye-es, sir."

"And why?"

"He's an awful rotter, sir, and he's no right here! We helped Gosling turn him out half an hour ago, and he came back, by getting over the wall from the road. So—so—so we collared him."

"Extraordinary!" exclaimed Mr. Quelch. "The man can scarcely be a burglar! He must be intoxicated! Is this the man I heard calling for help?"

"I—I suppose so, sir."

"Wharton! You were concealing this man here. Explain to me at once why you were trying to keep his presence here from my knowledge!"

The captain of the Remove was dumb. But Jerry Hawke had recovered his voice by this time, and it was not necessary for Wharton to speak.

"I'll 'ave the lor of yer!" howled Mr. Hawke, staggering to his feet. "I come 'ere to collect a debt, and I've been treated like this 'ere! I'm going to see the 'Ead! P'r'aps you'll try and stop me now, you young 'ounds!"

"Have you prevented this man from calling on Dr. Locke, Wharton?"

"Yes, sir," said Harry desperately. "Gosling turned him out once, and he came in like a burglar, so we collared him!"

"That does not explain your concealing him here, Wharton! The man should be handed over to the police if he has forced an entrance into the school. Hawke, if that is your name, what is your object in intruding here?"

"Master Bunter owes me money!" roared the angry sharper. "These coves were trying to keep me from speaking to the 'Ead, because they knew young Bunter came to see me at the Cross Keys, and borrowed money of me."

"Good heavens!" exclaimed Mr. Quelch.

He understood now.

Harry Wharton & Co. were silent. They had done all they could, but they had failed, and the Owl of the Remove had to face the music now.

There was a brief silence. Then Mr. Quelch said quietly:

"So you were trying to shield your Form-fellow, Wharton?

"Yes, sir," said Harry. "That awful rascal induced Bunter somehow to play the fool. He's more to blame than Bunter. I—I hope, sir, you'll remember that Bunter is a silly idiot—ahem!"

"I shall deal with you boys later," said Mr. Quelch. "As for you, Mr. Hawke, you deserve the rough treatment you have received for forcing your way into this school. You will now follow me to Dr. Locke, to whom you will make your statement. Wingate, kindly bring Bunter to Dr. Locke's study."

Mr. Quelch whisked out of the shed, and Jerry Hawke, with a vaunting leer at the juniors, followed him. Harry Wharton & Co. left the wood-shed more slowly.

"Nothing doing!" said Bob Cherry. "Bunter's in for it now. I—I suppose it was bound to come."

"We've done our best," said Harry.

And that was the only consolation of the heroes of the Remove.

THE TWELFTH CHAPTER.
Facing the Music!

"BUNTER!"

Wingate rapped out the name in the doorway of Study No. 7.

Wally Bunter rose to his feet with a resigned expression.

"Yes, Wingate?"

"You're wanted in the Head's study!"

"All right."

"Come along, you young ass!"

The fat junior followed Wingate downstairs. At the foot of the staircase he met the Co. coming in.

"We tried to keep the man away, Bunter," said Wharton in a low voice. "It was no go, though."

"Thanks, all the same!" said Wally.

"Bunter, old man, you're in for it. Do take my advice, and tell the Head the truth!" said Wharton earnestly. "You're clean bowled out, and it's no good lying. Do tell the truth, kid!"

Wally gave him rather a peculiar look.

"I will!" he said.

"That's good advice, Bunter," said Wingate. "Tell the truth and stick to it. Come on!"

The captain of Greyfriars led Bunter to the Head's study, pushed him in, and retired. Wally Bunter advanced towards the writing-table where Dr. Locke sat with a severely frowning countenance. Mr. Quelch was standing with his hand resting on the table, and Jerry Hawke was facing the two masters, with an impudent leer on his face.

On the table lay the "bit of writing." That paper, with Billy Bunter's scrawled signature upon it, was Jerry Hawke's trump card. His hopes of fingering the money it represented were very slight, but he flattered himself that it was sufficient to ruin the junior he had failed to bully and blackmail.

"Bunter!" said the Head in a deep voice.

"Yes, sir?"

Wally Bunter pulled himself together. What Billy Bunter would have done in such a position he could not guess. But the matter was, in fact, much easier for Wally than for Billy, for he had not signed that paper, and he could say so with perfect truth.

The Head pointed to the incriminating document.

"Look at that paper, Bunter!"

Wally looked at it.

"Is that your signature?" asked the Head in a terrifying voice.

"No, sir!"

"What?"

"No, sir!" repeated Wally firmly.

He had never seen the paper before, though he knew now that Billy must have signed it. But he was not Billy, though he was supposed to be Billy.

Jerry Hawke started, and his yellow teeth came together. Rogue as the man was himself, it had not occurred to him that Bunter would be rogue enough to deny his own signature. He blinked at the fat junior.

"He's lying!" he roared savagely. "He signed the paper. Let 'im write 'is name 'ere, and compare the two!"

"Bunter, do you mean to say that that paper is a forgery?" exclaimed the Head.

"I can't say anything about it, sir, excepting that I never signed it, and I've never seen it before," said Wally.

Jerry Hawke spluttered with wrath.

"Have you ever had any dealings with this man, Bunter?"

"Never, sir, except that I knocked his hat off on Saturday when he tried to speak to me in the lane, and pitched into him this afternoon because he bothered me," answered Wally.

"Ahem! You have never—ahem!—visited the place he comes from—a very disreputable public-house in Friardale?"

"Certainly not, sir!"

"You have not borrowed money from this man?"

"No, sir!"

Splutter from Jerry Hawke.

"Take that pen, Bunter, and write your usual signature," said the Head.

Wally obeyed. He wrote "W. G. Bunter," which, if the Head had only known it, stood for Walter Gilbert Bunter. But the Head did not know that.

Dr. Locke picked up the paper, and compared it with the "bit of writing." The handwriting was very similar, but there was a difference. Wally's hand was not exactly like Billy's.

"Look at these papers, Mr. Quelch. Is that Bunter's usual signature?"

Mr. Quelch pursed his lips.

"In point of fact, sir, this signature is more like Bunter's usual style than the one he has just written, but they are very similar," he said. "The writing, of course, is easy to imitate—a childish, round hand. But——"

Mr. Quelch paused, quite at a loss. Both masters searched Wally's face, but his fat face was calm and sedate.

"There is only one conclusion I can come to," said the Head at last. "You, Mr. Hawke, are a self-confessed sharper and swindler! On your own statement, you have induced a foolish schoolboy to enter into money transactions with you. Whether you have done worse than that, whether you have imitated his signature to extort money from him under threats, I cannot say for certain. But in this case of doubt I am bound to accept the word of a Greyfriars boy against that of a man of your utterly base character. If Bunter were speaking falsely, I have little doubt that I should detect him; but he appears to be speaking the truth. You, on the other hand, are evidently false to the very core, and actuated by spite and malice!"

Mr. Hawke spluttered.

"The matter therefore drops here," said the Head. "I shall destroy this paper. If you retain it I shall communicate with the police at once, and prosecute you as a blackmailer. Will you leave it here?"

Jerry Hawke gasped. He was equal to nothing else. All the wind had been taken out of his sails. The trump card he had counted on had failed him owing to circumstances of which he was ignorant.

As he did not reply, the Head pointed to the door.

"Go!" he said. "Let me learn on any future occasion that you have approached any boy belonging to this school, and I will pursue you with the utmost rigour of the law! Go!"

Still gasping, Mr. Hawke limped out of the study.

A couple of minutes later there was a sound of scuffling and hurrying in the misty quad. Some of the Remove were escorting Mr. Hawke to the gate—not gently.

"Bunter, I have accepted your word," said the Head quietly. "I think you have spoken the truth. I hope so. You may go."

"Thank you, sir!" said Wally.

And he went.

Harry Wharton & Co. came in rather breathlessly from the quad, and met the fat junior at the foot of the staircase.

"Sacked?" asked Bob Cherry.

"Not a bit!" answered Wally cheerfully.

"Going to be flogged?" asked Wharton.

"Oh, no!"

"Then what's happened?"

Wally grinned.

"I took your advice, old top, and told the truth," he answered. "All serene—right as rain. Time I got on with my prep."

(Don't miss "A DOG WITH A BAD NAME!"—next Monday's grand complete story of Harry Wharton & Co., by Frank Richards.)

Extracts from "THE GREYFRIARS HERALD" and "TOM MERRY'S WEEKLY."

THE GHOSTLY REVELLERS.

A Story of Holiday-time. By ROBERT DONALD OGILVY.

I.

"OH, yes, I'm game!" I said.

"I don't know whether you'll really care about it, Don," said Dick Russell, with what seemed to me rather unnecessary anxiety.

For why should any fellow doubt that any other fellow whom he knows to be keen on footer would care about a game, even with a village team that very likely did not know a heap about it?

I was staying for a week or two with Dick, before going home to the Highlands, where he was to go with me. We had had no end of a jolly Christmas, with snow and skating to provide amusement. But, with the festive season fairly over, a change had come in the weather, and the outlook was chiefly mud.

But who minds mud when there's footer to be had?

"Well, they're rather a rough lot," Dick explained, when I asked him the reason for his doubts.

"I can be rough myself, come to that. I don't mind a barging game, as long as it's clean and fair."

"Can't give any guarantee that it will be that."

"Anyway, it's the other side we shall be playing, not your local ruffians."

"Yes. But we shall be playing for the ruffians, old top!"

"Don't you want to play, Dick?"

"I do. I'd be as keen as anything on it if it wasn't that—well, see here, Don, you've got a pretty bad impression of this place, and I don't want it made worse."

"Rats!" I answered. "It isn't the village that matters to me; it's your folks. And if you say that I've anything but the highest opinion of them—why, I'll punch your silly head!"

But I knew just what Dick meant.

The village in which the Russells live is an out-of-the-way place, separated by miles of muddy roads from everywhere; and most of the people in it were not exactly nice.

The parson was an old man, feeble in body and mind; the schoolmaster was a kind of bad-tempered hermit; and Mr. Russell was the only other person in the place who had any influence. And he had lost most of his through losing most of his money—which shows in itself what sort of people he had to deal with. For he had never grudged anything he could do for them when he was well-to-do; and now that he had less cash he tried to do even more in other ways. But they preferred the cash.

Dick came to the conclusion that we might as well chance it. He would not have minded so much if the match had been at home; but it was at another village ten miles or so away. And the Russells had no car, not even a pony-trap, these days.

We should have to travel with the rest of the team in a big char-a-banc affair which some local merchant had on hire. And Dick seemed to think I shouldn't like it.

I laughed at him. I am not exactly a young lady, you know.

But Dick was right.

I did not like it. Neither did he.

Those village chaps really were the limit. It did not matter much that they should smoke, though most of them were under eighteen, and, anyway, smoking isn't good for the wind. I could have stood their swearing, though they might just as well have cut it out; but swearing was not the worst of their language, by long odds. And when they brought out great jars of beer and proceeded to prepare for the game by soaking themselves, I began to wonder whether all the Huns were in Germany.

"Have a drop, young Russell?" said the captain, a big brute who worked at a brick-field.

"No, thanks!" replied Dick curtly.

"Tote?"

"Yes, I suppose so. Anyway, beer isn't in my line."

"'E'd rather 'ave clarick an' all that sort of thin muck! That's what they tipples at the Warren 'Ouse!" sneered the goalkeeper, a fellow with a club foot, a squint, and ever so many worse characteristics.

"Not now they don't," said a third. "Them wines costs money, Bart; an' there ain't a fat lot of that at the Warren House these times."

"Oh, shut up!" I snapped, for I had seen good old Dick flush. He is very sensitive.

They glared at me.

"Wants a drop 'isself," said Bart, the goalkeeper.

"He's welcome," said the skipper.

He tried to force the great jar on to me. But, of course, I wasn't having any of that.

"D'ye s'pose as his lordship could drink arter chaps like us?" sneered Bart.

"They say he's one of them Highland chiefs when he's at home—goes about in kilts an' bagpipes an'—an' wigwams an' things," remarked another, with a leer at me.

I grinned. At home I may wear the tartan—well, then, I do wear it, and what is there against it? But I certainly don't go about in bagpipes and wigwams, though I plead guilty to "things."

But Dick did not grin. He was angry.

"Stop!" he said sharply to the driver.

The man pulled up.

"'Ere, what's the bloomin' row?" inquired Bart.

"I don't like your sneers at me," said Dick. "But I won't have your sneers at my guest—that's flat! You ought to be dashed well ashamed of yourselves! We'll get out and go back!"

"What, an' leave us two men short, after promisin' to play, an' us lookin' to your clever college footer tricks to pull us through?" roared the brickmaker.

"Yes—that!" snapped Dick.

"Call that playin' of the game?"

"Is it only Ogilvy and I who ought to play the game, Waites?" asked Dick.

"I don't see what we've done to make a song an' dance about."

"I do. I suppose you don't know how to be decently polite and friendly, but you might be civil!"

"Sit on Bart's head, some of you!" shouted Waites. "He's the chap who ain't civil. Drive on, Bill! The young gent don't mean it!"

Bill drove on. Dick did not object to that. But I saw that his mouth was set hard; and during all the rest of that muddy drive he never spoke another word. I didn't, either. And no one said anything to us, though some of them whispered things about us.

They wanted us. Neither Dick nor myself can claim a regular place in the Remove footer team; but Harry Wharton & Co. would have made rings round Wistham village, and I suppose we were well above the average of Waites and his crowd.

I wondered whether they would be able to play at all after the beer they lowered on the journey. But I suppose the brewers have not started making it strong again yet; and I am not sure that it's a bad thing they have not. Anyway, the chaps tumbled out of the char-a-banc apparently not much the worse for it.

II.

THE ground we had to play on turned out to be a regular Dismal Swamp, up to one's ankles in mud in some places. But the team against us was a heap more decent than the team we were playing for.

If you have ever played footer under such conditions you may be able to understand how sick it makes you feel after a bit.

It is all very well to argue that the foulness and brutality of your side is not your fault—that it is only an accident that you are on it—but you can't really feel like that about it.

Waites put Dick and me on the right wing together, and we were glad of that. He played at centre. I can't say we were glad of that.

I never saw a rougher player. But I saw several fouler players that day, and they were all on our side!

You would say that a goalkeeper does not get much chance to foul. But Bart fouled like blazes. I suppose he made his chances when they didn't come to him ready-made.

The two backs were as bad as Bart. The centre-half was the worst of the crew. He wore boots that were absolutely illegal, and he rapped opponents' ankles with the beastly things as if that was what he lived for. And the referee never seemed to see anything!

There was precious little enjoyment in that game for us, I can tell you. A quarter of an hour before half-time we did do a kind of wade down our wing, and finished up by scoring a goal, Dick putting to me a sodden ball with about half a stone of mud on it, which I drove somehow between the posts. But after that we only saw the ball at a distance.

It might have been different if the other side had been on top. Our help would have been wanted then.

But our hooligans were having the best of the game all through the first hour, at the end of which they were three goals up.

Then something went wrong with Bart. I think it was the beer in him.

Anyway, he began to fumble and mis-kick. In ten minutes he had let three through.

Then our hooligans got frightfully wild. All that they had done in the way of fouling and barging before was eclipsed now. Dick was sick, and I felt ratty.

At last the skipper of the Wistham team, a very decent, quiet chap, who played the kind of game we had been used to at Greyfriars, though he was a brickmaker, like our cad Waites, spoke to Dick.

"Mr. Russell," he said, "couldn't you speak to them?"

Dick went as red as a tomato.

"I can, Brown," he said, "and I will! But it won't be a scrap of use. If I hadn't been sure of that I'd have spoken long ago. What's the matter with your ref?"

"Oh, he's scared of them! See here, sir, don't you speak if you'd rather not. But I should just like to say that all of us know that you an' the other young gent don't cotton to their dirty tricks, an' that we've nothing against you."

Pretty decent of him, wasn't it? We should have been glad enough to play for Wistham, I can tell you. Perhaps we may next Christmas.

Dick spoke to Waites. Waites guffawed at him, and Bart and the cad at centre-half jeered.

"There's only one thing to do, Don," said Dick quietly. "When we see the next foul we go off the field!"

Waites and Bart and most of the rest heard that. But it made no difference.

We went off within a minute and a half. Our own team hissed us. The Wistham chaps cheered. The referee snuffled and looked at his toes.

Wistham won by the odd goal in seven. Serve our cads right!

"D'ye think you're goin' back with us, young Russell?" sneered the villainous Bart.

"We wouldn't!" snapped Dick.

But we were in rather a tight place. Dick wouldn't let me pay for the hire of a trap. The dear old chap is so proud that I had to give in to him. And he couldn't afford to pay for the hire of one himself. I am not at all sure that it would have been easy to get one, anyway.

That decent chap Brown helped us out. He lent Dick his own bike, and he borrowed one for me.

We shook hands with him and started off. The rest of our team had gone to the Cat and Fiddle. It sounded like a thousand cats and a hundred or so fiddles—all played by people who couldn't—as we went past.

"Gay lot!" said Dick. "My hat, Don, I wish I lived somewhere else—anywhere else!"

III.

I CAN'T say that bike-ride was enjoyable even at the start.

There was not half a mile of really decent road between the two villages. But there were ten miles in all to be covered; and, some way or another, it had to be done.

We plugged on, with the wind right in our teeth, and black clouds blowing up. We did not talk much; but we weren't feeling morose with one another, and neither of us grumbled when the other chap had to stop for prising mud from between the wheels and the guards, or tightening a loose pedal, or some little amusement of that sort. It was about once in every four hundred yards or so that we had to do that. But it never seemed the right time for both of us at once.

Then the snow began.

It did not just drift down. It swirled and eddied and beat upon us till we lost almost all sense of direction, and kept getting off the road and not finding it out until we were in the ditch. And it was so confusing that we barged into one another through not being able to see the other chap, you know. But we did not get snapping at one another. If it had been anybody but Dick with me, or anybody but me with Dick, I guess the fur would have flown a bit, though.

"If only we could get shelter somewhere for a time this might stop," I said. "Anyway, we want a rest."

"There's nowhere near," declared Dick.

But even as he spoke a building loomed up darkly through the snow on our right.

"What's that?" I asked.

"I'd forgotten it," Dick answered. "But it's no go—nobody's lived there for ages. Not a single giddy light, you see. And it's haunted!"

"Haunted be hanged!" I said. "You don't believe in such rot, I'm sure!"

"Well, no," Dick said. "There's nothing in it, I suppose; but pretty nearly everyone round here believes it, all the same. Care to try it if we can find a way in?"

"Oh, rather! It's shelter, anyway," I told him.

We were both about fagged out, and the snow and wind were worse than ever.

It wasn't at all difficult to get in. A door round at the side was half off its hinges. We left our borrowed bikes under the shelter of a lee wall, and took the lamps with us.

Beastly place inside—ugh! Cobwebs and dirt and creeping things and mildew—all sorts of unearthly noises—but no ghosts on show.

"Let's go upstairs," said Dick. "It may be a trifle less damp there."

The stairs were rotting in places, and we picked our way up with care. It was drier on the first floor, though not much more cheerful. We found a seat in the bay of a window not far from the head of the stairs.

"What's the giddy yarn about this show?" I asked.

"Oh, it's rot, of course! But they say that on a certain night in the dead of winter the sounds of some awful sort of revelry come from here, and that if anyone had the nerve to look—but no one has in my time—they would find a whole crowd of ghosts carousing in the big hall below. This place used to belong to a squire who was known as 'Hellfire Harke,' and the yarn about the ghostly revelry has three murders in it—quite enough for one evening party, eh? But don't let's talk any more about it—don't! I'm not a funk, but——"

Dick stopped short, with a shrug of his shoulders and a kind of shudder. I am not a funk, either; but I must own that I was not very keen to hear any more of that horrible old story. I heard it all afterwards; but I am not going to tell it here. All I can say is that I don't wonder folks thought the place must be haunted, or that no one wanted to live in it!

IV.

THEN both our lamps went out, and it was no good trying to relight them, for we knew that the oil was gone.

The wind howled round that awful old house like a thousand demons shrieking, and the snow lashed against the window-panes as I have never known snow to do before. Dick thrust his arm through mine, and I was glad to feel something warm and alive close at hand.

Not too warm, for that matter. It was fairly parky there. But at least it was shelter.

We had about half a dozen matches; but we were saving those for the descent of the staircase, which was not the kind of thing it would be safe to try in the dark.

"Wonder what the pater and the mater and the girls will be thinking has become of us?" said Dick, after a long silence.

My mind had been busy with the same thing. Mrs. Russell and the girls would be worrying, I knew. I did not think Dick's father would. He is the sort of man who leaves the worrying until there is nothing practical to be done. What I feared was that he would start out to look for us; and I knew that he was not in a fit state of health to be out on a wild night like this.

How the wind roared!

Suddenly we heard a great crash, and Dick clutched me hard.

"W-w-what was that?" I muttered.

It was no use muttering. You had to shout to make yourself heard in that storm.

Dick did not hear; but I felt him dragging at my arm.

"Want to go down and see?" I yelled.

"Nunno!"

Well, I didn't, either.

We sat there holding on to each other like a couple of kids.

That crash had sounded frightfully eerie, because, somehow, the house seemed silent in a curious way in the midst of all the shrieking and noise outside.

I don't know how long we sat there without another word. Noises were in the house now—weird noises—muttering voices and footsteps. They did not make us feel any more comfortable. Dick and I had cold feet—there's no denying that!

Then there came another noise—a voice lifted in song.

"It's true, Don!" gasped Dick. The wind had died down for a moment, and I heard every word he said. "Those awful brutes—Hellfire Harke—the ghostly revellers! Oh!"

Upon my word, I believed it! Perhaps I was likelier to believe than Dick. We don't take much stock in spooks and things at Greyfriars, but at my home up in the Highlands it's different. I could tell you some weird tales about the family ghosts of the Ogilvies, and second-sight, and all that.

But that made it a bit easier for me than it was for Dick Russell. I never heard that his family had any ghosts of their own.

The wind seemed to be lulling; but the snow fell as fast as ever. It had drifted through a broken window, and there was a great pile of it on the floor a few yards from us. And we sat in that queer, glimmering half-light that snow gives and listened to that beastly singing, and fairly shivered.

We could not make out the words a bit; but the voice was a beast—the sort of voice you might expect a chap like Hellfire Harke to have. And now other voices were lifted; the revels were in full swing, and we had a nasty feeling that the murdering was going to begin all over again soon.

"I can't sit here any longer!" said Dick suddenly. And he dragged me towards the stairhead.

I don't think either of us remembered the danger of going through those rotten old stairs. I don't believe we realised that we were going down. There wasn't any good reason for going down, for neither of us thought of bolting.

We stood at the bottom of the staircase holding on to one another, and yet, somehow, less funked than we had been.

The noises came from the great hall to our left, and through its open door we caught a gleam of light. It was not an illumination by any means; there was not much more than our two cheap bike lamps had made before they chucked up making any.

I don't know which of us it was that made the first start towards that open door. If it was this child, I don't know why he did it; and if it was Dick, I don't know a bit more why. The way we were feeling you might have expected us to move in the other direction—and to move middling quickly.

But we went.

And then, all in a moment, our fright was over, and we knew the truth.

For we looked in at that open door and saw that the light was that of the lamps from the char-a-banc, and that the ghostly revellers were Waites and Bart and the rest of that crew.

Was it Dick or I that let out the wild yell that sent them all scattering, bolting as if for their lives? I don't know; but I am sure that neither of us had any notion at the moment of trying to give them a fright.

They rushed past us in the dark passage without seeing us—or, if they did see us, they took us for spooks. They were gone inside ten seconds—out of the haunted house into the snow and the wind—howling with fear as they went. A door crashed to behind them, and Dick leaned up against the wall and laughed hysterically.

Behind them they left their lamps, their beer, their pipes, even one or two of their greatcoats.

But they left more behind than that. When, a few minutes later, we reconnoitred, we found that the char-a-banc, with its two horses, had also been deserted. They were bolting for the village on foot, forgetting all about that. Even Bill, the driver, had forgotten.

Of course, they had sheltered from the storm like us, probably—not quite like us—not minding if they made a night of it.

"Shelby will expect to see that brake back," said Dick, half an hour or so later, when the storm had slackened.

"Right-ho!" I replied. "No reason why he shouldn't have it."

And we stowed the borrowed bikes in, and drove the shivering horses home.

That's all!

THE END.

Printed and published weekly by the Proprietors at The Fleetway House, Farringdon Street, London, E.C. 4, England. Subscription, 8s. 10d. per annum. Agents for Australasia: Gordon & Gotch, Melbourne, Sydney, Adelaide, Brisbane, and Wellington, N.Z. South Africa: The Central News Agency, Ltd., Cape Town and Johannesburg. Saturday, January 18th, 1919.

THE RAID ON THE UPPER FOURTH DORMITORY.

By W. H. O. KNOZOO.

It was bold Harry Wharton who spoke unto his men:
"We'll beard the Temple in his lair, the lion in his den!
Take each your deadly bolster, and let each man fight like ten!"

And every staunch Removite was keen, to try a fall—
Bob Cherry, Nugent, Johnny Bull, he whom we Inky call,
The Bounder, Squiff, and Peter Todd—they were ready, one and all!

Dick Russell and his Highland chum, Don Ogilvy, the wary,
And Morgan from the hills of Wales, and one who's never chary
Of running risks when mischief calls—Desmond from Tipperary.

Piet Delarey, from Afric's shores, and Taranaki Brown,
And burly Percy Bolsover, with his most ferocious frown,
Tom Redwing and Mark Linley, Kipps, of conjuring renown;

And Hazeldene and Penfold, and Newland and Dick Rake,
With Hilary and Bulstrode, the giddy war-path take.
E'en deaf Tom Dutton hears the call; e'en Mauly is awake!

Wibley, Treluce, and Trevor, Smith (Robert Fortescue),
Wun Lung and Jimmy Vivian, they're to the colours true;
And in the rear come gingerly the craven-hearted few—

Sly Fish and crafty Skinner, and Sidney Snoop and Stott,
And that stout porpoise, Bunter, least war-like of the lot.
If aught had hung on Bunter's pluck, our chance had gone to pot!

Like a tiger on its hapless prey, like Britons on the Hun,
We burst into the Fourth Form dorm, and took each mother's son
Therein completely by surprise. Like a shot out of a gun

Our Wharton dashed at Temple and smote him on the head—
A mighty blow!—ere he could guess who stood beside his bed;
But quick jumped Temple to his feet, with angry face and red.

And they rallied to him gamely, Dabney and Fry and Scott,
And Murphy and MacDougall, and all the giddy lot;
And a most tremendous battle was waged around the spot

Where Cecil Reginald and our bold Harry Wharton whacked
Hard at each other's craniums. No doughty champion slacked.
(Though Bunter crawled beneath a bed, that statement's still a fact!)

And in the midst of all someone came in, and on his napper
Bob Cherry brought his bolster down—then saw 'twas Mr. Capper!
And Bob, dismayed, could only stammer: "It was—er—a mishap—er!"

. . . .

(And the rest cannot be told in rhyme. It wasn't a bit poetical. Capper has no soul for poetry or for war. Let's put it in one line—Swish, swish, swish!—and more swish!)

THE GREYFRIARS GALLERY.

No. 102—THE REST OF THEM.

THIS is the final article of a series which has proved amazingly popular. Of course, I expected it to be popular, or I should not have started it. But I never guessed how enthusiastic my readers would be about it.

Some of them would like it to go on for a long time yet. But I think the time has come to close it up.

Of the characters who really matter to the stories scarcely any remain undealt with, and the few who could be classed as of any importance have figured for so short a time that they do not offer much chance of interesting treatment.

Perhaps the most outstanding figure among them is that of Aubrey Angel. But it is only a few months ago that we first read about Angel, and we all know what he is—a wrong 'un through and through, possibly the worst fellow at Greyfriars. There is his pal Kenney. But Paul Kenney is another Stott—vicious enough, but with little go in him.

There is little Napoleon Dupont, Bolsover major's stable companion, of whom we may hear more yet. And there is Dick Hilary, the son of the erstwhile Conchy. Very good fellow, Hilary—fellow with a conscience and courage. But we know all about him, don't we?

TREVOR AND TRELUCE.

Then there are quite a lot of fellows who have never figured at all prominently, such as Trevor and Treluce, Smith minor and Glenn in the Remove; Faulkner and Hammersley and North in the Sixth; Bland and Fitzgerald and Hilton and Smith major and Price and Tomlinson major in the Fifth; Scott and Tomlinson minor and others in the Upper Fourth; Castle and Pettifer and Marsden in the Second; some in the Shell and the Third also.

But what is there one can say of any of them, beyond a line or two? For the most part they are merely members of the chorus, so to speak.

Bland is Blundell's special chum, and stood by him loyally when Hilton made a bid for the captaincy of the Fifth. That is about the only thing ever recorded of Hilton, whose own chum is Tomlinson major. Terence Fitzgerald is a genial Irishman. Scott, of the Upper Fourth, is a level-headed North Briton, who would probably make a better skipper for the Form than Temple, who is really a bit of an ass in many ways. Trevor and Treluce don't amount to much; they are never found cutting a dash. On the whole, they are inclined to lean to the wrong side when the Form divides itself on any question. But they only lean; they don't push hard. Glenn—who has gone now—and Smith minor may be set down as quiet fellows with no harm in them. Marsden aspires to be the humorist of the Second; but the fags have no craving for a verbal humorist—the kind of humour that appeals to those young gentlemen is of the practical joking type.

There are people at Highcliffe who might have been dealt with. The Head, Dr. Voysey, for instance; but when one has said of him that he is a weak, irresolute man, with a tendency to snobbishness, one has said all that matters. Arthur de Bohun Langley, the Highcliffe skipper, is a very likeable sort indeed, but slack and easy-going, and with some tastes that are no good either to himself or to the school. The other Sixth-Formers there, as far as we know them, are all rather slack and rather doggish. Monson major of the Fifth is a hulking bully; his younger brother of the Fourth—he might have been given an article to himself, but really he has never done anything much but follow Ponsonby's lead—is one of the nuts, rather sulky, but with something better in him than either Gadsby or Vavasour. Drury is another nut, but less decidedly of the Pon faction than Monson minor. Pelham and Blades also follow Pon's lead at times. But Smithson and Yates and Jones minor and Benson are all Courtenayites, and very decent fellows.

Except for Dick Trumper and Solly Lazarus the Courtfield boys do not matter a great deal. But Dicky Brown and Walter Grahame may be mentioned here—both all right, you know.

At Cliff House there is only little Molly Gray, the red-headed junior with the lisp, who is a good chum of Merton's, and a favourite with Marjorie & Co. But about Cliff House it is more than likely that you will have the chance to learn a great deal more within a few months. There is a surprise in store in that connection.

The Rev. Mr. LAMBE.

There are relatives of the boys at Greyfriars who might have been dealt with, as Johnny Bull's aunt and uncle, and dear Horace's Aunt Judy, and Colonel Wharton, and Major Cherry, and Uncle Benjamin Todd, and Sir Reginald Brooke, and Josiah Snoop, have all been. But there is not much to tell you about Frank Nugent's father and mother except that he is quick-tempered and she is wrong-headed and injudicious; nor much about Harry Wharton's gentle Aunt Mary, except that she is the sort of aunt any fellow would be proud to have; nor much about Mr. Hiram K. Fish, except that he is very much Fishy's father; nor much about Mr. Abraham Sylvester, except that he seems a good sort, although a millionaire. There are Mark Linley's father, a fine specimen of the best kind of British working-man, and Mark's sister, Mabel, a nice girl, and his wayward younger brother, Gerald, who does not amount to much. There are also Mrs. Locke, the Head's wife; nothing but good to be said about her, and not much to be said anyway. Percy Locke, nephew of the Head, would offer more scope; but he only appeared in one story, and the chief thing one remembers about him is that Gosling, who is not a very affectionate person, seemed fond of him. I had nearly forgotten Dick Penfold's good old father—a cobbler and a gentleman! Mr. Joseph Banks and Captain Punter are other characters outside the school walls; but these two have closer connection with St. Jim's, and may be dealt with in the "Gem" later.

The Rev. Orlando Beale Lambe, Vicar of Friardale, of whom we have a portrait, remains. It was Mr. Lambe who got the jumping crackers which the Famous Five, taken in by the Bounder, meant for Gosling, reported to be coming along in the dusk. And it was Mr. Lambe who, at the Friardale Bazaar, dropped hard on to innocent Harry Wharton for what was really the sinful Bunter, practising his ventriloquism at Mr. Lambe's expense.

Of course, there have been quite a number of boys who have figured in a story or two, and then disappeared from the scene. At every school boys come and go; Greyfriars is no exception to that rule.

Let us recall some of them—I cannot pretend to remember quite all.

There was Arthur Brandreth, whose father came so near to suffering for the crime of Josiah Snoop. A good sort, Brandreth, older than his years in some ways, loyal and plucky, and most forgiving. Then do any of you remember Theophilus Flipps, who talked a bit like Skimpole of St. Jim's, and was great on hygiene—"The Young Health-Seeker," and all that—and did the weirdest things? Theophilus was not the kind of boy any Form-master would want to keep; but I should not mind seeing him back for a while. Then there was Arthur Jolly, who changed places with Peter Potts, the new page—young dog, Jolly, but amusing. Poor Potts in the Form-room! Clive Cholmondeley never came to the school; his place was taken by Tom Handley, the ship's boy who wanted an education. Con Fitzpatrick came only to run away to sea; the sea called Con, and he could not be deaf to that call. Jack Verney, the efficient and audacious, took the place for a brief time, by the help of making-up, of Archie Drake, the would-be Admirable Crichton. Herbert Spring, a young scoundrel, came in the name of his young brother; but Conrad Spring turned up, and Herbert went. We may hear more of them.

Do you remember Cecil Leigh, whose real name was Henry Hopkins, and who was ashamed of his father, the worthy old publican who had saved to make a gentleman of him? And Cyril Vane, Bob Cherry's cousin, rather a young pup, though he improved before he left? And Algy Darrell, whose secret gave trouble during his short stay? He had been sacked from his former school because he had shielded a guilty chum. And Jack Holt, the boy from the farm, supposed to be Sir Harry Beauclerc, but really a very much better fellow than that atrocious young bounder and cad, who did not misplace his aspirates, but had hardly any other redeeming quality? And Paul Sidney, the protege of Ferrers Locke, who had been a thief, but had put his past behind him, only to find it rise up against him? And Rupprecht von Rattenstein, that haughty Hun, a lovely specimen of the German race, rotten to the core? And Heath, cruel and treacherous?

Dalton Hawke was scarcely a genuine "boy." Ferrers Locke sent him along to play detective, and he went when his task was accomplished. But in another sense he was quite a genuine boy, for Greyfriars suited him and he Greyfriars.

This is not all, I know. There were the fellows known as "the Terrible Two"; but they also were not genuine boys. There was Gadsby—no relation to him of Highcliffe, I believe—who was sacked for the theft of a valuable postage-stamp. No doubt there were others; but I cannot pretend to give an exhaustive list. It is quite a little world, this of the Greyfriars stories, and I have forgotten the very names of some of its many inhabitants.

Something must be said about the members of the school staff, tutorial and domestic, who have not been dealt with. But the only thing I can recall about Mr. Kelly, lately away in the Army, is that he sent Sammy Bunter, as a new boy, to wash his nasty, grubby paws, and that Sammy did not like it a little bit. And what can be said about Mr. Eusebius Twigg and his brother, Mr. Bernard Morrison Twigg, save that they are there, and no doubt doing their duty as per catechism?

Mrs. Kebble is an efficient matron—at least, I know nothing to the contrary. We don't see much of her; the Second may see more. Joseph Mimble is the husband of Jessie, the dame of the tuckshop; Joseph tends the Head's garden, and is not fond of boys. And that's all!

DALTON HAWKE.

****

THE EDITOR'S CHAT.

For Next Monday:

"A DOG WITH A BAD NAME!"

By Frank Richards.

Wally Bunter is the dog with the bad name, of course.

It really is rough on Wally. Apart from his looks and his big appetite, he has no more in common with his cousin Billy than Harry Wharton or Bob Cherry has.

But to Greyfriars he is Billy, and the burden of Billy's sins is heavy upon his shoulders.

He fancied that staying on at Greyfriars would mean playing for the junior footer team. But he had forgotten that his form on the field did not count. It was Billy's want of form—Billy's crass ineptitude, rather, that counted.

He thought, too—poor old Wally!—that the friendly terms he had established with Harry Wharton and his circle would continue. But when Wally became Billy—well, you can see how it altered everything!

W. G. B. AT ST. JIM'S!

Meanwhile, if you don't read the "Gem," you are losing your Billy Bunter—and missing some of the finest school stories ever written! No good writing to me to complain about the transfer of the egregious Billy to the "Gem"! I shall not show the least sympathy. I am enjoying both sets of stories too much for that. Wally, burdened with Billy's sin, is a fine substitute for Billy at Greyfriars; and Billy at St. Jim's is too funny for words!

ABUSE!

I have received two abusive letters from a reader whose initials are M. G.—he gives his name, but I have no great confidence in its being his right one—and whose address is "London." I don't know whether he expected an answer. I don't know why he reads the papers, which plainly don't satisfy him now. He pours unmeasured abuse on the long stories, the short stories, and the Chat. I can always find room, he says, for the piffle I call short sermons. He is wrong. It may or may not be piffle; I fear that to a fellow of his type anything about playing the game and being decent would seem piffle. But I don't write for fellows of his type; and it very often happens that I cannot find room for what I want to say.

He is sure that the circulations of the papers are decreasing; and he is very far wrong again there. The circulation figures bear out what I gather from the general tone of my correspondence—that the very great majority of readers are absolutely satisfied.

It is so very easy to drop a paper if it does not suit you. It is never worth while to abuse an editor on that account, for the chances are that he has never set out to please the kind of person you unhappily are.

M. G. is under the foolish delusion that Messrs. Clifford and Richards "control" the papers. This in itself is a fairly clear proof of his general ignorance. In spite of that ignorance, I should not mind civil criticism from him. But abuse is not criticism; and hopes that the two papers are going all to pot come very badly from one who assumes a right to say what should or should not be in them. Perhaps M. G. would like to come along and edit them?

But on the whole I cannot offer him the job. I have no confidence in his judgment—not so much because it differs from mine as because it differs from that of nearly all his fellow-readers.

He says he knows that both papers are doing badly—that is why I ask for more readers, he is sure. It does not occur to him, I suppose, that every editor always wants more readers. As a matter of fact, the MAGNET and "Gem" alike are going great guns. Our circulation is very well indeed, thank you!

YOUR EDITOR.

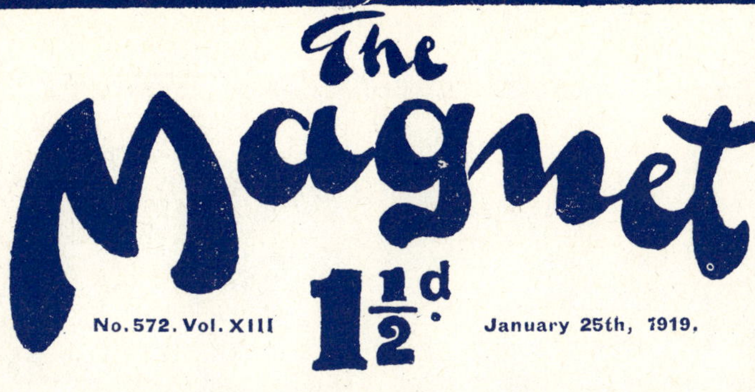

A DOG WITH A BAD NAME!

BUNTER'S BUCKSHEE BATH!

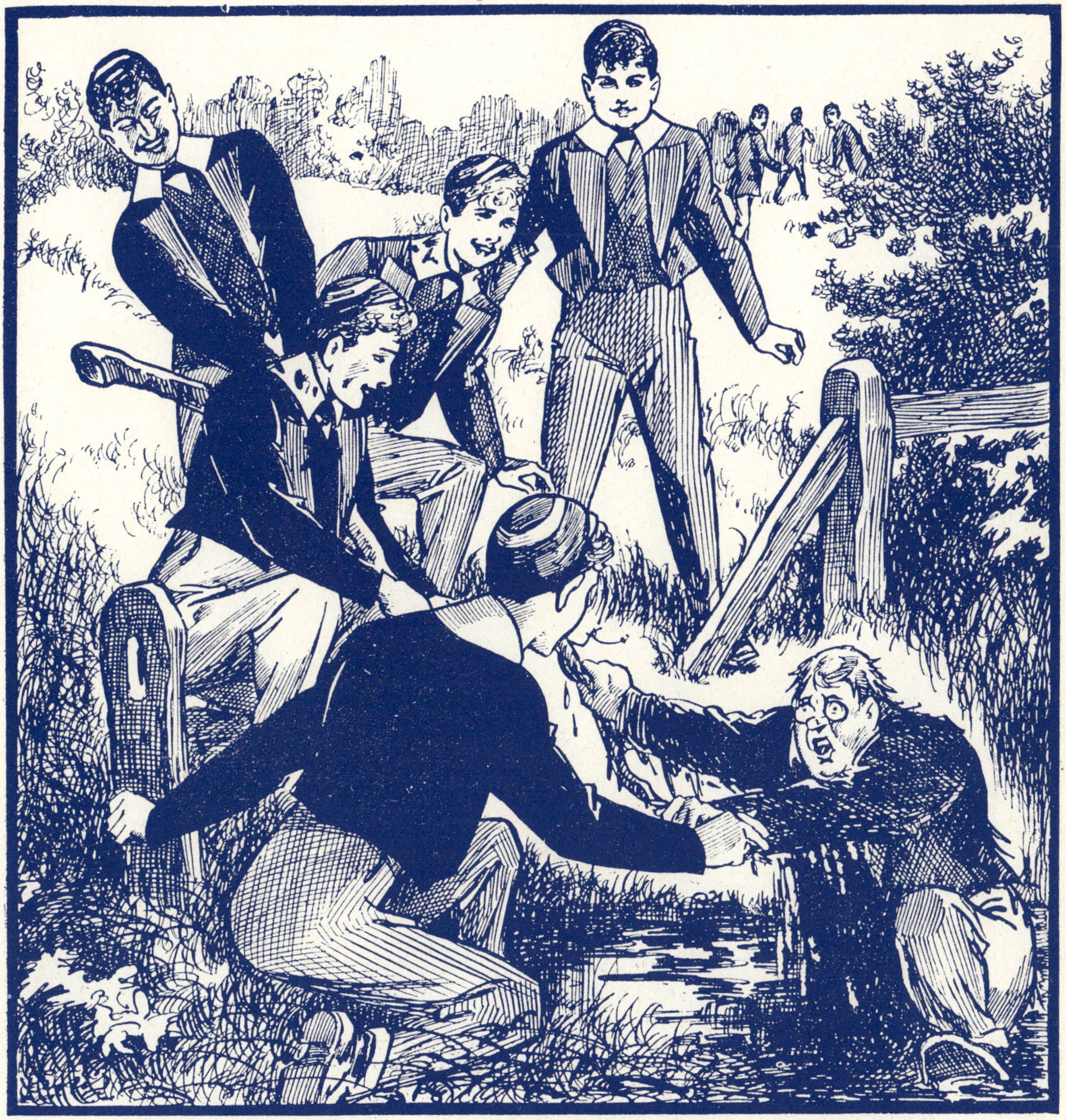

A Dog with a Bad Name!

A Laughable, Long Story of Harry Wharton & Co. at Greyfriars.

BY

FRANK RICHARDS.

THE FIRST CHAPTER.
No Change for Bunter!

"HOOK it!"

Three or four voices uttered that command at once, as a fat face looked into Study No. 1 in the Remove passage.

There was an important discussion going on in that famous study; and Harry Wharton & Co. did not seem desirous of Bunter's company.

"Cut!" said Wharton, pointing to the doorway. "We're busy, Bunter."

"Look here——"

"Don't you understand English?" asked Bob Cherry. "I'll put it in German if you like. Getten-sie out!"

"Ha, ha, ha!"

Bob Cherry's meaning was clear; but his German would certainly have made a Hun smile—if any Hun is capable of a smile in these days.

"Look here, you fellows——" persisted the fat junior.

"Hook it!"

"You're fixing up for the Highcliffe match, I understand——" went on Bunter.

"You understand?" said Vernon-Smith, the Bounder of Greyfriars, in a tone of great surprise.

"Yes. Isn't it so?"

"Oh, yes, it's so," agreed the Bounder. "But it's rather new for you to understand anything, Bunty."

"You silly ass——"

"Cut off, Bunter!" said Harry Wharton impatiently. "You know you mustn't interrupt the footer committee."

"But I want——"

"Never mind what you want. Get out!"

"But I want——"

"Buzz!"

"I tell you——"

"Scat!"

"Look here, you silly idiots——" roared the fat junior wrathfully.

"My hat! If he doesn't understand English, perhaps he will understand this cush!" exclaimed Bob Cherry.

He grasped a cushion and hurled it, and Bunter jumped out into the passage just in time.

The cushion bounced on the opposite wall, and fell to the floor.

"That's cleared him," grinned Bob. "Hallo, hallo, hallo! What? Oh!"

Whiz!

The heavy cushion came back.

It caught Bob Cherry under the chin as he jumped up, and he sat down again in a hurry, just missing his chair.

There was a loud bump as Bob landed on the carpet, and a louder yell followed. Bunter grinned in at the doorway.

"Go it!" he said. "I'll keep it up as long as you do, fathead!"

Bob Cherry gasped.

"I—I—I'll slaughter him! I'll spiflicate him! You wait a tick for me, Bunter, you Owl!"

Bob Cherry jumped up and rushed for the door. But the fat junior did not wait. He melted away in the passage.

"Hold on, Bob!" called out Harry Wharton. "We've got to wind up before tea, you know."

Bob Cherry grunted, and came back into the study.

"There'll be a dead Owl found lying about Greyfriars one of these days," he said darkly. "I'm getting fed up with Bunter."

"Well, about the Highcliffe match," said Vernon-Smith. "I really think Redwing ought to be put in the front line. Of course, it's for you to settle, Wharton. But Redwing is really good stuff, you know."

The captain of the Remove smiled.

Smithy was rather given to urging the claims of his chum, in season and out of season.

"He's good man," admitted Wharton. "But——"

"One of the best," urged the Bounder.

"Admitted; but the Highcliffe match is rather a corker," said Harry. "We can't afford to run risks with it. Courtenay's team is in tip-top form. We want to send our very best men over there on Saturday."

"That's what I'm getting at," remarked Smithy.

"H'm! But——"

"You haven't finally settled the front line yet?"

"No; but——"

"Hallo, hallo, hallo! Here's that fat bounder again!" exclaimed Bob Cherry, in tones of great exasperation.

The door of No. 1 had reopened, and the fat face and glimmering glasses looked in again. Bunter held up a fat hand.

"Hold on!" he said. "Can't you let a chap speak a word? It's really important, Wharton."

"Hook it!" roared Bob.

"I want to play on Saturday——"

"What?"

"Give me a chance in the Highcliffe match——"

"You—you silly Owl!"

"Fathead!"

"Ass!"

"Look here! You ought to give a chap a chance," urged the fat junior. "You've seen me at practice lately. You want a man in the front line. Well, I'm your man. What's the good of my sticking at footer if I never have a chance in a match?"

"You silly ass!" exclaimed Wharton impatiently. "You know you can't play footer. You play a sillier game than Coker of the Fifth—if possible. You hardly know a footer from a footer-boot! Buzz off!"

"You've seen me——"

"I know you've picked up at practice," said Harry, with a nod. "That's surprising enough, in a fat slacker like you——"

"Who's a slacker?"

"You are, you lazy Owl! The fattest and laziest slacker at Greyfriars!"

"Look here——"

"Next time we're playing a home for idiots we'll put you in the team, if you like," said Wharton. "Until then, go and eat coke! Now buzz off!"

"I want you to understand——"

"Cut!"

"You see——"

"'Nuff said!" exclaimed Bob Cherry. "This is where the silly Owl gets it in the neck! Fed up!"

He made a rush at the Owl of the Remove as he spoke, and this time Bunter did not dodge quickly enough. Bob Cherry's powerful grasp closed on him.

"Frog's march!" cried Wharton.

"Collar him!" exclaimed Squiff, the Australian member of the committee.

The juniors collared Bunter on all sides. His weight was considerable; but many hands made light work, and he was swept off the floor, roaring.

"Carry him home!" grinned Smithy.

"Yaroooh! Leggo!"

Bunter, yelling, was rushed into the passage, and along it to No. 7. He was tapped on the floor half a dozen times before No. 7 was reached; and at each tap he let out a terrific yell. Smithy kicked open the door of No. 7, and the fat junior was rushed in.

Bump!

Bunter landed on the study table with a concussion that made it dance.

"Now, you come back, and next time we'll shove your head in the coal-locker!" panted Bob Cherry.

"Yarooooh!"

Harry Wharton & Co. left No. 7 and returned to their quarters. The footer discussion was resumed, without any further interruption from Bunter. That plump youth sat up on the table in No. 7 gasping for breath.

"Ow-ow-ow! Grooogh!" he gasped. "Silly asses! Oh, dear! Yow-ow-ow! I'm jolly well going to get into the team somehow, all the same! Oh, dear! I wish I'd never changed places with Billy—I might have got some footer at St. Jim's at least! Ow!"

That reflection came rather late in the day to Wally Bunter, who had taken the place of his cousin Billy at Greyfriars, unknown to anyone else in the school.

Billy Bunter, who couldn't play footer for toffee, had gone to St. Jim's with Wally's' footer reputation; and Wally, his cousin and double, was at Greyfriars, with Billy's happy reputation of being a duffer at everything in general, and football in particular.

And Wally Bunter had the exasperating consciousness of being as good a footballer as any fellow in the Remove—and the absolute certainty of never playing a match so long as he was supposed to be Billy Bunter!

It was really too thick for words, and the worst of it was that it couldn't be helped unless Wally owned up that he wasn't Billy, in which case he couldn't have stayed at Greyfriars at all.

If Harry Wharton & Co. had only known——

But they didn't know!

THE SECOND CHAPTER.
A Dog With a Bad Name!

"HA, ha, ha!"

"Here comes the merry footballer!"

"Bunter's latest!"

"Ha, ha, ha!"

There was a general chortle in the junior Common-room that evening when Bunter of the Remove rolled in.

Bunter's demand for a place in the Remove Eleven had tickled the Remove no end, as they expressed it themselves.

There were good footballers in the Remove who had no chance of figuring in the Highcliffe match, which was one of the three toughest fixtures in the list, the other two being the matches with St. Jim's and Rookwood. For Bunter to demand a place in the team for that match, of all others, struck the Remove as being the joke of the season.

Wally Bunter grunted as he found himself the centre of the general merriment.

It was really his own fault. He was playing the part of Billy Bunter of his own accord, that being the only way of gratifying his keen desire to belong to Greyfriars. But certainly he had not realised the estimation in which his cousin Billy was held at the school.

No wonder Billy had been anxious to change places, and get a fresh start at St. Jim's, where he was not quite so well known! Wally was beginning to wonder whether he could keep up that change of identity for a whole term, as he had arranged with Billy.

At every step he was up against Billy's unenviable reputation, and it seemed a hopeless task to attempt to live it down.

"Good old Bunter!" chuckled Johnny Bull. "He does these things to cheer us up, and make us forget the rations."

"The cheerfulness is terrific!" remarked Hurree Singh. "Without the esteemed fatheaded Bunter there would be no smilefulness."

"Bunter a footballer!" roared Bolsover major. "Ha, ha, ha!"

"I'd undertake to play your head off, anyway!" grunted Wally.

"The playfulness would be terrific!"

"If Wharton had any sense he would put me in the team!" growled Wally.

Harry Wharton laughed.

"I haven't that kind of sense, my fat infant," he replied. "Ask me something easier."

"Cheeky ass!" said Hazeldene. "You're not good enough for a match with the Second Form, let alone with Highcliffe."

"Oh, rats!"

"Don't be an ass, Bunty, old scout!" said Peter Todd good-naturedly. "You can't play footer or cricket; you can't do anything but guzzle, and borrow bobs, and tell whoppers! That's your line. Stick to it!"

"Who tells whoppers?" howled Wally.

"You do, my fat tulip; mountains of them!" said Peter, in surprise. "I suppose you're not going to claim to be a Georgie Washington as well as a footballer, are you?"

"Ha, ha, ha!"

"Oh, you're a silly ass!" growled Wally resentfully. "I could prove to you that I'm a good man for the Form Eleven if I liked!"

"Ha ha! Go ahead and do it!"

"Only—only I can't——"

"Ha, ha, ha!"

Wally's eyes sparkled over his cousin Billy's spectacles. He was strongly tempted at that moment to speak out and announce that he was not Billy Bunter at all, but he checked himself in time. Even with Billy Bunter's unenviable reputation to struggle against he wanted to remain at Greyfriars, and he did not despair of yet making himself respected in the Remove, in spite of everything.

He sat down silently near the fire and took up a book. It was a Latin book, and some of the juniors who noticed that grinned. Billy Bunter was a slacker at work as well as at play, and the sight of the fat junior reading Latin for his own entertainment struck them as comic.

Billy Bunter was the last fellow in the world to set up as a swot, and the juniors concluded that the Latin book was some new stunt of the Owl of the Remove.

Bolsover major looked over his shoulder and grinned.

"I suppose you understand that, Bunter?" he asked.

"Yes."

"What is it?"

"Cicero."

"We don't have Cicero in the Remove," said Frank Nugent. "You've taken up Cicero on your own—what?"

"Why shouldn't I?" asked Wally.

"Ha, ha! No reason why you shouldn't if you want to, but don't expect fellows to swallow it, old top. What's the game?"

"Br-r-r-r!"

"Oh, I know the game!" grinned Skinner. "I've played that stunt myself! You pick out some awfully hard stuff and con over it when the cheery old Form-master is likely to come across you. Form-master spots it, and thinks to himself what a terrific hard worker you are, and goes easy with you ever afterwards. That's it, isn't it, Bunter?"

"No, it isn't!" snapped Wally.

"I fancy it is," said Bob Cherry.

"Why, you Owl, you can't construe Cæsar without tripping up all the time, and you want us to believe that you're reading Cicero!"

"The Cicerofulness is not terrific," said Hurree Jamset Ram Singh, with a shake of his dusky head, "but the spooffulness is great!"

Wally's fat face flushed over his book.

He was really a hard worker, and he had a taste for study. He had worked for his bread before his good luck came along and he had a chance of going to St. Jim's—and had chosen Greyfriars instead under such peculiar circumstances. He was anxious to get on with his studies, and he really found an attraction in reading Cicero in the original. But again Bunter's reputation was up against him, and all the fellows took it for spoof.

"Let's make him construe!" grinned Snoop. "Make him stand up and construe Cicero, same as in class."

"Good egg!"

"Right-ho!" exclaimed Bolsover major. The bully of the Remove picked up a ruler, in imitation of Mr. Quelch's pointer. "Bunter!"

"Hallo?" grunted Wally.

"Stand up, Bunter!"

"Rats!"

"Stand up and construe!" roared Bolsover major.

"Go and eat coke!"

"He can't construe Cicero!" said Wharton. "What's the good of asking him? It's only spoof!"

"It's not spoof!" howled Wally. "I'll construe fast enough if you want to listen to it!"

"Ha, ha! Go ahead!"

"Pile in!" grinned Squiff. "What's the book?"

"'In Verrem'!" snapped Wally. "'De signis.'"

"My hat! That sounds learned enough!" chuckled Tom Brown. "What's it about, Bunty?"

The Removites chuckled. Fully convinced that the fat junior's study of Cicero's orations was merely a stunt, they did not expect him to be able to state what the book was about. But Wally answered cheerfully enough.

"It's old Cicero gassing about Verres, who played the goat in Sicily like the Huns in Belgium," he said. "You ought to know that. This is 'Liber Quartus.' I'll go on if you like."

"Go it!" came a chorus.

"Ha, ha, ha!"

"Silence for the swot!" roared Bolsover major. "Now, then, Bunter, get on with your 'Liber Quartus,' and if you don't construe right up to the mark you're going to get a licking, same as in class."

"Thats only fair!" agreed Wharton. "Begin, Bunter!"

"Oh, I don't mind," said Wally.

And he started from "Venio nunc ad istus . . . ," and, to the amazement of the Removites and the Fourth-Formers in the Common-room, he went ahead without a fault. Wharton looked over his shoulder at the book, and he looked very puzzled. Bunter, who bungled Cæsar, seemed quite at home with Cicero.

"My only hat!" ejaculated the captain of the Remove at last. "He's really doing it!"

"He's got it by heart out of a crib!" sneered Skinner.

"I haven't!" roared Wally indignantly. "Wharton can see that I'm doing it from the book."

"It really seems like it," admitted Wharton. "It beats me. Of course, he may have got it up in advance, to spoof us."

"But fancy Bunter being able to mug up Cicero at all!" ejaculated Nugent. "Who'd have thought it?"

"I believe he's spoofing, all the same," said Bolsover major. "Go on from another part, Bunter."

"All right!"

Bolsover major turned the leaf himself, and pointed out a new place to begin. Wally went on cheerily from "Pro deum hominumque fidem." Bolsover major could only stare. He had selected that place for Wally to begin, and the fat junior could not be supposed to have mugged up the whole of the volume.

"Well, my hat!" ejaculated Bolsover.

"Well done, Bunter!" said a deep, quiet voice.

The juniors spun round.

Mr. Quelch, the master of the Remove, stood in the doorway, with a very approving smile on his somewhat severe face.

The Remove-master had been passing the junior Common-room, when he heard the very unusual sound of a fellow reading out Cicero within. Naturally, it had struck his ear, and he had stopped to give attention, unnoticed by the juniors, who were all watching Wally Bunter.

Wally started and coloured, and lowered the book hastily, as he heard the Form-master's voice.

Mr. Quelch gave him quite a benignant look.

"I congratulate you, Bunter!" he said. "You have made advances in your studies that I was certainly not aware of. You will be a credit to your Form, Bunter!"

"Oh, sir!" gasped Wally.

The Remove-master walked out into the passage, evidently well pleased. But the Removites did not look pleased.

They gave the fat junior accusing glances.

"You knew Quelchy was there!" said Skinner. "What did I tell you fellows! It's a stunt to curry favour with the masters!"

"I didn't know he was there!" shouted Wally angrily.

"Rats!"

"Rot!"

"Spoof!"

"How could I have known he was there?" shrieked Wally. "You silly asses, I hadn't the faintest idea——"

"Rats!"

"Spoof!"

"Dry up!"

"Don't tell any more whoppers, Bunter! Can't you see you're bowled out, you spoofing worm?"

Wally Bunter gave it up. Once more Billy Bunter's reputation had risen up and smitten him, as it were; and it was useless for him to protest.

THE THIRD CHAPTER.

Six on the War-path!

"HALLO, hallo, hallo! Wherefore this thusness?" exclaimed Bob Cherry.

Hurree Jamset Singh came in at the gates of Greyfriars—or, to be more accurate, he hopped in.

The Nabob of Bhanipur presented an extraordinary sight.

His right leg was tied up, being bent at the knee, and his dusky wrists were fastened together with a length of cart-rope. On his olive visage were several large dabs of white paint. His cap had been put on backwards, and his jacket turned inside-out.

Bob Cherry stared at him blankly.

"Inky, you ass! What the thump have——"

"Hallo! What's the matter with Inky?"

Harry Wharton and Johnny Bull and Nugent came racing up. They all stared at the nabob.

"Inky, old scout——"

"What the merry dickens——"

"Oh, dear!" gasped the nabob. "Yow-ow! I am an unhappyful victim, my esteemed chums!"

He hopped in, and leaned on the open gate, gasping for breath. Gosling came out of his lodge and blinked at him, with high scorn. Gosling evidently did not approve of proceedings of this sort.

"My heye!" said Gosling. "Pretty goings hon! Wot I says is this 'ere, I shall report this!"

"My esteemed chums, I begfully demand to be released!" gasped Hurree Singh. "I have fallen into the hands of the disgusting Philistines."

"The Highcliffe rotters?" asked Wharton.

"Ow! Yes! I have suffered a terrific ragging."

"The rotters!" exclaimed Bob wrathfully.

"What the dickens did you let them handle you like that for?" asked Wally Bunter, who had come up with a dozen other fellows by this time.

"The esteemed rotters were six to one!" groaned Hurree Singh. "I have punched Ponsonby's esteemed nose, and dotted the worthy Gadsby in his ridiculous eye. But the too-muchfulness was terrific."

Hurree Singh's chums were cutting him loose from the rope already. But it was not an easy task. The Highcliffians had done their work well.

Most of the juniors were grinning. Hurree Jamset Ram Singh's misadventure had its comic side.

"The cheeky rotters!" exclaimed Wharton. "Where are they, Inky?"

"I fell in with the disgusting bounders at the corner of Redclyffe Lane as I returnfully came from Friardale," gasped the nabob. "There were Ponsonby and Gadsby, and Monson and Vavasour, and Drury and another esteemed beast. And they seized me collarfully."

Wharton knitted his brows.

The footer-match with Frank Courtenay's team at Highcliffe was almost due, and Wharton would willingly have avoided rags with the Highcliffe fellows just then. But Ponsonby, Courtenay's rival at Highcliffe, kept up all his old enmity towards Greyfriars, and he had been glad of the chance of causing trouble just before the match.

"I suppose they've cleared off by this time," said Johnny Bull, "otherwise we'd go out and mop them up!"

"The esteemed Pon declarefully remarked that he would wait for us, if we cared to come out," said the nabob.

"Then we'll jolly well go!" exclaimed Bob Cherry.

"Five of us will be enough," said Wharton. "Five of Greyfriars are good enough for six Highcliffe nuts."

"Hear, hear!"

"Better take another man," said Wally Bunter. "I'll come."

"Ha, ha, ha!"

"Look here——"

"Don't be funny, Bunter. This isn't a time for your little jokes," said Wharton. "Come on, you chaps! You feel up to tackling them again, Inky?"

"The tacklefulness will be terrific, my esteemed Wharton," said the nabob, dabbing at the paint on his face with his handkerchief. "I will come with enormous pleasure."

"Come on, then!"

And the Famous Five started at once, the nabob still dabbing at his face, which had a queer, mottled appearance. Wally Bunter cheerfully rolled out of the gates after the Co.

"Hallo, hallo, hallo! There's that fat slug crawling after us!" exclaimed Bob Cherry, as he noticed Bunter coming on behind.

Wharton looked round.

"Cut off, Bunter!" he said.

"Rot!" answered Wally. "There's six of the Highcliffe bounders, and you'll want another man."

"Cut off, you duffer!" exclaimed Bob Cherry impatiently. "You'll cut off fast enough when you see the Highcliffe chaps."

"Rats!"

"Look here, what game are you playing?" demanded Johnny Bull. "You know you're funky even of the Highcliffe cads!"

"You'll see!" growled Wally.

And he kept pace with the Famous Five as they marched forward on the war-path.

Wally was determined. This seemed really a good opportunity to retrieve his reputation—or, rather, his cousin Billy's reputation. He was a handy fellow with his hands, fat as they were, and he had no end of courage; and he was quite ready for a scrap with any number of Highcliffians. After seeing him put up a really good fight the juniors would not be able to deny that Bunter was worthy of respect, or at least civility.

Harry Wharton & Co. did not heed him further. They did not quite understand Bunter of late; but they had no doubt whatever that he was simply spoofing, as usual, and that he would flee at the first sign of the enemy.

The chums of the Remove walked quickly, and were not long in reaching the corner where Redclyffe Lane turned off from the Friardale Road.

There was a high bank beside the lane, with a fence at the top, and on top of the fence Ponsonby & Co. were seated in a row.

The nuts of Highcliffe grinned down at the new arrivals.

It was a half-holiday that afternoon, and Ponsonby & Co. were out looking for trouble, as they frequently were. Hurree Jamset Ram Singh had fallen a victim to heavy odds, and the nuts had enjoyed ragging him; but Pon's offer to wait there till his friends came along had rather surprised his comrades. They were not looking for a battle royal on fair terms.

But Ponsonby was in a wilful humour, and he had his way. There was a good deal more of the fighting-man in Pon than in his comrades. And he had taken some precautions. On top of the steep bank the Highcliffians were in a strong position, and they had cut sticks from the hedge for use if required. So they felt a rather unusual confidence.

The Famous Five and Wally Bunter halted, and looked up at them.

"Here they are!" said Frank Nugent.

"And here we are!" said Bob. "We're looking for you, Ponsonby."

"You've found me!" remarked Pon agreeably.

"Blessed if I thought you'd really stay!" said Johnny Bull. "I thought you'd have bunked for safety."

"Oh, we're ready to lick you, if you're yearning for a dashed lickin'," said Pon carelessly. "Bounders have to be kept in their place; and the best way is by lickin' 'em, I suppose."

"Oh, rather!" agreed Gadsby.

"Absolutely!" grinned Vavasour.

"Well, we're ready for the licking," remarked Harry Wharton. "Chuck those sticks away, and come down here, and begin."

"Come and fetch us, dear boy!"

"We'll soon do that, if you don't come down!" growled Johnny Bull.

"Well, we're waitin'."

"Screw up your merry courage to the stickin' point, old beans!" grinned Monson. "Have a little pluck!"

The Co. gave them a grim look. They either had to begin the combat under very disadvantageous terms, or clear off and leave the Highcliffians to crow. And the latter alternative was not to be thought of.

Harry Wharton glanced at his comrades.

"Ready?" he asked.

"You bet!"

"Yes, rather!" said Bunter.

"You keep off the grass, you fat duffer! Come on, kids!"

And Harry Wharton led the way up the steep bank with a rush, his comrades close after him. And after them scrambled Wally Bunter, though, as the Removites did not look back, they were not aware that the fat junior was at their heels.

THE FOURTH CHAPTER.

Hors de Combat!

"GO for 'em!"

"Give 'em socks!"

"The sockfulness will be terrific!"

Ponsonby & Co. slid off the fence and grasped their sticks.

The bank was steep, and the rush upward was rather breathless. As the attacking party came within reach the Highcliffians lashed and lunged with the sticks, and there were loud gasps and yells.

"Yaroooh!"

"You rotters, use your fists!"

"Ha, ha!" roared Ponsonby. "Give them jip!"

The Famous Five came on valiantly; but the Highcliffe nuts were hitting hard, and the lashing of the sticks was no joke. The rush stopped, and the Removites receded a little.

"Come on!" grinned Ponsonby.

"Absolutely! Come and have some more!" yelled Vavasour, brandishing his stick. "Yah! Funks!"

"Use your fists, you rotters!" panted Bob Cherry.

"Shift them!" exclaimed Ponsonby. "Charge!"

The Highcliffians came rushing down the steep bank, lashing out reckless blows.

The Removites were driven down the slope.

Nugent lost his footing and rolled down, narrowly escaping pitching into the ditch at the bottom. Bob Cherry closed with Monson, and rolled down the bank with him.

Johnny Bull crashed into Bunter, who was close behind him, and sent the fat junior rolling.

"Yoop!" roared Wally. "You clumsy ass! Oh!"

Squash!

The ditch along the lane was narrow but it was rather deep; and though there was little water in it, there was plenty of mud. Bunter sat fairly in the middle of it, and his fat legs disappeared, the mud squashing up round his waist.

He struggled frantically to extricate himself.

"Lend me a hand, you fellows!" he yelled.

But the Co. were too busy to heed Bunter.

Bob Cherry had Monson down, and had wrested his stick from him. He jumped up, and gave Monson the benefit of his weapon with such effect that the Highcliffian howled with anguish.

The other four of the Co. had been driven back to the lane, their fists proving futile against Ponsonby & Co.'s weapons. Pon and his friends crowded round Bob Cherry as he thrashed Monson.

"Down him!" shouted Pon.

Bob turned on the Highcliffians like an enraged lion.

He had a stick in each hand now, and though he was one against five, he did not hesitate. He rushed at them, lashing out as recklessly as Pon & Co. themselves had done.

Ponsonby uttered a wild yell as he received a crack on the head, and Gadsby roared as he caught a lunge with his chin. In a second the Highcliffians were backing away. Reckless lashes of a stick were not to their taste when directed against themselves.

Vavasour clambered over the fence, and started at a run across the field behind, evidently having had enough, though Bob had not reached him yet.

"Come on!" roared Bob.

Harry Wharton & Co. were already returning to the charge.

Bob's reckless attack scattered the Highcliffians; Pelham got over the fence and bolted after Vavasour.

But Pon and the rest were too hard pressed to be able to get away, and they dodged and scrambled on the bank in dire apprehension.

Meanwhile, Wally Bunter, deeply embedded in the mud, and completely winded, gasped out appeals for help that were not heeded, as he strove to drag himself out.

But his efforts were in vain; the thick, deep mud held him in its grip, his own weight adding to its tenacity. There was nothing to catch hold of, and he squashed and wriggled in vain in the clinging mud.

He was completely out of the fight; not that his companions had expected for a moment that Bunter would be in it.

But the fight was nearly over now.

Drury got across the fence and fled, and Ponsonby, Gadsy, and Monson were surrounded. They still had their sticks; but Bob Cherry's lashing blows were too much for them.

"Hold on!" gasped Ponsonby. "We give you best!"

"Pax!" quavered Gadsby.

"Put down those sticks, then, you cowardly rotters!" exclaimed Harry Wharton savagely. "You're going into the ditch!"

"That's the terms of the giddy armistice!" grinned Bob Cherry.

"Look here——"

"That's enough! You can give in or fight it out, and you've got one second to decide in!" exclaimed the captain of the Remove roughly.

Bob Cherry took a tighter grip on his stick, ready for a charge; and the Highcliffians did not risk it. They threw down their weapons.

"I—I say, let us off, you know," pleaded Monson. "We—we've given in!"

"My dear chap," said Bob Cherry, "we're up against Highcliffe militarism, and you're going to get the knock-out. Into the ditch—that's the terms of the armistice!"

And the three remaining Highcliffians were collared and rolled bodily down the bank.

"Look out!" yelled Wally Bunter. "Don't pitch the beasts on me!"

"Hallo, hallo, hallo! Bunter's sticking in the mud!" roared Bob Cherry. "Ha, ha, ha!"

"Lend a fellow a hand, you cackling dummy!"

"Ha, ha, ha!"

"Look here, you silly chumps——"

Squash!

Ponsonby landed in the ditch, and after him went Monson and Gadsby. The splashes of mud spattered Bunter as he sat within a few feet of them, and he roared again.

Ponsonby & Co. scrambled out actively on the other side, but Bunter's weight was against him. He was still struggling in vain.

"Poor old Bunty!" grinned Bob Cherry. "What a giddy conquering hero!"

"Help, you fathead!"

"Blessed if I know how we're to get him out!" chuckled Nugent. "Anybody got a steam crane in his pocket?"

"Ha, ha, ha!"

"Catch hold, and pull me out!" raved Wally. "I'm sinking deeper. I'm in a deep place. Yow-ow-ow!"

The Removites roared. Ponsonby & Co. even grinned as they looked at the fat junior. They were muddy enough themselves, but their state was quite natty in comparison with Bunter's.

The three Highcliffians beat a retreat, squelching out mud as they went, while Wally Bunter yelled for aid.

The grinning Removites gathered round him, and a branch, broken off a tree near at hand, was extended to him. Wally grasped it, and by the combined efforts of the Famous Five he was extracted from the ditch, a good deal like a cork from a bottle.

Bunter in a new light! (*See Chapter* 2.)

"Yow-ow-ow-wooooop! I'm muddy! Ow!"

"The mudfulness is terrific," grinned Hurree Jamset Singh. "The esteemed Bunter should have stayed at home. The new stuntfulness was not the proper caper."

"Grooogh!"

"Ow!" said Bob Cherry. "I've got nineteen bumps on my napper, more or less. Those funky rotters——"

"Never mind; we've licked the Huns," said Wharton. "Let's get off. You'd better dive into the river before you come home, Bunter. You're a bit smelly with that mud."

"Grooh! Ow-ow-ow!" mumbled the unhappy Bunter. "All Bull's fault, the silly ass, for bumping into me!"

"What were you behind me for, you thumping ass?" answered Johnny Bull.

"Yow-ow! I was trying to get at the Highcliffe cads, wasn't I?"

"Rot!"

"Why, you silly ass, what do you think I was doing?" roared Bunter.

Johnny Bull shrugged his shoulders.

"What's the good of telling us you're not a funk when we know you are?" he demanded. "I dare say you sat in the ditch on purpose to keep out of the scrap. Just one of your tricks."

"Why, you—you—you——" spluttered Wally.

Words failed him.

He sat in the grass by the road and gasped.

Harry Wharton & Co. walked away towards Greyfriars, leaving the fat junior still spluttering. Wally scrambled up, and scraped himself down, and rubbed off as much mud as he could with bunches of grass. But he was still in a parlous state when he followed in the footsteps of the Co. to Greyfriars.

And, worst of all, he had quite failed to convince the chums of the Remove that he had meant business in taking part in the scrap. The tumble into the ditch had kept him out of it, and it was too like one of Billy Bunter's tricks not to be supposed one. Wally Bunter's reflections were dismal as he tramped home to Greyfriars.

It really seemed that there was no hope for it, and that he was destined to remain a dog with a bad name.

THE FIFTH CHAPTER.
Major and Minor!

"OH, dear! Ow-ow-yow!"

Those dismal ejaculations proceeded from Sammy Bunter of the Second Form at Greyfriars.

Wally Bunter heard them as he came slowly up the lane towards the school, after cleaning all the mud he could off his person. Harry Wharton & Co. were long out of sight.

The fat junior paused.

Bunter minor was his cousin, and the fat fag looked as if he had been in the wars. He was gasping and groaning, and making frantic efforts to extract his cap from down his back.

"Hallo, tubby!" said Wally, halting.

Sammy Bunter blinked round through his big spectacles.

"Oh! You!" he said. "Why, couldn't you come along before, and lend me a hand, Billy, you fat idiot?"

Wally grinned at that brotherly greeting. He did not mind Sammy's lack of Chesterfieldian polish, so long as Sammy continued to believe that he was his brother Billy.

"Help me get this cap out, Billy, you grinning Owl!" howled the fag. "What are you standing sniggering for, you image?"

Wally obligingly extracted the cap.

"No need to suffocate me!" gasped Sammy. "You always were a clumsy Owl, Billy!"

"All serene now?" asked Wally.

"No!" growled the fat fag. "I'm not all serene! I'm winded, and I'm hurt. Any other fellow's major wouldn't see him ragged by a Fourth Form cad. Yah!"

"Fourth Form chap been ragging you?" asked Wally.

"Yow-ow! Yes."

"Angel, perhaps? He's a bit of a bully," said Wally, his eyes gleaming over Billy Bunter's spectacles.

Wally had been far from pleased by some glances and words from Aubrey Angel, the dandy of the Fourth, and he was feeling inclined for a row with somebody. He was prepared at that moment to call on Angel of the Fourth, and bestow upon him what was really due to Ponsonby & Co.—on good cause being shown, of course.

But Sammy shook his head.

"'Twasn't Angel," he said. "Angel's down on me owing to your swindling him——"

"What?"

"I suppose you haven't forgotten swindling Angel of the Fourth?" asked Sammy sarcastically. "Why, lots of the fellows know about it. I heard Tubb and Paget of the Third chin-wagging about it. You betted with him on a footer-match——"

"I didn't!" shouted Wally indignantly. "I've never betted on a footer-match in my life."

"Gammon!" said Sammy. "Why, you mentioned that to me yourself."

"Eh?"

"And you lost, and tossed Angel double or quits, and never paid up," continued the fag. "You owe him the money now."

"Oh, my only aunt!" groaned the unhappy Wally.

He wondered how many more of his cousin's sins he was to be called upon to answer for.

"Angel's down on me whenever he sees me, and it's all your fault," said the fat fag. "But it wasn't Angel this time."

"Well, who was it?" asked Wally. "As your—your major, I'll take it up for you, if the chap's too big for you. Who is he, and what's he done?"

"Oh, come off!" said Sammy, with incredulous contempt. "You're afraid to look Temple in the face, let alone punch him!"

"Temple of the Fourth?" asked Wally.

"Yes, the swanking cad! I wasn't doing anything, really," groaned Sammy. "He came along with Fry and Dabney, and they sat me down, and stuffed my cap down my back, and Fry said it was because I belonged to the Second, and the Second ought to be suppressed."

"Ha, ha, ha!"

"Why, what are you cackling at, you image?" roared Sammy, in great wrath. "Nothing funny in Fry's silly cheek, I suppose?"

"Well, on general principles, the Second ought to be suppressed," said Wally, with all the lofty pride of a Removite. "Still, I'm not going to have my cousin—I—I—I mean——"

"What are you talking about?"

"I'm not going to have my minor ragged by the Fourth. I'll make Temple apologise!"

"He, he, he!" It seemed to be Sammy's turn to cackle. "Don't be such a funny idiot, Billy! Swank doesn't suit you."

"I'll make him apologise, or lick him," said Wally firmly. "There's too much swank about Temple, and he ought to be sat on a bit."

"Catch you sitting on him. You'd run like a Hun if he made a face at you!" grunted Sammy.

"You'll see."

"Oh, come off!" said the fat fag impatiently. "You can't spoof me, if you can other chaps. Don't I know you, Billy?"

"Not so well as you think, perhaps," said Wally, with a grin.

"You look as if you've been ragged yourself," said Sammy, blinking at him. "You're muddy all over."

"That was a scrap with the Highcliffe rotters."

"Lots of scrapping you did, I don't think!" scoffed Sammy Bunter.

"I got stuck in a ditch, and couldn't help——"

"He, he, he!"

"Oh, dry up your cackling!" growled Wally. "Which way was Temple going? I'll go after him."

"He was going back to Greyfriars."

"Well, you come with me, and you'll see me beard the giddy lion in his den," said the fat Removite.

"I'll see you climb down, and swallow all your dashed swank!" grunted Sammy; "and I'll come along specially to see you do it, you gassing duffer!"

And the fat fag rolled along towards Greyfriars with his major. Evidently Sammy had no faith in the fat Removite's warlike intentions.

"I had a letter from Bessie this morning," said Sammy, blinking up at Wally as they came towards the school gates.

"Bessie?" repeated Wally.

"Yes. She says you haven't sent her the half-crown you borrowed from her when you were home last time on the holidays!"

"D-d-does she?"

"Yes. She's written to you four times for it already."

"Has she?" groaned Wally.

"Yes. And she says you're a fat beast not to pay up!"

"Oh!"

"And she says if you don't send her the half-crown she'll come and see you at school, and make you square up!" continued Sammy, with a grin.

Wally jumped.

"C-c-come and s-s-see me!" he ejaculated.

"So she says. I don't believe she would spend the money on the railway-ticket, though!" said Sammy. "She's mean. She's as mean as you are, Billy, in money matters. Nugent minor, of my Form, gets tips from his sister when he goes home; but Bessie's never stood me anything. Didn't even pay for my ticket at the cinema!"

"Did you want her to?" grunted Wally.

"Of course I did, and so did you!" said Sammy warmly. "You know jolly well you whispered to me to let Bessie go in first and take the tickets, and she was too fly!"

"D-d-did I?"

"You know you did!"

Wally was silent. He knew his cousin Bessie only slightly, but he was aware that that young lady was very like her brothers Sammy and Billy. If Billy owed her half-a-crown, the matter was never likely to come to a finish till the half-crown was paid; but it would be Wally who would receive the next dunning letter from Miss Bunter. And it was worth half-a-crown to avoid the danger of Bessie Bunter looking in at Greyfriars. Wally had a well founded fear of feminine sharpness, and he thought that Miss Bessie's eyes might detect what was invisible to Sammy's.

Already a considerable amount of Wally's pocket-money had gone in settling small debts left behind by Billy Bunter. This was another to put on the list. Wally was beginning to feel that one of the greatest pleasures in life would be to get within hitting distance of his absent cousin's nose.

The two Bunters came in at the gates, and Sammy blinked towards the School House, and grinned at Wally.

"There's Temple!" he said.

Temple, Dabney, and Fry were chatting in the quadrangle, and they grinned as they looked towards the Bunters. Wally walked on towards them.

"Now's your chance!" giggled Sammy.

"I'm taking it!" answered Wally Bunter.

"Oh, cheese it! You're not going to row with Temple, I know that!"

"Come and see!"

"He, he, he!" chortled the sceptical Sammy.

He rolled on after Wally, who marched straight up to the group of Fourth-Formers.

"Hallo, here's Fat Jack of the Bonehouse!" remarked Fry. "What do you want, Falstaff?"

"I want a word with Temple!" said Wally. "You've been ragging my minor, Temple!"

Cecil Reginald Temple glanced at him loftily.

"Yaas, I believe I did bump the fat little beast!" he yawned "He looked so jolly sticky I thought it would do him good. I'm goin' to bump him every day till he washes his neck!"

"Ha, ha, ha!" chorussed Temple's chums.

"I don't allow my minor to be ragged by Fourth Form bounders!" said Wally.

"Dear me! Here's Bunter beginnin' as a humorist!" said Temple. "The dear man doesn't allow! How are you goin' to prevent it, fatty?"

"I'm going to lick you!" explained Wally.

"Eh?"

"Lick you!"

"Ha, ha, ha!" roared Temple in great merriment. And Dabney and Fry burst into a yell.

Sammy Bunter blinked at his major in great amazement. Really, it looked as if Bunter of the Remove meant business.

THE SIXTH CHAPTER.

Bunter's Challenge!

"HALLO, hallo, hallo!"

"Bunter on the war-path again!"

"The warfulness of the ludicrous Bunter is terrific!"

Harry Wharton & Co. came along from the tuckshop, where they had been refreshing themselves with ginger-beer after the scrap with Highcliffe. They were greatly entertained by Bunter's belligerent looks, all the five being quite convinced that the fat junior had sat in the ditch in order to avoid conflict with Ponsonby & Co.

And here he was defying Temple of the Fourth, who was more than a head taller than himself, and who was rather a good fighting-man, in spite of his dandified ways. The chums of the Remove did not believe for a moment that he intended to tackle Cecil Reginald; but they were rather interested to see how he would manage to squirm out of it after delivering his defiance.

"Go it, Bunter!" chuckled Bob Cherry. "Go for his nose!"

"He's been ragging Sammy!" said Wally.

"Well, the fat little beast can do with a ragging!" remarked Johnny Bull. "But let's see you wallop Temple, Billy!"

"I'm going to——"

"Ha, ha, ha!"

"Are you ready, Temple?" demanded Bunter.

"Ha, ha, ha!" roared Temple. "Don't be so funny, Bunty! You're givin' me a pain in the ribs. You are, really!"

"I'm going to give you a pain in the eye if you don't put your paws up!" grunted Wally.

"Ha, ha, ha!"

"Isn't Bunter a corker?" chuckled Skinner. "He knows that Capper's at his study window, and there can't be a fight here, so he's as brave as a lion. This is as good as his working off cheery old Cicero when he knew Quelchy was at the door!"

"I didn't see Capper, you rotter!" howled Wally.

"Gammon!"

"Cheese it, Bunty!"

Wally breathed hard through his fat little nose. True it was that Mr. Capper, the master of the Fourth, was at his study window reading, and that the group were within full view of that window. Fighting was certainly out of the question under a Form-master's eyes.

"I knew you were spoofing, Billy!" said Sammy Bunter. "Dash it all, everybody knows you're spoofing! Chuck it!"

"I'm going to fight Temple!" said Wally.

"Ha, ha, ha!"

"I can't fight him here——"

"Of course you can't!" said Harry Wharton, laughing. "That's why you're asking him to fight, you fat Owl!"

"It isn't!" shrieked Wally. "I'll jolly well lick you, too, Wharton, if I have much more of your cheek!"

There was a roar of laughter.

Wally stared round angrily at the merry juniors. Temple was almost doubled up with merriment.

"Look here, Temple, what time and place will suit you?" demanded the fat junior. "I mean business!"

"Ha, ha, ha!"

"Will you be behind the wood-shed in a quarter of an hour?" asked Wally. "I've got to get this mud off, and then I'll be there! Gloves or not, just as you like!"

"Oh, don't be such a funny ass!" implored Temple.

"Will you be there?"

"Of course I won't! What's the good of my waitin' behind the wood-shed while you're hidin' in a corner somewhere?" grinned Temple.

"I tell you I'll be there!" said Wally. "And if you don't come, Temple, I'll give you the coward's blow!"

"Draw it mild, fatty, or I shall squash you here and now!" said Cecil Reginald, frowning.

"I mean business!"

"Oh, go and eat coke!"

"Funk!" said Wally.

"Wha-a-at?"

"Rotten funk!"

Temple's face flushed. He did not like being called a funk, even by so egregious a person as the Owl of the Remove.

"If you want me to wring your fat neck——" he began.

"You'll meet me behind the wood-shed, or else I'll start on you now!" said Wally

Temple clenched his hands, but Edward Fry tapped him warningly on the arm.

"Look out! Capper's got his eye on you!" he murmured.

"That's why that fat cad is cheekin' me!" said Temple, frowning. "Look here, Bunter, I've had enough of your foolin'. I'll be at the wood-shed in a quarter of an hour, and if you're not there I'll look for you with a cricket-stump, and give you the lickin' of your life! Savvy?"

"Done!" said Wally.

"And if you are there, I'll roll you over and nearly burst you!" said Temple.

"You're welcome, if you can do it!" said Wally cheerfully.

And he walked on to the House, leaving Temple looking very angry, and most of the fellows grinning.

That Bunter would turn up at the rendezvous nobody believed for a moment. Temple did not expect to find him there; and he was grimly determined that, if he failed to keep the appointment, the Owl of the Remove should have a record stumping for his impudence.

But at the appointed time Temple, Dabney & Co. sauntered round to the wood-shed, and some of the Remove went with them. They wondered whether Bunter might possibly carry his bluff to the length of turning up there. Meanwhile, Wally was in the Remove dormitory, cleaning off the mud from his clothes and his person, and looking forward quite cheerfully to the encounter with the captain of the Fourth.

THE SEVENTH CHAPTER.

Stumped!

"BUNTER!"

Wally Bunter was coming downstairs at a great rate, to keep his appointment with Temple of the Fourth, when Mr. Quelch called to him.

Mr. Quelch was standing in the hall, in company with Mr. Capper. The latter wore a portentous frown.

"Yes, sir?" said Wally, meekly approaching the two Form-masters.

"Mr. Capper informs me that you have been quarrelling with a boy in his form——"

"Oh, sir!"

"With Temple," said Mr. Capper. "I was surprised, and shocked, to see Bunter actually threatening Temple, almost under my study windows, without the slightest provocation. Temple kept his temper admirably—quite admirably! He is a well-behaved boy."

And Mr. Capper frowned very severely at Wally.

"You have been quarrelling with Temple, Bunter?"

"In—in a way, sir."

"Don't prevaricate, Bunter!"

Wally flushed crimson. He had not meant to prevaricate; but Mr. Quelch had been accustomed to prevarication from the Owl of the Remove.

"Oh, no, sir!" he stammered. "I didn't mean——"

"Have you quarrelled with Temple?" snapped the Remove-master.

"Well, ye-es, sir!"

"And where were you rushing in such a hurry when I called to you?"

"I—I was going out, sir."

"To meet Temple probably?" remarked Mr. Quelch drily.

"I—I was going to see him, sir."

"You need tell me no more, Bunter. This means, of course, that a fight has been arranged."

Wally was silent.

"You are a ridiculous boy, Bunter," said Mr. Quelch severely. "I had not observed before that you were quarrelsome. "You must be very quarrelsome, however, to pick a dispute with a boy in another Form, and a boy with whom you certainly have no chance of success in an encounter. I forbid you to carry this foolish dispute further!"

"Oh, sir!" gasped Wally.

Mr. Quelch raised his forefinger in severe admonition.

"You are not to fight with Temple, Bunter! Doubtless you would be very severely treated if you did; but I shall not allow it. If I hear, Bunter, that you have fought with Temple, I shall send you to Dr. Locke, with a request that you shall be flogged!"

"Oh, sir!"

"I require your promise, Bunter."

"I—I——"

"I am waiting, Bunter!" snapped Mr. Quelch. "Give me your word at once not to fight with Temple!"

There was no help for it.

"Very well sir," said Wally. "I—I give it, sir."

"That will do. I advise you, Bunter, not to be quarrelsome, and not to be ridiculous," said Mr. Quelch.

And the Remove-master turned away with Mr. Capper, leaving the fat junior to his own devices.

Wally Bunter left the School House very slowly.

It was cruel luck!

He was on his way to meet Temple of the Fourth at the appointed place; and he had had to promise not to fight Temple.

He could guess that Mr. Quelch, apart from his disapproval of such methods of settling a dispute, regarded it as ridiculous of him to have challenged the captain of the Fourth, and probably desired to save him from the severe handling he had provoked by his challenge.

If Mr. Quelch's motive had been that, Wally was not at all grateful for his kindness. He was exasperated.

Luck seemed to be against him all along the line. He could imagine the chuckle with which he would be greeted when he stated that he was forbidden to fight Temple.

He had given his word; and, unlike Billy Bunter, with Wally his word was his bond. And a flogging by the Head in case of disobedience was rather too serious a punishment to be lightly faced.

Wally was not feeling happy as he made his way to the wood-shed

Owing to the talk with his Form-master he was a few minutes late, and the juniors on the spot had already given him up.

"I knew he wouldn't come!" said Cecil Reginald Temple. "I said so! And I said I'd stump him if he didn't—an' I jolly well will, too!"

"Oh, rather!" said Dabney.

"Give him five minutes," said Harry Wharton.

"What's the good?"

"Hallo, hallo, hallo! Here he comes!" shouted Bob Cherry, as a fat figure came round the wood-shed.

"Ha, ha! Here's Bunter!"

"See the conquering hero comes!"

"Ha, ha, ha!"

"Go it, Bunter!"

"Now, I wonder what yarn he's goin' to spin to keep out of fightin' me?" remarked Cecil Reginald.

Wally Bunter came up with a troubled face. The juniors all regarded him with curious inquiry.

"Off with your jacket, Bunty!" grinned Bob Cherry. "I've got the gloves here."

"The—the fact is——" began Wally haltingly.

There was a roar laughter. Everybody had expected the fat junior to begin with some excuse; and here he was beginning.

"Well, what's the yarn?" roared Bob. "Got a pain somewhere?"

"Suddenly remembered an appointment with the Prime Minister?" asked Frank Nugent.

"Or is your postal-order coming, and are you going to maffick?" inquired the Bounder.

"Ha, ha, ha!"

"The—the fact is, I—I can't!" stammered Wally.

"Oh, we know you can't!" chortled Fry. "We never expected you would! But what whopper are you going to tell?"

"Spin the yarn, Bunty! Let's hear the facts!"

"The facts!" roared Bob. "Ha, ha ha!"

"The fact is, I can't fight Temple to-day!" said Wally, with a scarlet face. "It seems that old Capper was watching us from his window——"

"You knew he was when you started jawin' me," said Temple.

"I didn't!" yelled Wally.

"Rats!"

"That's why you did it!" grinned Fry. "Own up, fatty!"

"Old Capper saw us, and he's spoken to Quelchy," said Wally Bunter. "And—and Quelchy——"

"Ha, ha, ha!"

"Oh, don't cackle! Quelchy's jawed me, and made me promise not to fight Temple!" panted Wally.

"And you didn't want to promise?" chuckled Bob Cherry. "You did it quite against your will, of course?"

"Of course!" said Wally.

"Ha, ha, ha!"

The juniors roared.

"And Bunter's a slave to his word!" said Johnny Bull gravely. "We all know that! He wouldn't break a promise for a ton of toffee!"

"Of course I wouldn't!" yelled Wally indignantly.

"Not when it keeps you out of a scrap!" grinned Bob.

"I tell you I want to fight Temple, but——"

"Go ahead, then!" chortled Temple.

"But I've promised Mr. Quelch——"

"There was bound to be a 'but,'" said Harry Wharton, laughing.

"The butfulness is terrific!"

"This is rather bright of Bunter," remarked Vernon-Smith. "He picks a quarrel with a chap who could mop him up with one hand, where a Form-master can see him—and manages to promise not to fight the chap—and is bound by a promise for the first time in his life——"

"Ha, ha, ha!"

"So he reaps plenty of glory, and all Greyfriars can see what a hero he is—or would be if he hadn't promised!"

"I tell you——" shrieked Wally, as the juniors roared.

"Well, it may be bright of him," said Cecil Reginald Temple, with a nod. "Rather clever, I've no doubt! But I've made a promise, too, and I'm quite as much a slave of my word as Bunter is. I've promised him a stumpin' if he brought me here for nothin'. Are you ready, Bunter?"

"Look here——"

"You brought the stump, Dab?"

"Oh, rather!" said Dabney. "Here you are, old top!"

Temple took the cricket-stump in his hand, and advanced towards the fat junior. Wally Bunter backed away in alarm.

"Look here, Temple——" he exclaimed.

"I'm going to stump you, dear boy. You can fight if you like, of course."

"I've promised——"

"That may be true, or it may not, but you never intended business in any case, an' you know it! What's the good of lyin'?"

"I tell you——"

"You needn't tell me anythin', old scout. You can get ready for a stumpin'," said Temple. "You're not goin' to waste my time for nothin'!"

Wally jumped back.

"Keep off, you rotter! I say, Wharton——"

"It's your look-out, Bunty," said the captain of the Remove, with a shake of the head. "You shouldn't go in for heroics, you know, when you haven't the pluck of a bunny-rabbit!"

"You cheeky rotter—— Yarooooh!" roared Wally, as Cecil Reginald got in a starter with the stump.

"Ha, ha, ha!"

Wally jumped and dodged. He could not fight Temple, that was certain, with both a flogging and a promise in the way. It looked as if he would have to take the stumping. Nobody was inclined to interfere. The general opinion was that the fat junior had asked for it, and they did not see any reason why he should not get it.

Temple was larruping the fat Removite heartily now, and Wally bounded to and fro in frantic efforts to dodge the stump, amid shrieks of laughter.

He fairly fled at last. It was not much use to stay there and be stumped.

"After him!" roared Dabney.

"Ha, ha, ha!"

"By gad! I'm after him!" grinned Temple. "Don't you worry!"

The dandy of the Fourth was after Bunter like a shot. The fat junior put on an unexpected speed, but Temple kept close behind, lunging with the stump, and at every lunge there was a terrific yell.

Wally vanished round the wood-shed and fled for the quadrangle, and Temple stopped as they came in sight of the School House windows. The unhappy Bunter disappeared from sight, unpursued further.

Temple panted for breath as he halted at last. There was a roar of merriment from the following crowd.

"See the conquering hero goes!" roared Bob Cherry.

"Ha, ha, ha!"

"By gad! I fancy it will be a long time before that cheeky fag starts challengin' the Fourth again!" chuckled Temple. And he walked away with Dabney and Fry in great good humour.

The crowd broke up, chortling. The affair had ended just as they expected it to end, and they had found it entertaining. And in Study No. 7 in the Remove Wally Bunter dolefully rubbed the places where the stump had smitten, and bemoaned his bad luck.

THE EIGHTH CHAPTER.
Up Against It!

PETER TODD indulged in a chuckle when he came into Study No. 7 to tea with Tom Dutton. Wally Bunter was there, and he was not looking happy. Temple had smitten with the stump—perhaps not wisely, but certainly too well

Wally blinked dolefully at his study-mates over Billy Bunter's glasses. But it was evident that they had no sympathy to waste on him.

"Feeling bad, Fatty?" asked Peter.

"Ow! Yes."

"Serves you right, doesn't it, my fat tulip?"

"Br-r-r-r!"

"You shouldn't do these humorous turns, you know," said Peter. "You're too funny, Bunter! You'll be challenging Coker of the Fifth next, and promising somebody not to fight him!"

"Don't you believe I promised Quelchy, you rotter?"

"You may have, or you may not. Your statement on the subject, my fat pippin, doesn't affect the matter one way or the other."

"Oh!" stuttered Wally.

It was not much use being angry with Peter Todd. Peter supposed that he was talking to Billy Bunter, and Billy Bunter had a reputation for untruthfulness that would have made Ananias green with envy.

"You're a young ass, Bunter!" said Tom Dutton. "You've made this study look silly with your rot!"

"Can't look much sillier than it is!" retorted Wally.

"Eh?" said Dutton, putting his hand to his ear.

"Oh, rats!" grunted Wally. His temper was rather morose just then. "Get an ear-trumpet, or get me a megaphone, or don't talk."

"Pork?" said Tom Dutton, in astonishment.

"Br-r-r-r!"

"Do you mean for tea?" asked the deaf junior. "Where did you get it from? Can you get pork without a coupon now?"

"Fathead! Who's talking about pork?" roared Wally.

"Why, you are!"

"I'm not!"

"Hot?" said Dutton. "Certainly I like pork hot; but the question is, have you got any pork? You're such a spoofer——"

"Oh, help!" gasped Wally.

"If we're going to have pork for tea, well and good," said Dutton. "I'm hungry after footer practice. What are you opening the sardines for, Peter?"

"Tea!" yelled Peter.

"But Bunter says we're going to have pork."

"There isn't any pork!"

"All right. Where's the corkscrew?" asked Dutton.

"Corkscrew!" howled Peter. "What do you want a corkscrew for?"

"Didn't you ask me to draw a cork?"

"Oh, my hat! No!" roared Peter.

"You needn't roar at me, Peter Todd! I'm not deaf! Blessed if this study doesn't seem to me like a lunatic asylum sometimes!" grunted Dutton. "You and Bunter talk the most awful rot sometimes. If you don't want me to draw a cork, what do you want me to do, then?"

"Only hold your jaw, old chap, for mercy's sake!"

"All right," said Dutton.

He turned to the study cupboard, and then looked round at Peter.

"I can't see it here, Toddy."

"Can't see what?"

"The cake."

"Cake?" repeated Peter dazedly.

"Yes. Where is it?"

"Ha, ha, ha!" roared Wally.

"I don't see anything to cackle at, Bunter! If you are pulling my leg, Todd, talking about a cake——"

Peter did not answer. He was apparently deaf. Conversation with Tom Dutton sometimes became too strenuous even for the energetic Peter.

"I don't believe there's a cake at all!" said Dutton warmly. "And as for the pork, I can't see any pork!"

And as he received no reply, Tom Dutton sniffed, and settled down to sardines.

Wally Bunter ate his tea in silence. He was still feeling sore, both in body and mind, and he could not see how he was to set himself right with his Form. Even in his own study he was an object of derision. That might suit Billy Bunter, but it did not suit Wally in the least. But how he was to alter it was a puzzle to the fat Removite.

He succeeded in surprising his study-mates by producing a bag of biscuits to wind up the meal.

"Whose are they?" asked Peter.

"Mine!" snorted Wally.

"Whose were they before they became yours, then?"

"I bought them from Mrs. Mimble."

"My hat! Has Mrs. Mimble started you on tick?"

"I've paid for them."

"My only Aunt Selina Jane!" said Peter Todd. "And you're going to whack them out in the study?"

"Oh, rats!" said Wally crossly. And he left the study, closing the door after him with a slam.

Peter Todd shook his head seriously. He really could not understand Bunter of late. There were very marked signs of improvement in the fat junior, but—there was a big but!

The Remove fellows knew Billy Bunter too well. It was a case of once bitten and twice shy.

Peter's belief was that Bunter was on some new stunt which was intended to turn out to his personal profit in some way; but he had to confess that he did not quite understand.

"Give a dog a bad name, and hang him," is an old saying; and it certainly fitted the case of the unfortunate Wally.

Can it be Bunter? (*See Chapter* **11.**)

"Of course!"

"I suppose I'm dreaming!" remarked Peter Todd. "I may as well dream that I'm eating biscuits, though!" He helped himself, and started. "Quite good, Bunty! Doesn't it give you a pain to be whacking them out?"

"No, you rotter!"

"And some ass said the age of miracles was past!" said Peter Todd. "You're not ill, Bunty?"

"Oh, don't be an ass!"

"Well, you beat me!" said Peter Todd. "You've been paying your footing in the study for some days now——"

"Ever since I've been here!" howled Wally indignantly.

"Oh, come off! You started paying your footing the day after your cousin left—that was the first time!"

"Oh! Ah! Yes! Of—of course! That—that's what I meant!"

"And do you know, we haven't heard anything since then of your postal-order or your titled relations!" said Peter.

"Oh, bother!" said Wally. "You know I haven't any titled relations!"

"Quite so! But you always spoofed that you had!"

"Br-r-r-r!"

"But the question arises," said Peter, "what little stunt are you on now? What have you started telling the truth for? Is it a game, or are you ill, or what is it? I'd really like to know!"

THE NINTH CHAPTER.
Coker Asks For It!

"CHERRY!"

"Hallo, hallo, hallo!"

"Where's Bunter?" asked Coker of the Fifth. "Now, then, sharp's the word! I've no time to waste!"

Bob Cherry grinned.

Coker of the Fifth not only had no time to waste, but apparently he had no manners to waste on the Remove. Which was not the best method of getting his questions answered promptly.

"Do you hear me?" snapped Coker.

"My dear man, I could hear you if I were in Friardale!" answered Bob. "Only I shouldn't be sure whether it was you talking, Coker, or the town bull roaring!"

Coker made a threatening movement towards Bob Cherry. But Bob was on the Remove landing, and there were reinforcements within call; and Coker thought better of it. It was not safe for even the Fifth to rag the Remove in their own stronghold.

"I asked you where Bunter was!" said Coker sulphurously. "I want to see Billy Bunter!"

"What a peculiar taste!" yawned Bob. "You're about the only fellow in Greyfriars who does!"

"Where is he?" roared Coker.

"You really want to know?"

"Yes, you young ass!"

"Then you'd better inquire!" said Bob cheerily. And he strolled away up the Remove passage. But he kindly remarked over his shoulder as he went: "And inquire civilly, old nut! You may get an answer then!"

Bob strolled into his study, leaving Coker breathing hard through his nose. There was no one else visible in the Remove passage, and Coker went along to investigate on his own. He looked into Study No. 6, and found four juniors at home there—Racke and Morgan and Wibley and Micky Desmond. They looked at Coker inquiringly, and rather warily.

"Is this Bunter's study?" growled Coker.

"Does it look as if it was?" asked Wibley.

"Answer me, you little idiot!"

"Go and eat coke, you big idiot!"

"If you want a licking all round——" roared Coker.

"We do!" chuckled Dick Rake.

"We does!" grinned Micky Desmond.

Again Coker of the Fifth nearly committed assault and battery; and again he remembered that he was in the enemy's country, and restrained his just wrath. He went out and slammed the door, and looked into the next study. He found Tom Dutton there.

"Is this Bunter's study?" he demanded, frowning.

"Eh?"

"Is this Billy Bunter's study?"

"Oh! Has he tumbled off his bike?" asked Dutton.

"What? Who?"

"Bunter."

"How the thump should I know?" roared Coker in surprise.

"Well, you said Bunter was muddy! How did he get muddy, then?"

"Oh, my hat! I asked you if this was Bunter's study!" roared Coker. "Can't you hear, you deaf ass?"

"Eh?"

"Where's Bunter—Billy Bunter?"

"It's no good mumbling at me, Coker! If you want an answer, you'd better speak clearly, not mumble!"

"I'm looking for Billy Bunter!" shrieked Coker. "Isn't this his study?"

"Oh! Yes. This is his study. You needn't yell! I can hear you when you don't mumble!"

"Well, where is he?"

"You'd better ask him, if you want him to tea——"

"Oh, crikey!"

"Still, I'll give him a message from you, if you like, when he comes down from the box-room!" said Dutton. "Shall I tell him you want him to come to tea?"

"Is he in the box-room?"

"Eh?"

Coker snorted and strode out of No. 7. He fancied it would be less trouble to look into the box-room than to elicit further information from Tom Dutton.

Tom looked after him in surprise.

"Bad-tempered beast!" he commented. "I've a jolly good mind not to give Bunter his message! Still, I think I will—it will clear Bunter off for tea, anyway!"

Horace Coker strode up to the end of the Remove passage, where there was a little stair that led up to the box-room. Coker stamped up that stair, and looked into the room above. Wally Bunter was there, and there was a sound of cracking wood. The fat junior was dislocating an old packing-case for firewood in the study.

"Oh, here you are, Bunter!" growled Coker.

"Here I am, as large as life and twice as natural!" answered Wally cheerfully. "Have you come to help me break up this wood? That's kind of you, Coker!"

"No, I haven't, you cheeky fag!"

"Then take your face away, old sport; it's a bit of a worry!"

Coker's eyes gleamed. But he had his temper under unusual restraint that day.

"I want you to come to my study presently, Bunter!" he said.

"Tea?" asked Wally.

"After tea."

"Oh! Afraid I sha'n't have time!"

"You're a bit of a ventriloquist," went on Coker, unheeding. "Now, old Prout is coming to my study to jaw me—my Form-master, you know! I've heard you play your tricks with your silly voice, and I want you to spring it on old Prout! Make a dog growl under his chair, and all that, you know!"

"Oh!" ejaculated Wally.

"You can do it," said Coker. "I've heard you play such tricks. You've played them on me, like a cheeky young sweep. Prout says he is going to talk to me seriously—he's not satisfied with me in class."

"No wonder!" commented Wally.

"None of your cheek, Bunter! Prout's an old donkey—he doesn't know when he's got a really good pupil under him. He makes no end of mistakes, especially in spelling! He actually put two g's in 'agglomerate' to-day! It was no good my objecting—he had to have his way!"

"Ha, ha, ha!"

"I didn't come here to be cackled at, Bunter!" said Coker darkly. "Now, I want you to be in my study when he comes and worry him with ventriloquism—then he'll cut it short, and give a chap a rest! I thought this rather a good idea!"

Wally grinned.

It really was rather a good idea, for Coker. And Billy Bunter would certainly have jumped at it—on condition that Coker handed him certain coin of the realm by way of reward for his trouble.

But it was not in the power of Billy Bunter's double to oblige, for he did not share Billy's weird gift of ventriloquism.

"Of course, I don't want you to do it for nothing!" snapped Croker. "I know what a mercenary little beast you are!"

"Look here——"

"I'll stand you half-a-crown."

"Nothing doing!" said Wally.

"If you think you're going to stick me for more than half-a-crown you're mistaken!" roared Coker.

"Sorry I can't oblige," answered Wally.

"If you clear Prout off in five minutes I'll make it three bob," said Coker generously.

"I'm afraid I can't undertake to clear Prout off at all, old bean," answered Wally.

"You greedy young Shylock, how much do you want?"

"Nix!"

"Do you mean to say you won't ventriloquise at all for me when I ask you?" demanded Croker.

"Can't be did. Sorry!"

"Why not?"

"I don't think I could do it to-day if I tried," said Wally, very truthfully. "Couldn't do it to save my life."

"Utter rot!"

"Well, there it is, old top!"

And Wally went on cracking up the packing-case, while Coker regarded him wrathfully.

"I suppose you mean that you want five bob?" growled Coker at last. "It's not worth it, and you know it."

"I don't mean that."

"What do you mean, then?"

"Can't be did!"

Coker pushed back his cuffs.

"I'm not used to being cheeked by fags," he said. "I've made you a fair offer, Billy Bunter, and I expect you to do as I want."

Wally whistled. He would willingly have obliged Coker if he had been able to do so; but he wasn't, and that settled it. And he certainly did not intend to explain the reason to Coker.

"Do you hear me?" roared Coker.

"Good-bye, old scout!" said Wally. "Take your voice away with you, and mind the step!"

"Otherwise," said Coker, "I shall lick you. I suppose you understand that?"

"Nice afternoon, isn't it?" said Wally.

"What?"

"But it will be wet if it rains," went on Wally, with owl-like gravity, while Coker stared at him, perplexed.

Coker's mighty brain worked slowly, and it always took him some time to realise that his leg was being pulled.

"I suppose you think that's funny?" he said at last.

"On the other hand, it will be fine if the rain holds off," said Wally. "Don't you think so, Coker?"

Coker's reply was not in words. He jumped at Wally Bunter. The unusual self-control he had been displaying deserted him. It was pretty clear that the fat junior was not going to oblige him in the matter of the ventriloquism, and Horace Coker decided to take it out of his hide, as he would have expressed it.

Wally dodged round the packing-cases, catching up a broken stave as he did so.

"Hands off!" he exclaimed warmly. "Now, then—— Yaroooh!"

"Yoop!" roared Coker.

They yelled simultaneously, as Coker's grasp fastened on Wally's neck, and Wally's stave smote Coker on the head.

"Now, you cheeky little beast——"

"Leggo!"

"I'll give you the licking of your life, you—— Yaroooop!"

Somehow—Coker never knew how—a fat leg was twined with his own, and he stumbled and went down with a crash. And before he knew what was happening next two fat hands had seized his ankles and lifted them into the air, and Coker was helpless.

The astounded Coker lay on his back, gasping, and catching at the floor with his hands, while Bunter held his ankles in a grip that seemed like iron. It was amazing that the podgy hands had so much strength in them.

"Leggo!" howled Coker, in his turn.

Instead of letting go, Wally whisked him doorward. Coker's back and the back of his head slid along the box-room floor.

"Oh, crumbs! Oh, my hat! Yooooop!"

Coker went sliding out on the landing, drawn by his ankles, and he gave a terrific yell as he was swept off the edge and down on the little staircase that led into the Remove passage. His head bumped on the second step, and then on the next, and he clutched wildly round for a hold.

"Now, are you going to make it pax?" gasped Wally.

"Yarooh! I'll smash you!"

"Then down you go!"

And with a powerful shove Wally sent Coker of the Fifth rolling down. With a bump and a clump Coker rolled into the Remove passage, and he lay there roaring.

Wally went back rather breathlessly into the box-room, and took the precaution of turning the key in the lock.

In the Remove passage Horace Coker roared and spluttered, and spluttered and roared, and a crowd of Removites came racing to the spot.

THE TENTH CHAPTER.

Doubting Thomases!

"HALLO, hallo, hallo!"

"Coker!"

"The Cokerfulness is terrific!"

Coker of the Fifth sat up. He was dusty and dishevelled, and crimson with wrath. He had more bumps than he could have counted.

"Ow! Oh! Ow! I'll smash him!" he panted.

"Coker——"

"I'll pulverise the cheeky fag!" howled Coker.

"My dear man, we do all the pulverising in this passage!" said Harry Wharton, laughing. "Collar him!"

"Leggo! I—I'll——"

"Frog's march!" shouted Bob Cherry.

"Ha, ha! Bump him!"

"Down with the Fifth!"

Coker found himself struggling in about a dozen pairs of hands. He had succeeded in awakening a hornets'-nest—as he often did. The Removites did not care in the least whom it was that Coker was disputing with, or what the dispute was about. That did not matter at all. It was a matter of principle, and the principle was that Fifth-Formers couldn't kick up a shindy in the Remove passage without being frog's-marched out of that delectable quarter.

It was useless for the unfortunate Horace to struggle, though he did struggle strenuously.

He went down the Remove passage in the clutch of many hands, and various parts of him smote the floor, a dozen times at least, before the big staircase was reached.

Then he went down the stairs.

On each stair Coker rapped hard, and at each rap he let out a terrifice yell.

On the next landing he was left, gasping. That was out of the Remove precincts, and Coker was at liberty to crawl away if he liked. As he sat up, breathless and furious, the Remove stairway above him was crammed with laughing juniors.

"Come up again, Coker!" called out Bob Cherry invitingly.

"Ha, ha, ha!"

"Come and have some more, Coker!"

"The morefulness will be terrific, my esteemed, fatheaded Coker!"

"Yarooooh!"

"'Oh, listen to the band!'" sang Bob Cherry.

"Ha, ha, ha!"

Coker staggered up. Coker was a fighting-man, but he was not feeling inclined to try conclusions with half the Remove at once. He shook his fist at the yelling juniors, and limped away down the lower staircase, followed by howls of derision.

"Dear old Horace!" chuckled Bob Cherry. "Always shoving his foot into it, and always getting it stamped on!"

"What was he up to here, though?" asked Wharton. "He seems to have been rowing with somebody in the box-room."

"Somebody pitched him down," said Rake. "He came up here inquiring after Bunter; but it can't have been Bunter."

"Ha, ha! Not likely!"

The Removites ran back along the passage, and up the box-room stairs, to ascertain who it was that had pitched Coker out of that apartment. It was rather a hefty job, pitching out Coker of the Fifth anywhere, and they were rather curious.

The box-room door was locked, and Bob Cherry thumped on it.

"Oh, get off!" came a fat voice from within.

"Hallo, hallo, hallo! Is that you, Bunter?"

"Yes, ass!"

"Let us in, you Owl!"

"All serene! I thought it was Coker coming back."

Wally Bunter unlocked the door, and the Removites crowded into the box-room. They looked round the room—but only Wally was there.

"Where is he?" asked Wharton.

"Who—Coker?"

"No; the fellow who pitched Coker out!"

"Here!"

"Where? There's nobody here but you, that I can see," said the captain of the Remove, puzzled.

"I'm the chap."

"What?" roared the juniors.

"You pitched Coker out of the room and down into the Remove passage?" yelled Peter Todd.

"Yes."

"Well, my hat! Of all the thumping liars——"

"Draw it mild, Bunty!"

"Give us an easier one, Bunty!" implored Bob Cherry. "That one's too steep! Do give us something easier."

Wally Bunter blinked at the Removites in great exasperation. Not one of them thought for a moment of believing his statement.

"I tell you I pitched Coker out!" he shouted.

"Ha, ha, ha!"

"Picked him up with one hand and tossed him out like a cricket-ball, I suppose?" said Squiff humorously.

"I yanked him out by the ankles——"

"I don't think!"

"You didn't sling him out with one hand?" grinned Tom Brown.

"No; I couldn't—could I, you ass?"

"Of course you couldn't; but that's no reason why you shouldn't say you did, is it?"

"Look here——"

"But who was the chap who did do it?" said Bob Cherry, coming back to the subject. "Coker's rather a hefty chap to handle. Who was here with you, Bunter?"

"Nobody."

"But there must have been somebody, as Coker was chucked out!"

"I chucked him out."

"Oh, don't sing that over again to us!" said Bob impatiently. "What's the good? Tell us who was here with you? Was it Bolsover major?"

"There was nobody——"

"Look here, give the chap a name!" exclaimed Squiff. "Why should you want to keep it dark? Hobson of the Shell, perhaps——"

"It wasn't!"

"Then, who was it?"

"Me!"

"Gentlemen, chaps, and fellows," said Bob Cherry, "the chap who pitched Coker out on his neck deserves well of his country. We want to know who it was, and this fat Owl persists in telling us whoppers. I vote bumping him till he yaps out the name!"

"Hear, hear!"

"I've told you!" hooted Wally. "I—I—— Hands off, you chumps! I'll jolly well—— Oh, my hat! Leggo!"

But half a dozen of the grinning juniors collared the unfortunate double of Billy Bunter, and he was swept off the floor.

"Now, this is your last chance!" said Bob. "Who slung Coker out?"

"I did!"

"Go it!" said Bob.

Bump!

"Yoooooop!"

"Second time of asking," said Bob Cherry. "Who was it slung Coker out on his neck, Bunty?"

"I did!"

Bump!

"Third time of asking—who was it, you spoofing fat Owl?"

"Yow-ow-woop!"

"That isn't a name!"

"Ha, ha, ha!"

"Why won't you tell us, Bunter?" exclaimed Harry Wharton.

"Yow-ow! I've told you! Ow!"

Bump!

"Oh, crumbs!"

The juniors gave it up at that; and they streamed out of the box-room, leaving Wally Bunter sitting on the floor gasping for breath. He gasped and panted, and wondered whether the time would ever come when he would not have to answer for Billy Bunter's sins.

When Wally limped into Study No. 7 half an hour later Tom Dutton had a message for him.

"Coker's been here, Bunter. He wants you to go to tea with him."

Wally grinned faintly. Whether Coker had left that message or not, he was not likely to go to tea with Horace.

"Aren't you going?" asked Dutton, as the fat junior sat down.

Wally shook his head.

"Better go, you know."

"Rats!"

And Wally stayed.

THE ELEVENTH CHAPTER.

Amazing!

"THE coast's clear!" remarked Aubrey Angel of the Fourth.

It was Wednesday afternoon, and Harry Wharton & Co. were hard at work on Little Side, keeping in form for the approaching football match with Highcliffe School. Most of the Remove fellows were out of doors; and when Angel and Kenney of the Fourth Form came up the Remove staircase they found it and the passage beyond deserted.

"Sure Bunter's at home, though?" asked Kenney.

"Yes; I've made inquiries. The fat young beast's got lines, and he's staying in to do them."

"He will get done, as well as the lines—or instead of them!" grinned Kenney.

"Unless he squares!" said Angel.

The two black sheep of the Fourth walked on to Study No. 7. Angel had a dog-whip under his arm, and a grim expression on his handsome face.

Ever since Bunter had spoofed him in a bet on a footer-match Angel had been very much down on the Owl of the Remove. He wanted Bunter to square up, and that was the last thing in the world Billy Bunter was ever likely to do.

Naturally, Wally Bunter did not consider himself liable; he was using his cousin's name, but he had not undertaken to pay his gambling debts.

Wally was alone in Study No. 7. He had lines that afternoon from Loder of the Sixth, and he had been warned to bring them in by tea-time. He was keen enough on footer, but Little Side had few attractions for him under the circumstances; there was no chance of Bunter practising with the eleven.

The fat junior was scribbling away industriously when the study door opened and the two Fourth-Formers came in.

Wally Bunter jumped up at once. He did not need telling that the visit was a hostile one. The whip under Angel's arm was proof enough of that.

"Shut the door, Kenney!" said Angel.

Slam!

Kenney set his back to the door, and grinned at Bunter.

The Fourth-Formers expected the fat junior to look alarmed; but he did not. Billy Bunter would certainly have been alarmed; but Wally was made of sterner stuff.

"You're making rather free in my study, aren't you?" Wally remarked cheerfully.

"We've called on business," explained Angel.

"Thanks; I don't want any tips for the races, or to back any team on a footer-match!" answered Wally sarcastically. "I suppose you fellows will be spreading yourselves, now there's peace and plenty of racing. But it's not in my line."

"You owe me money."

"Rats!"

"You laid a bet on a footer-match with me, an' lost," said Angel. "You tossed me double or quits, an' lost again. Then it came out that you hadn't any money!"

"Oh!" ejaculated Wally.

"I was an ass to be taken in—but you were spoofing about havin' a tenner, and I swallowed it," said Angel. "You'd have touched my money fast enough if you'd won, by gad!"

Wally was silent. There was nothing for him to say, excepting that he was not Billy; and that he must not say!

"Of course, I know you can't pay whole quids in a lump!" continued Angel. "I thought you could—but I find you can't! But you can square up in time—on the merry instalment plan, you know. You've been spending money lately—I've seen you. How much can you stand this afternoon?"

"Nix!"

"Make it half a quid, and I'll be satisfied till you're in funds again!" said Angel, with the air of a fellow being very generous.

"My dear man, I owe you nothing, and I'm going to pay you exactly that amount and no more!" said Wally.

"You lost the money to me——"

"I didn't—ahem!—I mean——"

"Wouldn't you have taken my tin if I'd lost?"

"No!"

"What?" exclaimed Angel.

Wally shook his head.

"I certainly shouldn't have touched your money!" he said, quite truthfully. Billy Bunter would have touched it, certainly; but that was quite a different matter, which it was not convenient for Wally to mention.

"That's a dashed lie!" said Angel.

"Go and eat coke, dear boy!"

"Are you goin' to pay up?"

"No!"

"Then I'm goin' to take it out of your hide, you fat swindler!"

"Hold on!" said Wally quietly, though his eyes glittered. "I don't choose to explain to you how the matter stands, but I'm not responsible for the money. Besides, you're a gambling cad, Angel, and if you make bets with a chap in the Lower Fourth you deserve to be dished. You oughtn't to be paid in any case—and you won't be! Now, get out of my study!"

"I rather expected this!" remarked Angel. "And, as I said, if you don't pay up I'm goin' to take it out of your podgy hide, Bunter!"

"You can try, if you like!" grinned Wally.

"No good yellin', my fat beauty!" sneered Kenney. "The Remove are all out of doors, as we happen to know!"

"What difference does that make?"

"Only that you're goin' to have a thumpin' lickin', with nobody to interfere!"

"Bless your innocent little heart, I don't want anybody to interfere!" said Wally Bunter coolly. "If I can't handle two sneaking, smoking, gambling cads like you fellows, you can dog-whip me as much as you like!"

Angel and Kenney stared at him.

That was not exactly the language they expected from the Owl of the Remove, and it surprised them.

"The fat Owl thinks there's somebody to help him, I suppose!" said Angel, after a pause. "Look out in the passage, Kenney."

Kenney glanced out of the study.

"Only Mauleverer!" he said. "He's amblin' along—he can't do anythin'!"

"Never mind him! Now, Bunter——"

Angel started round the table, and Kenney stood ready to head Bunter off when he dodged.

But Wally Bunter did not dodge. He stood cheerfully facing Angel, who lashed out with the dog-whip as soon as he was close.

The fat junior jumped quickly back, just escaping the slash. Before Aubrey Angel could lift the whip again Wally darted forward like an arrow from a bow.

His plump arms were thrown round Angel, and they closed.

Angel grinned as he gripped the fat junior, intending to pitch him on the carpet, and there lash him at his ease.

But the grin died off his face immediately. For the fat arms were closing on him like a vice, with a grip that took his breath away, and in a moment more his leg was hooked from under him, and he went to the floor with a crash.

"My hat!" exclaimed Kenney, in astonishment.

Angel lay gasping on the carpet, while the astounded Kenney blinked at Wally Bunter.

"Ow!" gasped Angel. "Oh! Ah! Oooooooop!"

Wally came round the table at great speed, making for Kenney. Kenney faced him, and they closed. In spite of what he had just seen, Kenney could not believe that the Owl of the Remove was a dangerous adversary.

But he was soon undeceived. He found himself spun off his feet and tossed on the carpet like a sack of potatoes.

Crash!

"Yooop!"

"Oh, begad!" came a voice from the passage, and the door opened and Lord Mauleverer glanced in. "Anythin' wrong here, dear boys? Somebody committin' a murder? Oh, gad!"

Mauleverer stared blankly at the astounding scene in the study—Angel and Kenney gasping on their backs, and Wally grinning down at them over his glasses.

"Oh, gad! I'm dreamin'!" ejaculated his lordship.

Angel scrambled up furiously.

"Collar him, Kenney!" he yelled.

He rushed fiercely at Bunter. Kenney sprang up and followed him. They attacked the fat junior together.

"Here, hold on!" exclaimed Lord Mauleverer. "Fair play's a jewel! Back up, Bunter! I'm comin' to help you!"

But Lord Mauleverer's help was not wanted.

Wally stood up coolly to the two Fourth-Formers. Angel caught his right with his chin, and went down with a crash; and Kenney, after a moment or two of sparring, captured Wally's left with his eye, and was strewn across Angel, yelling.

Wally picked up the dog-whip.

"There's the door, my pippins!" he said cheerily. "I'm going to thrash you till you travel——"

Whack, whack, whack!

"Yaroooh!"

"Stoppit!"

"Yow-ow-ow-wooop!"

Angel and Kenney squirmed wildly to escape the vigorous lashes. They were not thinking of fisticuffs any longer—they only wanted to escape. The lashing of the dog-whip followed them to the door, where the astounded Mauleverer jumped aside to give them room to pass.

Yelling widly, Angel and Kenney fled into the passage. They sped for the stairs, with Wally behind, lashing away merrily. Down the Remove staircase went the two Fourth-Formers, and Wally, stopping on the landing, threw the dog-whip after them.

He returned rather breathlessly to his study, grinning. He thought it probable that he had heard the last of Aubrey Angel's claim against Billy Bunter.

Lord Mauleverer tapped him on the shoulder.

"Bunter, dear man——"

"Hallo, fathead!"

"Am I dreamin' this?" asked Mauleverer dazedly.

"See if you wake up when I pinch you!" answered Wally.

"Yarooooh!"

Lord Mauleverer was satisfied that he was awake.

* * * * * *

Harry Wharton & Co. blinked when they heard the news.

Had they heard it from Bunter they would have chuckled. But it was from Mauleverer that they heard it.

There was no doubt about it. The Owl of the Remove had licked Angel and Kenney together in combat, and had chased them down the Remove passage in full flight. Curious youths who looked into Angel's study that evening found him nursing his chin and Kenney nursing his eye.

It was astounding, but it was true!

"Bunter a fighting-man!" said Bob Cherry blankly. "Bunter standing up to two fellows at once—Bunter! And beating them, too! My hat! As the poet remarks, 'Are things what they seem, or is visions about?'"

"It beats me!" confessed Wharton.

And Hurree Jamset Ram Singh declared that the beatfulness was terrific!

"If this is so—and it seems so—it may have been the truth about Coker, and Temple, and—and even in the scrap with the Highcliffe fellows!" said Frank Nugent. "Bunter's changed—the giddy leopard has changed his spots, and the Ethiopian his skin! I wouldn't have believed it without an eye-witness!"

"Bunter was a dog with a bad name!" said Wharton, laughing. "But—but—well, I can't make it out!"

Nobody in the Remove could make it out; but there it was. Even Peter Todd showed a new respect for his fat study-mate. Wally Bunter wore a cheerful grin that evening. He had shown his mettle at last; and he was no longer A Dog With a Bad Name.

(Don't miss "THE AMAZING BUNTER!"—next Monday's Grand Complete Story of Harry Wharton & Co., by FRANK RICHARDS.)

NOTICES.

Back Numbers Wanted by:

H. Banfield, 33, King's Avenue, New Malden, Surrey—"Gem," 469, "Passing it On." 6d. offered.

Edgar Hanson, 50, Wood Bank, Manchester Road, Slaithwaite, near Huddersfield—two GEMS, any sort, between 300 and 400.

John Chew, 24, Sycamore Road, Blackburn—Double Numbers of "Gem" and MAGNET, Christmas, 1913-14-15. 3d. each offered.

E. Roblin, Ailfryn Cottage, Bryn Road, Lougher, Glam, South Wales—any "Gems" before 400, 3d. each; before 200, 4d. each; also 516 and 519. Write first.

Trevor Jenkins, 5, Highland Place, Aberdare, Glam—"Bob Cherry's Barring-Out," "Loyal to the Last." 6d. each offered.

Extracts from "THE GREYFRIARS HERALD" and "TOM MERRY'S WEEKLY."

THE LUCK OF THE BRAVE!

By TOM REDWING.

Foes at Midnight!

THE shades of night had fallen over the forest.

Except for the occasional cry of some prowling wild beast, no sound disturbed the silence. Yet in that region of perpetual gloom and solitude human life was stirring, as any traveller might have surmised from the dancing light of a camp-fire that burned in a natural clearing amongst the trees.

Facing each other across the fire were two white men, one a youth of about eighteen, and the other nearly twice that age. They both looked hard and fit, and their sun-burned faces, even in repose, expressed the keen watchfulness and instant readiness for danger that come from a life of constant peril and hardship.

"I'll turn in for an hour or two, Dan," said the elder of the two, yawning as he knocked the ashes from his pipe. "I'm sleepy. Wake me up when you're tired, and don't let the fire go out, or we'll have a jaguar or two sniffing around, and I never fancied the near company of those creatures."

Dan Morgan laughed, and then looked a trifle serious.

"There are worse things than jaguars to be feared, Steve," he said. "The stuff in our packs wouldn't tempt all the jaguars in this country, but it would be a mighty fine draw for some of the natives."

The other shrugged his broad shoulders.

"Shucks!" he exclaimed. "Those johnnies haven't got the pluck to try and rob us. The very sight of our rifles would scare 'em."

"Not the real Indians," said Morgan. "They don't know what fear is."

"So I've heard before," was the reply; "but that isn't any reason why I should believe it."

Having delivered himself of this opinion, Stephen Roach, wrapping himself in his blanket and oilskin covering sheet, stretched his long limbs and was quickly plunged into a deep slumber.

Left entirely to the company of his own thoughts, Dan Morgan stared reflectively into the glowing embers of the fire. He and Roach, comrades now for many months, had braved innumerable dangers in the pursuit of a quest as remarkable as any ever undertaken by mortal man.

Two of a shipwrecked crew landed at a small port far up the South American western coast, they had starved and suffered for weeks while vainly endeavouring to get into touch with the British Consul at the nearest town, which was over a thousand miles away. At last, despairing, utterly at the end of their slender resources, they set out on foot to reach civilisation again.

One night, a week later, they stopped at the first house they had seen in the course of their lonely and perilous journey. The owner of the place, an old Spanish settler, was lying at the point of death. His last hours on earth were comforted by the two comrades, who were the first white men he had seen for years, and before he died he imparted to them information of immense value.

This related to buried treasure whose resting-place was known to him alone. His knowledge he passed on to the comrades, who, fired by his story, determined to go and search for the hidden treasure. To do this was rendered easier by the circumstance that their benefactor placed his resources at their command, so that, after his death and burial, they were able to set out fully equipped for the venture.

It was a hazardous journey that they made through wild and inhospitable country; but fortune favoured them. They found the treasure concealed beneath a rock at the foot of a high cliff. It had been there for over a century, and it consisted of gold and precious stones of every description. By their discovery the comrades jumped from poverty to wealth in a single bound.

Since then they had travelled a considerable distance on the return journey to the coast, but many days had still to pass before they could hope to reach their objective. Here, in the mighty forest that stretched away for endless leagues on every side of them, they were apparently the only white men.

The howling cry of some forest wild-cat aroused Dan Morgan from the reverie into which he had fallen. Picking up some loose sticks, he flung them on the fire, which blazed up again with a flaming crackle of dry wood. The lad resumed his seat, only to leap amazedly to his feet the next moment, while his lips parted in a sharp exclamation of surprise.

Near to him stood the motionless figure of an Indian chief. Proud, warlike in dress and appearance, the new-comer regarded the British youth with a calm yet fiercely threatening stare that was hard to meet. He wore the costume of a Mexican hunter, and the silver buckled belt round his waist held a couple of revolvers and a long-bladed knife that glittered like frosted glass in the firelight.

"The dickens!" said Morgan. "Who are you?"

The Indian pointed proudly to the curling white eagle's feather that rose like a plume above his head.

"White Eagle," he said, in a harsh tone. "And you?"

"Well," Morgan answered, "if you really want to know it, Dan Morgan's my name."

White Eagle gravely bent his head.

"Ha!" he said. "Then you and the other paleface"—glancing at Roach's recumbent form, "are those who took the buried treasure from its hiding-place in the shadows of Black Mountain. It were better for you had you never found it."

"How's that?" came Morgan's quick inqury.

"Because all your time and labour have been wasted," White Eagle rejoined. "The young men of my tribe know that you have the gold, and they claim it."

There was a sudden rustle. At the sound the Indian spun round, to find himself looking down the barrel of a rifle pointed at him by Roach, whose bronzed, weather-beaten face was crimson with rage.

"Claim it, do they?" cried the incensed Britisher, his eyes, closed in peaceful sleep but a few moments before, now sparkling with fiery anger. "Then they'll have to fight for it, the thieving coyotes! Hands up, you ugly son of a gun, or I'll drill a hole through your carcase!"

White Eagle did not move a muscle. With unshakable intrepidity, his lips parted in a haughty smile, he stared at the white man.

"Hands up!" Roach cried again, his finger tightening on the trigger. "D'you hear me?"

A mocking laugh came from the Indian chief. At the same moment he bounded high into the air. Then Roach fired, once, twice, the double report echoing far and wide. He stared in front of him with a puzzled frown on his brow. There was no sign of White Eagle anywhere.

"Where is the hound?" he asked.

"Gone back to his warriors," answered Morgan. "He was too quick for you. And now, I guess, we're up against it with a vengeance."

Silent and grim, Roach slipped another two cartridges into the magazine of his rifle.

Fighting for Life!

THERE was an ominous stillness in the forest that, to Dan Morgan and his comrade, was more nerve-straining than any visible danger. Beyond the flickering light cast by the fire was an impenetrable gloom, where peril lurked in readiness to spring out upon them.

The Indian chief had gone; but they knew that he would return with his savage followers. What chance would they have then? They were armed with a magazine rifle and a bandolier of cartridges apiece, but such defensive power would avail them little against the tactics of men accustomed all their lives to forest warfare.

The foes they had to contend against were the descendants of the formidable Red Indian tribes who, rather than submit to the domination of the white man in the northern territories of the great American continent, had made the long trek southwards to the mountains and forests of Mexico and Brazil. Often though Dan Morgan and his companion had heard of these fierce, proud outlaws, they had never before come into actual contact with them.

"I'm thinking," said Roach at last, breaking the silence, "that you were right, Dan, in saying that there were worse things than jaguars to be feared. We're in a queer fix, and I don't see how we are to get out of it. Of course, we could give up the treasure, but that's not to be thought of, for it's our own."

"You bet!" agreed Morgan. "I'd sooner die than hand it over to a lot of Redskins! Say, old chap," he continued, "I've thought of a plan. No doubt we're being watched like a cat watches a mouse, but we ought to be smart enough to slip away and throw the Redskins off our track for several minutes."

"What would be the good?"

"Why this," Morgan answered. "In that time we could double back to the river we crossed this afternoon and reach the island, where we'd be able to beat off any attack made against us."

Roach cogitated in silence for a moment or two. Then he gave a nod of assent to the suggestion.

"It's a sporting chance, anyhow, and something good may come of it," he said. "We'll take it."

The camp-fire had died down, and its waning light threw but a feeble glimmer on the massed black shadows in the background. Cautiously but swiftly the comrades slung the packbags over their shoulders, and made every preparation for departure. Now all was ready for the fateful move.

"You go first!" whispered Roach, his rifle ready for instant use in case the Redskins should become aware of what was happening and rush them. "Keep as near as you can to the track we made. I'll follow you close."

Fortune favoured them. Threading an intricate way through the vast stretch of tangled undergrowth, they reached the banks of a broad and swiftly-flowing river. The island, long and narrow, was in mid-stream, and the dark, irregular mass of it was but faintly discernible in the night-gloom.

With rifles firmly strapped to their packs the comrades lowered themselves into the water and struck out for the island. The strength of the current made it impossible for them to swim a straight course, and before reaching land they were carried two hundred yards down the stream. Exhausted but triumphant, they scrambled ashore.

"That's one more point in the game to us," said Roach, vigorously shaking the water from his head and shoulders, "and I reckon that White Eagle and his friends won't tumble to it until the morning. They'll find we're missing soon enough, no doubt, but they aren't at all likely to track us here before daylight."

"In that case," Morgan replied, "we'll both have a good sleep. We shall want to be wide awake when they do find us here."

Undeterred by thought of poisonous reptile or savage beast, they made the swampy, reed-grown ground their couch, and were quickly oblivious to the perils that beset them. awn came, and found them still soundly sleeping.

The sun shone out, and the life of the

forest made itself heard in a thousand different voices. Wakened up by the bright light, Dan Morgan opened his eyes, rubbed them hard, and, yawning lazily, sat up and looked round at his companion.

Instantly his whole body stiffened, and into his eyes crept a look of unutterable horror and alarm. Lying easily on his back, with both hands clasped at the back of his head, Roach was asleep, in blissful unconsciousness of the fact that a huge swamp-adder was coiled up on his chest.

The reptile had snuggled down there for warmth. Its flat, ugly head was pointed straight at Roach's throat. The slightest movement on the part of the sleeping man would inevitably arouse and irritate the adder, with tragic consequences.

Irresolute, undecided how to act for the best, Morgan stared fixedly at the hideous thing. Suddenly Roach moved, and the closely-knit coils of the reptile's body loosened and stirred with quivering activity. Again the man shifted his position, raising his knees and moving one hand from the back of his head. He was awake.

With inconceivable rapidity the adder uncoiled itself and drew back its head to strike a venomous blow at the doomed man. There was no help for Roach. He saw what threatened him, and the fearsome reptile paralysed his every nerve.

Not so Morgan. Galvanised into feverish action by the frightful peril threatening his comrade, he snatched up his rifle and fired. Speeding true to its mark, the bullet smashed the adder's head to a pulp, and the writhing, twisting body rolled and floundered to the ground, and disappeared with noisy rustling amongst the reeds.

Roach, shaken and pale of face, rose to his feet.

"Thankee, Dan!" he said, a trifle unsteadily. "That shot saved my life."

The other gave a grim little laugh.

"'Twas mighty unfortunate I had to fire, though," he said, "for the report has betrayed our whereabouts to the Redskins. Look yonder!"

The river-bank was dotted with savages. More came running each moment from amongst the trees and bushes. A conspicuous figure was White Eagle, who, with one hand shading his eyes from the sun, looked long and intently at the island.

"Sure enough, they've spotted us!" said Roach. "We'll get back a little under cover."

As they moved away a flight of arrows whistled all about them, piercing the bark of trees and tearing bunches of leaves from the bushes. Picking one up, Roach examined it.

"These barbs are dipped in poison," he said. "The slightest scratch from one would be fatal."

They took shelter behind the broad trunk of an enormous banyan, which, a veritable monarch of the forest, towered high above great masses of tropical undergrowth of every kind. The arrows shot across the river continued searching for them. Suddenly a long, blood-curdling yell rang out, and a score of Redskins plunged into the stream and headed for the island.

"It's the real show beginning now," said Roach. "Don't waste a single shot, Dan. Hit your man every time."

The bobbing heads of the swimmers were easily distinguishable. They were not close together, but spread widely out. Looking out from behind the banyan, Roach fired at one of the leading savages. Instantly two or three arrows, shot by Redskins keeping watch on the far bank, came perilously near to him, and he darted back into safety.

"Here they come!" cried Dan.

The first men to reach the island climbed lithely up the bank, the water running from their oiled bodies, and dived amongst the reeds and long grass. After the first rustle of the disturbed verdure had subsided there was no sound or movement. But the comrades knew that their foes were creeping stealthily towards them, and that they would speedily be fighting for their very lives.

In a rift of the foliage a fierce, painted face and a gleaming pair of eyes appeared for a moment, and Roach fired. A dreadful cry followed. Then on every side the Redskins sprang to their feet, and advanced with a furious rush, yelling, and whirling knives and tomahawks in a frenzy of hate and excitement.

The comrades poured in a rapid fire from their rifles. Every bullet found its mark. The attack weakened and recoiled. With startling abruptness the sounds of conflict ceased. The Redskins who had survived fell back and scuttled deep amongst the undergrowth with the quickness of hunted wolves.

"Hurrah!" cried Dan. "They've had enough of it!"

"For the present," said Roach; "but they'll come back again. Now they know what we can do they'll alter their tactics. We must do the same, and be beforehand with them."

He glanced upward at the far-spreading branches of the banyan-tree.

"That's where we'll stand to," he said. "There's room enough there for a whole regiment to hide. Up you get!"

One after the other they climbed the tree. It was not a difficult task, for there was a multitude of branches to cling to, and in a few minutes they were fifty or sixty feet above the ground. So thick and strong were the interlacing boughs that they were able to walk about as on a platform, and the density of the foliage, which was added to by the leaves of innumerable parasitic creepers, concealed them like an enveloping cloud.

Recharging their empty magazines with fresh cartridges, they listened silently for some sound betokening a fresh advance by their foes. But no warning signal came to their ears. The suspense threatened to become unbearable.

"I'll take a peep down below," said Dan Morgan. "Hold on to my rifle for a moment."

Scarcely moving the leaves, so slow and cautious was he, the lad lowered himself to a branch from which he was able to command a clear view of the ground below. No sign of human life was to be seen. But, stay! What was that object which moved ever so lightly as to escape the notice of any but the keenest eye? It looked like a green bush.

Yet Dan Morgan knew that bushes were stationary things. This particular one advanced into the little open space where he and Roach had camped during the night.

"Gee-whiz!" muttered the lad. "It's a disguised Redskin!"

At the same moment something caught hold of his hair and gave it a vicious pull. Startled and furious, he glanced up, to see on the branch above him a large monkey, who, stretching down its paw, had seized hold of his head. He tried to free himself, and the ape, chattering excitedly, snatched so hard at his scalp that he could not refrain from uttering a shout and striking a wild blow with his fist at his mischievous opponent.

The monkey, jabbering and grinning, skipped away. Immediately afterwards Morgan remembered the walking bush, and, with a feeling of mingled apprehension and dismay, looked for it again. It had vanished.

"Of course!" he said ruefully. "The fellow spotted me, and has gone to tell his mates about it!"

Returning quickly to Roach, he told the other of what had taken place.

"Don't blame yourself," said his companion, not without a laugh of amused interest. "You couldn't help the monkey collaring hold of you. I should have hallooed just the same if I had been in your place. All the same," he added, "it's made things more serious for us. They know where we are now."

Even as Roach finished speaking an arrow hissed past his head, and stuck quivering in an upright branch a foot or two away. Impulsively he fired in the direction whence the deadly missile had come, and the sound of a heavy body was heard as it crashed through the foliage and then fell to the ground with a dull thud.

"That was a lucky shot," said Roach, as he peered down and caught sight of the lifeless body of the Redskin who had fallen a victim to his rifle. "He was close on us, the varmint, when he strung that arrow!"

"Yes," rejoined Morgan. "And he didn't climb our tree, but the next one. The branches of all these trees meet and intermingle, and the beggars can reach us from all sides at once."

The other's grim face looked grimmer than ever.

"It's bad," he said. "But they sha'n't catch us napping, anyhow."

Lying flat on his chest along the bough, he rested the barrel of his rifle in a wide fork that allowed him a free-and-easy movement of the weapon. His bandolier he laid flat by his side, so that he could reload the magazine with cartridges in the quickest possible time.

"This is where they're most likely to try and get at us," he said. "You stand nearer the trunk and keep a general look-out. I'll give you a shout if I want you."

Going to the post indicated, Morgan kept vigilant watch and guard. Twenty minutes passed, and he saw nothing to arrest his attention, although the occasional crack of Roach's rifle told him that his comrade was busily engaged elsewhere.

Then a tiny piece of bark-peeling fell silently, and brushed his cheek in its descent. He looked up, and his heart gave a mad leap of excitement. About fifteen feet above him a dark-brown hand was holding back a foliaged bough, and through the opening thus made two burning eyes, set in a cruel, proud face, stared down at the British lad.

"Snakes alive!" said Morgan aloud. "It's White Eagle!"

Acting on an instant's swift, unbidden warning, he pressed close against the tree-trunk.

Just in time! Even as he did so a heavy, broad-bladed stabbing-knife hurled downwards through the empty space where he had been exposing himself a moment before.

To the River!

QUICK as lightning Morgan held up his rifle, and fired twice. He heard the bullets slashing through the leaves, but no sound to indicate that White Eagle was struck. Once more he fired, with the same result as before.

"Guess the cunning rascal has saved his skin!" he muttered. "How I'd like to have one shot at him out in the open! He'd never wear head-feathers again!"

In tense expectancy of another attack, he stood stiff and motionless where he was. But his unseen foe gave no sign. He began to fidget with growing impatience. At last, unable to control himself any longer, he moved forward a step, and glanced up in search of the Indian chief.

A quick look round satisfied him that White Eagle was not there. Had the other moved to a place of safety, or was he still watching the young Britisher from some near coign of vantage? In either case he was still to be reckoned with—a fierce, vindictive foe, who would show the comrades no mercy should they fall into his clutches.

Hearing Roach calling to him, he quickly joined his comrade.

"D'you see that smoke?" said the elder man. "Well, what do you make of it?"

Thin, curling wisps of smoke were rising from the ground. There was also a strong smell of burning grass and bush-growth in the air. Startled and alarmed, Morgan stared at his companion, the expression of whose face was very stern and grave.

"Great Scott!" exclaimed the lad. "They've started a fire!"

Roach nodded his head.

"They have!" he replied. "The beggars mean to smoke us out!"

The smoke rapidly increased in volume and density. It came from all sides. Soon the comrades could hear the crackle of dry wood as the fire seized upon it, and the spluttering hiss of scorched leaves. Sparks ascended, and were blown hither and thither by the breeze, setting alight to the topmost foliage of the trees, and starting conflagrations in a hundred different places.

"We must get down out of this," said Roach, coughing back the smoke that filled his throat. "It's better to die fighting than to stay here and be roasted alive."

"Then we'll strike back towards the river," Morgan declared. "We may stand a better chance."

Roach shook his head.

"We must make for the stream on the far side of the island," he said. "The Redskins won't be looking for us there. They'll be mostly watching the way we came."

Having made the packs containing the treasure firm and secure, the comrades descended the giant banyan where they had taken their precarious refuge. They were almost blinded and suffocated by the hot, swirling smoke that rose to meet them. But terrible though it was to endure, it at any rate screened them from the notice of the savages.

More by luck than through any sense of

Printed and published weekly by the Proprietors at The Fleetway House, Farringdon Street, London, E.C. 4, England. Subscription, 8s. 10d. per annum Agents for Australasia: Gordon & Gotch, Melbourne, Sydney, Adelaide, Brisbane, and Wellington, N.Z. South Africa: The Central News Agency, Ltd. Cape Town and Johannesburg. Saturday, January 25th, 1919.

direction they struck the course they were seeking. It was not a great distance across the island, and, after a journey that left them more dead than alive, they reached the riverside. Here a great crowd of monkeys, driven from their haunts by the flames and smoke, had assembled, and the babel of sounds made by this strange host was deafening.

"Look!" shouted Morgan, seizing his companion by the arm. "We're saved!"

What he saw was a native boat, a light but strongly-built craft, capable of seating four persons, floating on the still waters of a small creek that formed an irregular inlet of the river.

Almost wild with joy, he and Roach raced towards it. The boat, which had evidently been abandoned and left there a long while since, was in serviceable condition.

Losing no time, the comrades stowed away their packs, and then, jumping in, pushed off into the main stream with a long pole that Roach had found lying in the grass.

Caught by the rapid current, the little vessel was quickly carried away from the island, which was now almost blotted from sight by a huge pall of smoke rising slowly to the sky. The red glare of leaping flames grew brighter and brighter. The island and everything on it was doomed to destruction.

"Those Redskins were a bit too reckless, I'm thinking," said Roach. "In seeking to make cinders of us they'll make cinders of themselves, unless they get a quick move on."

"Expect they've done a bunk already," Morgan answered, "and swum back to the mainland."

"Not all of them," said Roach, an eager note in his voice. "See that party there?"

He pointed towards the island. Running along the bank were three of the savages—White Eagle and two of his followers. Catching sight of the boat, they knelt down, and, fixing arrows to their bows, shot at it.

The feathered barbs fell short, and Roach, standing upright and waving his hand, uttered a loud, mocking laugh. Instantly Morgan pulled him down, for White Eagle, throwing aside his useless bow, picked up a rifle and fired it. The bullet hummed over the boat, and Roach had again to bless the promptitude of his young companion in saving his life.

"The ugly snake!" he gritted out between his clenched teeth. "I'll do better than him, anyway!"

Levelling his own rifle, he returned the fire. But haste made his aim uncertain, and the Indian chief was untouched by the bullet. Before he could fire a second shot a rolling cloud of smoke hid White Eagle from his sight.

"Ah, well," he remarked, "I guess the fire will do for him, and it'll only be justice! He set it going for our special benefit. Now he'll feel what it's like himself!"

Dan Morgan gave a merry laugh.

"It doesn't matter what happens to him and his fighting-men now!" he said. "They can't do us any more harm. And we've still got the treasure, old man. That's the main point."

Roach chuckled, and blinked his smoke-reddened eyes.

"Yes," he agreed; "I guess that's the main point right enough, Dan. All we've got to hope for now is that our luck will hold to the end."

Their luck did hold to the end. Late in the day they were picked up by a river steamer, and a fortnight afterwards they reached Valparaiso. There they were able to dispose of the treasure they had gone through so many dangers and hardships to secure, and returned home to England with the inspiring knowledge that they would be rich for the remainder of their lives.

THE END.

GUSSY'S LATEST LOVE-AFFAIR!

By ROBERT ARTHUR DIGBY.

I.

"WOULD you chaps care to come over to Topham with us to-morrow afternoon?" Cardew asked us after lessons on Tuesday afternoon.

"What's the wheeze?" Herries growled.

"Skating, old top," said Clive. "Just you four and us three. We are seven, you know."

"That would be wipping!" D'Arcy exclaimed. "I have ten shillin's left from the last fivah my patah sent me. We could get a scwumptious tea at Topham."

"Good old Gussy!" laughed Blake. "He never forgets the deserving poor."

"I don't wegard my fwiends as objects of chawity," said Arthur Augustus solemnly. It's so easy to pull Gussy's leg that it's hardly worth doing.

"Well, if Gussy provides the grub I don't mind going," Herries said. "It will do Towser good to have a run."

"That beast coming, too?" Levison gasped in dismay. "He will be under our feet all the blessed time!"

"Shut up, you ass!" Herries growled politely. "He's as much right on the ice as you have, and he's a jolly sight more ornamental!"

"Pax, my brothers!" Blake put in gently. "There's no reason why Towser shouldn't go, if Herries particularly wants to take him. I suppose you chaps don't object?" he added, turning to Clive, Cardew, D'Arcy, and myself.

"Not at all," Clive said politely.

"Yaas, do take the brute," Cardew drawled. "Herries can buy us some new togs if Towser should happen to get hungry an' mistake our bags for dog-biscuits."

D'Arcy wasn't very enthusiastic at the suggestion, but was too polite to say so, as he would, in a sense, be the host. Towser has such an unfortunate predilection for Gussy's "twousahs."

Of course, I made no objection. We of Study No. 6 are used to having Towser about with us, but some of the chaps get quite nervy if he gives a friendly little growl or playfully snaps at their legs.

After prep was finished for the evening we hunted up our skates and cleaned and adjusted them, so that there would be nothing to prevent our starting immediately after dinner on the following day.

"I wish I had some skates for Towser," sighed Herries, as he gave a final oiling to his own. "I'm sure he knows he's going. Have you noticed how playful and excited he is getting?" he added, as Towser gave a friendly little snap at Gussy's nether garments.

"I do wish you would keep Towsah undah contwol!" Arthur Augustus complained. "He vewy neahly spoilt my new twousahs!"

"Ha, ha, ha!" we yelled. D'Arcy is one of the best, but he's worse than a girl where clothes are concerned.

"Rats to your old trousers!" Herries snapped. "You shouldn't wear clothes that attract the dog's notice. It's your own fault if you insist on irritating Towser's artistic sense."

"Weally, Hewwies," D'Arcy started, "I wegard your wemarks about my clothes——"

"Chuck it, you fatheads!" said Blake, in an exasperated voice. "It's like living in the monkey-house at the Zoo to share a study with you!"

II.

"WHAT luck!" exclaimed Cardew. "There's practically nobody on the ice!"

We had just come in sight of the flooded fields at Topham, where we had decided to spend the afternoon.

Three or four village boys were sliding along one side of the field, and in the far corner a young lady was skating alone. Otherwise, we had the whole stretch of ice to ourselves.

"It's absolutely ripping!" Blake called, as he took a trial run while we were fixing our skates. "It's as smooth as glass and very thick! Hurry up, you chaps, and don't waste the daylight!"

In another minute we were all on the ice, accompanied by Towser, who, in his excitement, was in everybody's way.

"Keep Towser over your side, there's a good fellow," Clive said, as he narrowly escaped coming a cropper over Towser's head. "I'm afraid he'll get trodden on."

Herries looked at him coldly.

"Here, Towser!" he called, and skated over to the other side of the ice with the bulldog at his heels. Herries hates anyone to suggest that Towser could ever be in the way.

For some time peace reigned over the scene, broken occasionally by yells from the village boys as one or other of them toppled over on the slide.

The air was keenly exhilarating, and life seemed to all of us very well worth living, especially with the prospect of Gussy's spread when it became too dark for skating.

"Hallo! What was that?" Cardew exclaimed, as a sudden, sharp cry rang across the ice.

"Look! Towser has knocked that girl over!" said Blake excitedly.

At some distance from us we could see a muddled heap of dog and girl. Towser appeared to think that the young lady had some designs upon his person, and was growling in a menacing manner.

"Herries should never have brought the dog," Levison said. "I pointed out what a nuisance he would be, but Herries wouldn't listen, and you all backed him up."

"Well, how were we to know the dog would get into trouble?" Blake asked, with some heat.

D'Arcy, meanwhile, wasted no time in words, but skated over to the scene of the accident as quickly as his legs could carry him.

Herries was engaged with Towser, and he left it to D'Arcy to help the young lady to her feet. It was just as well, for Herries is no lady's man, whereas Arthur Augustus was born to rescue distressed damsels. He has the chivalrous soul of a twelfth century knight.

"What a chance for Gussy!" Blake laughed. "Behold him once again falling in love!"

D'Arcy certainly seemed to be getting along exceedingly well, considering that he had never seen the young lady before. Presently he and the girl came skating towards us hand-in-hand.

"By Jove!" ejaculated Cardew, as they drew near. "I'm blessed if it isn't Norah Anketell, Clive! What a lark! Don't tell Gussy I know her."

With that he went to meet them.

"May I intwoduce my fwiend Cardew, Miss Anketell?" Gussy asked.

Cardew favoured Miss Anketell with a sly wink, and was duly introduced.

"That boundah Towsah wan into Miss Anketell," Gussy explained. "I am afwaid she is wathah badly shaken up. I pwopose we go stwaight away and have some tea. You will come and have some, too, won't you, Miss Anketell?"

Norah Anketell looked at Cardew before replying. He gave a scarcely perceptible nod.

"Yaas, do come, Miss Anketell," he urged aloud. "We owe you a tea, you know, because it was our dog, or, anyway, old Hewwies'—same thing, y'know—that knocked you over."

Norah Anketell smiled upon Gussy.

"I think I would like to come if you are sure I shall not be in the way," she said sweetly.

"If you will excuse me I will just let the other fellows know we are goin' on," D'Arcy said, and skated off, leaving Cardew and Miss Anketell together.

Cardew seized the opportunity of D'Arcy's absence to explain the joke to Norah, and she entered into it with a great deal of zest.

When Gussy returned she was talking with great animation to Cardew, and scarcely deigned to notice the presence of the Honourable Augustus.

"Er—Miss Anketell, do you feel well enough to start yet?" D'Arcy inquired. "I am afwaid you will feel howwibly shaken after your fall."

"I am quite all right, thank you," Norah Anketell replied. "Mr. Cardew has offered to help me to the village. I think my ankle is slightly sprained."

And without another word she tucked her arm in Cardew's, and the two started towards the village.

D'Arcy stood petrified with surprise and chagrin that Cardew should cut in like that and carry off the girl under his very nose!

"Hallo, Gussy! What's up? Lost a shilling and found a threepenny-bit?"

Blake broke in upon his meditations.

The rest of the party had come up, hugely delighted at the success of their little plot.

"I would pwefer not to discuss the mattah!" D'Arcy replied with dignity. "I am vewy suwpwised at Cardew, and vewy disappointed in Miss Anketell!"

"Why, what's the matter? What have they done?" Blake inquired in mock surprise.

"I wefuse to say anything furthah about it," Arthur Augustus repeated. "If you fellows are quite weady we will go to the village and ordah tea."

"Right-ho, old bean!" Herries said. "Towser is famished, and I feel that I could do with a crumb or so myself."

III.

The tea was a huge success, from everybody's point of view but D'Arcy's. As host he, of course, fulfilled his duties punctiliously, but his whole joy of life had gone since Norah had so basely deserted him for Cardew.

"Cardew, deah boy, forgive my intewwuptin' you, but will you ask Miss Anketell if she will have some more tea?" he asked, with laboured politeness.

A ripple of laughter came from Norah Anketell.

"Thanks awfully, Mr. D'Arcy!" she said cheerfully. "Mr. Cardew makes me laugh so much that I am as dry as a fish!"

In stony silence Gussy passed the refilled cup to her. She acknowledged it with a smile, but the next moment turned again to Cardew, and continued an animated conversation with him.

"If evewybody has finished, I pwopose we see about getting back to the station," D'Arcy said after tea.

"Yaas, deah boy!" Cardew replied. "I think you ought to be making a move. Miss Anketell is allowing me to drive her to the station, as her ankle is still rather painful."

D'Arcy bit his lip to stifle an exclamation of vexation, and looked unutterable things at Cardew. Clive and Levison looked rather anxiously at Cardew. They knew from experience what a reckless driver Ralph Reckness Cardew was.

"Cardew, I should be glad if you would see me this evenin' in my studay!" Gussy said pompously.

"Well, deah boy, I expect I shall see you before the evenin's over, anyway," Cardew replied casually. "Nothin' in that. Why this thusness?"

"There is something vewy important I must say to you," D'Arcy continued. "And I should pwefer to see you alone."

"Right-ho, old top!" Cardew said breezily. "Swords or pistols? All the same to you, y'know. Are you ready yet?" he added, turning to Norah.

As it would take us longer to walk to the station than it would for the others to drive, we started straight away, Cardew and Miss Anketell leaving at the same time for the livery stables to arrange for the trap.

"Done in the eye this time, old top!" Blake said laughingly.

"I fail to undahstand what you mean, Blake!" D'Arcy replied, with icy hauteur.

"I can't imagine how any girl could resist Gussy's new waistcoat!" I remarked.

"Dig, you uttah ass——"

"Or that gorgeous tie," Clive put in.

"And you've had so much practice, too!" Blake jeered. "We shouldn't be surprised if Cardew did cut us out. But you!"

"You wottahs! Pway do not wefer to the subject again!" gasped Arthur Augustus, walking rapidly ahead.

"Come back, you silly fathead!" Blake called.

But D'Arcy, like "The Cat Who Walked by Himself," walked on in dignified silence alone.

About half-way to the station Cardew drove past us with pretty little Norah Anketell beside him.

She favoured us with a smile, and Cardew was passing with a "Cheerio!" when he suddenly noticed that Gussy was not with us.

"He's going at a pretty fine rate!" Clive remarked. "He should be more careful when he is driving a lady."

At that moment Cardew turned round in the trap and shouted back to us.

"What have you done with Gussy?"

"He's walking on ahead," Levison answered.

"He has just turned the bend in the road," Blake added.

"Look out, Cardew!" howled Herries.

But the warning was too late. With a hoot of the horn a car turned the bend of the road which Cardew was approaching.

The horse shied, reared, and plunged ahead. Cardew tugged at the reins for all he was worth, but it had no effect at all upon the horse.

We all raced down the road at top speed, and a second later the car passed us. The occupants were evidently quite unaware of the effect their car had had upon Cardew's horse.

"By Jove! Somebody has stopped the horse!" Herries panted.

"Yes! It's Gussy!" Clive gasped.

We quickly reached the spot. Cardew had got down from the trap, and was vigorously engaged in brushing Gussy's clothes.

"Any damage, old man?" I inquired.

"No, deah boy," Gussy said politely, endeavouring to screw half an eyeglass into his eye; "but I've bwoken my beastly eyeglass, an' can't keep it in my eye!"

"Ha, ha, ha!"

We yelled with delight. It certainly looked as though he had been rather badly handled.

Gussy, the immaculate, presented a somewhat unusual sight. His collar was broken, and half of it flapped out in the breeze. His clothes were dusty and dishevelled, whilst a gaping hole appeared at the knee of his trousers.

Miss Anketell, however, was quite blind to any imperfections. She clambered down the trap, and, seizing both of Gussy's hands, tried to thank him.

"But for your courage we might both have been killed, Mr. D'Arcy!" she said, with tears of gratitude in her eyes.

"D'Arcy, old man, I'm sorry I played the giddy goat with you," Cardew said contritely. "As a matter of fact, we were only pulling your leg. I have known Miss Anketell for years. Clive has met her before, too. Haven't you, Clive?"

"I had that pleasure some time ago," Cilve replied.

"But—but I don't undahstand!" Gussy said in a tone of bewilderment. "Did you weally know Cardew before to-day, Miss Anketell?"

"Yes; I've known him for ages!" Norah laughed. "They told me you were rather—well, keen on girls, and I offered to cure you by making you hate me."

"Oh, weally!" Gussy objected. "You could nevah make me do that, you know!"

"I think we had better take Mr. D'Arcy along with us the rest of the way, Ralph," Norah Anketell suggested. "I am afraid he is scarcely up to walking after being dragged along the road for about a dozen yards."

"Yaas, do hop in, old top!" Cardew urged. "There's loads of room."

We seized our hero and barged him up into the trap. We gave three cheers for Gussy. Cardew drove off, and we continued our journey soberly to the station.

Gussy makes you think jolly hard sometimes. He's a bit of an ass, and an awful dandy, and he's as soft as soft can be about girls; but he's all there when pluck is wanted, and—well, there's only one Gussy, and we wouldn't spare him to anybody!

THE END.

The Editor's Chat.

For Next Monday:

"THE AMAZING BUNTER!"

By Frank Richards.

The Bunter now at Greyfriars is, of course, Walter Gilbert, not William George.

And the two, alike as they are in person, are as unlike in most of their characteristics as any two fellows well could be.

Billy is—well, you all know what Billy is!

Wally, despite his fat, is essentially the same sort of fellow as any of the Famous Five, as Squiff, or Ogilvy. All of these differ in some ways from one another, of course; but they are all alike in more ways.

They are all capable and straight and decent. They can do the things worth doing; and they don't care about the things one should not do. I do not mean that they are perfect; but they are emphatically decent. And Wally is like that.

So it is that he finds his cousin Billy's legacy of trouble very hard to bear. For the things Billy has done are the kind of things honest Wally hates—mean and dishonest things, right off the rails. And Wally is supposed to have done them; and the fact that he is now behaving like a decent fellow is looked upon as amazing.

Next week's story finds him in contact with the Courtfield Council School crowd, of whom we have heard little lately. They know Bunter well, of course; but it is Billy Bunter whom they know. Nice for Wally, again!

Skinner, Stott, and Snoop also come into the story. The Famous Five play rather smaller parts than usual. Some readers may regret this fact; others will not. It is a bit of a change, anyway.

BILLY BUNTER AT ST. JIM'S!

If you are not getting the "Gem" you are making a big mistake.

And it is not my fault.

I have been telling you to get it, you know.

The yarns of Billy Bunter in his new quarters are the funniest I have ever read.

"Bunter of the New House" is this week's story, and it shows us W. G. B. in close association with Figgins & Co., who are most completely fed up with him before the story ends.

They think he is Wally, you know; and they have seen Wally play footer. Now they see Billy play—no, that's wrong. He can't! But they see him doing what he fancies to be playing footer.

'Nuff said!

GET THE "GEM"!

NOTICES.

Correspondence Wanted By:

Herbert Foondhere, Ashfield House, Thornton, Bradford, Yorks—with readers anywhere—17-18. Stamped addressed envelope.

The Misses Mary and Helen Harkins, Sinclair Street, Milngavie, Scotland—with girl readers between 18 and 19.

J. Robinson, Maise Street, Longstone, near Bakewell Derbyshire—with readers anywhere.

Davis Zartz, 198, Queen Street, Port Elizabeth, South Africa—with readers overseas.

D. McGrath, c/o P.O., Box 231, Port Elizabeth, South Africa—with readers overseas.

Miss Doreen Cohen, 32, Queen Street, Port Elizabeth, South Africa—with girl readers anywhere—14-17.

Frank McGrath, P.O., Box 169, Port Elizabeth, South Africa—with readers anywhere.

Gideon Smit, 117, Sir Lowry Road, Cape Town, South Africa—with readers in Ireland, India, Hong Kong, Egypt, U.S.A., or New Zealand.

Edward MacPherson, c/o Mangold Bros., P.O., Box 311, Port Elizabeth, South Africa—with readers overseas.

Miss Eileen Quinn, 15, Dollery Street, Port Elizabeth, South Africa—with readers anywhere.

Claude Whitehead, 51, Market Square, Pocklington, Yorks, wants more members for MAGNET and "Gem" Correspondence Club; magazine printed regularly.

YOUR EDITOR.

The GEM 1½d

No. 571. Vol. 13. January 18th, 1919.

BILLY BUNTER AT ST. JIM'S.

A PIG IN CLOVER!

WILLIAM GEORGE BUNTER

BILLY BUNTER AT ST. JIM'S.

By MARTIN CLIFFORD.

A Magnificent, Long, Complete Story of Tom Merry & Co.

CHAPTER 1.
Up to Study No. 6.

"AHEM!"

"Well?"

"Ahem!"

Blake and Herries and Digby looked rather curiously at their noble chum, Arthur Augustus D'Arcy of the Fourth.

Arthur Augustus' face was very serious; and he looked as if he were about to utter something of the greatest importance. But there was a curious hesitation in his manner. Apparently he feared for some reason the effect of his forthcoming remarks upon his study-mates.

"What have you got on your chest?" asked Jack Blake.

"Ahem!"

"Got a cold?" asked Digby.

"Wats! No."

"You seem to be coughing a lot," said Herries suspiciously. "If you're getting the 'flu, Gussy, you'd better buzz off to sanny at once. You don't want to give it to the whole study."

"I am not gettin' the 'flue, Hewwies. I was about to say somethin' wathah important to you chaps."

"Well, say it, old scout, and get it over," suggested Blake. "What is it?"

"Ahem!"

"Wake me up when you begin," yawned Digby.

"Ahem! I—I say, this studay is wathah a good size for a juniah studay, don't you fellows think so?" asked Arthur Augustus.

"Not bad," said Blake, in great wonder. "Is that what you were going to say? Sapient remarks on the size of the study?"

"N-no—no! We weally have a lot of space heah, more than they have in some of the studies."

"None too much space, with your dashed hatboxes and necktie-boxes and things about."

"Wats! I admit that it was wathah a cwowd when Twimble was put in heah—he's such a fat boundah—when he first came to St. Jim's. I admit that it was much more comfy when we got wid of Twimble."

"Passed unanimously," agreed Blake. "What about it?"

"Howevah, we could weally make woom for five, at a pinch."

"We could, I dare say, but we're jolly well not going to!" said Blake. "None of the studies has five in it. And you can bet your Sunday hat that this study isn't going to. What are you driving at, anyway? Do you want to ask Clive or Roylance to dig in here? If so, no's the answer. They're charming fellows, but a good deal more charming outside than inside."

"Hear, hear!" said Herries and Dig together.

"Weally, Blake——"

"So that's what you're humming and hawing about!" exclaimed Blake warmly. "You want to stick another fellow in the study along with us. You must be off your rocker!"

"Silly ass!" commented Herries.

"Weally, Hewwies——"

"Nothing doing!" said Blake. "Go home and think it out again. Besides, I don't suppose any fellow is keen on changing into this study, and crowding us out. What rot!"

"A new fellow——"

"Well, of all the cheek, to think of planting a new fellow here!" exclaimed Blake, in great exasperation. "There's No. 2, with only Trimble and Mellish in it. There's No. 3, with only Bates and Macdonald. Let the new fellow go there!"

"But——"

"Rot!" said three voices together.

"But this new fellow is somethin' wathah special!" pleaded Arthur Augustus. "I am alludin' to Buntah——"

"Bunter?"

"Walter Buntah, you know—the chap we met at Gweyfwiahs. You wemembah him—a cousin of that fat boundah Billy Buntah."

"I remember him," said Blake. "We were a man short, owing to Tom Merry playing a Shell duffer when he might have had a Fourth Form chap—and Wally Bunter was there, and he played for us."

"And kicked the winnin' goal, deah boy!" said Arthur Augustus persuasively.

"I dare say somebody else would have kicked it if he hadn't," said Blake. "Besides he didn't kick it—he headed it."

"It comes to the same thing, deah boy."

"I dare say it does; but that's no reason why he should come into this study when he comes to St. Jim's. You can ask him to tea if you like!" added Blake liberally.

"If he brings his own rations," said Digby thoughtfully.

Arthur Augustus paused. He polished his eyeglass carefully, jammed it into his noble eye, and resumed the attack.

"Wally Buntah is a weally good sort, Blake, and he did me a gweat service while we were at Gweyfwiahs. I was set on by a pair of young wuffians while I was out walkin', an' they were goin' to stick me in a ditch, an' wuin my clobbah. Wally Buntah wushed to the wescue."

"And saved your clobber at the risk of his life?" grinned Herries.

"He saved my clobbah, at all events. It was a genewous action. We became gweat fwiends."

"No reason why you shouldn't be friends; but you're not going to plant your new friends on your old pals," said Blake. "Five in a study is too much of a good thing. No takers!"

"He is a wippin' footballah——"

"We don't play footer in the study."

"He will be vewy useful in the team against the New House," said D'Arcy. "We have agweed that we are goin' to give the New House the kybosh at footah this season. Young Buntah will help."

"He can help without digging in this study."

"The New House would be glad to bag him, to play for their wotten old show," said D'Arcy. "It is weally a stwoke of luck for us that he is goin' to be a School House chap."

"Room for him in the School House without invading this study," answered Jack Blake inexorably.

Herries and Digby nodded assent. They were prepared to be quite cordial to the new fellow at St. Jim's.

True, they did not think much of Billy Bunter of Greyfriars; but they were ready to believe that his cousin Wally was the real white article, so to speak.

But they were not willing to extend hospitality to the point of being crowded in their study by a new-comer. Four was enough; indeed, Blake had remarked that what with Gussy's toppers, and Herries' boots, four was too large an allowance.

Certainly there was no room for five. Arthur Augustus, in his desire to be obliging to the new fellow, was really not displaying his usual tact and judgment.

The swell of St. Jim's surveyed his inflexible study-mates through his celebrated monocle more in sorrow than in anger.

"Then you wefuse to have my fwiend Wally in the studay?" he asked.

"I'd as soon have your young brother Wally—and that's saying quite a lot," replied Blake. "These Wallies are a nuisance."

"Wats!"

"Let it go at that!" said Blake. "Now, speaking of the House match next Saturday, we've got to persuade Tom Merry, somehow, to put in enough of the Fourth. We want to make a sure thing of it."

"Yaas; but about young Buntah——"

"Give us a rest, old chap! We're pretty certain to beat Figgins & Co., anyway," continued Blake. "They can't really make up an eleven to stand against us. But if Tom Merry persists in playing a crowd of the Shell——"

"About Buntah——"

"Give Bunter a rest!" roared Blake.

"I wefuse to give Buntah a west, Blake," answered Arthur Augustus firmly. "I weally think it is up to us to invite him to dig in this studay, and I am goin' to persuade you somehow to agwee."

Blake glared at his noble chum. Gussy was displaying once more the firmness which his chums likened unto the obstinacy of a mule.

"That means that you're going to wag your jaw till you've talked us silly?" inquired Blake.

"I wegard that as a beastlay way of puttin' it, Blake; but I am certainly not goin' to let the mattah dwop. I wegard it as bein' up to us. Now, about young Buntah——"

"Will you let Bunter drop?"

"Certainly not!"

"Well," said Blake, "you won't persuade us, but we shall persuade you. If you say Bunter once more—only once, mind—your head goes into the cinders!"

"Good egg!" said Dig and Herries.

"Weally, Blake, I am bound to mention Buntah, as—— Yawooooh!"

"That does it!"

Arthur Augustus' chums seemed fed up with the subject of Bunter. They jumped at Gussy as if moved by the same spring. Arthur Augustus leaped for the door, but three pairs of hands yanked him back. The next moment his noble head was exploring the fender.

"Yawooh!" roared Arthur Augustus, struggling frantically. "You howwid wottahs! Yawooh! Welease me!"

"Will you dry up on Bunter?"

"Ow! No! Yooop! Leggo! Oh deah! Bai Jove! Ow!"

"Rub his head in the cinders," said Blake. "Rake out some more ashes for him, Dig! Lucky for him the fire's not alight!"

"Gwoogh! Yooop!"

"Will you let Bunter drop?" grinned Blake.

"Gwoogh! No! Yaas! Yaas, wathah! Oh, cwumbs!"

Arthur Augustus scrambled away, his noble head of hair streaming ashes. He shook his fist at his grinning studymates.

"You uttah wottahs!" he roared.

"About the House-match——"

"I have a gweat mind to give you a feahful thwashin' all wound——"

"We'd better point out to Tom Merry that he can't do better than play, say, eight or nine of the Fourth. That leaves two or three places for the Shell; quite enough, in my opinion."

"You feahful wuffians——"

"Hallo, there's Gussy still wagging his chin! Collar him, and we'll put his head into the coal-locker next!"

But Arthur Augustus did not wait for the coal-locker. As his chums started towards him he hastily retired from Study No. 6, and the door of that celebrated apartment closed with a bang.

Blake & Co. grinned, and resumed the interesting football discussion which had been interrupted by the mention of Wally Bunter. It appeared to be settled that Wally would not become an occupant of Study No. 6 in the Fourth!

CHAPTER 2.

Kerr Thinks It Out!

"ANYHOW, we're jolly strong in goal!"

George Figgins made that pronouncement in his study in the New House at tea.

His chums, Kerr and Wynn, nodded assent.

Fatty Wynn, especially, had no doubt on the point. For Fatty Wynn was goalkeeper for the New House Junior Eleven.

"They can't dig up a goalie anything like ours," went on Figgins. "That's one comfort. Mind you're at the top of your form on Saturday, Fatty!"

"Rely on me!" said Fatty Wynn. "Pass the pilchards, old chap!"

"Of course," went on Figgins reflectively, "taking it all in all, we're better footballers in this House than they are in the School House."

"Hear, hear!" smiled Kerr.

"I don't think there's any getting around that," said Figgins.

"I say, Figgy——"

"I suppose you agree with me, Fatty?"

"Yes; but——"

"But what?"

"You haven't passed the pilchards!"

"Oh, bother!" grunted Figgins. "I'm talking about the House match, not about dashed pilchards!"

"You pass them, Kerr, old chap," said Fatty Wynn. "Don't you fellows think I'm greedy! I'm simply thinking of keeping myself in form for the House match. You can't do better than lay a solid foundation."

"A week ahead?" grinned Kerr.

"Well, suppose a chap gets run down, how's he going to keep goal?" asked Fatty Wynn warmly. "I think that Figgins, as skipper, ought to be grateful to me for thinking so much about keeping in form for the match."

"Oh, rats!" said Figgins ungratefully. "As I was saying, we're better footballers than they are; but where the rub comes in is this—they're a bigger House, and have more men to pick from. We're limited in numbers."

"Little but good!" suggested Kerr.

"That's it! And I don't deny," said Figgins, "that I wish we were a bit stronger in the front line."

Kerr looked thoughtful.

"They have all the luck, really," went on Figgins. "There's a new chap coming to St. Jim's on Monday, who's a regular corker on the footer-field. You remember that chap, Wally Bunter, at Greyfriars—he played for our side when we were there. He's coming on Monday, and I hear that he's going into the School House. If he were coming into the New House I'd be glad to play him next Saturday. It's really too bad!"

"I think——" began Fatty Wynn.

Figgins turned to his plump chum.

"If you've got a suggestion to make, Fatty, go ahead!" he remarked cordially.

"Well, I have, Figgy, if you won't jump on a chap."

"I like that!" exclaimed Figgins. "Haven't I asked you both for advice every time I make up a team? Why, you fat bounder, you know I'm always willing to listen to advice, and act on it, too! What do you think, then?"

"Well, I really think——"

"Go ahead!"

"I think we might as well have the sausages for tea——"

"What?"

"What's the good of keeping them for supper?" said Fatty Wynn argumentatively. "Lots of things may happen before supper-time. Let's have them to finish up tea, and chance it."

Figgins glared at Fatty Wynn, while Kerr chuckled.

"You—you—you're thinking about sosses!" roared Figgins. "I thought you were going to make suggestion about the eleven!"

"Blessed if you're not always jawing footer, Figgy! Now, about those sosses. If we have them for tea——"

"Dry up!" howled Figgins. "Here am I, trying to make up a team to beat Tom Merry's crowd, and you think of nothing but pilchards and sosses, and Kerr sits like a graven image without saying a word!"

"I've been thinking," said Kerr mildly.

"Well, what's the good of thinking if nothing comes of it?" demanded Figgins gruffly.

"Something may come of it, old top," said Kerr placably. "I've been thinking about that new kid, Bunter."

"No good thinking about him—he's going into the School House. He'll play against us next Saturday most likely."

"It's certain he's going into the School House?" asked Kerr.

"D'Arcy says so; he knows pretty well, I think. They made friends when we were over at Greyfriars for the match."

"I suppose the chap doesn't know much about this school," remarked Kerr. "He can't know that New House is cock house of St. Jim's, or he'd try to squeeze in here. From what I've seen and heard of him he's a really good sort, and plays a splendid game of footer, though he's fat as Fatty——"

"Fatter!" grunted Fatty Wynn.

"Fatter!" agreed Kerr amiably. "But he's a topping sort, and the New House is just the place for him. Why shouldn't he change his mind and come into the New House? We could bag him for our eleven then."

Figgins stared.

"I suppose his people have arranged his House for him," he answered.

"Yes; but if he specially wanted to come into this House his people couldn't object, I should think. Suppose he settled down here, and wrote his pater a very earnest letter, saying how much nicer it was in the New House. That would work the oracle, I think."

"But he wouldn't!"

"He might! He's coming on Monday," said Kerr. "Suppose he was met somewhere on the way here, and persuaded. Three very nice fellows might meet him, with their best manners on—us, for example——"

"May come during lesson-time," said Figgins doubtfully.

"Then we should have to get off lessons somehow. We'll find that out. We'll talk to him all the way to St. Jim's. We'll put it to him nicely. He's a bit of a gormandiser, I believe, like his cousin. Well, we'll spin him a yarn about this House being a land flowing with milk and honey, and so forth. We'll get something decent to feed him on, as an example. We'll make him as happy as a Hun with a dish of sauer-kraut, and swear eternal friendship. And we'll bag him for this House, and spring him on Tom Merry next Saturday at footer—what?"

Figgins grinned.

"It might work!" he said.

"Jolly good idea!" said Fatty Wynn heartily. "Especially the idea of standing him a feed. That's bound to touch any fellow's heart if he's at all decent!"

"You remember when that fat bounder Trimble came," said Kerr. "They didn't want him in the School House, and they tried to plant him on us, and very nearly succeeded. Well, one good turn deserves another; we'll bag Bunter, by way of a Roland for an Oliver."

"Kerr, old man, I give in!" said Figgins. "You've really got a brain on you. That chap kicked the winning goal for us at Greyfriars, playing as a raw recruit. After a week's practice in our front line he would be worth no end to us. It's a go!"

"After all, he's bound to prefer this House when he knows what's what," said Kerr.

"Yes, rather!"

"We'll even let him share this study with us, if he likes!"

"Oh!"

"I—I say!" murmured Fatty Wynn, in dismay. "If he's got an appetite anything like his cousin Billy's, I'd rather he was in some other study. We're on rations, you know."

"Rats!"

"It's a go!" said Figgins, rubbing his hands, and quite unheeding Fatty Wynn and his misgivings. "If he'll come, we'll bag him. And why shouldn't he? It's an honour to him to be asked into the New House. We've got to find out exactly when he's coming, and wangle to met him somewhere."

"We can get that out of Tom Merry."

"Mind he doesn't suspect what you're up to, Kerr!" exclaimed Figgins, in alarm. "If those bounders smell a rat——"

"They won't!" said Kerr, rising from the table. "I'll cut across and see Tom Merry now. Nothing like striking the iron while it's hot."

And George Francis Kerr left the study and the New House, and strolled across the quadrangle in the dusk.

Figgins remained in thought for some moments, and Fatty Wynn watched him with a peculiar expression on his face.

Figgins strolled out of the study at last; and then Fatty Wynn jumped up.

A minute later there was an appetising savour of frying sausages in the study.

The question of the footer eleven for the House match was not quite settled yet, but the more pressing question of the sosses was settled beyond recall.

CHAPTER 3.

Tact!

TOM MERRY came into his study on the Shell passage in the School House with a slight frown upon his sunny face.

Manners and Lowther looked at him inquiringly.

"Anything doing?" asked Lowther.

"No."

"Rotten!" remarked Manners.

"Linton is a hard old case!" growled Tom Merry. "For some weird and mysterious reason he sticks Form work before everything else."

"Perhaps because he's a Form-master!" suggested Monty Lowther. "These Form-masters are trying."

"Br-r-r-r! I pointed out to him that Wally Bunter is coming along with his tutor man on Monday afternoon, when we shall be at lessons. I said as persuasively as I could that, in the circumstances, we should like to meet him at the station. I said it would be polite."

"And what did Linton say?"

There was a snort from the captain of the Shell.

"He said that if I could meet Bunter at the station without infringing upon the time devoted to Form work I was at liberty to do so."

Lowther grinned.

"Linton's a dry old bird!" he remarked. "He was pulling your leg, Thomas."

"I suppose he was," agreed Tom. "But I didn't give in at that. I mentioned that Wally Bunter was a total stranger in the locality, and might miss his way to St. Jim's."

"And he said——"

"He asked if Bunter was dumb."

"Dumb!" repeated Manners and Lowther.

"Yes. He said that unless Bunter was dumb he would doubtless be able to inquire his way to the school."

"Ha, ha, ha!"

Tom Merry joined in the laugh. Mr. Linton, the master of the Shell, was humorous in his dry way, and he had received Tom Merry's modest request in a mildly sarcastic humour.

"We sha'n't get off lessons on Monday afternoon, then," said Lowther. "I dare say old Linton guessed that we were thinking more about that than about Bunter."

"Bet you he did!" grinned Manners. "He's a downy old bird. It's rotten, though. I was going to take my camera out."

"But I'd really have liked to show Bunter some attention," said Tom. "Of course, we sha'n't see much of the kid, as he's going into the Fourth. But I liked him at Greyfriars, when we met him there, and I'd like to give him a welcome here. But Linton's a hard-shell old Hun. He doesn't see it."

"Well, I never really expected him to," said Lowther. "It was only a chance. Lathom may be a bit more amenable to reason, and some of the Fourth may get off to meet Bunter."

There was a tap at the half-open door and Kerr of the Fourth came in.

The Terrible Three nodded to him cheerily.

Although the School House and New House juniors were deadly rivals, they managed to keep on very good terms with one another when there was not a House row going on.

"Trot in, old scout!" said Tom Merry. "We were just talking about that chap Bunter. You remember meeting him?"

"Yes; ripping chap," said Kerr. "Not very like that cousin of his."

"Well, they're as alike as two peas to look at," said Tom. "Blest if I could tell t'other from which! But they're not alike in anything else. I've just asked Linton to let us off on Monday to meet him at Wayland, and Linton has been giving me some of his sarc."

"I was going to speak about him," said Kerr blandly. "It would be only civil to show him some attention. Pity you fellows can't get off—a great pity! Some of us in the Fourth might manage it. Is he coming while lessons are on, then?"

"Yes. I've asked Gussy, who seems to know all about it. He's getting to Wayland by the three train on Monday afternoon," said Tom unsuspiciously.

"Coming alone?" asked Kerr carelessly.

"Oh, no; there's a tutor wallah with him, a chap named Shinbones or something——"

"Slimson," said Manners.

"That's it, Slimson. It seems that this chap Wally Bunter hasn't been to a public school before, and he's been prepared by a tutor for the Fourth here. His father's on war work somewhere, and the tutor man is bringing him to St. Jim's, this side up, with care."

"Well, he ought to be met at the station," said Kerr decidedly. "It's up to us to be a bit civil, as he played for our side at Greyfriars when we met him there."

"Just what I was thinking."

"I was going to take my camera!" said Manners regretfully.

"Lathom is a good little beast," remarked Kerr thoughtfully. "I don't see why he shouldn't give permission. If a fellow with some tact pitched it to him nicely——"

"You try!" said Tom, smiling. "You've got lots of tact. Of course, he ought to be met by School House chaps, as he's coming into this House."

"He certainly ought to be met by fellows belonging to the House he's going to belong to," assented Kerr. "That's settled."

"Well, try it on Lathom," said Tom.

"I will!"

Kerr left the study, having thus easily discovered what he had come to learn. He made his way at once to Mr. Lathom's study. The master of the Fourth had his quarters in the School House.

The Terrible Three, having been disappointed in that little scheme for getting an extra half-holiday on Monday, settled down to prep, and dismissed Wally Bunter from their minds; while Kerr of the Fourth proceeded to interview his Form-master.

"Come in!" said Mr. Lathom's mild voice, as the Scottish junior tapped at his study door.

Kerr entered, and the Fourth Form-master blinked at him kindly over his spectacles. Kerr was persona grata there; he was one of the keenest pupils and hardest workers in Mr. Lathom's Form, and a Form-master naturally liked a pupil who liked study for its own sake, and did not merely grind through it as a painful duty. Not that Kerr was a swot merely; he played as hard as he worked, and he was one of the best men in the New House eleven.

"If you please, sir——" began Kerr meekly.

"Yes, my boy," said Mr. Lathom benevolently.

"I—I was going to ask you a favour, sir," said Kerr, with becoming hesitation.

"Proceed, Kerr."

"There's a new fellow coming to St. Jim's on Monday afternoon, sir——"

"Yes, Walter Bunter; he will be your Form-fellow, Kerr," said Mr. Lathom, with a nod.

"I happen to know him, sir; some of us met him at Greyfriars, where he was visiting his cousin, while we were there for a football match. He's a very good fellow, sir."

"Indeed!" said Mr. Lathom, rather puzzled.

"We—we thought, sir," said Kerr submissively, "that as he's a—a new-comer we——"

"A new boy is naturally a new-comer, Kerr."

"Ye-e-es, quite so, sir—yes, of course! But—as—I mean, if you would give us permission, sir, we should like to meet him at the station on Monday afternoon."

"I am afraid that that will be impossible, Kerr, as he arrives while lessons are in progress."

"Ahem! We—we thought, sir, that, under the—the circumstances——"

"I was not aware that there were any unusual circumstances in connection with this new boy, Kerr."

"There—there are, sir," murmured Kerr. "He's a really splendid chap, and —and he has worked in an office as a clerk or something. It's possible, sir, that he may feel a little—a little diffident, thinking perhaps that some fellow might be inclined to be a bit snobbish on account of his having been at work as a boy. If some of us met him at the station in a friendly way, it would put him at his ease to begin with. Don't you think so, sir?"

Mr. Lathom beamed at Kerr over his spectacles.

"My dear lad, that is very, very thoughtful of you!" he exclaimed.

Kerr coloured a little. But, in fact, Kerr was quite sincere in what he said. That consideration had been in his mind before he had thought of bagging Wally Bunter for the New House Junior Eleven. There were fellows at St. Jim's, like Racke and Crooke of the Shell, and Trimble and Chowle of the Fourth, who were quite likely to display snobbishness towards Wally Bunter, and make him uncomfortable if they could; and if Wally's first experience of St. Jim's happened to be with Racke & Co., certainly he was likely to be made to feel discomfort. Kerr was very thoughtful for others, and he really deserved Mr. Lathom's commendation.

It was evident that he had gained his point.

"You wish to be excused lessons on Monday afternoon, then, is that it?" asked the Form-master.

"Yes, sir, if you would let Figgins and Wynn and myself go—ahem!——"

Mr. Lathom looked thoughtful for a moment.

"Very well," he said. "It is certainly very thoughtful of you, Kerr; and you are so conscientious a pupil that I cannot suspect you of wishing to avoid Form-work. I will grant leave to the three of you for Monday afternoon."

"Thank you, sir!" said Kerr, delighted.

"Not at all, my boy," said Mr. Lathom graciously.

And Kerr left the study in a mood of great satisfaction, and returned to the New House with his good news. He found George Figgins waiting for him in the doorway, and he imparted his news, which made Figgins chortle with satisfaction, too. Then they went up to the study to inform Fatty Wynn.

They found that plump youth reclining in the armchair, with a very shiny look on his face. There was a scent of recent cooking in the room, and half a sausage lay on a plate. It was all that remained.

"We've got leave to meet Bunter on Monday, Fatty!" announced Figgins.

"Oh!"

"All three of us!"

"Ow!"

"And we're going to bag him."

"Grooogh!"

"What on earth's the matter with the image?" asked Figgins.

"Gurrrg!"

"He's bolted the sosses!" exclaimed Kerr wrathfully.

"Not all the lot, surely?" said Figgins, aghast. "My only hat! No wonder he looks like a prize porker!"

"Groogh!"

"Is this how you keep fit for footer?" roared Figgins.

"I—I was so jolly hungry!" moaned Fatty Wynn. "There's n-n-nothing like laying a s-s-solid foundation. I—I get so jolly hungry at this time of the year. Ow! I—I never meant to bag the lot! I just went on without noticing them. Groogh! I—I think perhaps I've overdone it. Ow!"

"I think perhaps you have!" grunted Figgins. "And I think you're jolly well going to be bumped for overdoing it, too!"

"Ow! D-d-don't touch me!" gasped Fatty Wynn. "D-d-don't touch me! I—I say, I—I wish I'd left the last three, I do really! Ow!"

Fatty Wynn was left unbumped; he was evidently not in a state for it. His chums left him to his sufferings. When they came up later to prep, they expected to find Fatty Wynn pale and worn and languid. But they didn't. As they came into the study, his first remark was:

"I say, Figgins, what are we going to have for supper?"

"Supper!" yelled Figgins.

"Yes. There's no sosses now. What are we going to have?"

Figgins stared at him a moment, and then he said:

"I know what you're going to have, Fatty; you're going to have that bumping! That's what you want, and what you're going to get!"

"I—I say! Here, hold on! Leggo! Yoooop!"

Bump!

CHAPTER 4.

The Wrong Bunter.

BILLY BUNTER sat in the corner of the railway-carriage and grunted. His fat face expressed discontent.

In the opposite seat was Mr. Slimson, the tutor, and they had the carriage to themselves on the train that was running on to Wayland Junction.

Mr. Slimson was perusing a pocket edition of Horace, from which he glanced across at Bunter occasionally with disapproval.

He was not pleased with Bunter, and Bunter was not pleased with him.

Mr. Slimson was a gentleman of great attainments in the scholastic line, and he was accustomed to the work of cramming hapless youths, and he had found Wally Bunter a very apt and bright pupil, and his work had been unusually easy up to the time that Wally visited his cousin Billy at Greyfriars School.

From that time Mr. Slimson's task had not been an easy or a pleasant one.

What had come over his pupil he did not know, but he was only too painfully aware that there was a great difference.

Walter Bunter was being sent to St. Jim's by his former employer, Mr. Penman, of Canterbury; a reward for the courage Wally had shown in defeating the designs of burglars who had broken into his office. Wally had visited Greyfriars full of the good news, to tell his cousin Billy. And Billy Bunter had then been struck with the tremendous idea he was now carrying out.

Unlike as the cousins were in nature, in appearance they were as alike as two peas from the same pod. Only Billy's spectacles distinguished him from Wally.

Billy was in hot water at Greyfriars in many ways. He had earned the wrath of his Form-master for slacking; he had earned lines from the prefects; he owed money to nearly every member of his Form; and he had landed himself in trouble with a racing sharper owing to his desire to have a little flutter. And it seemed to Billy Bunter a tremendously good idea to change places with his cousin Wally and go to St. Jim's, leaving the hapless Wally to shoulder all the troubles he left behind at Greyfriars.

It was impossible for the trick to be detected so long as the two fat juniors kept their own counsel. And Wally, who was friendly with the Greyfriars fellows, was keen to stay there, and so he had agreed at last to Billy's remarkable suggestion.

A change of clothes was made on the way to the station, when Wally's visit at Greyfriars terminated, and the trick was done.

Wally had returned to Greyriars as Billy; Billy had left by the train as Wally.

As Wally was passing the last few days, before going to school, at his tutor's house in London, Billy had not had to meet Wally's family, though he would have done so with perfect confidence. At Mr. Slimson's house he was received without the slightest suspicion as Wally.

Mr. Slimson had noticed a change, but he never dreamed what that change really was.

Instead of a bright pupil, he found that Bunter had become excessively dense. Instead of a keen, alert fellow, he found a slow, obtuse, and short-sighted fellow, for Billy had given up his glasses to carry out the imposture. There had been a visit to an oculist, and glasses were ordered for Bunter, the professional gentleman expressing surprise that he had not been ordered glasses before.

Mr. Slimson had rather liked Wally; but after a day or two of Billy he became exceedingly anxious to land his pupil at St. Jim's and wash his hands of him. His former good opinion of Wally was quite gone now.

Indeed, the worthy tutor had confided to his wife that the boy really did not seem the same boy at all since his visit to Greyfriars, little dreaming how near to the facts his remark was.

Bunter repaid his aversion with interest. Billy Bunter hated work, and his feelings towards people who wanted him to work were Hunnish. Besides, he didn't need preparing for the Fourth Form at St. Jim's; he had been in the Remove at Greyfriars, and knew the Form-work well enough to pass. The Remove was the Lower Fourth at Greyfriars; but the standard of work was higher there, and it corresponded to the Fourth Form at St. Jim's. Bunter was quite content with his attainments, such as they were, and he was not looking for scholastic distinction, as Mr. Slimson soon found.

Mr. Slimson found other things, too. Wally had had a formidable appetite, but compared with Billy's it was as moonlight unto sunlight, as water unto wine.

Bunter scoffed everything he could lay hands on in Mr. Slimson's house. He robbed the pantry, and he haunted the precincts of the kitchen at every opportunity, like a lion seeking what he might devour.

Bunter Gets It In the Neck.
(See Chapter 9.)

Now that they were on the way to St. Jim's Mr. Slimson was looking forward with great keenness to landing his hopeful pupil, and having done with him; and so he was trying to keep good-tempered.

But Bunter was very trying. At every station he wanted to get out and scout in the buffet, and twice he had nearly lost the train. He sucked aniseed-balls, he chewed bullseyes, he produced eatables from all his pockets, and he was sticky. Mr. Slimson wondered how he could ever possibly have liked his pupil.

Mr. Slimson put away his book at last.

"Wayland is the next station, Bunter," he said.

"Is it?" grunted Bunter.

His manner was not very respectful. Unlike Wally, Billy Bunter did not see any reason for wasting respect on a "blessed tutor."

"It is!" said Mr. Slimson quietly. "Please don't suck your thumb, Bunter!"

Grunt!

"And wipe that stickiness off your mouth," said Mr. Slimson. "You must have been eating toffee again!"

"I'm hungry."

"You had a very substantial lunch, Bunter."

"That was over an hour ago."

"Bless my soul!" said Mr. Slimson.

Bunter blinked out of the window through his big spectacles, and grunted. He was more than fed up with Mr. Slimson, and anxious to get rid of him. He wondered if Arthur Augustus D'Arcy would be at the station to meet him. D'Arcy had made friends with Wally Bunter, and he had a deep aversion towards Billy; but that did not matter, as he was going to receive Billy as Wally.

Billy Bunter was looking forward to a great time at St. Jim's. Wally had made an excellent impression upon Tom Merry & Co., and Billy was going to reap the fruits of it.

"I—I say, Mr. Slimson——" began Bunter, after a pause.

"Yes?"

"I—I was expecting a postal-order before starting for school," said Bunter, blinking at him. "Somehow it didn't come. I—I suppose you could let me have the ten shillings, Mr. Slimson, and I'll send you the postal-order when it comes?"

Mr. Slimson's face was like unto that of a graven image.

"I understand that you have received your first week's allowance from Mr. Penman," he replied.

"That's gone!"

"If it has gone, Bunter, you can only have expended it upon indigestible comestibles!" said Mr. Slimson severely.

"I'm rather hard up, as it happens," said Bunter. "I don't want to arrive in my new school without a brown in my bags. Of course, I should send the postal-order on immediately!"

Mr. Slimson looked at him fixedly.

He had never been to Greyfriars, and he had never heard of Billy Bunter's celebrated postal-order, which was always expected, but never arrived.

After some thought, he extracted a ten-shilling note from his purse.

"Very well, Bunter. Take this. I shall expect to be reimbursed before the end of the week."

"To-morrow!" said Bunter. "My postal-order's sure to come to-morrow! It's from one of my titled relations, you know."

Mr. Slimson looked hard at him.

"I will give you a word of counsel before you begin at your new school, Bunter," he said quietly. "You have, I understand, worked in an office, and it is by the kindness of your late employer that you are sent to St. Jim's. This is all to your credit. It is very creditable of you to have supported yourself at so early an age, and relieved your parents, whose means are straitened. But you must not forget the facts."

"The—the facts?" murmured Bunter, suppressing a grin. Mr. Slimson's "facts" were only facts in regard to Wally Bunter, to whom he supposed he was speaking.

"You have several times," resumed Mr. Slimson, "spoken to me of your titled relations during the past few days. Now, you certainly have no titled relations, Bunter!"

"Wha-a-at?"

"I repeat that it is all to your credit that you have supported yourself at an early age, Bunter. But it is a clear proof that you do not possess the wealthy and influential connections, all on cordial terms with you, that you would claim."

"Oh!" gasped Bunter.

"I have only noticed that absurd snobbishness in you since your visit to Greyfriars. I conclude that at that school you picked up some of the ways of speaking of some more wealthy boy. This is ridiculous in a lad in your position, Bunter, and if you persist in it it is likely to bring you into ridicule in your new school. I am speakng entirely from kindness, Bunter, in order that you may not bring yourself into discredit."

Billy Bunter gave the tutor a glare that bade fair to crack his spectacles. Evidently he did not appreciate Mr. Slimson's kindness in the least.

"You have nothing to be ashamed of, unless you indulge in foolish brag, which is something to be very much ashamed of indeed," added Mr. Slimson. "I trust you will bear this in mind, Bunter."

"Well, of all the cheek!" ejaculated Bunter.

"What?"

"Cheek!" retorted Bunter independently. "Sheer cheek! That's what I call it—cheek! Neck, in fact!"

Mr. Slimson gazed at him speechlessly. He had given advice to pupils before, but he had never heard it characterised as neck before. His hand wandered to his umbrella. Billy Bunter came very near at that moment to getting what he had really been asking for ever since he had been with the tutor.

But Mr. Slimson restrained his wrath, comforted by the reflection that he would soon be rid of his hopeful pupil for good. They sat in grim silence, while the train ran on to Wayland, save for an occasional snort of indignant contempt from Bunter.

The train stopped at last.

"Wayland Junction! Change for Rylcombe and Abbotsford!"

Billy Bunter threw open the door, and, taking no heed of his elderly companion, jumped out on to the platform. Then he blinked this way and that way, in the hope of beholding the elegant figure of Arthur Augustus D'Arcy, whose best pal he was going to be at St. Jim's—perhaps!

CHAPTER 5.
No Chance for Gussy.

"WOTTEN!"

Arthur Augustus D'Arcy made that remark after dinner that day at St. Jim's. He spoke in tones of deep indignation, and several fellows kindly inquired what it was that was rotten.

"Wotten!" repeated Arthur Augustus. "I have asked Mr. Lathom for permish to meet my fwiend, Wallay Buntah, at the station. He has wefused."

"Well, Mr. Linton refused us!" said Tom Merry cheerily. "It's rotten, but there you are! Can't be helped."

"Yaas; but he has alweady given permish to othah fellows—New House boundahs!" exclaimed Arthur Augustus wrathfully. "Now, as Wallay Buntah is comin' into the School House, oughtn't he to be met by School House fellows, if at all? I appeal to evewy gentleman pwesent."

"Yes, rather!" said Blake. "I'd have been glad of an afternoon off myself."

"Hear, hear!" chimed in Herries and Dig.

They weren't specially interested in Wally Bunter, perhaps; but they would have been very glad to spend that clear, sunny afternoon outside the Form-room.

"Who's got leave?" asked Dick Julian.

"Figgins & Co. of the New House."

"Cheek!" said Roylance.

"Awful nerve!" exclaimed Manners. "Why, that bounder Kerr——"

"So that's why he was so jolly interested in the new chap the other day!" exclaimed Monty Lowther. "Why, he said himself that Bunter ought to be met by chaps from his own House!"

"The blessed spoofer!" exclaimed Tom Merry. "So those three bounders have got an afternoon off!"

"I wegard it as wotten! I was not thinkin' in the least of an aftahnoon off. I was thinkin' of Buntah. I got vewy fwiendly with him at Gweyfwiahs, and he will expect me to meet him if poss. But Mr. Lathom says he has alweady given leave for Figgins and Kerr and Wynn, an' he cannot welease the whole Form fwom lessons. I twied to point out to him that I did not constitute the whole Form, but he intewwupted me quite sharply."

"Go hon!"

"He did, weally, deah boys! Now, I wegad this as wotten. The New House boundahs are wedgin' in where they have no wight. There is only one thing to be done!" said Arthur Augustus firmly.

"And what's that?" asked Levison.

"Figgins & Co. must wesign in my favah. I wegard it as bein' up to them."

"Ha, ha, ha!"

"I see no weason whatever for laughtah! I am goin' to put it to Figgins, an' if he does not agwee I shall expwess my opinion vewy stwongly!"

"And that will do the trick, of course!" remarked Cardew of the Fourth. "Fix him with your glittering eye, you know, and——"

"Wats!"

Arthur Augustus, in great indignation, started in search of Figgins & Co. It was not till close on time for afternoon classes that he found them; and then they were on their way to the gates.

Figgins & Co. looked very cheerful, as was natural in the circumstances. Even apart from their little scheme of bagging Bunter, it was very pleasant out of doors on that clear, cold day; certainly a great improvement on the Form-room.

They smiled sweetly as Arthur Augustus bore down on them, with stately wrath in his aspect.

"Pway stop, you fellows!" began Gussy.

"Certainly, old top!" answered Figgins affably. "We're off to meet a train; but we'd risk losing it for the sake of hearing your beautiful accent! Pile in!"

"I wegard that wemark as asinine, Figgins! I undahstand that you are goin' to meet Buntah at Wayland!" said D'Arcy loftily.

"Do you?" exclaimed Figgins in astonishment.

"Yaas, wathah!"

"Well, my hat!" ejaculated George Figgins.

"Is it not the case, Figgins?"

"Oh, yes, it's the case!"

"Then I fail to see anythin' to be surpwised at in my makin' the wemark!"

"My dear man, you said you understood it!" explained Figgins. "You'll admit yourself that there's something very surprising in your understanding anything. Now, be candid!"

"You uttah ass——"

"Eh?"

"You cwass duffah——"

"Go it!"

"You—you feahful chump——"

"Ain't he eloquent?" said Figgins admiringly. "This is how he is going to pitch it at them in the House of Lords some day! But look out, Gussy; there'll be ladies in the House of Lords by the time you get there, and you'll have to use much nicer expressions. That's a tip!"

"I wegard you——"

"I say, we've got to call in at Mrs. Murphy's on the way," said Fatty Wynn anxiously. "Come on!"

"Right-ho! Walk out of the way, Gussy!"

"I wefuse to allow you to pwoceed, Figgins, until this mattah has been settled. Buntah is a School House fellow, and therefore he ought to be met by me, who am his fwiend. Therefore——"

"Ergo!" said Kerr encouragingly.

"Therefore I wequest you to wesign in my favah, an' to go to Mr. Lathom an' tell him so!"

"What a nice afternoon!" said Figgins.

"What?"

"It doesn't look like rain, does it?"

"I am not talkin' about the weathah, Figgins!"

"But I am, old scout!"

"You are delibewately beggin' the question, Figgins, an' I wefuse to weply to iwwelevant wemarks. You are not goin' to meet Buntah. I wegard you as baggin' my leave."

"He regards us as bagging his leave!" said Figgins sorrowfully. "Do you really mean that seriously, Gussy?"

"Yaas, wathah!"

"He means it seriously, you fellows! And if we bag your leave, will you regard us with terrific scorn?"

"Yaas!"

"He will regard us with terrific scorn!" said Figgins sadly. "And if you regard us with terrific scorn, Gussy, will it matter in any way?"

"Ha, ha, ha!" roared Kerr and Wynn, quite entertained by the expression on Arthur Augustus' noble countenance.

"Figgins! You—you jokin' wottah, I'll——"

"There goes the bell for classes!" said Fatty Wynn. "You'd better cut, D'Arcy!"

"I wefuse to cut——"

"Gussy!" roared Blake.

"I wepeat, Figgins——"

"You'll be late!" hinted Kerr. "Lathom will comb your hair!"

"Figgins, I wepeat——"

"Gussy!" raved Blake. "Get a move on! Do you want to be detained, you ass?"

"Undah the circs, Figgins——"

"We mustn't keep Gussy any longer, or Lathom will be wrathy with him!" said Figgins considerately. "Sit down, Gussy, and we'll go on!"

"I wefuse to sit down! I—— Yawooooh!"

Gussy refused; but his refusal did not count for much, as the three chortling New House juniors seized him and sat him down gently in the quad. Then they hurried on to the gates, leaving the swell of St. Jim's gasping.

"Gwoogh! You feahful wuffians! Yooop!"

"Gussy, you ass!" Jack Blake rushed up and helped D'Arcy to his feet, taking hold of his ear to do so. "Come on——"

"Yawooop!"

"Come on, you duffer! You're late already!"

"I wefuse to come on, Blake, until I have thwashed Figgins!"

"This way!"

"Leggo! Blake, you feahful wuffian, I—— Oh, cwumbs!"

Arthur Augustus, with a grip of iron on his arm, was rushed away to the School House. He turned up in the Fourth Form-room only a minute late; and Figgins — unthrashed — proceeded merrily on his way with Kerr and Wynn.

Arthur Augustus' noble brow wore a cloud that afternoon in class. He was indignant, and he was wrathful. He was heard to murmur several times dark hints concerning a "feahful thwashin'." Apparently something very serious was impending over the devoted head of George Figgins after lessons.

And Figgins, quite regardless of the impending storm, was proceeding cheerily on his way to Wayland with his chums, to meet Wally Bunter, as he thought, and to bag a first-rate footballer for his eleven—and, as a matter of fact, to meet Billy Bunter, and bag the worst footballer that ever muffed a kick. If he had only known! But, fortunately, he did not know! It was a case where ignorance was bliss!

CHAPTER 6.
Bagging Bunter.

"HALLO, Bunter!"

"How do you do, old scout?"

"Jolly glad to see you, Bunter, old top!"

Those three cordial remarks, fired off at once, greeted William George Bunter as he blinked round the station platform at Wayland. Three cheery juniors were waiting on the platform, and they rushed up as soon as they saw Bunter. A podgy hand was shaken thrice.

Billy Bunter blinked at Figgins & Co. He remembered them as members of Tom Merry's eleven in the Greyfriars match—Fatty Wynn especially. He understood that they had come to meet him, but he was disappointed. It was Arthur Augustus D'Arcy he wanted to see. The wealthy and elegant swell of St. Jim's was marked down, as it were, as his prey.

"Hallo!" said Bunter, rather offhandedly. "Is D'Arcy here?"

He was so accustomed, by this time, to playing the part of Wally Bunter that he almost believed he was Wally, and there was not the slightest hesitation in his manner.

"D'Arcy!" repeated Figgins. "Ahem! He—he would have come, but he wasn't able to get off lessons!"

"Rotten!" said Bunter discontentedly.

Figgins coughed.

Bunter's manner was not gracious. Figgins & Co. did not know him very well, certainly; but they had not expected Wally Bunter to act quite like this. And they were right. Wally wouldn't have acted like that.

"Blessed if I see why he couldn't get off, if you got off!" said Bunter, with a grunt. "I expected him."

"Ahem!"

Mr. Slimson had stepped from the train by this time. The St. Jim's juniors raised their caps to him respectfully. They were aware that Bunter was to be accompanied to St. Jim's by his tutor.

"We're friends of Bunter's, sir," explained Kerr. "We've come to meet him and see him to the school."

"That is very kind of you," said Mr. Slimson. "Perhaps you can direct us to the platform for Rylcombe."

"Certainly, sir! Half an hour to wait," said Fatty Wynn. "There's a buffet at this station, if you'd care to step into it."

Billy Bunter's eyes glistened behind his spectacles; but Mr. Slimson seemed impervious to the attractions of the buffet. He shook his head.

"I say, you fellows, I think I'll look in at the buffet," said Billy Bunter eagerly. "I'm famished!"

"You had better come with me at once, Bunter," said Mr. Slimson, with asperity.

Bunter looked obstinate.

"Plenty of time," he said. "I want something to eat."

"Half an hour before the train, sir," murmured Figgins.

Mr. Slimson tightened his lips.

"Very well. Follow me to the local platform in time for the train, Bunter."

"Oh, certainly!" said Bunter carelessly.

The tutor marched off towards the bridge over the line, probably glad to be rid of the Owl of Greyfriars for a time, though annoyed by Bunter's want of respect.

Bunter was glad to see him go.

"Awful crusty old stick, that blessed old fogy!" he confided to the St. Jim's juniors. "Nagging a chap all the time!"

"Hard lines!" muttered Kerr.

"I'm fed up with him," said Bunter, with a sniff. "Blessed if I see what he wanted to come to the school with me for at all! I suppose I can find my way about without him."

"I should think so," said Figgins.

"I say, you fellows, we might leave him on the platform, and get off without him," suggested Bunter. "Rather a lark to leave him mooching about the station looking for me—what?"

And he chuckled a fat chuckle at the idea.

Figgins & Co. exchanged a quick glance.

As a matter of fact, the presence of the "tutor-wallah" was rather a difficulty in their path. If Bunter arrived at St. Jim's in charge of Mr. Slimson it would not be easy to inveigle him into the New House, and land him there like a fish, so to speak.

Figgins had already been turning over in his mind the question whether there was any means of dropping the tutor en route.

Bunter's suggestion came as a way out of the difficulty.

"What a ripping idea!" said Figgins. "Jolly good wheeze, I think! After all, it won't hurt him to catch the next train."

"He, he, he!"

"Topping!" said Kerr.

"I say, you fellows, where's the buffet?"

"This way," said Fatty Wynn.

The four juniors went along the platform. Figgins relieved Bunter of the bag he carried. His box, being labelled for Rylcombe, did not need looking after.

Outside the buffet Figgins paused.

"If we're going to dodge the tutor man, we'd better hop out of the station and walk," he suggested.

"Much of a walk?" asked Bunter.

"Oh, a short cut through the wood, you know."

"Good idea, then."

"Then we'd better not stop here," suggested Figgins.

Bunter gave him a freezing look.

"I'm hungry," he answered.

"Yes, we'd better drop in, Figgy,"

urged Fatty Wynn, quite agreeing with Bunter. "I can do with a snack myself just now."

"Is there any time when you couldn't do with a snack?" grunted Figgins.

"Well, Bunter's hungry, too, you know."

Bunter settled the matter by rolling into the buffet, and the St. Jim's trio followed him. There was only a wartime display in the buffet, and Bunter gave a disparaging glance round.

But Fatty Wynn, who was well acquainted with the resources of the place, gave the orders, and Bunter was soon tucking in at a great rate. Fatty Wynn followed his example, while Figgins and Kerr looked on and waited.

After a quarter of an hour George Figgins became restive.

"The tutor man will be looking for you soon, Bunter," he remarked.

"'Nother quarter of an hour," said Bunter, glancing up at the clock.

"But he'll expect you on the local platform."

"Oh, bother him! These buns ain't bad," said Bunter. "I'll have some more."

And he had some more.

Five minutes more passed, and Fatty Wynn was ready to move; but the Owl of Greyfriars was not. He was still going strong, in the happy knowledge that Figgins & Co. were going to settle the bill.

"Look here, Mr. Slimson will be coming back for you," said Figgins at last. "We sha'n't get out of the station, Bunter, if we don't get a move on."

Bunter gave in at last. His snack had assumed, and exceeded, the proportions of a square meal, but he condescended to slide off the stool at the counter at last.

"I'm ready," he remarked.

Figgins footed the bill, after a hasty collection from Kerr and Wynn to help him out. Then they left the buffet. On the opposite platform Mr. Slimson was seen, and he waved his umbrella across at Bunter.

"Bunter, make haste!" he called out across the line. "The train is due in a few minutes."

"I'm coming!" called back Bunter.

He rolled along the platform with the three St. Jim's juniors, but not in the direction of the bridge. Mr. Slimson called out again.

"That is not the way, Bunter. Cross by the bridge. Bless my soul! Bunter! Bunter!"

Bunter & Co. disappeared among a crowd of passengers, and Mr. Slimson did not see the Owl again.

Figgins & Co. emerged from the station with the prize, and started walking at a good rate, fearful of seeing the tutor dodge out of the station in pursuit.

Fortunately, Mr. Slimson had no suspicion that Bunter had left the station, with the amiable intention of leaving him stranded, and he waited on the local platform, with growing anxiety and impatience, till the local train came in. The train came, but Bunter did not. While Mr. Slimson fumed, Bunter was rolling out of Wayland with Figgins & Co., and starting on the walk to St. Jim's through the wood.

CHAPTER 7.

Bunter Makes Up His Mind.

BILLY BUNTER'S fat face wore an expression of satisfaction now.

He had satisfied—or almost satisfied—his unearthly appetite, and it had not cost him anything, which was all to the good. And he had left Mr. Slimson stranded.

He cordially disliked Mr. Slimson, and he was much entertained at the idea of the unhappy tutor searching up and down the station for a fellow who was not there.

He chuckled several times as they started through the wood.

"When's the next train to Rylcombe, you fellows?" he asked.

"An hour," said Kerr.

"He, he, he! That old bounder will have to wait, then."

"Ahem! I suppose so."

"Serve him jolly well right!" said Bunter.

"H'm!"

Figgins & Co., to tell the truth, were rather remorseful about the trick that was being played on Mr. Slimson. It was only because the success of their little scheme demanded it that they had made a sacrifice of the unoffending gentleman. They were far from sharing Bunter's satisfaction, and they did not sympathise with it.

"Find that bag heavy, old scout?" asked Bunter, as Figgins changed it from one hand to the other.

"Nunno! Not very."

"There's some tommy in it," said Bunter. "I bagged a cold chicken last night."

"D-d-did did you?"

"Yes. And you should have heard Mrs. Slimson after it this morning," grinned Bunter. "She couldn't guess what had become of it."

"Oh!"

"There's a cake, too," said Bunter. "A jolly good cake! Mrs. Slimson could make cakes. I'll say that for her, though she was rather a cat."

"Nice of her to give you a cake, anyway," remarked Fatty Wynn. "That's what I call a real womanly action."

Bunter chuckled.

"He, he! She didn't give it to me; I bagged it."

"Oh!"

"I felt entitled to bag anything I could, you see," explained Bunter. "I never had enough to eat at Slimson's show. If he takes in pupils for cramming, he ought to feed them, oughtn't he?"

"Certainly!" said Fatty Wynn warmly.

"What's a crammer if he doesn't cram?" asked Kerr.

"I never had enough to eat at Greyfriars, either," said Bunter incautiously. "I hope it's better at St. Jim's."

"At—at Greyfriars!" repeated Figgins. Did you stay long at Greyfriars?"

"Oh! Ah! Ahem! I—I mean my—my visit there," stammered Bunter.

"I see."

"I'm a bit anxious about the feeding at St. Jim's," went on Bunter. "What is it like, you fellows?"

Figgins & Co. smiled at one another. This was an opening.

"Well, that depends a good deal on the House you enter," said Kerr. "In the New House we rub along all right. But I've heard Trimble, of the School House, say that he's half starved."

Bunter looked alarmed.

"I—I say, you fellows, I'm booked for the School House!" he exclaimed. "That's rather rotten. Are you New House?"

"Yes, rather!" said Figgins, with proud emphasis.

"And they feed you well?"

"Quite as much as we want," said Kerr.

"I wish I'd been put down for the New House, then," grunted Bunter. "I was glad it was School House, because my old pal Gussy is there. But I suppose I could chum with D'Arcy just the same if I was in the other House."

"Quite easily," said Figgins. "Is D'Arcy an old friend of yours?"

"Bosom pals," said Bunter.

"Well, you'd see as much of him as you wanted to if you were in our House. Speaking as a friend," said Figgins solemnly, "I should advise you to get into the New House if you could."

"You see, it's the cock house of St. Jim's," explained Kerr. "There's a certain amount of distinction in belonging to the New House."

"My hat!" said Bunter. "Isn't the New House the place the other chaps speak of as an old casual ward?"

"Ahem!"

"I heard Lowther speaking about it at Greyfriars; he was arguing with a chap named Redfern, I think," said Bunter. "He said the New House was a home for idiots."

"Oh!"

"That—that was only School House swank," said Kerr. "Poor old Lowther is School House, and he pretends to like it—they all do. But the New House is IT. F'rinstance, we practically win all the footer matches for the school, and in House matches we walk all over that crowd."

"We'd like you to play in the Junior House Eleven, if you belonged to our House, Bunter," remarked Figgins. "Of course, a new chap never is given his cap for the eleven; but we'd make an exception in your favour."

Bunter nodded.

"I expect that, of course," he said. "A footballer like me would make the fortune of any junior side."

"Oh!"

"Rather hard cheese on Tom Merry's lot, though," grinned Bunter. "They'll be beaten to the wide if I play against them."

"Oh!" murmured Figgins again.

He was puzzled.

Conceit, as he knew very well, was not usually an attribute of a really good player; and on Bunter's words alone he would have set down the fat junior as a pretentious ass. But he remembered how he had seen Wally Bunter play in the match at Greyfriars, and his play had been simply first class. Naturally he was puzzled.

"Will Gussy be playing for the School House?" asked Bunter.

"Yes; he generally plays in House matches."

"H'm! I don't know whether I could agree to playing against my old pal Gussy, and putting the kybosh on him," said Bunter thoughtfully.

"D'Arcy wouldn't mind—he's a real sportsman."

"But, of course, the grub question comes first. I'm jolly well not going to be starved, I know that! Who's this Trimble you spoke of?"

"A School House chap," said Figgins. "I've certainly heard him say a dozen times that he's half starved."

"Ever heard a fellow in your House say so?"

"Never!"

"We often have little feeds in the study," remarked Kerr. "Wynn here is a topping cook. You should see the sosses he turns out!"

Bunter's eyes glistened behind his spectacles.

Those spectacles had attracted the notice of the St. Jim's juniors, as they remembered that Wally Bunter had not worn glasses like his cousin. But they had made no remark on the subject, from motives of politeness. It was easy enough to conclude that Wally was taking after his cousin in the matter of defective sight.

"Sosses!" said Bunter. "I'm rather fond of sosses."

"My dear chap, you can't do better than come into the New House," said Figgins. "A letter to your people will be enough——"

"Oh, that's all right; they wouldn't care either way!" said Bunter carelessly. "Never mind them. Do you get anything over the rations in your House?"

"We don't need to," said Kerr diplomatically. "We get plenty, and plenty is enough, isn't it? Look at Wynn here! He looks as if he has enough, doesn't he?"

"He does, and no mistake," said Bunter. "He's fat!"

Fatty Wynn breathed hard. He was not so fat as Bunter, at all events. But he made no remark. It was no time to tell Bunter what he thought of his manners.

"I suppose I could come into the New House if I liked," said Bunter thoughtfully. "In fact, I think I shall. What sort of a dinner do you get?"

"Well," said Kerr, "I don't know whether you care for sirloins——"

"Yes, rather!"

"And steak puddings——"

"Oh, good!"

"And puddings and pies and preserved fruits——"

"Phew!" gasped Bunter.

"And a Housemaster who keeps on urging you to take another helping," said Kerr recklessly.

"My dear chap, I'm coming into the New House!" gasped Bunter. "Not another word—I'm your man!"

And so it was settled.

What Bunter was likely to think the next day, when Kerr's attractive picture was put to the test, was another matter; by that time he would be installed in the New House.

Kerr, certainly, had not said that all those nice things were to be obtained in the New House; but that was the impression Bunter received from his remarks, and it made his mouth water.

He even quickened his pace a little, as if anxious to get to the delightful quarter where there were sirloins and steak puddings, and pies and preserved fruits galore, and a Housemaster who was so considerate as to urge fellows to take fresh helpings.

Figgins & Co. smiled serenely. They had bagged their game!

Fortunately, they were not aware yet of the variety of game they had bagged.

CHAPTER 8.
A Pig in Clover.

"HALLO! That merchant looks rather excited!" remarked Tom Merry.

The Terrible Three of the Shell were strolling in the quad after lessons, when a gentleman entered at the gates; no other than Mr. Slimson.

If he did not look excited, he certainly looked disturbed and angry.

He came along with great strides; but he stopped as he saw the Terrible Three, and spoke to them.

"Can you tell me whether a boy named Bunter has arrived here this afternoon?" he asked.

"Bunter!" said Tom Merry "I know he's expected; but I don't know if he's come; we're only just out of the Form-room."

"He was in my charge," said Mr. Slimson. "Somehow, he disappeared at Wayland Station. He must surely have come on to the school. There were three boys with him from this school, who met him at the station."

"I know them," said Tom. "They belong to the New House. I'll cut in and see if they brought Bunter here, if you like, sir."

"Thank you very much!" said Mr. Slimson. "I am most anxious about the boy. He is so stupid that he may have lost himself somewhere."

Tom Merry ran into the New House, leaving Mr. Slimson with Manners and Lowther

He hurried up to Figgins' study, to discover whether the Co. were there, rather puzzled by the tutor's story of the happening at Wayland.

There was a savoury smell proceeding from Figgins' study, though it was not yet tea-time. Tom Merry tapped at the door and looked in.

Figgins & Co. were there with their guest.

They had arrived at St. Jim's before lessons were over, and had entered the New House quite unobserved

Bunter was landed in Figgins' study, which was the first step in the carrying out of the little scheme.

The fat junior was seated at the table, with a plate of sausages and chips before him.

It was necessary for him to see the Housemaster as soon as possible; but Mr. Ratcliff was in the Fifth Form-room at present, and could not be seen till he returned to his quarters. Figgins & Co. were improving the shining hour by feeding Bunter. They had taken his measure pretty accurately in one respect at least, and they knew that the best way to appeal to him was through his inner Bunter.

They were doing it in great style. All the resources of the study were at the disposal of the guest. Piles of toast surrounded him, and the sosses and chips were done to a turn. Fatty Wynn, who could have cooked the head off a French chef, as Figgy put it, had done nobly, and the result was very pleasing to Bunter.

The Owl of Greyfriars was enjoying himself.

Figgins & Co. were enjoying themselves, too, in their own way; in the satisfaction of having secured that valuable prize, and dished the School House once more.

They looked rather warlike as Tom Merry came in. To tell the truth, they had forgotten all about the unfortunate tutor stranded at Wayland Junction, and they were hoping to keep Bunter dark till his name was entered as a regular inmate of the New House, which could only be done by Mr. Ratcliff, the Housemaster.

"Oh, here you are!" exclaimed Tom Merry.

"Here we are," said Figgins, rather gruffly. "Anything wanted?"

"Yes; Bunter's wanted."

"Oh!"

"Is that Wally Bunter?" asked Tom, perplexed.

"Of course it is!"

"Oh!"

Tom Merry had wondered for a moment whether it was Billy Bunter, at sight of the big glasses.

The Owl of Greyfriars looked up with an agreeable grin.

The Lordly Bunter!
(See Chapter 11.)

"I'm the man!" he said. "Glad to see you, Tom Merry! You haven't forgotten me—what? I kicked goals for you—eh?"

"I've not forgotten you, old son!" said Tom. "I—I wasn't aware——"

"Oh, the specs," said Bunter calmly. "I found I had to have 'em, you know. Put it off as long as I could; but it had to come. Runs in the family, you know, as a matter of fact. My cousin Billy's just the same."

Tom Merry nodded.

It was not surprising that another Bunter had taken to glasses; but certainly this youth looked the living image of Billy Bunter as he remembered him.

"Well, Wally, old son, you seem to have lost your tutor at the station," said the captain of the Shell. "He's just arrived, in a state of flutter.

"Oh, old Slimson!"

"Yes; I'll tell him you've arrived all right. How did you come to miss him?" asked Tom.

Bunter chuckled.

"Left him waiting for a train, while we walked," he answered. "Never mind him. He's a silly old ass. Tell him to go and eat coke!"

"Wha-a-at?"

"No need to waste politeness on him," said Bunter. "He's only a paid tutor, you know."

"Oh!"

"He can tell the Head I've come, and take himself off," said Bunter. "Bother him! Tell him I said so."

"I don't think I could give him a message like that, Bunter," said Tom Merry quietly. "You'd better come to him, hadn't you?"

"How can I, when I'm having tea?"

"He will expect——"

"Let him expect, and be blowed!"

"But, really, Bunter——"

"Look here," said Bunter. "I'm jolly hungry—I've only had a snack at Wayland since lunch. I'm having tea, and I wouldn't leave this spread if there was an air-raid. That's flat! Bother the man!"

"B-b-but——"

Bunter settled down with knife and fork again, evidently with no intention of stirring.

"These sosses are prime," he said. "What a bit of luck that you can get sosses without coupons now! I say, Wynn, you can cook!"

"Can't I?" said Fatty Wynn, beaming.

"You ought to have the O.B.E. for it," said Bunter. "They give the O.B.E. for much lesser things."

Fatty Wynn grinned an appreciative grin. Next to eating the sosses himself, it was enjoyable to see them thoroughly enjoyed by a fellow who knew what good cooking was. He felt quite chummy towards Bunter just then.

Tom Merry stood undecided. He liked Wally Bunter; but it was only too clear that the new junior's manners left much to be desired.

"Well, what am I to say to the tutor man?" he asked at last.

"Pass the salt!" said Bunter.

"Couldn't you keep him busy a bit, while Bunter's finishing his tea?" asked Figgins. "Mr. Ratcliff will be back in a few minutes——"

"Eh? What's Mr. Ratcliff got to do with it?"

"Ahem! Ah! D-d-did I say Mr. Ratcliff?" stammered Figgins. "I—I mean that Bunter's hungry, you know, and he's simply got to finish his tea. Take the tutor man for a walk."

"I can't, you ass!"

"Take him into the School House, and tell him Bunter's coming," said Kerr.

"Well, I suppose I can do that," said Tom Merry.

And he left the study.

"I'm jolly well not going yet, though, you fellows!" said Bunter.

"No fear!" said Kerr. "The man can wait a bit."

"He's paid!" said Bunter. "Let him wait!"

"Ahem! Another cup of coffee?"

"Yes, rather!"

"Try the cake next?"

"Thanks; I'll finish the sosses first. Lots of time for the cake."

And Billy Bunter went on with his gastronomic performances, which Figgins and Kerr watched almost with awe—and even Fatty Wynn with growing amazement.

CHAPTER 9.

Bunter of the New House.

"COME in!" snapped Mr. Ratcliff.

Figgins opened the door of his Housemaster's study, and ushered William George Bunter into his presence.

Mr. Horace Ratcliff glanced at Bunter, and glanced at Figgins.

Figgy's manner was very meek. He knew that this was a matter that required tact.

"Well, Figgins?" said Mr. Ratcliff acidly. His tone generally was acid.

Figgins & Co. had warned Bunter that Mr. Ratcliff's manner was against him, and that his good qualities were not to be seen on the surface. They did not consider it judicious to add that a microscope would have been required to see his good qualities at all.

"If you please, sir, this is the new boy in the Fourth Form," said Figgins—"Walter Bunter, sir."

"I do not see why you have brought him here, Figgins."

"As he is coming into this House, sir——"

"You are mistaken, Figgins. I have not been informed that a new boy is expected in this House."

"No, sir?" exclaimed Figgins, looking surprised.

"Probably Bunter is intended for the School House," said Mr. Ratcliff. "You had better take him there."

"But—but he really is coming into this House, sir—aren't you, Bunter?"

"Certainly!" said Bunter promptly. "It's a mistake about my going into the School House, sir. I really don't know how such a mistake could have arisen—it's very extraordinary. My father—h'm!—is very particular about my being in the New House."

Mr. Ratcliff thawed a little.

"Dear me!" he said.

"I have a letter from my father to the Head, sir, specially mentioning that he desires me to be placed in the New House."

"That should certainly settle the matter," said Mr. Ratcliff. "Pray, show me the letter."

"Certainly, sir!"

Bunter began to go elaborately through his pockets.

Figgins watched him, dumbfounded. As Bunter certainly was intended for the School House, Figgins could not see how he could have had such a letter in his possession. It did not occur to Figgy's simple mind for the moment that Bunter was lying.

Bunter went through one pocket after another.

"Did you see what I did with that letter, Figgins?" he asked.

"Nunno!" stuttered Figgins.

"I read it out to you in the study, you know."

"D-d-did you?" stammered the amazed Figgins.

"I must have lost it," said Bunter. "It's very annoying. I'm very sorry indeed, sir, that I've lost my father's letter."

"It was very careless of you, Bunter!" said Mr. Ratcliff snappishly. "However, I will speak to the House-dame, and you may take up your quarters in this House for the present."

"Thank you, sir!"

"May Bunter come into our study, sir?" asked Figgins meekly. "We can make room for four."

"Certainly!"

"Perhaps you'd speak to the Head, sir," suggested Bunter. "There seems to be a mistake about my House."

"I will mention the matter to Dr. Holmes. Have you seen your Form-master yet?"

"Not yet, sir."

"You had better take Bunter to Mr. Lathom, Figgins!"

"Yes, sir."

Figgins left the study with Bunter, very pleased at the result of the visit. The matter had gone more easily than he had anticipated; partly, perhaps, because he had not anticipated barefaced lying on Bunter's part.

In the passage Bunter gave him a fat wink.

"I pulled his leg a treat—what?" he remarked.

"Did you?"

"Yes—about that letter! He, he, he!"

"You haven't got a letter from your pater?"

"Of course not!"

"You—you only pretended to have lost it?" ejaculated Figgins, understanding at last.

"He, he, he!" was Bunter's reply.

"You'd better come and see Lathom," said Figgins abruptly. He was not so pleased with his prize now as he had expected to be.

"Who's Lathom?"

"Our Form-master."

"Oh, all right!"

Figgins piloted Bunter across the quad to the School House, feeling sure of him now. There was an exclamation as he came in with him.

"Bai Jove! Heah you are, Buntah!"

Arthur Augustus D'Arcy advanced to meet his old friend of Greyfriars.

"Hallo, Gussy, old top!" exclaimed Bunter, shaking hands very heartily with the swell of St. Jim's. "Jolly glad to see you!"

"It is a gweat pleasuah to meet you heah, Wally!" said Arthur Augustus. "It appeahs that your tutah awwived without you."

"He, he, he! I stranded him at the station!"

"Oh, bai Jove!"

Tom Merry came up.

"Your tutor's in Mr. Railton's study," he said. "You'd better go in, Bunter. He's a bit ratty!"

"Bother him!" answered Bunter.

"You will have to see Wailton, Wally, to weport yourself," said Arthur Augustus. "He will give you a study heah, you know!"

Arthur Augustus would have liked to add that he wanted Bunter in Study No. 6; but Blake & Co. had already settled that matter. They were present, and they gave him significant looks.

The swell of the Fourth gave his chums a reproachful glance. He was failing to keep up the high standard of hospitality he had marked out in advance, and it was due to their objection to being crowded in No. 6.

"Bunter's got his study already!" remarked Figgins casually.

"Bai Jove! What studay, deah boy?"

"Mine!"

Arthur Augustus turned his eyeglass upon Figgins in great surprise.

"Weally, Figgins, I do not see how Buntah can share your studay, as it is in the New House!" he said.

"Quite easily," said Figgins. "Bunter's a New House chap."

"Wats!"

"Fact!" grinned Figgins. "He's reported to Ratty, and it's settled."

"Wubbish! Buntah's a School House chap!"

"Nothing of the kind!"

"Look here," exclaimed Tom Merry, "you're making a mistake, Figgins! Bunter certainly was coming into this House; I heard so from Mr. Lathom."

"Even Form-masters make mistakes sometimes!" answered Figgins cheerily. "It turns out that Bunter's booked for the New House."

"Weally, Figgins——"

"Well, ask the kid himself!" said Blake. "I suppose he knows!"

"Yaas, wathah! You are comin' into the School House, Buntah?"

The Owl of Greyfriars hesitated. It was very flattering to be sought after in this way; though, as a matter of fact, it was not he who was being sought after, but his cousin Wally. Bunter took it all to himself; and he began to doubt whether he had done so wisely as he had supposed in planting himself in the New House.

Figgins noted his expression, and he caught the Owl of Greyfriars by a fat arm.

"Come on!" he said. "You've got to see Lathom!"

"Weally, Figgins——"

"This way, Bunter!"

"I—I say, you fellows——" began Bunter.

There was a step in the passage, and Mr. Slimson's voice broke in.

"Oh, you are here, Bunter!"

Bunter blinked at him.

"Here I am!" he answered.

"You left me at the station!" exclaimed Mr. Slimson sharply.

"Did I? Sorry!"

"You deliberately left me there, while you walked to the school, leaving me to suppose that you had lost yourself!" exclaimed the tutor.

"Ahem! Not at all, sir!"

"Then why did you leave me?"

"Forgot all about you!" said Bunter coolly.

Mr. Slimson stared at him, and seemed to swallow something with difficulty. The juniors looked hard at Bunter. Arthur Augustus murmured "Bai Jove!" under his breath.

"Follow me, Bunter!" said Mr. Slimson, at last. "I will take you to your Housemaster, and wash my hands of you!"

"I've seen my Housemaster!" answered Bunter. "You needn't bother any further! The fact is, I don't want you any longer!"

"Buntah!" murmured D'Arcy, in distress.

Mr. Slimson blinked at Bunter, and then took him by the collar. His temper was failing—which was not surprising in the circumstances.

"Come!" he snapped.

And Bunter had to go. The tutor led him into Mr. Railton's study.

"This is the lad Bunter, Mr. Railton," said the tutor. "I place him in your charge; and, with your permission, I will now take my leave."

The School Housemaster gave him a rather curious look. He did not fail to note the signs of suppressed wrath in the tutor's face. He then glanced at the fat, self-satisfied face of Bunter.

"Ah! This is Bunter?" he said. "Where have you been all this time, Bunter?"

"Having my tea, sir."

"What!" exclaimed Mr. Railton. "Are you aware that Mr. Slimson has been waiting for you for upwards of half an hour?"

"Never thought about it, sir!"

"You should have thought about it, Bunter!" said Mr. Railton, frowning. "Have you never learned to treat your elders with respect?"

Bunter grunted as a suitable reply to that.

"And how comes it that you missed Mr. Slimson at the station, and left him under the impression that you were lost?" asked the Housemaster.

"I decided to walk."

"Without informing Mr. Slimson?"

"I forgot him."

"You must learn to have a better memory, Bunter, and a great deal less impertinence!" said Mr. Railton sternly, and his hand strayed to a cane.

Mr. Slimson interposed.

"Pray do not pursue the matter on my account," he said. "You will excuse me now; I have little time to spare for my train. Good-afternoon, Mr. Railton!"

Mr. Railton accompanied the tutor to the door, where he shook hands with him, and Mr. Slimson went his way. The Housemaster returned to the study, where Bunter was waiting

He fixed his eyes upon the fat junior.

"Bunter, you have treated Mr. Slimson very disrespectfully!" he said.

"Have I?" said Bunter.

"You have, boy!"

"He's paid!" said the Owl of Greyfriars.

"What?"

"He's paid for it all, you know, sir!" explained Bunter.

"Boy! I am sorry, Bunter, that your first experience here should be a caning, but you leave me no other resource," said Mr. Railton. "Such impertinence as this cannot pass unpunished! Hold out your hand!"

"Oh!" ejaculated Bunter.

He blinked at the Housemaster in alarm as Mr. Railton picked up a cane. Mr. Railton was really angry. The Owl of Greyfriars was a new experience to him, and not an agreeable one.

Bunter did not hold out his fat hand. The interview with the Housemaster had quite fixed his desire to belong to the New House; he had already taken a cordial dislike to Mr. Railton.

"You hear me, Bunter?" rapped out the School Housemaster.

Bunter backed away a step.

"Oh, really, sir!" he exclaimed. "As I don't belong to this House——"

"What?"

"I'm a New House chap!" said Bunter. "Figgins says the chaps are only punished by their own Housemasters!"

"That is the case," said Mr. Railton, looking at him. "But you are under a mistaken impression, Bunter; your name has been given me by Dr. Holmes, as an inmate of this House."

"That's a mistake, sir," said Bunter cheerfully. "I've already put down my name in the New House, and Mr. Ratcliff has given me a study there."

"Bless my soul!" said Mr. Railton, perplexed.

He laid down the cane.

"Mr. Ratcliff told me I was to go to my Form-master, sir," said Bunter, pursuing his advantage. "I'm bound to do as Mr. Ratcliff tells me, as he's my Housemaster. Can I go now, sir?"

"Figgins!" called out Mr. Railton, catching sight of the New House junior hovering outside the doorway.

"Yes, sir?" said Figgins.

"You heard what Bunter said. Are you aware——"

"Oh, yes, sir," said Figgins. "Bunter's been to Mr. Ratcliff already, sir—he's for the New House."

"A mistake has apparently been made," said Mr. Railton. "If Mr. Ratcliff has made arrangements to receive this boy in his House——"

"He has, sir."

"Very well! You may go, Bunter!"

And Bunter went.

Cadet Notes.

During the last three years the lads who have reached military age have shown themselves as a whole anxious to join the Army and do their bit. We do not believe that they needed any compulsion to bring them in; and many. we are sure, regretted that the Military Service Act prevented their joining earlier. The younger boys have been looking forward to the time when they would be called, but now that is suspended. If a boy joins the Regular Army under the new peace conditions, or the Volunteers, he has to give all his time to it and to be bound for a certain number of years. For the boys between 14 and 18 there is a great chance. They can join Cadet Corps, which are to be found in every part of the country, under the most favourable conditions. There are no whole-time workers. They attend on a few evenings in the week. The cost to them is nominal, and if, having joined up, they do not like it, they can resign. No doubt many boys would be only too pleased to get some military instruction and discipline in a way which did not interfere with their regular work. A boy can join a Cadet Corps, and then, if he finds he likes the work, he can join the Regular Forces later, knowing to a certain extent what to expect. Most of the Cadet Corps are infantry, but R.A.F. Instructional Corps are being formed, at present chiefly in the neighbourhood of London. A few corps have machine-gun companies, and in one or two places outside London there are Artillery Cadet Corps. Any boy who wants advice as to his nearest corps should write, stating his age, etc., to the C.A.V.R., Judges' Quadrangle, Law Courts, Strand, London, W.C. 2.

CHAPTER 10.
Diplomatic.

"WOTTAHS!"

Thus Arthur Augustus D'Arcy, the ornament of the Fourth Form, in the School House junior Common-room.

Arthur Augustus was wrathy.

His noble eye gleamed behind his eyeglass, and his countenance expressed the loftiest indignation; and Monty Lowther was moved to inquire what was biting him.

"Nothin' is bitin' me, Lowthah," answered Arthur Augustus. "I wegard the question as widic. I wepeat that they are wottahs!"

"Who are, dear man?" asked Manners.

"Those New House wuffians. I was goin' to give Figgins a feahful thwashin' for tweatin' me with gwoss diswespect this aftahnoon; an' I let him off because Buntah was with him, an' I did not want a wow in the pwesence of a new fellah. And what is my weward?"

"Echo answers what?" grinned Blake.

"The feahful wottahs have bagged Buntah!" continued Arthur Augustus. "That is why they went to the station to meet him! They bagged Buntah for their wascally old House!"

"There seems to have been a mistake of some sort," remarked Tom Merry.

"There was no mistake, Tom Mewwy. Those boundahs have induced Wally to change his mind an' go into the New House instead of comin' heah!"

"Oh, my hat!" ejaculated Monty Lowther. "That's what Kerr was after the other day. The bounder actually said that Bunter ought to be met by fellows belonging to his own House. They had planned it, then?"

"Yaas, wathah!"

"Well, what does it matter?" asked Herries. "If the chap prefers the New House it shows he's an ass; but it doesn't matter, that I can see."

"Wats! It mattahs a gweat deal, Hewwies. What do you think they have bagged him for?"

"Blessed if I know, unless it's to melt him down into tallow."

"Ha, ha, ha!"

"Weally, Hewwies——"

"Well, they do seem to have bagged him," said Tom Merry. "But they're welcome, so far as I can see. What did they want him for?"

"They have bagged him to spwing him on us in the House match, because he is a wipin' footballah!" said Arthur Augustus, with conviction.

"My hat!"

"Good old Gussy!" exclaimed Clive. "Gussy's hit it! They've bagged our new recruit!"

Tom Merry wrinkled his brows.

He had been rather perplexed by the happenings of that afternoon; but he saw light now. Already, in his own mind, he had assigned Wally Bunter a place in the School House Junior Eleven; and he had reflected with satisfaction what a rod in pickle he would prove for the enemy.

The case was altered now. It was the enemy who had bagged that brilliant forward. As a New House fellow, Bunter would play for Figgins' team—which, as it happened, specially needed strengthening in the front line.

"The awfully deep rotters!" exclaimed Manners indignantly. "We're not going to stand this, you fellows!"

"Wathah not!" said Arthur Augustus emphatically. "I wefuse to allow my fwiend Wally to be bagged in this unscwupulous mannah! He is entitled to the honah of belongin' to the cock house of St. Jim's—an' that is the School House. I wefuse to have him pwactically kidnapped in this way!"

"Hear, hear!"

"But he must be a silly ass to let those New House bounders pull his leg like that!" said Monty Lowther.

"The howwid boundahs have influenced him somehow, Lowthah. But we cannot take this feahful injahwy lyin' down!"

"No fear!"

Tom Merry nodded.

"I wanted Bunter for our eleven," he remarked. "We can beat the New House without him, of course; still, we're entitled to him, as he's our man. We can't have our players collared like this!"

"No feah!"

"And it's up against the School House," continued Tom. "The New House bounders will be cackling no end over dishing us in this way. We've got to get Bunter back, for the honour of the House!"

"Hear, hear!"

"Yaas, wathah! Follow me, deah boys, and we will waid the New House, and cawwy him off!" exclaimed Arthur Augustus.

"Ha, ha, ha!"

"I fail to see anythin' to cackle at in that suggestion!"

"Fathead!" said Blake politely. "Look here! What about asking him to supper in Study No. 6? Send him a polite note by a fag, and he's bound to come. Then we'll talk to him like Dutch uncles, and make him change his silly mind again."

"Yaas, wathah! That is not a bad ideah! Anyhow, I wefuse to allow the New House boundahs to bag him!"

Blake's suggestion was acted upon; and Tom Merry sat down to indite a very polite invitation to supper, addressed to W. Bunter. D'Arcy minor of the Third Form was requested to take the note over to the New House—in order not to excite suspicion on the part of Figgins & Co. D'Arcy minor cheerfully undertook the task, and scuttled over to Mr. Ratcliff's House on his errand.

Tom Merry & Co. waited with keen interest for his return.

Even fellows who were quite indifferent as to which House the new boy might join were keen on bagging him in turn from Figgins & Co. If the New House wanted him, that was a good reason why they shouldn't have him—from the point of view of their rivals in the School House.

D'Arcy minor looked into the Common-room in the New House, and, as neither Bunter nor Figgins & Co. were there, he went up to Figgins' study. There he found the new junior in company with the Co.

Bunter was talking; and Figgins & Co. were listening with expressions of great interest. Their object was to keep Bunter quiet and contented in the New House, so as to get him established there, as it were; and also to keep him out of reach of temptation from the School House side. As a matter of fact, Bunter's conversation was boring them almost to tears; but they endured it nobly.

Bunter's remarks consisted chiefly of self-satisfied references to himself and his exploits; the kind of praise, in fact, which according to the proverb is no recommendation.

He was quite charmed with Figgins & Co.; he had never been allowed to run on like this, with attentive and respectful listeners, at Greyfriars.

D'Arcy minor put his head in at the door.

"Hallo, Falstaff! Letter for you!" he called out, and he tossed Tom Merry's note to Bunter, and departed whistling.

Bunter caught the note, in some surprise, and opened it. A fat smile of satisfaction overspread his face as he read it, and Figgins & Co. regarded him with some anxiety.

"You fellows will excuse me?" said Bunter, rising.

"Ahem! Going somewhere?" asked Figgins.

"Yes; my friends in the School House have asked me to an early supper."

Figgins' eyes gleamed. He did not need telling that supper in the School House was only the bait that was being used to land this fat fish.

"But you're going to have supper with us," he urged. "Fatty's been making no end of preparations."

Bunter nodded.

"My dear man, I can do two suppers!" he answered. "I'll have supper with you when I come back."

"Oh, my hat! I—I mean——"

"Tom Merry says I'm expected at once, and there'll be all my friends at supper to meet me," said Bunter. "I'll get off. I'll be back in time for supper here—don't worry!"

"But—but—but—— I—I say!" stammered Figgins.

Bunter was moving to the door, and Figgins & Co. looked at one another. It was settled, certainly, that Bunter was a New House fellow, and it would not be easy for him to change back. But it was perfectly clear that Tom Merry & Co. meant to attempt to induce him to do so, and the result was uncertain.

Yet to keep Bunter in the New House by force was hardly feasible. While the Co. were debating it in their minds Bunter rolled out of the study.

"He—he's bound to come back!" said Figgins hesitatingly. "He's got his name down in this House now, and a Housemaster can't be played with like that. Even if he changes his mind, he'll have to stick here now."

"We'll call for him before bed-time, and make sure!" said Kerr.

"Good!"

Figgins & Co. felt confident; but their confidence was mixed with uneasiness. But they could only hope for the best. At all events, if Tom Merry & Co. attempted to bag their new recruit, they were determined that Bunter should be recaptured by hook or by crook—there was no doubt at all about that.

CHAPTER 11.
Won from the Enemy.

STUDY No. 6 was looking quite festive when Billy Bunter rolled into it in company with the Terrible Three.

Tom Merry, Manners, and Lowther had met him at the door of the School House, and they escorted him to No. 6 with great satisfaction.

Blake & Co. met him there with equal satisfaction.

As a matter of fact, the juniors should have been at prep just then, and it was not time for supper; but it was agreed on all hands to "blow prep," for the important purpose of foiling the knavish tricks of the New House.

Rations had been pooled, and every possible addition made to the festive board; and Bunter's eyes glistened at the sight of the spread table. How he was able to tackle that early supper after his feed in Figgins' study was a mystery; but it was clear that he was quite ready to try.

"I say, you fellows, this is really ripping of you!" said Bunter, as he took his seat at the table. "So glad to see you all again, too!"

"The pleasure's all on our side, old chap!" said Tom Merry solemnly.

"Yaas, wathah!"

"We've got lots of things to say to you, Bunter!" continued Tom Merry. "We'd like to settle about the footer, for one thing. We want you in our eleven, of course."

Bunter did not answer.

He was eating.

When he was eating all other matters faded into the background. But the chums of the School House were only too glad to see him contented, and they waited on him with great assiduity.

Even Bunter slacked down at last, however, and lay back in his chair with a fat grin of contentment.

Beaming faces surrounded him. Billy Bunter had the unusual feeling of being popular and sought after. It was very flattering and very pleasing, and he enjoyed it.

"There seems to have been a mistake made about your House here," remarked Tom Merry pleasantly. "You're really coming into this House, of course."

Bunter shook his head.

"Sorry, old scout; can't be done!" he said. "I couldn't stand the grub, you know!"

"The grub?" repeated Tom.

"Yes! Otherwise, of course, I'd have been glad to be with my old pals! But I'm bound to think of my health first."

"But the grub here is just the same as in the New House!" said Blake, rather puzzled.

Bunter stared at him.

"Eh? Ain't you half-starved here?" he exclaimed.

"Certainly not!"

"But—but Figgins said, and Kerr said that——"

"Bai Jove! The spoofin' wottahs!" exclaimed Arthur Augustus indignantly. "That is how they did the twick, then!"

"They said a School House chap named Trimble told them he was half starved in this House!" exclaimed Bunter.

"Trimble's a fat pig, and always grousing about the rations!" explained Tom Merry. "The truth is, we do better in this House than they do; our Housemaster is a good sort, and Ratcliff is a crusty old Hun. He glares at a chap who asks for a second helping."

"Like a tiger!" said Lowther.

"He's got a temper like Von Tirpitz!" said Manners.

"And he never sees a junior without caning him or giving him lines!" said Digby.

"Hardly ever!"

"Oh, crumbs!" said Bunter, in dismay.

"They were takin' you in, deah boy!" said Arthur Augustus D'Arcy. "But it's all wight! All you've got to do is to change back!"

Bunter swelled.

"This is what comes of being so much sought after!" he said. "It's the same wherever I go, especially with girls, too! They can never take their eyes off me!"

"Oh!"

"And you say the grub here is as good as in the other House?" asked Bunter cautiously.

"Better!"

"Well, this is a rather nice study," said Bunter, blinking round. "I could be comfortable here!"

Blake & Co. looked rather queer.

"Of course, my original intention was to dig with my old pal Gussy!" said Bunter. "Blessed if I don't do it!"

Blake and Herries and Digby opened their lips—and closed them again. Arthur Augustus gave them a stern look. The Terrible Three eyed them significantly.

If Bunter was to be bagged, and the New House foiled, it was no time for Blake & Co. to raise objections about crowding in No. 6. It was, in fact, a time for self-sacrifice; and Blake felt it. He gulped something down.

"Do!" he gasped.

"Oh, d-d-do!" mumbled Herries and Dig.

"Yaas, wathah!" said Arthur Augustus, with a grin. "Pway wemain and share this studay with us, Buntah!"

Bunter nodded affably.

"It's a go!" he said.

"Bravo!"

"I shall have to step back to the New House, though——"

"Eh? Why?"

"I've arranged to have supper with Figgins——"

"S-s-supper?"

"Yes! Can't break an engagement, can I?"

Tom Merry & Co. blinked at him. It really looked as if Bunter had determined to commit suicide by the painful method of bursting.

"Oh! Supper!" gasped Tom, at last. "B-b-but we're going to have another supper here! This—this is only a—a—a snack to go on with! We—we have supper after prep."

"My dear fellow, say no more!" said Bunter genially. "I'm staying! Rely on me!"

There was a tap at the door, and it opened, to display three rather grim faces. Figgins & Co. had arrived.

Grim looks met them.

"Just called in for Bunter!" said Figgins, as affably as possible. "Supper's nearly ready, Bunter!"

"Tell those boundahs what you think of them, Buntah, deah boy!" advised Arthur Augustus.

Bunter did not move. He was feeling rather too heavy and over-fed to want to move, in fact. He blinked loftily at the New House juniors through his big glasses, and merely waved a fat hand at them.

"You can cut!" he said.

"Wha-a-at?"

"I'm a School House chap!" said Bunter. "You spoofed me—took me in! I'm disgusted with you!"

"Why, you—you——"

"In fact, I rather despise you!" said Bunter. "You can cut! That's all!"

"Yaas, wathah!" chuckled Arthur Augustus.

Figgins & Co. stood transfixed for a moment. Then there was a roar from George Figgins.

"Why, you fat rotter——"

"Ordah!"

"You belong to the New House now!" exclaimed Kerr. "Come on, Bunter!"

Tom Merry made a sign to his comrades. He did not mean Bunter to be assailed by more temptations.

There was a sudden rush at Figgins & Co., and they went whirling out into the passage.

There followed a sound of yelling and of bumping on the stairs as the heroes of the New House departed.

And Billy Bunter, in Study No. 6, chuckled a fat chuckle!

THE END.

(Don't miss next Wednesday's Great Story of Tom Merry & Co. at St. Jim's—"BUNT R OF HE NEW HOUSE!"—by Martin C.ifford.)

Extracts from "THE GREYFRIARS HERALD" and "TOM MERRY'S WEEKLY."

GRUNDY TO THE RESCUE. By Tom Merry.

I.

"Why is it wet?
Because it's Wednesday!
Why is it Wednesday?
Because it's wet!
Brrrrrrrrr!"

THIS extraordinary specimen of poetry was furnished verbally, and on the spot, by Monty Lowther.

At least, I suppose it's poetry. It doesn't rhyme. The metre's out. The reasoning is fallacious. Therefore, I have hopes that it will go down to posterity as classic poetry.

But its use now is to make clear that the day was Wednesday, and the weather was wet.

It had rained all the morning during lessons—which didn't matter. But it was raining harder still now, and looked like keeping it up all the afternoon—which mattered much. For a rather important practice match had been arranged for that afternoon, and now had to be abandoned.

"Never mind; it'll do the crops good!" I said philosophically. (My ankle was strained, by the way, and I wouldn't have been able to play in any case.) "Good for the crops, you know!"

"In the middle of winter?" snorted Lowther. "Down it comes! Blow it! 'Tain't fit for a dog to play footer in!'

"Even old Grundy wouldn't be ass enough to go out into it!" remarked Manners.

Cardew sauntered up. And when Cardew has nothing to do—which is often the case—there is generally trouble brewing for someone."

"I rather think Grundy would, if he were asked nicely," he said easily, more for the sake of argument than anything else.

"Rats!"

"Think I couldn't persuade him to take a little walk—say, for four or five miles?"

"I'm jolly sure you couldn't!" said Manners emphatically.

"Then we'll make a bet on it," said Cardew pleasantly. "Here, Levison!"

Levison was standing by with Clive, and came up on being addressed.

"Well, Cardew?"

"Bear witness to this little bet of mine, old bean! When peace is finally declared, and all of us, of course, are old, old men with white beards and bald heads, we are to gather round a festive board groaning under the good things of the earth. And if I don't succeed in sendin' Grundy out into the wet to-day, I'm to pay for that future spread. If I do succeed, then I'm to gorge myself to the full at these fellows' expense."

Levison grinned.

"I bear witness to that!"

"But without telling Grundy an actual whopper, though," I put in. "For instance, you could say that his uncle was having a fit in the road. That would send him out like a shot, but——"

"I'll spin him no whoppers, old son!" promised Cardew. "But I'll want your help, Levison. You're rather pally with Grundy, aren't you? I hear he's been lookin' after you lately."

Levison frowned, and then laughed.

"The silly old ass! He means well enough, I dare say. But I wish he'd mind his own dashed business!"

"Anything on this afternoon?"

"Not now that footer's off," answered Levison. "By the way, though, I've some lines to do for Lathom before tea. I forgot those."

"Never mind them! Just trot along with me! Ta-ta, you fellows!"

And Cardew lounged out of the Common-room with Levison.

When he left the room he left our minds also. We took his bet with a pinch of salt, so to speak, and remained at the window watching the rain, and listening to Lowther's worst jokes—if any of them can be called worse than the rest.

Cardew and Levison, however, were not long in making their plans. The result was that a few minutes later they sought the study of George Alfred Grundy.

That remarkable man was busy hammering huge studs into a pair of huge footer-boots.

Cardew viewed this operation with great interest until it came to an end.

"If you haven't studied footer, Grundy, old bean," he remarked, "I can see that you've studded footer-boots!"

"Eh?" said Grundy.

Cardew didn't trouble to explain that very obvious pun. He felt he hadn't energy enough.

Levison drew a cigarette-case from his pocket, and proffered it to Cardew.

"Have a whiff, old man? Ahem!"

Seeing Grundy's questioning eyes upon him, he hastily put back the case with a great show of confusion.

"Hallo! Sliding back again, Levison?" exclaimed Grundy. "I thought you'd chucked that game, like a sensible chap!"

"Well, so I have," said Levison uncomfortably. "I—— Can I have a word with you in private, Grundy?"

"Certainly!" said Grundy magnanimously. "Speak out!"

His great mind overlooked for the moment the fact that private speaking is scarcely possible in the presence of company.

Levison turned to Ralph Reckness.

"Will you clear out, Cardew?"

"With pleasure, as you put it so very nicely!"

And Cardew went, apparently rather huffy.

Grundy looked approvingly at Levison.

"That's the way!" he said. "Don't get too thick with that chap! I don't think much of him! Now, what's the trouble?"

"I'd like to have your advice——"

Grundy beamed.

"Go ahead!"

"In fact, it's more than advice I want! It's help—active help. You remember how Selby was imprisoned in the Moat House, don't you?"

"I remember that."

"Well, Lathom, he's—he's——"

"Collared at the Moat House?"

"Nunno! Another place altogether. I'll tell you how to get to it in a minute. But he—he's locked in a room——"

"Eh? Who locked him in?"

"It was done by a—a man I knew," said Levison cautiously.

Grundy stare at him.

"Then why didn't you stop him, you ass?"

"You—you see," said Levison desperately, "he's got a kind of hold over me——"

Grundy snorted.

"One of your shady acquaintances?"

"I don't see why you should call him shady," said Levison sullenly.

"Cut that! Who is he?"

"Never mind his name!" said Levison hastily. "If I give him away he might—well, he's already reported me to the Head for visiting the Green Man. I just scraped out of it with a licking!"

"Precious friend!" sniffed Grundy.

"He isn't a friend, really. But I'm under his thumb, in a way. I've had to do a lot of jobs for him that I haven't altogether liked—in fact, haven't liked at all. This afternoon I've something to do for him, and if I refuse it's ten to one he'll report me to the Head, and—and——"

Levison shrugged hopelessly.

"By Jove! He's locked Lathom in a room, you say?"

"Without food," said Levison miserably. "But the key's in the lock—I know that! It's just a matter of turning it, and Lathom's free. But I've this beastly job to do this afternoon for—you know, the fellow who locked him in—a job I detest; but—but I'm in his power——"

Levison paused.

"Where is this place?" demanded Grundy. "And what is it?"

"I can give you directions on a bit of paper. It'll mean a walk of four or five miles if you follow them. But if you think your legs could stand it——"

"My legs stand it!" exclaimed Grundy. "If there's a fellow at St. Jim's who's a patch on me at walking—beastly wet, though!" he said suddenly.

His spirits seemed damped for the moment. Then he asked:

"What kind of a place is it?"

"It's a kind of board-residence show, in a way, and people live there at a specified charge. I know the place well enough, and I think you will when you see it before you. It can't be missed if you follow these directions."

"Look here, then. If you'll promise me that you'll have no more shady transactions with this man—no gambling, smoking, drinking, and that rot——"

"Never, in future!"

"In spite of his power over you?"

"In spite of that," said Levison firmly.

"Then I'll free Lathom!" said Grundy magnificently. "That rotter ought to be imprisoned. I——"

"No!" broke in Levison. "Not that! I don't want him punished. But set Lathom free, and I promise you that he'll have nothing further to fear from the man who locked him in."

"Just as you like, so long as you keep your own promise."

"I'll keep that. In fact, I'll—I'll visit him this evening, and—and give him something, I can tell you!"

"Be advised by me, and break off with him," said Grundy encouragingly.

"But—but don't let it get about that I sent you. That—that fellow——"

Levison shuddered as he spoke, and broke off dramatically.

"He must be a Hun!" exclaimed Grundy. "I wish I could put my fist against his nose!"

"I'll scribble out the directions," said Levison quickly. "Lemme see!"

After a few minutes with the pencil, he handed the sheet of paper he had been working on to Grundy.

The latter read, and nodded approvingly. The directions were lucid enough:

"Follow Rylcombe Lane.
Take footpath across moor.
Reaching lane, turn to right.
At the end, again turn to right.
First turning on left.
First on right.
Second on right.
First on right—building in front."

"And then," explained Levison, "it's all quite simple. At the gates of the house you'll find a porter—one of the Taggles breed, you know. Take no notice of him, for the gates are open. Straight ahead is the door of the place—also kept open for the convenience of inmates, of course. Whether Lathom's gagged and bound—well, you can depend upon it he won't be making much noise. He's locked up in the end room of the first passage on the second floor. Remember that?"

"Second floor, first passage, end room," repeated Grundy, jotting it down on paper.

Then he looked dubiously at Levison.

"Look here, this is the solid truth you're giving me, ain't it? Lathom is locked up in this room?"

"I know it for a dead cert!" exclaimed Levison desperately. "How I know doesn't matter. But it's the truth."

"Right-ho! Then I'll be off. Lucky you asked my advice, young Levison."

"You're the only fellow I felt I could rely upon to do a job of this kind, Grundy!"

And Grundy departed upon his errand, greatly gratified.

. . . .

Cardew lounged into the Common-room, with Levison, grinning, behind him.

"Still here, old beans!" he remarked. "What behold ye, Sister Ann & Co.?"

"Rain!" snorted Monty Lowther. "Rain, rain; nothing but—— Hallo, Grundy!"

"Not really?" yawned Cardew.

Cap pulled down over his eyes, coat buttoned up to his ears, George Alfred Grundy squelched across the quad.

He stopped in the gateway, with the rain beating down upon him, and pulled a piece of paper from his pocket.

After referring to it for a moment he thrust it back again, and swung out of sight—behind a curtain of falling rain.

"When the pipin' times of peace come," Cardew reminded us, "I'll expect that spread. So don't squander your old-age pensions away!"

II.

GRUNDY set his jaws grimly as he strode down the road.

"Chaps like Levison were made to get into the clutches of scoundrels," he muttered. "I can't imagine anyone taking me in to that tune. Ha, ha! Ugh! What a beastly day! I wonder what the waster's like? Poor old Lathom!"

This, and much more, Grundy said to Grundy, as he tramped on through the wet and mud.

He was crossing Wayland Moor by now. This bleak and desolate expanse worked upon his imagination, and the abducting of Lathom seemed quite likely.

A hulking figure, roughly dressed, and carrying a huge stick under its arm, loomed up.

Grundy looked at the man suspiciously in passing.

The man evidently resented being looked at suspiciously. He returned the look with redoubled suspicion.

Grundy became more suspicious. He spun round when the man passed, and stared intently.

Then the man slung round, and returned the stare in a very aggressive manner.

A sudden thought struck Grundy. Suppose the man had had something to do with the imprisonment of Lathom? For, although there was no reason why he should have, there was still no reason why he shouldn't. Thus reasoned Grundy.

"I'll throw out a few hints," he thought. "He may let something drop unawares."

He looked harder at the man.

"When you've seed enough ov me I'll pass on!" growled the stranger.

"I want no impudence from you, my man!" said Grundy sharply. "As a matter of fact, I'm not so sure that I haven't seen you before!"

The stranger stared at him unpleasantly.

"'Ave you?"

"Mind," said Grundy, eyeing him narrowly, "I don't say that you've committed a robbery, or a murder, or anything like that——"

The man scowled.

"But there's such a thing as locking people in rooms," said Grundy meaningly. "Not to mention gagging and binding them!"

"Who's locked people in rooms?" exclaimed the man.

"Never mind! I make no accusations! But I hope I know a criminal when I see one!"

"Young 'ound!"

The man grasped his cudgel furiously.

"Look here! Blustering won't do any good! I've done a bit of detective work in my time——"

"Take that!"

"Yaroooogh!" roared Grundy, as the stick descended sharply upon his head. "My hat! Ow!"

"And that!"

Whack!

Grundy fled, howling, and the stranger shook his fist after him.

Grundy met many equally suspicious-looking characters after that, but he did not accost them. He had had enough.

In the lane he made further reference to the paper.

"Turn to the right!" he murmured.

Grundy trudged along the muddy lane, getting wetter and wetter.

At the end, according to the instructions, he again took the road to the right.

"This seems to be a roundabout way of Levison's," he grumbled, when at last he came to the turning on the left. "It would have been much shorter to have taken the road behind the school."

He went quite a long distance now before he came to a road shooting off from the right.

Grundy walked on.

The roads became worse, but he plodded on manfully.

Grundy frowned when the time came to act upon the direction "Second on the right."

"It strikes me," he exclaimed, "that I'll pass jolly near to St. Jim's! That fool Levison——"

He didn't finish, but plodded on, his frown deepening.

Twenty minutes' further walking, and Grundy came to the "first on right."

The "building in front" was St. Jim's!

Gradually, very gradually, it dawned upon Grundy's great mind that something was wrong. It had, in fact, been dawning upon his mind for some time.

Going through the gates he passed the porter, indisputably of the Taggles breed, and set off across the quad, bewildered and bedraggled. As yet he hadn't quite grasped the situation.

A few of us were on the steps of the School House now, for it had almost ceased to rain at last.

"Hallo!" yawned Cardew. "Didn't expect Grundy back so soon, by gad!"

Levison made himself scarce. But Grundy didn't seem to want him.

As if in a dream, he was murmuring, "Second floor; first passage; end room!"

He followed these directions, and we followed him.

They brought him to Lathom's study.

What prompted him to try the door I don't know. Even his slow brain must have grasped the fact that the "abducting" bizney was off.

Anyway, he tried it; and it was locked. But Lathom was inside, and he unlocked and opened the door.

"Well?" he snapped. "I am very busy! What is it, Grundy?"

"I—I—— You're not kidnapped, sir?" stammered Grundy.

"What?"

"I—I mean, not gagged and bound—that is—I—I—a rotter hasn't locked you in this room—a room—— Oh, crumbs!"

"Is this a joke, Grundy?"

"Nunno, sir! I——"

"You ridiculous boy! Come into the room!"

He dragged poor Grundy in as he spoke.

Let us draw a kindly veil.

. . . .

"You rotten liar, Levison!"

George Alfred Grundy, his hands tucked under his armpits, glowered at Levison.

"I say, go easy, Grundy!" I exclaimed. "You can't call a fellow a liar for nothing, you know!"

"For nothing!" hooted Grundy. "He told me Lathom had been locked in a room by—by——"

"By himself!" said Levison calmly.

"By a chap whose power you were in!" roared Grundy.

Levison nodded.

"So I am, in a sense. I said he makes me do jobs that I detest. Well, he gave me some lines to do this afternoon, and that ain't pleasant, is it?"

"You—you—— Grundy was almost speechless. "You said he was locked in a room miles from St. Jim's!"

"Not at all! I merely showed you one way of getting to Lathom's room. It was rather a long way round, I admit. But it was a walk, you know!"

Grundy rushed at him. But we collared him promptly, and held him back.

"Well, I give you best, Levison!" he said ruefully. "But to bamboozle me, you know! Me! My hat! You're cleverer than I thought, Levison!"

"Thanks awfully!"

Printed and published weekly by the Proprietors at The Fleetway House, Farringdon Street, London, E.C. 4, England. Subscription, 8s. 10d. per annum. Agents for Australasia: Gordon & Gotch, Melbourne, Sydney, Adelaide, Brisbane, and Wellington, N.Z. South Africa: The Central News Agency, Ltd., Cape Town and Johannesburg. Saturday, January 19th, 1918.

THE ST. JIM'S GALLERY.

No. 32.—Richard Henry Redfern.

DICK REDFERN is quite one of the heftiest fellows among the St. Jim's juniors, and popular exceedingly. Richard is brainy, but he is muscular also. Among the best of Mr. Lathom's pupils, he is also among the most prominent members of the Fourth Form on the playing-fields. He ranks with Figgins and Kerr and Fatty Wynn in the New House elevens. Those four are worth very nearly as much as the other seven, though there are good men among the seven.

Redfern came to St. Jim's as a scholarship boy, and with him came his chums Owen and Lawrence. They were all from a County Council school, and the attitude of the juniors generally towards them was not entirely a welcoming one. The first St. Jim's fellow they met was Arthur Augustus D'Arcy. Now, Gussy has not an ounce of snobbery in him, and when he let out the fact that his chums were rather expecting to see three doubtful specimens he had no intention at all of hurting the feelings of Redfern & Co. Gussy offered to protect them. They did not feel that they wanted protecting; but what he had said gave Redfern an idea.

The fruit of that idea was the appearance at the old school of three awful ragamuffins. If that was the kind of thing St. Jim's expected, let St. Jim's have it! Mr. Wiggs, at Wayland, supplied the necessary clobber, and Redfern, Owen, and Lawrence supplied a Cockney accent that one might have cut with a knife, and remarks that did not represent the real tone of their minds. They were thicker than anything the juniors had dreamed of. "If you coves are goin' to put on any side there will be trouble," said Redfern. "We ain't goin' to be put on because we came from Slum Alley." That, of course, is not Redfern's usual language. It fairly took aback Figgins & Co., for it was to the New House that the three new fellows came. Gussy gave the game away, and the fellows who had been just a little inclined to be snobbish felt a bit ashamed of themselves. They had certainly been fairly scored off.

Reddy & Co. were up against Figgins & Co. from the outset. They were the New Firm, they said, and they meant to make the New House cock House at St. Jim's.

"I'm sorry to ruffle his Majesty King Figgins, but we've decided to start an independent republic in the new study," Redfern told Tom Merry & Co.

Figgy and his chums got in the Terrible Three to help them handle the New Firm after the New Firm had scored very distinctly in a wheeze which had to do with pies and sawdust and things. But even with such illustrious aid Figgy & Co. failed to pull it off. It was plain that the New Firm were fellows of more than common resource.

It was Redfern who led the revolt against Mr. Ratcliff which culminated in a barring-out. Other things had happened before the New House juniors took that very drastic step, however.

The trouble arose over the food question. There is no getting away from the fact that Mr. Ratcliff is mean. For a long time before this complaint had been made of the quality and quantity of the grub—the official grub—in the New House, which compared very unfavourably with that in the School House. Fatty Wynn found it less bearable than ever when the Housemaster confiscated his private supplies and called him a greedy young rascal. Arthur Augustus D'Arcy, always sympathetic, helped Fatty to recover the stuff from the pantry. If it was not precisely the same stuff, it was equally good stuff, anyway; and a fair robbery is no exchange—no, that's wrong. It was a fair robbery, and it was an exchange—at least, so Fatty Wynn thought.

Mr. Ratcliff did not agree with Fatty. He put the prefects on to inquire about what he called the robbery. They were not keen on the job. Monteith and Baker and Webb all chucked it after a bit; but Sefton held on—he liked anything with a touch of bullying in it. Before Monteith had gone out of the game Redfern had had him quite nicely. The three new boys were questioned as to what they had had for tea. Redfern confessed to having had a tongue at tea. Asked where he got it, he said he had brought it to St. Jim's with him. Monteith said that it could not have kept good so long unless it was a tinned tongue. But Reddy said it wasn't tinned. He had kept it in a safe place. Monteith asked him where, and his reply was "In my mouth!"

As nothing definite was discovered by Sefton, the juniors were put on short commons. Now, this was plainly unfair. Many were to suffer for one or two, and to suffer in a way that is not fair punishment. It may be a very effective way of getting at a growing boy to cut his food supply down; but it is a wrong way—bad for the boy.

Figgins got up a protest against it. Every New House Fourth-Former stood up at the tea-table to protest, and every one of them got five hundred lines of Virgil for his audacity.

Then Redfern did something much more audacious. He took all the New House juniors down to the bunshop at Rylcombe for the biggest spread that the place could provide—and he had the bill sent in to Ratty!

There was trouble, of course. Redfern was

sent for by the furious master. The rest would not let him go alone. At least twenty followed him—Owen and Lawrence, of course, and Figgy & Co., and also Pratt and French and Thompson and Clarke, among others. The Housemaster said that the bill would be sent to Redfern's parents. Reddy told him coolly that his father could not possibly pay it. Then Mr. Ratcliff ordered that each boy who had taken part in the "disgusting orgy" should pay his share—or, rather, that their parents or guardians should do so. Kerr stepped forward at that. If it was attempted, he said, his father would certainly make a counter-claim against Mr. Ratcliff for food charged for in the term's bills and not supplied. All the juniors were willing to go to the Head; but Ratty did not want that. Dr. Holmes is the last man to agree with starvation as a penal measure. So they were ordered into Hall, and the angry master came down with a birch in his hand. Hall was empty! It was open rebellion now.

Monteith and Sefton were summoned, and told to fetch the six ringleaders—Redfern, Owen, Lawrence, Figgins, Kerr, and Wynn. They were authorised to use force if necessary. Monteith did not care about doing that. Sefton rather liked it—until he found what the results were.

He got handled then, and at dinner he got it worse. The juniors were completely out of hand. They collared grub meant for the senior table; they pelted the unpopular Sefton with vegetables. Ratty did not show his nose. But during the afternoon he sent for Redfern, and Mr. Lathom, who knew nothing of the trouble, told the junior to go. Reddy did not go to Mr. Ratcliff; he was discovered by that gentleman walking the quad, and informed that he would be expelled. He was captured with Sefton's aid, and cruelly birched by the master while the bullying prefect held him. Figgy led an attempt at rescue; but the juniors could not get in to save Reddy, and the upshot of it all was that Mr. Ratcliff was hustled out of his own House, and it was barred against him.

Then the Head stepped in. He dealt with the rebels himself; but he dealt with Mr. Ratcliff also. That gentleman had to take a holiday of several weeks' duration. He came near to resigning in his wrath; but, unluckily, he thought better—or worse—of that.

Redfern's leadership in this affair naturally increased his prestige among the juniors of the New House. But the New Firm, hefty as they were, never quite got on top of Figgy & Co., and, though they may try again, are never likely to.

The rivalry led to at least one big row, however. The New Firm were informed by Figgins that they had to toe the line; and they did so—in seeming. But it was only in seeming, and the results of the pretended obedience were not welcome to Figgy & Co. Mr. Ratcliff sent for Redfern and his two chums, and told them, before he caned them, what amounted to a direct lie. It is true that his words could have been so construed as to avoid the implication that Figgins had sneaked to him; but that was the only construction any boy would have put upon them, and one can have no doubt that it was the construction Ratty meant to have put.

Redfern was in a fury. He went straight to Figgins and accused him of sneaking. That accusation is one that a fellow of Figgy's type—honest as the day—is sure to resent hotly. They got to blows at once, and, though separated by Kildare, fought it out later behind the chapel.

It was a tough fight. Figgins was on top when Ratty intervened. He might have had Redfern knocked out but for his chivalry. It was not in Figgins to go for a fellow as he staggered up from a nasty fall. The laws of the Ring allow it; but George Figgins has a higher sense of fair play than that. He stood aside and let Reddy rise unhampered—waited for him to get breath and start again. Good old Figgy! But just so would Redfern have done had the positions been reversed.

The Head had to clear up this mess, too. And again he had to rebuke Mr. Ratcliff. It was obvious to the Head that Ratty had been at least careless in his handling of the truth. Probably Dr. Holmes did not suspect that behind that seeming carelessness lay meditated spite. But we know Ratty, and I, for one, have no doubt whatever that he meant to make bad blood between those two, both of whom he hated.

On the whole, with occasional squabbles and some constant rivalry, Redfern and Figgins have been the best of friends since that.

But Redfern has had one other big fight. Quite lately we found him, through the machinations of Racke and Crooke, hard up against Tom Merry. Tom carried too many guns for him, and he was licked. But Reddy can take a licking. The nasty suspicions hurt him far more than that did; but a few words from Tom made amends for them. Two fellows of so much the same type as Richard Henry Redfern and the junior captain of St. Jim's could not be at feud long after there had been a fair chance of clearing up matters.

How thoroughly popular Dick Redfern is was well shown when Cardew displayed the snobbishness of which mention was made a couple of weeks ago. Not only the New

House juniors invited to Cardew's spread, but those of his own House, too, walked out when they heard him insult the three scholarship boys. He made amends later; but one need not tell that story over again.

Redfern's journalistic proclivities have not been mentioned. He means to be a journalist when he leaves school; but that did not quite justify him in running away to be one, as he did once. He got a job, and did very well at it, too. But he had to come back to St. Jim's, and was glad to come. Do you remember how, later on, he was asked to report a meeting at Wayland, and found Mr. Ratcliff getting up to make an anti-war speech, and turned out the gas to save St. Jim's the disgrace which he considered would have been brought upon the school by such a speech from one of its masters?

Dick Julian owes something to his New House namesake. There was a time when Julian was accused by Hake, the rascally New House Sixth-Former, of theft; and the evidence against him seemed very strong. Redfern was certain of Julian's innocence, and set out to prove it. The fact that it must have been a fellow from his own House, if not Julian, did not choke him off. By a clever ruse he showed Hake to be the dishonest rotter he was, and eventually Hake confessed the earlier theft—for Redfern's ruse had involved tempting him to another—and Julian was completely cleared.

One of the very best. Redfern, frank, honest, full of fun, full of mischief, too, but never wicked mischief; an all-round athlete of rare calibre, cricketer, footballer, runner swimmer; with first-class brains in addition. Floreat!

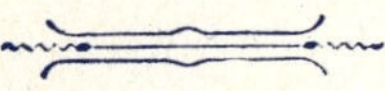

The Editor's Chat.

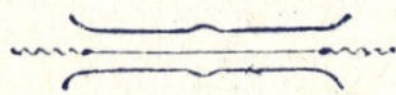

For Next Wednesday:

"BUNTER OF THE NEW HOUSE!"

By Martin Clifford.

You know Bunter now, all of you.

How do you like him?

Nice, unselfish, sportsmanlike, winning kind of chap, isn't he?

But he really is funny—you cannot deny that.

And the stories dealing with his doings at St. Jim's are some of the very best I ever read.

Quite a lot of the St. Jim's fellows know Billy Bunter. They don't know him quite as Greyfriars knows him, of course. But they know him to be greedy and vain and untruthful.

They don't know, however, that the fellow who has come to St. Jim's is Billy Bunter. They think he is Wally, Billy's cousin. And Wally is a decent fellow in every way—one of the very best.

So Billy makes a start at St. Jim's with a clean slate; and we see how soon he begins to make it dirty.

And poor old Wally—at Greyfriars, with all Billy's misdemeanours piled on his poor, innocent shoulders!

But if you want to know—as I am sure you do—what happened to Wally, you must get the "Magnet."

"FALKIRK'S" CRITICS.

I have had scores of letters about my Falkirk correspondent's last communication. Not one of the writers agrees with him! He was greatly incensed because I did not take much notice of the one Scot who did. But that particular Scot was so very un-Scotlike.

So is "Falkirk." Most of those who write about his communications are of his own race; but their tone is as different from his as anything can be. They don't talk rot about Bannockburn; their blood does not boil because George Francis Kerr has red hair and freckles; they don't hate the English or feel sure that I hate the Scots; they don't say silly things about Americans.

My own experience is that very few Scots have any dislike for England, or for English things and people. There is much of this in Ireland; it is fostered artificially by Sinn Fein and such movements. But Scotland is so very different. In the great old fighting days England and Scotland learned mutual respect. I can think of Bannockburn in exactly the same way as of Flodden, save that there was none dead at Bannockburn whom one could regret as one finds it easy to regret that gallant, knightly Scots James who died on Flodden field with all his nobles around him. Do you know Aytoun's "Edinburgh after Flodden"? Do you remember how the man who came back alone to Edinburgh told of those stark Scots warriors?

"Of the brave and gallant-hearted
Whom ye sent with pride away
Not a single man departed
From his monarch yesterday!"

But they all died round their King, who lay there "keeping royal state and semblance still," with two of his bravest lords at his head and at his feet a slain English knight.

There are thousands—many thousands—of English people who are as full of pride in the deeds of the Highland regiments as any Scot can be. For myself, brought up as I was on Sir Walter Scott's ringing verse and manly stories, I am as keen as any Scot can be. The average Englishman, I am sure, is not a man who has any of this feeling of sectional jealousy. He is ready to consider Scot or Irishman or Welshman as a brother; it is hardly his fault if they feel otherwise. But I do not believe, and I will not believe, that the Scots or the Welsh, or, indeed, many of the Irish, do feel otherwise.

AN ISSUE THAT WILL BE REMEMBERED.

I hope every reader of the GEM has ordered his copy of the "Penny Popular," which will reappear on Friday, January 24th. If you have not done so you would be well advised to place an order with your newsagent immediately, as failure to do so is liable to bring you bitter disappointment.

With this magnificent issue of the "Penny Popular"

A MAGNIFICENT PLATE

of Billy Bunter will be given free, whilst in the issue dated February 1st, and on sale the previous day, a splendid plate of

ARTHUR AUGUSTUS D'ARCY

showing the swell of St. Jim's in various positions, will be

GIVEN FREE.

The above is a small reproduction of this plate. When I tell you that the size of each of these plates will be 10in. by 6½in. you will see that there will be nothing cheap about them, and that they will be well worth framing.

In the issue of the "Penny Popular" dated January 25th there will be a long complete tale dealing with the early adventures of the chums of St. Jim's, and entitled "D'Arcy's Delusion!" In this story Gussy falls in love with the girl at the tobacconist's, and—— Well, I do not think I need say more to prove that the story will be one of the very best.

There will be two more stories in this number. One is entitled "Billy Bunter's Postal-Order!" by Frank Richards; and the other is "Rivals of Rookwood!" by Owen Conquest.

There is going to be a big demand for this Bumper Number of the "Penny Popular," so take my advice and

PLACE AN ORDER

with your newsagent at once. Don't leave it until the end of the week. Do it now!"

NOTICES.

Correspondence, etc., Wanted by—

G. R. Abraham, 110, Silverleigh Road, Thornton Heath, Surrey, wants members for correspondence society.

J. W. Mayer, 556, Oldham Road, Bardsley, Ashton-under-Lyne, wants members for Book and Exchange Club.

J. Saxton, 98, Sneinton Road, Nottingham, wants writers, over 14, for amateur magazine.

H. Swindells, 10, Vernon Street, Buxton Road, Macclesfield, wants to correspond with readers anywhere. He is willing to supply all information as to names and numbers of Companion Papers. He would like to hear from readers who are interested in ventriloquism. Stamped addressed envelope.

YOUR EDITOR.

EXTRACTS FROM THE DIARY OF A FAG.

MONDAY.—Rising-bell? Oh, 'tain't right! Why can't they let a chap sleep on for a few hours? Somebody'll catch it, though, to-day. The fellows are calling from the quad—no time to get washed. I'll see about it in the morning—if I've time. Just kicked a football through old Ratty's window. Now for fireworks! The old rotter's always ratty in the morning, so I expect I shall catch it. Curly Gibson says it serves me right; he says it stops the game. Perhaps it does, but I'll settle with him soon, though. Just "interviewed" that old beast Ratty. Oh ain't life worth living!

TUESDAY.—Just had a wash. That's worth putting down here. It wasn't exactly a bath. But what's the use? Chap'll only get dirty again, so it's a waste of soap, and it ain't patriotic to waste anything, they say. I always was a patriotic chap. Darrel has just told me I'm to fag for him to-morrow. That's good! Plenty of tuck now. Hurrah!

WEDNESDAY.—Just brought a herring away that Darrel doesn't want. Jolly funny! He says its smell is strong enough to stop one of our tanks. I s'pose he doesn't know what a nice-flavoured herring is like. He's a good chap, though, old Darrel! I'm having a fine time!

THURSDAY.—Just made a booby-trap for that rotter Knox. When he walks into his study down it'll come right on the top of his napper. Serve the beast jolly well right! What's he want to cane me for, anyhow? Just for sliding down the banisters and bumping into him at the bottom and knocking him spinning, that's all, the rotter! Ha, ha, ha! It was funny, though. I mean his sitting on the floor, not my being caned. That booby-trap has just acted. What a row the rotter's making! He'll never know who's done it, though. Three cheers for the Third!

FRIDAY.—Just had four fights. Won 'em all. Nothing much the matter with me, though. Only a few teeth missing, and a swollen eye, and a nose like two. But the other chaps are in the sanny—for good, I think. Can't write any more to-day. I feel a bit queer, though not from the fights, mind you.

SATURDAY.—We play a footer match to-day. I'm centre-forward. It's been raining like billy-ho all the morning, and the ground's like a giddy pond; we're kicking with the tide, though. Just finished the match. We've won, eight to six. But ain't we in a lovely state! We'll all be in the sanny soon. Wally D'Arcy says that doesn't matter at all, though, because he says we shall jolly well be out for next Saturday's match. Old Wally knows that for sure, because he's just whispered that if we're not better we're jolly well going to do a bolt. Good old Wally! Football is a grand game, ain't it?

N

The GEM 1½d

No. 572. Vol. 13. January 25th 1919.

LOOK!

IN THIS ISSUE: **FREE PLATE OF BILLY BUNTER!**

"The Penny Popular" Will Reappear on Friday, January 24th Order Your Copy at Once!

BILLY BUNTER'S POSTAL-ORDER ARRIVES—AT LAST!

This Magnificent Plate will be GIVEN FREE with the Issue of "The Penny Popular" dated February 1st.

OUT THIS WEEK!

BUNTER OF THE NEW HOUSE!

By MARTIN CLIFFORD.

A Magnificent, Long, Complete Story of Tom Merry & Co.

WILLIAM GEORGE BUNTER

CHAPTER 1.
Billy Bunter of St. Jim's.

"I SAY, you fellows!"

Billy Bunter sat up in the armchair in Study No. 6 in the School House at St. Jim's.

He had been asleep, and for some time his unmelodious snore had resounded through the study.

Blake & Co., who were at their prep round the table, had worked to that unmusical accompaniment.

Bunter rubbed his eyes, and set his spectacles straight on his fat little nose, and blinked round him.

He had been dreaming of Greyfriars as he snored in Blake's armchair, and he expected for a moment to find himself in his old Greyfriars study when he awakened.

But the sight of Blake and Herries, Digby and D'Arcy, working at the study table, recalled him to himself.

He remembered that he was no longer Billy Bunter of Greyfriars, but Wally Bunter of St. Jim's; that, at all events, St. Jim's had accepted him as Wally Bunter without a suspicion.

Bunter grinned a fat grin as he looked at the four busy Fourth-Formers.

He had no prep to do, as it was his first day at St. Jim's, and he had improved the shining hour by taking a nap in the armchair.

When he was not eating Billy Bunter was always ready to sleep.

"I say, you fellows!"

Arthur Augustus D'Arcy glanced up as the snore ceased to resound.

He met Bunter's blink, and nodded affably.

"Hallo! Wakin' up, deah boy?" he remarked.

"Had a good nap?" asked Blake. "I suppose you were tired after your journey down, old fellow?"

Bunter nodded.

He was not so much tired after his journey to St. Jim's as after his exertions at an early supper in Study No. 6. His performances at that early supper had amazed the study. But Bunter had awakened, refreshed by sleep, ready for further efforts, like a giant refreshed with wine.

"Yes," he said. "What about supper?"

"Eh?"

"Must be getting towards bed-time," remarked Bunter. "I suppose you have some supper here?"

"Bai Jove!"

"Oh, yes; certainly," said Jack Blake hastily. "In fact, the Shell bounders are coming in to supper, and they're going to bring some supplies. I suppose you're pretty sharp set?"

There was a hidden sarcasm in this remark which was quite lost on William George Bunter.

"Yes," he said, "I've a fairly good appetite, you know. That chap Figgins asked me to supper in the New House——"

"Oh, never mind Figgins!"

"Fatty Wynn has been making some preparations," remarked Bunter. "Perhaps I ought to go over."

"My dear chap, you can't pay visits to the New House at this hour," said Blake. "Only half an hour to bed-time. Besides, we're going to have supper here."

"Kerr was very pressing, too——"

"You fellows done your prep?" asked Blake, looking round. "Tom Merry will be here in a minute or two."

"Neahly, deah boy."

"Buck up, then!"

"I'll get the fire going, if you like," said Bunter. "It's gone out. Don't mind me; I'd like to make myself useful."

Blake hesitated a moment. Coal rations were very short in junior studies. But he nodded. Politeness to that distinguished guest came before all other considerations.

"Go ahead, old nut!" he replied

Bunter detached himself from the armchair.

How he could possibly be hungry again in so short a time was a deep mystery to Study No. 6; but it was evident that Bunter was keen on supper.

He looked round for materials for a fire.

Firewood was lacking, but fortunately there was some of Jack Blake's fretwork at hand, and Bunter proceeded to crack it up and build a fire.

Paper seemed short, too, but some pages from a Latin grammar supplied the deficiency.

Bunter was not particular

The fire was soon going strong, and he heaped on it what coal remained in the locker.

It was quite a successful fire. Blake & Co., having finished their prep, rose from the table, and surveyed the fire with some satisfaction. It was a cold night.

"Good!" said Herries, warming his hands.

"Yaas, waihah!" said Arthur Augustus D'Arcy. "Vewy good indeed."

"Oh, I can light fires," said Bunter. "I can do pretty nearly anything, if you come to that. At Greyfriars——" He paused in time. "Time those chaps were here for supper. Hallo! Anything wrong, Blake?"

Jack Blake was gazing with a stony gaze at some fragments of fretwork in the fender. Busy with prep, he had not observed Bunter gathering the materials for the fire.

"That—that—that's part of my letter-rack!" he gasped. "And—and where's the photo-frames, and—and——"

"You didn't mind my using that rubbish for the fire, Blake?"

"Rubbish?" repeated Blake faintly.

"And I suppose that old book was no good?"

Herries' expression became quite extraordinary as he looked at what was left of the "old book."

"That's my Latin grammar!" he said, in a grinding voice.

"Bai Jove!"

"Here they come!" said Bunter cheerfully, as the door was thrown open and Tom Merry, Manners, and Lowther, of the Shell, made their appearance.

The Terrible Three came in with cheery smiles—and parcels.

Tom Merry & Co. were in high feather that evening.

For had they not triumphed over the New House, and beaten Figgins & Co. to the wide? Had not Figgins & Co. planned to bag Bunter for the New House, on the score of his football reputation—a reputation which, by the way, belonged to his cousin Wally—and had not the School House fellows frustrated their knavish tricks, and bagged Bunter in their turn? Naturally, the Co. were feeling very pleased with themselves.

True, they did not yet know exactly the kind of prize they had bagged. Had they known their Bunter better they would probably have made the New House fellows very welcome to him.

But for the present they were triumphant, and they were satisfied, and everything in the garden, so to speak, was lovely.

"Here we are again!" said Tom Merry cheerily. "You fellows finished prep? Good! Ready for supper—what?"

"Yes, rather!" said Bunter. "Anything to cook? I'm rather a dab at cooking, you know, and I've got a good fire going."

"Ahem! It's a—a cold collation," said Tom Merry. "Ham and hard-boiled eggs, and a cake."

"My dear chap, don't mench!" said Bunter. "Almost anything is good enough for me. So long as the stuff's good, and there's plenty of it, I'm easily satisfied."

Bunter's earlier performances had exhausted the resources of Study No. 6, but the Terrible Three had come to the rescue. The fat junior's little, round eyes glistened behind his glasses as he surveyed the contents of the packages. Books and papers were cleared away, and the study table laid for supper.

Blake's glance wandered occasionally to the remnants of his fretwork, and Herries seemed a little thoughtful, perhaps on the subject of his Latin grammar. Study No. 6 had accepted Bunter as an inmate, to keep him out of the clutches of their old rivals of the New House. But they were beginning to think already that they had paid too high a price for the baffling of Figgins & Co.

However, so far, all was cheery politeness. They had to take Bunter as they found him; and if they did not find him quite as they had expected it could not be helped.

Supper was going strong when there came a tap at the door, and Talbot of the Shell glanced in.

"Bunter here?" he asked. "That new chap? Oh, here he is!"

"Here I am," said Bunter, blinking at him.

"Pretty nearly time Bunter got to his own House," said Talbot. "Mr. Ratcliff has just come across looking for him."

"Oh!" ejaculated Tom Merry.

"Ratty seems rather cross," said Talbot. "Bunter had better slip out before the old bird nails him."

"Can't!" said Bunter. "I haven't finished supper. Besides, I'm a School House chap, you know. I was sent here for the School House."

"Yaas, wathah!" said Arthur Augustus.

"Oh!" said Talbot, puzzled. "I understood that that was a mistake, and that you have been entered at the New House."

"I've changed my mind," said Bunter.

"Figgins & Co. bamboozled him into entering in the New House," explained Tom Merry. "They wanted to bag him for their House Eleven, you know. We've put it to Bunter, and he's sticking to us, after all."

Talbot whistled.

"Ratty will have something to say about that," he remarked. "I don't think a fellow can change after a Housemaster's put his name down."

There was a step in the passage.

"Here comes Kildare!"

The captain of St. Jim's came along to the door of No. 6.

"Talbot, have you seen that new kid Bunter——"

"Ahem!"

"Oh, here he is! Bunter, get back to your own House; you're not allowed to stay here so late."

"Oh, really, you know——"

"Cut off!" said Kildare.

Tom Merry & Co. exchanged glances. This was a new complication, and it began to look doubtful whether they would succeed in bagging Bunter, after all. Blake glanced at the fragments of his fretwork, and took comfort.

"The—the fact is, Kildare——" began Tom.

"Well?"

"Bunter belongs to the School House," explained Tom. "It—it was a —a mistake his name being put down in the New House——"

"Better explain that to his Housemaster," said Kildare. "Mr. Ratcliff is in Mr. Railton's study. You can go there with Bunter, if you like."

"Oh, all right!"

"I haven't finished my supper," said Bunter.

"Ahem! Housemasters can't wait while you finish your supper," said Tom Merry. "Better come along, Bunter."

"But there's the cake——"

"Get a move on!" snapped Kildare. "Do you want me to take you by the ear?"

Bunter blinked at the captain of St. Jim's, and decided to get a move on. With a discontented grunt, he followed Tom Merry from the study and down the stairs.

CHAPTER 2.

Mr. Ratcliff Puts His Foot Down.

MR. RATCLIFF, the master of the New House, wore a frown, as he often did.

He was in Mr. Railton's study, and he had declined the School House master's offer of a chair.

He was annoyed.

His sharp little eyes glittered as Tom Merry entered the study with the Owl of Greyfriars.

"Here is the boy!" he snapped.

"Bunter, you should not have stayed so late in this House," said Mr. Railton mildly. "You have given your Housemaster the trouble of coming over for you."

"For which you will be duly punished, Bunter!" snapped Mr. Ratcliff. "Follow me!"

"If you please——" began Tom Merry.

"You have nothing to do with this matter, Merry," grunted the New House master. "Follow me at once, Bunter!"

Bunter stood where he was. He did not like the look in Mr. Horace Ratcliff's greenish eyes.

"Bunter is a new boy, Mr. Ratcliff," remarked the School House master. "Doubtless he is unacquainted with House rules, so far——"

"Merry is perfectly well acquainted with them, and he appears to have kept Bunter here," said Mr. Ratcliff sourly. "Perhaps you are right, and the punishment should fall upon Merry instead of Bunter."

"Will you let me explain, sir?" exclaimed Tom Merry. "Bunter belongs to the School House!"

"Nonsense!"

"It's a fact, sir," said Tom, addressing Mr. Railton. "His father sent him here for the School House. The Head knows."

"I was under that impression, Merry," said Mr. Railton. "But Bunter himself explained to me that it was a mistake, and he applied personally to Mr. Ratcliff to have his name entered at the New House."

"Oh!" ejaculated Tom.

"That—that was a mistake, sir," stammered Bunter, liking less and less the look in Mr. Ratcliff's eye.

"Indeed! Another mistake, Bunter?"

"I was spoofed, sir," said Bunter. "Figgins spoofed me—— Yarooooh!"

"Bunter, what do you mean by shouting out in that manner?"

"Yow-ow-ow! That idiot Merry stamped on my foot! Yooop!"

Tom Merry's face became crimson as Mr. Railton gave him a stern look.

"Merry, are you attempting to keep Bunter from explaining the matter to me?"

"I—I—ahem!"

"You may retire, Merry; your presence is not required."

"But, sir——"

"Go!"

There was no possible answer to that, and Tom Merry went.

He haunted the passage, however, in a troubled state of mind. Evidently Bunter was going to give away the little game Figgins & Co. had played; which was against all the rules from the junior point of view.

Tom hardly liked to believe that Bunter was a sneak; he had liked and respected Wally Bunter, and he believed Billy to be Wally. He waited in the passage in a state of great uneasiness.

"Now, Bunter, explain yourself!" said Mr. Railton severely.

"I was spoofed, sir," said Bunter. "Figgins spun me yarns about chaps being half-starved in this House——"

"What?"

"So I joined the New House, sir, under a—a—a misapprehension," said Bunter. "But I'm a School House chap, sir. It's not my fault that I'm so much sought after. It comes of being so popular."

"Then your statement to me that a mistake had been made was a falsehood!" exclaimed Mr. Railton.

"Ahem! Nunno!"

"Then what was it?"

"It—it—it was a figure of speech, sir!" gasped Bunter.

"After the prevarication you have been guilty of, Bunter, I shall certainly refuse to rely upon any statements you make," said the Housemaster. "The matter must be settled by reference to your father. For the present you belong to Mr. Ratcliff's House, as your name is entered there, and you will go to your House at once!"

"I am waiting for you, Bunter!" said Mr. Ratcliff, in a voice that Von Tirpitz might have envied.

Billy Bunter blinked in dismay.

"But—but I don't want to go!" he spluttered. "I—I mean—— Yoooop!"

A loud howl escaped Bunter as Mr. Ratcliff's finger and thumb closed on his ear like a vice.

"Come!" said the New House master.

"Yow-ow-ow!"

"Silence!"

Mr. Ratcliff led Bunter from the study. In the passage he blinked dismally at Tom Merry as he was led away.

"I—I say, Merry——"

"Come!" rasped Mr. Ratcliff.

The dismayed Owl of Greyfriars was led out of the School House into the darkness of the quadrangle.

"Well, my hat!" murmured Tom Merry.

He returned rather dismally to Study No. 6, where he found his chums anxious for news.

"Where's Buntah, deah boy?" asked Arthur Augustus.

"Ratcliff's taken him away."

"Bai Jove! But he has no wight to take away a School House chap!" exclaimed the swell of St. Jim's warmly.

"Can't say I'm sorry," remarked Herries.

"Weally, Hewwies——"

"Look at my Latin grammar!"

"Bothah your Latin gwammah, Hewwies! I wefuse to allow Buntah to be kidnapped in this way by old Watty!"

"Well, it's his own fault," said Tom Merry. "He let Figgins spoof him, and——"

"He is wathah inexpewienced, Tom Mewwy."

"And he seems to have told Railton a lot of thumping lies!" said the captain of the Shell grimly.

"I wefuse to think so!"

"He's burned my Latin grammer," said Herries.

"Bai Jove! I weally think we shall nevah heah the end of that Latin gwammah. Buntah was vewy kind to light the fiah for us, and he was bound to use somethin'."

"Well, I'll change with you," said Herries. "I'll have your Latin grammar, and you can have mine—what's left of it."

"Pway, don't be an unweasonable ass, Hewwies!"

"So the New House has bagged Bunter, after all," said Manners. "He'll be playing against us in the House match on Saturday. That's what those New House bounders wanted all along."

"It's going to be settled by the Head writing to Bunter's pater," said Tom Merry.

"Good!" said Arthur Augustus. "That means that he will come into the School House, aftah all! Vewy good indeed!"

"Well, we'll be glad to have him," said Tom. "I liked him well enough when I met him at Greyfriars, when he was visiting his cousin Billy at the time of our footer-match there. We don't seem to have seen him at his best today."

"He is a weally wippin' fellow," said Arthur Augustus. "I made fwiends with him, an' I am not goin' back on a fwiend."

"He's given Figgins & Co. away to the Housemasters."

"Bai Jove! I am suah he did so inadvertently, Tom Mewwy; he could not have meant to give them away."

Tom Merry laughed.

"All serene, Gussy; we'll think the

best we can of him. Hallo! Here comes Darrell to rout us out to the dorm!"

Tom Merry & Co. went up to bed rather puzzled about Bunter, and not quite knowing what to make of him. Certainly, so far he had not borne out their previous high opinion of Wally Bunter. But they were willing to be charitable, and to think the best they could of him; and that was all they could do.

Meanwhile, the Owl of Greyfriars was not having a happy time in the New House!

CHAPTER 3.
Going Through It.

"FIGGINS! Kerr! Wynn!"

Monteith of the Sixth looked into the Common-room in the New House, and rapped out those three names in succession.

Figgins & Co. looked round, ceasing a rather excited football argument with Redfern and Lawrence. Monteith was looking grim.

"Yes, Monteith?"

"Mr. Ratcliff wants you three in his study," said Monteith. "Cut off at once!"

"Oh! Anything up?" asked Kerr.

"To judge by Mr. Ratcliff's expression, something certainly is up," said the prefect drily. "I advise you to hurry."

"Right-ho!"

The three juniors started for the Housemaster's study not in a happy mood. Nobody in the New House enjoyed being called on the carpet by Mr. Ratcliff.

"What the dickens is the row?" murmured Fatty Wynn uneasily. "We haven't trodden on Ratty's corns that I know of. He can't have heard of the rabbit-pie in the study, I suppose? If he has, it's not his bizney. 'Tain't over the rations."

"It isn't the rabbit-pie, fathead!" said Kerr. "May be something to do with that new kid Bunter."

"I don't see how it can be," said Figgins. "He's gone into the School House, after all. We could spring Ratty on them, and get him to claim the fat bounder as a New House fellow, only—only——"

"Only we can't!" said Kerr, with a grin. "That's not in the game. It looks as if we've lost Bunter, after all. But I wonder what's the matter with Ratty?"

Kerr rubbed his hands with painful anticipation.

The three juniors presented themselves in Mr. Ratcliff's study. Bunter was already there. He was standing with an expression of mingled indignation and apprehension on his fat face. He blinked wrathfully at the Co. as they came in. He attributed his present plight to them and to their little scheme of bagging him for their House.

Mr. Ratcliff eyed the juniors grimly.

"You—you sent for us, sir?" faltered George Figgins.

"I sent for you, Figgins, to question you with regard to this boy Bunter. It appears that the matter has been misrepresented to me——"

"Oh, sir!"

"Bunter, it appears, was sent here to the School House, and he spoke falsely in informing me that a mistake had been made."

Figgins & Co. were silent.

It was not their fault that Billy Bunter had departed from the strict line of veracity. They had not wanted him to.

"Bunter spoke falsely owing, apparently, to your persuasions," said Mr. Ratcliffe. "You induced hm to come into this House when he was intended for the other."

"We—we wanted him here, sir."

"You were aware that he was intended for the School House?"

"Ahem! Yes, sir! But—but we thought he might as well suit himself, our House being the—the best House," explained Figgins.

"You had no right whatever to interfere, Figgins!"

"Ahem!"

"I was deceived by this boy, who certainly uttered a falsehood."

"Oh, really, sir——" came from Bunter. "I must say, sir——"

"Silence! The boy's name has been entered in this House, and the House-dame has been given the trouble of making arrangements for him," said Mr. Ratcliff. "I also have been put to trouble. He is now to remain here till his father has been written to. All this trouble, Figgins, has been caused by your reckless deception!"

"Ahem!"

"According to Bunter's statements, you deceived him——"

"What?"

"So you did!" exclaimed Bunter, blinking at Figgins. "You spoofed me! You were entirely to blame! You don't deny that. It was your fault all along!"

Figgins stared at him.

"You can't deny it!" hooted Bunter.

"I don't want to!" said Figgins contemptuously. "If I'd known you were a sneaking cad I wouldn't have troubled my head about you!"

"Oh, really, Figgins——"

"Figgins! How dare you use such expressions!" thundered Mr. Ratcliff. "I shall punish you three juniors for the trick you have played."

He picked up his cane.

Figgins & Co. said no more.

The little scheme they had played was really a harmless one, due to their rivalry with Tom Merry & Co. of the other House; but it was useless to attempt to explain all that to Mr. Ratcliff. They had been sent for to be punished, and they had to go through it.

They went through it in the next few minutes, with all the fortitude they could muster.

Swish, swish, swish!

Billy Bunter blinked on, wondering whether his turn was coming He was soon enlightened.

"Now, Bunter!" said Mr. Ratcliff.

Bunter started back.

"If—if you please, sir——"

"Hold out your hand!"

"I—I should like to point out, sir, that I wasn't to blame!" gasped Bunter. "I—I—I—it was Figgins all the time, sir, and—and Kerr, and—and Wynn. "I'm shocked at them, sir; in fact, disgusted that——"

"Hold out your hand, Bunter!"

"I—I despise them, sir! I believe they're thoroughly bad," said Bunter. "I—I wasn't to blame in the least! They'll bear me out in that!"

"Do you hear me, Bunter?"

"Ye-es, sir! Certainly! But——"

"If you do not hold out your hand at once, Bunter, you shall be flogged instead of caned!" thundered Mr. Ratcliff.

"Oh, dear!"

Billy Bunter's fat hand came gingerly out.

Mr. Ratcliff's expression was quite Hunnish as he took aim with the cane. Evidently it was going to be a terrific swish, and the acid-tempered master was putting his beef into it.

Bunter's heart failed him as he saw it coming. Without stopping to think, he jerked back his hand as the cane descended.

Whack!

Naturally, as the cane met with no resistance, it continued its career, and was stopped by Mr. Ratcliff's own leg.

"Yoop!" roared Mr. Ratcliff, as he caught it. And he hopped on the other leg in anguish.

Figgins & Co. gasped.

Billy Bunter blinked at the Housemaster in utter dismay. He had certainly not intended that to happen, and he was too terrified to move as he saw the Housemaster hopping on one leg.

"Oh, dear!" he gasped.

"Ow! Oh! Yaw-woop! Ugh! Ooooop!" came from Mr. Ratcliff. "You—you young rascal! Oooooop! You young scoundrel! Yooop!"

"I—I say, sir—— I—I—— Oh, crumbs! Leggo! Yarooooh!"

Mr. Ratcliff's left hand fastened on Bunter's collar. The cane rose in his right, and descended.

Swish, swish, swish, swish!

Bunter's yells rang through the study. Figgins & Co. retreated into the passage, not wishing to catch Mr. Ratcliff's eye again. But the Housemaster was not thinking of them. All his attention was devoted to Bunter, and the unhappy Owl of Greyfriars was going through it with a vengeance.

The terrific yells that rang from Mr. Ratcliff's study drew fellows to the passage outside, and they listened in awe—without venturing too near the door, however.

Billy Bunter came forth at last.

He came at a run; and the study door closed behind him with a slam.

"Yow-ow-ow-ow-ow-wooooop!" roared Bunter.

"Had it bad?" asked Redfern sympathetically. It was rather an unnecessary question.

"Yoop! Yah! I won't stay here!" howled Bunter. "Oh, dear! I wish I was at Greyfriars! Ow-ow-ow!"

"Shut up that row, Bunter!" said Monteith, coming along the corridor. "Bed-time, you fags! Get off to your dormitory!"

"Yow-ow-ow!"

"This way, Bunter!" said Figgins.

"Yah! Beast! Yow-ow-ow-ow!"

Billy Bunter gave the Co. a glare, and rolled away. He was not feeling friendly towards Figgins & Co. just then.

In the dormitory he turned a deaf ear to words of consolation. He was still grunting and snorting when Monteith put the light out, and he grunted and snorted himself to sleep at last.

CHAPTER 4.
Well Matched.

TOM MERRY & CO. looked for Bunter when they came down the following morning. They were rather curious to know how he had got on with Mr. Ratcliff. But they did not find the fat junior in the quad before breakfast. They found Figgins & Co. taking a brisk walk; but the new junior was not to be seen.

"Where's Bunter?" asked Tom Merry.

Figgins gave a grunt.

"Still in the dorm! He didn't turn out at rising-bell."

"Lazybones!" explained Fatty Wynn.

"Did he catch it from Ratty?"

"Yes; can't say I'm very sorry," said Figgins candidly. "He isn't exactly the fellow I thought him."

Tom Merry smiled. That was exactly his own impression of Bunter.

"He seemed a really decent chap when we met him at Greyfriars," remarked Monty Lowther.

"He seems to have changed a bit," said Kerr. "He doesn't seem to have the faintest idea of playing the game. I can't understand how we were so taken in by him."

"Sorry you bagged him?" grinned Manners.

Kerr laughed. His little scheme had turned out a success in a way, after all. Bunter had been bagged—at least for the present. But the Scottish junior was beginning to doubt whether the prize was worth the trouble.

"You can have him back, so far as I'm concerned," he answered.

"Keep him, old chap!" said Tom Merry affably. "I make you a present of him."

And the Terrible Three strolled on, smiling.

"After all, we've got him," said Figgins. "He seems to be a bit of a worm in some respects, but he's a footballer; we know that, because we've seen him play at Greyfriars. And he's a rod in pickle for those School House bounders on Saturday."

"Yes, there's that!" agreed Kerr.

"After all, we must remember he's a new kid, and—and he dropped in under rather unusual circumstances," said Figgins tolerantly. "We ought to make allowances for him."

"Oh, certainly!" said Kerr, rather drily.

"He's got his good points," said Fatty Wynn. "He knows how to cook, and he's a judge of cooking. He doesn't eat a thing without looking at it or caring what it is, like you, Figgy."

Figgins chuckled.

"Well, as he's got his good points, we'll make the best of him," he said. "At least he's a good forward, and he will be no end of use in the House Eleven on Saturday. Make the best of him, and keep friendly with the chap, and he may turn out all right, after all."

Kerr nodded without speaking.

He was not so sure of the possibility of making friends with a fellow like Bunter; but he was loyally prepared to back up Figgins, and see what could be done.

After all, Bunter could not very well be dropped like a hot potato, after being taken up with so much enthusiasm. It was only fair play to give him a chance.

At breakfast in the New House, therefore, Figgins & Co. smiled genially at the Owl of Greyfriars.

They received a glare in response.

Apparently Bunter wasn't prepared to receive their friendly overtures in a friendly spirit.

He had not forgotten his licking yet; and he could not forgive Figgins & Co. for having landed him, like a fat fish, in the New House.

True, he owed his punishment to his own untruthfulness, for which Figgins & Co. certainly were not responsible; but he visited it all upon their heads. Moreover, he was separated from Arthur Augustus D'Arcy, and he had looked upon that wealthy youth as a prospective goldmine.

After breakfast Figgins & Co. joined him, and walked out with him, Bunter wearing a lofty and disdainful expression.

He was going out to look for D'Arcy, as a matter of fact, and he had no use for the New House chums.

"Like to come and see my rabbits, Bunter?" asked Figgins affably.

Bunter thawed a little.

"I don't mind cooking rabbits for you after lessons," he said.

"Ahem! I don't meant that. White rabbits, you know."

"They can be eaten all right," said Bunter.

"Mine can't!" answered Figgins shortly.

Bunter sniffed.

"We'll show you round the school a bit," said Kerr amicably. "You haven't really seen St. Jim's yet."

"You needn't trouble."

"Ahem!"

"The fact is, I'm going to speak to my old pal D'Arcy," said Bunter. "You fellows needn't worry about me!"

And he rolled away, leaving Figgins & Co. staring. Figgins breathed hard through his nose.

Figgy was not accustomed to wasting much attention upon a mere new kid; and to have his friendly attention turned down in this way was rather a facer for him.

"Never mind; he's got his back up," he said. "We must make allowances."

"Hum!" said Kerr.

Bunter succeeded in discovering Arthur Augustus D'Arcy. He attached himself to that noble youth until lessons, and came into the Form-room with him.

It is possible that the noble Gussy did not find himself so much at ease with the new fellow as he had expected to be with Wally Bunter; but if that was so, he would not admit it even to himself. Loyalty was Gussy's strongest trait; he had made a friend of Bunter, and he was going to stick to him—so long as he could, at all events.

Mr. Lathom, the master of the Fourth, eyed Bunter a good deal in class that morning. Even Baggy Trimble was not denser than Bunter; and the fat junior's denseness was accompanied by a self-satisfaction which was a little exasperating However, Mr. Lathom was very lenient with a new boy, and Bunter got through the morning.

Tom Merry & Co. rushed Arthur Augustus away to footer-practice the moment the juniors were dismissed, and Bunter was not able to nail him. He did not feel any inclination whatever to follow the juniors to the footer-ground.

He was blinking about him in the doorway when Baggy Trimble came up, with a friendly grin on his fat face.

Bunter eyed him.

Baggy Trimble was a youth whose rotundity of figure rivalled Bunter's own, and, indeed, he resembled Bunter in a good many other respects.

But Trimble had his sweetest smile on now.

"I've been going to speak to you, Bunter," he remarked. "I hear that you're quite a terrific footballer."

"That's me!" said Bunter cheerfully.

"Well, I'll tell you what I was thinking," said Baggy. "At home—at Trimble Hall——"

"Where?"

"Trimble Hall—my home, you know," said Baggy affably. "At Trimble Hall we're going to do rather big things this Easter. The pater's keeping open house for a lot of wounded officers, chiefly generals, and we're doing a lot to entertain them. Among other things, the pater's asked me to bring a crowd of fellows home."

"Has he?" said Bunter.

"He has! We're going to get up two footer elevens, and play matches, and all that—sort of football week, you know," said Baggy. "Hearing that you were a great gun at footer, I determined to ask you."

Taking a Pig by the Ear!
(See Chapter 2.)

Bunter blinked at him. This was really flattering, and the Owl of Greyfriars began to swell.

"I'd like to ask you to captain one team, if you would," said Trimble. "Of course, there's not only footer. There'll be a lot going on, in one way or another. Care for shooting?"

"I'm a dab at it."

"Then you'll like Trimble Hall. Skate?"

"Like a bird!"

"I—I've never seen a bird skate!" said Trimble, staring.

"I mean, I skate jolly well. Precious few things I don't do well, if you come to that," said Bunter.

"I can quite believe it," said Trimble cordially. "You're a dancing-man, I can see that. A fellow with your figure would be bound to dance. Care for it?"

"Yes, rather! You should have seen me when they gave a dance at Cliff

House!" said Bunter. "The girls couldn't take their eyes off me."

"I'm not surprised at it—not at all. Shall I put you down on my list, then?" asked Trimble. "I've only got fifteen fellows down so far—D'Arcy and Tom Merry and Blake, and Talbot and Cutts of the Fifth, and some others."

"Put me down, by all means," said Bunter. "If you give parties and so on, you can depend on me to make them go."

"I will! The pater will be delighted to see you!" said Trimble heartily. "You'll meet some fairly decent people at my place—Lord French, you know, and Robertson. I don't know if you care for military men——"

"Certainly!"

"And some rather big political johnnies," said Trimble carelessly—"Asquith and Lloyd George, and that lot, you know. We bar Lansdowne. I don't care much for them myself. I find Asquith rather a bore."

"D-d-do you?"

"He talks too much," said Trimble. "I suppose you won't feel nervous if you meet Royalty?"

"N-n-not at all!" gasped Bunter.

"We're rather expecting King George for a few days at Easter. I'm so glad you're coming, Bunter!"

"Rely on me."

"By the way," said Trimble confidentially, "my remittance hasn't come to hand yet—a tenner I was expecting from my pater."

"Oh!" said Bunter, his manner changing a little.

"It's rather a nuisance, because I've lent D'Arcy my last quid. Could you lend me half-a-sov till the next post, old chap?"

Bunter blinked at him.

Trimble had come down to facts at last.

"Certainly," said Bunter. "I'm expecting a postal-order, and as soon as it comes just remind me, will you?"

"The fact is," said Trimble, "I'm actually hard up at the present moment. It's rather absurd—ha, ha!—but there you are. These things happen."

"They do!" agreed Bunter.

"If you could lend me a bob till the post comes in——"

"Certainly!" said Bunter.

He drove his hand into his pocket, and Trimble's eyes glistened. But the fat hand came out empty.

"I remember now," said Bunter calmly. "I left my purse in Figgins' study. So sorry!"

He rolled out into the quadrangle, leaving Baggy Trimble staring after him. Trimble could not make up his mind whether Bunter was the biggest fool he had ever met, or whether he wasn't!

He determined, at all events, to be on hand when Bunter's postal-order arrived. He was not aware that his schooldays were likely to be over and forgotten by that time.

CHAPTER 5.
Making Himself at Home.

"COMING down to footer, old fellow?"

Figgins asked that question after dinner, tapping Bunter on the shoulder quite cordially.

Bunter blinked at him through his big glasses.

"No!" he answered.

"Ahem!" murmured Figgins.

"I don't care for racing about after a ball just after dinner. It's not good for the inside."

"Oh, it's not regular practice, you know—just punting the ball about a bit."

"Well, I 'm not coming! You haven't treated me well," said Bunter distantly. "You told me fellows were half-starved in the School House——"

"I told you Trimble said he was half-starved there," corrected Figgins. "So he did. He says so every day."

"Twice a day!" remarked Kerr.

"More like a dozen times!" said Fatty Wynn, with a grin. "Trimble's a fat, greedy bounder!"

"You told me the New House master always asked a fellow to take a second helping, and a third," pursued Bunter warmly. "That was you, Kerr."

"Not at all!" answered Kerr. "I asked you what you thought of a House-master who did so. Quite a different thing."

Bunter snorted.

"Old Ratcliff is a stingy beast!" he said. "He sticks an eye like a gimlet on a chap who wants enough to eat."

"You didn't do badly."

"Why, I'm simply famished!" said Bunter indignantly.

"My dear man, the grub's the same in both Houses, so you'd be famished anyway," said Figgins. "Besides, you can get things at the tuckshop to eke it out if you like."

Bunter brightened up.

"Well, that's a good idea," he said. "But I'm in rather a difficulty there. My postal-order hasn't arrived."

"Were you expecting one?"

"Of course! It ought to have been here by the first post this morning; in fact, I dare say it has come, and hasn't been handed out yet. If you'd care to lend me the ten bob, Figgins——"

"What ten bob?"

"The postal-order's for ten. Then I'd hand it to you as soon as I get the letter. It comes to the same thing, doesn't it?"

"Quite!" agreed Figgins. "Only I——"

"Only what?" grunted Bunter.

"Only I haven't got ten bob," explained Figgins.

Grunt.

"Half-a-crown any good?" asked Figgins.

Smile.

"My dear chap, you're a Briton!" said Bunter affectionately. "I'll settle this out of my postal-order."

"Right you are!"

With half-a-crown in his podgy paw, Bunter started for Dame Taggles' little shop. At Greyfriars Bunter spent a portion of each day trying to obtain extra supplies of rationed food at the school shop, never daunted by continual failure. He was wondering whether he would have better luck at St. Jim's.

But Dame Taggles uttered that disagreeable word coupons at once when Bunter demanded a tin of beef and a pot of jam, and the Owl of Greyfriars had to come down to unrationed articles.

However, he found considerable satisfaction in expending Figgins' half-crown, and he looked rather shiny and smeary when he turned up for afternoon lessons.

After lessons, as there was still light enough for some footer practice, most of the juniors were on Little Side, whither Bunter did not follow.

With his football reputation it was rather odd that he did not seem in a hurry to touch the game; and Figgins, who was anxious to see the form he was in, was getting rather impatient about it. But Bunter declined, and the Co. left him to himself.

Baggy Trimble joined him as he was making for the New House, with a genial smile, but a suspicious eye.

"The post's in," he remarked.

"I know."

"Did your postal-order come?"

"There's been some delay in the post," said Bunter, with a grunt. "For some reason it hasn't turned up. To-morrow morning, I expect. Did you get your remittance from Trimble Hall?"

Trimble nodded.

"Oh, yes!" he answered carelessly.

"A tenner?" exclaimed Bunter, his round eyes growing rounder behind his spectacles.

"Yes," assented Trimble. "I rather expected a pony, but the pater made it a tenner after all. He's getting rather close with money."

"I—I say, Trimble!" Bunter almost gasped. "My postal-order's sure to come in the morning. Could you lend me——"

"How much, old fellow?"

"Ten bob!"

"Why didn't you ask me ten minutes ago?" said Trimble regretfully. "I've just settled my bill at the tuckshop, and then Tom Merry borrowed what I had left—cleared me right out. It's really too bad, isn't it?"

Billy Bunter grunted, and rolled on to the New House without replying. As a matter of fact, Bunter and Trimble were well matched, and both of them were beginning to realise it.

Bunter found his study—Figgins' study—empty, which did not displease him. He intended to have an early tea before Figgins & Co. came in.

He blinked into the study cupboard, and his face brightened.

In five minutes he was seated at the table, and the cold rabbit that was intended to furnish a tea for four was furnishing a tea for one.

Figgy's supply of sardines followed it, and Fatty Wynn's cake.

The cupboard was in the state of the celebrated Mrs. Hubbard's when Bunter had finished.

He was feeling a little better now, though still, like Alexander, sighing for fresh worlds to conquer, when Figgins & Co. came tramping in, ruddy and hungry from footer.

"Hallo, here you are!" exclaimed Figgins cheerily. "Ready for tea, Bunter?"

"Yes, rather!" assented Bunter. "I was wondering when you fellows would come in."

"Well, here we are! Not a jiffy now," said Figgins, going to the cupboard. "Are you hungry, old chap?"

"Famished!"

"You might have taken a snack," said Fatty Wynn, who could feel for a fellow who was famished.

"Well, I have," said Bunter. "I've had a snack, but I'm ready for tea."

"Hallo! Where's that rabbit?" exclaimed Figgins, staring into the empty cupboard.

"And the sardines?" asked Kerr.

"And my cake?" boomed Fatty Wynn, staring over Figgy's shoulder with quite a horrified expression. "Some awful rotter has boned our grub!"

"I—I say, you fellows——"

Figgins & Co. looked at Bunter. They remembered that he had had a snack.

"D-d-did you——" stuttered Fatty Wynn.

"I finished the rabbit," said Bunter calmly. "It was a rotten small one."

"And the sardines?"

"Yes; I thought I'd better, as I was going to wait for tea till you fellows came in."

"You—you—you've scoffed my cake!" gasped Fatty Wynn.

"Well, it wasn't much of a cake," said Bunter. "But I managed to get it down. I'm not a particular chap."

"You—you—you——" stuttered Fatty Wynn, at a loss for words.

There were no words in the English language, or even the Welsh, that could have expressed his feelings at that moment. Even German would not have done justice to them.

Bunter blinked cheerfully at the petrified Co. They were hungry from footer, and there was nothing for tea. Even the war-bread had vanished, almost to the last crumb.

"Well, what are we going to have for tea?" asked Bunter.

"You've scoffed our tea!" roared Figgins at last.

"You—you—you fat Hun!" howled Fatty Wynn.

"Fat!" repeated Bunter. "Well, I like that! I suppose you weigh about a ton!"

"Well, it can't be helped now," began Figgins pacifically. "But you'll have to learn not to bag all the grub in the study, Bunter. That's a bit too thick."

"I'm going to scalp him!" hooted Fatty Wynn.

"Shush!"

Bunter's lip curled in disdain.

"If you're worried about a measly old rabbit and a tin or two of sardines, I'll pay for them!" he said scornfully.

"Oh, dry up! You're not wanted to pay for them," growled Figgins. "Only go easy on other fellows' grub."

"As you make a fuss about such a trifling matter, I shall insist upon paying for the things!" said Bunter loftily.

"Let him do it, then!" hooted Fatty Wynn. "We can get something or other at the shop, and we're all stony!"

"Oh, rats!" said Figgins uneasily. "The fat bounder's not going to pay us anything!"

"Rot! Let him stand a tea, as he's bagged our tommy!" exclaimed Fatty. "I'm hungry! Hungry, I tell you! We've missed tea in Hall!"

"Yes, let him pay up!" said Kerr, who was looking very keenly at the Owl of Greyfriars. "Why not?"

"What's the amount?" asked Bunter contemptuously. "Will five bob cover it?"

"Make it five bob," said Kerr quietly.

"Then I'll settle up—as soon as my postal-order comes."

"I guessed that was coming," said Kerr. "That's why I spoke. You don't intend to settle up, Bunter. You're not expecting a remittance at all; and you're a fat, lying, spoofing bounder!"

"Kerr, old chap——" murmured Figgins.

"I won't lick you, Kerr——" began Bunter.

"Oh, do!" said Kerr.

"But I shall certainly decline to remain in this study if I'm not treated with civility."

"Get out of it, then!" hooted Fatty Wynn.

"Oh, really, Wynn——"

"Shush!" said Figgins. "Look here, Bunter——"

Bunter gave him a lofty blink.

"You needn't speak to me, Figgins!" he said. "As you're not having tea in this study, I shall go to tea with my old pal D'Arcy. I must say I think this is a rotten House, and I shall be glad to change over!"

With that Bunter rolled out of the study, and slammed the door after him.

"I—I—I'll go after him and pulverise him!" hissed Fatty Wynn.

"You won't!" grinned Figgins. "Let's go along and see if Reddy's got anything for tea. After all, the chap's going to play footer for us on Saturday, and help us beat the School House!"

"Oh, blow footer!" growled Fatty Wynn. "I want my tea! Besides, the fat bounder has been fighting shy of footer, and I shouldn't wonder if he's no good at all!"

"Rats! You saw him play at Greyfriars."

"Well, he's a fat rotter, and doesn't look like a footballer!" said Wynn. "He's too jolly fat to put up much of a game!"

"Ha, ha, ha!"

"What are you cackling at now?" demanded the Falstaff of the New House.

"Nothing, old son! Come and see Reddy!" grinned Figgins.

And Figgins & Co. started on a voyage of discovery in quest of tea, what time Billy Bunter was calling on his friends in the School House with the same object in view.

CHAPTER 6.
Very Short Commons.

"TWOT in, deah boy!"

Arthur Augustus D'Arcy smiled genially as a fat face and spectacles glimmered in the doorway of Study No. 6.

Blake and Herries and Digby did not look enthusiastic, but they contrived to smile.

Study No. 6 were about to have tea, and Blake & Co. did not need telling that that was why Bunter had given them a look-in.

Supplies were short in Study No. 6, however, the state of the money market being tight.

Blake wondered what Bunter would think of the tea.

"I thought I'd drop in, old nuts!" said Bunter affably. "I'm really a School House chap, you know. I feel more at home here. Kindred spirits, you know."

"That's wight!"

"Figgins & Co. pressed me to stay to tea, but I felt bound to decline," said Bunter. "I told Figgins I was sorry, but I couldn't leave my pals in the lurch."

"Good man!" said Arthur Augustus approvingly. "I wish we had somethin' bettah to offah you, Buntah; but war-time, you know. I'm suah you don't mind."

"Not at all!" answered Bunter. "So long as there's good stuff, and plenty of it, you won't find me complaining."

"Oh, bai Jove!"

Blake & Co. wore rather curious expressions as they laid out the frugal tea-table.

There was bread; fortunately, no shortage of that. There was one tin of pilchards—a small tin. There was coffee—rather weak—plenty of water, but a limited supply of the stimulating bean. Such as it was, Bunter was welcome to share it.

Supplies might be limited, but the hospitality of Study No. 6 was unbounded. The question was, how Bunter would enjoy the hospitality without the supplies? Arthur Augustus felt a little concerned; though his concern would probably have been relieved if he had been aware of how exceedingly well Bunter had already done himself in the New House.

Bunter's expression, too, became rather odd as he blinked at the tea-table. He had led himself to expect that Study No. 6 was a land flowing with milk and honey.

War-time restrictions could be got round by a fellow with plenty of money, and as D'Arcy was the son of a wealthy nobleman Bunter did not see why there should be frugality in No. 6. Gussy's great maxim of "Noblesse oblige" did not appeal to the Owl of Greyfriars in the least.

"Short commons—what?" remarked Bunter, as he took the tin-opener from Dig and started on the pilchards.

"Yaas, old fellow, wathah!"

"War-time, you know," remarked Blake.

"Oh, all serene!" said Bunter. "Luckily, I'm not what you'd call a hungry chap. I've always had rather a delicate appetite."

He opened the tin quite deftly, and turned out the pilchards into a plate. He sat before that plate, and took up a fork.

The Fourth-Formers watched him with curious looks.

"Pass the bread, Blake!"

"Oh, yes! Here you are!"

"Any butter?"

"Nunno."

"Never mind. I can rough it," said Bunter. "These pilchards are not bad. What are you fellows going to have, though?"

"Eh?"

"Not at all bad," went on Bunter. "Is that coffee? I'll take a cup, please. I take both sugar and milk—plenty of sugar, please."

"Oh!" gasped Blake.

There were five lumps of sugar in the mustard-tin, which was all that remained of the study's supply. Bunter blinked at them.

"Sugar limited?" he asked.

"Yes-es."

"Then I'll have only one cup of coffee, please."

And Bunter cheerfully ladled the five lumps into his one cup of coffee, somewhat to the consternation of Study No. 6.

"You fellows don't take sugar?" he asked affably.

"Oh! Ah! Nunno!"

"Not to-day, at all events," grunted Herries.

"You're really better without it," said Bunter comfortingly. "Sugar isn't what it used to be. Besides, you don't need sugar if you have plenty of honey."

"But we haven't any honey," said Herries.

"Ah! That's a mistake," said Bunter. "You should get it, you know."

"All sweetstuffs are rationed now."

"But you had time to lay in a supply before that," said Bunter. "It's only a question of money."

"Bai Jove!"

"That's hoarding," said Herries.

"Weally, Hewwies——" murmured Arthur Augustus, in distress.

"Well, isn't that hoarding?" demanded Herries, who was getting very restive, and had an expression on his rugged face that reminded his study-mates of Towser. "What do you call it?"

"I am suah Buntah was only jokin'," said Arthur Augustus.

Bunter gave him a quick blink.

"Oh, of course!" he said. "I suppose you could see, Herries, that my remark was simply a joke?"

"Oh, was it?" grunted Herries.

"If you think I would hoard——" began Bunter warmly.

"Hewwies does not think so, old chap," said Arthur Augustus soothingly. But Herries did not speak. He gave a subdued snort.

"You fellows ain't eating anything," said Bunter, when the pilchards were gone. "Not hungry—what?" He rose from the table. "If you'll excuse me, I'll look in on Tom Merry. I'm really sorry I can't stay longer; but a chap has to portion out his time, as it were, when he's a great deal sought after. Ta-ta!"

And Bunter rolled out of Study No. 6, leaving a deep silence there—a silence that was more expressive than words.

The fat junior rolled along to the Shell passage, and looked in at Tom Merry's study.

The Terrible Three were at tea, and they gave Bunter a genial welcome.

"Trot in, old scout!" said Tom Merry. "Had your tea?"

"Not yet," said Bunter. "I don't mind joining you fellows."

"Sit down, kid," said Manners.

Bunter sat down. The study table was rather well supplied, as it happened, and Bunter blinked over it with great satisfaction.

He did not waste much time on conversation. He travelled through the provisions at express speed, and the Terrible Three, constrained by politeness, did not enter into competition with him.

The pot of home-made jam, from Tom Merry's old governess, Miss Priscilla, was untouched when Bunter arrived, and after he arrived nobody else had a chance of touching it. Quite odd expressions grew on the faces of the Shell fellows as the Owl of Greyfriars proceeded. He finished when a single crumb did not remain on the table.

"Time this blessed war ended, I think!" said Bunter at last. "I'm getting fed up with rations. Short commons once in a way ain't so bad; but short commons all the time get on a fellow's nerves. It's bad for the health. Don't you think so?"

"Ye-es!" gasped Tom Merry. "I—I suppose so."

"Not that I complain," said Bunter magnanimously. "I'm patriotic, I hope. A snack like this will see me through, if there's nothing better going."

"Oh!" said Lowther.

"You fellows finished?" asked Bunter.

"Ye-es."

"Well, I'll be getting along," remarked the Owl of Greyfriars, as it became clear that no fresh supplies were to be produced. "I've got to see Talbot."

He gave the Terrible Three a gracious nod, and rolled out, leaving them blinking at one another.

"Mum-mum-my hat!" murmured Monty Lowther.

Tom Merry burst into a laugh.

"Come to think of it," remarked Manners, "I don't envy Figgins & Co. their prize! I rather think it will be a good thing for this House if Bunter stays over there."

"I wonder how he gets on with Fatty Wynn?" grinned Lowther.

"Ha, ha, ha!"

"Hallo! What's that?" exclaimed Manners a minute later, as a loud roar came from the passage.

"Yarooh!"

"You fat rotter! That's my marmalade!"

"Yoop!"

Bump!

The Terrible Three rushed into the passage.

CHAPTER 7.

Arthur Augustus Receives a Shock.

BILLY BUNTER was sitting on the floor clutching at his glasses, which had slid down his fat little nose. Over him towered George Gore of the Shell, his face red with wrath.

"What's the row, Gore?" exclaimed Tom Merry.

"Look at him!" roared Gore furiously. "Just caught him coming out of my study with my marmalade under his arm!"

"Yaroooh!"

"Oh, my hat!" ejaculated Lowther. "Bunter, my fat pippin——"

"Yoop! Keep him off! Yaroooh!"

"My marmalade!" roared Gore. "The very last lot! And that fat pig——"

"Shush!" murmured Tom Merry. "Here's your blessed marmalade. Don't make such a terrific row, old scout!"

The jar of marmalade had rolled along when Bunter sat down. Tom Merry picked it up.

"I say, you fellows, that's mine!" howled Bunter.

"What?" shouted Gore, in amazement and wrath. "You just brought it out of my study!"

"I—I say, you fellows——" Bunter scrambled up. "Look here, that's mine! I hope you don't think, Tom Merry, that I'd touch another fellow's marmalade?"

Tom Merry stared at him.

"Gore says you brought it out of his study," he answered.

"I happened to have it under my arm, because I'd stepped in to speak to Talbot," explained Bunter.

"You—you had it with you?" ejaculated Manners.

"Yes; exactly."

The Terrible Three fairly blinked at Bunter. It was only a few minutes since he had left their study, and they had seen no sign of marmalade about him while he was there.

Cadet Notes.

Did you make any resolutions for New Year and, if so, have you kept them? If you have not, I am going to suggest some resolutions for you. Let those boys who have not yet joined a Cadet Corps find out where the nearest Corps is, and if they are eligible, let them become members. If a boy joins now he will be able to make himself efficient during the winter months, so as to take his share of the larger duties in the summer. He will probably get a holiday in camp somewhere in the country, and is certain of some good exercise in the open air.

Some boys still appear to confuse the Cadets with the Regular Army. For their benefit we will repeat that a Cadet Corps is only for boys between the ages of 14 and 18, and takes up a little of their spare time only, and requires but a small subscription from its members. Most Corps teach Infantry Drill; some also give Machine-Gun and Engineering Instruction. Members wear uniform and learn to shoot. In the winter most of the training is done indoors in the evening, with occasional outdoor parades at the week-ends. In the summer most of the work is out of doors, and most Corps go away to camp for a short time. Any lad who does not belong to a Cadet Corps is missing a great opportunity of making himself healthy, smart, and efficient. It costs practically nothing, and its advantages are enormous, and we believe that it is only ignorance which keeps so many lads from joining. Any boy who would like to know the nearest Corps should write, stating age, etc., to the C.A.V.R., Judges' Quadrangle, Law Courts, Strand, London, W.C. 2.

Gore seemed speechless.

"You had it with you!" repeated Tom Merry blankly. "But you hadn't it with you in our study, Bunter."

Bunter started a little.

"Yes, I—I had," he stammered. "The fact is, I brought it over to—to offer you fellows for tea, but—but I forgot it."

"You lying Hun!" roared Gore.

"Oh, really, you know——"

"Look here, Bunter——" began Tom.

"I say, you fellows, it's mine, you know! Gimme my marmalade, Tom Merry!" hooted Bunter.

"But—but you couldn't have had it when you were in our study!" roared Monty Lowther. "We should have seen it if you had."

"I—I had it in my pocket."

"In your pip-pip-pocket?"

"Yes, of course!"

"A three-pound jar of marmalade in your pocket!" yelled Manners.

"I—I—I mean, I hadn't it exactly in my pocket!" stammered Bunter. "I—I really meant to say I should have had it in my pocket if my pocket had been big enough. See?"

"Oh, my hat! And where did you have it, then, while you were in our study?" demanded Manners.

Bunter paused a moment. That really required thinking out.

"I—I left it out in the passage, now I come to think of it," he replied. "I dropped it, and forgot it."

"You didn't hear it drop?" asked Lowther sarcastically.

"Exactly—I didn't! I—I saw it as I came out, and picked it up again. See? Give me my marmalade, Tom Merry!"

"Well, my only sainted Aunt Jane!" ejaculated Tom Merry. "Here's your marm, Gore."

George Gore grabbed the jar.

"It's mine!" hooted Bunter.

"Don't be funny, old scout!" said Tom Merry. "I suppose this is some sort of a joke of yours, Bunter. Chuck it!"

"I say, you fellows——"

"Bai Jove! What's the mattah?" Arthur Augustus D'Arcy came along the passage. "I twust you fellows are not waggin' Buntah?"

"He jolly well ought to be ragged!" snorted Gore. "A chap who bags a fellow's marmalade, and tells lies about it——"

"Weally, Goah——"

"I appeal to Gussy!" said Bunter. "Gussy, you remember that I had a jar of marmalade under my arm when I came into your study?"

"Bai Jove, I don't, Buntah!"

"You must have noticed it!" urged the Owl of Greyfriars.

"I should have noticed it if it had been there, Buntah," said Arthur Augustus innocently. "But it wasn't, deah boy!"

"Are you asking D'Arcy to tell lies for you?" hooted Gore.

"I wegard that wemark as uttahly wotten, Goah!" said the swell of St. Jim's severely. "Buntah is incapable of such a thing."

"He's capable of stealing grub and lying about it, anyway!" growled Gore. And he marched into his study with his recaptured jar.

Bunter gave it a mournful blink as it vanished from his sight. That marmalade was gone from his gaze like a beautiful dream.

Arthur Augustus gave him a rather doubtful look. Bunter was surprising him again.

"I say, you fellows, is that chap going to be allowed to keep my marmalade?" asked the Owl of Greyfriars reproachfully.

"Br-r-r-r!" was Tom Merry's reply. And the Terrible Three went back into their study. They had had enough of Bunter.

The fat junior went down the passage with Arthur Augustus, who was still looking puzzled and uncertain.

"You were an ass!" grunted Bunter discontentedly.

"Weally, Buntah——"

"Why couldn't you back me up?"

"B-b-back you up, Buntah?"

"Yes. The fellows would have taken your word if you'd said it was my marmalade."

"Vewy pwobably, Buntah; but I couldn't say it was your marmalade when it wasn't your marmalade, could I?" exclaimed Arthur Augustus, in blank astonishment.

"Oh, you're a duffer!" grunted Bunter. And he rolled away down the stairs, leaving the swell of St. Jim's staring.

"Bai Jove!" murmured Arthur Augustus. And then, after a moment or two, he murmured again, "Bai Jove!"

Then he returned to Study No. 6, with a very, very thoughtful expression upon his face.

CHAPTER 8.
No Footer for Bunter.

"CERTAINLY not!" W. G. Bunter spoke in a tone of finality.

It was Wednesday, a half-holiday at St. Jim's, and a clear, cold afternoon, and naturally most fellows' thoughts were turning to football.

That afternoon Figgins' eleven was going to be put through its paces, and Figgins, of course, wanted Bunter in the ranks.

Bunter had been bagged by the New House chiefly as a rod in pickle for the School House when the House match came off on Saturday. Figgins had not forgotten the great form Wally Bunter had displayed in the great game at Greyfriars.

But, good as his new recruit was supposed to be, Figgins wanted him to practise as much as possible with the team. He looked on his new man as a tower of strength, and that consideration made him more patient with Bunter than he would otherwise have been.

But the fat junior's dislike to footer practice puzzled and irritated him. Wally Bunter had been as keen as mustard, but he seemed to have changed, somehow.

Figgins was pointing out to Bunter now that he was expected to turn out with the team that afternoon, and show what he could do. The fat junior's reply was a most emphatic negative.

"I don't care about it this afternoon," he went on, while Figgins & Co. glared at him. "Besides, I'm not at all sure that I shall play for you on Saturday, Figgins."

"What?" roared the New House leader.

"I haven't been treated well in this House," said Bunter. "I'm not treated well in the study. A fuss is made over a measly rabbit. There's a lot of jaw over a tin of sardines. I despise that kind of thing. It's mean!"

"Never mind the rabbit now," said Figgins. "I've got you down for my eleven on Saturday."

"Well, I may play," said Bunter. "I don't say I won't. But if I'm going to win matches for you I've got to be treated a lot more civilly. I tell you that plain."

"Look here——"

"As for practice," pursued Bunter, "I don't need it. Without any practice I could play the heads off anybody you've got here. I don't think much of St. Jim's footer."

"Wh-a-a-a-t?"

"Not in my style, you know; in fact, it's fumbling. You don't mind my mentioning it, I'm sure, but really, you know, your footer here is enough to make a cat laugh!" said Bunter agreeably.

"To mum-mum-make a kik-kik-cat laugh?" stammered Figgins dazedly.

"Yes; not at all the sort of game I'm used to. I play it, you know—not fool at it!"

"My hat!"

"If you don't mind my speaking plainly, Figgins, you're a pretty rotten player!"

"Am I?" gasped Figgins.

"Oh, yes; and Kerr is a dud—simply a dud!"

"I—I'm a dud!" breathed Kerr.

"And look at Wynn in goal!" said Bunter disparagingly.

"Well, what about me in goal?" asked Fatty Wynn, with an expression on his face that was quite extraordinary.

"Poor—very poor!" said Bunter cheerily. "You're too fat, for one thing!"

"Fuf-fuf-fat!"

"Yes; and clumsy!"

"Clumsy!" breathed Fatty Wynn.

"Like a blessed hippopotamus, if you want me to be quite candid!" said Bunter. "You'll have to improve, you know. If I join your eleven I can't be let down in the game. I shall want you to play up."

"Oh!" gasped Figgins.

"Stick to practice," said Bunter encouragingly. "If I have time I'll look in and give you some coaching. I may not have time, though. A fellow with so many engagements——"

"You're coming down to practice this afternoon?" gasped Figgins at last.

"Sorry; can't be done!"

Billy Bunter rolled off with that, and the Co. looked at one another.

"Don't play that fool at all, Figgy," advised Fatty Wynn. "I've told you already that he's too podgy to play."

"But we've seen him play!" exclaimed Figgins. "Didn't he play for us that time at Greyfriars when Tom Merry was a man short for the match? He played up like a giddy International!"

"Well, so he did; but, all the same, I dare say that was only a fluke. Look at the fat idiot now!"

"Fathead!" answered Figgins. "It wasn't a fluke, and couldn't have been. He played up splendidly from start to finish, and practically won the match for us."

Fatty Wynn grunted.

He could not deny that Wally Bunter had played a wonderful game on that great occasion; and yet he felt he was ri ht, and that the fat, self-satisfied Owl was no footballer.

How to reconcile those two things was rather a puzzle, though there would have been no difficulty in the matter if he could have guessed that Billy Bunter had taken his cousin Wally's place at St. Jim's.

But nobody at St. Jim's dreamed of that.

"We've got to play him," said Figgins decidedly. "That's why we bagged him from the School House; and we should look asses if we didn't play him after all. Goodness knows, he's got no recommendation excepting his footer! If we've got to put up with the fat beast, it would be silly not to make use of him where we want him."

"That's so," agreed Kerr. "But it's queer how he steers clear of footer since he's been here."

"I'll jolly well make him practise!" exclaimed Figgins wrathfully. "Of all the conceited chumps——"

"Conceited chumps don't usually play good footer," remarked Fatty Wynn sapiently.

"He does," answered Figgins. "I wouldn't believe it if I hadn't seen him; but I have seen him do it, and that settles it."

"Well, I suppose it does. All the same——"

Gore the Bully!
(See Chapter 7.)

"A lot of the chaps have been growling at me about putting him in the eleven," growled Figgins. "They think he's no player, to look at him; and, goodness knows, he doesn't look like a footballer! But a chap can believe his own eyes, I suppose? He's going to play in the House match if I have to yank him to Little Side by his fat ears. After that he can go and eat coke!"

Figgins was in an exasperated mood, which was not surprising under the circumstances.

The New House chums had taken no end of trouble to bag Bunter for their House, and it had earned them a licking. They found him unendurable in the study, yet they put up with him. But all would have been in vain if he did not turn up trumps on the footer-ground in the House match.

On that point Figgins was determined. Bunter had to play for his House.

There would never be another opportunity, so far as they went; for Figgins was aware that Bunter would be shifted to the School House after a time. So long as the New House had him they were going to get the benefit of him.

And after that the School House could have him as soon as they liked; and certainly Figgins & Co. were not likely to weep when he shook the dust of their study from his feet.

But it was easier to determine that Bunter should practise with the team than to make him do it. When the New House footballers were ready to begin the Owl of Greyfriars had vanished.

Bunter was the biggest duffer at footer that ever muffed a kick, but he was firmly persuaded that he was a first-class man.

The fact that he had been excluded from the Remove Eleven at Greyfriars he attributed to jealousy of his great prowess.

Still, he could not fail to be aware that fellows who saw him play had no desire to avail themselves of his services. Along with his conceit he had a great gift of cunning. He was fully resolved to enjoy the distinction of playing in a House match; and, in spite of his conceit, he realised that if Figgins saw him play Figgins would never have him in his eleven.

That was the chief cause of his disdainful attitude. Nobody at St. Jim's was going to see him play footer till they saw him in the New House team for the big match, when it would be too late for Figgins to change his mind. For, whether it was jealousy of his powers or not, Bunter was aware that Figgins would drop him like a hot potato if he once saw him play.

It was necessary, therefore, to avoid the practice game of that afternoon, and Bunter avoided it by going out of gates. He had another attraction out of gates. Racke & Co. of the School House were going out, and the Owl of Greyfriars had calmly decided to attach himself to them.

In his few days at St. Jim's Bunter had learned something of Racke and his set.

In fact, there were few things that the Peeping Tom of Greyfriars did not nose out sooner or later.

Bunter wasn't shocked at the black sheep of the School House. The Owl rather prided himself on being a blade. It was the disastrous result of playing the gay dog that had made him so anxious to get away from Greyfriars, and leave the penalty for his cousin Wally to pay. But the fatuous Owl was ready to play the gay dog again.

When Racke and Crooke and Scrope strolled out of gates Bunter strolled after them, and he had been gone half an hour when the New House footballers went down to practice, and Figgins sought for him to round him up.

Figgins, naturally, sought him in vain. The chief of the New House juniors was in a rather excited and wrathful frame of mind when he came down to Little Side without Bunter. He called to Arthur Augustus D'Arcy, who was there with Study No. 6.

"Seen Bunter, D'Arcy?"

"Yaas, wathah, deah boy!"

"Oh, good!" exclaimed Figgins, in relief. "I believe he's dodging the footer. Where is he?"

"I weally do not see why he should dodge the footah, Figgins. Wally Buntah is wathah a keen footballah."

"Well, where is he, anyhow?" asked Figgins.

"I am sowwy I do not know his pwesent whereabouts, Figgins."

"You said you'd seen him!" hooted the exasperated Figgins.

"Yaas, so I have. In class, you know."

"Ass!" shrieked Figgins.

"Weally, Figgins——"

"I saw him in classes, fathead!" howled Figgins.

Arthur Augustus nodded.

"I have no doubt you did, Figgay, as you are in the same Form."

"Oh, you—you chump! Have you seen him since lessons?"

"I wefuse to be called a chump, Figgins."

"Have you seen that fat burbler since lessons?" yelled Figgins.

"Weally, Figgins, I wish you would not woah at me. It thwows me into quite a fluttah when a fellow woars at me."

"You—you—you——"

"Howevah, I have not seen him since lessons," added Arthur Augustus. And he walked away.

"Come on, Figgy," said Kerr, with a grin. "We'd better begin without the fat bounder. He's gone out, I expect."

"I—I'll burst him when he comes in!" growled Figgins. "Fancy, a new kid, only came on Monday, and he's offered a place in the House team, and he turns up his fat nose at it! If he tries to dodge us on Saturday I'll—I'll—I'll——"

"Are we ever going to begin?" asked Redfern, with an air of martyr-like patience.

"Oh, get going, and be blowed!" snapped Figgins.

And the New House footballers got going without Bunter. That valued youth was otherwise engaged just then—very otherwise.

CHAPTER 9.
A Gay Time.

"I SAY, you fellows!"

Racke & Co. looked round.

They had left Rylcombe Lane, and crossed a field and entered an old barn, where the sportive youths expected to be free from observation.

Since Racke's man had cleared out of the neighbourhood the festive Aubrey had lost the headquarters where he had been accustomed to resort for a little game. But a little game was a necessity to a fellow of Racke's shady tastes. While the other fellows were more strenuously engaged, Racke & Co. were planning to enjoy a quiet game of poker in the barn.

Aubrey had introduced poker to his cheery set. It had the advantage that it was a much more reckless form of gambling than nap or banker.

The three black sheep stared grimly at Bunter as his fat form was framed in the doorway of the old barn. They were not glad to see him.

"Well, what do you want, barrel?" asked Crooke surlily.

"Oh, really, you know——"

"Fourth Form fags not wanted here!" growled Scrope. "Cut it!"

"I'm not talking to you," said Bunter with dignity. "I simply wanted to ask Racke if he could change a banknote for me."

"I could," said Racke; "but I want my change. Ask somebody else."

"Well, you see, I've asked at the tuckshop, but Mrs. Taggles couldn't change a ten-pound note," said Bunter. "I could ask my Housemaster, but old Ratty would be down on me, as likely as not, for having a tenner at all."

Racke & Co. exchanged a quick glance.

They had come there to gamble among themselves, but they were not at all averse from devoting some little time to relieving a new fellow of his pocket-money. If Bunter had a tenner he was quite welcome in that select circle so long as the tenner lasted.

Three agreeable smiles were turned on Bunter as if by magic.

"Well, I don't know that I could change it," said Racke. "I'm rather short of money to-day—only about seven or eight pounds about me."

Crooke and Scrope sneered. It was like Racke to remark that he was short of money when he had twice as much as either of them.

"Well, I dare say I can get it changed in the village," said Bunter. "You fellows going that way?"

"Well, you see——"

"I say, are they cards you've got there?" asked Bunter, blinking at Racke's hand. "I'll tell you what, you chaps! If you care for banker, or nap, I'm your man!"

Bunter's fat face did not betray that he knew perfectly well that the shady trio had come there for the especial purpose of playing cards. He preferred to let them suppose that he was an unsuspicious new fellow, with tastes like their own.

"Well, mum's the word," said Racke. "We were going to play poker."

"Ripping game!" said Bunter.

"Oh, you play it?" asked Crooke.

"Yes, rather! I learned it from Angel of the Fourth. He's a gory chap at Greyfriars," said Bunter.

"Never heard of him," yawned Crooke. "But if you'd like to take a hand, Bunter, you're welcome."

"Quite welcome," said Scrope. "I can see that you're a sportsman, Bunter."

"That's me all over!" answered Bunter. "I hope you fellows don't play for bob stakes, though. I'm accustomed to something rather big."

"No limit?" asked Racke.

"That's my style."

"We'll see you through, then."

Another quick glance was exchanged among the young rascals. It was tacitly agreed that they were to skin Bunter before their own game began.

The fat junior sat down on a beam, and Racke upturned an old bucket to serve as a card-table. Deal fell to Aubrey, and he handed round the cards, five to each.

Billy Bunter blinked at his cards. He knew the rules of poker, though he was a hopeless duffer at that game as well as at more manly games. His eyes glistened behind his glasses as he found himself in possession of four queens and an ace.

"Draw any?" yawned Racke.

Crooke and Scrope drew cards, but Bunter shook his head. With such a hand as that he knew it was best to "play pat."

The betting began with shillings, and Bunter dropped in one shilling. It belonged to Redfern, from whom he had borrowed it that morning.

The stake was raised to half-a-crown, and again Bunter came in, with a half-crown that had formerly been the property of Arthur Augustus D'Arcy. After that Racke put in four shillings with a flourish. The three looked at Bunter.

The fat junior half-drew a pocket-book from his inside pocket, but let it slip back again.

"Can't cut up a tenner," he grinned. "I'll put in I O U's till the finish, and redeem them afterwards."

Racke nodded assent.

Billy Bunter scribbled "10s., W. G. B." on a fragment of an old letter and dropped it into the pool.

"My hat! You're going it!" remarked Crooke. "But I'll see you!"

And Gerald Crooke dropped in a red ten-shilling note.

His comrades followed his example, and Bunter followed on with a pound in paper.

Scrope passed, but Crooke and Racke continued. They grinned at one another.

Anyone less obtuse than W. G. Bunter would have divined that Racke had planted a good hand on him with the intention of drawing him on, having provided himself with a better one. But Bunter was too busy with his own game of spoof to realise that he also was being spoofed.

Pounds dropped freely into the pool, and Crooke passed out of the game, still grinning. The three were to recover their stakes and share the plunder afterwards, and Crooke and Scrope had only passed to keep up appearances.

Pound after pound dropped in, till Bunter had written paper to the value of ten pounds in the pool.

Then Racke called.

"Four of a kind," he remarked carelessly as he laid four kings and an ace face upward on the old bucket.

Bunter stared at the cards, and gasped.

Four kings, of course, beat four queens, and Racke had won the pot.

"Oh!" gasped Bunter.

"What's yours?" smiled Racke.

"Quick - quick - queens!" stuttered Bunter.

"Well, that was a near thing," said Racke agreeably. "You're a real sport, Bunter, to go in so deep on four queens. I rather think I take the pool."

"Oh, dear!"

Racke turned out the pool and counted up Bunter's paper.

"Nine-pounds-ten," he said coolly. "Chuck over the tenner, dear boy, and I'll give you ten shillings change."

"The — the tenner!" stammered Bunter.

"Yes."

"Oh, I—I say, you fellows, I think that's D'Arcy calling me!" exclaimed Bunter hastily.

He jumped up and made for the door.

With a spring a good deal like that of a tiger Racke of the Shell was after him, and he grasped the fat junior by the shoulder and yanked him back.

"No, you don't!" he said grimly. "You settle up first, my pippin!"

"Oh, really, Racke——"

"Trot out that tenner!" said Racke roughly.

"I—I say, you know, the—the fact is——"

"You fat swindler, pay up!"

"If you call me names, Racke, I shall decline to pay up!" said Bunter, with dignity.

"We'll see about that!" said Aubrey Racke. "Now, then, are you going to hand over what you've lost, you dashed fat thief?"

"Be a sport, Bunter!" urged Crooke. "You've lost, you know!"

Billy Bunter cast a longing look towards the doorway.

"I—I say, you fellows," he gasped, "I—I'm going to settle, of course. The—the fact is, I'm expecting a postal-order, and the——"

"What?"

"The minute it comes I'll settle up!" gasped Bunter. "I—I mean, I'm expecting a tenner, you know, from—from one of my titled relations. The minute it comes I'll hand it over——"

"You'll hand over the one you've got about you, you fat rotter!"

"My hat!" exclaimed Crooke, as a sudden light dawned on him. "He hasn't got a tenner at all! He's been spoofing us!"

"What?" yelled Racke.

"Oh, really, you know——" mumbled Bunter feebly.

The truth dawned upon Aubrey Racke. That innocent question of Bunter's, as to whether he "could change a tenner," had been intended to give him the impression that Bunter had a ten-pound note when he hadn't!

All the cash he had possessed—Redfern's shilling and D'Arcy's half-crown—was in the pool, and the fragments of paper with figures scribled on them were worth their weight as wastepaper, and no more!

Racke of the Shell, who prided himself on being the sharpest customer and keenest bird at St. Jim's, had been taken in by this fat Owl as easily as a baby!

Indeed, if he hadn't taken the precaution of cheating Bunter he might have had to hand over hard cash, while Bunter was risking in the game nothing but fragments of old letters!

For a full minute Racke stared at Bunter with wrath gathering in his face, hardly able to believe that he had been taken in like this.

Then the storm burst.

"You—you—you fat thief!" he howled. "You—you've got no money at all!"

"Oh, really, Racke! I—I'm expecting a postal-order——"

"I—I'll smash you!" roared Racke.

"Yaroooh! Help! Fire! Murder! Yoooooop!"

Bunter hardly knew what happened in the next five minutes. In that brief space of time—which did not seem brief to him—he paid for all his sins.

He sat up in the barn and blinked after Racke & Co., who were walking away. He gasped and sputtered, and sputtered and gasped, and groped down his back for his spectacles, and groaned deeply.

When the enterprising Owl of Greyfriars tottered out of the barn he was feeling that life was not worth living. He limped home to St. Jim's with a gasp and a groan at every step.

Billy Bunter had set out for a sportive afternoon. He was not feeling sportive when he limped in, at last, at the gates of St. Jim's. The way of the transgressor had turned out to be hard!

CHAPTER 10.
Not Popular.

TOM MERRY & CO. had the pleasure—or otherwise—of seeing a great deal of Billy Bunter during the next few days.

Figgy's determination to get him along to footer practice gave the Owl a great deal of dodging to do.

He bestowed the honour of his company upon the chums of the School House to a considerable extent. As he confided to them, he was going to be a School House chap—as soon as his father was heard from.

His father, as a matter of fact, hadn't the faintest idea that William George was anywhere near St. Jim's. It was Wally's father Bunter referred to.

Wally Bunter's father was away from home on war-work, and it was some days before the Head received a reply from him. And that reply was only to refer Dr. Holmes to Mr. Penman, of Canterbury, who had sent Wally Bunter to school. So the Head had to write again; and, meanwhile, Bunter remained an inmate of the New House—heartily sick of it, in truth, though not so sick of the House as the House was of him.

Mr. Ratcliff, when he deigned to notice Bunter's existence at all, generally did so with a snap, and the fat junior's podgy fingers were often smarting. Figgins & Co. barely tolerated him in the study; but the saving grace of being a good footballer—or being supposed to be one—saved Bunter from complete contempt there. What they would think of him after the House match was a very interesting question.

With Study No. 6 open to receive him, Bunter was quite anxious to be transferred, but for the present he was New House. Blake & Co. did not view the prospect with any joy. Even Arthur Augustus, perhaps, had some slight doubts as to whether Bunter would be enjoyable company in No. 6. But Arthur Augustus was not a fellow to go back on his word.

Meanwhile, Bunter spent a good deal of time in Study No. 6, which, as it happened, had the effect of making that study less and less keen to have him there permanently.

"That fellow Figgins is after me for footer!" he said, as he dropped in after lessons on Friday. "I've told him it's too dark."

"There is some light, Buntah!" remarked Arthur Augustus, who was getting tea. "Blake and Hewwies and Dig have gone down."

"Let 'em!" replied Bunter. "I don't need all that practice, you know. You—ahem!—you've seen me play footer!"

"Yaas, wathah; and it was wippin'!"

"Footer's my strong point!" remarked Bunter, blinking at him. "Cricket, of course, I play well, and other games; but I must say I'm a dab at footer. It's really my game!"

"Yaas?"

"I'm not at all sure I shall play for Figgins on Saturday," said Bunter loftily. "His team ain't up to my form!"

"But weally, Buntah, you are bound to play for your House if you are wanted!"

"Well, I dare say I shall be good-natured!" said Bunter. "That's a fault of mine—I'm always too good-natured; always thinking of others, you know! Are you going to have tea now?"

"When Blake comes in, Buntah!"

"May as well begin now!"

"Blake is goin' to bwing in the gwub, dear boy! There isn't much!"

"Blessed if I see what you go short for!" said Bunter. "You've got plenty of tin, and a chap with plenty of tin can always get round the rations, with a bit of gumption!"

"I twust, Buntah, that I shall nevah have that kind of gumption!" said Arthur Augustus sternly.

"Ahem! I—I mean, of—of course, you——"

"Bai Jove! I weally think I'll go down to the footah befoah tea! It is weally quite light!" said Arthur Augustus. "Will you come, Buntah?"

"No fear! Figgins will nail me!"

"But why not do some pwactice, deah boy?"

"I don't need it!"

"Pwactice makes perfect, you know!" suggested D'Arcy.

"Oh, yes; but I'm perfect already, so far as footer goes!" explained the Owl of Greyfriars.

"Oh!"

And Arthur Augustus went alone. And he did not admit, even to himself, that he had gone in order to escape from Bunter's fascinating society.

Billy Bunter blinked round the study discontentedly. He blinked into the cupboard, found a jar of calves'-foot jelly there, and ate it—the jelly, not the jar; though really he looked as if he could almost have eaten the jar, too.

Then he went along to Tom Merry's study. The Terrible Three were out, and the cupboard door was locked.

"Suspicious beasts!" muttered Bunter in disgust. "Just as if they're afraid that a chap might be after their grub! Pah!"

He looked into Racke's study next, and found Racke and Crooke there. They scowled at him over the tea-table.

"Get out!" snapped Racke, reaching for a missile.

Bunter eyed him warily as he came into the study.

"I'm sorry to say, Racke, that you're booked for trouble!" he remarked.

"What do you mean, you fat chump?" growled Aubrey uneasily. Racke lived under a constant dread of his shady exploits coming to light. That was one of the drawbacks of being a merry blade.

"I've been thinking over what happened on Wednesday!" said Bunter. "I'm shocked at you, Racke!"

"What?"

"You were gambling, and you drew me into it—me, an innocent new chap!" said Bunter. "It was really disgusting, Racke! I wonder you can look me in the face afterwards!"

"Why, you—you——"

"I feel bound to ask the Housemaster's advice about it!" said Bunter.

"You fat worm!" hissed Racke. "Does that mean that you are going to sneak?"

"I'm afraid it's my duty, Racke!"

"Well, go and sneak! And I shall deny the whole yarn!" said Racke. "Crooke and Scrope will bear me out!"

"I don't want to be unfriendly, old scout!" said Bunter. "The fact is, I'm prepared to stand by you as a pal! But I must explain how the matter stands! I'm expecting a postal-order——"

"Wha-a-at?"

"A postal-order! It's been delayed in the post. Now, as a pal, I think you might lend me the ten bob, and take the postal-order when it comes. What do you think of the idea?"

Racke stared at him.

"If you treat me as a pal, of course, I'm prepared to stand by you," said Bunter. "But, mind, I expect to be treated well! That's only fair! If you like to lend me the fifteen shillings—— Yarooooh!"

Whiz!

A cushion flew across the study, and caught Bunter under the fat chin.

The Owl of Greyfriars spun back into the doorway with a yell, and sat down there, hard.

"Give me that hassock, Crooke!" shouted Racke.

"Here you are!"

But Billy Bunter did not wait for the hassock; the cushion had been enough for him. He flew.

The hassock whizzed out into the passage after him. But Bunter was first, and he just escaped.

"Oh, crumbs!" gasped Bunter, as he scuttled down the staircase. "Oh, crikey! The beast! Oh! Ow! Oh, my hat!"

Crash! The Owl of the Remove rushed into Grundy of the Shell, who was coming upstairs.

Grundy gave a gasp, and grasped the Owl by one fat ear. There was a dismal yell from Bunter.

"Yow-ow-ow! Leggo, Tom Merry, you beast! Yow-ow!"

"Where are you running to?" demanded Grundy. "I'm not Tom Merry, you blind owl!"

"Yarooh! Leggo!"

Grundy sat him down on the stairs, snorted, and went on. Bunter shook a fat fist after him.

"Yah! Beast! Come back, and I'll lick you!" he howled.

George Alfred Grundy swung round, and started back. According to the proverb, second thoughts are best; and on second thoughts Bunter decided not to lick Grundy. He scudded out of the School House instead.

His fat face wore a frown when he came into Figgins' study in the New House and found the Co. at tea.

"Is that all there is for tea?" he snorted.

"That's all!" snapped Fatty Wynn. "There'd be more if you stood your whack, as any decent fellow would!"

"Oh, really, Wynn——"

"You could have tea in Hall, you know," suggested Kerr.

"I've had tea in Hall," grunted Bunter.

And he sat down to take the lion's share of what was going in the study. After tea Figgins referred to the subject of football.

"You've dodged footer practice all the week, Bunter," he said.

"Oh, don't worry!"

"You're playing for the House tomorrow," said Figgins, controlling his wrath. "I want you to put up a good game."

Bunter sniffed.

"There won't be a fellow there to touch me," he said. "I'll play—just to show you fellows what footer's really like."

"Well, if you can show us anything we don't know, we'll be glad to learn," said Figgins mildly. "But no dodging off after dinner! I may as well say that I shall keep an eye on you."

Figgins did keep an eye on Bunter after lessons the next day. But as it happened it was not needed.

The Owl of Greyfriars was quite ready to spread himself in a House match. When the junior footballers went down to Little Side Bunter went with them; and he rolled on to the field with an air of supreme self-satisfaction in his footer rig—looking as if he were on the point of bursting through at all quarters.

CHAPTER 11.
Bunter's Goal.

PHEEP!

Lefevre of the Fifth blew the whistle.

Two good junior teams were in the field. Tom Merry's eleven was good all through; and Figgy's eleven, like the egg in the story, was good in parts. The New House had a smaller number of players to choose from; but that deficiency, Figgins hoped, was made up by the bagging of that distinguished player Bunter. If Bunter put up such a game as Wally Bunter had played at Greyfriars he would certainly be a tower of strength to his side; and Figgins felt that, in that case, he could forgive him all his faults and failings.

There was a good crowd round the field to see the House match, and Bunter drew a good many glances. Fellows who had seen Wally Bunter play expected great things of him. Other fellows wondered what made Figgy so crass an ass as to play the Owl in the match at all. Certainly, as he stood blinking in the front line, he did not look much like a topping footballer.

Bunter had demanded the place of centre-forward, and Figgins had conceded it. The Owl of Greyfriars had a fixed belief that he looked the very thing, as he stood there, with his podgy nose elevated and a lofty expression on his fat face.

Figgins had suggested that he should remove his glasses for the match, in case of accidents; but Bunter declined. As a matter of fact, the Owl of Greyfriars would have been quite helpless without them—though probably that would not have made much difference to the quality of his footer.

The New House got away with a rush from the whistle, and Figgins' forwards bore down through the enemy—with the exception of the centre man. He laboured after the rest, puffing and blowing.

There was a yell from New House fellows round the ropes.

"Get a move on, porpoise!"

"Roll on, barrel!"

"Yah! Wake him up!"

"Bai Jove!" murmured Arthur Augustus D'Arcy. "I weally thought Wally Buntah was a footballah! This is vewy wemarkable!"

There was a long and hard tussle in the School House half, in which Bunter did not take part—excepting for one effort to take the ball away from Kerr, which fortunately failed. School House rallied, and drove the enemy back into their own territory, and a fat figure was strewn on the field behind them as they advanced.

It was Billy Bunter, gasping and grunting, and clutching around for his spectacles.

The School House pressed on, and the ball went in from Tom Merry's foot, and there was a delighted roar from School House partisans.

"Goal!"

Billy Bunter scrambled to his feet with the help of a grasp from George Figgins. Figgins was looking at him as if he would eat him

"Bunter!" he gasped.

"Yow! Leggo!"

"Why don't you play up?" howled Figgins.

"Why don't you?" retorted Bunter. "How can a chap play up in a gang of fumblers like this? Call this football?"

"You—you clumsy, fatheaded Hun!" roared Figgins. "You've taken us in somehow! You can't play footer!"

"Fat lot you know about footer! Why, the Second Form at Greyfriars would cackle at this!" snorted Bunter.

"You—you—you——"

"Line up!"

Figgins controlled his feelings. He was amazed as well as enraged. For it was evident to the veriest tyro on the field that Bunter could not play footer—and it was on his football reputation that Figgins & Co. had bagged him.

And this was a House match—and Figgins had put that hopeless dud into the centre of his front line expecting huge things of him there!

The ball was kicked off again, Figgins suppressing feelings that were too deep for words. Bunter did not kick off; Redfern was shifted to centre.

Billy Bunter's eyes gleamed behind his glasses. The New House players had dropped him out of account; they played as if he were not there. But that did not suit Bunter. He was going to distinguish himself.

He rushed into the fray.

Tom Merry & Co. had brought the ball up to the New House goal. Redfern bagged it from D'Arcy, and was about to clear, when Bunter took him in flank.

As Reddy was not expecting an attack from one of his own side he was naturally taken by surprise. Bunter captured the ball, leaving Redfern in a dazed condition, and rushed it for goal—but, unfortunately, owing to short sight and general obtuseness, he mistook the goals, and rushed for the New House citadel. Before Fatty Wynn could realise that a New House forward was kicking for the New House goal, the ball shot in.

There was an almost hysterical yell round the field.

"Goal! Goal!"

"Ha, ha, ha!"

"Bravo, Bunter!"

"Well kicked! Ha, ha, ha!"

Fatty Wynn seemed frozen. So did Figgins, for a moment or two. Then, as the whole field yelled, he rushed upon Bunter and grasped him by the back of the neck.

"Yarooh! Leggo!" howled Bunter. "There's a goal for you, you fumblers! That's the way to play footer!"

"Ha, ha, ha!"

"Oh, crikey!"

"It's our goal!" shrieked Figgins. "You've kicked a goal against us! You—you unspeakable toad! You fat villain! You cringing Hun! You—you—you—— Get off the field! You—you yahoo, bunk!"

"I—I say, you fellows—— Yow-ow-woooop!"

The enraged Figgins, with an iron grip on Bunter's neck, fairly ran him off the field, finishing with a powerful drive from a rather large football boot which landed the fat junior among the howling spectators.

Bunter did not appear on the field of play again; and the School House won the game, although the New House fellows played up desperately.

. . . . .

"Ha, ha, ha!"

A terrific burst of merriment greeted Billy Bunter when he put his fat face into Study No. 6, where Tom Merry & Co. were celebrating their victory over their old rivals.

"I—I say, you fellows——"

"Ha, ha, ha!"

"Bai Jove, Buntah, you are a corkah, you know!"

"Oh, really, Gussy——"

"What a stroke of luck that the New House bagged you, Bunter!" roared Tom Merry. "Otherwise, I should have put you in my eleven! What an escape!"

"I shall be able to play for you now, Merry," said Bunter, blinking at him. "I'm not going back to the New House——"

"I shouldn't think your life would be safe there if you did," chuckled Blake.

"I've just seen Railton," went on Bunter. "That blessed letter has come at last; and the Head says I'm to be in the School House. I'm jolly glad to have done with Figgins & Co. They're a rotten lot."

"Weally, Buntah——"

"I can't say I think much of their footer, either."

"Ha, ha, ha!"

"So you can put me down for your eleven, Tom Merry!"

"I'll put you down fast enough, and hard enough, if you come anywhere near my eleven!" grinned Tom Merry. "Not taking any, my pippin! You've played in your last House match here, Bunter."

"I hardly expected this jealousy from you, Tom Merry——"

"Ha, ha, ha!"

A roar of laughter drowned Bunter's further remarks. It was pretty certain that the Owl of Greyfriars would never figure in Tom Merry's eleven—but, at least, he was to be an inmate of Study No. 6 in the School House; there was no help for that.

Blake & Co. wondered how they would be able to stand him—and even Arthur Augustus wondered a little.

But Billy Bunter had no doubts. He fully expected to be popular—being a fellow of so much charm!

That evening his belongings were transferred to the School House; and he confided to Arthur Augustus that from that date they were going to be simply inseparable—to which Arthur Augustus replied, in faltering tones:

"Yaas, wathah!"

THE END

(Don't miss next Wednesday's Great Story of Tom Merry & Co. at St. Jim's — "SPOOF!" — by Martin Clifford.)

Extracts from "THE GREYFRIARS HERALD" and "TOM MERRY'S WEEKLY."

THE MYSTERY OF CLIVE. By Ernest Levison.

CARDEW'S an ass—an awful ass!

Oh, I know very well it's been said before—lots of times. I don't claim any originality for the statement.

And I know he's a clever ass. All of us in No. 9 have brains, for that matter.

Clive's are the ordinary sort of brains—good enough, but not remarkable.

Mine are—well, if I said what mine really are I might be accused of swank.

But Cardew's are extraordinary. I don't mean in quantity, or yet exactly in quality, but in kind. They aren't a bit like those of anyone else I ever met.

It was a kind of shock to both Cardew and me when Clive got mysterious.

You see, he is not that sort of chap. Cardew can make mysteries out of almost nothing. But Clive is generally as easy to see through as a pane of glass.

So I was no end surprised when Clive answered my query as to whether he was coming along to the Grammar School ground to see us play Gay's crowd by saying that he had an engagement elsewhere.

He almost blushed when he said it, and looked quite confused. Cardew stared at him hard. Cardew says he has the eyes of a lynx, you know.

It was only as a matter of form I had put the question. I really had not felt any doubt about the answer. Clive and Cardew always do come along when I am playing, unless the match is too far off for followers of the team to be allowed.

Study No. 9 is not quite as well represented in the St. Jim's Junior Eleven as I consider it should be.

I am a fixture in the team, so I can't grumble personally. Cardew slacks, so he has no right to grumble; but I maintain that he might be in the first half-dozen if he would only take the game seriously.

But Clive—well, I know that Tom Merry honestly considers Lowther a shade better than our man; but I honestly don't. And there are one or two others about whom I have my doubts.

Clive never grumbles; he is not that sort. But I know that he does feel sometimes that watching a game in which he might be playing is rather dull work.

All the same, I was surprised when he said he was not coming along to see us put it over the Grammarians.

"Got an engagement, Sidney?" said Cardew sweetly. "Oh, good! I'm tired of spectatin', y'know. I'll toddle along with you."

Clive really blushed then.

"Sorry, old chap!" he mumbled. "But—— Oh, well, I can't take you, and that's all about it!"

Cardew wagged a reproving finger at him.

"Naughty, naughty!" he said.

"You silly fathead! What do you mean?" roared Clive.

"Cherchez la femme!" replied Cardew, looking ever so knowing.

"You potty idiot! You may trot round looking for girls——"

"I am glad you say 'may,' Sidney, for you must admit that, as a matter of fact, I don't. It is true that they sometimes pursue me. But my fatal beauty, my extraordinary fascination—these things are misfortunes, not faults. And it is hard to be reproached with one's misfortunes—hard, indeed!"

"You chump! I'm not reproaching you with your beauty or your fascination—never knew you had them, and don't believe it now. And if you don't run after girls I believe it's only because you're too slack and lazy——"

"Not because he has your extremely proper views on the subject, Clive," I put in, grinning.

"Well, I do think it's rot for chaps of our age. Look at Gussy, now——"

"But you an' I an' Gussy are not all the same age, dear boy," said Cardew, looking quite serious.

"Ass! There isn't six months' difference between any two of us!"

"Years, old gun—decades! Gussy is about twelve, for any practical purpose. You are—shall we say a rather youthful thirteen? I—I am forty, at least, an' beginnin' to feel old age creepin' upon me like a giddy thief in the night, y'know."

"Rot! You know what I mean. All that sort of thing is all very well at its right time; but I don't expect to have any time to spare to fall in love before I'm twenty-five at least," said Clive.

"An' the image thinks that fellows fall in love in their spare time!" gibed Cardew. "Why, Sidney, dear, innocent lad, a chap in love positively hasn't any spare time! It's all taken up with runnin' after the fair one an' meditatin' upon her extraordinary perfections—see?"

"Rot!" snapped Clive again.

"But I really ·ieve the dear Sidney has succumbed to the shafts of the archer," Cardew said to me later, when Clive had gone out.

"Eh? Succumbed to what?" I asked, not catching on.

"Don't you ever read the classics, dear boy?"

"Only when I have to."

"Even that should have been enough to put you wise to Cupid with his bow—Cupid, son of Venus—called Eros by the Greeks."

"Oh, that piffle!" I said. "Chuck it, Cardew! Clive is about the last chap I know to get potty about a girl."

"Ernest, ingenuous youth, are you not aware that it is just the very last chap likely to fall in love who does it—souses in right up to his giddy neck?"

"Rot! Why, by that I might go doing it!"

"I can think of nothin' more extremely probable!" drawled that silly ass.

He was all wrong, of course. Don't I fancy I can see myself? Not much!

And Cardew did not really believe it of me. But he stuck to his notion about Clive.

II.

"I DESIRE the inestimable privilege of your company this afternoon, cousin George," said Cardew to Durrance an hour or two later.

Durrance is a level-headed chap in most ways; but Cardew can lead him into playing the fool sometimes. Durrance is no end fond of Cardew—partly, I suppose, because he had no people of his own till it was found out that he was Commander Durrance's son, and our silly ass's cousin.

"Right-ho!" said Durrance. "Are we going to see our chaps smash up the Grammarians?"

Cardew yawned.

"Nothin' so dull an' trite, dear boy," he answered languidly.

"I don't call that dull, you know."

"'Tot homines, tot sententiæ,'" said Cardew.

He will trot out this classical stuff when the fit takes him, though he's always getting into rows with Lathom for not preparing his construes. When we have Cicero to do he will stick his head into the "Æneid," and gas about old Publius Virgilius Maro being a great poet; but when it's Virgil that ought to be done he reads O. Henry or Mark Twain.

"Eh?" said Durrance.

In the Fourth we don't let on that we understand any Latin at all outside the hours of classics and prep. Of course, Cardew is an exception to that, as to all other rules. But I've known him to pretend that he could not translate "Homo sum" when it happened to suit him to take the usual attitude.

"Let every galoot think as he durned well

pleases. That's an up-to-date translation," Cardew explained.

"Well, where are we going?" inquired Durrance.

"My dear man, I don't know in the very least!"

Durrance stared, as well he might.

"But——"

"I know what we are goin' to do. Whither it will lead us is another matter, oh, my cousin!"

"I see," said Durrance.

But he didn't, and Cardew saw that he didn't.

"We are goin' to follow the dear Clive, cousin George."

"Eh? Follow him where? Do you mean go with him?"

"Cousin, cousin, there have been times when I have suspected you of intelligence! I regret to say that those times must now be consigned to the limbo of the past."

"You do talk such silly rot, Ralph!"

"On the contrary, all my utterances are concise, perspicuous, and——"

"Now you're talking like Skimmy!"

"Am I, by Jove! That won't do. Let me try a fresh line. How, cousin George, could we follow Clive an' at the same time go with him?"

"Ask me another! What licks me is what you should want to follow the chap for."

"That is an easy one. Clive confesses to a mysterious engagement this afternoon."

"I say, you know, Cardew, we can't go butting in like that!"

"For Sidney's own good, dear George—for his own good, y'know. Hang it all, man, what's the good of your bein' named George if you can't be pious an' interferin'?"

Durrance stared again.

"George is a good boy's name—I don't know why. I can't argue the matter. I should find myself up against Georgius Quartus, some time the Prince Regent, who was not the very cleanest of potatoes. But there were George Washington an' George Herbert—holy George Herbert—you've heard of him, old bean?"

"I haven't, and I don't want to. I want to know what all this rot about spying on old Clive is."

"Don't call it spyin', George dear! Let us say seein' that the dear youth doesn't get into mischief."

"Rot! Clive isn't that sort."

"Should you be surprised to hear, cousin George, that the inocent Sidney was in love?" yawned Cardew.

"Ha, ha, ha!" chortled Durrance.

It struck him as funny for the moment. But then he saw the other side of it.

"If you mean that he's going to meet a girl, I'm dashed if I'm going to dog him!" he said.

"But surely you don't agree with his doin' such things, George? Our Sidney—our sweet, ingenuous youth, who might almost be a George himself, so high does he——"

"Oh, cut out all that rot, Ralph! It's a jape you're after, I know; but somehow I can't quite see it your way."

But in the long run Durrance was induced to see it Cardew's way. Of course, he knows how really chummy Cardew and Clive are; but I fancy the real reason why he gave in was because he was jolly sure Cardew was wrong.

III.

"LOOK here, Cardew, I must go," said Clive impatiently.

We had already gone off to the Grammar School ground, and most of the Fourth and Shell had gone with us. Skimmy was left behind, likewise Baggy and Mellish, and a few more slackers and rotters. But Clive must have been rather surprised to see that Durrance had not gone, and he may have felt so about Cardew, though by this time he ought to have given up being surprised at anything Cardew does or doesn't.

Cardew had kept him talking—about nothing in particular. Now the cool bounder asked:

"Go? Where to, old top? You're not playing, are you?"

"Tom Merry asked me to be reserve, but I told him I'd rather not," replied Clive.

He flushed slightly as he spoke, and it occurred to Durrance that he rather evaded the question whether he was playing footer.

Durrance is pretty keen, you know.

"You amaze me, Sidney! Why, if you had taken on that honourable position there might have been—let's see—perhaps one chance in ten thousand of gettin' a game. The dear Levison might break his neck on the way there——"

"I don't want Levison to break his neck just to give me a game, you cheap ass!" snorted Clive. "Besides, if that happened, the match would be off, of course."

"Don't be so dashed literal, Sidney, old gun! A minor accident, now——"

"I'm not keen on one chance in ten thousand," grunted Clive. "It's hardly good enough. I'm going, Cardew, so leave go of my jacket!"

"But where to?" persisted Cardew.

"Didn't I tell you I had an engagement for the afternoon, dummy?"

"Oh! Ah! Yes, now that you mention it, you did casually refer to somethin' of the kind."

"Casually refer! Why, we argued about it for ever so long, you maniac!" hooted Clive.

"That's a failin' of yours, my boy—that tendency to unnecessary argument," said Cardew sweetly. "You should try to overcome it. It may grow upon you."

Clive only grunted at that.

"Would you care for the company of myself an' cousin George?" asked Cardew.

"No, I jolly well wouldn't!" roared Clive. "No offence, Durrance, old chap; but this lunatic knows already that I don't want anyone with me."

And with that Clive hurried off.

"Clear case, eh, Georgie?" said Cardew.

"Hang it all, don't call me Georgie, ass! I draw the line at that," said Durrance. "Clear case of what?"

"Goin' to meet a charmer—eh, what?"

"I don't a bit believe it."

"Well, well! Nous verrons. Anyway, I've made the dear Sidney so late in startin' that he will ride at a breakneck pace an' never give a glance behind. Which, as the sleuth-hounds will be upon his trail, is all to the good—eh, dear cousin George?"

Clive rushed for the bike-shed, ran his machine up to the gates, jumped on, and was off in the direction of Wayland in about two twos.

But Durrance thought that it was queer he should carry a bag on his handle-bars if he were really going to meet a girl.

Cardew and Durrance got out their bikes and pursued Clive over Wayland Moor.

Clive never once looked round. So far Cardew was right.

But Durrance felt pretty sure that he was wrong otherwise.

Cardew always pretends that he doesn't like riding hard; but he rode hard enough then. It was about as much as Durrance could do to keep up with him.

When they got to Wayland Cardew made out that he was frightfully pumped; but he wasn't a bit really, Durrance says.

"By Jove! This is worse than my blackest dreams!" exclaimed Cardew.

And even Durrance was rather taken aback. For Clive had wheeled his machine into the yard of a pub, and they saw him go into the place by a side door in the yard!

I say a pub, but that's not quite fair. It was a highly respectable hotel, and within a minute Durrance had seen through it all.

For a small crowd of other fellows, from fifteen to eighteen or so, all with bags, passed into the hotel by the front door.

"Footer team, gone in to change," said Durrance. "Same with Clive, I'll bet. He's playing footer here this afternoon, though why he wanted to make a mystery about a simple thing like that licks me, I'll own."

"What an unimaginative mind you have, cousin George!" said Cardew, in scornful sorrow.

"Right-ho, chappie! We shall see," said Durrance.

Two or three more fellows went in, all ready togged for the game.

"Some of the local team," said Durrance. "The others would be the visiting side, and this place is the team's headquarters. Nothing in that. But I suppose your theory is that Clive is spoony on some barmaid here. Got gifts for her in that bag—ha, ha!"

"Wait an' see, my infant!" said Cardew oracularly.

"Meanwhile, we might put up our bikes," Durrance remarked. "If old Clive's playing in a game here we may as well watch it, though I'd rather have seen the Grammar School match, I'll own."

IV.

CLIVE came out with a good-looking fellow two or three years older than himself just as the two returned from stabling their machines.

He did not see them. They followed.

And within three minutes something happened that made Durrance doubtful, and Cardew even more cocksure than ever.

A very pretty girl, fair-haired and blue-eyed, stopped and greeted the two—or, rather, greeted Clive, for she shook hands with him, while she only gave his companion a nod.

"The charmer! Nice, too, cousin George!" said Cardew. "Ah, see! The other fellow feels himself in the way. He's going on."

It was even so. Clive's companion quickened his pace, and left the two, while Clive and the girl walked on more slowly.

"Now, what saith the sapient cousin George?" asked Cardew.

"Well, it looks a bit like it," admitted Durrance. "But I wouldn't be dead sure, even now. A fellow can walk by the side of a girl without being in love with her, I suppose?"

"Can he, by gad?" returned Cardew sceptically.

"Well, can't he?" said Durrance impatiently. "You couldn't, I dare say—you're a bit of an ass, Ralph—but I could."

"Clive couldn't, though—not a girl like that," said Cardew solemnly. "It would be worse for him than for Gussy. Gussy's had the disease before. Georgie, I have an idea!"

"It's sure to be something mad," said Durrance doubtfully.

"You disappoint me. I thought you were an admirer of mine."

"Oh, rats! What's the brilliant idea, anyway?"

"I am going to save Clive!" replied Cardew dramatically.

"Chump! I can't see what he needs saving from."

"From that siren, dear boy."

"Well, what's the gadget?"

"That you will see presently."

Durrance was interested—and mystified. He remonstrated when Cardew led him in the

Printed and published weekly by the Proprietors at The Fleetway House, Farringdon Street, London, E.C. 4, England. Subscription, 8s. 10d. per annum. Agents for Australasia: Gordon & Gotch, Melbourne, Sydney, Adelaide, Brisbane, and Wellington, N.Z. South Africa: The Central News Agency, Ltd., Cape Town and Johannesburg. Saturday, January 25th, 1919.

opposite direction from that which Clive and the fair lady had taken.

"We don't know where they are going," he said. "And I want to see Clive play. That will be better value than your fat-headed idea!"

"They are going to the Sports Ground, of course!" answered Cardew. "I am not a stranger in Wayland. Come on, Georgie-Porgie!"

"Oh, you blithering idiot!" groaned Durrance. But he followed.

Cardew led him to a shop where theatrical costumes were sold or let on hire.

"Could you—er—transform me into a fairly presentable young lady?" he asked the proprietor.

The man looked him over critically.

"With a little make-up, sir, I could turn you into quite a handsome one," he said, without the quiver of a muscle in his solemn face.

"An' my friend here?" asked Cardew. "Of course, in his case there are natural disadvantages to contend with, y'know, but——"

"Not for Joseph!" snapped Durrance.

"You mean for Georgie, don't you, dear boy? Well, I let you off. You shall be my devoted escort. But in that capacity, I warn you, you will have to fade out of the picture the moment I say 'Vanish!' For you, Georgie dear, would give the giddy game away."

"We'll see about that," said Durrance.

He waited in the shop while Cardew went into a back room.

He had been there twenty minutes or so when a girl came out, and stopped before him.

"Oh, you duck!" she said. "I really must kiss you!"

Durrance admits that he very nearly cut and run at that. But before he could make up his mind the drawling voice of Ralph Reckness said:

"On second thoughts, no! Cousin George, was your washin' this mornin' quite on the customary scale of thoroughness?"

"You awful ass!" gasped Durrance. "You don't think I'm coming along with you like that, do you?"

"No, Georgie—no! You will come as the very ordinary schoolboy you are. I have given up hope of any transformation of you into the nice, modest sort of maiden you see before you!"

"That's as well," said Durrance, "for I wouldn't make a fool of myself like that for an admiral's pension! And as for the modest—hang it all, Ralph, you look beastly fast, if you ask me. That chap's overdone the paint-and-powder bizney."

But Cardew was quite satisfied with himself—habit of his, by the way. And, somehow, he persuaded Durrance to come along with him to the Sports Ground. I fancy the curiosity Durrance felt helped to make the persuading easier.

Cardew would not say what he intended to do. It was easy to guess that it would be something pretty wild; and Durrance seemed to remember having heard that there were penalties for male persons who wore female clobber in public.

But Durrance went along. And I think that I should have done the same had I been there.

V.

WAYLAND SWIFTS were the team Clive was playing for, and their opponents were a side from Westwood. It was a good, clean, fast game, and Clive, at centre-half, put up a first-class show.

But all that does not matter much to the story. I am not going to describe the match. It would be more to the purpose for me to tell you just exactly how, some miles away, we put it across Gordon Gay & Co. to the tune of four to two.

(Yes—I think not! But Levison kicked the last two goals for us—jolly good ones, both of them; and I suppose this is really what he wanted to get in.—T. M.)

At half-time the score was two all—at Wayland, that is, not at Rylcombe—and when Clive came off the field he went straight to the young lady with whom he had walked to the ground.

Durrance really thought then that it was a case!

"Vanish!" said Cardew, in a stage-whisper.

Durrance did not exactly vanish; but he hung back. He would have done that, anyway, without being told.

Cardew, with a flutter of skirts—Durrance says—and a ghastly leer—I should say—swept up to Clive and the girl.

"Oh, Sidney, Sidney, my own, have I found you at last?" he squeaked.

(He denies squeaking. He says he didn't leer—it was a look between smiles and tears that he gave Clive. He was playing the part of the deserted sweetheart, you know.)

Clive went as red as a beetroot.

"Look here, you know, you're making a silly mistake!" he said confusedly. "I don't know you from Adam!"

"The young lady seems to know you, though," said the fair girl.

She smiled, as if a good deal amused. But Clive wasn't amused at all.

"Oh, Sidney—darling Sidney——"

"Gerraway!" howled Clive.

Then if that ass Cardew didn't fall on his neck before everybody!

"Oh, my hat! Stoppit! You're making a mistake! You must take me for someone else! Look here, I don't want to be rude to a girl, but——"

"No mistake at all, Clive, old bean!" breathed Cardew in his ear. "But I fancy the fair charmer will be rather off you after this, y'know."

"Cardew! Oh, you silly ass!"

And then Clive burst into a roar of laughter. The people round must have thought him hysterical. But he wasn't—not a bit of it!

Our Sidney is not a dull person, for all Cardew may say when he is ragging him. He saw through the game directly Cardew said that.

And he turned to the girl.

"Mrs. Wilmot," he said, "you're partly responsible for this. Let me introduce my chum Cardew, who has been idiot enough to dress up as a girl to—well, I suppose it was to—er—to—he thought he could make me out a—a kind of a gay deceiver, you know, and choke you off me!"

Durrance came up in time to hear the girl's silvery laugh and to catch her reply.

"Really, your chum Cardew seems to have taken a lot of trouble quite needlessly, Mr. Clive!" she said. "I wonder what my husband would say? But Mr. Cardew makes such a charming girl that in your place I should insist upon his maintaining his role until the end of the match, at least."

But that did not suit Cardew. No, he wasn't taken aback. You don't know him if you think that likely—anyway, if you think it likely he would show it. But he hurried off to the pavilion, and got out of his girl's clobber, and made it all up in a parcel. He had his own things on underneath, of course.

And I'm hanged if he didn't go back to Mrs. Wilmot as bold as brass, and stand by her side during the whole of the second half, and talk to her as if he had known her for years! Durrance said he seemed to forget that he had neither cap nor overcoat in his enthusiasm. But I fancy it was not really so much enthusiasm as his way of brazening the thing out.

Wayland Swifts won by three goals, and Clive showed up well from first to last. And on the way home he told Cardew and Durrance all about it.

"You remember we played against them last term?" he said. "Gray—that's their skipper—chap you saw me with—and I happened to get yarning, and I let out that I was only playing as a reserve, and he said that they'd be glad to have me in their team when I had nothing else on. So I played for them a fortnight ago—when Levison was at Westwood with the team, and you'd gone off on some potty bizney of your own, ass! And I was keen to play to-day, because the return with our fellows is next week, and if I don't play for St. Jim's I want to play for the other side."

"On your form to-day," said Durrance, "you ought——"

"Oh, I'm not grumbling! I know Merry's absolutely fair. But I should like to show him I'm a trifle better than he thinks me."

"But all this doesn't explain the charmin' Mrs. Wilmot," said Cardew.

"She? Oh, there's no need to explain her, is there? Gray took me home to tea with him last time. She's Gray's married sister; her husband's in the Army, and out in France. She was interested in me because I'm South African, and so's he, and after the war she's going back with him to live there. You potty idiot! She's ten years older than I am!"

"That's no odds!" drawled Cardew. "Ask Gussy! An' she doesn't look it!"

"Married, too!" snorted Clive.

"H'm! That's not much odds, either!" replied that ass Cardew.

But, of course, he did not mean that. He only wanted to shock Clive and Durrance. That's Cardew's way.

We called him "Miss Cardew" for a week or two afterwards. But it fell flat. The bounder didn't mind a bit!

THE END.

NOTICES.

Correspondence, etc., Wanted by—

S. Inglis, 20, Tinsley Street, Liverpool, wants members for correspondence club. Stamped addressed envelope. New system.

S. P. Hannan, 6, Bell Street, Newsome Road, Huddersfield—with readers, 15-17, preferably in Yorkshire.

Edward H. Edwards, 117, Constantine Road, Hampstead, N.W. 3, wants readers, about 17, to co-operate in amateur magazine.

Ernest T. Acott, 57, White Lion Street, Angel, Islington, N. 1, wants to hear from readers anywhere to form a club, take charge of foreign branches, etc. Stamped addressed envelope.

D. Rutter, 33, Charminster Road, Bournemouth, Hants, with readers abroad re film-acting and travelling.

C. Pescia, 75, Glenferrie Road, Glenferrie, Victoria, Australia—with readers, 11-13, willing to join correspondence club.

Miss P. S. Gardner, Beverley, Victoria Street, Roseville, New South Wales, Australia—with another girl of different country, 15-16.

E. A. Pridmore, Main Road, Misterton-cum-Walcote, near Lutterworth, Leicestershire—members wanted to start a club with Colonial branches.

Miss Edna McGrath, Yarunga, O'Sullivan Road, Woollahra, Sydney, N.S.W., Australia—with girl readers, 18, in United Kingdom, America, and Canada.

Wm. Forsyth, 23, Friars Goose, Felling-on-Tyne—with readers, 15-16, keen on going on stage.

A. P. Wybrow, 417, York Road, Wandsworth, S.W. 18—with readers interested in foreign stamps.

A. E. Duncan, 25, Beechfield Street, Cheetham Hill, Manchester, wants more members for stamp exchange; overseas readers specially invited.

M. Banner, 25, Salisbury Street, Long Eaton, Derbyshire, England, asks Dave Duncan, Albert Park, Australia, to write. No reply came from last letter, which must have been lost.

Harry Gibson, 1, Eleanor Street, Hall Lane, Armley, Leeds—with readers interested in Meccano.

Patrick Moore, 7, Artane Cottages, co. Dublin—with readers anywhere.

T. H. Brazier, 54, Institution Street, Woodhouse, Leeds, wants cigarette-cards—Gallaher's War Series, giving Rev. Capt. Addison, V.C. S.C.F. 1s. offered.

H. M. Norris, 221, Westcombe Hill, Blackheath, S.E. 3—with readers anywhere.

Miss Gladys Dove, Chandos Lodge, Ellenborough Park, Weston-super-Mare—with girl readers, 17-18.

Thomas Newson, 50, Laburnum Street, Kingsland Road, London, E. 2—with any reader with foreign stamps for sale. Best prices for stamps in good condition.

G. W. Blamphin, care of James Bacon & Sons, 17-19, Basnett Street, Liverpool—with readers, 14, anywhere.

Wm. Leedham, 25, Park Lane, London, W. 1—with readers interested in amateur theatricals.

F. Wirty, 12, Tavistock Place, W.C. 1, wants members for his correspondence club—amateur magazine. Stamped addressed envelope.

Basil G. W. Bayley, 24, Reynard Road, Chorlton-cum-Hardy, Manchester — with foreign and Colonial readers.

W. Stubbs, 13, Sandmere Road, Bedford Road, Clapham, S.W. 4, wants members, 14-16, for stamp club; Colonials specially invited. Stamped addressed envelope.

Miss Ailsa Hay, Blackwood Road, Bunbury, Western Australia, will be glad to hear again from the driver in the R.F.A., France.

J. W. Connolly, 203, Westgarth Street, Melbourne, Victoria, Australia—with readers, 14-15, in England.

Eddie Davidson, Elmfield, Haydon Bridge, Northumberland—with readers, 12-13, anywhere.

C. B. Arahill, 30, Louis Street, Redfern, Sydney, New South Wales, Australia—with readers anywhere. Wishes to obtain back numbers.

F. Paweusky, care of Messrs. J. W. Jagger & Co., Main Street, Port Elizabeth, South Africa—with readers in England.

G. Duckett, 33a, Edgwick Road, Foleshill, Coventry—with readers anywhere.

Max Nochimovitz, P.O., Box 126, Oudtshoorn, Cape Province, South Africa—with readers, 12-14, anywhere.

G. H. Blewett, 1, Balsam Street, St. John's, Newfoundland—with readers in New Zealand, Tasmania, Australia, and Africa. All letters answered.

BUNTER OF THE NEW HOUSE.

BUNTER AND BAGGY.

The Editor's Chat.

For Next Wednesday:

"SPOOF!"

By Martin Clifford.

Next week's story is positively gorgeous.

I laughed over it till I almost cried.

Bunter plants himself upon No. 6, thanks to the weakness of Gussy.

No, that's hardly fair.

There is something much higher than weakness in Gussy's politeness.

Billy Bunter is Wally to St. Jim's; and Wally had done Gussy a service, and Gussy liked Wally very much.

So Billy gets into No. 6, though already he had shown pretty plainly the cloven hoof.

And Billy is got out of No. 6—got out by one of the most elaborate games of spoof ever played at St. Jim's.

I am not going to tell you all about it here; but I don't mind letting you know that Baggy Trimble and Mellish come into it on one side, and on the other, besides Blake & Co., the Terrible Three and the chums of No. 9.

The game is a game after Cardew's own heart, and he takes a most effective hand in it.

Don't on any account miss this story!

WALLY BUNTER AT GREYFRIARS.

And don't miss, either, the fine stories appearing in the "Magnet," in which you can read how Billy's cousin, Wally Bunter, who ought to have gone to St. Jim's, fares at Greyfriars, loaded down, like the scapegoat of old, with sins not his own!

We have never had anything in the two papers quite like this double Bunter series—never, to my mind, anything better, if anything as good.

AN UNFOUNDED COMPLAINT.

A Welsh boy, signing himself "Cymro Glan," writes from Manselton, Swansea, to complain that there is no Welsh boy at St. Jim's. He has been reading the GEM for over two years, and not once has he seen a Welsh name appear in it!

Rub your eyes, "Cymro Glan," and look out for the name of David Llewellyn Wynn!

YOUR EDITOR.

N

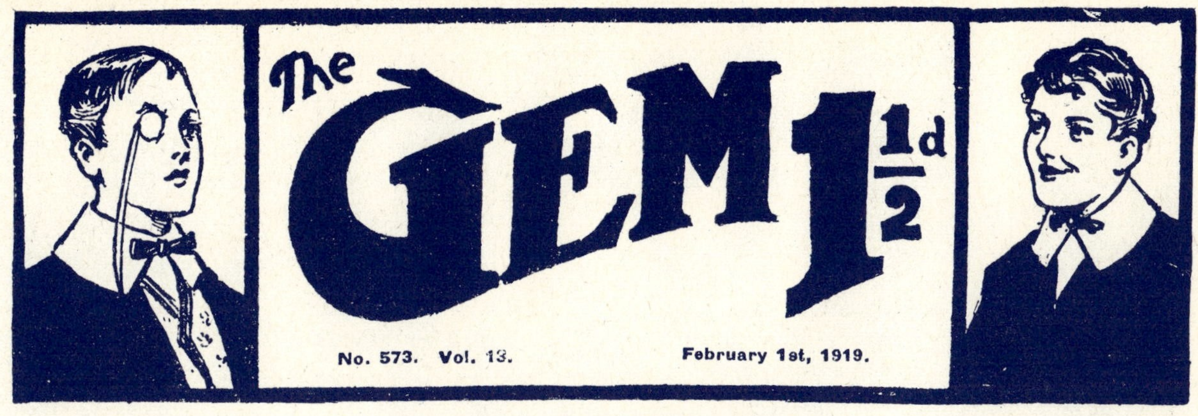

SPOOF!

BUNTER TAKES THE CAKE!

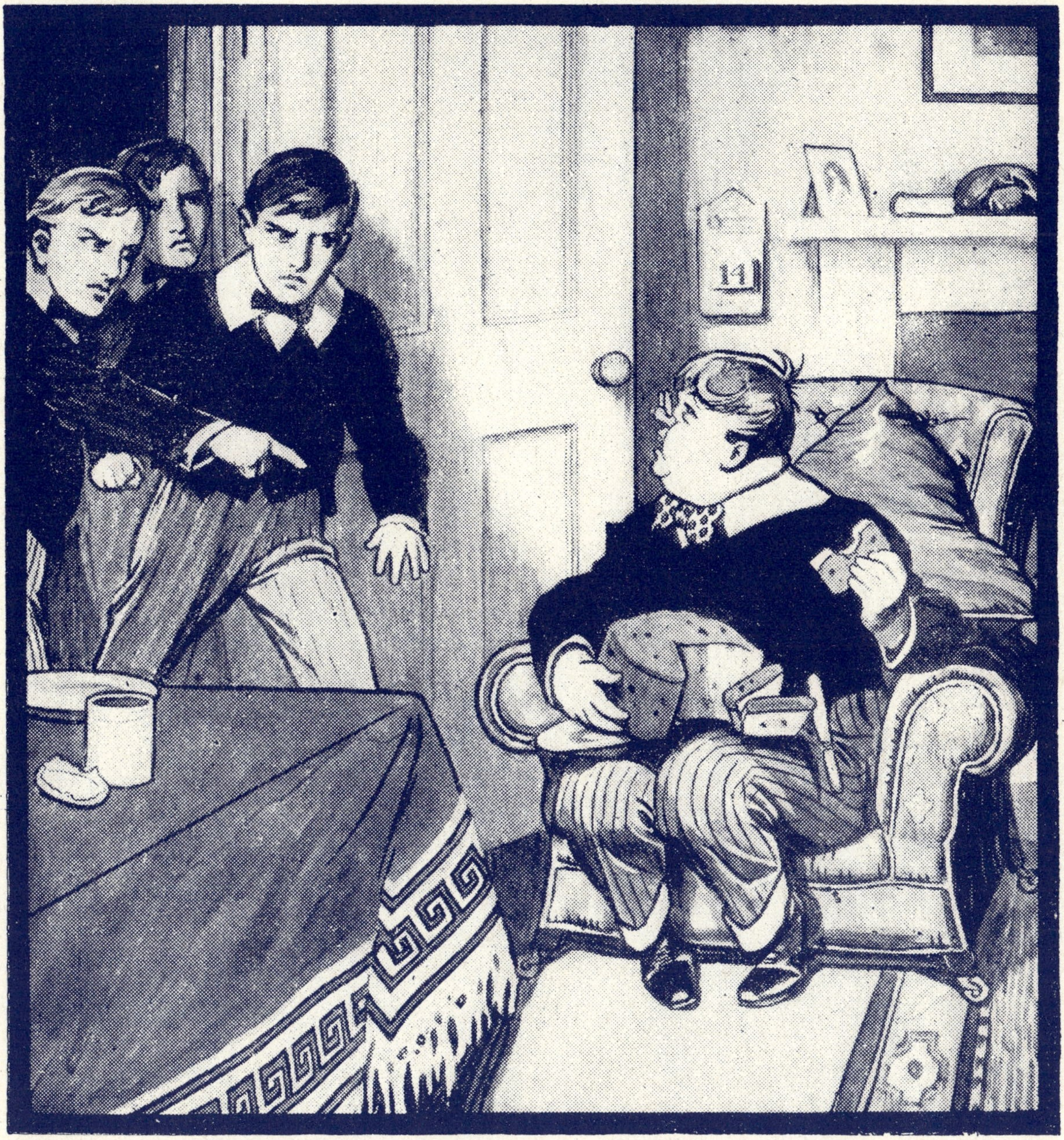

1-2-19

SPOOF!

A Magnificent, New, Long, Complete School Story of Tom Merry & Co. at St. Jim's.

By MARTIN CLIFFORD.

CHAPTER 1.
The Troubles of Study No. 6.

Tom Merry was looking into his study cupboard with a perplexed expression upon his face when Blake of the Fourth came along.

Blake did not appear happy.

He glanced into the study, where Monty Lowther was slicing bread, and supplying Manners, who was on his knees before the study fire making toast.

Tom Merry turned from the cupboard, and was about to speak to his study-mate, when he observed Blake in the doorway.

"Hallo! Trot in, kid!" he said.

Blake came in.

"Just in time for tea," said Tom Merry cheerily. "Anything up, old scout? You look as if you've been hunting for trouble and finding it."

"I've found it without looking for it," grunted Blake. "I'll have tea with you, if you fellows don't mind."

"Not a bit—in fact, it's a pleasure," said Monty Lowther solemnly. "Trot out the cake, Tommy."

"Anything wrong in Study No. 6?" asked Tom.

"Yes."

"What's happened?"

"Bunter!"

"Oh!" said the Terrible Three together.

They understood.

"It's Gussy's fault," said Blake glumly. "He would have that fat bounder planted in our study. It's no good trying to stand him; we can't do it. Dig's gone to tea with Julian, and Herries has dropped in to see Lumley-Lumley. I've come along here to sponge on you chaps."

"My dear kid, you're as welcome as the flowers in May. Where's D'Arcy?"

"Oh, he's staying in No. 6—standing Bunter! It's what he calls 'Noblesse oblige.'"

Tom Merry laughed.

"That fellow Bunter is the limit," said Blake. "I admit I rather liked him when we met him at Greyfriars; he didn't seem much like that toad of a cousin of his, Billy Bunter. Since he's come to St. Jim's he seems just Billy Bunter over again, to the life."

"I've noticed it," assented Tom.

"He's the limit," said Blake. "It's no good; we can't stand him! I was wondering whether you fellows could make any suggestion for getting him out of our study."

"Ask him to change."

"I've done that."

"And what does he say?"

"He says he wouldn't leave his old pal Gussy for anything. He says I can change out if I like—in fact, he'd be glad if I would." Blake breathed hard through his nose. "Me, you know—out of Study No. 6! I know I shall slaughter him some day!"

"We've been rather taken in over that chap," remarked Manners. "We thought he was a footballer; but he plays like a born idiot!"

"He's a toad!" said Blake. "A horrible toad! He tells lies—beastly lies! He brags. He—he does everything he shouldn't. You fellows wouldn't care to have him in this study, I suppose?"

"The Fourth don't dig with the Shell," said Tom Merry, laughing.

"That might be arranged—for once."

"Ha, ha! No jolly fear!"

"It's a pity he couldn't be planted on the New House," remarked Lowther.

"Even the New House is too good for him," said Blake. "No. 6 simply isn't fit to live in since Bunter came. Why couldn't he go to Greyfriars, like his cousin? No need for him to come to St. Jim's that I know of."

"And you can't even have tea with him in the study?" said Tom Merry sympathetically.

"There isn't any tea!" grunted Blake. "We came in famished after footer, and found that the fat bounder had had his tea—and ours, too! He'd scoffed the whole shoot!"

"Oh, my hat!"

"Now he's turned up with a big cake," said Blake. "I thought he'd brought it in for the study."

"A big cake?" repeated Tom Merry.

"Yes; a whacking big sultana cake—looked quite nice! And what do you think he's doing? Sitting in the arm-chair bolting it—all of it!"

There was a peculiar expression on Tom Merry's face.

"A whacking big sultana cake?" he repeated.

"Never mind, we've got a whacking big sultana cake, too," said Monty Lowther comfortingly. "Miss Priscilla sent it to Tommy, and it's come along just at the right time. Why don't you trot it out, Tommy?"

"It's not there," said Tom.

"You put it in the cupboard."

"I know that."

"Well, then, it's there, isn't it?"

"The trouble is that it isn't!" answered Tom Merry grimly. "And so I think I can guess where Bunter got his big sultanan cake from!"

"Our cake!" shouted Lowther.

"My hat!" ejaculated Blake. "I wondered where he'd got it. He's bagged your cake as well as our tea!"

Manners rose from the fireplace.

"We're not standing this," he said. "I think we'd better trot along to No. 6 and see Bunter."

"I rather think so!" said Lowther emphatically.

"You make the coffee while we're gone, Blake," said Tom Merry.

"Right you are," assented Blake. "You can kill him, if you like. I don't mind. In fact, I'd rather you did."

The Terrible Three hurried out of the study and along to the Fourth Form quarters.

They were naturally wrathy.

Miss Priscilla Fawcett's sultana cake was a thing of beauty, if not a joy for ever, in the eyes of the hungry juniors. Bunter of the Fourth had to learn to let other fellows' provender alone, and the Terrible Three were quite prepared to give him the necessary lessons.

They had liked Wally Bunter. His outward resemblance to his cousin Billy was startling, but inwardly he had not seemed to resemble the Owl of Greyfriars at all. But since the new junior had been at St. Jim's the eyes of Tom Merry & Co. had been opened on that subject. And now they did not like Bunter a little bit.

Arthur Augustus D'Arcy, the ornament of the Fourth, stepped out of Study No. 6 as the Terrible Three reached that celebrated apartment.

He gave the Shell fellows a rather troubled smile.

Arthur Auguustus had made friends with Wally Bunter, and he was not a fellow to go back on his friendships. But he had found the fat junior very trying.

"Anythin' up, you fellows?" he asked, noting the expression of the Terrible Three.

"We want Bunter!"

"I twust, Tom Mewwy, that you are not thinkin' of waggin' Buntah? Buntah is a fwiend of mine."

"If you don't want your friends ragged, Gussy, you'd better instruct them not to bone other fellows' cakes."

"Bai Jove! Buntah has a cake."

"He's burgled ours!"

"Oh!"

"And we're going to talk to him," said Tom Merry. "You run away and play, Gussy, if you don't think you can stand the harrowing scene. We're going to strew Study No. 6 with his bones!"

"Weally, Tom Mewwy——"

"Run away, old scout!"

"But pewwaps it is not your cake, aftah all."

"We shall see, old top. Get out of the way, there's a good kid!"

"Undah the circs, Tom Mewwy——"

"My dear gramophone, the cake will be all gone if we wait till you've run off all your records," said Monty Lowther.

"I wefuse to be called a gwamophone, Lowther!"

"Hop it!"

"I wepeat—— Yawoooooh!"

The Terrible Three grasped Arthur Augustus D'Arcy, and gently but firmly lifted him aside. Then they strode into the study.

CHAPTER 2.
Whose Cake?

BILLY BUNTER was enjoying himself.

He had had quite a good time since he had come to St. Jim's. The fellows, certainly, were finding out the true inwardness, so to speak, of his nature; but no one had guessed the well-kept secret that he was Billy Bunter of Greyfriars, passing under the name of his cousin Wally.

And though he was wearing out even the great patience of Arthur Augustus D'Arcy, he was still regarded with some toleration—as Wally!

Wally Bunter's reputation, in fact, had stood Billy in good stead; it had saved him, so far, from a good many study raggings, though how long it would continue to shield him was a question.

He was enjoying himself, in his own way, immensely at the present moment. He had had a tea for four—much to the exasperation of Study No. 6. Now he was travelling through an enormous cake, a special gift from Tom Merry's old governess—and Miss Priscilla's cakes had grown more appetising than ever since the advent of the piping times of peace.

He blinked up through his big glasses as the Terrible Three appeared in the doorway.

For a moment there was a guilty look on Bunter's fat face; but the next moment he gave the Shell fellows an affable nod.

"I say, you fellows——" he began, with his mouth full.

"Where did you get that cake?" demanded Tom Merry, pointing an accusing forefinger at the big cake, which was reduced already to half its original size. But it was still recognisable as the property of Study No. 10 in the Shell.

"That—that cake?"

"Yes; that cake, you fat burglar!"

"Oh, really, Merry——"

"Stop wolfing it!" roared Lowther.

"Oh, really, Lowther——"

Monty Lowther grabbed the cake, and rescued it from Billy Bunter's fat paws. The Owl of Greyfriars jumped up.

"I say, you fellows, that's my cake! Gimme my cake!"

"Where did you get it?"

"My—my pater sent it to me!" explained Bunter. "It—it arrived by this afternoon's post!"

"Weally, Tom Mewwy, it is quite poss that you are in ewwah," said Arthur Augustus, his eyeglass gleaming in at the doorway. "Buntah asserts that it is his cake——"

"I should jolly well think so!" exclaimed Bunter indignantly. "I can show you the letter my aunt wrote with it——"

"Your aunt?" exclaimed Tom Merry.

"Yes; and——"

"So your pater sent you the cake, and your aunt wrote a letter with it?"

"I—I mean my—my uncle—that is to say, my pater wrote the letter—that's what I really meant to say. I can show you the letter," added Bunter loftily.

"Show it, then!"

"I could, if I choose; but I decline to have my word doubted——"

"What?"

"Under the circumstances, I refuse to show you the letter!" said Bunter firmly.

"You spoofing Ananias!" exclaimed Tom. "There isn't any letter, and that's not your cake!"

"If you doubt my word, Merry, this discussion had better cease! Gimme my cake, Lowther, you beast!"

"Buntah is within his wights in wefusin' to have his word doubted!" said Arthur Augustus hesitatingly.

"Yes, rather!" chimed in Bunter. "I should jolly well say so! Besides, Gussy can bear witness that he saw me unpack the cake in this very study!"

"Oh!" ejaculated Tom, staggered for a moment. "In that case——"

"Bai Jove! I do not wemembah seein' you unpack the cake, Buntah!" exclaimed Arthur Augustus in astonishment.

Bunter closed one eye at him—a sign which Arthur Augustus did not in the least comprehend. It did not occur to Gussy's noble brain that Bunter was calling upon him to bear false witness.

"My hat! He's winking at Gussy!" ejaculated Manners.

"Oh, really, Manners——"

"Bai Jove! Why should Buntah wink at me, deah boy?"

"Because he wants you to back up his lies, you ass!"

"Gweat Scott!"

"N-n-nothing of the kind!" gasped Bunter. I—I wasn't winking——"

"What were you doing, then?"

"I—I—I was—was—in fact, I—I was——" Bunter stammered.

"Exactly!" said Tom Merry. "Now, the fat bounder has scoffed half the cake. Are we going to hang and quarter him, or boil him in oil?"

"Oh, really, Tom Merry——"

"Boil him in oil!" said Monty Lowther. "Or, as there isn't any oil handy, bump him on the carpet, and jump on him!"

"I say, you fellows——"

"Collar him!"

"Weally, deah boys——" objected Arthur Augustus.

"You're dead in this act, Gussy; travel off!" said Monty Lowther.

"I wefuse to twavel off, Lowthah! I considah——"

Billy Bunter dodged round the armchair in great alarm.

"Stand by a pal, Gussy!" he exclaimed. "I say——"

"Wely on me, Buntah!"

"That's my cake!" went on Bunter, blinking over the top of the chair-back. "I can produce my uncle's letter if necessary——"

"Your uncle's!" roared Manners.

"Yes."

"It was your pater's a minute ago!"

"I—I really meant my uncle—my Uncle James!" said Bunter, apparently thinking the uncle would be more convincing if the name were given. "My Uncle James, who lost his leg on the Somme, you know."

"More likely lost his head, if he was there at all!" remarked Lowther. "I can guess what a Bunter would do with his legs if he found himself in danger."

"Bai Jove! That is weally a wotten wemark, Lowthah, considewin' that Buntah's uncle was a fightin'-man——"

"I should think so!" said Billy Bunter warmly. "I'll bet that none of your relations helped so much to beat the Huns, Lowther, as my Uncle Peter——"

"Uncle what?"

"I mean, James!" said Bunter hastily.

"Liars should have good memories," remarked Manners, repeating an old proverb which Billy Bunter would really have done well to bear in mind.

"If you call me a liar, Manners, I'll—I'll——"

"Well, what will you do?" asked Manners.

"I'll treat you with utter contempt!"

"Ha, ha, ha!"

"Well, we've got the cake—what's left of it!" said Tom Merry. "Let the fat bounder off!"

"He ought to be bumped!" said Lowther warmly.

"I wefuse to allow Buntah to be bumped, Lowthah! I do not wegard your claim to that cake as pwoved at all!" said Arthur Augustus D'Arcy.

"I know it by sight, don't I?" demanded Tom Merry.

"So do I!" exclaimed Bunter, at once.

"I've got the wrappings it came in, in my study, addressed to me!" added the captain of the Shell.

"So have I!" said Bunter.

"Bai Jove! Pwoduce the w'appin's, Buntah, and that will pwove to these fellows that you weally weceived a cake by post!"

"Yes; produce them!" said Tom.

"So I would, only I happen to have used them to light the fire with!" said Bunter. "Otherwise, I'd produce them with pleasure. I suppose you can take my word?"

"Wouldn't take it at a gift!" said Lowther. "I suppose you can see that the fat rotter is lying now, D'Arcy?"

"Weally, Lowthah——"

"None so blind as those who won't see!" said Manners. "Will you clear off, Gussy, while we slaughter this fat burglar?"

Arthur Augustus shook his head.

"I wefuse to do anythin' of the sort, Mannahs!"

"Well, shall we slaughter Gussy first, or let that rotter off?" asked Monty Lowther. "I leave it to the meeting."

"Oh, come on!" said Tom.

The Terrible Three were unwilling to slaughter the Honourable Arthur Augustus, though keen to deal out drastic punishment to the fat Owl of the Fourth. But Arthur Augustus stood in the way, and evidently did not mean to desert his pal.

So the Shell fellows gave it up, and walked out of the study, carrying the remnant of the cake.

Billy Bunter's spectacles glimmered after it till it was gone. Then he gave a deep sigh.

"If you are weally sure that that is your cake, Buntah——" said Arthur Augustus hesitatingly.

"Of course it is!" said Bunter peevishly. "Haven't I told you it was sent to me specially by my aunt?"

"You said your patah, Buntah, and then your uncle——"

"I—I mean my pater—that is to say, my uncle. I hope you don't doubt my word, Gussy?" said Bunter loftily.

"N-n-no!"

"I should certainly refuse to be friendly with a fellow who doubted my word."

"That is quite wight, Buntah."

"I'm still hungry," said Bunter, changing the subject. "The worst of it is that I'm stony broke. My postal-order hasn't come."

"Were you expectin' a postal-order, Buntah?"

"Yes—from a titled relation of mine," said Bunter. "I suppose you couldn't lend me five bob till it comes?"

Arthur Augustus gazed fixedly at Bunter for a moment or two. He had already cashed several postal-orders for the new junior, and somehow none of them had arrived at St. Jim's. Even Arthur Augustus, careless as he was in money matters, was beginning to think that Bunter ought to wait for the arrival of his remittances before he asked fellows to cash them.

However, he slid his hand into his pocket, and Bunter's eyes glistened behind his spectacles. Bunter had looked upon Arthur Augustus as a prospective gold-mine when he came to St. Jim's in the place of his cousin Wally, and so far Arthur Augustus was panning out remarkably well.

Five shillings clinked into Bunter's fat hand.

Arthur Augustus watched him rather curiously as he rolled out of the study, en route to Dame Taggles' tuckshop.

The swell of St. Jim's remained alone in the study, with a very thoughtful expression on his face.

CHAPTER 3.
Plotting a Plot.

TOM MERRY & Co. sat down cheerfully to tea.

Blake, however, was looking sombre.

The addition of Bunter to the happy family in Study No. 6 seemed to weigh upon Jack Blake's cheery spirits, which was not surprising.

"It's too bad!" said Tom Merry, guessing Blake's thoughts. "We were mistaken in that fellow Bunter. Can't you fire him out of your study somehow?"

Blake shook his head glumly.

"He's planted there!" he said. "He won't move. It's really all Gussy's fault; he's so soft. Just the same as when Trimble came here. He planted himself on our study by getting round Gussy. We got rid of him. But Bunter is a fixture. He makes a regular income out of Gussy, you see. Wild horses wouldn't drag him away."

"He seems an awful rotter!" said Manners.

"He is!" said Blake dismally. "Why, every day some fellow comes nosing into the study after something that Bunter has scoffed. He has no mercy on anybody's rations. And the way he tells lies——"

"I should think Gussy would be fed up."

"I believe he is, but he won't own up," growled Blake. "Can't you fellows make some suggestion? How can we boot him out of the study?"

"Blessed if I see!" said Tom Merry thoughtfully. "Gussy asked the Housemaster for Bunter to be put there, with your consent. After that you can't ask for him to be changed out."

"That's impossible. And he won't go of his own accord," said Blake, helping himself dismally to cake.

"You might persuade him, somehow," said Lowther. "Suppose you asked him to change into No. 2, with Trimble and Mellish? They're a pair of wriggling worms, and would suit him."

"They wouldn't have him at any price."

"Well, they can't be blamed for that," said Tom Merry, laughing.

"Both of them rather made up to Bunter at first," said Blake. "They thought there might be something in his yarns about his people being wealthy. But they seem to have found out it's all bunkum. They let him alone now."

The Terrible Three chuckled.

"And Bunter was rather taken with Trimble, too," said Blake, his face relaxing into a grin. "I suppose he thought there might be something in Baggy's yarns about Trimble Hall. But he's let him alone since."

Tom Merry wrinkled his brows thoughtfully.

"Suppose——" he began, and paused.

"Well?"

"I've got a wheeze!"

"Go ahead!" said Blake, not very hopefully. His expression implied that he did not think very much of Shell wheezes.

"Suppose Bunter's yarns about his wealthy people were true, and that he did get some remittances, Trimble and Mellish would make up to him no end," said the captain of the Shell.

"But they're not."

"And suppose," said Tom, unheeding, "that Bunter believed in Trimble Hall, and the terrific wealth of the Trimble family, then he would jump at the chance of sucking up to Baggy."

"But he doesn't."

"And then," said Tom, "they'd click, and Bunter could ask Railton to let him migrate into No. 2, and once he was landed there you'd be done with him!"

"But——"

"My dear man, you're dense!" said Tom Merry patiently. "Nobody takes any stock in Trimble's yarns. But suppose some very important persons—us, for example—began to listen to Baggy with very great respect——"

"Oh!"

"Also to Bunter on the same lines——"

"Ah!"

"Isn't it very likely that they'd succeed in spoofing one another——"

"Ha, ha, ha!" roared Blake.

"The difficulty is that it would cost some tin," said Tom. "If we believe their yarns, they'll expect us to shell out small loans. Is it worth it?"

"It's worth a small fortune to squeeze Bunter out of No. 6!"

"Besides, Gussy does squeeze out money now," said Manners. "Bunter plunders him right and left."

"That's so," agreed Blake. "I wonder——"

"It's a case of shoulder to shoulder," said Tom Merry. "We're bound to help. In fact, we're partly responsible. We were taken in by Bunter, and that helped Gussy to get taken in, and that planted Bunter on you. We'll all stand in and help. Besides, it will be fun to see those two spoofing bounders trying to chisel one another."

"Ha, ha, ha!"

"Good egg!" said Blake heartily. "I say, I'll call Dig and Herries, and we'll talk it over."

"What about Gussy?"

Blake shook his head.

"Leave Gussy out! Gussy's too good for this world. He feels that it's up to him to stick to Bunter, because he made friends with him once, and he shuts his eyes to the plain facts. Besides, Gussy tries hard to believe in Bunter, anyway. He will back us up without knowing it."

"Ha, ha!"

Blake left the study, and returned with George Herries and Robert Arthur Digby of the Fourth. Miss Priscilla's cake was finished by the whole party while an animated discussion went on.

Herries and Dig entered heartily into the scheme. They were as fed up with their new study-mate as Blake was.

The plot was plotted, and, details having been arranged, several more fellows were called into the study—Kangaroo of the Shell, Julian and Roylance of the Fourth, and Cardew, Clive, and Levison from Study No. 9.

They all gave in their adherence cheerfully. They had seen enough of Bunter to sympathise with the unhappy plight of Study No. 6, and they were willing and ready to do all they could to relieve that celebrated study of its incubus.

When the discussion and the cake were finished, the party broke up, and as they came down the passage from Tom Merry's study they sighted Baggy Trimble of the Fourth.

Baggy was leaving Racke's study in rather a hasty manner, and for a moment a boot was visible in the doorway ere the door closed after him.

Apparently Baggy had invited himself to tea with Racke and Crooke, and had been given the order of the boot.

He was shaking a fat fist at the closed door when Tom Merry & Co. came along.

"Hallo, kid!" said Tom Merry cheerfully. "What's the trouble?"

"That cad Racke!" gasped Trimble. "He's actually kicked me—me, you know, because—because"—Baggy hesitated a moment—"because I refused to lend him a fiver!"

"Oh, my hat!"

"Well, you might have lent a chap a fiver," said Monty Lowther, closing one eye at his comrades. "A fellow like you, rolling in fivers——"

"Wallowing in them," said Manners.

Trimble stared at the chums of the School House. This was rather a new view for them to take, and he suspected for a moment that they were pulling his podgy leg. But their faces were quite grave.

"Well, I've got plenty of money, of course," said Trimble. "But I don't see why I should lend it to Racke."

"Better keep out of that study, Trimble," said Kangaroo solemnly. "They play banker and nap there. It's really not safe for a wealthy fellow like you."

The juniors passed on, feeling that that was enough to begin with. Baggy Trimble looked after them rather uncertainly.

It was rather gratifying to be recognised like this as a wealthy fellow, and warned to be careful of his ample wealth. Trimble jingled a French penny and a bad halfpenny in his pocket, and strutted as he went down the passage. He felt as if he were coming into his own.

If this was the opinion the School House juniors had of him, it looked as if the negotiations of small loans—date of repayment uncertain—would be an easier matter in the future. Baggy Trimble resolved to put that matter to the test at a very early date.

CHAPTER 4.
Cardew Begins.

BILLY BUNTER pricked up his ears.

It was the following day, and morning lessons were over. A very important matter occupied Bunter's mind—how and where a snack was to be obtained before dinner-time. That deep problem was filling the fat junior's mind as he sat on a bench under the old elms. Arthur Augustus D'Arcy had been trotted in vain. He was stony, partly owing to Bunter's previous extractions. Blake and Herries and Dig he had not cared to approach. He had received such very emphatic replies from them on previous occasions.

Bunter was thinking out the problem when Baggy Trimble and Cardew of the Fourth came strolling along under the leafless trees.

There was an almost comical expression of fat gratification on Baggy Trimble's face. Many a time and oft had he striven to get on chummy terms with the grandson of Lord Reckness, who had endless titled connections and heaps of money. And Ralph Reckness had coolly kept him at arm's-length—or further off than that—all the time.

Now there was a change. Cardew was displaying the most cordial urbanity towards the fat Fourth-Former, and Baggy was basking, as it were, in his smiles. Baggy was not aware, naturally, that Cardew had entered whole-heartedly into Tom Merry's wheeze. Baggy knew nothing of the wheeze.

Cardew was likely to carry the game much further than Tom Merry dreamed; anything in the nature of spoof appealed to his peculiar nature. And it amused him hugely to pull Baggy Trimble's egregious leg.

"The Easter vac?" Cardew was saying, as they came within Billy Bunter's hearing. "You're really very kind, Trimble."

"Not at all, old fellow," said Trimble

affectionately. "We'd be glad to have you for the holidays."

"Well, I've never seen Trimble Hall," said Cardew thoughtfully. "I must say I'd like to see Trimble Hall."

"Then make it a fixture," said Trimble. "I'm making up a party for the holidays, Cardew. I'd be glad to have you. I'll put your name down."

"Thanks no end, old fellow!"

"Not a bit of it."

The two juniors had stopped quite near Bunter, apparently not observing him. Or, rather, Cardew had stopped, and Trimble followed his example. The Owl of Greyfriars blinked at them in surprise.

Bunter had heard all about Trimble Hall—it was impossible to be in the same form as Baggy Trimble without hearing all about it. Bunter had taken that magnificent establishment with a very large grain of salt—as he had observed that the other fellows did.

It astonished him to find Cardew taking it quite seriously in this way.

It interested him, too. Cardew, he knew, was a keen fellow, and quite at home in that elevated sphere where viscounts and marquises are as common as blackberries. If Cardew took stock in Trimble Hall, that was as good evidence as could be asked for that Trimble Hall was not merely a figment of Baggy's fertile brain.

"How shall we get down to the Hall, by the way?" asked Cardew. "What's your station, Trimble?"

"Oh, the pater's car will come for us!" said Trimble airily. "Now the war's over, you know, that's all right."

"But if you're taking a large party down——"

"About a dozen," said Baggy carelessly.

"Will the car take the lot?"

"Oh, yes. I'll 'phone my pater to send the biggest Rolls-Royce," said Trimble. "Rather pleasant, you know, to go down in a party by road. I never did care for railway travelling."

"Well, you do things in style at Trimble Hall, an' no mistake!" said Cardew admiringly.

"Always did, you know. What's the good of being a millionaire if you don't spend your money?" said Baggy fatuously. "That's how my pater looks at it."

"You must have a good time when you're at home."

"Topping!" said Baggy. "Of course, there'll be some people there you mayn't care for—big political johnnies—the Prime Minister, and some of the War Office big guns, and so on. But they needn't bother you."

"I sha'n't let them," said Cardew gravely.

"My pater likes that kind of society. He's going in for a title, you know, and those things have to be wangled," said Trimble. "But——"

"I should rather like to meet the Prime Minister," remarked Cardew. "I suppose you could get me an introduction?"

"Certainly. I'll make a note of it," said Baggy. "I'm afraid you'll find him a bit of a bore. I do."

"Oh! You—you do?" gasped Cardew.

"Yes. Still, one has to meet such people."

"Of—of course!"

"I think you'll enjoy yourself at Trimble Hall," said Baggy, beaming. "I don't brag of my wealth, you know. Doocid bad form. But there it is. We're millionaires, and we live up to it."

"Well, of course, anybody could see that much, from the thumpin' remittances you got."

"Oh, it goes!" said Trimble. "Money simply flies, you know, when a fellow's as open-handed as I am. I lent my last tenner to Figgins of the New House."

"D-d-did you?"

"And the pater's got rather ratty about my asking him for money again so soon," sighed Trimble.

"No wonder, if you blue it a tenner at a time!"

"Well, I never was mean, you know, and I simply can't refuse a pal a loan when he asks for it. The worst of it is the pater's written to say that, as I've had twenty pounds in the last week, he's not going to send me any more till the end of the term."

"You really can't expect him to," said Cardew gravely.

But it comes awkward," said Trimble, watching Cardew's grave face eagerly. "I'm to have a tenner on the last day of the term——"

"That will set you up."

"Yes; but in the meantime——"

"My dear fellow," said Cardew cordially, "if you're short of tin in the meantime, you've got plenty of friends who'll stand by you. F'rinstance, I should be very much offended if you forgot me when you happened to be short of tin."

"W-w-would you?" gasped Trimble, hardly able to believe his fat ears.

"Certainly. I really hope that you won't forget to mention it to me, Trimble, if you happen to be short."

"I—I won't——"

"If a half-sov would be any use to you at the present moment——"

"It—it would."

"Say no more, old nut. Here you are!"

"Ralph Reckness Cardew strolled away, leaving Baggy Trimble staring, with a fixed and astonished gaze, at the money in his fat palm.

Billy Bunter blinked at him, with new and wonderful respect in his blink. "Money talks," it is said, and if Cardew was lending Trimble money because he knew all about the unlimited wealth of the Trimbles, that was evidence quite good enough for Bunter.

And the fat Owl could have kicked himself for not having welcomed the advances Trimble had made on his arrival at St. Jim's.

This wealthy fellow, son of a millionaire—a fellow who mixed with Prime Ministers at home—had been quite friendly at first, and Bunter had let the chance slip.

He resolved to make up for lost time at once.

Trimble was still staring almost dazedly at his plunder when Bunter rolled towards him and joined him.

A Temporary Loan!
(See Chapter 2.)

"Trimble, old chap!" said Bunter affectionately.

Trimble stared at him—not a welcoming stare.

He was on pally terms with the dandy of the Fourth now, and he had no use for Bunter. Besides, a few days had been enough to convince him that Bunter's brag was as unfounded as his own.

"Hallo!" he said coldly.

"I've been looking for you," said Bunter, with determined cordiality.

"I dare say you have," answered Trimble coolly. "And you can look a little farther!"

He walked away.

"Oh!" murmured Bunter. "Fat beast!"

But Billy Bunter was not so easily beaten as all that. A little later Tom Merry & Co., from the steps of the School House, observed quite an interesting scene.

Baggy Trimble, with a smear of jam round his fat mouth, was coming in to dinner. Billy Bunter joined him in the quad, and walked with him.

THE GEM LIBRARY.—No. 573.

Trimble gave him a haughty look.

"I say, Trimble, old chap," said Bunter coaxingly, "I'll tell you what——"

"You needn't!"

"The fact is, Trimble, I was going to ask you to tea——"

"I'm going to tea in Study No. 9, thanks," answered Trimble. "Levison's asked me to tea with him and Cardew."

"To-morrow, then——"

"To-morrow I've promised Manners."

"Oh!" murmured Bunter.

Trimble seemed a very much sought-after person all of a sudden. Billy Bunter could have kicked himself once more, and quite hard, for not having seized the opportunity of palling with him.

"The fact is, Trimble," murmured Bunter, "I—I'm not very comfy in No. 6—rather crowded, you know——"

"No bizney of mine."

"Plenty of room in No. 2, though," said Bunter. "I really wanted to come into it before, only D'Arcy over-persuaded me——"

"Jolly glad he did!"

"Ahem! I—I'm thinking of asking the Housemaster to change me into No. 2, as there's more room there——"

"I'll jolly well roll you out if you wedge into my study, Bunter! And I'll see Railton about it, if you do!" said Trimble. "You're not going to loot my study as you do No. 6."

"Oh, really, Trimble——"

"Scat!" said Trimble.

He walked on alone. But Billy Bunter hurried after him, and joined him in the doorway.

"I say, Trimble, old chap——"

"Oh, go and eat coke!" snapped Trimble. "Hang on to somebody who wants your company—I don't!"

And Trimble rolled away, sniffing. Tom Merry & Co. exchanged a cheery grin. Evidently the plot was working!

CHAPTER 5.
Gussy is Puzzled.

Arthur Augustus D'Arcy was surprised.

He could not quite make it out.

When he came into Study No. 6, and found Blake and Herries and Digby listening to Bunter with respectful attention, he could scarcely believe his noble eyes.

Bunter was rather surprised himself—but not much. His view was that Study No. 6 was doing him simple justice at last. He was a fine fellow; he was a fascinating personality; and they hadn't recognised it. Now they seemed alive to their error, and were making up for lost time. That was what it looked like—to Bunter.

When Billy Bunter could obtain an audience he was accustomed to spreading himself. And once Study No. 6 had become respectfully attentive Bunter's spreading grew tremendous.

The glories of the Bunter home equalled, if they did not excel, those of Trimble Hall; indeed, as Herries remarked privately, when it came to lying, Bunter and Trimble were neck and neck.

In expatiating upon those glories Bunter almost forgot that he was, for the nonce, Wally Bunter—but he was not in danger of betraying himself, for no one really heeded or compared his various statements—his habitual untruthfulness was well known now, and nobody expected him to keep anywhere near the facts.

Bunter's yarns generally wound up with the confidential statement that, owing to unforeseen circumstances, a postal-order he had been expecting had not arrived. But, to his great satisfaction, he found that even the postal-order was swallowed, as it were—and Blake and Herries and Digby, in turn, cashed it for him in advance.

With the ultimate object of ridding the study of the intolerable Owl, they felt that it was money well spent.

Arthur Augustus was surprised—he was puzzled—and he was a little suspicious.

He was pleased at first; but it dawned upon his noble brain that his chums were pulling Bunter's leg, and that was rather annoying.

Tom Merry's little scheme had been at work for a couple of days when D'Arcy tackled his chums on the subject. Bunter had just left the study with a half-crown he had extracted from Dig—on account of a remittance hourly expected.

"You fellows seem to be gettin' on bettah with Buntah," Arthur Augustus remarked casually.

"Yes, looks like it, doesn't it?" said Blake.

"I twust you are not pullin' his leg?"

"How?"

"Well, you have vewy fwequently wemarked that you do not believe his statements wegardin' his home and people, Blake."

"But you did, Gussy."

"I could not possibly doubt the word of a fwiend, Blake."

"Even when he tells whoppers?" grinned Blake.

"Weally, you know——"

"Well, now we're following your noble example, Gussy. We're making it a point to believe everything Bunter says."

"I twust you weally believe him, Blake."

"Can't do better than our best, can we?"

"I suppose not. But the wemarkable thing is that you are tweatin' Twimble in the same way."

"Trimble!" yawned Blake. "What about Trimble?"

"I have seen you listenin' to his widiculous yarns about Twimble Hall, just as if you didn't know he was lyin'."

Blake shook an admonitory finger at the swell of St. Jim's.

"Gussy!" he exclaimed, in a tone more of sorrow than of anger. "Really, I'm shocked at you!"

"Weally, Blake——"

"How do you know that Trimble isn't telling the truth as much as Bunter?" demanded Blake.

"Weally——"

"Trimble Hall is just as likely to exist as Bunter Court," remarked Digby. "Millionaire Trimble is as likely a person as Lord Bunter de Bunter."

"Yaas, but——"

"We've all accepted Trimble's invitations home for the next vac," said Blake. "So has Cardew. So we're bound to be civil."

"Yes, rather," grinned Herries.

"You know vewy well, Blake, that Twimble is spoofin', and that he does not weally mean to take anybody home for the vac"

"Gussy!"

"Bai Jove! I wefuse to be addwessed as if you were shocked at me, Blake!" exclaimed the swell of St. Jim's.

"But I am shocked at you, Gussy! You're getting suspicious in your old age!" said Blake sorrowfully.

"I wefuse to admit for one moment that I am suspicious. I wegard suspiciousness as wotten bad form!" exclaimed D'Arcy hotly. "But we know the facts about Twimble. Didn't he ask a lot of fellows home once befoah, and hedge at the last minute? Did anybody go to his place? Didn't he contwive to wiggle out of it?"

"Well, it did look like that," grinned Blake. "But he may mean business this time."

"Wats!"

"Now, look here, Gussy——"

"I wepeat—wats! You are pullin' Twimble's leg, and Buntah's leg. I weally do not see what you are doin' it for."

"'Noblesse oblige'!" said Dig. "We're bound to take their word, ain't we? We're not suspicious, Gussy."

"If you think that I am suspicious, Dig——"

"Besides, Trimble is a chap worth knowing, like Bunter," remarked Herries. "I'd like you to be a bit more civil to Trimble, Gussy."

"I wefuse to be civil to Twimble."

"But the son of a millionaire might be jolly useful——"

"I do not cwedit for one moment that his patah is a millionaire; and I should certainly wefuse to be civil to him on that account, even if I did cwedit it."

"Well, we're not so jolly disinterested," said Blake. "We're going to cultivate Trimble—for his money, you know."

"I suppose you are jokin', Blake?"

"Sober as a judge, old man! There's a lot of delightful traits in Trimble's character—if a chap could only see them."

"I have nevah been able to see them."

"You're prejudiced, Gussy. Hallo!" Blake glanced at the study clock. "Time I was off, or I shall keep Trimble waiting."

"Bai Jove! Are you goin' out with Twimble, Blake?"

"Yes; he's asked me."

"You nevah cared for that boundah's company befoah!"

"I didn't believe then that he was rolling in money," explained Blake. "The case is altered now."

And Blake strolled out of the study.

"Bai Jove! I wefuse to believe that Blake cares a wap for Twimble's money, even if he has got any, which I don't cwedit for one moment!" exclaimed Arthur Augustus. "This is some wotten stunt!"

"Go hon!" murmured Dig.

"You are pullin' Twimble's leg, an' Buntah's leg, an' my leg!" exclaimed Arthur Augustus, with some excitement.

"My hat! What a lot of leg-pulling!" said Digby. "My dear man, if you don't believe Bunter's yarns, you can tell him so, but we're making it a point to believe in them in lumps. You ought to be pleased, as you're always standing up for that fat Owl—ahem!—I mean, that splendid chap."

"Wats!" was Arthur Augustus' reply.

He retired from the study, very much perplexed, leaving Herries and Dig chortling.

He was further suprised when he came out into the quadrangle. Jack Blake was walking down to the gates with Trimble, and Gussy caught a snatch of Trimble's conversation.

"You'll find everything tip-top at Trimble Hall——"

Arthur Augustus' feelings were expressed in a sniff.

Next his eyes fell upon Billy Bunter, who was in conversation with the Terrible Three. The Shell fellows were listening with as much respect as Blake & Co. had shown in the study.

"The difficulty is," Bunter was saying, "that my pater's sent me a cheque, the amount being rather too large for a postal-order. I don't quite know where to get it cashed."

"Oh, bai Jove!" murmured D'Arcy.

Trimble paused, and glanced round; he heard that remark of Bunter's as he passed. Perhaps Blake had led him past to hear it.

There was a scornful grin on Trimble's podgy face. He, for one, did not believe in Bunter's cheque. But he was surprised to see that Tom Merry & Co. took it with perfect seriousness.

"That's awkward, Bunter," said Tom Merry seriously.

"Dashed awkward!" agreed Bunter. "I suppose you fellows——"

"Is it for a large amount?" asked Tom.

"No; only for ten pounds," answered Bunter negligently.

"Oh! Ah! I say, Blake!" called out Tom Merry.

"Hallo?" said Blake, coming up, Trimble with him.

"Bunter's in rather a difficult position," said Tom gravely. "It seems that he's got a cheque from his pater. We never get cheques, and I'm blessed if I know how to get one cashed. What would you suggest?"

"Well, if it's an open cheque, Bunter can take it to the bank," said Blake, after some thought, while Baggy Trimble stood dumbfounded.

"It's a crossed cheque," said Bunter hastily.

"Oh, in that case, the Housemaster would cash it for you," said Blake. "He could pass it through his bank, you know."

"Why, of course!" said Tom Merry. "Mr. Railton would do it like a shot!"

"It might take some time," said Bunter, blinking at them. "Perhaps, while I'm waiting for it, you fellows could——"

"Go to the Housemaster and ask him," suggested Lowther. "If he can't cash it on the spot, we'll lend you some tin with pleasure!"

"Good!" said Bunter.

He rolled away to the School House with the Terrible Three. Blake turned away towards the gates again with Trimble.

"I—I say, Blake, do you think Bunter's really got a cheque for ten pounds?" breathed Trimble.

"He says he has," answered Blake, looking surprised. "I suppose he ought to know."

"I thought it was all gas——"

"My dear chap, that's a bit suspicious, isn't it?" said Blake reprovingly.

"Has he really gone to the Housemaster about it, I wonder?"

"Cut in and see," said Blake, laughing.

"By gad, I will!"

Baggy Trimble, intensely curious, ran quickly into the House. He found the Terrible Three lounging in the passage near Mr. Railtons' door.

"Where's Bunter?" he gasped.

Tom Merry nodded towards the Housemaster's study.

"Gone in to Railton?"

"Yes."

"Then—then he's really got the cheque?"

"Why shouldn't he?"

"Oh, my hat!" said Trimble.

He left the School House, and rejoined Blake, with a very thoughtful frown on his fat face. The Terrible Three grinned at one another.

"The plot thickens!" murmured Lowther.

Trimble's walk with Blake was cut rather short that afternoon—not at all to Blake's disappointment. Baggy was rather anxious to get back to St. Jim's—and see Bunter!

A fellow who asked a Housemaster to cash a cheque for ten pounds for him was a fellow worth cultivating. And Baggy Trimble by this time bitterly regretted that he had repulsed Bunter's friendly overtures. But that was an error that could be rectified!

CHAPTER 6.

A Chance for Mellish.

"WELL, Bunter?"

Billy Bunter blinked rather uneasily at the master of the School House.

The Terrible Three had accompanied him as far as the door of the Housemaster's study—to get his cheque cashed. The cheque, unfortunately, had no existence outside Bunter's fervid imagination, so he certainly could not ask Mr. Railton to cash it. But he had to enter the Housemaster's study with that pretended object in order to keep up appearances; and, once inside, he cudgelled his brains for an excuse to give Mr. Railton for his visit.

The School House master regarded him with surprise. He could not understand what the fat junior was blinking and hesitating for.

"Well?" he repeated.

"If—if you please, sir——" stammered Bunter, to gain time.

"Kindly come to the point, Bunter! My time is of value!" said Mr. Railton severely.

"Certainly, sir! I—I wouldn't waste your time for anything——"

"You are doing so, however! Why have you come to my study?"

"I—I—the fact is, sir——"

"Well?" exclaimed Mr. Railton impatiently.

"I—I'm expecting a postal-order, sir!" gasped Bunter.

"What?"

"It—it hasn't come, sir, and—and if you could advance me the ten shillings, sir——"

"Certainly not!" said Mr. Railton severely. "You are a very singular boy, Bunter, to come to your Housemaster with such a request. Leave my study at once!"

"Yes, sir!" gasped Bunter.

And he left the study, glad to escape Mr. Railton's keen eyes.

The Terrible Three were waiting in the passage. They came towards Bunter as he closed the Housemaster's door.

"All serene?" asked Tom Merry.

"Nunno! He—he can't cash the cheque!" gasped Bunter, blinking uneasily at the Terrible Three.

Bunter had a way of judging others by himself, and he wondered whether an inquisitive ear had been near the keyhole while he was talking to Mr. Railton within.

But he was soon relieved. The chums of the Shell looked sympathetic, and certainly unsuspicious.

"That's hard cheese!" said Manners.

"Yes, isn't it?" said Bunter, gathering confidence. "Awfully hard on a chap when he's got a cheque for ten quid, and——"

"We'll find somebody else," said Tom Merry musingly. "Perhaps Mrs. Taggles would change it at the tuckshop? Let's try!"

"I—I've left it with Railton," said Bunter hastily. "He—he's going to pass it through his bank, you see, and—and let me have the money when it comes. I—I shall have to wait."

"Oh!" said Tom gravely. "Well, that's really the best thing you could do with it, Bunter."

"Yes, but in the meantime——"

"I dare say Trimble could accommodate you in the meantime," said Monty Lowther, with the solemnity of an owl. "Trimble's simply gilt-edged, you know; he says so himself."

"Good! Let's go and see Trimble!" said Manners.

"He—he's gone out, hasn't he?" asked Bunter.

"He was here a minute ago, speaking to us. Let's look in his study, anyway."

"Oh, all right! But perhaps you fellows——"

"This way!" said Tom Merry, suddenly deaf.

The Terrible Three turned to the staircase, and Bunter rolled after them. They looked into Study No. 2 in the Fourth Form passage. Baggy Trimble was not there; but his study-mate, Percy Mellish, was in the room, busily occupied with lines—as the Terrible Three happened to know.

Mellish gave the chums of the Shell a sour look; but he honoured Bunter with a civil nod.

Mellish had heard Bunter's tales of magnificence—of which he would not have believed a word but for the fact that Tom Merry & Co. seemed to be taking them for granted. So far as Mellish could see, the Terrible Three and Study No. 6 were sucking up to Bunter for his money. Certainly there was no other way of accounting for their seeking Bunter's society. Bunter unadorned, so to speak, was not exactly fascinating; but if he was rich, that accounted for everything—in Percy Mellish's eyes.

"Trimble out?" asked Tom Merry.

"He's gone out with Blake, I believe," said Mellish, with a sneer. "Blake's been fishing for an invitation to Trimble's place, and he seems to have caught it. Blessed if I ever believed in Trimble Hall!"

"Oh, draw it mild!" exclaimed Tom. "Trimble's asked us there for the vac."

"And you're going?"

"We've accepted the invitation," said Tom gravely. "According to Trimble, a chap will get a topping time there."

"According to Trimble!" sneered Mellish. "I'll believe in his merry palace when I see it!"

"Perhaps Trimble hasn't asked you?" suggested Bunter, blinking at him.

"Go and eat coke!" was Mellish's reply, his civility to Bunter giving way under the strain of that remark.

"Well, never mind Trimble Hall," said Tom Merry. "Bunter's looking for Trimble to cash a cheque for him!"

"Ten pounds!" said Bunter loftily.

"You get cheques for ten pounds?" exclaimed Mellish, with wide-open eyes.

"That's nothing to me!" said Bunter.

"Gammon!"

"Oh, really, Mellish! These fellows saw me hand the cheque to Mr. Railton, who's promised to cash it for me, anyhow!"

"Phew!"

"Well, as Trimble's out, there's nothing doing here!" said Tom Merry hastily. "I dare say we can accommodate you, Bunter, till you get some cash in hand. Will five bob be any use?"

"Certainly, old chap!"

Mellish's eyes grew wider and wider as the Terrible Three sorted out sufficient silver to make up that sum.

"Of course, I know that's not much to a wealthy fellow like you, Bunter!" said Lowther. "But we're not all millionaires!"

"Don't mench, old chap!" said Bunter. "I'll let you have this back when I get the cash from Railton!"

"That's all right!"

The Terrible Three went out, and Bunter was following them, when Percy Mellish called to him.

"I say, Bunter, old chap——"

"Hallo?" said Bunter carelessly.

"Care for toffee?" asked Mellish amicably. "I've got some rather good toffee here!"

"Like a bird!" said Bunter.

The Owl's fat face beamed as he sampled Mellish's toffee—and he took a rather large sample. When the toffee was finished Bunter rolled away—having accepted an invitation from Mellish to come in to tea that week.

Mellish looked very thoughtful. The sneak of the Fourth was impecunious, and he was accustomed to hanging on to wealthy fellows like Racke and Crooke for the sake of the crumbs that fell from the rich man's table. Racke and Crooke patronised him, and disdained him. It occurred to Mellish that it would be more agreeable, and more profitable, to pay his court to this wealthy new junior, who had cheques for ten pounds at a time.

Evidently there was something in it, or why were Tom Merry & Co. so civil to the fat fellow? They must have an axe to grind, Mellish reflected. And when it came to flattery and toadery, Mellish felt that he could easily cut out Tom Merry & Co. He had great gifts in that line.

Mellish was thinking that over while the Terrible Three, having finished with Bunter, went down to football practice.

"It's working!" grinned Monty Lowther. "Next thing will be a close friendship between Bunter and Trimble—you'll see!"

"Bunter will be after Trimble's money, and Trimble will be after Bunter's; and, as neither of them has any, no harm will be done!"

"Ha, ha, ha!"

"Trimble's sure to try to get Bunter to chum with him in his study, and I fancy Mellish will second him. And Bunter's sure to jump at the chance, to get in close touch with Trimble's wealth!"

The Terrible Three roared.

The wheeze was working like a charm. The two incurable spoofers were succeeding in spoofing one another—with a little assistance from Tom Merry & Co.

It really looked as if Study No. 6 would be relieved of W. G. Bunter before very long!

CHAPTER 7.
Bosom Pals.

"I SAY, you fellows!"

Billy Bunter rolled into Study No. 6 at tea-time the next day, and found it rich and fragrant with the scent of frying herrings.

He sniffed.

"I say, you fellows, I've asked a friend to tea!" he said.

"Wight-ho, deah boy!" answered D'Arcy. "Any fwiend of yours is welcome! Vewy fortunately, we have some jam."

"Yes; that's lucky!" remarked Blake solemnly. "Who's your friend, Bunter—Tom Merry?"

"No!" said Bunter disdainfully.

Apparently he did not think very much of Tom Merry.

"Lowther or Manners?"

"Certainly not! It's Trimble!"

"Oh, Trimble!" said Herries, turning his face away to hide the grin that was overspreading it.

"Bai Jove! Twimble!"

"And I'd like something a bit decent for tea," said Bunter, with a very dissatisfied blink at the herrings. "Trimble's a rather decent chap!"

"Bai Jove!"

"I should like to be hospitable," said Bunter. "Blessed if I care about offering a friend fried fish for tea!"

"Cut down to the tuckshop," suggested Digby. "Dame Taggles has a lot of stuff in——"

"Railton hasn't changed my cheque yet," explained Bunter. "I'm still short of tin."

"Too bad!" said Blake seriously.

Arthur Augustus D'Arcy turned his eyeglass on Blake searchingly. Gussy was not suspicious. Suspicion and Gussy were as far as the poles asunder. But he had doubts about that cheque. He could not help having very strong doubts.

The amazing circumstance was that Blake & Co. appeared to swallow it whole. The story of the ten-pound cheque was a little too steep for Gussy, who was of quite a trusting disposition; and it would have taxed his credence to the utmost limit. He naturally expected his chums to express their opinions on the subject with Fourth Form candour. Instead of which they seemed to take the cheque for granted.

Arthur Augustus simply couldn't catch on. This unwearying politeness to Bunter was past his noble comprehension.

"Well, it would take a day or two for the cheque to pass through the bank," said Herries gravely. "It has to go through a clearing-house or something. I don't see why Railton can't advance you the money."

"Yes; why not ask him?" remarked Dig.

Bunter shook his head.

"I don't care to ask favours of him," he said. "He might have offered it. He didn't choose to, and I sha'n't ask him. I shall wait till the cheque is cashed."

Jack Blake looked at the Owl almost in wonder.

He knew perfectly well that there was no cheque in existence, and that Bunter had not therefore given it to Mr. Railton to change for him. Yet the fat junior spoke with calm assurance, as if he believed in it himself.

The fact was that Billy Bunter was so accustomed to talking out of his hat that he had almost lost the distinction between truth and falsehood. So long as his statements were believed, that was good enough for him; and he did not consider it necessary that they should have any relation to the facts.

Arthur Augustus looked very uncomfortable. He felt, rather than knew, that the Owl was lying, and it gave him a sense of great uneasiness.

Blake turned to the herrings again.

Spoofing Bunter was rather a joke, but Blake felt his patience approaching the limit sometimes.

Herries and Digby coughed, and went on laying the table. They, too, wondered how Bunter could do it. They almost expected him to choke, sometimes, when he rolled out such thumping whoppers. They did not know the Owl so well as he had been known in the Greyfriars Remove. Bunter was in no danger of choking.

"So—so Twimble is comin' to tea?" said Arthur Augustus, breaking a silence that was growing painful.

"Yes, my pal Trimble," said Bunter loftily.

"I was not awaah that Twimble was your pal, Buntah."

"You're aware of it now, then! I've chummed up with Trimble," explained Bunter, blinking at Gussy. "We've got a lot in common. In these days of Socialism and Bolshevism and things it's the duty of wealthy fellows to stick together. That's how I look at it."

"Oh!"

"I didn't know Trimble was wealthy—I mean, he didn't know I was wealthy—I—I—I mean, of course, that that really has nothing to do with it," stammered Bunter. "What I mean to say is, I like Trimble. I think he's a splendid chap—a really fine fellow."

"I do not agwee with you, Buntah."

"Oh, really, D'Arcy——"

"I do not think vewy much of Twimble."

"I don't like to hear a fellow run down behind his back!" said Bunter loftily.

"What?"

"You heard what I said. I'm not going to listen to anything against my pal Trimble."

Arthur Augustus' eye gleamed through his eyeglass.

"Buntah, if you imply that I am wunnin' a fellow down behind his back ——" he began, breathless with wrath.

"Well, what are you doing, then?" grunted Bunter.

"I am statin' a fact that Twimble is perfectly well awaah of—that I do not think much of him, and do not appwove of him," said Arthur Augustus, more quietly. "Holdin' that opinion of Twimble, I do not care to sit down to tea with him."

"He's jolly well coming here to tea!" said Bunter. "I've asked him. I suppose I have a right to ask a fellow to tea in my own study?"

"Certainly. And I have a wight to wetiah fwom the studay; and I shall pwoceed to do so."

And Arthur Augustus walked to the door.

"Suit yourself," said Bunter. "I don't care. In fact, it'll make more room for my pal Trimble."

Arthur Augustus did not reply to that. He walked along to Tom Merry's study in the Shell, where the Terrible Three gave him a hearty welcome.

Jack Blake closed one eye at his chums in Study No. 6.

Firmly imbued now with the belief that Trimble was a fellow of great wealth, and delighted with Trimble's readiness to make friends with him, Bunter was thinking of nothing but getting on the chummiest possible terms with his new pal.

He could not afford to consider Arthur Augustus at such a time. If all he heard of Trimble was correct, Baggy was a more valuable friend than Gussy. Bunter was already dreaming of the terrific good times in store for him at Trimble Hall. And certainly Trimble, personally, was more to his taste than Gussy. He had none of the notions which Bunter regarded as "high-falutin," such as Gussy had. He was greedy and bouncing and untruthful—in fact, a fellow after the Owl's own heart.

Bunter hardly heeded Gussy's departure from the study. He was giving his attention now to tea, which he hoped would make a good impression on

Trimble. He certainly was not satisfied with herrings for tea.

"What have you got beside that?" he asked, with a disparaging glance at Blake's frying-pan.

"There's jam," said Dig.

"Anything else?"

"Bread-and-butter."

"I should like something decent for Trimble. He's accustomed to something a bit more decent than fried fish."

"We must do our best for Trimble," said Blake gravely. "Cut along to the shop, Dig, and see what you can do."

"And bring in something fit for a gentleman to eat," said Bunter. "I'm blessed if I know how you fellows stand grubbing about in the study as you do. Of course, I can make allowances for your people being poor, and all that; but, really——"

"We can't all be as wealthy as you and Trimble," said Blake meekly.

"I know that, and I make allowances. Still, you ought to remember that you've got a fellow in the study now who's accustomed to decent living."

"Oh!" gasped Blake. "We—we'll try to."

Herries gripped a cushion, hard; but a look from Blake restrained him, and he dropped it again. Herries had come quite near spoiling the whole thing.

Dig hurried away to the tuckshop, and came back with quite a handsome supply. Bunter looked more satisfied as it was laid on the table.

"That's better," he said. "You might have got a cake, though."

"It wouldn't run to one of Dame Taggles' cakes," said Dig.

Bunter snorted.

"That's all very well; but I don't see why I should go short because I happen to be temporarily short of tin. Mrs. Taggles would let you have one on tick."

"We don't run tick at the tuckshop in this study."

Another snort.

"I may as well say out plain, Blake, that I expect to be treated well in this study," said Bunter.

"Oh!"

"I've been thinking of changing out," said Bunter loftily. "I believe I should get on better with Trimble. There's more room in his study, too. Of course, I don't want to throw you fellows over," added Bunter kindly.

"Oh, don't!" implored Blake.

"Don't!" gasped Digby.

Herries uttered an unintelligible sound, something like the growl of his bulldog Towser.

"Well, a chap has to consider himself," said Bunter fatuously. "It's all very well for you fellows, having a wealthy chap in the study, very convenient for you, and all that——"

"Oh! Exactly!"

"But if you want to keep me here you will have to treat me decently, that's all," said Bunter, in a tone of finality. "In fact, I may as well tell you what I want, and what I shall expect, if I'm to stay in this study."

"Oh!"

"I've often found one of you planted in the armchair when I come in. Well, I don't mind that, so long as the chair's given up to me as soon as I want it. I'm not selfish."

"Oh!"

"And I expect something pretty decent at tea-time, especially when I bring a friend in to tea. Of course, I shall settle up for everything when my postal-order comes—I mean, when my cheque's cashed."

"Same thing!" murmured Blake.

"What did you say?"

"N-nothing! Go on, old scout!"

"Well, that's about all," said Bunter. "Just remember that I'm not tied to this study, and if I don't find things to my satisfaction I shall walk out of it. Bear that in mind!"

"We—we will."

"I want you to be civil to Trimble, too. Try to be as good-mannered as possible—not so much of your fag boisterousness."

"Oh!" gasped Blake.

"I'll go and fetch Trimble now. Have everything ready when I come back," said Bunter.

He rolled out of the study.

Blake & Co. looked at one another eloquently.

"D-d-d-did you ever?" gasped Dig.

"That's the kind of nice fellow Bunter is when he's given his head!" murmured Blake. "Isn't he delightful?"

to him on account of it; and, with that belief in his mind, Bunter was naturally haughty and uppish, showing all the charming qualities, in fact, of his fascinating nature.

But, while he was decidedly uppish to Study No. 6, he was all smiles and civility to Trimble—the wealthy Trimble, the distinguished son of the millionaire of Trimble Hall!

And Trimble, for precisely similar reasons, was all civility and smiles to Billy Bunter.

In fact, the friendship between them was quite touching to witness.

It really seemed to be a case of "Two souls with but a single thought, two hearts that beat as one."

At the tea-table they even restrained their greediness to some extent in order to impress one another favourably.

Mutual Toadying.
(See below.)

"I can't stand it much longer," said Herries, in a tone of suppressed rage. "If it doesn't come to a finish soon, Blake, I shall start on him."

"Patience, my son! It's worth a little trouble to get that fat beast out of the study for good."

Herries snorted.

"Look here, you don't want me here. I'll go over and see Figgins in the New House. I shall break out if that fat ruffian starts gassing again—and he will."

And Herries tramped out of the study in a boiling state. Dig looked inclined to follow him, but Blake called him back.

"Don't leave me to stand it alone, Dig."

"Oh, all right!" said Dig resignedly.

Blake and Digby were there when Billy Bunter came back with his esteemed pal Baggy Trimble.

Tea was ready, and everything was in apple-pie order. Blake had obeyed Bunter's instructions on that point. It did not surprise Bunter to find that his word was law in Study No. 6.

His belief was that Blake & Co. believed in his wealth, and were sucking up

"Have another egg, Trimble?"

"No, thanks, old chap."

"Like the jam-tarts, Trimble?"

"Yes, rather! I say, Bunter, you try these cream-puffs. No, don't mind me; you try them, old fellow."

Blake and Digby were left very much out in the cold. Their tea was somewhat meagre, but they drew Trimble out on the subject of the glories of Trimble Hall, and Baggy fairly spread himself in boasting.

Blake and Dig listened with profound and envious respect, watchful of the effect upon Bunter, whose manner to Trimble grew more and more sugary. Then they drew Bunter on the topic of his titled relations, his father's mansion and the family yacht, the shooting-box in Scotland and the villa at Nice, to all of which Trimble listened with open ears and open mouth, his feelings towards Bunter evidently those of a long-lost brother.

Blake and Digby left them to finish tea together. They breathed more freely when they were outside Study No. 6.

"My hat!" murmured Blake, as they

walked away. "I'd never have believed there could be two such terrific liars in existence. I thought Trimble was the one and only!"

"And they believe one another!" gasped Dig.

"Ha, ha, ha!"

When the last crumb had vanished in Study No. 6 Trimble and Bunter came out, arm-in-arm. Mellish of the Fourth joined them as they strolled into the quadrangle, eagerly polite and agreeable.

From his study window Tom Merry caught sight of the three, and he chuckled. His chuckle drew his studymates to the window.

"Touching picture of friendship!" grinned Monty Lowther.

"It is vewy wemarkable to me," said Arthur Augustus D'Arcy. "I weally do not see what Buntah sees in Twimble. I weally cannot stand Twimble myself. And—and—— Ahem!"

Gussy was about to say that he did not see what Trimble saw in Bunter either, but he refrained.

"Well, they're both immensely wealthy," remarked Tom Merry. "That's a sort of bond of union, isn't it?"

"But are they, deah boy?"

"Well, they say so, and they ought to know."

"Yaas, but——"

Arthur Augustus was silent, and said no more. But he was more and more puzzled. As his belief in Bunter declined, that of Tom Merry & Co. seemed to be increasing, which was very perplexing indeed.

CHAPTER 8.
Bunter is Sorry.

"I'M sorry!"

Bunter made that statement in Study No. 6 later in the evening.

The Terrible Three had dropped in to share a supper of baked chestnuts with Blake & Co. Bunter rolled in, and helped himself to the lion's share of the chestnuts, and then looked thoughtful for some moments. Then, with a very firm manner, he stated that he was sorry.

"Sowwy, Buntah?" repeated Arthur Augustus D'Arcy. "About what, deah boy?"

"Sorry that I sha'n't be able to share this study with you any longer," said Bunter firmly.

"Bai Jove!"

"I say, that's rather hard on these chaps, isn't it?" said Monty Lowther, with owl-like gravity. "Your presence here, Bunter, gives the study a sort of distinction——"

Tom Merry gave his chum a warning look, but it was not necessary. Flattery could never be laid on too thick for Bunter.

"Of course, I'm quite aware of that," said the fatuous Owl, "and I repeat, I'm sorry! But I must say that I've never been treated really well in this study, and the fellows can't expect me to stay."

Arthur Augustus turned his eyeglass on Bunter. In spite of his manful attempt to keep up the friendship he had formed with the fat junior, Gussy could not help his face brightening at the idea of the Owl clearing out of Study No. 6.

But Blake and Herries and Digby looked properly downcast.

"You're really going to leave us?" asked Blake sorrowfully.

Bunter nodded.

"But why?" asked Tom Merry. "What have these fellows done, Bunter, for you to desert them in this way?"

"It isn't exactly that," said Bunter. "There's too many in this study. I've suggested that Herries should change out, to give me more room here, but he hasn't done it."

Herries made a sound like Towser, but did not speak.

"I never get really enough tea, either," said Bunter. "I don't want to be personal, of course, but I am down on greediness and selfishness. Considering that I foot the bill, I ought to have enough."

"You—you foot the bill?" stuttered Blake.

"I mean, I'm going to when my remittance comes—I mean, when my cheque's cashed. It comes to the same thing."

"Oh, I—I see!"

Arthur Augustus D'Arcy breathed hard.

"I do not wegard it as comin' to the same thing," he said. "Buntah, I am sowwy to say it, but I do not cwedit your statement."

"What?"

"I am extwemely sowwy to say such a thing, but I do not believe you have had a cheque for ten pounds, and taken it to Wailton to cash," said Arthur Augustus firmly. "I have twied to believe it, but it is imposs. I cannot pwetend to believe that statement, Buntah!"

"Oh, my hat!" murmured Blake.

Bunter sneered.

"I might have expected something of this sort when I decided to turn you down, Gussy," he said.

"T-t-turn me down?" stuttered D'Arcy.

"Yes. It's jealousy!"

"Jealousy?" breathed Arthur Augustus.

"That's it. As for my cheque," said Bunter loftily, "Tom Merry came with me when I took it to Railton, and he knows."

"If that is the case, Buntah, I have made a mistake, and I am willin' to apologise. But I must wequest Tom Mewwy to confirm it."

"Oh, I went with him," said Tom. "I stayed—ahem!—outside the study while he was speaking to Railton."

"You did not see the cheque?"

"Ahem! No."

"Or hear it spoken of in the presence of Mr. Wailton?"

"No. Ahem!"

"Then your evidence is worth nothin', Tom Mewwy."

"Go hon!" murmured the captain of the Shell.

"I wepeat, Buntah, that I have twied vewy hard to cwedit your vawious statements, and I can do so no longah," said Arthur Augustus. "I feel in honah bound to tell you so."

"Oh, Gussy!" murmured Blake reproachfully.

"Some fellows are suspicious cads!" remarked Bunter casually.

"Bai Jove!"

Arthur Augustus jumped up.

"Buntah, I am sowwy, but I cannot allow that wemark to pass. I have twied to keep fwiendly with you because you saved my clobbah fwom bein' wuined by some wottahs when I was ovah at Gweyfwiahs. But it is weally imposs. Aftah that wemark, Buntah, I feel that I have no wesource but to give you a feahful thwashin'!"

"I say, you fellows——"

"Shush!" said Blake, pushing Arthur Augustus into his chair again. "Cheese it, Gussy!"

"Weally, Blake——"

"We're not going to allow you to quarrel with a fellow like Bunter. Suppose he was to use his influence with Trimble to keep us out of Trimble Hall?" said Blake severely.

"Oh, ewumbs!"

"Even if Bunter deserts this study, we shall always admire him and respect him as—as much as we do now," said Blake.

"Quite as much!" said Dig.

"I will wetiah fwom the studay," said Arthur Augustus, with dignity. "I will only wemark that I am vewy glad Buntah is goin'."

"Gammon!" said Bunter.

Arthur Augustus controlled his noble feelings, and retired from No. 6.

"I suppose D'Arcy feels it a little—he feels thrown over, of course," remarked Bunter. "But I can't help that! Trimble and Mellish have been pressing me to come into their study, and I'm jolly well going to. I'm sorry, as I said. Really sorry! But the fact is, I've stood you fellows pretty patiently, and I've never been treated really well here. You needn't try to talk me over—I'm going!"

"We could go to the Housemaster and protest," remarked Blake thoughtfully.

"Too late!" grinned Bunter. "Trimble and Mellish have been to him already, and he's given permission for me to change."

"Oh!"

"I'm going to see him myself now," added Bunter. "Later, Trimble's coming to help me move my things."

The Owl of Greyfriars cast a last blink round, and, seeing that there were no more chestnuts, he walked out of the study.

Tom Merry & Co. looked at one another in eloquent silence.

"He—he—he's gone!" gasped Blake.

"Actually gone!" murmured Dig. "It's too good to be true—but it's true!"

Tom Merry chuckled.

"What price my wheeze?" he asked. "My dear kids, when in doubt, always come to No. 10 in the Shell!"

"I can't quite believe it yet!" said Blake. "Not a word till the fat beast has asked the Housemaster to change him—then it'll be too late for him to change back."

And the chums of No. 6 waited—between hope and lingering doubt!

CHAPTER 9.
Exit Bunter!

BILLY BUNTER tapped at the door of Mr. Railton's study, and the School House master's deep voice bade him enter. Bunter opened the door and rolled in, and the Housemaster fixed his eyes upon him. Mr. Railton had observed Bunter a good deal since the Owl had come to St. Jim's. Bunter was rather a new thing in his experience.

"Well, Bunter?" said Mr. Railton.

"If you please, sir, I want to ask permission to change my study," said the Owl, blinking at him.

"For what reason, Bunter?"

"There's five of us in No. 6, sir, and it's rather a crowd," said Bunter. "There is more room in No. 2, and I have a very special friend there—Trimble."

"Quite so, Bunter! You would have been assigned to Study No. 2 when you came here but for your own request and D'Arcy's that you should be placed in No. 6. Have you any other motive for wishing to change?"

"Well, I don't get on very well in Study No. 6, sir," said Bunter. "I find it difficult to stand selfishness. The fellows are all right, in their way, but they're selfish—very thoughtless for others."

Mr. Railton looked at him very curiously.

"I hope you are able to avoid those faults, Bunter," he said.

"I hope so, sir," assented Bunter.

"Ahem! Well, there is no objection to your changing your study, Bunter, if the boys in Study No. 2 do not object to the change.

"Oh, they'll be glad sir!" said Bunter. "The fact is, I should be welcome in any study I selected!"

"Indeed!"

"Oh, yes, sir!" said Bunter confidently. "I've been begged to come into several studies; but, of course, I can't oblige everybody."

"You may send Mellish and Trimble here," said Mr. Railton abruptly.

"Very well, sir!"

Bunter rolled out, and hurried away to No. 2 in the Fourth, where he found Mellish and Trimble. They greeted him affectionately. From their manner it might have been supposed that Bunter was the apple of their eye.

Bunter's manner to the two was nicely discriminated, however. To Trimble, he was honeyed; to Mellish, he was lofty and patronising. There was nothing to be got out of Mellish.

There was, as a matter of fact, nothing to be got out of Trimble, either; but Bunter was as yet unaware of that important fact.

"I've spoken to Railton," he announced. "He wants to see you two fellows, to clinch it."

"Right-ho, old boy!" said Trimble. "We'll go at once!"

"Like a bird!" said Mellish.

"Don't call in at No. 6 as you go," said Bunter hastily.

"We're not likely to!" grinned Trimble. "But why?"

"I've told them you've asked the Housemaster already," explained Bunter. "They were actually suggesting asking Railton to keep me in No. 6."

"Great Scott!"

"After your money, the cads!" sneered Mellish. "They won't lose you if they can help it."

"That's it, of course," agreed Bunter. "They think—I mean, they know I'm rolling in oof, and they've made a good thing out of me already. I've practically stood all the exes of the study since I've been here; and, though I'm a generous chap, I'm getting tired of it. I own that."

"No wonder!" said Trimble. "They jolly well sha'n't keep you! We'll cut off and see Railton at once."

And Trimble and Mellish lost no time.

They repaired to the School House master's study, where Mr. Railton's consent to the change was duly obtained.

In great glee they returned to the Fourth Form passage.

Bunter was reclining, not to say sprawling, in the armchair in No. 2, and he blinked at them inquiringly over his big glasses as they came in.

"All serene!" said Mellish.

"Right as rain, old bird!" chuckled Trimble. "You belong to Study No. 2 now. I say, let's get your things moved in here!"

"We'll help," said Mellish.

"Oh, of course!" purred Trimble. "We'll help Bunter! It's a pleasure!"

Bunter grinned with satisfaction.

He had had the pleasure of turning down Study No. 6, and displaying what a popular and much-sought-after fellow he was; and he had planted himself in Trimble's study—on the chummiest possible terms with the son of the Trimble Hall millionaire!

No wonder he was satisfied.

The precious trio proceeded in company to Study No. 6, where Tom Merry & Co. were still chatting round the fire.

Arthur Augustus had rejoined the family circle by this time, and he looked a little restive as Bunter and Trimble and Mellish came in.

"No more chestnuts!" said Herries sarcastically.

Bunter sniffed.

"Do you think we want your mouldy old chestnuts?" he asked. "I've come to take my books and things away!"

"Really changing out?" asked Blake.

"I've spoken to Railton, and so have these chaps. I belong to Study No. 2 now," said Bunter loftily. "I'm sorry—I've said so—but——"

"Boo-hoo!" came from Jack Blake.

He was weeping.

Bunter blinked at him suspiciously. Even he could see that Jack Blake's grief was not quite genuine, especially as the other fellows were grinning.

He gave another snort, expressive of disdain.

"Help me with these things, you chaps," he said.

"Bai Jove! Don't take my Latin gwammar, Buntah!"

"Oh! Is that yours?"

"Yaas, wathah!"

"And that dic. is mine!" grunted Herries. "Let it alone! Your own rag is on the floor, where you left it!"

More sniffs from Bunter; but he was constrained to take only his own property, and he disappeared with it, followed by his new study-mates, also laden.

Bunter and his belongings were duly installed in Study No. 2.

"My only hat!" murmured Blake. "It really seems too good to be true!"

"Bai Jove! I cannot say I am sowwy that fat boundah has cleahed out!" confessed Arthur Augustus D'Arcy. "It is wathah bad taste for him to be so vewy uppish about it, though!"

"Nature of the beast!" explained Monty Lowther.

"It's because we've been so jolly civil!" chuckled Blake. "Bunter will always have those nice manners to anyone who's civil to him. You see, he thinks we're after his money."

"I do not believe he has any money, Blake."

"Same here!" said Blake cheerily. "He has about as much as Trimble!"

"Ha, ha, ha!"

Arthur Augustus D'Arcy turned his eyeglass upon his chums.

"I fail to undahstand you fellows," he said.

"Go hon!"

"For several days past," pursued Arthur Augustus warmly, "you have been makin' out that you believed Buntah's vewy impwobable yarns——"

"We've let him run on," assented Blake.

"And you have been doin' the same with Twimble——"

"Quite so!"

"And now, it appeahs, you have only been pullin' their sillay legs, and you do not believe a word of eithah of them!"

"Exactly, old bean!"

"And sevewal othah fellows, Cardew, and Levison, and Kangawoo, and some othahs, have been backin' you up in this widiculous game."

"You've got it!"

"And now, pway, what does it mean?" demanded Arthur Augustus. "I have a feelin' that somethin' has been goin' on behind the scenes which has not been confided to me."

"That's dawned on him at last!" said Monty Lowther admiringly. "With a brain like that, Gussy will wake 'em up in the House of Lords some day."

"Weally, Lowthah——"

"My dear old nut," said Blake, "can't you see? The little game was to make Bunter and Trimble to believe one another's yarns——"

"Bai Jove!"

"So that they would chum up——"

"Oh!" said Arthur Augustus slowly.

"And Bunter would be anxious to squeeze into Study No. 2, and Trimble and Mellish would be glad to get him there. See?"

"Oh!" ejaculated Gussy.

"It's worked like a charm," said Blake. "And I suggest a vote of thanks to Tom Merry, who thought of the wheeze."

"Hear, hear!"

"Bai Jove!" said D'Arcy. "I am not weally suah that I appwove——"

"Go hon!" Blake rose to his feet. "Let's see how those dear pals are getting on in No. 2."

"Ha, ha, ha!"

Tom Merry & Co. strolled along the passage and looked in at No. 2. Bunter and Trimble and Mellish were seated round the table there, doing their prep. They looked quite a happy family.

"Comfy here, Bunty?" asked Blake.

"Oh, yes, thanks," said Bunter, blinking at him. "By the way, Blake, I'll come to tea in No. 6 to-morrow, and bring Trimble——"

"Will you, by gad!"

"Yes; but it's got to be understood that there's something decent. You'll bear that in mind?"

"No," said Blake, with a chuckle: "I won't bear that in mind, Bunter! What I shall bear in mind is this—that if you show your overfed chivvy in Study No. 6, either to-morrow or any other day, you'll get a cushion on it!"

"Wha-a-at?"

"And a boot to help you travel!" grunted Herries.

Bunter blinked at the juniors as if he could scarcely believe his ears. Trimble and Mellish looked astounded. This was rather a change of tune, and they had not been prepared for it.

"I—I—I say, you fellows!" gasped Bunter. "I suppose you're joking?"

"You put your fat nose inside No. 6, and you'll see!" answered Blake.

Slam!

The door closed, and the Co. went their way. In Study No. 2 astonishment reigned.

Tom Merry & Co. chuckled as they departed; and even upon the calm and aristocratic visage of Arthur Augustus D'Arcy there dawned a grin.

CHAPTER 10.
Alas!

STUDY No. 6 was itself again. Blake & Co., the next day, were wearing cheerful smiles.

The Terrible Three shared their satisfaction. They felt that they had done a good deed in helping to relieve that celebrated study of the intolerable presence of Bunter.

But that day there was a deep shade of thought on Bunter's face.

Perhaps he was beginning to realise the truth.

The polite and respectful hearing given him by Tom Merry & Co. had vanished all of a sudden. For a couple of days he had been allowed to swank, brag, and to boast, and the Co. had lent him their ears, and even lent him their money.

Now there was a change.

That very morning Bunter generously bestowed his company on Study No. 6 in the quad after breakfast. Blake & Co. cheerfully turned their backs on him and walked away.

Bunter blinked after them in astonishment. This was certainly not the adulation due to his wealth. True, he hadn't any wealth; but he supposed that Blake & Co. believed he had—and he fancied they were after it—which came to the same thing.

"I say, you fellows!" he called out.

No answer.

Bunter hurried after them.

"Gussy, old chap——"

"I shall be obliged, Buntah, if you will not addwess me as Gussy!" said Arthur Augusuts, in his most stately way. "I am Gussy only to my friends."

"Oh, really, D'Arcy——"

"Pway welease my arm, Buntah!"

"Look here, you fellows——"

"Oh, buzz off!" grunted Herries.

"I—I say——"

"Bump him!" said Blake. "The fat rotter's given us enough trouble in the study, and still more trouble to get rid of him. Bump him!"

Billy Bunter did not stay to be bumped.

In a state of great indignation and astonishment, he hurried off. Naturally, he was very thoughtful that morning.

After morning lessons he looked for the Terrible Three; and ran down those cheery ornaments of the Shell.

"I say, you fellows——" he began, as he came up.

"Expecting a postal-order?" asked Monty Lowther gravely.

"Ye-es, exactly!"

"Short of tin?" asked Manners.

"Temporarily," said Bunter, his eyes gleaming behind his spectacles. "If you fellows could manage——"

"My dear chap, I can tell you what to do," said Tom Merry heartily.

"Eh? What?"

"Go to Railton, and ask him to hurry up with cashing that cheque of yours," said the captain of the Shell.

"That—that cheque?" stammered Bunter.

"Certainly."

"The—the fact is——"

"Dear old thing," said Lowther, "you needn't tell us the fact! We know the fact, my merry old bean! There isn't any cheque, and you thought you were spoofing us—and you weren't!"

"Oh, really, Lowther, if you doubt my word——"

"Ha, ha, ha!" roared the Terrible Three.

"I—I say, you fellows——"

"Stick Trimble for a loan, old bean," chortled Lowther. "Let him send for a cartload of banknotes from Trimble Hall. He can ask his pater to send them along in the Rolls-Royce, you know."

"I—I say——"

Tom Merry & Co. walked away, leaving Bunter stuttering. Apparently the general belief in his solvency had vanished all of a sudden—in fact, he began to realise that it had never existed, and that his fat leg had been pulled.

"Beasts!" murmured Bunter. "Lucky I've made friends with Trimble, after all. He's worth more to a chap than all that crowd."

And Bunter went to look for Trimble.

He found that podgy youth in talk with Cardew of the Fourth. But it was a Cardew quite different from the one Trimble had known for the past two days. Lord Reckness' grandson had been greatly entertained by the scheme of setting two impecunious spoofers to spoof one another; but the game was over now, as Trimble was learning rather suddenly.

Bunter jumped as he heard what the two were saying as the Owl came up.

"My dear fat pippin, I'll come to Trimble Hall—when the place is built," said Cardew, with a cheery smile. "Don't forget to let me know when it's goin' to be built."

"Wha-a-at do you mean?" stammered Trimble.

"And I'll lend you another ten bob, Trimble, when your pater's Rolls-Royce calls for us," added Cardew. "Not before then! When do you think that will be, old top?"

Cardew sauntered away, leaving Trimble speechless.

"I—I say, Baggy——" stuttered Bunter.

"I—I say, Bunter——" stuttered Trimble.

They looked at one another.

Perhaps the truth was dawning upon both of them

Bunter went on, after a pause.

"I—I say, Railton hasn't cashed my cheque yet, Trimble——"

"Hasn't he?" said Trimble. Trimble had heard a good many humorous remarks already that day about Bunter's cheque.

"Nunno!"

"Go and ask him about it," said Trimble, fixing his eyes on Bunter. "I'll come with you."

"I—I think I won't bother him! I—I was thinking that you might——"

"My pater isn't sending me anything more till the end of the term," said Trimble. "I've told you so—because I blued twenty pounds in one week."

"Wouldn't he if you asked him?"

"I don't care to."

Bunter's eyes began to gleam behind his spectacles.

"Suppose we telephoned him?" he said.

"It's a trunk-call," said Trimble hastily. "The number's not in the book here."

"But you know his number?"

"I—I've forgotten it." Trimble changed the subject. "I say, Bunter, I'll go to Railton and remind him about your cheque, if you like."

Bunter started.

"Not at all! Don't!" he exclaimed.

"Why, you ass——"

"Why not, if you've really asked him to cash a cheque for you?" said Trimble suspiciously.

"If you doubt my word, Trimble——"

"Well, a jolly good many fellows seem to doubt it!" said Trimble sourly. "I heard Levison say your cheque was the joke of the term. He was laughing over it no end, with Tom Merry and Blake——"

"Well, I heard Cardew say he'd come to Trimble Hall when it was built!" sneered Bunter. "Isn't it built yet?"

"That—that was only Cardew's little joke——"

"There seem to be a lot of little jokes about Trimble Hall——"

"Not so many as there are about your postal-orders and cheques and things, you——"

"Look here, Trimble——"

"Look here, Bunter——"

"My belief is, you've been spoofing me, and there isn't any Trimble Hall at all!"

"My belief is, you've been spoofing me, and there isn't any cheque at all, or any postal-orders, and you're a spoofing, sponging impostor!"

"You fat, cheeky rotter——"

"You fat cad——"

"I'll jolly well——"

"Yah!"

Fat fists were brandished in the air as the two podgy juniors glared at one another in great wrath.

"Hallo! A fight! A fight!" yelled Monty Lowther. "Roll up, ye cripples! Bunter and Trimble—the Great War over again!"

"Ha, ha, ha!"

There was a rush of juniors at once to see that sad and sudden ending of a sudden friendship.

"Go it, Trimble!"

"Pile in, Bunter!"

"I—I say, you fellows, I've a jolly good mind to mop him up!" said Bunter. "But—but he isn't worth it——"

"Oh, yes, he is!" urged Blake. "Quite worth it—ain't you, Trimble?"

"I've a jolly good mind to burst the fat rotter!" said Trimble disdainfully. "But—but it's just on dinner-time——"

"Ha, ha, ha!"

"Take 'em by the necks and make 'em begin!" exclaimed Grundy of the Shell. "You take Bunter, Tom Merry, and I'll take Trimble—— Hallo, they're off!"

There was a roar of laughter as the two heroes scudded off in different directions.

At dinner that day Bunter and Trimble scowled at one another from opposite sides of the table. Each had found the other out now, and friendship was off—most emphatically off.

And when Bunter came into Study No. 2 after lessons he found Percy Mellish there—not civil and honeyed, as of yore, but decidedly ratty.

"You fat cad!" was Mellish's greeting.

"Eh?" ejaculated Bunter.

"You spoofing rotter——"

"Oh, really, Mellish——"

"I know all about your cheque!" said Mellish. "You—you lying worm, you haven't a brown to bless yourself with, unless you've borrowed it of D'Arcy or some other silly ass!"

"Look here——"

"You're as big a spoofer as Trimble—and I thought he took the cake before you came!" snorted Mellish. "I was taken in. I thought Tom Merry and the rest were making up to you for your money. What could a chap think, the way they were going on?"

"So—so they were!"

"You fat idiot! They were pulling your leg, to get you out of Study No. 6, and——"

"Wha-a-at?"

"And Trimble's leg, and my leg, to get us to have you in here!" howled Mellish. "I was taken in! Now we're landed with you, you—you—you fat pig! I've a jolly good mind to sling you out of the study!"

"Oh!" gasped Bunter.

He understood fully at last.

His little round eyes gleamed with rage behind his spectacles.

"I—I jolly well won't be spoofed out of my study!" he gasped. "I don't want to stay here! You're a needy cad, Mellish, and Trimble is a poverty-stricken bounder! I'm going back to No. 6!"

"They won't have you, you fat idiot! They've wangled this whole bizney to get rid of you!"

"I—I—I'll go to the Housemaster, and —and——"

"After going to him yesterday to ask to be changed here?" sneered Mellish. "It's too late, you fat chump! They wouldn't have given the game away if it hadn't been all safe!"

"Oh, dear!" gasped Bunter.

The Owl of Greyfriars felt that it was only too true. But he did not despair yet. He rolled along to Study No. 6, and, as that apartment was empty, he rolled in and ensconed himself in the armchair, to wait for Blake & Co. to come to tea.

When those cheery juniors arrived Bunter felt an inward trepidation, but he blinked towards the juniors in the doorway with a ghastly smile.

Tom Merry & Co. were there—seven hungry juniors, laden with packages, come into tea after footer.

"Buntah!" ejaculated Arthur Augustus.

"Bunter!" exclaimed Tom Merry.

"Bunter!" roared Blake.

"I—I say, you fellows," murmured Bunter, "I've come back, you know!"

"Where's your dog-whip, Herries?"

"I'm looking for it!"

"I say you fellows, I know you're only joking. I—I wouldn't desert you, you know—not my old pals—especially Gussy! Gussy, old chap——"

"I wefuse to speak to you, Buntah!"

"He, he, he!"

"Hallo! What are you he-he-heing about?" asked Dig.

"Gussy's little joke," said Bunter feebly. "I can take a joke with anybody. He, he, he!"

"You'll take something else in a minute!" remarked Blake. "Buck up with that dog-whip, Herries!"

"Wha-a-at do you want the dog-whip for, Blake?" stammered Bunter.

"To lay round a fat rascal!"

"I—I say, you know——"

"Here it is!" said Herries. "You needn't trouble, Blake! I'll lay it on!"

"I say, you fellows—— Yarooooooh!"

Billy Bunter made a wild bound for the door. But he was not quite quick enough. There was another wild yell as Herries got in with the dog-whip.

"Ha, ha, ha!"

Bunter vanished down the passage, with Herries close behind. Wild yells were heard in the distance. Herries came back in a few minutes, rather breathless, but with a satisfied expression upon his face.

. . . .

And Bunter did not come back to Study No. 6!

THE END.

(Don't miss next Wednesday's Great Story of Tom Merry & Co. at St. Jim's — "BUNTER IN SEARCH OF A STUDY!" — by Martin Clifford.)

THE ST. JIM'S GALLERY.

No. 33.—George Richard Bruce Darrel.

IT is only in the natural order of things that the St. Jim's stories should have more to do with the Forms of the Middle School than with those of either the Higher or the Lower. There is plenty of interest in the Third, for the matter of that; but one would get tired of the cheery fags if one met them every week. Their activities are just a trifle too juvenile to bear weekly recountal. With the Sixth and the Fifth it is otherwise. Most of what they do would be too sedate and commonplace to be really interesting to most readers. Now and then, of course, things happen in the higher Forms; but they do not happen so often there as in the Shell and Fourth.

Thus far Eric Kildare, the genial and popular skipper, is the only Sixth-Former we have had in the St. Jim's Gallery. But this week Darrel is added to the list; and there will be two or three more to come—certainly Monteith and Baker and Knox, possibly others.

Darrel is Kildare's greatest chum, and every bit as good, sound, sportsmanlike, chivalrous a fellow as the captain of St. Jim's.

There has never been any break in their friendship. They were fags together—though we have no record of their fagging days. They went up the school together; and no doubt they had as high old times when in the Fourth and the Shell as Jack Blake & Co. and Tom Merry & Co. now have. As prefects, with a good deal of responsibility for the maintenance of discipline thrown upon their still youthful shoulders, they stand side by side.

Darrel is a fellow a bit off the usual lines, with more resolution and balance than the average boy of his age. He showed this in the course of his dealings with Mr. Ratcliff, narrated in that fine story, "The Fighting Prefect!"

Mr. Ratcliff had taken upon himself to gird at the Terrible Three in a manner that they considered distinctly off—and they were not far wrong, either. He threatened to cane them for impudence. They had not really been impudent, though possibly Lowther had been rather cool and off-hand with him. But then, he was running down Mr. Railton and Mr. Railton's methods to them; and they could not stand that. When he persisted in the caning notion they appealed to Darrel, who happened to be passing, and the prefect backed them up. He reminded Mr. Ratcliff that he had no right to punish a School House boy; his proper method was by complaint to Mr. Railton. Mr. Ratcliff was very angry indeed; but he could do nothing more effective than register a score against Darrel, with a view to paying it off later.

He got his chance; but, after all, he was not able to avail himself of it. For there were circumstances that gave Darrel the upper hand at the moment when the sour Ratty seemed to have him quite at his mercy.

An old St. Jim's boy named Stoker, who had suffered in his day under Mr. Ratcliff, was visiting the neighbourhood in a professional capacity. Mr. Herbert Stoker had taken to professional pugilism, and was starring at the Wayland Hall. It occurred to him that it would be quite a hefty idea to run over to St. Jim's and give Ratty a hiding. He was obliging enough to call up the New House master on the telephone and tell him of this kindly intention.

The juniors heard of it, and were keenly anticipative of Mr. Stoker's visit. The First Eleven were playing away from home, though Darrel, who was badly under the weather for private reasons, had not gone with the team. The Head and Mr. Railton were both absent that afternoon. Mr. Linton was also out. It was not to be expected that aid should come for Ratty from Lathom, Mr. Selby, Monsieur Morny, or Herr Schneider. So, on the whole, it looked warm for the New House tyrant, unless Darrel took up the cudgels for him. And, after the row between them, this hardly seemed a likely contingency.

Mr. Stoker came along. He was quite pleasant and friendly with the juniors; but he would not be turned back by Taggles. He said that he would be grieved to have to chuck a gentleman of a hundred years of age into his lodge on his neck; but he made it clear that he would bear that grief if necessary. He did not actually chuck him in; he merely carried him in, and put him down gently.

Then the Old Boy forced his way into Mr. Ratcliff's presence, and commanded that gentleman to hold out his hand for the cane. Ratty would not do that; he took flight out of his study window. Mr. Stoker pursued, lashing at him. He chased Ratty into the School House. The juniors did not see their way to interfere; Toby, the page, was not having any; Cutts of the Fifth stood by, refusing to lend a hand.

But Darrel chipped in. He refused to let Stoker touch Mr. Ratcliff. Stoker had already done a bit in that way; but that was not Darrel's fault.

There was a fight—a stern fight—and Darrel won. He is a boxer of more than put through it. He wanted to detain Stoker, bore no malice. He needed assistance to get back to Wayland; but he was very anxious that Darrel should not get into trouble with the Head.

That seemed likely enough. For Ratty had become brave when once his enemy had been put through it. He wanted to detain Stoker, and give him in charge for assault. Darrel would not have that; and Mr. Lathom agreed with Darrel. So Ratty reported Darrel to the Head. But he got no change out of that. Dr. Holmes is a gentleman and a sportsman.

Darrel was badly in need of twenty pounds. It was not for himself that he wanted it. He could not borrow it; but he thought he saw a way of making it Mr. Stoker's manager had offered a purse of twenty pounds to any amateur who could stand up to Stoker for ten rounds. Darrel went for that purse. Mr. Ratcliff got on his track, and saw his chance. Boxing in public for money is a heavy offence in a prefect's case, of course; and Ratty waited until Darrel had committed himself, and, incidentally, had fairly knocked out Stoker, before he made a move.

Then he told Darrel that he would report him to the Head, and the Sixth-Former knew what that meant—expulsion! But while they were talking Stoker appeared, still keen on his notion of giving his dear old Housemaster a hiding. Ratty appealed frantically to Darrel for aid. Darrel refused—unless he gave his word of honour to withhold the report. And Ratty gave it. After that there was no need for Darrel to do anything forcible in the way of defence. Mr. Stoker had been licked twice by Darrel, and he frankly said that he was not looking for a third licking. But he uttered dire threats against Ratty if that specimen went back on his word. Darrel had little faith in the master's word of honour. But Ratty kept it—probably because of his dread of Stoker.

It was for a woman that Darrel had wanted that twenty pounds. Some time before he had fallen deeply in love with Signorina Colonna, who was acting at the Wayland Theatre Royal. He had made her acquaintance in London, and he was most desperately in earnest. He was willing to wait five years—ten years—any time—if only she would give him hope—after the way of boys of his age. But there was more in it than in most attacks of calf-love. Darrel did not forget easily—he still cared very much for Pauline Colonna, even after she had married and gone to America with her husband, although he never knew that it was chiefly for his sake—to cure him of his infatuation—that she went, refusing a much better offer from a London syndicate.

"Young as he was, boyish in so many ways, he was yet a man in others, and in truth and depth of feeling quite a man. The signorina was the first woman upon whom he had bestowed a thought in this way, and she, with her beauty and grace, had won him at a glance. Foolish he might be, blind to obvious impossibilities, yet he was sincere and true, and there was something noble in the boy's love for the beautiful singer—a love founded as much on his instinctive knowledge of her goodness and true womanliness as upon anything else, as the signorina knew."

This is a quotation from the story in which Darrel's love-affair was told. Those who read it will recall the accident to Signorina Colonna on the stage, and how the seniors were going to Redclyffe to play, and how Darrel got Tom Merry to go to the post-office at Rylcombe and send a telegram to Wayland and await the reply. They will recall, too, how Tom and his chums rode their hardest to Redclyffe, and how the news was bad, and how Darrel borrowed Tom's bike and rushed off to Wayland, leaving a gap in the team which Tom filled with credit.

There was something like a quarrel between Kildare and Darrel over that, for Kildare did not know the whole story, or, indeed, much of it. And to Kildare, of course, the desertion of the team just before a match is an offence not easily to be condoned. But Kildare is not the fellow to be lacking in sympathy for a chum. And when he came into Darrel's study and found the fighting prefect with his elbows on the table, his face in his hands, and his whole frame shaken by heavy sobs, all bitterness left his heart. He never had a full explanation. "Next day Darrel was very pale and quiet, but quite himself. He had a sorrow in his heart, but he had courage there, too. He had his battle to fight, but he had the pluck to face it."

"It's all over, old chap," he said. "That letter was the finish. I shall never see her again! Perhaps I may tell you about it some day—not now."

That was enough for Kildare. "And if Darrel's heart ached when he read in the papers that Signorina Colonna had sailed for America, he said nothing about it. And time, as Pauline well knew, had power to heal the wound—in time nothing would remain of the boyish love but a memory tinged with sadness."

It might be so, but at least Darrel did not forget easily.

When he tried to borrow twenty pounds, and eventually made that sum by knocking out the cheery Stoker, it was for Pauline he wanted it. He told Kildare about it.

"You remember—once—there was a girl—an actress I knew—she was older than I—but I thought an awful lot of her," he said. "I've heard from her once or twice. She—she married. Well, I haven't heard from her lately. But I've had news from another quarter—news of her, and it's bad news. She's had bad luck. They—she and her husband, you know—started a touring theatrical company, and they've been done in. There was a fire, and they lost everything. They were almost on their uppers, and there's a subscription being raised among the people who knew them to help them on their feet again. They don't know that I know anything about it. But—but I want to help. You see, I could send a subscription to the fund without their knowing that it came from me."

There are other things one might tell about Darrel—minor things, but worth telling were it not for the fact that these two stories are quite enough to show his character. He has always been nearly as popular with the juniors as Kildare himself. Who could help liking so generous and plucky a fellow?

But in his dealings with Ratty and Stoker, in his hopeless love affair, Darrel stands sufficiently revealed—brave and knightly, with a man's heart in a boy's body. There is much courage that is mere animal courage, with something of the brute in it—even so, not to be despised, for courage always matters. But Darrel's is of a higher type than that; and, thinking of it, one remembers Bayard Taylor's words in that pathetic poem which tells of how the brave men in the chilly Crimean trenches sang "Annie Laurie":

"The bravest are the tenderest,
The loving are the daring!"

Extracts from "THE GREYFRIARS HERALD" and "TOM MERRY'S WEEKLY."

HARDLY A SUCCESS! By Clifton Dane.

I.

"SKIMMY, you raving lunatic, if you don't throw that beastly, stinking stuff through the window I'll jolly well pitch it out, and you with it, you—you potty ass!"

"My dear Gore——" Herbert Skimpole raised a hot and perspiring face from the fireplace, where he was stirring a thick, milky-white mixture in a large saucepan, and blinked through the steamy haze that filled the study. "My dear Gore," he began again, in a mildly indignant tone, "pray control yourself! I must refuse most emphatically to throw this extremely valuable composition through the window! I am surprised and pained at you, Gore, for making such an extraordinary and ridiculous request! In the glorious cause of Science——"

"Science be hanged!" roared George Gore. "I'm about fed up with you! Do you think I'm going to stand my study being made into a stinking chemical laboratory with your piffling experiments, you ass? What are you trying to make, anyhow—treacle-toffee, or what?"

Gore's query was obviously a piece of sarcasm. Whatever the genius of the Shell was making—or trying to make—it certainly was not treacle-toffee. The stuff smelled like a mixture of calcium carbide and burning india-rubber.

Sarcasm, however, was lost on Skimpole. He fixed a half-reproachful, half-pitying glare upon his questioner.

"Certainly not, Gore! As you ought to be perfectly well aware from your daily association with me, I have neither the time nor the inclination to attempt such an essentially frivolous and childish pursuit as making treacle-toffee! Indeed, I——"

"Then what is it, you—you giddy Anarchist? Give the beastly stuff a name, and then bury it, for goodness' sake!" gasped Gore, with a cough of disgust. "Why, it's enough to lift the giddy roof! The blessed study reeks like a bone works!"

Skimpole wagged a bony forefinger admonishingly at his angry study-mate.

"My dear friend, in the interests of scientific investigation all personal feelings and considerations should be sacrificed. I am perfectly well aware, my dear Gore, that my experiments are somewhat—er—unpleasant, and, indeed, obnoxious. But if you were so fortunate as to possess the intellectual ability necessary to undertake an investigation into the histories of great investigations you would discover that all inventors were inconvenienced by these essentially trivial details, which——"

"Oh, it's one of your piffling inventions, is it?" snorted Gore. "Well, cut the cackle and get on with the washing, you ass!"

"Washing? What an utterly absurd remark, Gore! I confess that I fail to see any possible connection between my great invention and—er—washing. This valuable compound," proceeded Skimpole earnestly, "is the Skimpole Patent Dust-Layer. It will, I am proud to say, revolutionise modern, but futile, methods of laying the dust; it will solve a problem that has occupied the brains of the greatest scientists of the century. It will abolish water-carts. People will, I modestly affirm, acclaim me as the greatest scientist and public benefactor of the age. I intend to test my invention on the road this afternoon. Afterwards I propose to offer the invention to the Government. If, however, they are so short-sighted as to refuse it, I shall float a public company and——"

"And make your giddy fortune!" sniffed Gore. "Then you'd drop your blessed Socialism and become a bloated capitalist—what?"

"Certainly not, Gore!" protested Skimpole. "I have no desire whatever to make my fortune. I must admit, however, that I cherish the intention of retaining the sum of fifty pounds for my personal use. That, my dear friend, I require to purchase books. I have for some considerable time strongly desired to possess the complete set of Professor Balmycrumpet's great work, 'From Monkey to Man.' I am already happy in the possession of two volumes. The remaining forty-eight volumes I—— Dear, dear, Gore! What ever is the matter, my friend?"

Something undoubtedly was the matter. Gore, who had been curiously examining the mixture, suddenly gave a fiendish yell, and began to prance about the room with his hand to his mouth. The solution had boiled over, and Gore had got a splash on his hand.

"Hang you and your blessed muck!" he bellowed. "Ow! I'm scalded! Wow! Oh, hang!"

Pouncing on the saucepan, Gore dashed to the window.

"For laying dust, is it?" he growled. "Then here goes to lay the giddy dust in the quad! Out of the way, Skimmy, you raving maniac!"

For Skimpole, with a wild cry of anguish, grabbed his angry study-mate's arm.

"Gore! I implore you, my dear Gore! I am exceedingly sorry for such a deplorable accident! But I beg of you, in the cause of humanity——"

"Humanity be jiggered!" yelled Gore, flinging open the window.

Then he hesitated. Gore was by no means so tolerant of Skimpole's little ways as his other study-mate, Talbot, was. But even in his anger Gore could hardly fail to see the obvious distress on Skimpole's face.

"All right, you silly idiot!" he growled. "Here's your precious stuff! Look here, Skimmy, my son. I'm off to the Grammar School match now. But if that filthy stuff isn't cleared out of this study by my return I'll—I'll ram your wooden head into the saucepan!"

With that terrifying threat, Gore, still nursing his hand, snatched his cap and left the study.

"Dear me!" gasped Skimpole. "What an exceedingly violent and headstrong youth!"

And, shaking his head sadly, the genius of the Shell treated his steaming preparation to a last vigorous stir, and lowered the saucepan on to the hearth.

Still reflecting on the frailty of human nature, the earnest scientist rummaged round the study until, from the recesses of the cupboard, he brought forth a large bottle. This, after much tribulation—for the stuff was hot—and the upsetting of about half a pint of the sticky stuff on the study floor, he managed to fill. Even then there remained a considerable quantity in the saucepan.

Skimpole paused, and, with one bony forefinger pressed to a still bonier forehead, frowned thoughtfully.

"Dear me!" he murmured. "I shall require a much larger receptacle than that to hold the solution. How exceedingly thoughtless of me not to have provided for such an obvious necessity! However, I will now proceed to the kitchen and endeavour to obtain from the cook a pickle-jar, or some such domestic utensil."

And, with that intention, the earnest enthusiast marched away, leaving the still dripping bottle to drain its sticky overflow on to the study tablecloth.

Printed and published weekly by the Proprietors at The Fleetway House, Farringdon Street, London, E.C. 4, England. Subscription, 8s. 10d. per annum. Agents for Australasia: Gordon & Gotch, Melbourne, Sydney, Adelaide, Brisbane, and Wellington, N.Z. South Africa: The Central News Agency, Ltd., Cape Town and Johannesburg. Saturday, February 1st, 1919.

II.

BAGGY TRIMBLE sniffed suspiciously. Baggy Trimble, when he wasn't actually eating or sleeping, usually was sniffing. But this afternoon his sniffs were unusually loud, and, had anyone been near him, would have been exceptionally objectionable. But the Shell passage was deserted save for Baggy. So that youth sniffed loud and long to his heart's content.

From Study No. 9 came a most extraordinary and alarming smell. It was the smell that had, earlier in the afternoon, been the compelling factor in driving George Gore into temporary exile—or, at least, had decided him to choose the school match with Greyfriars to an afternoon in the unsalubrious atmosphere of Study No. 9.

But to Baggy Trimble that selfsame smell had an entirely opposite effect, which explains why that over-curious youth was sneaking so cautiously along the passage—to investigate.

Sniffing hard, Baggy reached the door of Study No. 9, and peered inside. His little, piggy eyes glistened as they fell upon the still steaming saucepan. Cautiously and suspiciously Baggy tiptoed across the room, and poked a snubby nose over the thick, milky liquid.

Trimble was puzzled—frankly puzzled. He was also hungry—very hungry. But he hesitated. The thick substance steaming in the saucepan looked appetising enough, certainly. It might be grub—toffee—anything good to eat!

But the smell!

Still sniffing, Baggy lifted his podgy nose, and pondered a moment. Then, very slowly and warily, he dipped a grimy finger into the liquid. He withdrew it again with astonishing briskness, and danced about rubbing his finger frantically on his trousers.

"Wow!" groaned Baggy. "It's hot! Wow! I'm scalded to death! Oh, dear!"

Baggy stopped suddenly as his eyes fell upon the bottle on the table. Despite the fact that he was scalded to death, he withdrew the cork, and took a cautious sip.

After that Baggy Trimble's contortions were remarkable, and could have been more aptly portrayed on the cinema screen than described in mere words. His mouth, cheeks, and eyebrows went up and down like old bellows, while he gulped and spluttered in an alarming manner. Apparently Skimpole's patent dust-layer tasted as unpleasant as it smelled.

"Groough! Pah! Oh dear, the beastly stuff!" gasped Baggy.

Then, for the first time, he spotted the inscription, "HAIR-OIL" printed on the label, and his podgy features went a sickly white.

"Oh, crumbs! I'm poisoned! Grough! Hair-oil—the beastly stuff! Oh, help!" he groaned, with a horrible grimace

For fully a minute Boggy spluttered and gasped. After a while, however, he began to feel better. Then, disappointed and still hungry, he was moodily making a bee-line for the door, when he hesitated. With his cunning eyes twinkling greedily, he returned to the table. Replacing the cork, he left the study with the bottle of Skimpole's preparation hidden beneath his coat.

At Racke's study Baggy stopped, and entered without the formality of knocking. Chatting round the table were Racke, Crooke, Mellish, and Scrope. From the fact that Racke crammed the pink paper he was reading under the table on Trimble's entrance, it was plain that the topic of conversation was not cows. When Racke recognised the visitor, however, he jumped to his feet with a growl of anger.

"Well, by gad! You cheeky, fat beast!" he yelled. "What the dickens do you mean by barging into my study without knockin'? Why, you fat toad, if you don't clear out I'll dashed well——"

"He, he, he!" cackled Baggy Trimble, pretending to take the unkindly welcome as a joke, but keeping a wary eye on Racke. "He, he, he!"

Then, apparently thinking it wisest to get to business at once, the fat youth held up the bottle of mixture triumphantly.

"What do you think about that, Racke, old man? Hair-oil! Good stuff, too! Don't you wish you had it?"

"Get out, you fat beast, an'-take your filthy stuff with you!" roared Racke. "Hair-oil! Pah! I can niff the stuff here!"

"Oh, I say! Look here, old fellow!" protested Trimble. "Why, it was only this morning you were saying you hadn't a drop of hair-oil left—said you'd give anything to get hold of some. I bought this specially for you. Look here, five bob, and the stuff's yours! That's jolly——"

Baggy stopped, and retreated a step. Racke did not appear to be in a mood for business. Suddenly the fat youth had a brilliant inspiration.

"Mix it with brilliantine—like D'Arcy does," he suggested persuasively. "That does the trick! Takes all the smell away! Look here, say four bob——"

"Will you clear——" Racke was beginning, when he paused.

Trimble's cunning reference to D'Arcy looked like working! The well-groomed Arthur Augustus D'Arcy's perfectly-parted hair was a "thing of beauty and a joy for ever." It was one of the features of the immaculate Gussy Racke envied. Surely if D'Arcy used it——

"Here, let's see the stuff! I expect you've boned it from D'Arcy's study, you fat thief!" sneered Racke.

Trimble sniggered knowingly, and handed over the bottle. Racke examined it. The stuff did not look like hair-oil—not a bit. But it smelled—quite a lot. Perhaps it was a secret preparation of D'Arcy's thought Racke. Then he examined the label, which bore the name of a well-known toilet manufacturer. That settled Racke's doubts.

"Here you are, you thieving rotter!" he snapped, handing over five shillings to the smirking Trimble. "Now scat, or——"

Baggy pocketed the cash with alacrity, and bolted.

When he had gone Racke again examined the bottle.

"Good biz!" he laughed. "Hair-oil's beastly scarce these days! Wonder if that tailor's dummy D'Arcy will miss the stuff? Phew! Doesn't it just niff! Perhaps it won't, though, when applied to the hair. Anyhow, I mean to try the stuff. Hanged if I don't try some now! You chaps can try it if you like—this bottle will last for ages!"

And Racke, chuckling over his deal, went to the glass and commenced to apply the Skimpole Patent Dust-Layer to his hair!

Down in the tuckshop Baggy Trimble was endeavouring—with some measure of success, judging from the smirk of satisfaction on his fat face—to remove the taste of that same solution from his mouth with Mrs. Taggles' jam-tarts.

III.

"MY dear fellows!"

It was half an hour later. Tom Merry, Monty Lowther, and Manners looked up moodily at the sound of Skimpole's mild voice from the doorway.

"Come in, fathead!" growled Tom Merry.

Skimpole, a relieved look on his studious face, entered, and closed the door.

"Ah, my dear fellows!" he observed, blinking earnestly through his spectacles. "I am exceedingly gratified to find you here! I have come——"

"Good!" murmured Monty Lowther. "And now you have accomplished so much, I suggest your going—shut the door after you—there's a good chap!"

Skimpole blinked perplexedly at Lowther.

"Really, my dear Lowther, I fail to perceive any reason or object in your suggestion. It would be manifestedly absurd were I to depart without explaining my object in coming. I am urgently in need of assistance, and——"

How much?" demanded Lowther generously, diving into his pocket and producing twopence-halfpenny and a bad threepenny-bit. "Don't hesitate to say!"

"Dear me! You misunderstand me, Lowther. I am not in need of pecuniary assistance. Certainly not! However, possibly it has come to your knowledge that I have invented a patent dust-layer."

"A what—what-ter?" gasped three voices simultaneously.

"The Skimpole Patent Dust-Layer," explained Skimpole, with conscious pride. "I regret that time will not permit me to elaborate the details of my invention. It will suffice to say that not only will it revolutionise the dusty condition of the fair lanes and roads of this land of ours, but—ahem!—it will also cause the name of Skimpole to go down to posterity as one of the—— My dear Lowther, why do you hold aloft that cushion in such an extraordinary way?"

"To biff at a silly ass with too much gas!" roared Lowther. "Cut the giddy cackle, Skimmy, you idiot! What's your blessed trouble?"

"I am endeavouring to be as explicit as posible, my dear Lowther," protested Skimpole. "But, as I was about to observe, I intend this afternoon to test the composition on the road outside the gates. Not that I have any doubt as to its efficacy. Quite the contrary! But I have arrived at the conclusion that an ocular demonstration would be eminently——"

Skimpole paused as Lowther raised the cushion suggestively.

"Ahem! But to come to the point. I had intended to borrow the Rylcombe Urban Council's watercart for the experiment. On reflection, however, I have come to the conclusion that the hand-engine and hose in the woodshed will equally suit my purpose. It will, however, be a physical impossibility for one individual to manipulate the pump and direct the hose. That, my dear friends, is precisely my reason for this visit—to solicit your assistance."

The Terrible Three winked solemnly at each other. But they hesitated only for a moment. Study No. 1 were never known to refuse help to anyone.

"We're your men, Skimmy, old top!" grinned Tom Merry cheerfully. "Lead on, Edison Secundus!"

Five minutes later a little procession wended its way towards the woodshed. Skimpole led the way, staggering under the weight of a half-gallon jar. At the woodshed the party stopped. Tom Merry and Lowther hauled the antiquated old engine out of the shed. The tank was half full of water, as it happened, which suited Skimpole's purpose admirably.

"Heave-yo, me hearties!" grinned Monty Lowther, grabbing the handles of the engine. Then, with Tom Merry pushing behind, and Manners, who had a slightly sprained ankle, limping along with Skimmy in the rear, the party rumbled to the gates. Skimpole smiled beamingly as a billowy cloud of dust swirled round him in the roadway.

Lifting the lid of the tank, the inventor emptied the contents of the jar into the water.

"Phew! Pah!" gasped Lowther, getting a niff of the solution for the first time. "My giddy aunt! Dust-layer, is it? Why, the stuff's strong enough to lay bricks! Phew!"

"That," said Skimpole, "is an unfortunate but trivial detail. I shall be grateful, my friends, if you will kindly manipulate the pump when my preparations with the hose-pipe are completed."

After a little trouble, owing to the enthusiastic inventor getting himself wrapped up and nearly strangled with the hosepipe, things were at last got into working order. Amid the clanking of the pump Skimpole sprayed the road for quite a hundred yards, until the tank was empty. Then the inventor gave a sigh of satisfaction.

"You will now see, my dear friends, though in a small measure, what a benefit the Skimpole preparation for laying dust has conferred upon mankind," observed Skimpole.

Tom Merry and Lowther, however, decided that it was wisest to house the engine and hose before waiting to see the benefits of Simpole's experiment. They were only away at the woodshed three minutes, but they returned to find Manners bent double and roaring with laughter. Skimpole, a look of the wildest bewilderment on his face, was staring at the roadway with bulging eyes.

And no wonder! The road was free from dust, certainly. Skimpole's patent dust-layer had indeed done its work well—too well, apparently, for the road was rapidly turning a vivid green!

"Ha, ha, ha!" roared Monty Lowther. Then he lowered one foot gingerly into the green wetness, and withdrew it with difficulty. "Why—— Ha, ha, ha! The stuff's like treacle! Oh, my only pink pyjamas, what a mess!"

"Extraordinary!" gasped Skimpole, in amazement. "I must have mixed in some wrong ingredient! Dear me, how extraordinary!"

Suddenly Manners gave a roar, and pointed up the road.

"Oh, my hat! Look at Towser! Ha, ha, ha!"

Herries' bulldog was in difficulties. He was staggering along in the middle of the road, and whining dismally. At almost every step he stopped, and, lifting a paw, eyed the green, sticky mess dripping from it with a ludicrous look of astonishment. A little higher up was Cornelius, the school cat, whom Towser had evidently been chasing when they struck that verdant patch of green. He was mewing pathetically, and also in evident distress. Higher up the road still half a dozen ducks were tottering along like bluebottles on a fly-paper.

"Oh, dear!" murmured Skimpole, in tragic dismay. "How unfortunate! I fear——"

Skimpole stopped and shivered, for at that moment Mr. Ratcliff, his thin, sour face looking more irritable than usual, appeared at the gates. He eyed the four juniors suspiciously. The laughter of the Terrible Three ceased as if by magic.

"Boys, have you seen the postman yet?" he snapped.

"No, sir," replied Tom Merry meekly.

Mr. Ratcliff grunted, and stamped angrily.

"The man ought to have been here an hour ago," he snorted. "It is disgraceful! I shall certainly write——"

What the master was about to say Skimpole and the Terrible Three will never know. They saw Mr. Ratcliff stop before he had taken half a dozen steps, and eye his boots in amazement. Then he gasped audibly, and, bending down, gazed as if fascinated at the green-carpeted road.

"Good gracious!" he ejaculated, in bewilderment. "Good gracious!"

For a full minute he stood thus. Doubtless he would have spent longer so occupied but for the arrival just then of the postman. And his arrival, though expected, proved most unexpected.

Only a moment before he had cycled down Rylcombe Lane whistling cheerfully as if he hadn't a care in the world. A few yards behind him cycled Cutts, Gilmore, and St. Leger.

The four cyclists struck Skimpole's preparation at a fair speed. But they didn't keep it up—Skimpole's dust-layer saw to that.

The postman stopped whistling, and stared with goggly eyes at his front wheel, which was sending up a fountain of green slush. After which he turned in his saddle and subjected his back wheel to a similar absorbing scrutiny. Behind him the three seniors were also engaged in examining the remarkable phenomenon.

"Look out!" yelled Tom Merry suddenly.

After that things happened quickly. Tom's warning shout caused Mr. Ratcliff to look up suddenly. The four cyclists brought their study of the Skimpole dust-layer to an abrupt conclusion, and looked round in alarm. But too late!

The postman jammed on his brakes hard—too hard, for the bike stopped dead, and its unfortunate rider soared over the handle-bars. Luckily, however—for the postman—Mr. Ratcliff stopped his flight.

"Poof!" gasped Mr. Ratcliff, sitting down with a thump. "Poof!"

That was all the master said just then, for Cutts, Gilmore, and St. Leger had arrived. And all Mr. Ratcliff's time and energies for the next few moments were occupied in getting out of the mix-up that ensued.

"Oh, dear!" groaned Skimpole, gazing helplessly at the confused mass of arms, legs, and bicycle wheels. "How exceedingly unfortunate!"

The Terrible Three realised from the grunts, yells, and gasps that proceeded from the scrum that someone was getting hurt, and, being more practical than Skimpole, they braved the terrors of the treacly mass and went to the rescue.

With their help the struggling figures gradually sorted themselves out. Mr. Ratcliff, his face black with fury and his gown green with Skimpole's preparation, staggered slowly to his feet. Then he waded—so to speak—towards the shore.

There he appeared to find his breath, also his tongue. And the three seniors and the postman got the benefit of both. For quite five minutes the angry master raved. Then, suddenly becoming aware of his undignified condition, he was turning to enter the gateway, when he stopped.

From down the road sounded a loud cheer, and a waggonette containing the returning footballers, and escorted by a score of cyclists, appeared in sight.

"Oh, my only Sunday tile! The show isn't over yet!" groaned Tom Merry. "Good old Skimmy!"

IV.

THE cyclists were the first to become aware of the state of the road. In blank astonishment they stared at the thick, sticky mess as it clung lovingly to the revolving wheels. But when the filthy stuff began to bespatter their machines and clothes they dismounted hurriedly, and, with handkerchiefs to noses, made a bee-line for dry land.

With a final cheer the waggonette rolled up to the gates. Grundy, who was hanging on to the steps behind, was the first to come into touch with Skimpole's invention. Trust Grundy to find any trouble that's knocking around!

"Hurrah! We've won!" he yelled enthusiastically. "Three goals to one! Hurhur——"

Grundy's powerful voice ended in a smothered howl as he jumped from the steps, staggered a couple of paces, and measured his length on the sticky road.

"Ha, ha, ha!" roared the crowd of lordly seniors in the waggonette. The laughter tailed off very quickly, however, when they saw the cause of the great Grundy's downfall, and found they had to paddle through the green, sticky mess themselves.

"What ever does it all mean?" gasped Kildare, stamping up to Mr. Ratcliff with an astonished face and his handkerchief to his nose. "What is—— Oh, I say, sir, what a state you are in!"

"That," snarled Mr. Ratcliff, his voice quivering with anger, "is what I should like to discover, Kildare! It is outrageous—simply outrageous! If the District Council are responsible—— Good gracious! What ever is the matter now?"

Something evidently was the matter. Across the quad, yelling in terror, his short fat legs fairly twinkling under him, came Baggy Trimble. Behind him, armed with cricket-bats and stumps, came Racke, Crooke, Mellish, and Scrope. They seemed to be particularly excited about something, and also to be particularly anxious to get into touch with the flying Baggy.

"Help!" shrieked Trimble, taking refuge behind the stalwart form of Kildare. "Help! Save me!"

"Let me get at him!" roared Racke, running up with slaughter in his eyes. "I'll smash the filthy beast!"

Then Racke & Co. stopped suddenly as they noticed Mr. Ratcliff and Kildare. And just as suddenly a roar of laughter went up from the crowd of onlookers. Mr. Ratcliff did not see the reason for a moment. When he did he almost fainted.

For the heads of Racke and his shady pals were, if possible, more brilliantly green than the surface of the road outside! Their hair stuck out in matted clumps, like tufts of coarse, green grass. They presented a truly terrifying appearance.

"Bless my soul! Am I going mad?" muttered Mr. Ratcliff. "Green—everything's green!"

"Look at us! Look at our hair!" raved Racke, pointing to his head despairingly. "Look what that fat rotter's done! And it won't wash off! And it's all that fat beast's fault!"

"Racke, how dare you speak to me like that!" thundered the master. "Do you mean to say that Trimble is responsible for the filthy condition of your hair? Explain yourself at once, boy!"

Stuttering with fury, Racke related the story of his deal in "hair-oil" with the rascally Trimble. When he had finished, Mr. Ratcliff, his brain in a whirl, was turning to question the still shivering Baggy, when an interruption occurred. Skimpole, who had been listening in amazement to Racke's tragic story, stepped forward, his mild features very pale, but very determined.

"Excuse me, sir," he began politely but firmly, "I believe I am in a position to elucidate what at present appears to be somewhat of a mystery to you. Possibly you have observed that the colour and consistency of the preparation with which my unfortunate schoolfellows' heads are anointed resembles the solution at present covering a portion of the road outside the gates. The—ahem!—effluvium also, I would point out, is somewhat——"

"That, you foolish boy, is obvious to anyone but an idiot!" snapped Mr. Ratcliff testily. "Tell me at once what you know of this extraordinary business, and pray do not be so ridiculously long-winded!"

"Certainly, sir! I will endeavour to be as precise and explicit as possible. Possibly you are unaware that for some considerable time I have been engaged upon a new invention—namely, a patent preparation for laying dust. However, this afternoon, my investigations and experiments being completed, I emptied a quantity of the solution—in the absence of a more suitable receptacle—into a bottle, which, from the inscription on the label, had previously contained hair-oil. The bottle, however, unaccountably disappeared from the study during my absence. After listening to Racke's narrative, I am compelled to the obvious conclusion that my unfortunate schoolfellows have become possessed of the bottle of dust-laying solution, and have applied it to their hair under the impression that it was hair-oil. That, sir——"

"Ha, ha, ha!"

"Silence!" thundered Mr. Ratcliff, glaring around on the laughing crowd. Then the master turned suddenly to Skimpole, his eyes gleaming triumphantly.

"Is it possible? Dust-laying preparation? Do you actually mean to say—— Is it possible, Skimpole, you wretched boy, that you are responsible for the disgusting state of the road outside?"

"That," observed Skimpole, "I was also about to explain, sir. The result of my experiment is, I admit, most regrettable, and, as you will realise, is a great disappointment to me personally. But the present failure is entirely due to a slight error in the mixing of the ingredients. However, I hope to——"

"Enough!" thundered Mr. Ratcliff. "You will come with me at once, Skimpole! Dr. Holmes will, I have no doubt, be more interested in your explanations. Trimble, Racke, Cooke, Mellish, and Scrope will also accompany me, when we shall probably get to the bottom of this astounding business. What is it, Merry?"

Mr. Ratcliff stopped as the Terrible Three stepped forward.

"Skimpole is not alone to blame for what has happened, sir," said Tom Merry meekly. "We also had a hand—that is, we helped him, and are as much to blame as he."

"Oh, indeed!" replied Mr. Ratcliff in malicious exultation. "Ah, I might have suspected as much! Three of Mr. Railton's most promising pupils, too! Very good! You three boys will also accompany me."

With dignified stride—the effect of which was somewhat spoiled by his green-bespattered attire—Mr. Ratcliff led the way indoors, followed by the unfortunate eight juniors, and followed also by a yell of laughter which Kildare tried in vain to quell.

To relate in full the proceedings of that court of inquiry—what the Head said, what Mr. Ratcliff said, what Tom Merry & Co. said, what Trimble said—the frozen truth, of course—what Racke & Co. said, and in particular what Skimpole said—would fill considerably more than the rationed columns of the "Weekly," or even of the GEM.

Sufficient it is to say that Dr. Holmes did get very nearly to the bottom of the business. And as it happened, and to Mr. Ratcliff's utter disgust, the Head took a far more lenient view of Skimpole's little experiment than was expected. Possibly, had the Head known then that there was hardly an inch of St. Jim's—class-rooms, studies, dormitories, and even his own study carpet—where the Skimpole Patent Dust-Layer had not already penetrated, the punishments would have been more severe.

Anyhow, poor Skimpole got a good half-dozen of the best, and was gated for a month. Trimble got four stiff ones—more for telling lies than for anything else—while Racke & Co. were let off with a lecture on the advisability of looking before leaping. All the same, there is no doubt they came off worst of all.

As for Tom Merry & Co.—well, they received four strokes each, despite the fact that Skimpole—good old Skimmy!—protested vigorously against their punishment, and pleaded in vain to take the full responsibility for the business upon his own puny shoulders. Good old Skimmy!

The Editor's Chat.

For Next Wednesday:

"BUNTER IN SEARCH OF A STUDY!"

By Martin Clifford.

This week's story tells how Bunter, wangled out of No. 6, finds but a very temporary resting-place in No. 2.

Next week's will tell of his desperate endeavours to get a footing elsewhere. He tries Tom Merry & Co.—N.G. Julian & Co. are not having any. In No. 9 he is kindly allowed to stick to the armchair; but that is all. Mulvaney minor and Tompkins are surprised by his generosity; but there is a catch about that, of course. There always is a catch about it when Bunter makes a display of good qualities.

At the end of the story Bunter is still an outcast!

YOUR EDITOR.

N

The GEM 1½d

No. 574. Vol. 13. February 8th, 1919.

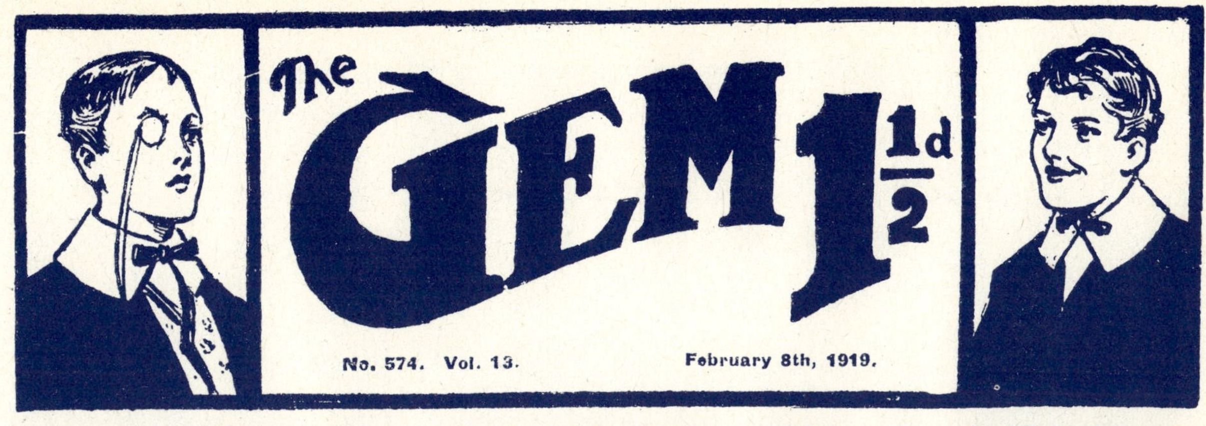

BUNTER IN SEARCH OF A STUDY.

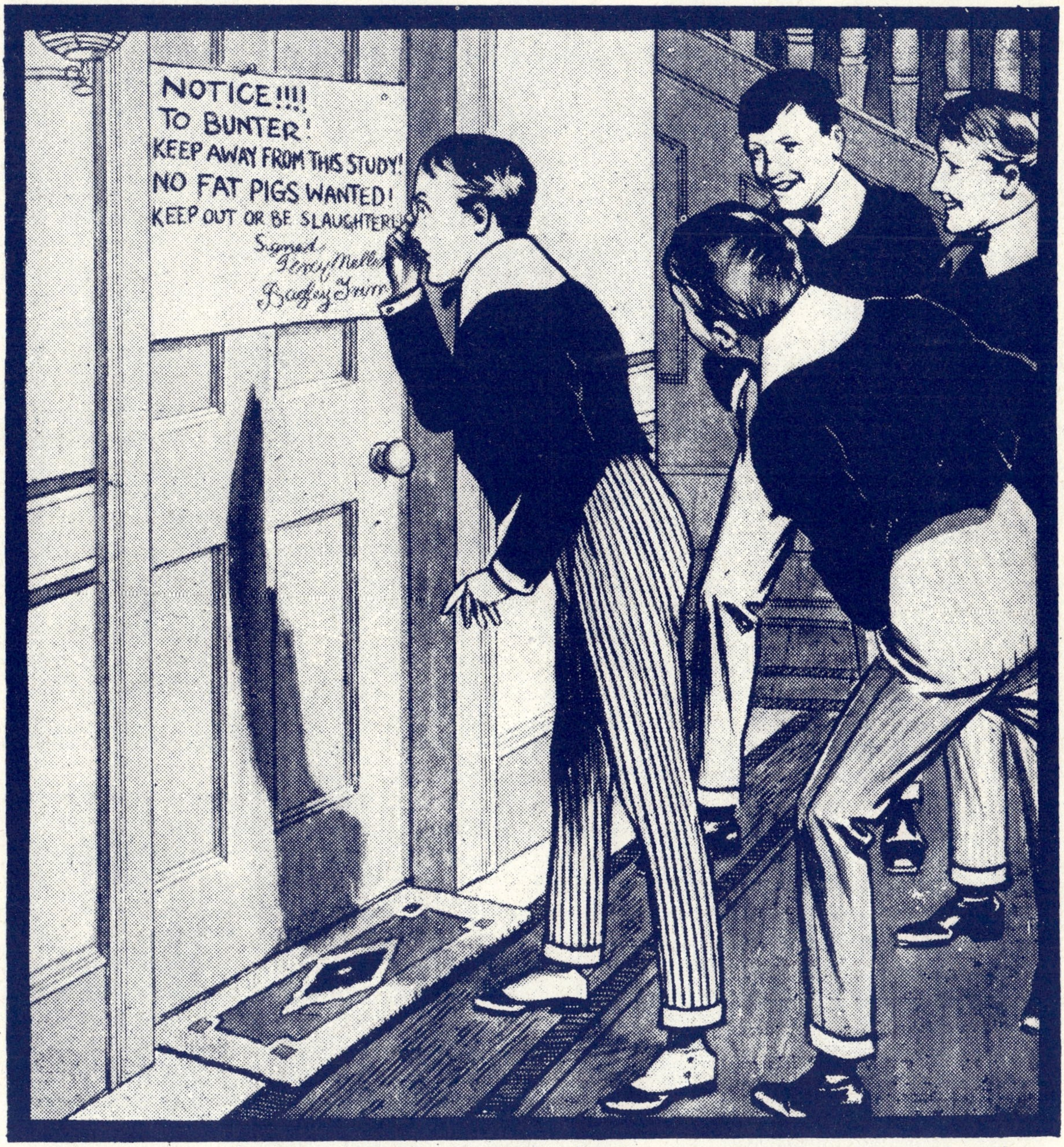

BUNTER GETS THE O.B.E. (Order of the Boot Everywhere).

 8-2-19

A MAGNIFICENT NEW, LONG, COMPLETE SCHOOL STORY OF TOM MERRY & CO. AT ST JIM'S.

BUNTER IN SEARCH OF A STUDY.

By MARTIN CLIFFORD.

CHAPTER 1.
Notice to Quit!

"BAI Jove! That is wathah wuff!"

"Serve him jolly well right!" said Jack Blake.

"Yaas, pewwaps so! But it is wathah wuff," said Arthur Augustus D'Arcy, with a shake of the head.

Blake & Co. of the Fourth were on their way to Study No. 6 when their attention was attracted by a notice pinned on the door of the second study in the Fourth Form passage.

It was a large sheet of cardboard, apparently the lid of an old box, and a rather surprising inscription was daubed upon it in capital letters with a brush.

Blake and Herries and Digby grinned as they looked at it. Arthur Augustus D'Arcy looked rather serious.

The notice ran, in sprawling capitals:

"NOTICE!!!!
TO BUNTER!
KEEP AWAY FROM THIS STUDY!
NO FAT PIGS WANTED!
KEEP OUT OR BE
SLAUGHTERED!
(Signed)
PERCY MELLISH.
BAGLEY TRIMBLE."

Perhaps it was rather rough, as D'Arcy remarked. But Mellish and Trimble, of Study No. 2, were not the only fellows in the School House who were "fed-up" with Bunter, the new junior of the Fourth Form. Blake & Co. had succeeded in getting rid of the fat junior from Study No. 6. Now, apparently, Study No. 2 was on the same tack.

"Serve him right!" said Herries. "We couldn't stand the rotter! Why should they stand him?"

"Yaas, but——"

"Bunter must roost somewhere," remarked Dig, with a grin.

"Yaas, wathah! And, aftah all, this is his studay," said Arthur Augustus. "I wegard this pwoceedin' as wathah high-handed. What do you fellows think of this?" added the swell of St. Jim's, as Tom Merry & Co. came along from the staircase.

The Terrible Three halted, and grinned as they read the notice.

"Not surprised," remarked Tom Merry.

"Not at all," said Manners. "Of course, Mellish and Trimble ain't much better than Bunter, if you come to that. Still, they're not quite such worms."

"They asked the Housemastah to have Buntah in their studay, deah boy."

"That was when they thought he was wealthy," grinned Monty Lowther. "Wealth covers a multitude of sins. Now they know he isn't it makes a difference."

"It ought not to make a diffewence, Lowthah."

"Quite so, old scout. But lots of things that oughtn't to happen do happen. F'rinstance, Wally Bunter oughtn't to have turned out such an awful outsider, when we all liked him on a short acquaintance before he came here. But he did."

"Yaas, he certainly did not come up to expectations," admitted Arthur Augustus. "He disappointed me vewy sewiously. I weally liked the fellow when I met him ovah at Gweyfwiars."

"We might have known, though," said Blake sagely. "He's exactly like his cousin, Billy Bunter, to look at, so we might have guessed that he would be like him in other ways."

"Talk of angels!" murmured Monty Lowther. "Here he comes!"

There was a grunt and a heavy tread in the passage.

Bunter of the Fourth came rolling along from the stairs towards his study, and he blinked at the little crowd of smiling juniors over his big glasses.

"I say, you fellows, anything on?" he asked.

"Ahem!"

Bunter blinked at them rather suspiciously. The fat junior had quite worn out the hearty welcome he had received when he came to St. Jim's. Tom Merry & Co. had been patient with him, for they had really liked Wally Bunter, whom they had met while on a visit to Greyfriars. But Bunter had exhausted their patience at last. And they had not the faintest suspicion that the new junior was not Wally Bunter at all, but Billy Bunter of Greyfriars, who had come there in his cousin's place, taking advantage of the likeness between them to make a fresh start at St. Jim's, and to leave on Wally's shoulders a heap of troubles he had collected at his old school.

Bunter had expected to be quite a success at St. Jim's—in Wally's name, and with his own fascinating personality to back up Wally's reputation. But it hadn't worked out like that, and he was growing discontented. Still, he was not tired of St. Jim's yet. He found himself more comfortable there than at Greyfriars—where he was too well known and understood for his comfort.

"I say, Gussy, I was looking for you," he remarked, after a suspicious blink round at the smiling faces.

"Weally, Buntah——"

"I've been disappointed about a postal-order," said Bunter. "More delay in the post, you know. I really think that the postal service ought to buck up a bit now the war's over—don't you?"

"Even then, your postal-order might still be delayed," remarked Monty Lowther, with great gravity.

Bunter was deaf to that remark.

"I suppose you could let me have the five bob, D'Arcy, and take the postal-order when it comes?" he said.

Arthur Augustus hesitated.

How many postal-orders he had already cashed in advance for Bunter he really did not know, but the number was considerable.

"Hold on a minute!" said Blake grimly. "Which postal-order are you referring to, Bunter?"

"Eh?"

"Do you mean the one Gussy cashed for you on Saturday, and which never came?"

"Ahem!"

"Or the one Dig cashed for you on Friday, which never came——"

"Oh, really, Blake——"

"Or the one Talbot cashed for you the other evening in the Common-room which——"

"Look here——"

"Or the one——"

"Bai Jove! Upon weflection, Buntah, I think I will wait till that postal-ordah comes befoah I cash it!"

"I hardly expected this meanness from you, D'Arcy. However, I dare say Tom Merry will cash my postal-order——"

"Certainly, when I see it!" said Tom, laughing.

"If you don't trust me, Tom Merry, you——"

"Not an inch, old scout! Not a quarter of an inch!"

"I decline to accept any favour at your hands, Tom Merry. No; you needn't say anything. I decline, and that's an end of it!"

And Billy Bunter turned haughtily away to his study.

Then he saw the notice on the door.

He halted, blinking at it in amazement, while the juniors watched him with grinning faces, wondering what effect it would have on him. Bunter blinked round at them.

"I say, you fellows, what does this mean? Who put this silly rot here?"

"Pwobably your studay mates, Buntah."

"Cheek!" said Bunter warmly. "They want to keep me out of my own study. I like that!"

"Well, if you like it, there's nothing to complain of," remarked Blake, with a chuckle.

"Of course, I shall take no notice of it," said Bunter loftily. "This is because I've declined to ask Trimble and Mellish home to Bunter Court, you know."

"Oh, my hat!"

"That was rather hard," said Monty Lowther gravely, "as Trimble, I believe, asked you home to Trimble Hall."

"Ha, ha, ha!"

"I'll jolly soon show them whether I'll keep out of the study!" exclaimed Bunter; and he threw open the door and rolled in wrathfully.

"Now for the merry circus!" grinned Blake.

And Tom Merry & Co. stood round the doorway and waited for the "circus."

CHAPTER 2.
Evicted!

"BUNTER!"

"Outside!"

Trimble and Mellish were in the study.

They seemed to be prepared for Bunter's arrival. Baggy Trimble had a wooden foil in his fat hand. Percy Mellish had a cushion handy, which he picked up as the fat junior rolled in.

Billy Bunter blinked at them through his big spectacles in great wrath and indignation.

"I say, you fellows——" he began.

"Outside!"

"Do you think I'm going to be turned out of my own study?" bawled Bunter.

Mellish nodded coolly.

"Yes, I do! We don't want you here!"

"Why, you asked the Housemaster to let me come here——"

"Because you spoofed us, you fat rotter!" said Baggy Trimble. "You spoofed us with your yarns about——"

"Never mind that," said Mellish hastily. "We don't want the fat bounder here, and we're not going to have him!"

"We don't want a chap who wolfs all the grub!" said Trimble.

"And snores in the armchair!" said Mellish.

"And tell lies!" said Trimble, with virtuous indignation.

"And uses other fellows' books to light the fire!"

"Outside!"

"You cheeky rotters!" howled Bunter. "I've a jolly good mind to lick the pair of you!"

"Go ahead!"

"I regard you with contempt! You're not worth touching!"

"Well, you're not worth touching!" said Mellish. "But we're going to touch you hard if you don't keep outside this study!"

"He, he, he!"

"Hallo! What are you he-he-heing about?"

"He, he! I can take a joke," said Bunter. "Now, what about tea? I can't stand anything to-day, as I've been disappointed about a postal-order, and D'Arcy has treated me with disgusting meanness."

"Bai Jove!" came from the passage.

"You can take a joke, can you?" said Mellish. "Well, you'll take this cushion, too, if you don't clear!"

"Oh, really Mellish——"

"And this foil!" said Trimble. "Now, where will you have it?"

"Oh, really, Trimble—— Yaroooh!" roared Bunter, as he got the foil and the cushion together.

Bump!

Billy Bunter sat down in the doorway, and roared.

Mellish fielded the cushion.

"Now, watch me bowl him fairly over," he said, poising it in the air.

The Owl of Greyfriars did not wait to be bowled fairly over. He squirmed wildly out into the passage, and the cushion missed him by an inch.

"Ha, ha, ha!"

Slam!

"Ow-ow! I'm hurt!" he gasped. you fellows—— Yoop! Can't you give a chap a hand up, you cackling dummies? Ow!"

Arthur Augustus D'Arcy kindly gave Bunter a hand up. The fat junior was landed on his feet, gasping for breath.

"Ow! Ow! I'm hurt!" he gasped "My backbone's broken!"

"Ha, ha, ha!"

"I mean, sprained! Ow! I say, you fellows, come in and back me up, and see me mop up those cheeky rotters!" gasped Bunter.

"My dear porpoise, it isn't our business!" said Tom Merry, laughing. "You shouldn't scoff their grub, you know!"

"A few sardines, and some tarts, and a cake!" said Bunter scornfully. "Just like them to make a fuss over a trifle like that! Ow! I'm not going to stand it!"

"I wouldn't!" chuckled Blake. "Go in and win, Bunter! We'll see fair play while you tackle 'em one at a time!"

"Yaas, wathah!"

"I could lick the pair of them!" gasped Bunter.

"Pile in, then!" said Lowther encouragingly. "Chuck them out of the study! We'll wait here and count 'em as they drop!"

"Ha, ha, ha!"

"They're both funks, you know!" said Manners. "Pile in!"

"Well, I shall help Bunter if you chip in! That's a tip!" said Tom. "You can pile in when he's done with Trimble!"

And Tom Merry stepped back into the passage.

His warning was enough. Mellish laid down the cushion. He did not want to tackle the captain of the Shell, who could have made rings round three or four Mellishes.

"Go it, Trimble!" he said. "You can handle that fat funk!"

"Yah!" said Bunter, in a very warlike tone. He was encouraged by the fact that Trimble was backing away instead of advancing.

"Go for him, I tell you!" exclaimed Mellish. "Do you want me to start on you, Trimble?"

"The—the fact it——" gasped Trimble.

"Yah!" hooted Bunter, more than ever warlike. "You're afraid! Yah! I'll jolly well mop up the study with you, Trimble!"

Bunter Gets It Hot.

Bunter hesitated for a moment. But he was hurt, and he was wrathy; and he screwed up his courage to the sticking-point.

"I'll jolly well do it!" he exclaimed. "You fellows keep Mellish off while I throw Trimble out!"

"Yaas, wathah!"

"Done!"

Billy Bunter drew a deep breath, set his glasses straight on his fat little nose, and hurled open the door of the study.

"Now, then, you rotters!" he gasped.

"Hallo, here he is again!" exclaimed Mellish. "Jump on him!"

Tom Merry looked in, and raised his hand.

"Fair play!" he said. "One at a time! Bunter's going to slaughter Trimble first. Hands off, Mellish!"

"Mind your own business!" hooted Mellish.

"Do you want me to help Bunter?" asked the captain of the Shell.

"I want you to mind your own business!" snapped Mellish.

And the Owl of Greyfriars advanced with his fat fists up; and Baggy Trimble retreated farther. Mellish stopped his retreat, however, by seizing him by the shoulders and spinning him at Bunter.

"Now go it!" he snapped.

Crash!

The two fat juniors collided, and both reeled back, gasping. Mellish gave Trimble another shove, and he sprawled at Bunter. One of his fat fists, sweeping the air wildly, landed on Bunter's nose, and there was a howl from the Owl of Greyfriars.

"Yaroooh!"

"Give him another!" shouted Mellish.

Billy Bunter jumped back. He did not want another. And Trimble, encouraged in his turn, came on with a rush, hitting out valiantly. Billy Bunter dodged hurriedly into the passage.

"Hallo! That's Bunter, not Trimble!"

exclaimed Monty Lowther. "Have you chucked yourself out, Bunter?"

"Ow!"

"Let him come in again, that's all!" roared Baggy Trimble victoriously.

"Go in and win, Bunter!"

"Ow-ow! I—I forgot that—that Kildare's asked me to tea!" gasped Bunter. "Can't keep a Sixth Form chap waiting!"

And Bunter rolled away hurriedly to the stairs. Baggy Trimble, victorious and triumphant, and brave as a lion now, blocked the doorway of the study with his podgy form, and roared:

"Yah! Funk! Come back! Yah!"

"Ha, ha, ha!"

Bunter vanished down the staircase.

"Well done, Trimble!" chortled Blake.

"I'm a pretty good fighting-man, you know!" said Baggy, puffing. "I could make rings round that fat duffer! Let him come back, that's all! I'm just spoiling for a fight!"

"My dear man, you sha'n't be disappointed then!" said Blake. "I'll fight you, if you like!"

Slam!

The study door closed.

Tom Merry & Co. went their way chuckling.

CHAPTER 3
A Kind Offer Declined.

TAP!

An interesting discussion was going on in Tom Merry's study, and the juniors did not heed the tap at the door.

"We want to beat them," said Tom Merry. "We beat them on their own ground, and we want to beat them here!"

"We do—we does!" agreed Monty Lowther.

"Oh, we'll beat them all right," said Manners. "That is, if you put me in the eleven, Tommy! I'll undertake to bag goals for you!"

"Hum!" said Tom.

"They're a good team, though," remarked Talbot of the Shell. "They've got some good men, especially Wharton, Cherry, and Vernon-Smith, I remember."

The Terrible Three were discussing the return match with Greyfriars School, which was due shortly. Talbot had come in to discuss tea and football at the same time. The door opened while Talbot was speaking, and a fat face and a large pair of spectacles glimmered in.

"I say, you fellows! Just in time!" said Bunter cheerfully.

"Just in time to buzz off," said Manners pointedly. "Shut the door after you, Bunter!"

Bunter shut the door, but he remained on the inside of it. There was an ingratiating smile on his face, but a very wary look in his eyes.

"He, he, he!"

"My hat! Is the alarm-clock going off?" exclaimed Monty Lowther.

"Oh, really, Lowthah——"

"Was it you, Bunter?"

"You know it was!" hooted Bunter.

"Is this an entertainment, then? Have you come here to give us an imitation of an alarm-clock on active service?"

"He, he, he!"

"There he goes again!"

"I can take a little joke," said Bunter. "He, he, he! If you fellows haven't finished tea, I don't mind joining you."

"We've finished!" said the Terrible Three, with one voice.

"Then you won't want this cake. I'll sample it, if you've finished," said Bunter; and he took a large sample.

The Terrible Three fixed their eyes upon him. Talbot smiled.

"I say, you fellows, this is jolly good cake!" said Bunter, with his mouth full.

"I'm glad you like it!" said Tom sarcastically.

"Well, of course, it's not like the cakes I get from home. Still, it's fairly good, and since you're so pressing, old chap, I'll finish it."

"My hat!"

Bunter finished the cake, while the Terrible Three sat and regarded him, not quite knowing whether to laugh or to sling Bunter into the passage for his cheek.

"Not at all bad," said Bunter patronisingly. "Did you get that cake from home, Tom Merry?"

"Yes," said Tom shortly.

"You should see the cakes I get from home," said Bunter, blinking at him. "Much better than this."

"Oh!"

"You see, we've got a French chef," said Bunter. "You only find these really first-rate cooks in really wealthy establishments, of course. That's how it is."

"Oh!"

"I hope I'm not interrupting you fellows——"

"You are!" said Manners grimly. "We were talking footer when you came in, and we want to go on, Bunter."

"Go on, old chap—don't mind me," said Bunter affably. "If you're in doubt about any point in connection with the game, put it before me. I'll give you my advice. If there's one thing I know inside-out it's footer."

"Oh!" gasped Manners.

"In fact, you'll find me useful in this study," said Bunter.

"Useful!" repeated Tom Merry.

"Yes, very. You see, I'm a jolly good cook—a dab at it. Then we've got tastes in common, too—my being a footballer, you know. I should be willing to give you fellows some coaching at the game——"

"Kik-kik-coaching?"

"Yes. I can give you no end of tips, too, to improve your form."

The Terrible Three were beginning to glare. Bunter had played in one match since he had been at St. Jim's, and in that match he had kicked the ball through his own goal. The Shell fellows did not want to learn that kind of footer.

"This study is bigger than my old one, too," pursued Bunter. "There will be room for me here."

"Room for you?"

"Yes. The only condition I make is that I have the armchair whenever I want it."

"The—the armchair?"

"But, of course, there'd be no objection to you fellows buying a second armchair if you wanted to. It would crowd the room a little, no doubt, but I never was selfish."

"Would you mind telling us what you happen to be burbling about, Bunter?" asked Tom Merry, with great politeness.

"The fact is, old chap——"

"Not too much of your old chap, please!"

"The fact is, I'm going to dig in this study," said Bunter. "I can't stand those chaps Mellish and Trimble. I'm surprised to find such fellows at this school. In fact, they're low. Low is the word."

"You're going to—to—to——" stuttered Lowther.

"Exactly. I've decided to have nothing whatever to do with Mellish and Trimble. On reflection, I've decided, too, not to go back to Study No. 6——"

"Blake's boot rather heavy?" asked Lowther sympathetically.

"Ahem! And so, you see, I've come here," rattled on Bunter. "This study will suit me! Not a word, old chap—I've decided."

"You—you—you've decided to dig in this study?" gasped Tom Merry.

"That's it! Where shall I put my books? I dare say you chaps will help me bring them along?"

"Well, my hat!" murmured Talbot.

The Terrible Three stared at Bunter as if frozen to their seats by his astounding cheek. They could hardly realise the nerve of it at first. Evidently the fat junior intended to "plant" himself there by sheer cheek—if he could.

The question was, whether he could! The probability was that he couldn't!

Tom Merry found his voice at last.

"Fourth Form doesn't dig with the Shell, Bunter," he said. "The Forms are never mixed in the studies. So it wouldn't do, you see."

Tom Merry thought that that was a politer form of refusal than pitching Bunter out on his neck. But it was evidently not plain enough for the Owl.

"My dear chap, that doesn't matter," said Bunter affably. "If you ask the Housemaster as a special favour, I'm sure he'll agree."

"Ask Railton as—as a special favour to—to have YOU in this study?" stuttered Tom Merry.

"That's the idea! I'm sure he'll say 'Yes.' You can point out what pals we are——"

"Pip-pip-pals!"

"Yes, and how splendidly we pull together, and all that. Then I'm sure Railton will say 'Yes,'" said Bunter. "In fact, you can consider it as settled. Now, who's going to help me bring my things here? Don't all speak at once."

The Terrible Three did not speak at all.

They exchanged a look, and rose to their feet. Speaking to Bunter, they felt, would not meet the situation; he wanted something plainer than words, and he was going to get it.

"No need for all of you," said Bunter, misunderstanding their motive. "You can come and help me with my books, Tom Merry, if you like. You other chaps can clear a place for them. I—— Oh! Ah! Yah! Wharrer you at? Leggo!"

Bunter roared, in surprise and wrath, as three pairs of hands were laid on him. Weighty as he was, the fat junior was swept off his feet.

"Oh, my hat! He weighs something!" gasped Manners. "Lend a hand, Talbot!"

"Certainly!" said Talbot, laughing.

Another pair of hands was added. With the four of them grasping his fat person, the Owl of Greyfriars was rushed to the door, with his arms and legs flying wildly in the air.

"Yarooh! Help! Fire! Murder!" roared Bunter. "Wharrer you up to? I won't come into this study if you play these silly tricks! Yooooop!"

Tom Merry released one hand to open the door. Then Bunter was rushed into the passage.

"Help! Yoooop! Yah! Oh!"

"Hallo! You fellows killing a pig?" called out Cardew, of the Fourth from the corner of the passage.

"Yoooop! Help!"

"Take him home!" gasped Tom Merry.

"Yaroooh!"

Down the passage went Bunter, with a rush, with arms and legs still flying. Tom Merry kicked open the door of No. 2 in the Fourth, and Bunter was rushed in.

Mellish and Trimble jumped up from their tea-table in surprise.

"What the thump——"

Bump!

Bunter landed on the hearthrug with a considerable concussion. He rolled over there and roared.

"There!" gasped Merry. "There, you fat bounder! There, you podgy porpoise! Next time you roll into our study we'll rub your head in the coal-locker before we roll you out!"

"Yaroooh!"

The Shell fellows retreated, breathless from their exertions. And as they returned to the Shell quarters they were followed by sounds of woe. Mellish and Trimble were rolling Bunter out of No. 2. The door of that study slammed on him, and Bunter was left sitting in the passage, gasping for breath—and still homeless.

— —

CHAPTER 4.

A Chance for No. 9.

LEVISON and Clive of the Fourth were at prep in Study No. 9 when Cardew came in, with a grin on his face. The two looked up.

"What's the joke?" asked Levison.

"Bunter!" said Cardew, with a chuckle. "That fellow is a corker! He's been booted out of his study, and he tried to plant himself on Tom Merry."

"My hat!"

"And now he's tried No. 5," grinned Cardew. "He started making himself agreeable to Julian. He told him he hadn't any prejudice against Jews, and could overlook Julian being a blessed Sheeny."

"Ha, ha, ha!" roared Levison and Clive.

Cardew chortled.

"It was so tactful," he said. "Bunter seemed to expect it to please Julian, and he seemed quite surprised when Julian knocked his head against the wall. I left him rubbing his head."

"Ha, ha, ha!"

"Now for prep," said Cardew, with a sigh. "I'd much rather watch Bunter in search of a study. He's no end entertainin'. I wonder if he'll give us a look in here?"

"He'll get the business end of a boot if he does!" grunted Clive.

"More than one boot," remarked Levison.

Tap!

"Well, by gad!" ejaculated Cardew, as the door opened and revealed a fat face and big glasses. "Who said I wasn't a prophet? Hallo, Bunter! Roll in, old tub!"

"Roll out!" snapped Levison.

"And sharp!" added Clive.

Bunter gave the chums of No. 9 an affable blink. He decided that, of the three, he would heed Cardew, and he rolled in.

"I say, you fellows——" he began.

"Dear old chap!" said Cardew affectionately. "What a pleasure to see you! You're looking well, Bunter."

Billy Bunter blinked at him in some surprise and a great deal of satisfaction. More than once he tried to attach himself to Cardew, who was the grandson of a noble lord, and rolling in money. He had been kept at a very severe distance hitherto. Now, all of a sudden, Cardew had changed.

Bunter was not aware of the peculiar disposition of the dandy of the Fourth, or of his exceedingly peculiar sense of humour. If he had been he would not have felt quite so satisfied.

"Look here, Cardew, we're doing prep," said Levison. "You'd better do yours, too, if you don't want Lathom to rag you in the morning."

"My dear man, I like to see Lathom raggin'; he's so entertainin'. Besides, I can't do prep when I'm talkin' to a distinguished visitor, can I? It's so kind of Bunter to drop in like this, without waitin' for the formality of an invitation. I call it friendly."

"The fact is, old chap, I mean to be friendly," said Bunter.

Levison grunted, and went on with his work; and Clive, grinning, followed his example. If Cardew wanted to pull Bunter's fat leg, and Bunter, apparently, wanted to have it pulled, it was not their concern.

"Dear old thing!" said Cardew. "Won't you sit down, Bunter?"

"Thanks, old fellow, I will!"

"Wait a tick! I'll give you the armchair. I've heard that you like armchairs," said Cardew, jumping up.

He spun the armchair round for Bunter, and dusted the seat very carefully. Bunter watched him with growing satisfaction. These attentions from the grandson of a lord were very gratifying. He was not aware that, while dusting the chair, Cardew had picked up a tube of seccotine, and was squeezing it out in streaks over the leather seat.

"There you are, old chap," said Cardew, concealing the empty tube in the duster as he presented the chair to Bunter.

Billy Bunter sank into the chair with a grunt of satisfaction.

"So awfully kind of you to give us a call, Bunter. I take it as a real favour. Eh—what?"

"Is this chair damp?"

"Damp! My dear chap, do you think I would give you a damp chair?" Cardew reproachfully. "I was sitting in it a minute ago, and it wasn't damp then. I hear you're looking for a study, Bunter."

"Yes. I've decided to cut No. 2," said Bunter, with a nod. "Tom Merry wanted me to dig with him, but I had to tell him it couldn't be done. Can't dig with the Shell, you know."

Levison and Clive looked up for a moment, and looked down again. Cardew's face was very grave.

"That was hard cheese on Tom Merry," he said. "A bitter disappointment to him, in fact."

"Well, I was sorry," said Bunter. "But it really couldn't be done. I told him so plainly. Same with Julian."

"Did Julian want you, too?" asked Cardew sweetly.

"Begged of me, almost with tears in his eyes," said Bunter. "But it couldn't be done. I was sorry, but I had to tell him I couldn't stand Sheenys."

"Oh!" gasped Cardew.

"The fact is, I was thinking of this study," went on Bunter, encouraged by Cardew's friendly manner. "I could get on here, I think."

"Could you?" said Levison, looking up.

"Oh, yes! I shall pull all right with you, Levison. I'm a bit of a sport myself," said Bunter, with a fat wink.

"A what?"

"I hear that you've been turning over a new leaf, Levison," grinned the Owl. "That will do for the masters and prefects; but you can confide in me, you know. I won't give you away. I know what you were at Greyfriars, before you came here. He, he, he!"

"I don't see how you know anything about me at Greyfriars!" snapped Levison.

"Ahem!" Bunter remembered himself. "I—I mean—I've heard——"

"Your cousin, Billy Bunter, of the Greyfriars Remove, has been chattering to you, I suppose?" interjected Levison savagely.

"He, he! Exactly."

"The fat rascal!"

"Oh, really, Levison——"

"Well, whatever Billy Bunter may have said to you," said Levison, little dreaming that he was speaking to Billy Bunter—"whatever that fat Owl may have told you, I don't want to hear anything about it. And if you talk to me about being a sport I'll pull your silly nose!"

Bunter winked again.

"All serene, old scout; I'll keep it dark," he said. "In fact, I'll back you up. I'll come with you on your little excursions. I'll see you through, old man. I'm fly, and a bit rorty at times!"

"You silly chump!" roared Levison. "Dry up!"

"I don't mind having a quid or two on the next footer-match, if you care for it," continued Bunter, unheeding. "Remind you of old times—what?"

Levison half-rose to his feet.

But Cardew gently pushed him back into his chair. He was not done with Bunter yet. He wanted the seccotine to set before the fat junior took his departure—or tried to take it.

"Ernest, old scout, don't bother Bunter," he said. "Bunter's called in as a friend. I'm proud and happy to see him."

"Oh, rats!" snapped Levison; and he resumed his work with a dark brow.

"Just like he used to be at Greyfriars—suspicious and sulky, you know, and always biting a fellow's head off," said Bunter.

"Your cousin Billy seems to have told you a lot about Levison."

"Eh? Oh, yes! Of—of course. I shall get on all right with Levison when he sees it's no use trying to spoof me," said Bunter cheerily. "You'll pull with me all right, Clive."

"Shall I?" said the South African junior grimly.

"Oh, yes! I'll look after you, and bring you out, you know. You're not a bad chap, only a bit dense."

"Oh!" ejaculated Sidney Clive.

"And I hope you'll get on all right with me, Bunter," said Cardew gently.

"Not a doubt about it," said Bunter brightly. "We've got a lot of things in common, you know."

"Have we?"

"Certainly. F'rinstance, we're both highly connected," said Bunter. "I'm not a snob, you know—far from it. But gentle birth is gentle birth, isn't it?"

"I believe it is," assented Cardew.

"There you are!" said Bunter. "It was really for that reason that I stood D'Arcy as long as I could—though, of course, the D'Arcys are not so old a family as the Bunters. There was a Bunter in——"

"Noah's Ark?" suggested Cardew.

"Nunno! I mean——"

"There should have been two Bunters there, though," said Cardew thoughtfully. "I think I remember reading that the animals went in two by two."

Bunter grinned feebly.

"Oh, really, Cardew! I was going to say, there was a Bunter in William the Conqueror's army when he came over——"

"That was before the Undesirable Aliens Act was passed," said Cardew gravely.

"Oh, really, you know! There was a Bunter at the signing of Magna Charta in the reign of Henry the Eighth."

"Of whom?"

"I—I mean Edward the Seventh," said Bunter hastily. "That is to say, Charles the First."

"Not King John, by any chance?" asked Clive sarcastically.

"Certainly not, Clive! You don't know anything about English history," said Bunter. "How could you, living out in Uganda——"

"Cape Colony, fathead!"

"What's the difference?"

"Oh my hat!"

"Fellows like ourselves, Cardew, have a lot in common—high connections, and titled relations, and so on," said the fatuous Owl. "We shall pull together rippingly, I think!"

"I'm sure we shall," said Cardew cordially. "Quite sure of it, Wally! You don't mind if I call you Wally, do you?"

"Do, my dear chap! I'll call you Ralph."

"Do!" said Cardew solemnly.

There was a tap at the door, and Dick Julian looked in. He started a little at the sight of Bunter in the armchair. Bunter waved a fat hand at him in a very lofty way.

"You can get out, Julian," he said. "I don't want your sort in my study. Excuse me speaking plainly!"

"Your study!" ejaculated Julian.

"Bunter has settled down in this study," explained Cardew airily. "He's made the offer, and we can't resist it—his manners are so charmin'."

"I looked in to see if your minor was here, Levison," said Julian, taking no further notice of the fat junior in the armchair. "I'm going to help him with a busted footer."

"He's in the Form-room, I expect," said Levison. "You can wring that fat cad's neck if you like—he doesn't belong to this study."

"Oh, really, Levison——"

"Thanks! I wouldn't touch his neck with a barge-pole!" answered Julian. "I'll look downstairs for Frank."

He left the study. Bunter had fixed his eyes sternly on Ernest Levison.

"Look here, Levison," he said, "I want none of your rot. I've accepted Cardew's pressing invitation to join this study. I remain here. That's settled. And I expect to be treated with civility!"

"Oh, rats!" grunted Levison.

"My dear Ernest, you might be civil to a chap's pal," said Cardew reproachfully. "Bunter's going to introduce me to his titled relations—isn't that so, Bunter?"

"Certainly, old chap!"

"You know what a snob I am, Levison. I'm after Bunter's titled relations like a Chicago millionaire," said Cardew. "I'm goin' home to Bunter Court about the same time that I pay a visit with Trimble to Trimble Hall. I hope you'll be quite comfy in this study, Bunter."

"Well, I shall make myself comfy, you know."

"And you'll stick to that armchair?" said Cardew sweetly.

"I was going to suggest it. I really must have an armchair to myself; otherwise, I don't think I could consent to come into the study at all. Of course, I shouldn't object to you fellows using it when I don't want it."

"You see what a generous chap Bunter is, Levison. Stick to that chair, Bunter—you don't mind?"

"Not at all. I'd like to."

"Well, you will!" said Cardew, smiling. "Do you mind if I get on with my prep for a bit, Bunter? You might care to sample a cake to pass the time while——"

"Where's the cake?"

"Don't get up! I'll get it for you."

Cardew placed the cake on Bunter's knees, and then started work. Billy Bunter was happily occupied for some time now. He toasted his toes before the study fire, and devoured the cake to the very last crumb—and it was a large one. All the time the seccotine was setting harder and harder between his trousers and the seat of the chair. There was no doubt that Bunter would stick to that chair—in the sense that Cardew intended.

Prep did not take Cardew so long as it took his study-mates. He timed it, in fact, to finish with the cake. When the last crumb had vanished, Cardew turned from his books.

"You're not done?" said Levison.

"Your mistake, old chap—I am," said Cardew. "Like to take a little nap in your armchair, Bunter?"

"Hasn't Bunter any prep to do?" asked Clive.

"I'm not doing any this evening," said the Owl. "I really don't need it as much as you fellows. I shall manage all right in the morning. I don't think I'll take a nap, though, Cardew; I'm thinking of supper."

"Sit where you are, old scout, and we'll wait on you."

"We won't do anything of the sort!" roared Levison. "Look here, Cardew, you've pulled Bunter's leg enough. Chuck it!"

Cardew cocked his eye reflectively at Bunter.

"Well, perhaps it's long enough," he conceded. "The seccotine must be well set by this time."

"That what?"

"Seccotine."

"What's that?" ejaculated Bunter.

"Sticky stuff, dear boy. Sticks like glue—only more so. I squeezed a whole tube into that chair for you."

"Wha-a-at?"

"You remember you thought it felt a little damp?" said Cardew urbanely. "Well, it was. But it's all right; it's not damp now. You said you didn't mind sticking to the chair, didn't you?"

Bunter's face was a study. There was a howl of laughter from Levison and Clive. The Owl of Greyfriars made a jump to get out of the chair. But he did not rise. He was glued where he sat, and he gasped with the unavailing effort.

"Ow!"

"May as well get down to the Common-room, if you fellows have finished," yawned Cardew. "Stick to it, Bunter!"

"Ha, ha, ha!"

"Ow!" spluttered Bunter.

He made a terrific effort to rise. The armchair rose an inch from the floor under him, and then landed on its castors again with a terrific clatter. And Bunter gasped once more.

"Ow! Wow!"

CHAPTER 5.
Sticking to It!

"HA, ha, ha!"

Three merry juniors were roaring with laughter in Study No. 9; and the sounds of merriment were not long in drawing attention. The door flew open, and the Terrible Three looked in.

"What's the merry joke?" asked Tom Merry.

"Bunter!"

"Ha, ha, ha!"

"Bai Jove! Are you fellows waggin' Buntah?" asked Arthur Augustus D'Arcy, arriving with Blake and Herries and Dig.

"Not at all!"

"Yarooh!" roared Bunter. "Lemme out of it! Oh, dear! You beast, Cardew! I refuse to share this study with you now! Yah! Oh!"

"What's the matter with him?" asked Tom Merry, in amazement.

The cause of Bunter's trouble was not visible to the eye, and the juniors did not quite see where the joke came in.

"Ow-ow! I'm stuck!" wailed Bunter. "Come and drag me out, somebody! Oh, dear!"

"Gweat Scott!"

"Bunter's idea was to stick to our armchair," explained Cardew. "So I put some nice, sticky stuff in it to help him. He's been sitting in it well over an hour, and it's well set. How he's going to get out I really don't know; I haven't thought that out!"

"Ha, ha, ha!"

"Bai Jove! It is weally too wuff!"

"Stick to it!" roared Blake, in great merriment. "He was always sticking to the armchair in our study, when he was there; but I never thought of this stunt. Go it, Bunter! You always were a sticker!"

"Ha, ha, ha!"

"Yow-ow! I want to gerrup!"

"Ha, ha, ha!"

More and more of the Shell and Fourth were crowding round Study No. 9 now, till the passage outside was crammed, and the study itself well filled. But Bunter was given plenty of room. The hilarious juniors wanted to see how he would negotiate the armchair. Bunter was much given to sticking to things that were not his own, and to see him sticking to Cardew's armchair in this new style was very entertaining. It was probable that by that time Bunter repented of his attempt to plant himself in No. 9. He was now not only planted, but rooted there.

The fat junior glared furiously at the chortling crowd of fellows, with a glare that bade fair to crack his spectacles. But the more he glared the louder they roared.

He made a desperate effort to tear himself from the chair, and again it rose off its castors, and landed with a terrific crash.

"Oh, you rotters!" howled Bunter. "Yah! Beasts! Do you think this is funny?"

"Yes, a little!" gasped Tom Merry, wiping his eyes. "It strikes me as funny. You've got no sense of humour, old scout."

"Stick to it, Bunter!"

"Ha, ha, ha!"

Crash!

Again a desperate effort to rise was followed by the crash of the castors on the floor. Bunter lay back in the chair and gasped for breath.

"Well, we may as well leave him to it," yawned Cardew. "Make yourself comfy in the study, Bunter. But I'm sure you'll do that. In fact, you said you would."

"Yarooh! Don't go away and leave me like this!" howled Bunter. "Help! Yaroooh! I kik-kik-can't move!"

"You'll have to go like a snail, with your shell behind you!" roared Monty Lowther.

"Ha, ha, ha!"

"I say, you fellows, help me out!" shrieked Bunter. "I can't stick here, you know!"

"Looks as if you can, Buntah, bai Jove!"

Dick Julian came along the passage with Frank Levison of the Third. Julian looked into the study as Bunter made another effort to rise, and crashed once more.

"What is it?" he asked.

"Seccotine—and Bunter sitting in it!"

"Ha, ha, ha!"

"I say, you fellows! I say, Julian, old chap! Lend me a hand, Julian——"

"My dear chap, you don't want a Sheeny to touch you," grinned Julian.

"I don't mind your being a Sheeny—I don't, really!" wailed Bunter. In—in fact, I like Sheenys, old chap!"

"Well, I don't like fat pigs, and I'm not touching you," said Julian, laughing.

"Yow-ow-ow! I say, you fellows, help——"

"Wrestle it out," said Blake. "Keep on long enough and something is bound to go, Bunter. It may be the chair, and it may be your bags. Put your beef into it!"

"Ha, ha, ha!"

The juniors, almost in hysterics, crowded out of the study. Billy Bunter howled to them in vain for help. He was left alone in the study, still struggling with the armchair.

"I say, you fellows! Come back, you rotters! I say, Levison, old chap! Cardew, you beast! Gussy—Gussy, old fellow! Yaroooh!"

Arthur Augustus halted in the doorway. He was good natured to a fault.

"Weally, Buntah, you asked for it," he said. "The way you twy to shove yourselves into fellows' studies is wathah pwovokin'."

"Yarooh! I didn't ask for jaw, you silly ass! Help me out of this blessed armchair, and don't stand there like a goat!" howled Bunter.

"Bai Jove! If that is what you call civil, Buntah——"

"Help me, you idiot!"

"I wefuse to be chawactewised as an idiot, Buntah!"

"You—you—you—you chump! Help me!" gasped Bunter. "You blinking, goggle-eyed idiot, lend me a hand!"

"I wegard all those expwessions as oppwobwious, Buntah, and I wefuse to have anythin' whatever to do with you. Your mannahs are simply wevoltin', Buntah!"

And Arthur Augustus D'Arcy walked away, with his noble nose in the air.

"Yow! Help! Fire!" roared Bunter.

"Ha, ha, ha!" came back from the passage. "Stick to it!"

Bunter made a terrific effort, and there was a sound of rending cloth. Something had given at last, but it was not the seccotine.

The fat junior rolled, gasping, out of the chair, with a further sound of rending.

"Oh dear! My bags! My word! Oh dear!" spluttered Bunter. "Oh, crumbs, it's jolly kik-kik-cold! Ow!"

He was free at last—free, not only of the armchair, but of a considerable portion of his nether garments. He rolled out into the passage, crimson with exertion and fury.

"Hallo! Here he is!"

"Not sticking to it, Bunter?"

"Yow! You rotters! I wish I was back at Greyfriars! Ow! Beasts! I—I say, you fellows, get me a coat, or something!" wailed Bunter.

"Bai Jove! What ever do you want a coat for indoors, Buntah?"

"Suppose—suppose I meet the Housedame, or somebody!" wailed Bunter. "Gimme a coat, or a blanket, or something——"

"Ha, ha, ha!"

The juniors shrieked. But Arthur Augustus D'Arcy, feeling that this was a want that really ought to be supplied, rushed away for a coat. Wrapped in the coat, Bunter bolted up the stairs to the dormitory—for a much-needed change. He was followed by hysterical yells.

"Bai Jove!" remarked Arthur Augustus D'Arcy, as he strolled away to the Common-room with his chums. "Buntah in search of a studay is wathah amusin'; but I weally don't think he will twy No. 9 again!"

And Gussy was right.

CHAPTER 6.
Dropped!

The next day Bunter of the Fourth was still without a study.

Tom Merry & Co. were rather interested in the fat junior's search for new quarters. Where he would ultimately land was an interesting question.

The proceedings of Mellish and Trimble in turning Bunter out of Study No. 2 were certainly high-handed, though nobody in the Fourth was inclined to blame them. An appeal to the Housemaster would have reinstated Bunter at once. But he hesitated to make it, for divers reasons. If he complained about being turned out, probably Mellish would complain in his turn of the raided rations and confiscated cakes. Moreover, Bunter was not at all keen to remain an inmate of No. 2 if he could obtain quarters elsewhere. It was the least desirable study in the Fourth—Mellish and Trimble being the least desirable study-mates.

Bunter had been glad to "dig" there, under the belief that Trimble, of Trimble Hall, was a wealthy fellow whom it was worth while to know. Trimble had welcomed Bunter under an equally erroneous belief. But the two "swankers" had found one another out now—with mutual disgust.

The Owl of Greyfriars would have been very pleased to change his quarters—quite as pleased as Mellish and Trimble would have been to get rid of him. But at present he had nowhere to lay his weary head.

Bunter had expected to be popular at St. Jim's—as Wally Bunter certainly would have been. But Billy Bunter had very quickly worn out Wally's welcome, so to speak.

His fascinating society was not sought after in the least; his presence in any study was not yearned for.

But Bunter was not beaten yet. There were a good many studies in the Fourth Form passage, most of them untried, so far, and all of them preferable to No. 2. And Bunter intended to try them—and "plant" himself in the best he could get—if he was allowed. There was one quality the Owl of Greyfriars possessed in superabundance, and that was "neck."

At morning lessons that day Bunter was in trouble with Mr. Lathom, the master of the Fourth, who speedily discovered that he had done no preparation the previous evening. Bunter was severely lectured, with a promise of the cane next time; all of which he took philosophically. He was not accustomed to looking ahead, and "next time" did not worry him.

In fact, he really hadn't much time to devote to Mr. Lathom's instructions that morning, anyway. He had the matter of the study to think out.

When the Fourth were dismissed Arthur Augustus D'Arcy spoke cheerily to the fat junior in the passage.

"I twust you are gettin' on all wight in your studay now, Buntah?"

Bunter blinked at him.

"I'm done with No. 2," he said. "I decline to go back there on any conditions whatever. I've told Mellish and Trimble it's quite useless to ask me. I simply refuse to do it!"

"Bai Jove!" said Arthur Augustus. "I twust you will find comfy quartahs elsewhere, deah boy."

"The fact is, I was thinking of No. 6——"

"Oh deah! I—I think Blake is callin' to me——"

The fat junior glared.

"I was thinking of No. 6," he went on calmly. "But I feel it wouldn't do. I couldn't stand your friends, D'Arcy."

"What?" ejaculated the swell of St. Jim's.

"I'd like to come there, for your sake; but I couldn't stand Blake—he's too much of a pig!" said Bunter calmly. "Herries, too—a regular ruffian!"

"Weally Buntah——"

"If you can get them to change out, Gussy, I'll come. Not otherwise."

"Look here, you fat boundah——"

Bunter waved a fat hand at him.

"It's no use, Gussy; I've said I'm sorry, and so I am. But unless Blake and Herries change out it's no good asking me to come to No. 6!"

"But I was not goin'——"

"My dear chap, urging me's no good! I'd do it if I could, to oblige you; but there's a limit."

"I was not goin' to ask you——"

"I repeat, I'm sorry, Gussy! But there you are!"

"Buntah, I wepeat that I should wefuse to allow you to——"

"Enough said, Gussy! I can't come—simply can't!"

And Billy Bunter turned and rolled away, leaving Arthur Augustus almost breathless with indignation.

"Bai Jove!" murmured D'Arcy. "I don't weally believe the fat boundah weally misundahstood me at all. Bai Jove, if he should poke his beastly nose into Studay No. 6, I should be vewy much tempted to stwike it violently!"

Billy Bunter rolled away with a grin on his fat face. He was looking for Hammond of the Fourth—having decided that Study No. 5 would suit him. That study was shared by four juniors—Hammond, Kerruish, Reilly, and Dick Julian. Julian had already declined the proposed honour, but Bunter was not a fellow to take no for an answer, if he could help it. He decided to try his luck with Harry Hammond.

He found that youth in the quadrangle, and joined him. Hammond gave him a good-natured grin.

"I've been looking for you, old chap!" said Bunter.

"'Ave you?" said Hammond, not very enthusiastically. As he hardly knew Bunter, he did not see any reason for the "old chap."

"Yes, I have, old scout!"

"Well, now you've found me!" remarked Hammond. "'Ere I am!"

The heir of the great firm which dealt in Hammond's High-class Hats had not yet conquered the difficulty of the aspirate. Billy Bunter smiled in a patronising way as he noted it.

"The fact is, Hammond, I rather like you!" he said loftily, his manner implying that this was a tremendous honour.

"You're very good," said Hammond.

"Not at all! I think we shall get on together!"

"I 'ope so, specially as we ain't likely to see much of each huther," said Hammond, moving on.

Bunter rolled along with him at once.

"The fact is, we shall see a good bit of each other, Hammond," he said. "I'm going to dig in your study."

"Oh!" ejaculated Hammond, understanding now. "Har you?"

"I ham!" said Bunter, playfully imitating Hammond's weird manner of speaking. "He, he, he!"

"Wot are you cackling at?" demanded Hammond gruffly.

"Ahem! I suppose you'll come and lend me a hand at getting my things to No. 5?"

Hammond stared at him. Whether Bunter was a crass duffer, or whether he was the cheekiest bounder he had ever come across, Hammond did not quite know. But he knew that the did not want Bunter for a study-mate.

"I thought Julian had told you you couldn't plant yourself in our study," he answered.

Bunter sniffed.

"Never mind Julian! I bar that fellow!"

"What!"

"Can't stand Sheenys!" said Bunter, with a shake of the head. "Mind, I'm not a snob. Far from it. F'rinstance, I'm going to be friendly with you, Hammond, but——"

"Are you?" said Hammond grimly.

"Oh, certainly! I don't mind the high-class hats!" grinned Bunter. "Of course, as a sensible chap, you'll bear in mind that there's a difference between us. But I'm not a snob—I don't care if you started life sweeping out the hatshop. In fact, I think it's up to a fellow like me to be kind to the lower classes when they're trying to improve themselves."

The Cockney schoolboy breathed hard.

"We shall get on all right," pursued Bunter, mistaking Hammond's silence. "I feel sure of that. Of course, I don't want a lot of dashed familiarity—you will keep your distance, and all that. But I mean to be friendly; and you can see what an advantage it will be to you to have me in the study."

"'Ow do you make that out?" gasped Hammond, who seemed to be on the verge of a volcanic explosion. But the short-sighted Owl of Greyfriars did not see the danger-signals, and he rattled on cheerfully.

"You see, it'll be no end of an advantage to you to have a gentleman to associate with. You'll be able to model yourself on me, and improve yourself generally, you know."

"Oh!"

"I'll give you some tips, too, about good manners and the way decent people behave," went on Bunter fatuously. "You can watch me, and do as I do, you know. It'll be no end of use to a fellow like you!"

Hammond gazed at him speechlessly.

"As for Julian, he's a dashed Sheeny, and I shall refuse to speak to him," said Bunter. "He has treated me with impertinence——"

"Julian's my pal!" said Hammond, in a sulphurous voice.

"Then I advise you to drop him, old fellow! In fact, I don't see how I can be friendly with you if you don't drop Julian!" said Bunter firmly.

"Well, I won't drop Julian!" said Hammond. "But I'll jolly well drop you, you fat, shiny, sneaking, grubby rotter—hard!"

"Here, I say—— Yarooooh!" roared Bunter, as the indignant Hammond seized him by the shoulders.

"Sit down, you fat image!"

"Yooop!"

Bunter sat down with a great concussion, roaring. Harry Hammond walked away, and left him sitting there.

"Ow, ow, ow!" roared Bunter. "Yooop! Grooh! Help! Ow!"

"Hallo! Bunter in trouble again!" exclaimed Monty Lowther, as the Terrible Three came along from the School House.

Tom Merry good-naturedly gave the fat junior a hand up. Bunter stood and gasped spasmodically.

"Ow, ow! Beast! I'll jolly well lick him! Where is he?"

"Where is who?" asked Tom, smiling.

"That beast Hammond!"

"Just yonder!" grinned Manners. "Shall I call him?"

"Nunno—never mind!" said Bunter hastily. "After all, it's rather beneath my dignity to soil my hands on him. Groooh! Fancy the beast cutting up rough because I—I—I refused to share his study!"

"Eh?"

"He begged me, almost with tears in his eyes, you know, but I told him it couldn't be done—I really couldn't stand a rotter like that—— Ow!"

"Ha, ha, ha!"

"Blessed if I see anything to cackle at! Ow, ow!"

The Terrible Three walked away, chuckling. Bunter rolled off in a disconsolate mood. He had failed once more, and he was still minus a study. And he was not consoled till dinner-time, when, with the third helping, calm and contentment once more returned to his fat visage.

Cadet Notes.

Now the Armistice has been signed and Peace is in prospect there is an idea amongst some boys that it it no use joining a Cadet Corps.

But Cadets are not merely a military corps; on the contrary, they form centres of social organisation, and give opportunities for boys to form friends and have a good time. Boys in factories and offices do not know what to do with their evenings, and find it difficult to get pals. A proper Cadet Corps has a club-room where bagatelle can be played, boxing can be learnt, and should give opportunities for other recreation. The best Cadet Corps have swimming clubs, football clubs, cricket clubs, etc. Classes should be organised for scouting, carpentry, as well as studies in geography, history, etc., where enough boys can be obtained. And uniform gives a smartness to the club that an ordinary club lacks.

If you do not belong to a Cadet unit, write to the Central Association. Letters addressed to the C.A.V.R., Judges' Quadrangle, Law Courts. London, W.C. 2, will find us.

During the War no lad has been unable to get a good job at a decent wage. But with demobilisation the competition for work is likely to be very keen, and the best jobs will go to the most qualified men. Education in the widest sense is likely to be the best testimonial for a boy applying for work. Cadet Corps provide a splendid centre for training. Drill adds inches to a boy's height and width of chest, and employers naturally get their first impression from a boy's appearance. Besides, it smartens him up, and generally quickens his inteligence. New corps are being formed everywhere, and some of the old ones are running recruiting campaigns. No. 7 Company (Stroud Green), 5th Bttn. Middlesex Regiment (Cadets) has vacancies for recruits, but if you do not know of any unit near you, apply to the C.A.V.R., Law Courts, London.

— —

CHAPTER 7.
A Feast of the Gods!

"PHWAT is ut intirely?"

Mulvaney minor of the Fourth was puzzled.

Dusk was falling, and the juniors who had been on the football-ground were coming in. Mulvaney minor and his study-mate, Clarence York Tompkins, were heading for No. 4 in the Fourth Form passage.

The door of that study was half-open, and from the room came a very appetising scent of cooking. It was a scent that was very grateful and comforting to two hungry juniors; but it was perplexing, too. For who could be cooking in No. 4, when its owners were both out, was a mystery.

"Somebody's in there!" said Tompkins.

"Bedad, and he's cooking, too!" said Mulvaney minor.

The Irish lad looked into the study in great surprise. Then he uttered an ejaculation.

"Bunter, bedad!"

There was a glowing fire in the grate, and before it Bunter was bending, watching the sausages that sizzled in a frying-pan. He turned a ruddy face to the two astonished juniors.

"Trot in, Mulvaney!" he said cheerily. "Come in, Tompkins, old fellow!"

The two juniors entered. They stared at Bunter blankly. The Owl of Greyfriars did not seem to observe their surprise.

"Like sosses—what?" he asked.

"Yis. But——"

"I thought you fellows would be hungry after footer," said Bunter; "so I thought I'd hop in and get tea ready for you."

"Howley Moses!"

"Well, my hat!" said Tompkins.

"There's plenty of sosses," said Bunter. "I've got some ham, too. And there's some ripping coffee. You fellows care for sultana cake?"

"Eh? Oh, yes! Rather!"

"Well, look at that one!"

"Begorra!" murmured the astounded Mulvaney.

There was a handsome cake on the table, as well as a loaf and several nice little pats of butter. Coffee was brewed, and the sausages were almost done. It was a really elegant spread; and it was being stood, apparently, by Bunter, for two fellows he hardly knew. Benevolence could hardly have gone further.

"Well, this is jolly good of you, Bunter!" said Tompkins, puzzled but gratified.

"Not at all, old chap," said Bunter.

Mulvaney minor grinned.

Tompkins was rather a simple youth: but Micky Mulvaney was not at all simple, and he thought he could guess Bunter's object. The fat junior was still in search of a study, and he was trying this as a new method. It was really more tactful than Bunter's methods usually were. Perhaps he was learning a lesson from his many rebuffs.

"Bunter, old top, you're a broth av a boy!" said Mulvaney minor.

"My dear chap, don't mention it," said Bunter, with a wave of his fat hand; "only too pleased!"

"I say, this is really good, you know," remarked Tompkins. "We hadn't anything for tea—nothing to speak of. I'm jolly hungry!"

"Same here, bedad!"

"Well, these sosses are just done," said Bunter. "There's lots of them, too—over a dozen."

"Bunter, me jewel, it's intirely dacent for you to be standing a spread like this!" said Micky Mulvaney.

"Not at all! What's the good of a fellow being rich if he doesn't spend it entertaining his friends?" said Bunter.

"Oh!"

"But we're not your friends," said Tompkins, perplexed.

"Oh, really, Tompkins——"

"Sure, I'm the frind of any chap who stands me a dish of sosses when I'm as hungry as a Hun," said Mulvaney minor.

"Bunter's a broth av a boy!"

The sosses sizzled cheerily as they were dished up. It was really a most appetising spread, especially after football in a keen wind. Clarence York Tompkins and Mulvaney minor sat down to it with great enjoyment. So did Billy Bunter. And, though Bunter took the lion's share, as usual, his companions at the festive board could not take exception to that under the circumstances. Besides, there was plenty for all.

It was, in fact, a feast of the gods in Study No. 4.

The sosses were disposed of to the very last one, and then the three juniors travelled cheerily through the big cake.

Bunter's fat face beamed over the table.

After this handsome spread, cooked by his own fair hands, so to speak, he felt that Mulvaney minor and Tompkins could scarcely decline the honour of receiving him as a study-mate. Refusal would come very awkwardly after they had partaken of his hospitality in this way.

The cake was finished at last, and Bunter gave a grunt of fat contentment.

"Not so bad—what?" he remarked.

"Topping, me boy!"

"I've got some grapes here," said Bunter.

"Oh, begorra! You must be rolling in tin, Bunter!" ejaculated Mulvaney, as Bunter produced a big bunch of hothouse grapes from a paper bag.

Tompkins opened his eyes wide. There were few juniors in the Fourth who could afford to grace the tea-table with hothouse grapes.

It was a big bunch, but it disappeared in record time. Mulvaney minor and Tompkins were feeling very kindly towards Bunter now. Really, it did look as if the fat Owl had his redeeming qualities.

It was rather puzzling, however, where the good things had come from. Only that morning Bunter had attempted to borrow a half-crown from Mulvaney—in vain—on the security of a postal-order he was expecting shortly. It looked as if the postal-order had come; and it must have been a big one, to judge by the spread in Study No. 4.

But Bunter was not finished yet. He produced a box, under the surprised eyes of his new friends, and opened it.

"You fellows care for chocs?" he asked.

"Oh, bedad! Yis, rather!"

"Help yourselves, dear boys!"

The dear boys helped themselves. Billy Bunter blinked at them as the chocolates began to disappear.

"I say, you fellows——"

"Ripping!" said Mulvaney minor.

"I was going to say——"

"Tip-top!" said Mickey heartily. "You're a jewel, Bunter—a rale jewel!"

"I was thinking——"

"You must come to tea with us tomorrow, Bunter, and we'll stand the spread," said Mulvaney.

Bunter blinked at him suspiciously. It really looked as if Mulvaney was seeking to avoid the topic Bunter was seeking to introduce. But the Owl of Greyfriars was not to be eluded.

"The fact is, how would you fellows like me to dig in this study with you?" he asked.

"Oh!"

"Hem!"

It was point-blank at last, and Tompkins and Mulvaney exchanged a look. It dawned upon the simple mind of Tompkins now why that gorgeous spread had taken place in No. 4.

"Ahem!" he said. "Hum! Ah!"

Which was not very intelligible, but expressed the feelings of Clarence York Tompkins.

"We should get on no end," said Bunter. "I like this study. I don't mind saying that I like you chaps."

"Oh!"

"Ah!"

"Done!" said Bunter, apparently interpreting those dismayed ejaculations as an answer in the affirmative. "It's settled, then."

"But——" began Tompkins.

"Not a word, old fellow; it's settled," said Bunter. "I'll tell you what, you can leave the catering for the study in my hands. I'm a dab at it. Simply place the money in my hands, and leave it to me."

"B-b-b-but——" stammered Mulvaney minor.

"We'll go and fetch my books and things along, when you've done with the chocs," said Bunter cheerily.

"Oh!"

"Um!"

"But——" began Tompkins.

Clarence York was interrupted. There was a sudden roar in the passage without—a roar which resembled that of an angry bull, but was only the powerful voice of Grundy of the Shell.

"Wilkins!" remarked Grundy pleasantly. "I suppose I'd better come."

And Grundy pushed Wilkins aside, and looked into the cupboard for the supplies he had placed there after unpacking the hamper.

Then his expression changed.

"Well, where are the things, Grundy, now you've come?" inquired Wilkins, in a slightly sarcastic tone.

"My hat!"

"You must have put 'em somewhere else."

"I didn't put 'em anywhere else!" roared Grundy. "I put 'em in this cupboard not an hour ago, and then I came down to get some footer with you chaps. They've been taken away!"

"Oh!"

The faces of Wilkins and Gunn fell.

Grundy's face was assuming an expression that was terrifying. That handsome bundle of sosses, that bunch of grapes, that box of chocolates—where

Bunter "Sticks To It!"

(See Chapter 4.)

CHAPTER 8.
Missing!

"ANYTHING for tea?" asked Wilkins.

"I should jolly well say so! I had a hamper this afternoon from my Uncle Grundy."

"Oh, good!" said Gunn.

"A real spread," said George Alfred Grundy, beaming on his study-mates. "I've put the things in the cupboard. Sosses and grapes and chocs—and things. Trot 'em out, Wilkins, old fellow, while I bung up the fire."

There was beaming satisfaction in Grundy's study in the Shell passage. A hamper from Uncle Grundy made the Shell fellows realise that the piping times of peace had really come at last.

"Where's the stuff?" asked Wilkins, looking into the cupboard.

"Under your nose," answered Grundy.

"Blessed if I can see it!"

"What an ass you are, George Wilkins!"

were they? And that splendid cake—that cake which was a real corker—whither had it vanished?

"Some rotter's been here!" gasped Grundy. "Even the butter-pat's gone! Some awful rotter! Trimble, very likely—he's that sort——"

Grundy gasped. His wrath was past words. He seized a cricket-stump which was fortunately at hand.

"I'm going to see Trimble!" he spluttered.

He dragged open the door, and rushed out of the study. There was a yell in the passage as he came into violent contact with three fellows there.

"Yaroooh!"

"You howling ass!"

"Ow!" gasped Grundy, staggering from the shock. "What are you getting in the way for, Tom Merry, when a chap's in a hurry?"

"You thumping chump!" roared Tom Merry wrathfully. "What are you bolting about like a mad bull for?"

"Bump him!" gasped Lowther, who had been hurled against the opposite wall. "Collar him! Squash him!"

"Look here——" roared Grundy.

"Hold on!" exclaimed Wilkins, interposing between Grundy and the Terrible Three. "Hold on! We've been raided—no end of tuck collared by somebody! Grundy's after him—see?"

"No reason why he should play Tank in the passage!" growled Tom Merry; but he refrained from collaring Grundy. "So you've been raided, too!"

"Eh? Have you?"

"Yes; some rotter has scoffed the butter out of our study," said Tom. "We were going to make inquiries. There's a loaf gone, too. That doesn't matter so much, but butter's butter."

"Same rotter, no doubt!" exclaimed Grundy. "I was going to see Trimble about——"

"We were going to see Bunter——"

"Hallo, Gore! You missed something?"

Gore came out of his study snorting.

"Somebody's got my butter!"

"Same beast!" howled Grundy. "Come on, and see me slaughter Trimble! I'm sure it was Trimble!"

George Alfred Grundy sped along the passage, and arrived breathless at No. 2 in the Fourth, stump in hand. The other fellows followed fast. Grundy hurled the door open, and burst in like a four-point-seven shell.

Mellish and Trimble were sitting down to tea, and they jumped up at this sudden interruption, in alarm.

"Hallo!" exclaimed Mellish. "What the——"

"I say——" began Trimble. "Yarooh! Leggo, Grundy! Wharrer you at? Oh, oh! Ow! Help!"

Grundy's powerful grip was on Trimble's collar, and he was yanked round his chair.

"Where's my tuck?" roared Grundy.

"Yaroooh!"

"Have you got it?"

"Yoooop!"

Whack, whack, whack!

"Hold on!" yelled Mellish. "What are you pitching into Trimble for?"

"He's raided my grub."

Whack, whack!

"But perhaps he hasn't!" exclaimed Tom Merry.

"Rot! If he hasn't, he can say he hasn't, can he? He doesn't dare to say so."

Whack, whack!

Tom Merry grasped Grundy's arm, and forcibly stopped the application of the stump. Baggy Trimble was yelling frantically.

"Let go!" howled Grundy. "Do you think I'm going to let him mop up my grub without making an example of him?"

"Yow-ow-wooop!"

"Let him speak first, you dangerous ass!" said Tom. "Trimble, have you been raiding our studies?"

"Yarooh! No! Yooop!"

"Stuff!" said Grundy. "Why couldn't he say that at once, I'd like to know."

"Yow-ow-ow! You didn't give me a chance, did you?" yelled Trimble. "Yow-ow! I'll go to the Housemaster about this! Yooop!"

"Well, who was it, if it wasn't Trimble?" demanded Grundy. "Mind, I don't believe yet that it wasn't! But I'm ready to investigate. If it wasn't you, Trimble, who was it?"

"Yow-ow! How should I know, you silly idiot?" hooted Trimble.

"There he goes—prevaricating again!" exclaimed Grundy. "He's guilty, of course, or he wouldn't prevaricate! I'll jolly well——"

"You jolly well won't," said Tom, shoving the incensed George Alfred back. "We'll find the right party first."

"I've found him! It's Trimble! He's done it before, hasn't he?" snorted Grundy. "Mellish is hand-in-glove with him, too. I'll give Mellish a jolly good hiding while I'm here!"

"Keep off, you mad idiot!" howled Mellish, dodging round the table in great alarm.

Wilkins and Gunn dragged Grundy back.

"Hold on, Grundy——"

"Look here——"

"Where's Bunter, Mellish?" asked Tom Merry.

"Don't know, and don't care!" growled Mellish. "He doesn't belong to this study now. Go and eat coke, the lot of you!"

"We'll find Bunter before we slaughter Trimble," said Tom. "Come on, Grundy! Keep your stump for the right party, fathead!"

Grundy glared round the study in search of some sign of the missing tuck. But it was not to be seen, and he allowed himself to be persuaded out of No. 2. The Shell fellows went along the passage inquiring for Bunter.

"Buntah?" said Arthur Augustus D'Arcy, when the inquirers looked into No. 6. "Buntah? I wemembah seein' him go up into the Shell passage about an hour ago; I haven't seen him since, deah boys. Pewwaps he has gone to tea with some Shell chap."

"It was Bunter, then!" exclaimed Grundy.

"Bai Jove! What was Buntah, Gwunday?"

Grundy did not stop to reply to that question. He rushed away in furious search for the Owl of Greyfriars. The searchers began at the first study in the passage, and went along study by study, in the hope of unearthing the fat junior sooner or later.

And so they came along to No. 4; and three startled juniors within that apartment heard the roar of George Alfred Grundy:

"I'll find him! I'll spiflicate him! My cake, my grapes—hothouse grapes, you know, from my Uncle Grundy! I'll squash that fat villain Bunter as flat as a pancake! I'll—I'll——"

"No. 4 next!" said Tom Merry. "Look in, Monty, and see if the fat bounder's there."

And the door of Study No. 4 was thrown open.

—

CHAPTER 9.
Trouble in No. 4.

BILLY BUNTER sat as if frozen to his seat as he heard the bull-voice of George Alfred Grundy in the passage outside. Mulvaney minor and Tompkins looked at him very expressively. It occurred to them whence had come that propitiatory spread.

"Oh!" gasped Bunter. "I—I say, you fellows——"

The handle of the door was turning. Then Bunter woke to life. He slipped from his chair and disappeared under the study table like a flash.

"I—I say, you fellows, not a word!" he breathed.

Then all was silent.

Mulvaney and Tompkins went on mechanically eating chocolates. The door was thrown open, and Lowther looked in. His glance travelled round the study.

"Not here!" he said

"Sure?" demanded Grundy, looking in over Lowther's shoulder, with a glare in his eyes. "You're rather an ass, you know——"

"You silly chump!"

"Let me look!" growled Grundy.

"Look and be blowed!"

Grundy strode into the study.

"Has Bunter been here?" he demanded.

"Look for him yerself, old top," answered Mulvaney minor diplomatically. He felt that he could not betray the fat junior, quivering under the table close by his boots, though he was much incensed at having been made, unwittingly, a party to a "grub raid."

"He's not there, old top," said Wilkins, in the doorway. "Let's get along. We shall never find him at this rate. What the dickens are you blinking at, Grundy?"

Grundy was blinking at the chocolate-box on the table, and his expression was terrific. He knew that chocolate-box.

"My chocs!" he gasped.

"Oh, begorra!" murmured Mulvaney minor.

Grundy strode up to the table and seized the chocolate-box, and held it up wrathfully in the air.

"Look at that!" he thundered. "That's my box! They're eating the chocs at this blessed minute!"

"Well, my hat!" ejaculated Wilkins. "So it wasn't Bunter after all! It was these fags!"

"Mulvaney!" exclaimed Tom Merry. "You!"

"Begorra, and I didn't know the stuff was Grundy's," said Micky in dismay, "though sure I might have guessed it was somebody's!"

"Where's my cake?" roared Grundy.

Mulvaney minor tapped his waistcoat.

"Inside, old top!" he answered. "You're a bit too late. You should have called earlier. You never were in time for anything, Grundy."

Grundy spluttered.

"I—I—I'll give you chocs! I'll give you——"

"Hold on!" shouted Mulvaney, dodging round the table as the muscular Shell fellow rushed at him. "I tell you I niver—— Oh, crikey!"

Twice round the table they went, Mulvaney dodging nimbly, and Grundy raging in pursuit. Clarence York Tompkins stood in a dazed state. But Grundy had not come there to chase an elusive junior round the table. He could not overtake the nimbler Fourth-Former, but he laid his powerful grasp on the study-table, and sent it whirling out of the way.

There was a terrific crash of tea-things as the table spun to the wall. Then there was a yell of surprise from Tom Merry & Co., answered by a louder yell from Billy Bunter, revealed squatting on the floor where the table had been.

"Bunter!"

"Yaroooh! I—I'm not here! Oh! Ow!"

"Bunter!" roared Grundy.

"Oh dear! I—I say, you fellows, I——"

"They're all in it!" shouted Grundy.

"Hold on!" interposed Tom Merry. "For goodness' sake, ring off a minute, Grundy! Give your jaw a rest! Mulvaney minor, tell us what this means, and sharp about it! We've been raided, and we find some of the plunder here. Now, what's it mean?"

"Sure, we didn't know," said Micky Mulvaney. "Hadn't the faintest idea where Bunter got the grub. We thought he was standing a spread."

"Oh!" exclaimed Tom. "You fat villain——"

"I didn't!" yelled Bunter.

"What?"

"I wasn't!"

"Wasn't! What do you mean? You weren't what?"

"I—I mean—I—I—that is to say, I—I——" stammered Bunter. "You—you see, it's like this. I've dropped in to see Mulvaney, only a minute ago——"

"Oh, begorra!"

"Did you raid my study?" roared Grundy.

"Certainly not!"

"Then who has?"

"I really don't know, Grundy. I never saw anybody raiding it when I was there——"

"So you were there, you fat spoofer?"

"Certainly not! Nowhere near the place!" gasped Bunter. "I—I don't even know your study from the others! You must remember I'm a new fellow here, Grundy. I——"

"You've just said you were there!" snapped Tom Merry.

"That—that was only—only a figure of speech. What I really meant was that I hadn't been anywhere near the place."

"Go it, Bunter!" said Monty Lowther admiringly. "Roll 'em out, old top! Have you got any relations named Ananias among your lofty connections?"

"Oh, really, Lowther——"

"It was Bunter right enough!" said Tom Merry, laughing. "He seems to have stood a feed with the loot; rather a new departure for him."

"Oh, dear!" gasped Tompkins. "What an awful rotter to bring his plunder here! We never knew."

"Begorra, we might have known!" said Mulvaney minor. "But we didn't! The baste said he was standing a spread!"

"That's all very well," said Grundy, with a snort. "But my prog's gone, and I want to know what I'm going to have for tea. My opinion is that you're a lot of young rascals, and I'm going to whop the lot of you!"

"Sure, I—— Oh, my hat!"

The next second Grundy and Mulvaney minor were waltzing round the study. Micky Mulvaney was not quite a match for the great Grundy, but he put up quite a creditable fight.

Tompkins was not a fighting-man, as a rule, but he loyally rushed to help his study-mate against his bulky adversary. Grundy got a grip on Mulvaney's collar, and a grip on Tompkins', after a struggle. Then he brought their heads together.

Crack!

"Yarooop!"

"Yah! Oh! Oooooop!"

"Hold on, Grundy——"

"Rats! You leave 'em to me!"

Crack!

Tom Merry & Co. rushed to intervene. The great Grundy was likely to do some more damage if given his head. There was a wild and whirling tussle in the study, for Grundy refused to part with his victims. Tompkins was swung round by the collar, and collided with Tom Merry and Gore, and sent them spinning against the overturned table. Manners and Lowther had hold of Grundy, but he was dragging them to and fro with him. Wilkins and Gunn tried to separate the combatants, and, like most peacemakers, they received a good many hard knocks from both parties.

Grundy was subdued at last, however, and bumped on the carpet. Mulvaney and Tompkins, gasping and dishevelled, retreated to a corner. The Terrible Three sat on Grundy.

"Lemme gerrup!" gasped George Alfred. "I'll spifflicate you! Wilkins—Gunn—lend me a hand, you silly chumps!"

"Oh, be quiet!" gasped Wilkins, rubbing his nose. "Some silly idiot has jammed a silly elbow on my nose! Ow!"

"Yow-ow-ow!" came from Gore. "It was my elbow, you fathead—yow-ow!—you jammed your fool napper on my elbow! Ow! My funny-bone! Ow-ow!"

"Lemme gerrup! Lemme——"

"Oh, keep quiet, you fatheaded Hun!" exclaimed Tom Merry. "Collar Bunter, somebody! That's the fat rotter who wants a ragging!"

"Where is Bunter?"

"What?"

"He's gone!"

"Oh, my hat!"

The Terrible Three rose from Grundy, who scrambled up, panting. They glared round the study for Bunter. But the Owl of Greyfriars, with great wisdom, had executed a strategic retreat during the scuffle, and he had vanished.

"You silly ass!" roared Grundy. "You've let that fat burglar get away!"

"You've let him get away, you mean, you chump!"

"I—I—I'll—I'll——"

Without stopping to be more explicit Grundy dashed from the study in search of Bunter. Wilkins and Gunn followed him. But Gore, nursing his funny-bone, and grunting, returned to his own quarters, and the Terrible Three followed his example. Mulvaney minor and Clarence York Tompkins looked at one another, and looked at their wrecked study.

"Oh, dear!" groaned Tompkins.

Micky Mulvaney brandished a fist in the air.

"Sure, the next toime I see Bunter—— Oh, begorra, sure I feel as if I'd been through a mangle! Ow-ow-ow!"

It was probable that, in spite of that handsome spread in No. 4, Bunter would not succeed in installing himself in that study.

CHAPTER 10.
The Way of the Transgressor!

"BAI Jove!"

The door of Study No. 6 opened suddenly, and Billy Bunter stepped in breathlessly, and closed the door behind him.

Blake & Co. stared at him as he turned the key in the lock and then leaned against the door, gasping for breath.

"Oh, crumbs!" gasped Bunter. "I say, you fellows——"

"What does that performance mean?" asked Jack Blake.

"What a vewy extwaordinary pwoceedin'," remarked Arthur Augustus D'Arcy, fixing his eyeglass on Bunter in great surprise. "Pway what do you mean by lockin' yourself in our studay, Buntah?"

"You fellows don't mind my staying here a bit?" said Bunter, blinking at them. "That beast Grundy's after me. He——"

"Good luck to him!" said Blake heartily. "I hope he'll catch you!"

"Oh, really, Blake——"

"You've been raiding his grub, I suppose, as usual?" said Herries, with a grunt.

"Not at all! There's a slight misunderstanding about a cake and some sosses," explained Bunter. "Grundy appears to have missed some from his study. Of course, I know nothing whatever about it!"

"Of course!" said Digby sarcastically.

"Yes, of course, old chap! Why Grundy should suppose I know anything about the matter I really don't know. You fellows know I'm not the chap to touch anybody's grub."

"Oh, my hat!"

Heavy footsteps passed the door of the study. Blake & Co. listened to them, grinning; Billy Bunter with breathless anxiety. But George Alfred Grundy's footsteps passed on.

"The beast doesn't know I'm here!" said Bunter in great relief. "I say, Blake, old chap, I wonder you don't lick Grundy!"

"Do you?" grunted Blake.

"Yes, really, old fellow! Look here, if you like to try, I'll hold your jacket!"

Jack Blake looked fixedly at Bunter. Then he rose to his feet and crossed to the door.

"I—I say, old fellow, what are you up to?" stammered Bunter.

The question was really unnecessary. Blake was unlocking the door. He threw it wide open.

"Travel!" he said briefly.

"I—I say, you fellows——"

"Do you want my boot?" asked Blake politely.

"Nunno!"

"You'll get it if you're not gone in one second!"

"Oh, really, old chap——"

Blake drew back his foot, and Bunter was gone in one second. Blake closed the door after him.

"Beast!" came through the keyhole.

Blake turned the handle again; and there was a patter of footsteps in the passage. The Owl was gone.

In the distance Bunter could see Grundy's broad back in the direction of the stairs. He did not venture in that direction. Frank Levison of the Third was just entering No. 9, farther up, and Bunter hurriedly followed him into that study, anxious to get out of sight before Grundy should turn his head.

Frank had come to tea with his major and Cardew and Clive. He looked surprised as Bunter followed him in—and so did Levison major and Sidney Clive. Cardew, however, nodded genially.

"Here's old Bunter!" he exclaimed. "How awfully good of you to give us a look-in, Bunter!"

"I—I say, you fellows!" stammered Bunter. "D-d-d-do you mind if I lock the door?"

"Not if you get on the other side of it first!" answered Levison.

"Oh, really, Levison——"

"My dear fellow, you're as welcome as the flowers in May!" exclaimed Cardew, jumping up. "I'll get a chair for you!"

"Oh, really, Cardew——"

Billy Bunter was not so gratified by Cardew's blandishments as he had been on the occasion of his previous visit. He had not forgotten his adventure with the armchair yet.

"Sit down, old nut!" said Cardew.

"I—I—I'd rather stand, thanks!"

"My dear fellow, I've got another tube of seccotine——"

"Wha-a-at?"

"And you're welcome to it! Won't you sit down?"

"Ha, ha, ha!"

"Nunno! I'll stand——"

"Can't possibly allow a guest to stand!" said Cardew, approaching him. Bunter backed towards the door in dismay. "Besides, I want to see you do your interesting armchair act again! It's no end funny! Now, old nut——"

"Look here——"

"This way, old fellow!" said Cardew, taking him by the arm.

Bunter jerked his arm away.

"I—I say, I—I won't sit down! Look here, you beast——"

Tramp, tramp! came the heavy footsteps of Grundy of the Shell outside. The door flew open.

"Here he is!" roared Grundy.

He rushed in. Bunter, with a howl of terror, dodged round Cardew, and the latter cheerfully put out a foot for George Alfred to stumble over. The Shell fellow landed on his hands and knees, with a roar.

"Hook it!" grinned Cardew.

Bunter took that good advice. He hooked it before Grundy could get on his feet again.

Wilkins and Gunn were coming up the passage in answer to Grundy's call, and they met Bunter in full career.

Wilkins flew to the right and Gunn

to the left, gasping, and Bunter rushed on, heading desperately for the stairs.

In Study No. 9 Grundy scrambled to his feet in red wrath.

"You tripped me up!" he roared.

"And you went down!" agreed Cardew. "Like to perform again, old top?"

"I'll—I'll——"

Levison and Clive, and Frank of the Third, jumped up to lend their aid as the Shell fellow advanced on Cardew; and Grundy changed his mind. He shook a big fist at the dandy of the Fourth, and tramped out of the study. He seemed surprised to find Wilkins and Gunn sitting in the passage.

"What are you doing there?" he demanded.

"Ow! That fat beast! Ow! I'm winded!" groaned Wilkins.

"You've let him pass you?" roared Grundy. "You silly chumps! You—you——"

"Oh, dry up!" grunted Wilkins. "I'm fed up with Bunter, and with you, too, Grundy! Go and eat coke!"

"What?"

"Coke!" snapped Wilkins. "Come on, Gunny!"

And Grundy's chums went back to their study. Grundy snorted disdainfully, and started for the stairs. Bunter was just disappearing down the second flight when Grundy reached the top landing.

"Got him now!" said George Alfred vengefully. "By Jove, I'll make shavings of him!"

And he rushed down the stairs in hot pursuit. Bunter flew. He came down the lower staircase with a rush, and at the bottom he was stopped by an iron grasp on his collar.

"Yarooh! Leggo, you idiot!" roared Bunter.

"Bunter!"

It was a terrifying voice. Bunter jumped as he recognised the tones of Mr. Railton, the Housemaster of the School House.

"Oh, crikey!" he gasped. "I—I didn't know it was you, sir! I—I thought it was some other idiot——"

"What?"

"I—I mean——"

On the staircase George Alfred Grundy had vanished from view at the sight of the Housemaster. He did not want to interview Mr. Railton.

"What are you rushing downstairs for in this absurd manner, Bunter? You might have rushed into me—you very nearly did so!" exclaimed Mr. Railton sternly.

"I—I was—was—was in rather a hurry, sir!" gasped Bunter. "I wasn't running away from Grundy, sir!"

"What?"

"Grundy's quite mistaken in thinking I know anything about his cake!"

"Is Grundy following you?"

Bunter blinked up the staircase.

"Oh, no, sir! Not at all! Nothing of the kind! I haven't seen Grundy since—since last week!"

Mr. Railton looked at the fat junior in perplexity. He did not know Bunter so well as his Form-master at Greyfriars knew him.

"Have you taken a cake belonging to Grundy?" he asked at last.

"Not at all, sir! I wouldn't do such a thing! Grundy is—is making a mistake—I told him so."

"You have just said you have not seen Grundy since last week, Bunter!"

"Oh! I—I mean I told him so last week, sir!"

Mr. Railton looked at the fat junior fixedly for some moments.

"You may go, Bunter!" he said at last.

And Bunter went, glad to escape. He rolled into the Common-room. A little later, when the coast was clear, the fat junior ventured up the staircase again, and looked into Study No. 4.

Mulvaney minor and Tompkins were still occupied in putting their study to rights. They ceased that occupation as Bunter blinked in, and fixed deadly looks upon him. The Owl of Greyfriars nodded cheerily, unobservant of the threatening storm.

"I say, you fellows, that beast Grundy's gone now!" he remarked. "You can come and help me bring my things to the study—— Why, what—— Whooop!"

As if moved by the same spring, Mulvaney minor and Clarence York Tompkins rushed at him. Even Bunter could not misunderstand that. He skipped into the passage.

"I—I say, you fellows——"

"Collar him!" yelled Mulvaney. "Bring me the poker, Tompkins!"

But Bunter was gone before the poker could arrive.

CHAPTER 11.
No Go!

THUMP!

Bang!

"Bai Jove! What's the wow, deah boys?" exclaimed D'Arcy of the Fourth.

Bang, bang!

Mellish and Trimble did not trouble to answer Gussy's query. They were thumping vigorously on the door of Study No. 2.

They looked ferocious.

It was the day following Bunter's unsuccessful attempt upon Study No. 4—and the fat junior was still homeless. But Bunter had been thinking during lessons that day. And now, at the hour of evening prep, Mellish and Trimble had arrived at No. 2, to find the door locked on the inside.

Outside was chalked, in big letters across the panels:

"NOTICE TO MELLISH AND TRIMBLE!
NOT WANTED!
KEEP OFF THE GRASS!
RATS!
(Signed)
W. G. BUNTER."

Which was pretty good evidence that it was W. G. Bunter who was in the study, and had locked the door against his former study-mates.

"You fat villain!" hissed Mellish through the keyhole. "Open this door, or we'll slaughter you! We've got our prep to do."

A fat chuckle came from within.

"Go to the Form-room, old top!"

"Open the door!"

"Rats!"

"Bai Jove! Buntah is turnin' the tables!" exclaimed Arthur Augustus. "This is weally faih play on you chaps, you know."

"I'll scalp him!" howled Mellish.

"I'll squash him!" roared Trimble. "Let us in, Bunter, you cad!"

Another fat chuckle.

"Go and eat coke!" came from within, after the chuckle.

W. G. Bunter evidently felt himself to be master of the situation.

Bunter's search of a study was over. Even the Owl had realised at last that it was futile; and that he would get more kicks than halfpence, so to speak, for his attempts to "plant" himself along the passage. So he had returned to his old quarters; and behind a locked door he bade defiance to Mellish and Trimble.

"We'll smash in the lock!" howled Mellish.

"You'll have the Housemaster up here if you do. What'll he say about turning a chap out of his study?" demanded Bunter.

"I—I—I'll——"

"Besides, I've got the table against the door," continued Bunter cheerily, from the inner side of the keyhole. "You can't get in, you know. Better make it pax!"

Thump, thump!

Bang!

The clamour at the door of No. 2 brought fellows along the passage from far and near. Tom Merry & Co. arrived from the Shell quarters, and Blake & Co. from Study No. 6. There was a roar of laughter in the passage. Bunter's device for regaining a footing in his own quarters rather tickled the juniors.

"Better not make too much row," advised Tom Merry. "There'll be trouble if you bring the prefects here."

"I—I'll smash him!" howled Mellish. "I've got to do my prep."

"Well, Bunter's got his prep to do, too," said Tom, laughing. "You've no right to keep him out of the study. The Housemaster wouldn't allow it if Bunter went to him."

"If he brings Railton down on us, we'll jolly well tell him about Bunter scoffing our ration."

"I say, you fellows," came from within No. 2, "I'm not going to sneak to Railton. As for the rations, I decline to enter into a paltry discussion about a pat of butter and a few measly sardines. I'm really surprised at you, Mellish. You shock me!"

Bang, bang!

"I don't mind letting you in," continued Bunter, "but it's understood that you've got to behave yourselves. Make it pax!"

"I'll—I'll—I'll——"

"I'll lay down my conditions," went on Bunter. "I'm to keep in the study, and I'm to have the armchair. I'm rather particular on that point. Do you agree to my having the armchair, Mellish?"

"I'll spiflicate you!" gasped Mellish.

"Of course, you fellows can have it when I'm not in the study. I'm not selfish, I hope."

"Ha, ha, ha!"

"Bai Jove! That chap Buntah is weally a corkah, you know."

"You fellows have got to promise, with Tom Merry as a witness. Otherwise, you don't come in. I may mention that if you don't come to terms I'm going to drop your books on the fire!"

"What?"

Bang, bang!

"I say, you fellows, it's no good banging at the door. By the way, I'm just going to start on the grub, Mellish. I suppose you meant the pilchards and the pineapple for my supper, didn't you?"

"Ha, ha, ha!"

"You fat rotter!" shrieked Mellish. "If you touch my pineapple——"

"If you touch my pilchards——" howled Baggy Trimble.

"Ha, ha, ha!"

Bang, bang! Thump! Kick! Bang!

There was a sound of a tin-opener at work in the study, and Mellish and Trimble were quite wild. There was a shout from Roylance on the stairs.

"Cave! Prefect!"

"Bai Jove! It's Knox!"

"Better clear," grinned Monty Lowther.

Knox, the bully of the Sixth, was coming up the stairs two at a time. The crowd of juniors melted away as if by magic. Nobody wanted to interview the Sixth Form bully if he could help it.

"What's this thundering row?" roared

Knox, as he strode into the Fourth Form passage.

But there was nobody left to answer. The only reply was shutting of doors and pattering feet in the distance. Knox stared at the chalked inscription on the door of No. 2, and shook the door-handle.

"What's this? What does this mean? Let me in at once!" exclaimed the prefect angrily.

"Oh, I say——"

"Bunter!"

"I—I'm not here, Knox. I—I mean, the—the door ain't locked—— That is to say—— Oh, dear!"

"Let me in!" thundered Knox, shaking the handle.

The key turned in the lock; there was no arguing with a prefect of the Sixth, especially when he had a temper like Knox's. The Sixth-Former threw the door open, and strode in, ashplant in hand; and Bunter retreated round the table in alarm.

"I—I say, Knox!" he gasped. "I—I wasn't making a row, you know——I—I was as silent as the tomb, you know! I really—— Yarooooh!"

The bully of the Sixth was not particular as to his victim, so long as he found one. The ashplant interrupted Bunter. With a wild yell, Bunter sprinted round the table, with Knox after him, laying it on.

"Yarooh! Help! Fire! Murder!" howled Bunter. "Stoppit, you beast! Oh, crikey! I tell you it wasn't me! I haven't—— I didn't—— I wasn't—— Oh, crumbs!"

Whack, whack, whack!

Bunter dodged out of the doorway at last and fled.

"Come back, Bunter!" roared Knox. "I haven't finished with you yet."

Bunter was not a very bright youth; but he was bright enough not to heed that command. He vanished up the dormitory staircase, and Knox, with a grunt, strode away.

A few minutes later, when Knox was safely gone, Mellish and Trimble came cautiously along to No. 2. They were grinning.

Mellish slipped the key of the study into his pocket.

"Now let that fat bounder come back!" he said. "I'll keep my cricket-bat handy for him."

And the bat was lying on the table when the two juniors sat down to prep, all ready for W. G. Bunter when he came—if he came.

When Bunter came, he came only as far as the doorway, and blinked in with great caution.

"I say, you fellows——" he began.

Mellish jumped up and seized the bat.

Slam!

The Owl of Greyfriars vanished, and did not reappear.

Billy Bunter was still In Search of a Study!

THE END.

(Don't miss next Wednesday's Great Story of Tom Merry & Co. at St. Jim's—"THE OWL'S NEST!"—by Martin Clifford.)

Extracts from "THE GREYFRIARS HERALD" and "TOM MERRY'S WEEKLY."

FIGGY AND THE FAGS. By George Francis Kerr.

I.

"GOT you!" ejaculated Figgy.

We had just come in from footer, ready for tea. Fatty, as usual, was more than ready. He had referred five times in three minutes to the rabbit-pie that was awaiting us, and had at last decided that we would have it hot—if he could manage to last out till it was made hot. I understood that that depended largely upon the state of the study fire. If it had got too low, the dear Fatty was sure that Figgy and I would never have patience to abide the slow heating of that pie.

Slow heating, mind you—don't overlook the aspirate. Take it away, and the process indicated by what would be left would certainly not be slow. As for the pie, none of that was likely to be left.

And Figgy, entering first, found young Jameson at our cupboard!

"I—I—— Oh, I say, Figgy, I wasn't doing anything!" said the kid.

"We're not going to have you doing nothing in our study!" rapped out Figgy.

It did look as though the kid was after that rabbit-pie. Jameson is a decent specimen of the fag tribe; but you can't treat them safely as if they were superior to temptation in the grub line.

"The cupboard isn't quite the best place to be doing nothing at, my young friend," I told Jameson.

"I should think not—not with a rabbit-pie there!" said Fatty warmly.

"Give me that cricket-stump, Kerr, old chap!" Figgy said.

"Look here, you're not going to stump me!" howled Jameson, wriggling hard.

He is a hefty kid—one of the biggest and strongest in the Third—but he found Figgy's grip a grip of iron.

"Your mistake!" growled Figgy. "I certainly am—unless you can give me a satisfactory explanation of what you were after. Mind, pie isn't a satisfactory one!"

"I wasn't after the pie, fathead!"

"Well, what was it, then?"

"You wouldn't believe me if I told you."

"P'r'aps—p'r'aps not. Better try me!" said Figgy.

"Well, then, I was after my lines!"

"Your—er—your which?"

"Lines. I've got two hundred to show up to Selby to-morrow morning."

"But what on earth made you come to our cupboard for them?" demanded Figgy, in natural amazement.

"I—I—— A chap said they were there!"

"Sounds a bit thin, Kerr—eh?"

"It's a rotten thumper!" said Fatty. "I didn't think you were such a young liar, Jam-face!"

"I'm not!" yelled Jameson.

"It's a queer yarn—so queer that it may be true," I remarked.

In my experience, the more unlikely a story of that sort is, when it's told by a fellow who does not make a habit of lying, the greater the chances are that it's true. If he were lying for once, he would most likely tell a better one.

This does not apply to fellows like Trimble and that chap Bunter we have had here the last few weeks. They do make a habit of lying; but I should not feel any inclination to believe their yarns on the score of their being improbable. They tell all sorts.

"Who was the chap, then?" snapped Figgy.

"I can't tell you."

"Of course he can't! There wasn't any chap," said Fatty. "Lemme come, Figgy! I shall know in a sec if he's been picking at that pie."

"It isn't sneaking to tell us, kid," I said, to give Jameson a chance.

And, of course, it was not. Telling us was quite a different thing from telling a master or a prefect. We have no authority—though we do know how to deal with grub-sneaks, all the same.

"That's what you say, Kerr," answered Jameson doggedly. "I say it is!"

"Don't we know better than you do?" said Figgy sharply.

"Not likely! You think you do, I dare say!"

"We do! It's like your giddy cheek to doubt it. You can either tell me the chap's name or take a stumping!"

"I won't tell you, and you jolly well aren't going to stump me! We'll make you sorry for it if you do!"

It was a silly threat. Jameson, as we all three understood perfectly well, was threatening us with vengeance at the hands of Wally D'Arcy & Co. He is the one New House member of the Wally tribe.

But, naturally, we are not exactly afraid of those seven young rips—not much!

Figgy was not in the best possible temper. He had heard that morning that Miss Cleveland—cousin Ethel, you know—was arriving by the midday train; but she had not come. Then someone had hacked him rather fiercely during the afternoon's play, and he was not at all sure that it was an accident, though, of course, he had to accept it as being so when the fellow apologised.

He shoved Jameson out at arm's-length, and brought that stump hard down across his shoulders.

The kid howled with rage, and kicked.

He landed Figgy right on the sore shin. Figgy let go of him. Jameson took the chance to bolt.

But Fatty was in the way, and not at all inclined to get out of it; and old Fatty is a pretty solid lump to get past.

Fatty stood still. Jameson dodged, and caught his left foot against a leg of the table. Figgy struck at that moment; and the stump, instead of getting the kid on the back, took him across the neck and cheek, leaving a great weal.

"Oh!" gasped Fatty.

"You rotten cad!" howled Jameson. "Oh, you foul cad!"

"Here, I say, kid, I'm frightfully sorry!" said old Figgy, his face white with dismay. "I never meant——"

"What did you go stumping me for, you beast? I wasn't doing any harm here, was I? Am I to be knocked about like this because I won't sneak?"

"I tell you I didn't mean——"

"You'd no right to touch me! Oh, you shall smart for this, you brute!"

"Easy does it, young 'un!" I said. "Figgy's not a brute, and you know that as well as I do. He's apologised. I don't see what more he can do. It's a nasty mark, I know, and, of course, it hurt. But do take it like a sportsman! Let me bathe——"

"I won't have one of you touch me, you cads! Three of you to one, and then to—— Boo-hoo!"

It was rage that made the kid cry, not pain. We all knew that. Young Jameson is not the sort to cry because he is hurt.

But I knew as he bolted from the room that if there was anything that could increase his bitterness against Figgy it was our having seen him break down like that. Wally's crowd hold crying a trick beneath contempt.

"I say, I've done it now!" groaned poor old Figgy. "Oh, I do hope Ethel doesn't see that kid's face!"

"She'll know that it was an accident, if she ever knows you did it," I told him. "But Jameson wouldn't tell her that."

"I—I couldn't face her if she knew anything about it, Kerr!"

Everbody knows how much good old Figgy thinks of Ethel Cleveland.

He isn't soft and sentimental about it, like Gussy when he gets gone on a girl. But he values her opinion more than anyone else's in the world; and it would almost break his heart if she believed him a funk or a bully.

"Well, she won't know," Fatty said soothingly. "Let's have tea."

"Tea!" snorted Figgy. "Who cares for tea?"

"Why, I do!" answered Fatty, opening his blue eyes very widely.

"Well, I don't!"

"That's a pity! Still, I dare say I can eat your share of the pie, old top!"

Fatty did, too. Figgy wouldn't touch a scrap of it. He just sat there and grizzled.

Cousin Ethel was coming next day—we knew that. And Wally is her cousin—really, not like the rest of us, except Gussy; we are only adopted cousins—and she likes all Wally's chums, and they like her. But they wouldn't tell her about a thing like that. Jameson would keep out of her way as long as it showed, I felt sure.

I could not get Figgy to believe it, though. He went to bed still uncomforted. He was ashamed of what he had done, anyway, for he knew he had struck in anger, though the blow's falling where it did was a pure accident. But it was the thought of Ethel Cleveland that made him feel it as a tragedy, instead of a mere "regrettable occurrence."

II.

"IT doesn't sound a bit like Figgins," said Frank Levison.

"Sound like him, you silly young fathead! It was him!" howled Jameson.

That youth had taken his bruised face and his injured spirit over to the School House, that his chums might comfort him and with him concert reprisals upon the enemy.

"Frank means that Figgy can't have meant to do it," said Wally D'Arcy. "I must say myself I'm surprised. But he did it. That's what matters."

"Oh, yes," admitted Frank. "I don't want Jam-face knocked about like that, of course. I think it's dead off. But if it was an accident——"

"Does it look like an accident?" snorted Jameson, with a hand to his bruised and smarting face.

"Not much!" returned Hobbs.

"I vote we give the rotter toko for this!" said Reggie Manners.

"Rather!" agreed Curly Gibson

"But old Figgy ain't a rotter," objected Frayne.

"That's just what I mean," Frank said.

Levison minor and Joe Frayne are far and away the most reasonable of Levison's band.

"He was in a tearing rage about something," Jameson said sulkily. "He let himself go. I know he doesn't often do that. But he did it this time—and just look at my mug!"

"What did you do to him?" asked Wally acutely.

And that was where Jameson went wrong. If he had admitted that he had kicked Figgy's shins it is very doubtful whether any of the other six—even Manners minor, who has been known to be guilty of that trick—would have gone whole-heartedly into a scheme of vengeance.

But he was ashamed to own up.

"Don't I tell you?" he said impatiently. "I was at their cupboard. That young sweep Gladwin had collared my lines, and he said he'd put them there."

"He was pulling your leg," said Wally.

"Well, he'll be jolly sorry he tried that on. I don't put up with having my leg pulled, I can tell you!"

No one commented on that. Gladwin is an inconspicuous fag on our side of the way, where the fags are rather down on Jameson, partly because all his chums are School House, and partly because he can lick any of the New House fags, and doesn't let them forget it. His giving Gladwin a hiding would be all in the day's work, and was not worth arguing about.

Figgy was a different matter. The kids all know what a jolly decent chap our old Figgy is, every way; and they had their doubts, I suppose.

But the law of Wally & Co. is each for all and all for each, and it was scarcely on the cards that Jameson's urgings to revenge should be fruitless.

"Well, anyway, we don't want to drag Kerr and Fatty Wynn into it," said Frank Levison.

"We certainly don't, old man," answered Wally, with a grin. "Unless we're going to get another half-dozen or so of our chaps in to help us."

"Game is to get Figgins somewhere alone, and jolly well put him through it," said Hobbs.

"But how are we going to get him alone?" asked Curly Gibson.

(I am reporting all this as if I had heard it, I know. I was not there, but I learned later about the deliberations, and you may take it from me that what I set down here is pretty accurate.—G. F. K.)

"I've got a notion for that—a ripping wheeze!" cried Manners minor.

Nobody seemed very enthusiastic. Somehow Reggie Manners is hardly taken at his own valuation in the Third. And that's just as well, for he is a swanky young ass, and often needs sitting upon.

"Well, we don't mind hearing it, though we know it will be a wash-out," said Wally.

"Rats! It will work like a charm! Do any of you know a dead sure way of fetching Figgins anywhere?"

"Tie him up and carry him there," suggested Hobbs, rather weakly.

"Ass! Unless you can get him somewhere you can't tie him up. Any place where you could tie him up you could rag him baldheaded—see?"

"How do you think you'd do it?" asked Wally.

"I don't think—I know!"

"Well, then, clever?"

"Send him a message from cousin Ethel!"

The six stared at Reggie. He had certainly though of something that would not have occurred to any of them.

"Dead off!" said Levison minor.

"Oh, you dry up! We don't want any of your pious notions!" snarled Reggie.

"I don't see that it's off," said Jameson.

"An' I can't see that Franky's notion's pious," Joe Frayne said. "I reckon as it's dead orf, too. We can't go draggin' of cousin Ethel into this 'ere bizney."

"Who wants to drag her into it?" shrilled Reggie. "I don't, you silly asses! I s'pose I—— Well, I think as much of her as any of you; and I wouldn't do a blessed thing to annoy her. But it wouldn't be dragging her in; she'd never even know."

"Seems a bit rough on old Figgy, though—trapping him that way," objected Curly Gibson.

"Well, if he goes and gets spoony on a girl——"

"It isn't a girl—it's cousin Ethel!"

"Young ass, you are, Levison! What is she if she isn't a girl?"

Frank could not explain. But some of them at least knew what he meant. Ethel Cleveland is to most of us something a good deal more than the ordinary girl, you see."

"An' I shouldn't exac'ly call it bein' spoony," said Frayne.

"Don't see what else you can call it," answered Wally. "And I don't see much against it myself. 'Tain't as if it was going to hurt Ethel in any way. I wouldn't have that."

"There you are, young Levison! And Wally really is her cousin!" said Manners minor triumphantly.

Wally's weight thrown into the scale turned it decisively.

The two dissentients had to give in. They agreed to share the enterprise, though they did not half like it. That is the law of the pack.

III

"WHAT do you want, Gladwin?"

Figgy was not in the study when Gladwin of the Third put in his tousled head.

"Ain't Figgins here?"

"You can look under the table if you like. Unless he's there, he can't very well be in the room without being visible."

"Oh, don't be funny, Kerr! It's serious."

"What's serious, kid?"

"What I've got to say to Figgy."

"Well, he'll be in before long."

"I—I say, Kerr, he'll be tearing mad with me. I shouldn't like him to give me a welt like he gave young Jam-face, you know."

"I don't think that's any way likely. But if you're afraid of it you can tell me, and I'll tell Figgy."

"I know what it is!" said Fatty.

I turned round sharply. I had supposed that Fatty was asleep.

"What, then?" I asked of him.

"That kid Jameson's yarn was true, though it did sound pretty thin. And this is the young sweep who put his impot in our cupboard!"

"No, I didn't," said Gladwin, looking rather relieved. "It wasn't put there at all. We only kidded the silly ass it was, that's all. It was my idea; that's why I came to own up."

"You've made a nice mess of things, I must say! What did you do it for?" said Fatty.

"Well, Jam-face thinks he's so jolly smart, and he kinds of looks down on us lot, and goes about with D'Arcy minor and that crowd. We like to take it out of him now and then. But—— Oh, I say, here's Figgy!"

And Gladwin bolted, leaving us to tell the tale.

Figgy didn't seem greatly interested, and he was not at all pleased.

"Makes it worse, if anything," he said. "I ought to have believed the kid. He's straight enough."

"Well, I didn't believe him," said Fatty slowly.

"You, porpoise? What's it matter what you think? You can't think, come to that! Kerr believed all right."

"No, Figgy, old son. I only thought it might be true because it sounded so blessed unlikely."

"What's bothering me is what cousin Ethel will say," said Figgy, frowning hard.

"Nothing at all, old top! She won't hear about it."

"I think she has heard. Anyway, I shall know in a few minutes, for I shall see her."

And Figgy started to put his tie straight and brush his clobber.

We did not ask him anything. We never do.

But I felt certain that Ethel Cleveland hadn't sent to say that she wanted to see him because she meant to rag him. That is not her way.

Matter of that, it's not her way to send him messages at all. We all know that she likes to see Figgy better than she does any of the rest of us, but that kind of thing is hardly in her line.

If she had sent for him, though, there was bound to be some reason for it. Figgy might have told us that Wally D'Arcy had given him the supposed message. I should have smelt a rat at once, though Wally is Ethel's cousin, for I felt sure that he and his crowd would want to get home on Figgy for the affair Jameson. But as it was I suspected nothing.

Figgy went off, looking distinctly neater than usual. He is hardly up to the mark of the admirable Arthur Augustus in the matter of appearance, you know, as a rule. He wasn't even then, for that matter.

He went off, and he fell right into the trap. An old bird like Figgy, too!

The seven were waiting for him behind a hedge half a mile or so from the school, and while he was looking round for cousin Ethel they pounced upon him as one man.

"Yooop!" howled Figgy, as he went down. "What's all this for, you young rotters?"

"Jam-face's mug," replied Wally briefly.

"You can't go doing beastly things like that without getting it in the neck for it," added Manners minor.

Figgy struggled desperately. He feared that at any moment cousin Ethel might be along, and it sent him nearly mad to think she might see him being handled like that by the fag tribe.

"If you don't let me go I'll——"

"Rats! We're too many for you, my beauty!" answered Wally. "What shall we do to him, you fellows?"

"He'll have to apologise to Jimmy, anyway!" said Hobbs.

"I'll do that," said Figgy at once. "I know now that the yarn he told was true. And I did apologise to him directly I'd done it. He knows it was an accident, and that's more than he can say about kicking my shin!"

"Did you do that, Jimmy?" snapped Levison minor, letting go of Figgy.

Jameson let go, too.

"Yes, I did," he growled. "I'm sorry now. But——"

"You ought to have told us!" said Wally severely.

"I know; but——"

"Oh, never mind that!" said Figgy hastily. "I can forgive it all serene. Let me get up, you kids. Look here, I'm expecting someone. You know that, Wally. I—I'll give myself up to you anywhere you like later on. Honest Injun, I will! Mind, I don't say I won't struggle or bash any of you; but, hang it all, you're seven to one! Surely it's a fair offer?"

"Ha, ha, ha!"

You can fancy how Figgy scowled at the riotous fags as they cackled.

It was no joke to poor old Figgy.

"You may be expecting someone, but she won't come," said Wally. "Why, you fat-

Printed and published weekly by the Proprietors at The Fleetway House, Farringdon Street, London, E.C. 4, England. Subscription, 8s. 10d. per annum. Agents for Australasia: Gordon & Gotch, Melbourne, Sydney, Adelaide, Brisbane, and Wellington, N.Z. South Africa: The Central News Agency, Ltd., Cape Town and Johannesburg. Saturday, February 8th, 1919.

head, don't you see it was all a spoof? Ethel didn't send you any message!"

"Then you are a rotten young liar!"

"No, Figgy, no! I only asked you if you'd meet cousin Ethel here. It was you who said you would. Your mistake. Ha, ha!"

"But I'm here, Wally!" said a voice. And there was Ethel Cleveland looking over the hedge at them!

They let Figgins go at once. He scrambled up, red and confused. But he was not redder or more confused than the fags. Levison minor told his major afterwards that he would have been jolly pleased if the earth had opened up and swallowed him. And what Manners major told his minor about thinking out caddish schemes I won't repeat, for I don't think any of the kids meant to be caddish.

"Mr. Selby's coming!" said Ethel.

"My hat!"

"Oh, crumbs!"

"What a squeak!"

Of course, old Selby has no love for George Figgins. But he is no end down on those seven, and it would have been a fine score for him if he had caught them at their ragging.

But all he saw when he stalked past was Ether Cleveland talking to one Fourth-Former and seven Third-Formers, and he just lifted his mortar-board to Ethel and scowled at her companions; and he went on.

"I don't understand this," said Ethel, looking straight at Wally.

"There's no need you should," said Reggie, who did not want her to know anything of his precious scheme.

"I spoke to my cousin, Reggie," she said quietly.

And she laid her hand on Figgins' arm. I don't think she knew she was doing it, and I am sure that it was not because she thought he needed protection. But it made Figgins feel happier at once; and somehow it impressed the fags, though it wouldn't have done if cousin Ethel had been anyone else.

"Well, I suppose I'll have to tell you," said Wally, drawing a deep breath. "You'll be mad, though. It wasn't just the most decent thing to do, I reskon, now."

And he told her of the trap into which Figgy had fallen.

She let her hand stay on Figgy's arm. Her face flushed as Wally told his tale, but she was not as angry as they had thought she would be.

"But what was it for?" she asked.

All the kids looked at Figgy. They were not going to answer that.

"I did that!" Figgy blurted out, pointing to Jameson's face.

"Oh, cheese it, Figgy! It was really my own fault!" protested Jameson.

"I'm sure it was an accident! I'm quite sure of that!" said cousin Ethel.

She was angry then, and hurt, too; and they all felt uncomfortable—none of them more so than Figgy.

"I didn't mean to hurt him like that, Ethel, of course," he said humbly. "But I was in a rage, and I did lash out at him."

"Well, I'd kicked your shins," growled Jameson.

"Let me look at it," said Ethel gently. Her fingers touched the red weal, and young Jameson went beet-root colour. But he liked it all the same; I am sure of that. For he knew that it meant the shin-kicking was overlooked, and it had cost him a pretty big effort to confess to that lapse.

"Girls are no end queer," said Wally, as he and five of the clan followed cousin Ethel and Figgy and young Jam-face.

They were more or less in disgrace, and they knew it; but those two weren't in the black books.

"Cousin Ethel isn't 'girls,' and I don't call it queer a bit!" said Levison minor stoutly.

"Oh, you're a young donkey!" snapped Reggie.

"And you're a young cad, Manners minor!" snorted Wally.

"Well, I like that! What are you, then?"

"Another of 'em! We all are—except Franky and Joe!"

But they are not, you know! Figgy says they are very decent kids. Cousin Ethel thinks them so. That proves it!

THE ST. JIM'S GALLERY.

No. 34.—The Hon. Walter Adolphus D'Arcy.

THAT is Wally's proper name, you know. But he does not insist on the use of it. In fact, the insistence is all the other way. Wally turns up his nose at the "Honourable," and is apt to put up his fists if anyone tries on the "Adolphus."

Which does not in the least imply that Wally is not honourable, in fact as well as in name.

He is as straight and essentially decent as any fellow at St. Jim's. He may poke fun at Arthur Augustus' high-flown ideas; but really Gussy and Wally are not so absolutely unlike as you might think to hear Wally talk. Their ways are different, but many of their characteristics are the same.

Wally is not a swell. There are times when Gussy finds it necessary to give him brotherly admonitions concerning clean collars and all that kind of thing. But a swell of thirteen or so is, as a rule, an almost unendurable specimen. At that important age there are so many other things for a fellow to think about, and his personal appearance is but a trifling matter. Two years later, when he has become aware of girls as girls, you know, it is different.

Like Gussy, Wally is ready to stand up for a fellow down on his luck. There have been many instances of this; some of them may crop up later in this article.

And, like Gussy, Wally has any amount of pluck, and is frank almost to a fault. You might say that he is franker than his major; for Wally will tell a fellow of his defects on purpose, whereas when Gussy does that the hostile criticism generally slips out more or less unawares. Wally is less tolerant than Gussy, who is always looking for the good that must be somewhere in every fellow. You would not catch Wally looking for the good points of, say, Piggott, or Racke, or Cutts. He is quite content to regard them as having none.

Study No. 6 went to meet Wally when he first came to St. Jim's, and Blake was particularly struck by his utter apparent want of resemblance to Gussy. Wally was very untidy indeed, and his jacket was covered with hairs. The hairs came from Pongo. As Wally explained, "That's the worst of Pongo! His wool does come off, and no mistake!"

"Hallo, kid! So you've come!" was Wally's greeting to Gussy at the station. "Same old Gussy! Same old window-pane!"

It is hardly needful to remark that Wally does not sport an eyeglass.

"I am sowwy!" Gussy told him, with dignity. "I will shake hands with you pwesently, when you have had a wash. I cannot have my gloves wuined!"

An inquiry after Wally's gloves elicited the fact that Pongo had gnawed one of them on the way, and the other had been left under the seat.

Jameson was cock of the Third at that date. In the Form-room Jameson was using two lockers. Mr. Selby told Wally he could have No. 10. Jameson told him he couldn't. It was plainly a case that could only be

settled by ordeal of battle, and everyone expected that Wally would be licked, not only because he was a mere new kid, but because Jameson was bigger and heftier, and had long swayed the Third.

But it turned out that Wally could have the key of the locker; and it also turned out before long that Jameson's reign over the Form was at an end.

Before Wally became cock of the Third, however, things had happened to him. He ran away. He had kicked a football right into the face of Mr. Selby—by accident, of course. But Mr. Selby did not believe that it was an accident, and he told Wally before the whole Form that he was lying in saying it was, and that he should cane him, not for the accident—or otherwise—but for the lie. Wally had had several other combats by this time, and had won them all. He was at the stage when he might look forward to being cock of the Form, but was not acknowledged as such, and was not exactly popular with the youngsters he had licked. They chortled at his getting a caning for telling a lie; and Wally determined to bolt rather than submit to the indignity.

Gussy refused to hear of his doing anything so foolish as bolting—offered to expostulate with Mr. Selby on his behalf—and lent him a couple of sovereigns. This gave Wally the chance to cut. Gussy had failed to perceive that; he does not always see all the way.

Wally went home to get together a few things before casting himself upon the world. His father, Lord Eastwood, was not there; but the butler wired to him, and locked Wally in his room to keep him safe.

Gussy came after him. But Wally eluded Gussy and did down Walker, and got clear away to London. Gussy, with Blake and Tom Merry, came to look for him, and found him—selling newspapers, or, rather, trying to establish his right by combat to a pitch wherefrom he might sell them.

He went back, and the trouble was cleared up. But Mr. Selby has never forgiven him, and probably never will.

Of the feud between master and boy much has been already told in the sketch of Mr. Selby. It has gone on without any real cessation ever since that early trouble. But it would, no doubt, have started in some other way if it had not started in that particular way. For to Mr Selby, who really dislikes all boys, a boy of Wally's type is specially objectionable. Wally is inclined to be cheeky; Mr. Selby considers him abominably impudent, and reads cheek into speeches quite harmless in intention. Wally is high-spirited and full of mischief; to Mr. Selby high spirits and mischief are only varied forms of original sin. It is safe to say that there is no boy in the Third for whom that Form's tyrant has the slightest liking; but Wally and Wally's chums are his special detestation.

In these days Wally has six staunch and loyal followers, all to be depended upon to back him up in emergencies, though they may kick over the traces at times. Reggie Manners, for instance, often does that. Frank Levison, the latest arrival of them all, is really Wally's best chum; but little Joe Frayne, the golden-hearted Cockney lad, stands very high in his regard. Perhaps that is because Wally has the strong fellow's natural liking for someone weaker than himself, someone who may now and then need standing up for. By which it is not in the least meant that Joe Frayne and Frank Levison cannot stand up for themselves. But they are gentler of nature than Reggie Manners, or than Hobbs, or than Jameson—enemy turned friend—or, perhaps, than Curly Gibson, though he is not quite of the same type as those three.

It is impossible to give much space here to the varied activities of the fag tribe—their japes—their feuds with the Fourth and the Shell—their cooking of kippers and bloaters on the fire in the Form-room—and all that sort of thing. By the way, the joke about the wangy herrings is only a joke; the Third do not really like them best that way. It is impossible to begin to recount the many tricks played upon Mr. Selby. It is impossible to tell of all the times in which Wally and Gussy have come into conflict over questions of behaviour and dress and graver matters. But it would be a big mistake to suppose that Wally, though he may constantly poke fun at Gussy, though he never treats him with the respect that Gussy considers his due, is not fond of his major—fond of him and proud of him, though he would never own to the pride.

There was another time when Wally ran away. It was more serious then. Piggott had plotted to make him seem guilty of theft, and many of the Form believed; and the evidence seemed so conclusive that the Head could not doubt. Lord Eastwood was sent for; but Wally would not wait to face his father. He bolted, and joined a boxing-booth as a very juvenile light-weight—with the added attraction of a mask. At Abbotsford Reuben Piggott, badly in need of money, faced Wally—whose identity was quite unguessed by him—in combat in the hope of making some. You will remember how the booth got on fire, and how Wally rescued his enemy. They are still enemies, in spite of that rescue; Wally and Piggott could never be friends.

At first there was trouble between Wally and Levison minor on account of Wally's very outspoken remarks about Levison major. But it was soon discovered in the Third what a first-rate little fellow in every way Frank is; and after that Wally & Co. went easier on the subject of "Ernie." Now there is no need for them to shun that subject; Levison major is an elder brother to be proud of. Afterwards trouble again arose through Frank's keen sense of honour. It developed to an extent that meant fighting; and they fought. Frank was licked, of course; he is not up to Wally's weight. But Wally's remorse when he found out how utterly in the wrong he had been made the bond of friendship between them stronger than ever.

Wally does not mind owning—once in a way—not often enough to make Tom conceited, you know—that he really has a good opinion of Tom Merry. When the row with Blake put Tom in the black books of his own Form and the Fourth, the Third stood by him loyally; and Wally was at the head of the Third in that, as in other matters.

Tom was master of the Third for a little while in the absence of Mr. Selby. And, of course, the Third gave Tom lots of trouble. To them his presence in a position of authority seemed no end of a joke. They called him "Mr. Merry" and "sir," and regarded the calling him so humorous. Wally, in spite of his real fondness for Tom, led the japing; and it was he who, pursued by Lowther and Manners, darted into Tom's study as a place of refuge, and said:

"Excuse me, sir, would you mind telling me exactly how many lines I have to do? You gave me so many this morning that I had forgotten. I know they were less than a million, sir, but I don't know exactly how many, sir."

Wally has his share of cheek, and a bit over—no doubt about that!

Do you remember how Wally stood up for Joe Frayne? So did Tom Merry, naturally, for it was through Tom that Joe came to the school. So did Gussy. Is not Gussy always to be counted upon by anyone down on his luck? But it was easier for them than for Wally; and Wally's championship was at closer quarters, and counted for more. But there will be more to tell about that when Joe comes to be dealt with. Wally could not stand it when Joe became a convert to Skimpole's Socialistic theories, however.

He stood up for Dudley, too. Dudley really was a bit of a rotter. Not quite a hopeless rotter—that was proved later. But Dudley had won Wally's heart by protecting Pongo; and it was through Wally that Dudley got a chance to make a fresh start.

Wally has done a good deal in the way of looking after Manners minor, too—a pretty thankless task. Reggie really is a handful, as was clearly indicated when he was dealt with in this series.

Don't imagine Wally as preaching or "pi." He is not that in the very least. But he has his standard of honour and decency, and he hates to see any of his chums fall below that standard. It is a tolerably simple one. According to Wally's code it is rotten to funk, sneak, tell lies, gamble, or smoke—and quite right, too! Piggott does all these things; and so Wally bars Piggott completely. Reggie has had lapses into most of them, if not all; but he is not barred completely, for they are only lapses.

Pongo—well, really, I think Pongo must be dealt with separately. It was doubtless something of a surprise to many readers to find Towser included in the Gallery. After that, the inclusion of Pongo will not surprise anyone; but I think it will interest most of you. There will, incidentally, be more about Wally then; but I feel sure none of you will mind that.

As might be guessed from his experiences as a runaway, Wally is a boxer of no mean order. In fact, he is quite a little champion for his age. It was no very difficult task for him to beat Racke, in spite of the Shell fellow's big superiority in height, weight, and reach. At cricket and footer Wally is also really good. He might fill a place at any time in the Junior Eleven at either game without any danger of letting the side down. He is unquestionably the best runner in the Third. In that connection one recalls more than one paper-chase, with reckless tearing-up of papers alleged to be valuable by their owners, for scent. And there is one paper-chase in particular which it is not easy to forget—that one in which Wally and Frank, as hares, went through the field with the bull in it—though Frank protested against the folly of that—and Reggie Manners, alone of the pack, followed.

Some of Wally's troubles with Mr. Selby have already been told of in dealing with that genial personage; and there would be little profit in recounting others. It must be admitted that Wally does not show up at his best in some of his encounters with the tyrant of the Third. But the odds are very heavily against him every time. Mr. Selby has the whip-hand, and it is hardly to be wondered at if Wally is rebellious and even sulky at times. I don't think he ever sulks with anyone else.

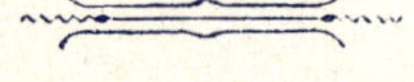

The Editor's Chat.

For Next Wednesday:

"THE OWL'S NEST!"

By Martin Clifford.

This week we have Bunter in search of a study. He does not find one—no one will take him in, though the whimsical Cardew may be said to have taken him in very completely in another sense.

In the next story Bunter is still searching. He does not find anyone willing to share a study with him; but—— Well, I must not tell too much. But the Owl does find a nest, of rather a strange sort; and out of that complications arise.

The Third Form comes into this yarn, and you will be amused by the feud between Billy Bunter and Wally & Co., I know.

CARDEW.

The mention of Cardew reminds me that I have had quite a number of letters of late about that enterprising and erratic youth. "Cardew's Pig" seems to have pleased many readers; and I have been asked for more stories in which Ralph Reckness figures prominently. Here and there someone—generally a very young reader—says that he cannot bear Cardew; but, on the other hand, with a large number he seems to have become almost first favourite.

Perhaps it is not surprising that the youngsters don't like him so well as the older readers. For essentially Cardew is older in his manner and his thoughts than most of the Fourth, just as Talbot is older than most of the Shell. And that makes him difficult for youngsters to understand. But I think even they cannot fail to appreciate the arm chair trick played on Bunter.

Yes, we shall be seeing quite a lot of Cardew in the near future, both in the long stories and in the short ones. It might be possible to get some yarns of his early days at Wodehouse. You can imagine, perhaps, what sort of a fag Cardew would have been!

TELL YOUR FRIENDS:

How do you like these Bunter stories? To me they seem as funny as anything I have ever read. I think they can hardly fail to strike you in much the same way.

Tell your chums about them! Don't keep a good thing to yourself—that's too Bunterish, you know.

Our circle of readers is growing every week; but we have room for lots more yet, as many more as you can gather in for us, in fact.

Most fellows have some sense of humour; and no one with a sense of humour could fail to appreciate the stories that Mr. Clifford is giving us just now.

I have often before urged upon my readers the fact that the best turn they can do me is to help in shoving up the circulation; and the response has always been good. But I hope that it will be better than ever this time.

NOTICES.

Correspondence Wanted.

F. Atkin, 160, Russell Street, Moss Side, Manchester—with readers anywhere, 15-17; friendly style.

Miss Evelyn M. Jones, 161, The Vale, Acton, W. 3—with readers anywhere, 14-16.

F. Burnage, 483, Chester Road, Old Trafford, Manchester, wants members for stamp club.

N. Outwin, Fernleigh, Reedness, Yorks, wants readers for free pass-round magazine.

Norman Griffiths, 10, Wote Street, Basingstoke, Hants, wants readers and contributors for the "Amateur World," 2d.

R. G. McCulloch, care of W. A. Cooper, 5, Barnflat Street, Rutherglen, near Glasgow—with readers interested in chemistry.

L. S. Patterson, 103, Parliament Street, Stockton-on-Tees, wants to hear of contributors to amateur magazines.

F. Bottomley, 46, Downhills Park Road, Philip Lane, Tottenham, N 13, wants contributor, about 12, for short stories for amateur magazine. Copy, 1½d.

Miss P. Lockey, 109A, Tottenham Road, Islington, London, N. 1—with girl readers in Colonies or America interested in stamps, books, etc.—aged 13-16.

H. Swindells, 10, Vernon Street, Buxton Road, Macclesfield, offers advice to readers on general subjects. Stamped envelope.

D. E. Strafford, Brampton House, 120, Weaste Lane, Pendleton—with readers anywhere.

R. Dunford, 406, Bowling Old Lane, Bradford—with readers, in their own languages, in France, Switzerland, Spain, South America and United States.

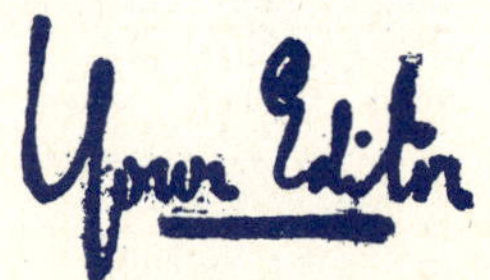

N

The GEM 1½d

No. 576. Vol. 13. February 22nd, 1919.

THE TWO BUNTERS.

WHICH IS WHICH?

22-2-19

A MAGNIFICENT NEW, LONG, COMPLETE SCHOOL STORY OF TOM MERRY & CO. AT ST JIM'S.

THE TWO BUNTERS.

By Martin Clifford.

CHAPTER 1.
A Shock for Bunter.

"HALT!"

Mr. Blagg, the Rylcombe postman, halted, with a grin, as the Terrible Three lined up a his path near the gates of St. Jim's.

"What is there for me?" inquired Tom Merry.

"Nothin', sir!"

"And me?" asked Lowther.

"Same as for Master Merry!" answered Mr. Blagg.

"And me?" demanded Manners. "Now, be careful, Blagg. I'm expecting a tip from my pater for some new films. Don't say he's forgotten it!"

Mr. Blagg's grin widened.

"I expect he have, Master Manners. Leastways, there isn't any letter for you."

"Alas!" said the Terrible Three tragically.

"I say, you fellows——"

Bunter of the Fourth rolled up.

"I say, is that the postman? I'm expecting a postal-order this afternoon——"

"The same one you've been expecting ever since you came to St. Jim's?" queried Monty Lowther, in a tone of gentle sarcasm.

"Oh, really, Lowther——"

"Roll out Bunter's remittances, Blagg," said Tom Merry. "We'll borrow a few hundred quids of Bunter, you fellows."

"Bunter!" repeated Mr. Blagg. "Yes, sir, there's a letter for Master Bunter."

Billy Bunter's fat face brightened.

Whether Bunter really expected a postal-order or not nobody at St. Jim's quite knew; but he certainly seemed to live in hopes of a remittance dropping in from somewhere.

He held out a fat hand.

"Hand it over!" he said. "I expect it's my postal-order, you fellows. It's been rather delayed."

"It has, and no mistake!" agreed Tom Merry.

Mr. Blagg obligingly went through his sack. Bunter watched him eagerly through his big glasses. The Terrible Three looked on, rather amused. They had heard a great deal about Bunter's postal-order since W. G. B. had honoured St. Jim's with his presence.

The letter was produced and handed over, and Mr. Blagg went on his way, sack on shoulder.

Bunter blinked at the letter.

It was addressed W. G. Bunter, at the school, in a firm, clear hand that Billy Bunter had never seen before.

The fat junior seemed to hesitate about opening it.

"Well, pile in!" said Monty Lowther. "Let us feast our eyes upon the wealth, Bunter, and it will console us for being stony."

"I—I suppose I can open it!" said Bunter hesitatingly.

"Eh? It's yours, isn't it?"

"Ye-es, of course, it—it's mine!"

"It's addressed to W. G. Bunter," said Tom Merry, glancing at the envelope. "Why shouldn't you open it?"

"Yes, why not?" agreed Bunter. "If there's a remittance in this letter it's mine, ain't it?"

"I suppose so," said Tom, in surprise.

"Yes, of course! It was understood ——" Bunter paused abruptly.

"What was understood?"

"Oh, nothing!"

Billy Bunter opened the letter at last by the simple process of jamming a fat thumb into the envelope.

The Terrible Three looked at him, perplexed.

Why Bunter should hesitate to open a letter addressed to himself, and should appear doubtful as to whether a remittance in it was his, was a mystery to the Shell fellows.

But there were many things about Bunter that perplexed Tom Merry & Co. His manners and customs were so unlike those of the Wally Bunter they had met, and were so like those of the Billy Bunter they had seen at Greyfriars!

Wally Bunter, they knew, was exactly like Billy to look at; but they had not known that the resemblance went further.

Naturally, they had no idea that the fat junior in the Fourth was not Wally Bunter at all, and that Wally's place at St. Jim's had been taken by Billy.

That was not likely to occur to them; though, if their acquaintance with the Bunters had been closer, they would probably have suspected something.

Billy Bunter's brief hesitation was over, and he opened the letter and unfolded it If there was a remittance for W. G. Bunter, it was certainly for Walter Gilbert Bunter, not for William George. But, after all, Billy was W. G. Bunter, too; and as he had taken his cousin's place at St. Jim's he was entitled to take his remittances, too. At all events, he decided that he was.

But there was no remittance in the letter. There was a closely-written page, and Bunter blinked at it discontentedly. But suddenly his blink became fixed and his jaw dropped.

His little round eyes almost bulged through his glasses as he stared at the letter.

"Oh dear!" he gasped, in utter dismay.

Tom Merry & Co. were turning away; but they turned back at that dismayed exclamation.

"Anything wrong, kid?" asked Tom good-naturedly.

"Oh dear!"

"Hasn't the postal-order come?" asked Monty Lowther sadly.

"Oh, crumbs!"

"Dry up, Monty! It looks like bad news," said Tom. He tapped Bunter kindly on the shoulder. "What's wrong, kid?"

"He's coming!" gasped Bunter.

"Who's coming? Your cousin Billy from Greyfriars?" asked Lowther, as if that would fully account for dismay at the prospect.

Bunter grinned faintly.

"Nunno! Oh dear! Why can't he keep away! What does he want to see Wally—I mean, why can't he mind his own business? I say, you fellows, what on earth is a fellow to do?" groaned Bunter.

"Well, what's the trouble?" asked Tom Merry. "If there's anything one can do, you've only got to say so."

"Oh dear! The silly old ass, why can't he keep away?" gasped Bunter. "No need for him to come here that I know of. Oh dear!"

"But what the deuce——"

Bunter recovered himself.

"I say, you fellows, don't you ask questions," he said, blinking at the Terrible Three. "I'm not going to tell you anything."

"What?" roared Tom Merry.

"You shouldn't be inquisitive, you you know," said Bunter, wagging his head at the incensed chums of the Shell. "This may be a letter from Mr. Penman, at Canterbury, and it may not. I'm not going to tell you anything about it."

"You fat, sneaking slug!" exclaimed Monty Lowther. "I—I'll——"

Tom Merry, with knitted brow, took Bunter by the collar.

"Yow-ow! Leggo! Wharrer at?"

"You fat rotter!" said Tom, in measured tones. "I asked you what was the matter because you were howling as if you were hurt. Do you think I care twopence about your affairs, you silly owl? Sit down!"

"Yoooop!"

Billy Bunter sat down—hard!

The Terrible Three walked away, leaving Bunter gasping on the hard road.

"Yah! Beast!" howled Bunter.

The chums of the Shell went in at the gates, unheeding. They were fed up with Bunter of the Fourth. Billy Bunter scrambled breathlessly to his feet, and shook a fat fist after them. Then he blinked again at the letter.

"Oh dear! What's a fellow to do? Mr. Penman—that's the mercantile beast who sent Wally to school—oh dear!—coming here to see how Wally's getting on—oh, crumbs!—and Wally's at Greyfriars, and I'm here—and he'll spot me at once. He's knows Wally better than these silly asses do. Oh, crikey!"

Billy Bunter rolled in at the gates in a state of dismay. The change of places with his cousin Wally had seemed to him a splendid idea at the time, and certainly it had extracted him from the peck of troubles he had accumulated at his old school.

But now——

It was all very well to face St. Jim's, where Wally was almost a stranger, in his cousin's name! But to face a man who knew Wally well, and had known him well for years—Billy Bunter's nerve was not quite equal to that!

But what was to be done?

CHAPTER 2.

The Troubles of an Impostor.

"BAI Jove! You look wathah wowwied, Buntah!"

Arthur Augustus D'Arcy of the Fourth paused as he came upon Bunter in the window recess in the Fourth Form passage.

The Owl of Greyfriars was standing there with a letter crumpled in his hand, and a lugubrious expression on his fat face.

He blinked dismally at D'Arcy over his big spectacles.

"Oh dear!" he said.

"Are you in twouble, deah boy?"

"Oh! Ow! Yes."

"I am weally sowwy to heah it, Buntah!"

Arthur Augustus was sympathetic. He had liked Wally Bunter once, and though he had soon been fed up with Wally's substitute he had not quite forgotten his former friendly feelings.

"Pewwaps I can help you?" he suggested. "If you would like me to advise you, Buntah——"

"Oh dear!"

"You can wely on me as a fellow of tact and judgment," said Arthur Augustus encouragingly.

Grunt!

"Are you coming in to tea, Gussy?" bawled Jack Blake from Study No. 6. "If you're not pretty quick there won't be any sosses for you!"

"Comin', deah boys!"

"Buck up, then!" called out Digby.

"I am wathah engaged at the pwesent moment, Dig."

Herries' voice came next.

"Do you mind if I give your whack in the sosses to Towser, D'Arcy?"

"Bai Jove! I object vewy stwongly, Hewwies. You can give your own sosses to Towsah if you like."

"Br-r-r-r!" was Herries' rejoinder to that.

Arthur Augustus D'Arcy made a step towards the study. But he stopped again, impelled by his kind heart, and turned towards Bunter.

"I twust it is nothin' sewious, deah boy?" he said.

"Yes, it is," grunted Bunter.

"If I can help you, Buntah, I am entiahly at your service."

"You can't prevent the old josser coming here, I suppose?" growled Bunter peevishly.

"Eh? Whom?"

"Never mind!"

"Are you expectin' a disagweeable visitah, deah boy?"

"Oh, no, nothing of the sort—not at all! In fact, there's nothing the matter —— I—I'm not worrying about anything," said Bunter.

Arthur Augustus blinked at him.

"Bai Jove!" was all he could say.

"The fact is, I'm as happy as—as a king!" said Bunter.

"That's all wight, then!" said Arthur Augustus, puzzled.

And he went on to his study in a mood of some perplexity. Bunter blinked after him darkly. He felt that his display of trouble was not judicious, and certainly if the cause of his trouble had become known it would have put a sudden end to his imposture at St. Jim's. But it was difficult for him to conceal the worry on his mind, and his looks did not bear out his statement that he was as happy as a king.

He rolled dismally away with so exceedingly troubled a fat visage that Julian of the Fourth stopped him as he came along.

"What's up?" he asked.

"Nothing."

"Oh, all right! Not catching 'flu?"

"Of course not, you ass!"

Bunter was rolling on, but he paused, and spoke to Dick Julian again.

"I say, Julian——"

"Go it!" said the junior good-humouredly.

"I—I say, you being a Sheeny, you know——"

"What?"

"I—I mean a Jew, you know, you must be a rather sharp chap," said Bunter. "All Jews are thundering sharp. I—I wonder whether you could give me a bit of advice?"

Dick Julian looked at him hard. Bunter's way of asking a favour was peculiarly his own, but Julian was a good-humoured fellow, and he smiled.

"Go ahead!" he said. "I'll try. I don't know about being thundering sharp, but I've got my wits about me. Pile in!"

"I can't tell you the circumstances of——"

"That makes it rather hard to advise, doesn't it?" asked Julian, with a stare.

"Well, I might put a case," said Bunter thoughtfully. "Suppose a chap——"

"Yes?"

"A—a—a chap, you know——"

"Yes, I've got that!" assented Julian. "A chap——"

"Suppose a chap had done a certain thing to oblige another chap. It might be his cousin, or it might not——" said Bunter cautiously.

"Ye-e-es?"

"And suppose they were keeping it dark——"

"Eh?"

"And suppose a man—it might be a business man from, say, Canterbury. It might be, and again it might not be. But suppose it was."

"Yes?" said the amazed Julian.

"Well, suppose he was coming to see a chap——"

"Which chap?"

"Oh, a—a chap, you know," said Bunter. "Suppose he was coming to see a chap, and a chap didn't want it to come out about having changed places——"

"Whatted?"

"I—I don't mean that!" gasped Bunter hastily. "Not changed places. Certainly not that. Nothing of the kind. I wonder what made me say that? I—I mean that the chap hadn't done anything of the sort. Is that clear?"

"Clear as mud!" said the perplexed Julian. "I think you'll have to make it a bit clearer. It sounds like a set of conundrums so far."

"You're a bit dense, Julian. I thought all Jews were jolly keen," said Bunter. "You don't seem to comprehend. Suppose, as I said, a chap—that is to say, suppose a man—say, a man at Canterbury——"

"Ye-e-es?"

"Suppose he was coming, then, and it might all come out. What would you do in that chap's place?"

Dick Julian gazed at the fat junior in wonder.

"Are you wandering in your mind?" he asked.

"Eh?"

"If not, what's the matter with you?"

"You silly ass! Haven't I made it clear?" demanded Bunter peevishly.

"Ha, ha! You'll have to make it clearer if you want my advice. I don't think Jew or Gentile could make head or tail of it so far," said Dick Julian, laughing.

"I'm not going to tell you my private affairs, Julian. Don't be inquisitive!"

"What?" yelled Julian.

"That's just like you Sheenies——"

"My—my—my hat!"

"I must say—— Yooooop!" roared Bunter, as Julian took him by the neck and proceeded to bump his head on the wall. "Leggo! Wharrer you at? You beast! Yarooooh!"

"There!" gasped Julian. "You fat worm, you can wriggle off now, and if you speak to me again I—I—I'll burst you!"

And Julian walked away in high dudgeon.

"Yow-ow-ow! Beast!" howled Bunter.

He rubbed his head, and rolled on dismally to Study No. 2, which he shared —or was supposed to share—with Mellish and Trimble. But Mellish and Trimble were fed up with Bunter, and they had given him the order of the boot from that study. Ever since then Bunter had been in search of a study, but nobody in the Fourth had shown the slightest desire to take him in.

The Owl of Greyfriars blinked in at No. 2.

"I say, you fellows——"

There were toast and toasted cheese on the tea-table, and Mellish and Baggy Trimble were sitting down to it. They jumped up as if moved by the same spring as Bunter looked in.

They did not waste any time in words. Mellish seized the poker, and Baggy Trimble the tongs.

Bunter did not wait.

Before they could reach the door he reached the staircase, and he went down the steps at great speed.

"Oh dear!" gasped Bunter, as he rolled out into the quadrangle. "I—I must have some tea. I've had nothing but tea in Hall and some sandwiches. I—I wish I was back at Greyfriars! Oh dear!"

He rolled away dismally to Dame Taggles' little shop. But he was in his usual state of impecuniosity, and the prospect of inducing Dame Taggles to extend tick to him was remote. The good dame had learned to know her Bunter in this time. There was already a considerable account due; and when Mrs. Taggles saw Bunter it was her habit to make remarks about that account—remarks which Bunter considered ill-timed and cross-grained.

Figgins & Co. of the New House were coming out of the tuckshop. They had plainly been shopping for tea in the study. Bunter joined them, with an ingratiating grin on his fat face.

"I say, you fellows——"

"Don't!" said Kerr.

"You buzz off!" said Fatty Wynn darkly. "You keep off the grass, you fat bounder!"

"But, I say, you fellows, I—I was thinking of coming to tea with you, for —for the sake of old times——"

"Do!" said Figgins genially. "Oh, do! We'll give you the frog's-march along the passage if we find you in the New House. Honour bright! Do come!"

Figgins & Co. walked on, but the Owl of Greyfriars did not follow them. He shook a fat fist after them instead.

CHAPTER 3.
The Only Way.

"I SAY, you fellows——"

The Terrible Three were at tea, and Bunter rolled into No. 10 in the Shell without waiting for the formality of an invitation.

Grim looks greeted him.

"Outside!" said Tom Merry curtly.

"I say, I'm in trouble!" urged Bunter. "As an old pal, Tom, old fellow, you——"

"If you call me 'Tom, old fellow,' I'll scalp you!" exclaimed the captain of the Shell.

"Oh, really, you know——"

"Keep your troubles to yourself, and be blowed!" said Monty Lowther. "And get out of this study!"

"I haven't had my tea yet—only tea in Hall, so far," said Bunter pathetically. "And—and just at a time, too, when I've got a fearful worry on my mind. I should think you might ask a chap to tea when he's down on his luck."

Tom Merry looked at him more attentively.

There certainly were signs of worry in Bunter's fat face. The impending visit of Mr. Penman, on the morrow, was worrying him considerably. How to deal with that threatened visit he did not know, though the problem had to be postponed while the more urgent matter of tea was dealt with.

Tom glanced at his chums after that survey of the Owl's fat face.

"Oh, just as you like!" grunted Manners, understanding his look. "You're a soft noodle, Tommy!"

"Thanks!" said Tom, laughing. "You can sit down, Bunter, if you like."

"Oh, do!" growled Lowther.

It was not a flattering invitation; but Bunter did not stand upon ceremony. He plumped down into a chair, his fat face brightening considerably.

"I say, you fellows, you've got cake?" he said. "And eggs—are these eggs new-laid?"

"So we heard. We didn't get a pedigree with them, though!"

"I'm rather fond of new-laid eggs. If I take four, can you chaps manage?"

"Oh, my hat!"

"Don't mind us!" said Lowther sardonically. There were only four eggs on the table.

"Right you are! I won't!" agreed Bunter. "I admit I'm rather hungry. I say, you fellows, these eggs are really good."

"Sorry there only four!" hissed Manners.

"Don't mench, old fellow! Of course, if you cared to cut down to the tuckshop and get some more I shouldn't object. In fact, I'd cook them. I admit I could do with a couple more."

Manners was silent; he really did not know what to say in reply to that. He contented himself with munching bread-and-butter and sardines.

Bunter made rapid work with the tea, and in the race for the cake he beat the Terrible Three hands down.

"I think we'll get out," remarked Tom Merry, the moment tea was over, as a hint to the guest to travel farther.

But hints were quite lost on William George Bunter of Greyfriars.

"I say, you fellows," he began, blinking amiably at the chums of the Shell, "I'm in rather a scrape."

"Keep in it!" said Lowther politely.

"I'm sure you'll help me out, Tom Merry, as an old pal——"

"Br-r-r-r-r!"

"You could if you wanted to, you know——"

"If it's cash," said Tom Merry bluntly, there's nothing doing!"

"'Tain't that! In fact, I expect to be in funds shortly!" said Bunter, with dignity. "I'm expecting a postal-order, in fact! I'm in a scrape——"

"Well?" grunted Tom impatiently.

"A man's coming to see me to-morrow afternoon——"

"Well?"

"It may be a man from Canterbury, or it may not," said Bunter cautiously.

"Well, a man from Canterbury's coming to see you!" exclaimed Tom. "I don't see any scrape in that!"

"It might be Mr. Penman, and it might not. Suppose it was Mr. Penman?"

"Who on earth's Mr. Penman?" grunted Manners.

"The man who—who I mean——"

"I remember the name," said Tom. "You were employed in an office at Canterbury, some time ago, and Mr. Penman was the head of the firm. Isn't that it?"

"Ye-e-es, exactly!"

"And he sent you to school," said Tom. "I know! Well, it's natural for him to come and see how you're getting on here, especially as he's an old St. Jim's man himself, so I hear. What are you grumbling about?"

"I—I don't want to see him!"

"Don't, then!"

"B-b-but I must if he comes! I—I want to dodge him!"

"What on earth for?" growled the captain of the Shell.

Bunter blinked at him.

"Now you're asking inquisitive questions——" he began.

"You fat idiot!" roared Tom, in great wrath. "I suppose you're too fatheaded to know what a silly ass you are; but if you don't travel out of this study you'll get chucked out! Have you sense enough to understand that?"

"Oh, really, Merry——"

"There's the door!"

"But I haven't finished yet, old chap!" said Bunter cheerfully. "What are you getting waxy about?"

Tom Merry laughed; he could not help it. Apparently Bunter did not realise that there was anything offensive in his remarks.

"I want to dodge the man," said Bunter, continuing; "and you can help me, Tom Merry. That's what I want you to do."

"Oh, go and eat coke!"

"You see, there's a football match played to-morrow, isn't there?" said Bunter.

"Yes; Abbotsford," said Tom. "They're coming over here to-morrow afternoon. What about the match?"

"I want you to play me."

"Eh?"

"I played in a House match when I came, you know——"

"And kicked the ball through your own goal!" roared Lowther.

"That—that was an accident——"

"There's not going to be any accidents about in our match to-morrow," said Tom Merry, laughing. "Nothing doing, Bunter! You took us in about footer, and it turns out that you can't play for toffee. The best thing you can do is to get some practice with the Third. D'Arcy minor, and Manners minor, and young Levison could teach you ten times as much as you know."

"Oh, really, Merry——"

Tom rose to his feet.

"Hold on a minute, Tom Merry! I want you to play me in the football match for a special reason. Not about football. Blow football! But, you see, if I'm playing in the match I shall be able to keep out of old Penman's way!"

"And you think I should play a hopeless dud in the Abbotsford match for a reason like that?" ejaculated Tom Merry, hardly able to believe his ears.

"Yes. You see——"

"Of all the fat idiots——" said Manners.

"Oh, really, Manners——"

"Well," said Tom Merry, "I'm not playing you, Bunter, for that reason or any other. And in any case, I wouldn't help you dodge Mr. Penman, and I don't see why you should want to. It seems to me you're an ungrateful bounder to speak like that about an old chap who's doing so much you for. And now, dear man, we're fed up with your fascinating society, since you force me to speak plain English. Travel!"

"I—I say, you fellows——"

"Buzz off!" said Lowther.

"Of course, if Tom Merry refuses to do the decent thing, I can't make him," said Bunter with dignity. "I may mention that I despise him——"

"Do you want my boot?"

"Nunno! I—I say, you fellows, if you won't help a chap in a scrape, you might at least lend me——"

"Nothing to lend, ass! Buzz off!"

"Lend me a——"

"We know all about the postal-order," said Lowther. "Wait till it comes, old chap! That will be a lesson in patience. You will be an old, old man by that time, and——"

"Lend me——"

"Oh, my hat! Stony!" shrieked Tom Merry.

"A stamp!" yelled Bunter.

"What?"

"A stamp!" snorted the Owl of Greyfriars. "I've got to write to my cousin. It's the only way now."

Tom Merry burst into a laugh.

"Well, I can give you a stamp," he said, opening his desk. "I've got one left, and you're welcome to it. "Here you are!"

"I said lend!" answered Bunter firmly.

"Lend or give, it doesn't matter!"

"It does matter!" said Bunter calmly. "I know some fellows are not so particular in money matters as I am. But I want it distinctly understood in this study that I certainly could not accept even so small as sum as three-ha'pence as a gift. Unless this is understood to be a loan, I——"

"Oh, my hat! A loan, if you like! Any old thing! And now, for goodness' sake, give us a rest!"

"Very well! If it's understood to be a loan I can accept it. Not otherwise. There's one other point——"

"There isn't! Buzz off!"

"There is! Will you have this three-ha'pence back out of my postal-order when it comes——"

"Eh?"

"Or could you make it convenient to wait till I get a cheque for a rather large sum that I'm expecting from a titled relation of mine?"

Bunter blinked at the Terrible Three with owlish seriousness as he asked that important question.

They stared at him for a moment. Then, with one accord, they fell on Bunter, their pent-up feelings finding expression at last.

"Yoop! Yowp! Yaroooh!" roared Bunter. And he fled frantically out of Study No. 10; and the question of the date of repayment of the three-halfpence remained unsettled—for ever!

CHAPTER 4.
All Clear!

THE next day Billy Bunter might have been seen, as a novelist would remark, looking a great deal more cheerful.

In fact, he seemed quite his old, self-satisfied self.

Whatever worry had been weighing upon his mind was apparently removed, and he was no longer dreading the visit of Mr. Penman, the mercantile gentleman from Canterbury.

The simple process of writing to his cousin at Greyfriars apparently had done the trick.

It was one of Billy Bunter's charming customs to shift his troubles off his own fat shoulders on to any shoulders that were handy; and, having done so, he felt at ease with himself and the world.

During morning lessons, while Mr. Lathom was attending to Levison's construe, Bunter whispered to Arthur Augustus D'Arcy.

"Gussy, old fellow——"

"Pway don't talk in class, Buntah! Mr. Lathom will be watty!"

"Blow Lathom!"

"That is a vewy diswespectful way of speakin' of a Form-mastah, Buntah!" said D'Arcy severely.

"You know all about the trains to Greyfriars," said Bunter, unheeding. "You've been over with the football eleven."

"Yaas!"

"Suppose my cousin was coming from Greyfriars to see me this afternoon," said Bunter. "Mind, I don't say he is. He might be. If he was, how long would it take him to get here?"

"That depends on the twain, Buntah."

"I know it does, fathead!"

"I have a stwong objection to bein' called a fathead, Buntah!"

"Suppose Wally——"

"Eh?"

"I mean, suppose Billy——"

"I do not quite follow you, Buntah!"

"Suppose my cousin cut dinner and got an express, he could get here pretty early in the afternoon, couldn't he?"

"Yaas, quite easily."

"Well, I've told him not to worry about dinner, under the circs," said Bunter thoughtfully.

"Bai Jove! Fwom what I wemembah of Billy Buntah, it is not much use tellin' him not to wowwy about dinnah!" smiled Arthur Augustus.

"If you mean that I'm greedy, D'Arcy, I'll——"

"I was speakin' of your cousin Billy."

"Oh! Ah! Yes! Of course! My mistake! Well, I suppose he'll have sense enough to cut dinner and catch an early express train, won't he? The trains are better since the war."

Mr. Lathom blinked round.

"Dear me! I am sure someone in the class is whispering!" he said. "Pray, who is whispering?"

Silence.

"You may proceed, Levison!"

Ernest Levison proceeded. Bunter remained silent, apparently satisfied on the subject of trains. His fat face was quite contented, at all events.

Tom Merry glanced at him with a smile when the juniors came in to dinner in the School House. He wondered whether Bunter was going to repeat his request to be played in the Abbotsford match that afternoon, as a means of dodging Mr. Penman of Canterbury.

But Bunter did not approach the subject when he saw the captain of the Shell. Tom tapped him on the shoulder when they came out of the dining-room.

"All serene now?" he asked.

"Eh? Oh, yes! What do you mean?"

"You were deep in trouble yesterday," said Tom.

"Oh, that's all right! By the way, though, Merry, I was going to make a suggestion——"

"Ha, ha! Do you want to captain the St. Jim's team this afternoon?"

"Under the circumstances, Merry, I decline to play for St. Jim's at all! On second thoughts, your junior play here is hardly up to my weight!"

"Your weight?" said Tom, with an amused glance at Bunter's ample figure. "Well, it wouldn't be easy to come up to your weight, would it?"

"I mean, my form, you ass!"

"My dear chap, your form is a thing of beauty and a joy for ever!"

"My form as a footballer, I mean! Not my figure, you chump! Though, if you come to that, there's precious few fellows in St. Jim's have a figure like mine!" said Bunter, with a sniff.

"Precious few!" agreed Tom. "Only Trimble and Fatty Wynn—and you beat them hollow."

"Oh, really, Merry——"

"Coming, Monty?"

"Hold on a minute! I was going to make a suggestion——"

"Buck up, then!"

"I'm expecting a postal-order——"

"What?"

"I was going to suggest that if you cared to hand me the money, I would—I wish you wouldn't walk away while I'm speaking, Merry!" howled Bunter.

But Tom Merry did so, in spite of Bunter's wish.

Billy Bunter grunted and rolled away. His celebrated postal-order was getting as well known at St. Jim's as it had been at Greyfriars. It really seemed doubtful whether Bunter would ever be able to raise any more loans on that postal-order.

The fat junior rolled out of gates at last, after an ineffectual attempt to raise the wind from Julian and Cardew and Roylance, and several other fellows in the Fourth. He ambled away down the lane to Rylcombe, and rolled in at the station there.

There he made inquiries from old Trumble, the porter, concerning trains from the east. He ensconced himself on the platform at last, to wait. The express trains stopped at Wayland Junction, and a local train brought passengers on to Rylcombe.

And Bunter's fat face brightened up at last when the local train came in and he spotted a fat face, remarkably like his own, at a window in it.

The train stopped, and Wally Bunter jumped out.

He glanced up and down the platform, and came quickly towards the Owl.

Old Trumble, who was wheeling a trolley along, stopped and stared at them in surprise.

"My heye!" he murmured.

The two fat juniors were so alike that they could scarcely have failed to attract a second glance anywhere.

Both were in Etons—Wally carrying a coat on his arm—and both wore glasses, though Wally wore his low on his nose so that he could see over them. He did not need glasses, but he had to adopt them

Bunter Hits Out.
(See Chapter 6.)

in order to keep up appearances while playing the part of Billy Bunter at Greyfriars School.

Seen closely, however, a difference between the two juniors could be observed; not in form or feature, but in health and fitness. Wally Bunter, fat as he was, was as fit as a fiddle, and he had a keenness in his eyes and a springiness in his step that were noticeably lacking in William George.

"Oh, here you are!" said Wally, not very amiably.

"And here you are!" said Billy.

"What do you mean by——"

"Let's get out of this," said Bunter hastily. "If we're seen together it will give the whole game away. That old porter beast is staring at us now!"

"You ought to have met me at Wayland, then. It wasn't safe for me to come and see you——"

"If you think I'm going to walk three miles, Wally——"

"Br-r-r-r!" grunted Wally.

"Come on, fathead!" said Billy Bunter, and he led the way hurriedly out of the station. The new-comer followed him, with an expression on his fat face that was far from amiable. It was pretty clear that Wally Bunter was not pleased by this sudden summons to St. Jim's.

CHAPTER 5.
The Two Bunters.

"AND now——" said Wally at last.

The cousins had separated outside the station, and Wally had followed Billy Bunter at a distance. Certainly any St. Jim's fellow who had seen them together would have been struck at once by their resemblance, and the imposture would have been in danger. Bunter had led the way into the wood, and he stopped there for Wally to come up.

"And now——" grinned Bunter, as his cousin paused.

"What does this mean?" growled Wally. "It was understood that we changed places, wasn't it? You asked me, and I wasn't half willing. Now you're running the risk of dishing the whole game by calling me here like this. I had to cut dinner at Greyfriars, and I've had nothing but some sandwiches in the train," added Wally, in a tone of deep grievance.

"Never mind that——"

"But I do mind that!" snapped Wally.

"It couldn't be helped, old chap. Old Penman's coming this afternoon at half-past three. Here's his letter."

Wally glanced at the letter.

"Well, I knew Mr. Penman would drop in sooner or later to see me at St. Jim's," he said. "You've taken my place there, and bamboozled everybody. Why couldn't you keep it up with Mr. Penman?"

"No jolly fear!" said Billy Bunter promptly. "Why, I don't even know the man by sight. And he knows you like a book. He would be bound to spot me."

"I—I suppose he might. But—but what's to be done, then? Do you want to change back?" Wally frowned. "It was agreed that you took my name at St. Jim's, and I took yours at Greyfriars, for a whole term. I didn't want to, and you know it—you talked me into it. And I know the reason now. You'd got into trouble with a dashed bookmaker, and you wanted to leave it all for me."

"Oh, really, Wally——"

"And I had no end of trouble with the man, too; and now it's blown over, and I'm getting on all right, you want to change back!" growled Wally. "Do you call that playing the game?"

"You're getting on with the fellows at Greyfriars?" asked Bunter curiously.

"First-rate, now."

"And they believe you're me?"

"Of course they do, fathead! I couldn't stay there if they didn't, could I?" grunted Wally. "And I suppose the St. Jim's fellows believe you're me?"

Bunter chuckled.

"Yes; it's working like a charm. I'm no end popular in the school——"

"Are you?" asked Wally, in surprise.

"Yes, I am!" roared William George.

"Well, I've found that you weren't so jolly popular at Greyfriars!" growled Wally. "You left a jolly juicy reputation behind you, and I came in for the benefit of it."

"Oh, really, Wally——"

"Half the fellows have been making out that I owe them money——"

"He, he, he!"

"It's all very well to cackle," said the incensed Wally. "But if I'd known how matters stood I jolly well wouldn't have agreed to your fat-headed scheme, I can tell you. I had a dog's life, at first—though the fellows have come round now. They think you're greatly improved."

And Wally groaned.

Bunter snorted.

"Oh, don't talk rot, Wally! They're a lot of asses to take you for me—a chap like you! Blessed if I can see it myself! You're not well-bred like me, for one thing——"

"Not like you, certainly!" said Wally Bunter drily. "And not a thumping liar like you, Billy! That's what surprises the fellows most of all."

"Look here——"

"Let's get to business. If you want to change back, I think you're being a toad—as you usually are. I'm getting on first-rate at Greyfriars now, and you ought to stick to the bargain."

"I don't want to change back—not yet, anyway. But I can't see old Penman this afternoon, and that's flat. You've got to do that."

"But—but——"

"It's easy enough," said Bunter. "You go to St. Jim's now, as me—or, rather, as yourself. He, he, he! The fellows don't know us one from another—unless they see us together, anyway. And the chaps who know you best—Tom Merry and that lot—will be playing footer."

"Footer!" said Wally, his face brightening. "I may get a game, then! I played for them when they came over to——"

"Rot! Tom Merry's refused me a place in the team, so he's hardly likely to play you—even if he knew it was you," sniffed Bunter.

Wally Bunter grinned.

"Well, never mind that," he said. "I suppose I can work it. I can meet Mr. Penman at the school. You'll have to keep out of sight."

"I'm going over to Abbotsford to keep out of the way—there's a matinee at the theatre there," said Bunter. "All I want you to do is to lend me some money."

"You have my allowance from Mr. Penman."

"Well, you have mine from my pater."

"A jolly small one, too—only half as much!"

"If you're going to be mean about money, Wally——"

Grunt from Wally.

"I made the arrangement wholly for your sake, as you know," said Bunter warmly. "You were so keen on going to Greyfriars instead of St. Jim's——"

"And you were keen on dodging out of the heap of scrapes you'd got into at Greyfriars——"

"Never mind that! I can do it on half-a-quid, if you can manage it."

"I can manage five bob."

"I call that mean!"

"You can call it what you like, Billy; and you can take it or leave it."

"Oh, I'll take it!" said Bunter, with a sniff. "I'm stony, owing to being disappointed about a postal-order. I may as well get off now."

"Hold on a minute!" exclaimed Wally. "You've got to give me some tips about St. Jim's. I'm a stranger there. You have a study, I suppose?"

"Yes; No. 2 in the Fourth."

"Any study-mates?"

"Yes; Mellish and Trimble."

"Friendly with them?"

"I despise them too much to be friendly with them!" said Bunter disdainfully. "Mellish is untruthful——"

"You wouldn't be able to stand that, of course!" said Wally, with deep sarcasm. "And what's the matter with Trimble?"

"He's fat and greedy."

"Ha, ha, ha!" roared Wally.

"Blessed if I can see anything to cackle at! You'd better keep clear of the study, Wally. Those two cads have turned me out, and they pitch into me if I go into my own study."

"My hat! What do you stand it for?"

"I disdain to soil my hands upon the cads!" said Bunter loftily.

"You don't disdain to soil them in other ways, though," remarked Wally, with a glance at his cousin's fat paws. "They could do with a wash."

"You cheeky rotter!" howled Bunter. "Look here, I'm not accustomed to being talked to like this by a poor relation——"

"Bow-wow! If you're kept out of your study, why don't you ask a prefect to interfere? You've a right to."

"Those miserable cads would make complaints about the grub if I did. They actually said so. A few sardines, you know, and some pilchards, and some sosses, and a cake or two, you know——"

"Yes; I know!" chuckled Wally. "I understand perfectly, my tulip. I shall have to use the study, though. Mr. Penman will expect to see my study."

"They may cut up rusty."

"Let 'em! They won't find me so jolly easy to shift out of the study," said Wally cheerfully. "Anything else to tell me?"

"Well, you might behave as decently as possible——"

"Eh?"

"And do me as much credit as you can. I am sure you don't mind my mentioning it, Wally, but you are rather low in some ways——"

"You fat idiot!"

"Why, you—you——"

"Am I going to see you again afterwards?" asked Wally gruffly.

"No need for that. Clear off after Old Penman's gone—he says he has to catch the six train back—and I shall come home from Abbotsford at half-past six, say—not earlier, to make sure of not meeting the old bounder. The fellows won't know there's been any change."

"They may notice that my neck is washed."

"Look here——"

"Well, I'll get off, then," said Wally.

"And bear in mind what I've said. Remember, you're taking a gentleman's place for the afternoon——"

"Ain't I going to take your place?"

"That's what I mean. Look here, Wally, I don't like your low jokes, and I'm not going to take any cheek from a fellow that's worked in an office, and who's sent to school by his dashed employer!" roared Bunter.

Wally's eyes sparkled.

"Mr. Penman undertook to send me to school because I saved him a big loss when his office was burgled," he said. "It was kindness itself. He's a really splendid man! And if you speak of him, Billy, you've got to speak of him a bit more respectfully."

"Catch me! A dashed old bounder who's made his money in trade——"

Bump!

"Yaroooop!"

Wally Bunter walked away through the wood, leaving Billy Bunter sitting in the grass, gasping for breath, and shaking a fat fist after him.

"Beast!" howled Bunter. "Yah! Beast!"

Wally walked on, unheeding; and the Owl of Greyfriars picked himself up, brandished his fat fist again, and then started for the railway-station. His fat face cleared as he rolled away.

He was going to have as good a time as possible in Abbotsford that afternoon, with Wally's five shillings to see him through; and Wally was going to encounter any difficulties that might crop up at St. Jim's.

So upon the whole William George Bunter felt satisfied.

CHAPTER 6.
Wally at St. Jim's.

WALLY BUNTER'S fat face was very thoughtful as he walked from the wood towards St. Jim's.

He had had his misgivings about that reckless scheme of changing places with his cousin Billy; but it had worked well so far.

At neither school was there the faintest suspicion of the change that had taken place.

Wally had his old wish—he was at Greyfriars with Harry Wharton & Co., the friends he had made earlier, and whose schoolfellow he had keenly wished to be.

And there was no harm in using Billy's name there, as he had given his own to Billy. He was succeeding, too, in living down the exceedingly unpleasant reputation Billy had left him as an inheritance at Greyfriars; and, in fact, he was happy at Greyfriars, and loth to think of leaving the school.

Billy Bunter's urgent letter, summoning him to St. Jim's in post-haste, had given him a very unpleasant shock. He knew the unreliable nature of the Owl, and the thought of changing back had dismayed him.

He was relieved now, however. Billy Bunter did not want to change back, so far, at all events.

And risky as another change was, for the afternoon Wally Bunter rather looked forward to spending a few hours at St. Jim's. There, at least, he would be under his own name, and he would see Tom Merry and D'Arcy, and other fellows he liked, who had been prepared to welcome him warmly when he became a St. Jim's fellow.

And he was rather tickled, too, at the thought of what would happen when Mellish and Trimble—whoever they were—taking him for the Bunter they knew, tried to evict him from Study No. 2 in the Fourth.

Something like an earthquake would happen to Mellish and Trimble if they tried that on. Wally was quite certain on that point, and he chuckled at the thought.

Racke and Crooke were lounging about the gates when Wally Bunter reached the school.

Most of the juniors were gathering on Little Side, as the Abbotsford team were expected soon; but Racke and Crooke were not attracted there. The two black sheep of the Shell did not care for footer, either to play or watch, unless they had bets on the game.

They were slacking, as usual; and as Bunter came up, Racke, in sheer idleness, reached out and knocked off his cap. It was safe enough to rag Billy Bunter.

"Hallo!" ejaculated Wally in surprise at that greeting.

"What are you wearing that rag for?" said Racke. "That's not a St. Jim's cap?"

Wally looked at him.

He was wearing an ordinary cap, having taken care not to bring with him anything distinctive of Greyfriars.

"You've knocked my cap off!" he said. "Will you have the kindness to pick it up for me?"

Racke chuckled.

"Not in these bags," he answered.

"I shall make you, then!"

"Eh?"

"Are you going to pick that cap up?"

"Hardly."

"Then here goes!" said Wally cheerfully.

He rushed at Aubrey Racke. Racke backed away in sheer astonishment.

"You fat idiot!" he ejaculated. "Do you want me to bump you on the ground and burst you?"

"Yes, if you can do it, old bean!"

"My hat!" said Crooke in wonder. "Bunter on the war-path! Mop up the quad with him, Racke!"

"I'm jolly well going to!" growled Racke.

He put up his hands savagely.

To his amazement, his clumsy hands were dashed aside with perfect ease, and he received a tap on the nose that made him blink. The next moment—how, Racke hardly knew—the fat junior had him by the collar, and, with a strength that Bunter had never been suspected of, he forced Aubrey to his knees.

"Pick up that cap, dear boy!" he said.

"Yow-ow! Leggo!" shrieked Racke.

"Are you going to pick up that cap?"

"No!" yelled Racke. "Help me, Crooke, you staring fool!"

Gerald Crooke ran to his aid. Wally's left came out like lightning, catching Crooke on the chin, and sending him spinning. Crooke spun into three juniors who were coming down to the gates to look for the Abbotsford brake. Tom Merry caught him by the shoulders and stopped him.

"Hallo, what's this game?" exclaimed the captain of the Shell.

"Ow-ow-ow!" moaned Crooke, clasping his chin and backing away. "Ow! My chin! Yow-ow-ow!"

"Leggo!" raved Racke. "You fat beast, I'll smash you! Yow-ow! Let me go!"

"When you've picked up my cap, old bean!" said Wally calmly.

Tom Merry & Co. looked on in utter wonder. Racke certainly was not a fighting-man, but Bunter was not supposed to be anything like a match for him, and he was nearly a head shorter than the black sheep of the Shell. And Bunter of the Fourth had not been famed at St. Jim's for courage; rather the reverse.

Yet here he was, handling Aubrey Racke as easily as a baby!

Racke was forced lower and lower, till his prominent nose almost touched the ground, and he wriggled and struggled furiously in the grip of the fat hand—in vain.

"Bunter!" gasped the captain of the Shell.

"Hallo, cocky!" said Wally, with a grin and a nod at Tom Merry, whom he knew well enough.

"What—what game are you playing, you fat bounder?" exclaimed Manners.

"This dear boy's knocked my cap off, and he's going to be obliging enough to pick it up, that's all."

"Well, my hat! I've seen a fag in the Third knock your cap off, and you never touched him."

"Bosh!"

"What?"

"I—I mean, I'm touching this dear boy, anyhow."

"Better pick up the cap, Racke," grinned Lowther. "You don't look as if you can handle Bunter."

"Ow! Help me, you fool, Crooke!"

"Ow-ow-ow!" was the only reply of George Gerald Cooke. He was busy with his chin.

Racke's nose was on the ground now, and Wally was gently but persistently rubbing it there. The Terrible Three grinned at they looked on. Racke clutched at the cap at last, and handed it up to Wally.

"Thanks, old bean!" said Wally Bunter cheerily. "You can sit down now!"

And Racke sat down—with Wally's assistance—hard.

"Well, my hat!" said Tom Merry. "Blessed if I thought Bunter could handle a Third Form fag like that, let alone a Shell chap!"

Racke rose to his feet, with a face like a demon.

But he did not approach Wally again. He was still aching from the iron grip that had been placed on him.

Panting for breath, he moved away with Crooke, who was still rubbing his chin ruefully. The two Shell fellows were not likely to rag Bunter of the Fourth again in a hurry.

Wally grinned cheerfully at the astonished faces of the Terrible Three. He put his cap on the back of his head.

"I'm jolly glad to see you again, Tom Merry," he remarked.

Tom stared at him.

"The gladness is all on your side, then!" he answered drily.

Wally started.

"What—what did you say? What the thump do you mean? If you call that civil——"

"I don't!" answered Tom. "But if you expect me to be glad to see you, Bunter, you must be wandering in your mind. And what the thump do you mean by speaking as if you hadn't seen me for a dog's age, when you saw me last at dinner?"

"At—at dinner!" Wally remembered himself in time. "I—I mean—ahem!—quite so! Yes—exactly! By the way, you're playing football this afternoon?"

"You know we are."

"Yes, yes, of course! Room for another man in the eleven?"

"Oh, don't be an ass! Are you beginning that again?" said Tom impatiently. "Don't talk out of your neck, Bunter; you make fellows tired!"

Tom Merry looked out at the gates. There was no sign yet of the Abbotsford brake, and he came in again. The Terrible Three walked away towards Little Side; and Wally, after a momentary hesitation, joined them.

CHAPTER 7.
Goal!

"HALLO, D'Arcy!"

Arthur Augustus, with an elegant overcoat and a handsome muffler over his equally elegant and handsome footer rig, was chatting with Blake on Little Side when Wally Bunter came up along with the Shell fellows.

The swell of St. Jim's extracted an eyeglass from some recess, jammed it into his eye, and surveyed Wally Bunter.

"Did you addwess me, Buntah?" he inquired.

"Of course I did, old bean!"

"I beg you not to do so, Buntah, in that exceedingly familiah way. I have wemarked befoah that I do not like it!"

"Oh!" said Wally.

He bit his lip.

It was something like his experience at Greyfriars over again. Billy Bunter had evidently left a far from pleasant state of affairs for him.

Wally Bunter had been quite chummy with Gussy · but it was pretty clear that Billy Bunter had made an end of anything like a feeling of friendship in Gussy's noble breast. And Wally was not exactly surprised.

It was rather difficult for Wally, who had just arrived from Greyfriars, to act as if he had been at St. Jim's all the time. But it was evidently necessary; and he kept on his guard.

Figgins & Co. came on the ground, and they grinned as they saw Bunter.

They had heard of the Owl's request for a place in the School Junior Eleven.

Wally was about to greet the three, whom he remembered well; but he paused in time.

"Time Abbotsford showed up," remarked Figgins.

"Well, kick-off's not till two-thirty," said Tom Merry. "Time yet. What do you want, Bunter?" he added, a little gruffly.

"I suppose you couldn't stretch a point. Mr. Penman's coming to see me this afternoon, and he's an old St. Jim's man—he used to play for St. Jim's thirty years ago. It would please him no end to see me playing for the School."

"Not if he's a footballer," said Tom Merry drily.

"Unless he's got a vewy wemarkable sense of humah, Buntah!" grinned Arthur Augustus D'Arcy.

"What rot! I played for you before, when you were short of a man at Greyfriars," said Wally. "You know I'm a player!"

"I know you played well that time," admitted Tom Merry. "It must have been some sort of a queer fluke, as you've proved yourself a fumbling idiot ever since you've been here."

"Oh, my hat!" mumbled Wally. "That fat idiot——"

"What!"

"N-n-nothing! I say, I can really play, you know," urged Wally. "I'll tell you what. You've got time before the match, as your visitors haven't arrived. Put a man in goal, and see if I can beat him."

"Fathead!"

"Ass!"

"Put Wynn in," said Wally determinedly. "Wynn's your best goalie, I believe. And if I beat Wynn——"

"Ha, ha, ha!"

"Mind, I don't want to bag another chap's place in the team," said Wally hastily. "I don't mean that. But I'd give a lot to let Mr. Penman see me playing for the School: I owe him a lot, and I'd like to please him. Some chap may offer to stand out for me."

The juniors stared at him.

"Are you quite potty?" asked Tom Merry at last. "You can't play footer, and you know you can't! Cheese it!"

"Ha, ha, ha!" roared Figgins. "If you can land a goal with Fatty between the posts, Bunter, I'll stand out for you."

"Done!" exclaimed Wally Bunter instantly.

"Ha, ha, ha!"

"You agree, Tom Merry, as skipper?" asked Wally, in a business-like tone.

Tom Merry laughed impatiently.

"What's the good of talking rot?" he said. "No need to be playing the fool on the field when Abbotsford comes along. Roll away and dry up!"

"Do you mean business, Figgins?" asked Wally.

"Ha, ha! Yes! Let him try, Tommy; it won't do any harm. It's funny to see that porpoise rolling after a ball."

"He can play the goat, if he likes," said Tom, with a shrug of the shoulders. "I don't mind!"

"And if I score a goal off Wynn Figgins can give me his place in the eleven?" asked the fat junior.

"Yes, ass: and he can give you his head, too, if he likes—and you can have mine along with it!"

"Done! I don't want your nappers, but I want a show in the game this afternoon, to please Mr. Penman. Will you trot into goal, Wynn?"

Fatty grinned.

"Any old thing!" he answered. "Go ahead!"

There was a general chortle as Fatty Wynn went into goal, and Figgins pitched out an old practice ball into the field for Bunter. Fatty Wynn grinned between the posts. But the chortling died away as Bunter took the ball up the field, dribbling it. Certainly the fat junior was dribbling the ball in a masterly way, as far as that went.

"I—I say, he isn't such a clumsy ass as he's always made out," said Figgins.

"He won't beat Fatty Wynn!"

"Ha, ha! No!"

A good man, with his best shooting-boots on, would not have had an easy task to beat the New House goalkeeper on his lonesome. Wally had set himself a hefty task, and he knew it. But he had some advantage in the fact that Fatty Wynn did not believe for a moment that the leather would come anywhere near him, and was certainly not on the alert as he would have been in a game.

Wally Bunter dribbled the ball up, and made a show of kicking, and Fatty Wynn grinned at him. In a flash Wally changed his feet, and the ball flew into the corner of the net before the fat goalkeeper knew what was happening. Fatty Wynn had fairly been caught napping!

"Goal!" stuttered Tom Merry blankly.

"Gig-gig-gig-goal!" spluttered Figgins.

"Goal!" murmured Kerr. "Oh, Figgy!"

Fatty Wynn stared round at the letter. There it was—there was no was no mistake about that! It was in the net, and that goal stood to Bunter's credit. As Fatty Wynn mechanically picked up the footer, Wally sauntered back to the astounded group of juniors by the ropes.

"Well?" he said.

"What does this mean?" exclaimed Tom Merry. "Fatty wasn't at his best, but that was a jolly clever kick. Have you been pulling our leg all this time, you fat rascal? You can play footer!"

"I told you I could."

"Yes, but——"

"Bai Jove! That was weally a vewy wemarkable kick!" said Arthur Augustus D'Arcy. "I weally did not think Buntah was capable of it."

Figgins' face was a study.

"Well, I can play," said Wally Bunter cheerfully. "The question is, can you make room for me?"

"Bai Jove! Figgay has settled that."

Tom Merry was silent. In his utter disbelief that Bunter could score off Fatty Wynn, he had given a careless assent to George Figgins' reckless offer. The assent had been careless, but he was a fellow of his word.

He looked rather queerly at Figgins.

Figgins was looking very queer indeed.

"Well, Figgins?" said Wally Bunter.

"You you—you've done it!" stammered Figgins.

"He's done it," said Kerr, "and he's done you, Figgy, you ass! You'll have to stand to it now, and so will Tom Merry. That fat bounder's dished the pair of you, to say nothing of the match."

"The match is all right," said Tom Merry. "I can see whether a chap's in form, and Bunter's in form all right. You remember how he played for us in the Greyfriars match that time. I suppose he's been spoofing us since. Anyhow, he can play footer."

"Yaas, wathah!"

"Well," said Figgins slowly, "I agree to that. I—I've been taken in."

"Taken in and done for!" grinned Blake.

"Hold on!" said Wally Bunter quickly. "I do want to play this afternoon, because Mr. Penman's coming, but I'm not going to diddle you, Figgins. If you want to call it off, I'm willing. I'll let you off, old boy!"

"Bai Jove!" murmured Arthur Augustus.

Tom Merry blinked.

This generous offer was quite like the old Wally Bunter—the Wally they had known before Bunter came to St. Jim's.

Figgins shook his head.

"If you play as you did that time at Greyfriars, you'll be as good a man in the team as I am," he said. "And a bargain's a bargain. I'm standing out. You agree, Tom Merry?"

"I've already agreed," said Tom.

"Then it's settled."

"I—I don't want to pin you down, Figgins, really," said Wally. "I withdraw my claim, if you like. There!"

Figgins grinned faintly.

"You're playing!" he answered. "Cut off and get into your rig, Bunter. The Abbotsford fellows will be along in a few minutes."

"Well, if you don't mind——"

"Buck up!" was Figgy's reply.

"Right you are, then!"

"Cut off!" said Tom Merry, as Wally Bunter hesitated. "There isn't too much time to change, and your things are indoors."

"I'm off!" said Wally.

His hesitation had a cause unknown to Tom Merry & Co. He did not know his way about the school, and had no idea where Bunter's footer outfit was kept. He was not even sure which was Bunter's House, of the two he could see in the distance. It was rather a difficult position, especially as he could not venture to let his doubts be observed.

He picked up his coat and started off. Tom Merry called after him, when he got to a little distance.

"Bunter, you owl!"

Wally looked round.

"Aren't you going to change?"

"Eh? Yes!"

"Well, your things are not in the New House, are they? Look here, if you're going to play, don't lose time."

"Oh, all right!"

Wally Bunter changed his direction, Tom having unsuspectingly given him his bearings. He trotted off cheerfully into the School House.

CHAPTER 8.
An Earthquake in Study No. 2.

"OH, my hat!" murmured Wally Bunter, as he entered the School House and looked round him over his glasses.

He knew there was no time to lose, as the visiting team were due already, but he was at a loss.

All he knew of Bunter's quarters was that the Owl belonged to Study No. 2 in the Fourth, and that his study-mates were named Mellish and Trimble. But where the Fourth Form quarters were was beyond him. He had to find them somehow.

As he stood blinking round him, three fags came along, and one of them Wally recognised by his likeness to the great Arthur Augustus D'Arcy. It was D'Arcy minor, of the Third Form. The other two were Frank Levison and Manners minor. D'Arcy minor had stopped to fasten an obstinate shoe-lace, and Frank Levison called out:

"Buck up, Wally. You'll be late for the match."

Wally Bunter started.

For the moment he naturally supposed that the fag's remark was addressed to him. But D'Arcy minor replied:

"Wait a minute, fathead!"

Evidently Arthur Augustus' young brother rejoiced in the same front name as Billy Bunter's cousin.

"Abbotsford ought to be here by this time," said Manners minor. "We sha'n't get a good place, Wally. There'll be a crowd."

"Oh, give us a rest, Reggie!"

At this point Wally Bunter had a brain-wave, so to speak. He gave a sudden stagger, and caught at Levison minor's shoulder for support. He selected Frank on account of his kind, good-natured looks, as the most likely to waste time on a fellow in distress.

"Oh!" he gasped.

"Here, roll off me, barrel!" said Frank.

"Ow! A—a sudden twinge!" gasped Wally Bunter. "I—I say, kid, help me to my study, will you?"

"Oh, my hat! I'm just off to the footer ground——"

"Rot!" snapped Manners minor. "Help yourself, you fat bounder! You've only been eating too much, I expect. Shove him off, Frank. Cheek!"

"Lend me a hand, there's a good kid!" murmured Wally Bunter.

"Come on!" called out D'Arcy minor, who, having finished his obstinate shoe-lace, was heading for the doorway.

Frank Levison hesitated.

"I'll come after you," he called back.

"More duffer you!" said Reggie Manners.

And he ran after D'Arcy minor.

"Come on, Bunter!" said Frank hurriedly. "I don't want to miss the kick-off. Get a move on, quick!"

He led the fat junior upstairs.

Wally Bunter kept a hand on his shoulder, as if for support, but he was not much trouble to Frank. All he really wanted was a guide.

Levison of the Fourth passed them on the stairs, with Cardew and Clive. Levison was in footer rig under his coat.

"Hallo! What are you rolling that tub about for, Frank?" called out Levison major.

"He's got a pain," said Frank.

"Serve him right!"

"Ow!" said Wally pathetically.

"Poor old Bunter!" said Cardew. "It was the hundredth sausage did it, I expect. Or was it the two hundredth, old bean?"

"Can I help you with my boot, old chap?" asked Sidney Clive. "If a really good shove behind would help you——"

Wally Bunter hurried on with Frank, and the three Fourth-Formers went down the stairs grinning.

"Here you are!" exclaimed Frank Levison, as they reached the door of No. 2 in the Fourth. "All right now?"

"Help me in."

"Oh, all right!" said Frank, manfully suppressing his impatience.

He was anxious to join his chums on Little Side.

He threw open the door of the study, and a scent of cigarette-smoke greeted him. Mellish and Trimble were there, and they had a guest in the study—Scrope of the Shell. The three young rascals were spending their half-holiday at banker, with cigarettes going. They stared at Frank Levison and the fat junior as they came in.

"Get out of this, Bunter!" snapped Mellish. "I've told you you're not to come here, haven't I?"

"Do you want another licking?" demanded Trimble.

Frank Levison grinned.

"Anything more I can do for you?" he asked.

"Hold on a minute," said Wally Bunter.

The fat junior had found Billy Bunter's study. But it was pretty clear that the football outfit was not kept there. All he was likely to find in the study was a scrap with Billy's study-mates. A "scrap" had no terrors for him, certainly, but he did not want one just then if it could be helped. He was anxious to get into Billy's football clobber and get back to the field.

"Well, what do you want, Bunter?" asked Frank. "I'm in a hurry, you know."

"I—I want my footer rig," said Wally.

"What on earth for?"

"I'm playing this afternoon for Tom Merry."

"Oh, don't be a funny ass, Bunter!" said Frank. "I haven't time to stay here and listen to fatheaded jokes."

And Frank Levison, not dreaming for a moment of taking Bunter's statement seriously, cut off, and went down the staircase on the banisters at great speed.

Wally Bunter had lost his guide.

Mellish, Trimble, and Scrope had risen to their feet, with threatening looks. They were angry at the interruption of their game. Mellish and Trimble were especially exasperated. They had not expected Bunter to make another attempt to establish his rights in the study; and they did not suspect that this was quite another Bunter they had to deal with.

"Take the fat beast by the neck," said Mellish.

"What-ho!" grinned Baggy Trimble.

"I'll lend you a hand," remarked Scrope. "Now, then, Bunter, out you go!"

Wally's eyes gleamed over his glasses.

"Hands off, you silly asses!" he snapped. "I've no time to waste on you!"

"We've a little to waste on you," said Mellish—"just enough to pitch you out on your neck!"

And the three juniors piled on Wally Bunter together.

What happened next was like an earthquake to them.

On previous occasions Billy Bunter had been handled easily enough. But the boot was on the other foot now, so to speak.

As their grasp was laid on the fat junior, two plump fists came up like lightning.

Scrope caught one of them with his nose, and Mellish caught the other with his eye.

Bump, bump!

The Shell fellow and the Fourth-Former reeled back, and sat down on the carpet. And Baggy Trimble, with a howl of surprise and terror, released Bunter as if the fat junior had suddenly become red-hot, and jumped back.

Wally grinned at them.

"Come and have some more!" he said.

"Oh!"

"Ow!"

"Oh dear!"

Scrope sat up and dabbed his nose dazedly. Mellish squirmed round the table before he ventured to get on his feet. Baggy Trimble dodged behind the armchair, as if to use it as a fortification.

W. G. B Was the Goal Bagger.
(See Chapter 7.)

They glared at Wally Bunter in blank dismay.

"Oh, I—I say!" gasped Trimble. "I—I say, Bunter, old chap——"

"Ow-ow-ow!" came from Mellish.

Scrope jumped up with a furious face, and rushed at Wally Bunter. The fat junior's hands shot up again, and Scrope was met with left and right, and, gasping and panting, he was driven out of the study into the passage. He was, perhaps, more amazed than hurt; but he was hurt, too, and he had plainly had enough by the time he was out of the study. He backed away in the passage, turned, and fled ingloriously.

Wally, grinning, turned back into the doorway, to find Mellish and Trimble regarding him with looks of amazement and apprehension.

"I—I say, keep off, you know!"

gasped Baggy Trimble. "I—I never wanted to turn you out, Bunter—never in my life! It—it was Mellish all the time. Mellish said——"

"Ow-ow!"

"Sure you don't want to turn me out?" grinned Wally.

"Not a bit, old chap. I—I like you too much!" gasped Trimble. "I—I have missed you awfully. Mellish remembers my saying so to him!"

"Yow-ow!"

"What do you say, Mellish, old buck?" asked Wally. He knew which was which of the two juniors now.

"Let me alone!" groaned Mellish. "Hang you!"

"Don't you want any more?"

"Ow! No!"

"Well, as we're so jolly friendly, you can do me a good turn," said Wally Bunter brightly. "I want my footer rig. Trimble, you can go and fetch it here for me, and help me change."

"With pleasure, old chap!" gasped Trimble, with a longing glance at the door.

His look showed rather plainly that if he was once safe outside the study he was not likely to come back with Bunter's footer rig.

"On second thoughts, I'll come with you," said Wally cheerfully. "Now, then, get a move on!"

"If you're going to the dorm yourself, you don't want me——"

"My dear chap, I'm enjoying your company. Shall I take your arm or your ear?"

"M-m-m-my arm, please!" stuttered Trimble.

"Come on, then!"

Wally Bunter left the study with Trimble, Mellish scowling after him savagely. Trimble, little dreaming that his companion did not know the way, headed for the Fourth Form dormitory.

"Get the things out for me!" said Wally autocratically.

"Look here, I'm not going to fag for you, Bunter——"

"Where will you have it?" asked Wally.

"I—I mean, I—I'm delighted to oblige you, old chap."

"That's better! Buck up!"

A minute more, and Wally Bunter was changing into Billy Bunter's football rig, and Trimble was allowed to go. He rolled off in a state of great amazement and disquiet. It was pretty clear now that Bunter would have to be allowed to resume his place in Study No. 2.

Wally had only succeeded in time; he had barely finished changing when D'Arcy looked into the dormitory.

"Weady Buntah? The Abbotsford fellows have awwived. Tom Mewwy sent me for you."

"Ready!" answered Wally cheerfully.

And he walked to the football-ground with Arthur Augustus.

CHAPTER 9.

The Abbotsford Match.

"ON the ball!"

"Play up, St. Jim's!"

Round Little Side there had gathered a big crowd of juniors. The Abbotsford match always drew a crowd; but the news that Bunter of the Fourth was playing for St. Jim's drew fellows from near and far.

"Bunter's playing!" said D'Arcy minor, to a group of the Third. "That means that Tom Merry's gone off his dot! The poor chap ought to be put under restraint."

"My only hat!" said Frank Levison. "The fat bounder told me he was playing, and I thought he was pulling my leg. Whose place has he got?"

"Figgy's," said Reggie Manners. "There's Figgy standing out."

"Well, my word!"

The surprise was general, for during the time he had been at St. Jim's, Billy Bunter had succeeded in convincing the Lower School that what he did not know about football would have filled whole volumes, if not libraries. Unless Tom Merry was indeed "off his dot," there was no accounting for it.

But the amazement increased when it was seen that the fat recruit was playing up for his side in great style.

He had a turn of speed that was not excelled even by the slim Arthur Augustus—in passing he was as accurate as Kerr or Redfern or Tom Merry himself. In a very few minutes all the on lookers knew that it was a very good man playing; and some of them rubbed their eyes.

"The fat idiot's been pulling our leg!" said Julian of the Fourth. "He made out he couldn't play footer."

"But, bedad, why should he?" said Reilly.

"Blessed if I know."

"Potty, I should think," remarked Kerruish. "Fatty degeneration of the brain."

"Anyhow, he can play!" said Julian. "Look at him now! He's got the ball away from Yorke—and Yorke's a good man."

"Pass, you barrel—pass!" roared Clive.

But Bunter did not need telling; he passed in to Tom Merry, who took the leather and rushed it on, with the whole forward line in full flight. There was a cheer as a hot attack on the visitors' goal followed.

The Abbotsford goalkeeper sent the ball back, once, twice, thrice, but the backs could not clear, and there was a sudden roar as the leather went into the net.

"Goal!"

"Bunter!"

"Goal!"

"Bravo, Bunter! Oh, crikey!"

It was a yell of astonishment round the field. The first goal in the match had fallen to St. Jim's, and it was Bunter of the Fourth who had kicked it.

"Well, my hat!" ejaculated George Figgins. "My only summer hat! I couldn't have done better than that! That fat duffer, you know—that blessed barrel—well, it beats me! Goal, goal, goal!"

"He's been spoofin' us all," said Cardew. "But what's he been doin' it for?"

"Goodness knows!"

"Good man, anyhow," remarked Clive, with satisfaction. "First goal to us, and we're going to win. Bravo, Bunter!"

Several of the team smacked Bunter's fat shoulder—Levison and D'Arcy and Tom Merry among them. The footballers had quite forgiven the Owl for his many sins now. They were astonished, but they were delighted.

"Bai Jove, that was a wippin' goal, Buntah! What have you been pwetendin' to be a sillay ass for?" inquired Arthur Augustus.

Wally grinned cheerfully.

"First-rate!" said Levison.

"Topping!" said Talbot of the Shell heartily.

The fat junior was on the best of terms with the team when they lined up again. It was clear that he was in the same topping form as on the historic occasion when he had filled a vacant place for Tom Merry at Greyfriars, and helped to beat the Remove there. The ineptitude shown by Billy Bunter was a perplexing puzzle. But that mattered little now; the new recruit was more than worth his salt.

The first half was drawing to its close when the station cab drove up the School House, and a stout gentleman stepped out. He was a ruddy-faced gentleman of middle age, with a good-humoured expression, and the way his glance turned towards the playing-fields, as he heard shouting from that direction, showed that he was an old player.

"Go it, Bunter! Put her through!"

"Bravo, Bunter!"

It was a roar from the football-ground, and the name reached the ears of the gentleman who had arrived in the cab.

Mr. Railton met him in the hall. The Housemaster was acquainted with Mr. Penman, who had visited St. Jim's many times as an Old Boy. He greeted the merchant warmly.

"I will send for Bunter," Mr. Railton remarked, after they had chatted a few moments in the Housemaster's study.

Mr. Penman smiled.

"I fancy Bunter is engaged at the present moment," he said. "I am very glad that he has turned out a footballer."

"A footballer?" repeated Mr. Railton.

"I heard the name shouted on the football-ground as I came in," said the gentleman from Canterbury.

"Bless my soul! I—I was not aware that Bunter of the Fourth was a foot baller of much account," said Mr. Railton, in surprise. "There is a junior match this afternoon, but surely Bunter is——"

He paused.

"Oh! There is perhaps another boy here of the same name?" said Mr. Penman, disappointed.

"No; no one of that name but Bunter of the Fourth. From what I have observed of him I should not have thought——"

Mr. Railton stepped to his window, and called to a junior in the quadrangle.

"Trimble!"

"Yes, sir?"

"Is Bunter playing for the School this afternoon?"

"Yes, sir," said Trimble.

"Bless my soul! You are right, Mr. Penman," said the Housemaster, turning back to the visitor. "Would you care to walk down to Little Side——"

"I was thinking that I should——"

"I will come with you."

The Housemaster and his visitor walked down to the football-ground together, and the shout they heard as they arrived showed that Bunter of the Fourth was not only playing for St. Jim's, but was winning golden opinions by his play.

"Bravo, Bunter!"

"Good man!"

St. Jim's were attacking again, and the Abbotsford defence was hard driven. Wally Bunter had taken the leather from a back striving to clear with an ease that astonished the Abbotsford man, and the next moment he was charged over. But in that second he centred to Tom Merry, who drove the ball home.

"Goal!"

"Well kicked, Tom Merry!"

Bunter sat up, blinking. His glasses were in his pocket now, and it was another surprise to the juniors that he did not seem at a loss without them.

Levison pulled him up.

"That was a jolly good pass, kid," said Levison. "Two up for us, by Jove!"

"Good man, Buntah!"

"Good man!" repeated Tom Merry. "You gave me that goal, Bunter. If you ever pretend again that you can't play footer I'll scalp you bald-headed!"

Wally chuckled breathlessly.

The whistle went a few minutes later, and the players came off, and Mr. Penman called to Wally Bunter. The fat junior ran up at once, and shook hands with his old employer. Mr. Penman's face was bright with satisfaction.

"In the Junior Eleven already—what?" he exclaimed. "I congratulate you, my boy! I'm more pleased than I can say."

"I congratulate you, too, Bunter," said Mr. Railton, with a rather puzzled look, however.

"Thank you, sir!" said Wally demurely.

"You will be a credit to the school, my boy," said Mr. Penman.

"Oh, sir!" murmured Wally.

He was devoutly thankful at that moment that he had come over from Greyfriars that day, and not risked Billy Bunter playing his part in the presence of his kind old friend.

Mr. Railton returned to the School House, but the gentleman from Canterbury remained on Little Side to watch the match to the end. And when play was resumed Mr. Penman's voice was as loud as any in the cheering.

Wally Bunter had played up well in the first half, but in the second he was fairly on his mettle. He owed much to Mr. Penman; and it was some sort of recompense to the old sportsman to see his protege playing for his old school with credit. The old gentleman's evident delight was an incentive to Wally to do his very best—and his very best was very good indeed.

Not that there was anything "pushing" in his play. He never kept the ball too much for himself, and never played a selfish game. No fresh goal fell to him; but his play was first-class all through, and when Talbot scored it was from a pass given him by Wally at inside-right. His play was rather good than showy. But the old sportsman was a good judge of play, and his face beamed with delight as he watched his protege.

Only once did Abbotsford succeed in getting through, and beating Fatty Wynn in goal. When the final whistle went St. Jim's stood three to one, and there was a terrific burst of cheering for the victors. And when the players came off George Figgins smacked Bunter on the shoulder with a terrific smack.

"Well done, tubby!" he said heartily. "Good man! Why, you're one of the best in the bunch!"

And Arthur Augustus D'Arcy chimed in:

"Yaas, wathah!"

CHAPTER 10.
Tea in Study No. 2.

TOM MERRY was puzzled.

After the Abbotsford fellows were gone the Terrible Three talked over the match by the fire in their study, and all three of them agreed that it was a puzzle.

Only that morning Bunter had been his most unpleasant self, and only a few days before he had displayed the most amazing ineptitude at footer. And now—now he had played a great game, as he had done once before to Tom Merry's knowledge—and not only that, but all his actions and words were those of a decent fellow. His grateful regard for Mr. Penman, for instance, was plain enough for anybody to see. But up to that afternoon Bunter had certainly not

given an impression of possessing such feelings. Tom remembered that Bunter had been annoyed by Mr. Penman's letter, and had actually spoken of "dodging" the old gentleman from Canterbury.

"It's a corker!" said Tom. "It almost seems as if Bunter's an entirely different fellow since dinner to-day."

"It does," agreed Monty Lowther, with a nod.

"And when he came here he seemed a different fellow from the chap we had met. Now he seems to have gone back to his old self. I don't think I'm specially dense," said Tom, "but it beats me hollow."

"It's a puzzle," said Manners thoughtfully. "I quite liked his way with old Mr. Penman. He seems to have quite

decent feelings. But only yesterday—well, my hat!"

The Terrible Three felt that they had to give it up. Bunter, with those sudden and surprising changes of character, was a complete puzzle to them. But they admitted that he wasn't by any means the toad they had recently supposed; and when a fat face and glimmering spectacles looked in at the door the chums of the Shell nodded genially, instead of bidding W. G. Bunter "buzz off" in uncompromising tones.

"I say, you chaps," said Wally Bunter, setting his glasses straight on his fat little nose, as if he found them uncomfortable—"I say, will you—will you come to tea with me?"

"We've had tea once, thanks!"

"Well, you needn't eat a lot, if you don't want to; but I wish you'd come."

"You can manage the lion's share, I suppose?" grinned Lowther.

"I could peck a bit," admitted Wally. "I generally can. I've a pretty good appetite."

"Ha, ha! You needn't tell us that! But we can't come, old scout," said Tom Merry. "We're hard up to-day."

The fat junior stared at them.

"What difference does that make?" he demanded. "I suppose you don't think I want you to pay for your tea, do you?"

"I suppose you want us to lend you the tin?" said Tom, opening his eyes.

"Well, I don't!" said Wally gruffly. "And if you call that a civil remark, Tom Merry, I don't agree with you."

"My dear ass," said Tom, "you generally mean that you want tin, if you ask a fellow to tea! You know it's the fact. What's the good of beating about the bush, Bunter? I don't quite understand you to-day."

Wally Bunter inwardly blessed his cousin Billy.

"Well, to-day I want you to drop in as friends," he said. "I've got a decent spread. I—I—I want you to come, you see. I'm really not sticking you for a loan—honour bright!"

"Oh!" said Tom.

"The fact is, Mr. Penman's in my study," said Wally Bunter. "He's having some tuck with me before he goes to catch his train. He used to be at St. Jim's, you know; and he's no end gone on grubbing in the study, and all that. He's asked me to ask in some of my friends—makes him think of his merry old schooldays, I suppose. I—I'd like you to come. D'Arcy says he will."

"All serene!" said Tom at once. "We'll back you up!"

"Thanks no end!"

"What about your study-mates, though?" asked Monty Lowther. "Have you settled with them about the study?"

"Oh, that's all right—they're keeping out!" said Wally. "They came along while I was getting tea—while Mr. Penman was with the Head, luckily. I knocked their heads together and scooted them."

"Oh, my hat!"

The Terrible Three, remembering what had happened to Aubrey Racke, could believe the statement—though the previous day they would have laughed at the idea of Bunter knocking together the heads of Mellish and Trimble. They followed Wally Bunter along to No. 2 in the Fourth.

Old Mr. Penman was there, his ruddy face glowing with good nature, and Arthur Augustus D'Arcy was in the study chatting with the old merchant. Jack Blake was there, too—Gussy had succeeded in persuading him to accept Bunter's invitation. Herries and Digby had declared that they would see Bunter "blowed" first, quite emphatically. They admitted that he had played a good game of footer that day; but in their opinion he was the same toad he had always been—which really was not quite correct, as it happened.

However, there was a sufficient party to make things move. Wally had been rather anxious about that; he wanted Mr. Penman to have a pleasant visit. He had five of the best in his study now, and they all found themselves on good terms with the Old Boy.

Over tea Mr. Penman told them the story of Wally's act of courage when the burglars had attempted to rob his office in Canterbury, Wally shifting uneasily in his seat while the story was related with great gusto by the old merchant. It raised Bunter in the estimation of the juniors, but it perplexed them, too. For

Bunter of St. Jim's hadn't shown that kind of courage, by any means; and, moreover, his modest diffidence while Mr. Penman told the story was strangely out of keeping with his usual "swank."

Still, the juniors were feeling quite cordial towards Bunter now; and they could only hope that the amazing change in him would last.

Mr. Penman glanced at his watch at last.

Wally was not sorry when that happened.

All had gone well so far, and he was anxious for the old gentleman to be clear of the school a good while before Billy Bunter returned. He trembled to think what might happen if Billy Bunter should "barge" in while Mr. Penman was there. But the old gentleman had his train to catch, and there was no danger of that.

When Mr. Penman left the School House in the dusk, Wally went with him to the station. Mr. Penman decided to walk, to chat with his protege on the way. Tom Merry & Co. saw them off at the gates.

They little dreamed that they were seeing the last of that particular Bunter.

Wally breathed more freely when he was outside the gates. It had been an entertaining afternoon, all things considered; but he was glad that it was over without any startling discoveries being made.

"You seem to be getting on excellently at my old school," Mr. Penman remarked genially, as they walked down the lane.

"Yes, sir," said Wally.

"You play a good game of football, my boy; and you seem to have some very agreeable friends."

"Ye-e-es!"

"Your Form-master's report of you is not exactly flattering, though."

"Oh!" ejaculated Wally

"You must work hard as well as play hard, my boy," said Mr. Penman kindly. "Keep up the games—they're useful; but don't neglect Form work. A sound mind in a sound body, you know—that's the idea! 'Mens sana in corpore sano'—what?" Mr. Penman chuckled. "That reminds me of my Fourth Form days. But I'm pleased with you—very pleased."

"I'm jolly glad of that, sir!" said Wally.

He was tempted, for the moment, to confide all to his kind friend; but he refrained. The old St. Jim's man would never have understood his keenness to go to Greyfriars, that was certain. Besides, there was his arrangement with Billy Bunter to be considered. Wally was silent.

At the station Mr. Penman shook hands cordially with his protege, and Wally saw him off in the train. The old gentleman departed greatly pleased with his visit to the school, and little dreaming what curious preparations had been made for that visit.

"And now for Greyfriars!" murmured Wally ruefully. "I shall just about do it by bed-time, I suppose—and what a thumping wigging I shall get when I get there! Well, it can't be helped!"

A quarter of an hour later Wally Bunter was on his way homeward to Greyfriars, with the pleasant prospect before him of a "wigging" for staying out late; and certainly he would not be able to give his Form-master the real reason of his having overstayed his time. And while the train bore Wally Bunter westwards, Billy Bunter was rolling home to St. Jim's, wondering what had happened there in his absence.

CHAPTER 11.
Laurels for Bunter.

"BUNTAH, deah boy!"

"Hallo?"

"Did you have to wait for the twain?"

"Train! What train?"

"I suppose you are awah that you have missed callin'-over, Buntah?"

"Can't be helped!" grunted Billy Bunter. "I suppose I've got to go in and be jawed by old Railton—what?"

Arthur Augustus D'Arcy turned his eyeglass curiously on Bunter. Already, somehow, there seemed a subtle change in the fat junior.

"You will have to weport to Wailton, Buntah. But it's all wight—he knows you went to the station to see Mr. Penman off."

"Oh, he's gone, then!"

"Eh?"

"I—I mean, of—of course!" stammered Bunter. "I—I say, I—I saw him off at the station, of—of course. I—I had to wait for the train; that—that's why I—I'm late in. See?"

"Yaas; I pwesumed that was the case, deah boy!"

"Oh, here you are, old top!" said Tom Merry, coming along the passage. "You've missed call-over."

"We had to wait at the station," said Bunter calmly. "I couldn't very well come back before Mr. Penman had started, could I?"

"No. That's all right, if you tell Railton."

Billy Bunter rolled away to the Housemaster's study, grinning. It was evident that there was no suspicion in the School House. He tapped at the door, and the Housemaster's voice bade him enter.

"I'm sorry I'm late for call-over, sir," said the Owl meekly. "There was a delay at the station. The train——"

"Very well, Bunter; I excuse you," said Mr. Railton genially. "Wait a moment, my boy. I am very glad, Bunter, to see that you play such a good game of football."

Bunter started.

"I—I'm a splendid footballer, sir!" he ventured. "If there's a thing I can really play, it's football!"

Mr. Railton's manner became a shade less genial.

"I had an impression, Bunter, that you were something of a slacker," he said. "I am glad I was mistaken."

"Oh, sir! The fact is, I ought to be in the Junior Eleven here," said Billy Bunter confidentially. "I offered my services to Tom Merry for the match to-day. He declined them."

Mr. Railton raised his eyebrows.

"But you played, Bunter!"

The Owl jumped.

"I—I played!" he stuttered. "Oh, ah! Yes! Certainly! The—the fact is——" It dawned upon Billy Bunter that Wally must have played in the Abbotsford match. "I—I certainly played—— Oh, yes, I——"

"You played a very good game, Bunter," said Mr. Railton, puzzled by the fat junior's confusion. "Mr. Penman was very pleased with you, and I am glad to correct my impression of you. I hope, Bunter, that you will endeavour to keep up to the mark, and not fall back into the habits of slacking, which I had previously observed."

"Oh, sir! Oh, certainly! Oh, yes, sir!" stammered Bunter.

He was glad to get outside the Housemaster's study. He was wondering what else Wally might have done while he was at St. Jim's, and was sorely nervous of putting his fat foot in it.

Baggy Trimble was waiting for him in the passage. Billy Bunter eyed him warily through his big spectacles.

But Trimble's manner was friendly, not to say effusive.

"I—I say, Bunter, old chap——" he began.

Bunter continued to eye him.

"You—you needn't be so jolly standoffish," murmured Trimble. "I—I say, old fellow, I'm really sorry there was any trouble in the study. It—it was all a misunderstanding. All Mellish's fault from beginning to end—and—and I really liked you all the time, you know."

Bunter wondered what on earth this might mean, and he judiciously kept silent. Evidently something else unknown to him had happened to account for this new friendliness from Baggy Trimble.

"Mellish won't cut up rusty any more," said Baggy.

"Won't he?"

"He, he! Not after you knocked him down in the study," grinned Trimble. "He doesn't want any more like that, I can tell you. You should see his eye now!"

Billy Bunter drew a deep breath.

"His eye!" he repeated.

"Beautiful mouse under it," chuckled Trimble. "Serve him right! I've told him it served him right! Cheek—trying to keep you out of the study—I've told him so. I never agreed to it! I—I was against it all the time, Bunter. I was, really, you know."

Bunter grinned.

What had happened was pretty clear now; his study-mates had fallen foul of Wally, and Billy was inheriting his cousin's reputation as a fighting-man!

The fat junior assumed a lofty manner at once. He gave Baggy Trimble a threatening blink.

"You tried to keep me out of the study as well as Mellish!" he exclaimed, in a bullying tone.

Trimble backed away.

"No, no, really, old scout!" he gasped. "I—I'm sorry—merely a misunderstanding, you know. I—I want you to come back to No. 2—I do, really! I—I've been looking to it no end."

"Well, I'm coming back," said Bunter. "I'm going up now, in fact. You can help me get my books from the Form-room."

"With pleasure, old man!" said Trimble affectionately.

"I've a jolly good mind to make you do your prep in the Form-room," said Bunter loftily. "Still, I'll let you off, Trimble. But if I ever have any more of your rot——"

"Never!" gasped Trimble, as Bunter doubled a fat fist. "I—I—I—apologise!"

"Well, that's all right. If you ever get your ears up again, you just remember what I gave Mellish!" said Bunter darkly.

"I—I will!"

Billy Bunter's manner was lofty, not to say swanky, as he rolled into Study No. 2, followed by Trimble, carrying his books.

Percy Mellish was there, bathing his eye for about the twentieth time, and he gave Bunter an angry scowl.

"Now, then, none of your sulks!" said Bunter, who almost believed by this time that it was really he who had given Mellish that eye. "If you want another eye to match that one, you've only got to say so, Mellish!"

Mellish scowled without replying.

"Do you hear me?" roared Bunter truculently.

"Yes!" snarled Mellish.

"Mind, I've half a mind to sling you out of the study," said Bunter aggressively. "If I let you stay here you've got to behave yourself. Understand that!"

Grunt!

"Do you understand it?" roared Bunter, clenching his fat fists.

"Yes!" gasped Mellish.

"That's all right, then. I want you to understand, too, that I'm head of this study," said Bunter, swelling almost visibly. "Bear that in mind! I'm not standing any cheek here. If I begin on you again you'll remember it. You too, Trimble."

"Certainly, old chap!" murmured Trimble.

"Make up the fire, Trimble!"

"Yes, Bunter."

"Put a cushion on the armchair for me, Mellish!"

Mellish gave Bunter a look that was only suited to a demon in a pantomime, and hesitated. But he decided to obey. Until he had recovered from that eye, at least, he was not likely to argue with Bunter.

Billy Bunter sat down in the armchair, grinning—monarch of all he surveyed. Study No. 2 really seemed large enough to hold the fat junior now.

. . . .

Tom Merry & Co. had been surprised by the change in Bunter that day.

But they were still more surprised by another change in him the next day.

Quite early in the morning Bunter, taking advantage of an unusual geniality in Arthur Augustus D'Arcy's manner, requested a loan in advance upon a postal-order he was expecting. It was, as he explained, from one of his titled relations.

Arthur Augustus made the loan. But his cordiality vanished, and did not return.

The same day Tom Merry took Bunter to football practice. Bunter's form seemed remarkably unequal at different times; but Tom had decided that he was a valuable reserve, at least, for the Junior Eleven.

Bunter went along cheerfully enough; bucked by the praise he had received for Wally's play, and quite convinced in his own fat mind that he could play Wally's head off, if it came to that.

But his performance on the field made Tom Merry rub his eyes.

Never had the captain of the Shell beheld so clumsy a dud on the football ground; excepting upon the occasions when he had seen Billy Bunter play before.

"My only hat!" was all Tom could say.

The wonderful form of the Abbotsford match was evidently a thing of the past; Bunter was himself again!

"Well, what do you think of me?" asked Bunter loftily. "Rather a cut above the footer you play here—what?"

"Oh, dear! I don't quite know how to tell you what I think of you," answered Tom. "Yesterday you played a splendid game; and to-day you play like a born idiot!"

"Oh, really, Merry——"

"I'm blessed if I understand it. Why, you can't even kick a footer to-day."

"I expected this jealousy, Merry—I'm acustomed to that sort of thing. I suppose I'm going to play regularly for the House and the School?" demanded Bunter loftily.

Tom Merry laughed.

"Not quite, old scout," he answered.

"Eh? When am I going to play in a match, then?"

"About the time of the Greek Kalends, I expect, my son—not while I'm football captain, at all events!"

"Oh, really, you know——"

Bunter did not play in a match. He offered his services several times—but they were declined without thanks. But the fat junior had one satisfaction at least—for a long time one of his chief topics was how he had played Abbotsford and beaten them. And in three or four days the juniors were wondering how they could ever possibly have imagined that Bunter of the Fourth was anything but a fat toad!

THE END.

(Don't miss next Wednesday's Great Story of Tom Merry & Co. at St. Jim's—"BUNTERS FUND!" — by Martin Clifford.)

THE ST. JIM'S GALLERY.

No. 36.—Mr. Philip G. Lathom.

Mr. Lathom can hardly be said to be quite one of the most important figures in the St. Jim's stories. Of masters, Mr. Railton, Mr. Ratcliff, Mr. Selby, and, of course, the Head, all figure more prominently. But all of these have already been dealt with, and of those who remain only Mr. Linton, Monsieur Morny, and Herr Schneider matter much besides the subject of the present sketch.

Messrs. Lathom and Linton, like the French and German masters, have very little to do with the discipline of the school outside their own Form-rooms. But perhaps what they have to do with it there is quite as much as they want.

The Fourth Form is not too easy to handle. Most of the fellows in it are very decent fellows indeed; but that does not mean that they never give Mr. Lathom trouble. Indeed, it is not certain that Arthur Augustus D'Arcy, for instance, quite one of the best of them, does not give him more trouble than Percy Mellish, who is, with the possible exception of Baggy Trimble, quite the worst. For Mellish is sly, and avoids, as a rule, coming too closely into contact with masters; while Gussy wants to argue matters with them, "as one gentleman with another," a thing which no master can really be expected to stand. Not because a man of Mr. Railton's type, or of Mr. Lathom's—they are essentially different, yet both the right sort—fails to recognise the fact that he is a gentleman and that all his pupils ought to be gentlemen as common ground. Where Gussy's theory slips up is on the fact that a master cannot permit a boy to argue with him.

Baggy gives Mr. Lathom trouble enough, no doubt. He is stupid and pig-headed. His construes are abominable, and his manners are revolting. But Baggy, again, is probably less trouble than Ralph Reckness Cardew, a fellow his superior in every way that matters, but not wholly pleasing to any master. Fatty Wynn is as good a fellow as there is in the Fourth, but his little habit of taking something into class in the way of a snack to keep him going through the long time between meals annoys Mr. Lathom a great deal—when he discovers it. In the days of my early boyhood I used to wonder why masters made so much fuss about such trifles as apples, chocolate, cocoanut-ice, or bullseyes in class. They did not prevent one from working. It might have been argued—had one been allowed to argue—that they helped one to get on with the work. But any and every master was down upon them. There came a

day when I myself was down upon them; but that was when I had become a master. I don't pretend to account for it; I did not think the matter out at all; I simply found that I had accepted the magisterial view of the matter—whence it followed that the boys I had to deal with must also accept it, or face trouble!

But I do not think such things really caused me the acute annoyance they caused Mr. Lathom. For I was never a mild little man, as Mr. Lathom is, and I had hardly such strict notions of propriety as he cherishes. I could never quite forget that I had been a boy myself, whereas Mr. Lathom probably seldom remembers that he was a boy. And no doubt he was a good boy. I wasn't.

Mr. Lathom has some of the defects that prevent any master from being quite a first-rate man for a very difficult job. But these matter less in the Form-room than they do outside. In a Form-room there must be a decent quietude, and japes are dead off—or should be. Sympathy with boys may help in class-work, but it is not indispensable; and there are men with sympathy who simply cannot teach at all.

As a Housemaster Mr. Lathom would probably be a pretty complete failure. But he would at least be more acceptable to the boys in his House than Mr. Ratcliff is. As a Form-master he is by no means a failure. His boys like him; not with enthusiasm, maybe, but still, they like him. They certainly respect him; they know that he always means to be just, and if he makes a mistake he does not shirk apologising for it. He does not sling around lines and canings with the liberality that characterises Messrs. Ratcliff and Selby; but, after all, no one wants him to. And he can punish when necessary; he is not too mild for that.

And he is a really good sort. Frank Levison could bear witness to that. Do you remember how Frank, hiding under the table in Mr. Selby's study, overheard a conversation between Messrs. Lathom and Linton that he should not have heard, and the trouble it caused by reason of his feeling that he had no right to repeat it, even though to do so would clear up a quarrel between him and his dearest chum? He went to Cardew for advice at last; and Cardew, who knows his Lathom well, suggested that he should make a clean breast of it to that gentleman. Mr. Lathom showed up well in that matter. He hates conflicts with Mr. Selby; the two men have nothing at all in common. But, to clear Frank, he risked the displeasure of his autocratic colleague; and what he said to Ernest Levison afterwards proved that he was capable of appreciating Frank's standpoint—quixotic as it might seem to some people.

Mr. Lathom is much easier to get round than most of the St. Jim's masters. When Wally Bunter was coming to the school—or was supposed to be coming, for, as you all know, it was Billy who really came—the Terrible Three asked leave from Mr. Linton to go and meet him at the station. Mr. Linton refused them curtly; he saw no reason why they should have leave during class-hours. But Kerr had no great difficulty in persuading Mr. Lathom to let him and Figgins and Wynn go. It is true that Kerr, while avoiding anything like a misstatement, played cunningly upon the Form-master's sympathies; but that only shows that he has sympathies to be played upon.

Kerr is one of Mr. Lathom's pupils who stands high in the master's regard, for, without being a swot, Kerr is a honest worker in class, and in several branches of study much above the average. But Mr. Lathom has been very angry with Kerr more than once, for the Scots junior has made up in the likeness of the Form-master, and has been caught out; and that is the kind of thing calculated to arouse any master's ire. Lathom is quite an easy one for a capable actor like Kerr. He is short, and his features are not too marked, while his little mannerisms are marked, and can readily be imitated. Do you remember how both Lowther and Kerr made up to represent the Fourth Form-master, and how Lowther took in the Fourth, but Kerr took in Lowther himself and most of the Shell? Two Mr. Lathoms were face to face then, and neither of them was the real one!

Mr. Lathom has been the master of the Fourth ever since stories of the St. Jim's Fourth have appeared. Mr. Railton came from Clavering; and one can remember Shell masters before Mr. Linton. But Mr. Lathom was always there. In the early days he used sometimes to take his pupils for a walk in the afternoon—girls' school fashion. They hated it, naturally. It was soon after the coming of Arthur Augustus that something occurred in connection with one of these walks that led to a fight between Kerr and D'Arcy, and proved the dandy's real mettle. Kerr had wangled out of the walk by checking Monteith, and getting lines which would occupy his time while it was being taken. At least, that was supposed to be Kerr's motive. It was not the real motive, however. He appeared during the walk made up as a ragged and h-less youth, who accosted Gussy as "Cousin Arty," and was repudiated with scorn. The Fourth had got hold of the exceedingly mistaken notion that Arthur Augustus was a snob. There is not a fellow in the Form who is less a snob than he is, as they know now. Gussy was naturally very angry with Kerr, and the two fought, and Kerr was licked. They have been good friends ever since, and Kerr probably understands the swell of the Fourth better than most, for he is capable of clearer understanding than most, and certainly likes him as well as almost anyone but his own three dearest chums. There is never any malice behind Kerr's chipping of Gussy.

But this has not very much to do with Mr. Lathom. He did not play at all a strong part when the trouble arose. There was, however, another occasion when he took the juniors out which has more bearing upon his character and tastes.

His tastes are scientific, and one of his pet studies is geology, which, of course, involves much more than the history of the earth's surface. One cannot get really interested in geology without also getting interested in the dim history of primitive man, which is so closely connected with it by reason of the many remains of primitive man found in certain strata of the earth.

The Fourth master tried to get the juniors interested in his own pet subject. Some of them may have been mildly interested; among nearly a hundred boys there are almost sure to be two or three who incline to the scientific. But only one was enthusiastic. That one was Herbert Skimpole. Skimmy backed up Mr. Lathom most loyally, but, of course, in his own queer way, and of course, believing that he himself was the fit and proper person to lead, rather than the mild, benevolent, bespectacled, and rather elderly gentleman who had initiated the business.

Trouble arose out of the excursions of the Junior Scientific Club. Some of it was accidental, and some—well, wasn't. It was quite an accident that Gordon Gay, Frank Monk, and Carboy, in a terrible state of stale egginess, knocked over Mr. Lathom in the High Street of Rylcombe, and left him sitting on the ground with much of the egginess transferred to him, to be accused by P.-c. Crump of being drunk and disorderly. The Grammarians would not have tumbled him over purposely, and Crump would never have laid that charge if he had recognised him.

But the affair of the beery Mr. Jones was no accident. The Terrible Three wickedly suborned Mr. Jones to play the part of a prehistoric man, in a hairy mask and a hairy skin that made him look very like a modern monkey. To find ever so small a relic of prehistoric man pleased Mr. Lathom no end, and Tom Merry & Co. naturally thought that he would be even more pleased to find a whole, live specimen of the article.

And Mr. Lathom was pleased—for a time.

"Amazing—incredible—unheard of, as it seems, the creature is living!" he cried, when Mr. Jones, in a drunken slumber, was lugged out of the cave. "Oh, if only the Royal Society were present now! Oh, Darwin, Huxley, Spencer, and Lodge, why are you not here at this moment?"

"Hoh! Hah! Grooogh! Whurrami?" muttered Mr. Jones.

"Listen, my boys!" said Mr. Lathom, in a whisper. "He is speaking in the unknown language of his period, before, probably, articulate words could be formed by human lips."

But when Mr. Jones—who was no ordinary tramp, but an artiste of sorts—said: "I'm the prehistoric man. I lived before the world began. I used to climb trees with the little chimpanzees, with a pretty, prehistoric Mary Ann"—then Mr. Lathom saw that he had been taken in, and called Mr. Jones an impostor, as he certainly was. But Mr. Jones did not like the term, and he went for the little master, and had to be dragged off him.

The same story which told of that scientific expedition told how Levison—a very different Levison from him of to-day—stole the famous and valuable fossil jawbone from its box in Mr. Lathom's study, and contrived to fasten the guilt of the theft upon Tom Merry, who was saved from expulsion in the event by the detective powers of Gussy! Gussy "worked it out in his bwain that the wottah" had hidden the fossil in Tom Merry's box; but that was not enough—his finding it there only seemed to make Tom's guilt more evident. But he fetched the locksmith who had made the key, and then Levison was bowled out.

It was Mr. Lathom who raised not too well-considered objections to the juniors reading such papers as the "Boys' Friend." You will remember how he came to reverse his decision, how he was rescued when a bull was chasing him, and talked afterwards with the man who had rescued him, and learned a few things from him. That incident shows him as a man with an open mind, at least, if not a remarkably strong one.

He has an open mind and a kindly nature, and no decent fellow could fail to respect and like him. The hero-worship which the few men of Victor Railton's type get is not for such as Mr. Lathom. But they do not want it; respect and some measure of affection will satisfy them.

Extracts from "THE GREYFRIARS HERALD" and "TOM MERRY'S WEEKLY."

WHEN THE GHOST WALKED.

A Tale of Wilton School.  By PETER TODD.

I.

"WHAT piffling rot! There are no such things as ghosts!"

Chumley paused in the middle of his thrilling ghost story and glared round the moonlit dormitory in righteous indignation.

"Who—what giddy bounder said that?" he spluttered angrily. "Why, I'll slay the—— My hat! Of all the blessed cheek, if it isn't that cocky new chap again!"

Chumley was distinctly annoyed. It was bad enough to be interrupted just when he was at the critical part of his hair-raising yarn. But to think that this new chap—a fellow who had only been at Wilton two days—should dare to chip in when he, Chumley, captain of the Fourth, was speaking—well, Chumley could not find words to express himself!

He appealed to the rest of the dormitory.

"Look here, you men, I put it to you. This new chap's too jolly cheeky by half! He wants putting in his place. Now, what shall we do with the rotter—bump him?"

The "men," who were sitting up in bed hugging their knees, simply grinned; so did Merton, the new boy. And this fact angered the great Chumley beyond measure.

Realising that his honour and prestige as head of the dormitory were at stake, he climbed impressively out of bed, and stalked with stately tread across the room.

"Now, you cocky new kid," he observed grimly, grabbing the bedclothes, "out you get! I'll jolly well give you piffling rot! Come out and take a hiding!"

Evidently a hiding did not appeal to the new boy. He held on to the sheets in apparent terror.

"Please don't touch me, sir!" he cried in terrified tones. "I won't do it again! Keep him off, you chaps! Oh, help!"

Laughter ran round the room, and Chumley's face flushed. Then, with a snort, he took a fresh grip of the sheets, and, putting his foot on the side of the bed, and began to pull savagely.

Amid the subdued cheers of the onlookers there followed an exciting tug-of-war. Merton, lying back in bed, easily held his own for some moments. Then quite suddenly he released his grip, and Chumley disappeared backwards amidst an avalanche of bedclothes.

"Ha, ha, ha!" roared the spectators.

"Help! Rescue!" came in muffled accents from the heaving bundle.

Huxley, a crony of Chumley's, was the first to answer the call.

"Come on, you fellows! Let's smash the cocky bounder!" he yelled, leaping out of bed.

The rest of the fellows now thought it high time to interfere. So far the affair had amused them vastly. Many were only too glad to see the lordly Chumley taken down a peg or two. But then, it wouldn't do at all

Printed and published weekly by the Proprietors at The Fleetway House, Farringdon Street, London, E.C. 4, England. Subscription, 8s. 10d. per annum. Agents for Australasia: Gordon & Gotch, Melbourne, Sydney, Adelaide, Brisbane, and Wellington, N.Z. South Africa: The Central News Agency, Ltd., Cape Town and Johannesburg. Saturday, February 22nd, 1919.

to let new chaps get too cheeky; and this chap certainly was.

A moment later the new boy was surrounded by a crowd of pyjama-clad forms. It looked as if he must be swamped. But evidently Merton was a fighter, for even such overwhelming odds did not daunt him. Grasping a pillow, he laid about him with a will.

There ensued a glorious mix-up of whirling pillows and waving legs and arms. In the dim light no one could be clearly recognised, and very soon Merton was forgotten in the general engagement.

For five minutes the battle raged, and the row was terrific. Then Chumley managed to disengage himself from the clinging sheets and the stamping feet. Breathing fire and slaughter, he joined the merry, smiting throng in search of Merton.

He found his quarry at last, and, with an exultant snort, charged. But Merton, a cheerful grin on his heated face, was ready. Next moment, locked in each other's arms, the two lurched about the room.

Suddenly they barged with a thump against a washstand. With an appalling crash and clatter the whole lot toppled over, and Merton and Chumley found themselves lying amid the ruins.

That ended it. The battle ceased by mutual consent, and the combatants sorted themselves out.

"Oh, my giddy grandmother's aunt, what a mess!" gasped Huxley in alarm. "Now you've done it, Chumley, you chump! Old Townley will be here in two ticks!"

"That's where you're wrong," replied Chumley, rising slowly, and rubbing himself tenderly. "I happened to hear our respected Form-master tell Cowley to keep an eye on our giddy selves—going to a whist-drive, or something, to-night, and won't be back until late. All the same, it's a wonder old Cowley hasn't dropped on us before this. For goodness' sake let's put things straight before he does pop in, you fellows!"

But it was too late. Hardly had two or three volunteers tackled the washstand when the door-knob rattled. Thereupon followed a wild scramble for beds, and for the second time that night the unlucky piece of furniture fell with a crash. Then Cowley—a tall, tired-looking senior—lounged into the room.

Some of the juniors produced some very artistic snores, though the majority rather overdid it. And, unfortunately, the peacefulness of the scene was not a little spoiled by the pillow-strewn floor, not to mention the fact that in the hurry four juniors had made a dash for the same bed, and had got a little mixed up in the process.

For some moments the senior eyed the room grimly. Then he looked at the washstand.

"Ah! Removing, apparently!" he observed at length. "Pray do not let me stop the important work! Chumley, I fancy I heard your melodious voice as I entered. Kindly awake! And perhaps Huxley and Masters will cease their snoring, and give you a hand to put this furniture back in its place."

Three minutes later the washstand had been lifted up and the room put into something like order. Then Cowley strolled back to the door.

"Each of you kids will bring me two hundred lines before prep to-morrow night. And if I hear another sound to-night, my sons—well, it will be the worse for some of you!"

With this terrible threat the senior vanished. When his footsteps had died away, Chumley sat up in bed with a snort of disgust.

II.

"THIS is your fault, you potty new ass!" he grumbled.

"No, it isn't old scout!" answered Merton. "I simply said there were no such things as ghosts. And there aren't! It's all imaginative rot!"

"Imaginative rot—eh? S'pose you'll say there aren't such things as burglars next. And"—went on Chumley, with heavy sarcasm—"I suppose you'll dispute the fact that this very school was broken into three nights ago? S'pose you call that imaginative rot—eh, you ass?"

Merton laughed. Considering the fact that the recent burglary at Wilton School was an undoubted fact, and that burglars had been the one absorbing topic since then, it wasn't likely he would dispute it. But he couldn't help laughing at Chumley's attempt at sarcasm.

"Go on, laugh, you rotter!" cried Chumley indignantly. "It's no joke, I can tell you. Of course, being a new ass, it doesn't worry you that the burglars not only got clear away with the old Head's silver-plate, but the footer-cup also—the footer-cup, mind you, that was only won outright last season! Why, you beastly rotter, I——"

"You utter ass!" broke in the new boy. "Of course, I'm as concerned about it as you are! But instead of quacking about it why don't some of you try to trace the thieving rotters. Anyway, what have burglars to do with ghosts? Any idiot knows that burglars are real enough. But as for ghosts—rot! I tell you I don't believe there are any such things!"

"But there are!" insisted Chumley. "What about Wilton Old Church? S'pose you'll say that ain't haunted next! Why, I myself have seen, or, rather, heard it! So have lots of other chaps."

"As I've never heard about it, I won't pass my valuable opinion," said Merton. "But, by the way, which is the church? Not the one I passed on my way from the station?"

"No, that's not it! The old church is about a quarter of a mile from here. It hasn't been used for years; condemned as unsafe—sinking, or something."

"I twig, then! Get on with the yarn! It can't be such drivelling rot as you were ladling out to us when I chipped in just now," observed Merton, with a grin.

"You needn't laugh," said Chumley earnestly. "It's quite true. Isn't it, you chaps? Although it isn't exactly a ghost, but one of those stone figures—gargoyles, or whatever they're called, representing the—well, his Satanic Majesty—stuck up just by the doorway of the church. The yarn is that if anyone runs around the chuch six times, the giddy thingumy,ig'll come down to 'em. Sounds a bit silly, I know; but Huxley and I were passing late one night, and heard it plainly enough walking on the flagstones round the church."

"I thought you said someone had to run round six times before it would come down!" sniffed Merton sceptically.

"So I did, ass! But that's how the yarn runs. Anyway, we've heard the footsteps—so have lots of other people. So there you are!"

"But hasn't anyone tried to do the trick?" persisted Merton; for, though he thought the yarn a bit tall, he was interested in it.

"Rather! Cowley tried it when he was in the Fourth, and they picked him up unconscious after he had run round four times. I know jolly well I wouldn't tackle such a job!"

Chumley didn't think it necessary to mention the fact that Cowley had caught his foot in a flagstone, and in falling had given his head a nasty knock against a gravestone. Even so, the new boy was not convinced.

"Of course it's all rot!" said Merton, when several more juniors had added a few thrilling touches to the yarn. "But I wouldn't mind having a go some time to see what would happen."

"Gas again—you're all gas!" sneered Chumley. "But if you're so jolly clever, why not lay the ghost to-night? Just the night for such a job! Townley's not about, and some of us will come with you. That's the ticket!"

"Hear, hear!" came an excited chorus from round the dorm.

For a moment the new boy hesitated. But he felt he had gone too far to draw out now.

"Right-ho! I'm not particular when!" he said coolly, leaping out of bed. "How do you get to the giddy haunted church?"

"Do you really mean it?" gasped several amazed voices.

"'Course I do," said Merton. "On this condition, though. If I succeed, Chumley must stand the dorm a feed to-morrow night. And if I fail—well, I'll stand one. That's fair enough!"

At this there was a unanimous chorus of approval. The conditions appealed to the fellows. They also appealed to Chumley, who never thought the new fellow would have the courage to carry out his task.

"Right, my pippin; I'm on!" he chuckled, slipping from beneath the sheets. "Buck up! Who's going with him?"

III.

"THERE'S the church!"

Chumley pointed across the playing-fields to where, on a slight hill, the square tower of Wilton Old Church showed, looking strangely silent and ghostly in the moonlight.

The three—Chumley, Huxley, and Merton—were standing on a flower-bed below the dormitory window. Only Chumley and Huxley had been willing to go with the new boy. The rest, though they had lent their aid in making a rope of twisted sheets, with which the adventurers had reached the ground, considered a warm bed preferable to ghost-hunting.

Keeping well in the shadows, the three reached the end of the school buildings, and then made a dash across the playing-fields. A few minutes' brisk running brought them to the boundary rails. Climbing these, the party found themselves in the Church Walk—a narrow path running between the churchyard wall and the rails, and leading to the school.

"No," said Chumley softly, "we'll stop here in the shadow of this tree while you do the trick, Merton, my boy! Half a mo, though! I vote we wait a bit, and see if the ghost's walking to-night. Keep quiet!"

As quiet as mice the three waited, listening intently. Everything was as silent as—well, as a churchyard should be. The wall was low, and beyond the tiers of gravestones the church gloomed dark and forbidding in the moonlight.

From where they crouched the church door could be plainly seen. Chumley was just trying to make out the figure of the gargoyle in the shadows, when suddenly a breath of wind stirred the branches above them, and simultaneously came a sound that made Chumley and Huxley give a startled gasp.

Tap, tap, tap!

"It's walking!" hissed Chumley thrillingly. "Listen!"

For a full minute there was silence. Then clear on the still air, but this time much louder, came the mysterious tapping, sounding remarkably like footsteps on the flagstones.

"It's coming nearer!" gasped Huxley, in alarm. "I'm off!"

Chumley had also heard as much of the ghost as he wished to hear, and followed the flying figure of his chum along the path. The new boy, however, stood firm, though he felt like bolting after the others. But he fought the inclination, and stood listening and watching, determined to find out the meaning of the strange sounds.

One thing he soon noticed. The tapping sounded simultaneously with the rustling of the wind in the trees. For a full minute he stood thus; then, with a chuckle, he turned and strolled along the walk schoolwards.

To his surprise, Chumley and Huxley were waiting some way down the path. Both looked somewhat ashamed of their inglorious flight.

"What the dickens did you scoot like that for?" demanded Merton. "Do you think I'm going to run round the blessed church when you're not there? Not likely! You'd say I'd not done it, then!"

"Why, do you still mean to do it?" gasped Chumley.

"Certainly! Come back, and let's get it over, you asses!"

"But the ghost!"

"Hang the giddy ghost! I don't believe in 'em! If you're not coming, say so! If you are, buck up!"

Chumley and Huxley hesitated a moment. Then they looked at the grinning face of the new boy, and decided that it was best for their reputation to go. And a few seconds later all three were standing once again in the shadow of the church wall.

Without a moment's hesitation Merton scaled the wall, and dropped over on the other side. Treading in and out among the grave-stones, he reached the church door. Then he glanced up, and saw the stone figure above his head.

The gargoyle was particularly ugly and grotesque. The face seemed to leer down with a fiendish grin, which almost made Merton shiver.

But he was determined to carry the thing through now he had started, and a second later he began the run.

As he trotted round his footsteps echoed hollowly to the watchers below; whilst Chumley counted the times Merton passed the church door, expecting every moment that something would happen.

Merton himself was beginning to feel rather nervous when he had completed the fifth round. Every time he passed the church door his eye caught the leering face of the gargoyle, and each time it seemed to leer more evilly.

Rounding the corner by the door for the last time, he barged into something—something particularly solid. And that something—or someone—carried a bulging sack!

For a moment he really thought the gargoyle had got him, and he gave vent to a stifled yell. But an instant later, as he staggered backwards from the impact, enlightenment came. For the man—he could see him clearly now—dropped the sack he was carrying with a clinking thud, and gave vent to a stream of particularly lurid language.

And Merton realised that it was no ghost! Even the busiest of ghosts doesn't usually carry bulging sacks, nor do ghosts use such bad language.

But he had not much time to ponder over these things. Next moment he was struggling in the rough, unghostly grip of two men. Punching and kicking, Merton fought hard to free himself. But the odds were too great, and a minute later he stood panting, firmly held by one of the men. The other stood back and eyed him curiously.

"Why, it's only a blessed kid, Bill!" he gasped, in surprise. "What shall we do with 'im?"

"Tie 'im up an' shove 'im in the church!" replied Bill roughly. "It's time we was off."

"Right y'are!" was the reply. "In with 'im!"

This project did not meet with Merton's approval. He did not argue the point, however.

He acted.

A quick back-heel on the shins of Bill caused that worthy to release his grip with a yell. Then Merton bent swiftly, and, butting Bill's companion below the chest, doubled him up and put him out of action.

After that Merton retreated according to plan.

IV.

He reached the churchyard wall safely, and, glancing back, saw that he was not pursued. Vaulting over, he found Chumley and Huxley still where he had left them. It was a surprise for Merton.

"Hallo! You've not run away, then?" he said breathlessly. "Frozen to the spot with terror I suppose?"

"Don't talk rot!" muttered Chumley excitedly. "I did get the wind up when I heard you yell out. But when I heard those brutes swearing—well, I may be afraid of ghosts, but this is a different thing. What the dickens is up? Who are the rotters?"

"Hanged if I know! There's something jolly rummy on. I'd like to know what's in that sack, too—yes, I'd like to know, by jingo!"

Whereupon Merton whispered his suspicions to his companions. When he had finished Chumley whistled softly.

"Cæsar! I believe you're right, old scout! But what shall we do?"

"Do? Why, tackle them, of course! They are there still—that is," added Merton, "if you're not afraid?"

"Afraid! Not me! I'm game for a scrap!"

"Right, then! Get down quickly. They're coming this way!" hissed Merton warningly.

All three crouched down beneath the shelter of the wall. A moment later gruff voices were heard. Then Bill appeared over the wall. And not until his companion had handed over the sack and dropped to the ground did the pair of ruffians notice the boys.

"Now!" hissed Merton, leaping swiftly on to Bill's back.

For a moment the ruffian staggered backwards in surprise. But he quickly recovered himself, and shook off the junior with ease.

Then began a rough time for the boys. Both men fought savagely, with much strong language and many angry threats. Chumley and Huxley bestowed their attention on Bill's comrade. But Merton had Bill all to himself—and Bill was a handful!

Merton leaned sick and giddy against the wall, where a nasty jab from his burly opponent had sent him. The ruffian was on the point of punching again, when a tall, athletic figure rushed upon the scene.

A straight left caught Bill neatly under the chin and dropped him heavily to the ground.

Then the new-comer turned to the other ruffian; but that worthy did not wait for his turn. He shook himself free from the two juniors' grasp, took to his heels, and fled. Bill stayed where he was, unable to get up, or deeming it safer not to do so.

"Oh, my hat!" gasped Chumley, in mingled relief and alarm. "It's Townley!"

It was! Fortunately for the boys, the master, on his way back from the whist-drive, had appeared just in time.

A moment Mr. Townley waited for the floored ruffian to rise. Then he stared at the boys grimly.

"What on earth is the meaning of this?" he demanded sternly. "What are you boys—— Hallo!"

The master stopped suddenly. From along the path came the sounds of a furious scuffle. Evidently Bill's friend had met trouble of some sort.

In silence the master and the boys—and Bill—waited. Then Bill's companion appeared and behind him a burly, uniformed figure, gripping the fugitive's arm in a ju-jitsu hold—a proceeding that individual evidently strongly resented.

"It's Jones, the bobby!" said Huxley. "My hat! What luck!"

"What's all this? Oh, good-evening, sir!" said P.-c. Jones, recognising Mr. Townley. "What is the matter?"

"That's what I wish to know," said the bewildered master. "Chumley, please explain this astonishing affair."

But it was Merton who explained. He had been examining the sack, and he now held up something that gleamed brightly in the moonlight.

"My aunt, the footer-cup!" breathed Chumley slowly.

"Looks like it," said Merton calmly. "These chaps are the burglars, and this is the swag!"

"If Mr. Townley did not grasp the situation just then, P.-c. Jones did. He had the handcuffs on the ruffian he was holding in a trice, and he stuck a big knee into the chest of Bill to keep that gentleman down.

"But what I cannot understand," said Mr. Townley, somewhat puzzled, "is what the men are doing here with the stuff now. It's three days since the burglary."

"Perhaps they had it hidden here, and have waited their chance to fetch it," suggested Merton quietly.

"H'm! I believe you're right," said the master. And the constable also agreed.

"And now, what are you boys doing out at this time of night?" asked Mr. Townley, turning upon the juniors suddenly.

None of the three was at all anxious to answer; but after a short silence Chumley spoke up.

"We were ghost-hunting, sir!"

"Ghost-hunting? What nonsense!"

"But we've heard the ghost, sir!" cried Chumley earnestly. "We—— Listen! There it is again, sir!"

Everyone listened. Above the moan of the wind in the trees came that weird tapping. Even the policeman and Mr. Townley were startled for the moment. Then the short silence was broken by Merton.

"It's all right. It's only the wind blowing the cord against the flagpole on the church tower!"

All looked up to where the flagpole showed gaunt and bare. And then they understood.

The constable laughed aloud, and Mr. Townley smiled in amusement. Chumley's face flushed redly, and if looks could have killed the new boy would have dropped dead.

"Come, boys!" said Mr. Townley. "Hurry back to school, now. I shall require a full explanation of this business in the morning. Constable, I will help you take your prisoners to the station."

Five minutes later the three adventurers climbed up the rope of sheets, and found the dormitory eagerly awaiting their return.

"Did he do it, Chumley? Hallo, your mouth's bleeding, Merton! Have you been scrapping?"

A chorus of questions and remarks were thrown at the three as the fellows began to n tice things. But Chumley was still sore about the flagpole business, and was too grumpy to answer. Merton and Huxley were busy at the washstands removing the traces of the conflict.

"We'll tell you all about it in the morning," said Huxley at last. "Old Townley will be here in a few secs."

"Yes; but tell us this, old man—who pays for the feed?"

"Chumley!" said Huxley shortly, as he scrambled into bed.

"Good old Chumley!" came the chorus.

Chumley's answer was a grunt, and he scowled across at Merton's grinning face.

"Never mind, Chumley old man!" said Merton consolingly, as he pulled back the sheets. "We'll let you have some—won't we, you chaps?"

. . . .

The next morning the three boys paid a visit by special request to the headmaster's study. But Dr. Reed, delighted at the recovery of his property—for beside the footer-cup all the valuables were found in the sack—took a lenient view of the juniors escapade, and let them off with a couple of hundred lines for breaking bounds.

But, of course, the heroes didn't mind that. And that night, after "lights out," the promised feed came off, and was a tremendous success. Even Chumley forgot his grievance under the benign influence of boundless tuck and conviviality, and joined heartily in drinking Merton's health in bottled ginger-beer.

The Editor's Chat.

For Next Wednesday:

"BUNTER'S FUND!"

By Martin Clifford.

If Bunter had tried to raise a fund for charitable purposes directly after the adventure of Nobody's Study it is hardly likely that he would have found many subscribers.

But the memory of the average boy is apt to be a short one. That is natural enough. The boy looks forward; it is old age that looks constantly back. And the average boy does not long cherish resentment. It has to be a fairly black deed that stamps a fellow once for all in the eyes of his circle.

Then, too, Wally Bunter has been along for a brief visit, and has made an impression that Billy could never have made. He handled Racke and Crooke, and Trimble and Mellish. It does not take a great deal to handle those four sweet youths; but the task is too big for William George. Wally has also played footer, and done great things in that line. Altogether his few hours at St. Jim's was almost enough to give his cousin a new lease of life there.

But if some of you fellows do not know what happens when Billy Bunter deals with trust funds, you can probably guess. And old "Magnet" readers know.

A VERY PLEASANT LETTER.

Most of the letters we get are pleasant; but that from which I am going to quote seems to me particularly so.

Of course, our papers are primarily for boys, secondarily for girls. They were not exactly intended for girls in the first place, but the girls have seized them, so to speak. They are not intended for grown-up readers. Yet we have a good many of these; people who have kept young hearts and a taste for schoolboy humour. The lady who wrote the letter quoted from below is evidently one of these. Her reference is to a paragraph in the "Magnet." But most of you read that paper, I know; and it does not matter, anyway.

"I am much amused by M. G.'s criticism," she writes. "Why, in the name of Fate, does he read the papers? I and my friend read them because we thoroughly enjoy them. We should not waste our time reading them if we did not consider them very clever and highly amusing. We are both grown-up readers—in fact, we have been grown-up for more years than we care to confess! We have read the papers on and off since they first appeared. I consider that, instead of deteriorating in course of time, as many paper do, the GEM and the 'Magnet' are as good as ever—even better.

"How Mr. Clifford and Mr. Richards always give us such clever stories passes my poor understanding.

"I have many friends at great public schools, and my late husband, who fell at Ypres in November, 1914, was a public school boy. He thoroughly enjoyed your papers.

"Do you not think that in M. G.'s case they are as pearls cast before swine? To understand such clever stories one requires a brain—and in M. G.'s case—— Well, 'nuff said!

"This is just to point out to you that sane and sensible people still thoroughly enjoy your stories, and recognise the principles held up in your papers.

"From my own experience of the errand-boy class of your readers, they are more honourable and better-mannered as a rule than non-readers. They all attempt to imitate the immortal Arthur Augustus."

My lady correspondent does not mean, I am sure, that the boys she mentions merely copy Gussy's unusual method of speech. She means that they try to be straight and candid and good-natured, as Gussy is. And they could hardly have a better example in that way.

Your Editor.

N

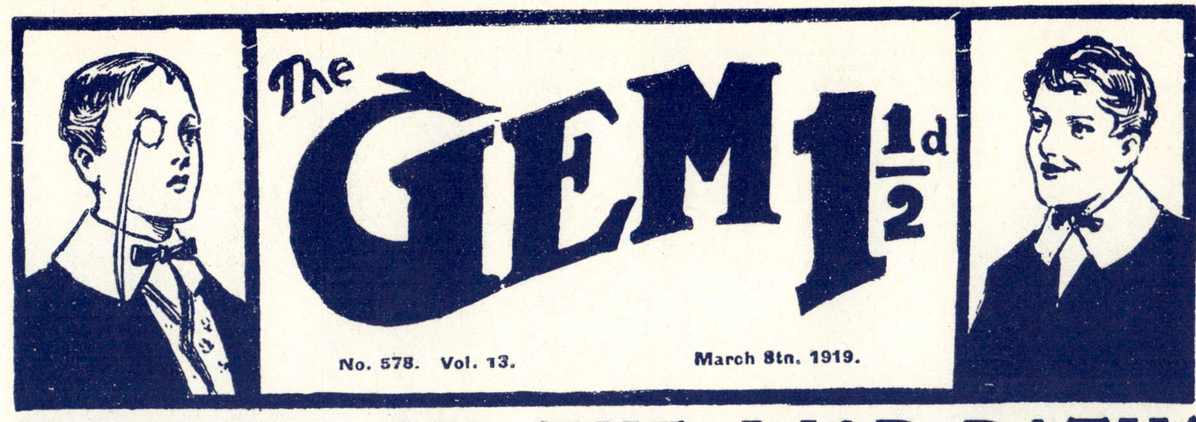

BUNTER ON THE WAR-PATH!

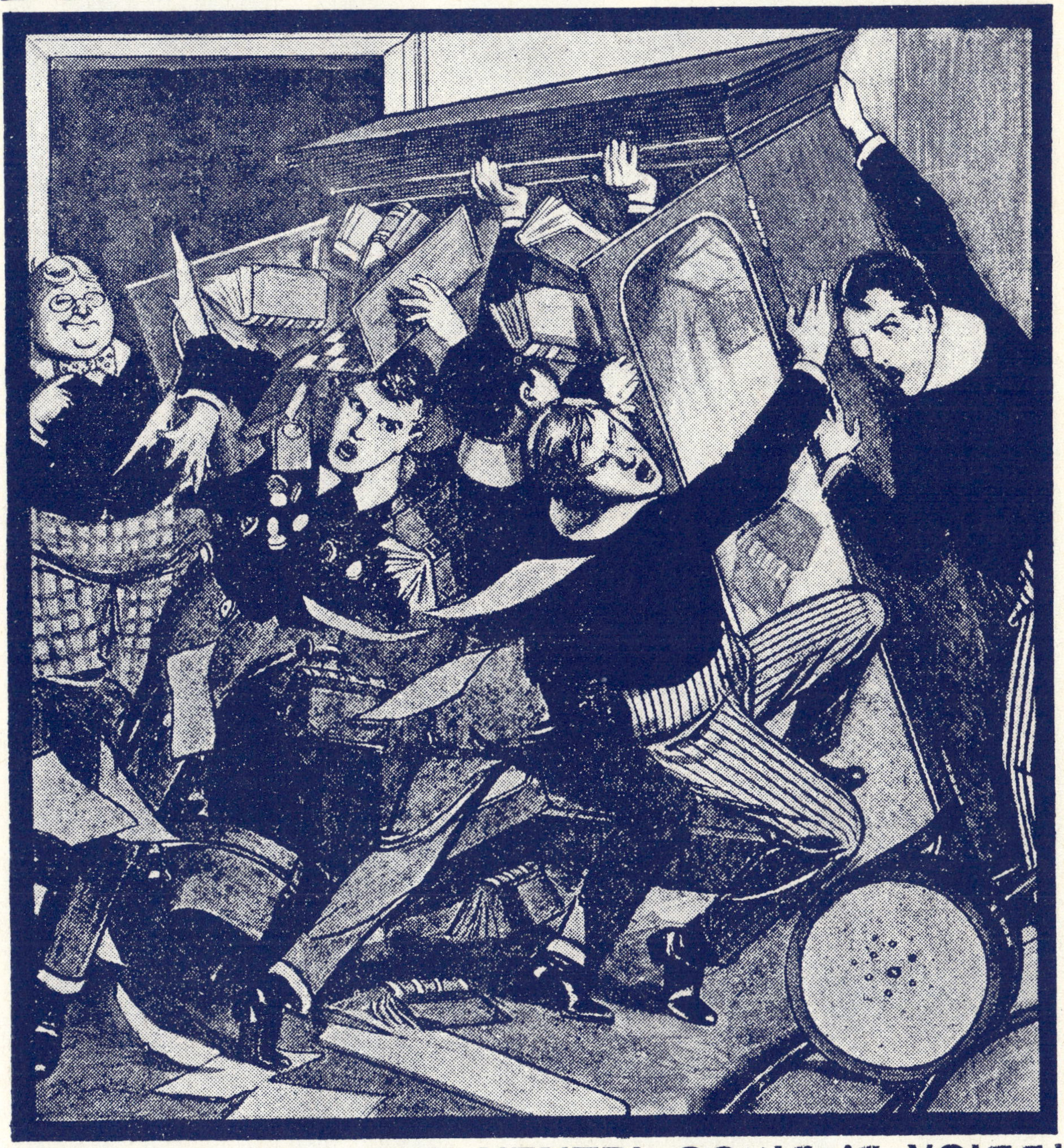

LOOKING FOR THE VENTRILOQUIST'S VOICE!

(A Screamingly Funny Scene in the Long, Complete School Story in this Number.) 8-3-19.

Bunter on the War-Path

A Magnificent, Long, Complete Story of the Chums of St. Jim's.

By MARTIN CLIFFORD.

CHAPTER 1.
After Bunter!

"WHERE'S that fat villain?"

"Eh?"

"Where's that podgy burglar?"

Tom Merry grinned.

Fatty Wynn, of the Fourth Form, was asking those questions, in tones that were simply sulphurous.

Fatty, who belonged to the New House at St. Jim's, had just come into the School House, and he met the Terrible Three in the doorway.

"Where's the fat rascal?" continued the Falstaff of the New House. "Have you seen him?"

"Which fat rascal?" asked Monty Lowther. "We've got two in this House—Trimble and Bunter."

"As well as one who comes visiting," remarked Manners blandly.

"Ha, ha, ha!"

Fatty Wynn snorted.

"I'm after Bunter—that fat rotter! I'm going to slaughter him! It's time he was slaughtered."

"High time," agreed Tom Merry. "Go ahead, and the School House will pass a vote of thanks. But what has Bunter been doing?"

"You'd hardly believe it," said Fatty Wynn, breathing hard. "There's a limit, you know, for everybody but Bunter. He's the very outside edge. What do you think of a fellow who bags another chap's aniseed-balls in the Form-room, where a chap can't make a row because there's a blessed Form-master present? Think of it!"

Fatty Wynn's voice almost failed him, in the excess of his wrath and indignation. It was evident that he regarded Bunter of the Fourth as having reached, and passed, the utmost limit of depravity.

"Awful!" said Tom Merry solemnly—as solemnly as he could. "People talk about the Kaiser. But what has the Kaiser done in comparison with that?"

"Echo answers what?" said Monty Lowther, with a nod.

Fatty Wynn gave another snort.

"Oh, don't be funny! I'm after Bunter—I'm going to boil him in oil. I'm going to spiflicate him! I'm going——"

"But what were you doing with aniseed-balls in the Form-room?" asked Manners severely. "Isn't that against the rules?"

"Of course it is, fathead! That's how Bunter was able to bag them Old Lathom fairly had his blinkers on us, when Bunter slipped his fat paw under my desk and bagged the whole lot. I couldn't say anything, of course, or Lathom would have been down on me for bringing tuck into the Form-room. Of course, the fat villain knew that."

"Ha, ha, ha!"

"It's all very well to cackle!" howled Fatty Wynn indignantly. "They weren't your aniseed-balls. You know how hungry I get in the morning—and I had a very light breakfast this morning, too—only a few sausages, besides the ordinary brekker, and a cake afterwards. I was depending on the aniseed-balls to see me through, and that fat brigand bagged them under my very nose."

The Terrible Three chortled.

They could imagine the feelings of Fatty Wynn at that awful moment, and they sympathised; but they were also able to see the humorous side of the affair, which was quite lost on Fatty.

"I told Figgins and Kerr, and they only chuckled," said Fatty Wynn. "They actually marched me off after lessons, and said I wasn't going for Bunter. I've only just got away from the silly asses. Now I'm after Bunter! I want to know where the fat villain is! I'm going——"

"I say, you fellows."

A fat junior—fatter than Fatty Wynn—rolled on the scene, blinking at the Shell fellows through a big pair of spectacles. He did not observe Fatty Wynn for the moment—but the New House junior observed him, and his eyes gleamed.

"Hallo, here he is!" exclaimed Tom Merry. "Wynn's just come over to see you, Bunter——"

"Oh!" gasped Bunter.

He gave Fatty Wynn one hurried blink, and made a spring for the stairs. The New House junior rushed after him.

"Put it on, Bunter!" yelled Lowther.

"Go it, Fatty!"

"Ha, ha, ha!"

Bunter of the Fourth made remarkable speed up the staircase, considering the weight he had to carry.

He blinked back on the first landing, and saw a fat and furious face behind him, and dashed on again frantically.

"Stop!" panted Fatty Wynn.

"Oh, dear!" gasped Bunter.

The fat junior came into the Fourth-Form passage with a wild burst of speed.

Blake and Co. were chatting outside their study, No. 6 in the Fourth. Blake and Herries and Digby spotted Bunter in time, and backed to the wall. But Arthur Augustus D'Arcy had his back to the new-comer; and, moreover, he was holding forth on the subject of the off-side rule, and he was deeply interested in his own remarks—perhaps the only fellow present who was. His first intimation of the arrival of Bunter was a terrific crash on his back which sent him spinning forward, to land on his hands and knees.

"Yawoooop!" yelled Arthur Augustus. "Oh, cwumbs! Wha-a-at's that?"

Bunter reeled back from the shock.

"Ow! Ah! Oh! Yooooop! Help!"

Before he could flee again Fatty Wynn was upon him.

"Yarooh!" roared Bunter, as the New House junior grasped him. "I say, you fellows—— Help! Murder! Fire! I never touched the aniseed-balls, you know! Yaroooh! Leggo my neck! I never knew there were any—I haven't eaten them all! Yarooh! Besides, there were only fifteen—— Yoooop!"

"Gweat Scott!" Arthur Augustus D'Arcy sat up dazedly. "What is it? Somethin' cwashed into me! Has the woof fallen in?"

"Ha, ha, ha!" roared Blake. "No, nothing's fallen in but Bunter."

"Yoop! Help! Draggimoff!"

"Oh dear! I have weceived a feahful shock! Look at the knees of my twousahs!" wailed Arthur Augustus.

"Yarooh! Help!"

"Take that!" gasped Fatty Wynn. "And that—and that! You fat rotter! I'll teach you to bag my tuck! I'll—I'll——"

"Yoop!"

Blake and Co., grinning, seized Fatty Wynn and dragged him off his victim. They had no doubt—none whatever—that Bunter deserved his punishment; but Bunter was School House and Wynn was New House, and so they laid hands on Fatty Wynn and yanked him away.

"Lemme gerrat him!" roared Wynn, struggling.

"Yow-ow-ow! I say, you fellows wallop him!" howled Bunter. "Yow-ow-ow! I'm hurt, you know! I'm injured! Yow-ow-ow! Wallop the beast!"

Blake and Herries and Dig held the struggling New House junior. Arthur Augustus had no attention to bestow on him. He was carefully dusting the knees of his trousers.

"Will you lemme get at the fat rotter?" breathed Fatty Wynn. "I tell you he bagged my aniseed-balls in the Form-room, under Lathom's nose. Why, you saw him yourself!"

"Don't you know that this is the School House, and dogs and New House chaps are not admitted?" demanded Blake.

"Fathead! Leggo!"

"Bump the fat beast!" howled Bunter.

"Yah! You fat rotter!" yelled Wynn.

"Ha, ha, ha!"

Even Arthur Augustus forgot his trousers for a moment, and chortled. It was very entertaining to Study No. 6 to hear Fatty Wynn and Bunter applying that adjective to one another.

"I never touched his aniseed-balls, you know," said Bunter, blinking at the chums of the Fourth. "Haven't tasted any for weeks, you know."

"Well, my hat!" ejaculated Digby. "There's a big scent of aniseed coming from somewhere when you open your mouth, anyway."

"Yaas, wathah!"

"Oh! I—I—that is, I——" Bunter stammered. "It—it isn't aniseed, you chaps, it's—it's onions!"

"Onions!" yelled Herries.

"Yes—no—I—I mean, it's—it's a—a tooth-powder I use. Smells a bit like aniseed."

"Bai Jove!" said Arthur Augustus. "You feahful fabwicatah, Buntah! Weally, you fellows, I think you had bettah let Wynn thwash him. I weally considah that a feahful thwashin' would do him good."

"Oh, really, D'Arcy——"

"Good idea!" assented Jack Blake. "Hallo, where are you going, Bunter?"

But Bunter was gone.

A door slammed along the passage, and a key clicked. The fat junior was safe from vengeance.

"Oh, you chumps!" snorted Fatty Wynn. "Lemme go! I'll——"

"Frog's-march!" said Blake.

"Hear, hear!"

"New House bounders mustn't come kicking up shindies in this, the respectable House of St. Jim's!" said Blake severely. "Give him the frog's-march!"

"Yaas, wathah!"

"Yah! School House rotters!" roared Fatty Wynn, struggling, as he went back to the stairs in the frog's-march. "I say, I'll—— Yaroooh! Oh, crikey!"

"Roll him down!"

"Ha, ha, ha!"

Fatty Wynn went rolling down, and on the lower landing the Terrible Three met him, and kindly rolled him farther. Fatty Wynn was hardly aware whether he was on his head or his heels by that time. Talbot of the Shell called up from the hall below.

"Cave!"

"Railton!" murmured Lowther. "Bunk!"

The School House juniors vanished. Fatty Wynn sat on the stairs and blinked at Mr. Railton. The School House master stared at him.

"What ever are you doing, Wynn? You have been making a great deal of noise."

"Oh!" gasped Fatty. "I—I—I rolled downstairs, sir."

"Have you hurt yourself?"

"Nunno, sir!"

"You should be more careful, Wynn."

The Housemaster gave rather a suspicious glance up the stairs; but there was no one to be seen. Fatty Wynn limped breathlessly out into the quadrangle. His chums, Figgins and Kerr, bore down on him there.

"Been in the wars?" grinned Figgins.

Fatty Wynn panted.

"Ow! I've been after Bunter! Wow! I've been frog's-marched——"

"Ha, ha!"

"You cackling duffers, I've been rolled downstairs——"

"Ha, ha! What did you expect?"

"Yow-ow-ow! And I haven't scalped Bunter!" gasped Fatty Wynn. "Yow-ow-ow! But I'm going to make him cringe! I've got an idea, too! You wait till we get into class this afternoon!" said Fatty Wynn darkly.

And Fatty Wynn limped home to the New House, still gasping for breath.

CHAPTER 2.

A Surprise for the Shell!

"OH, dear! I wish I'd stayed at Greyfriars!" mumbled Billy Bunter dolorously.

The fat junior was ensconced just inside the Shell Form-room.

It was time to gather for afternoon classes, and Bunter's place was in the Fourth Form-room. But Fatty Wynn's place also was there, and Bunter was extremely anxious not to meet Fatty Wynn. The aniseed-balls were really not worth the trouble they were causing him; but it was too late to think of that now.

In the circumstances Billy Bunter was feeling dismal.

It had seemed to him, at the time, such a ripping idea to change places with his cousin Wally, and come to St. Jim's in that plump youth's name and place; but somehow the scheme hadn't worked out as he expected.

Certainly, everybody believed that he was Wally. But he had worn out Wally's good reputation, and now he was judged on his merits.

And his merits really wanted looking for with a microscope.

The Owl of Greyfriars really felt that he might as well have stayed at his old school, where Wally Bunter was winning golden opinions in his place.

He had left a good many troubles at Greyfriars to fall upon Wally Bunter; but he was making a good many more for himself at St. Jim's, so it really came to the same thing, or nearly.

He blinked out of the doorway, hoping to see Fatty Wynn pass into the Form-room along the corridor, when the coast would be clear.

Some of the Fourth were going in, but Fatty Wynn was not among them.

Bunter drew back his head, and grunted.

"Beast!" he murmured. "Fat rotter, to kick up such a row over a few aniseed-balls. I told him I'd buy him a fresh lot when my postal-order comes, too! Can't take a fellow's word! Yah!"

"Hallo!"

Tom Merry came into the Shell-room with Manners and Lowther—the first to arrive for classes. They stared at Bunter.

"Got your remove into the Shell?" asked Monty Lowther. "I suppose I must expect that soon, from your general brilliance. I hear that you're a real credit to the Fourth, Bunty."

"I say, you fellows——"

"Hallo! Where did that fat frog blow in from?" asked Kangaroo, coming into the Form-room. "You'd better mizzle, Bunter. Linton will be here in two ticks."

"I say, you fellows, have you seen Fatty Wynn?" asked Bunter pathetically. "The fat beast is looking for me, you know. I'm not going to fight him. He's not worth it."

"I shouldn't," said Monty Lowther seriously. "As you are strong, be merciful, you know."

"That's just it," agreed Bunter. "If I lost my temper, you know, I should damage him. I don't want to do that. I'm rather a terrific fighting-man when I'm roused. That's how it is."

"Ha, ha, ha!"

"Shurrup!" came Talbot's voice at the door. "Here's Linton!"

There was sudden silence as Mr. Linton, the master of the Shell, came rustling into the Form-room. Mr. Linton glanced at Bunter.

"Bunter, what are you doing here?" he exclaimed. "You belong to the Fourth Form!"

"I—I—I just came to—to say good-afternoon to you, sir," stammered Bunter.

"What?"

"I—I—— It's nice weather, isn't it, sir?" mumbled the Owl of Greyfriars, wondering whether it was safe to venture into the corridor yet.

"Bunter!"

"I hope you're well this afternoon, sir?"

"My hat!" murmured Tom Merry.

Mr. Linton simply blinked at Bunter. He did not know that the fat junior was trying to gain time by that genial conversation. It looked to him like either impertinence or incipient insanity.

"Bunter, what do you mean?"

"Mum-mum-mean, sir?"

"Leave this Form-room at once!"

"Oh, certainly, sir!"

Mr. Linton turned snappishly away. But Bunter didn't. A blink into the corridor revealed Fatty Wynn coming along with Figgins and Kerr and Redfern. And Bunter drew back his head again with a jerk. The Shell fellows were coming in, and they all stared at Bunter, wondering what a Fourth-Former was doing there.

The master of the Shell had gone to his desk, and he glanced round and knitted his brows at the sight of Bunter still inside the doorway.

"Boy!" he thundered. "Bunter!"

The fat junior spun round.

"Ye-es, sir?"

"What do you mean? Are you out of your senses? Go to your own Form-room at once, Bunter!"

"Ye-e-es, sir! Oh, certainly!" gasped Bunter.

He made a movement to the doorway, and stopped again. Even Mr. Linton in the Form-room was not so dangerous as Fatty Wynn in the passage. Fatty Wynn robbed of his tuck was like unto a lioness robbed of her cubs. Billy Bunter's feet seemed really rooted to the floor inside the Shell Form-room.

Naturally, Mr. Linton did not understand. He picked up a cane from his desk and started towards Bunter. It was not usual for a Form-master to cane a fellow in another Form. But that unwritten law was about to be broken.

"The blessed ass!" murmured Manners. "Linton will scalp him if he doesn't go! I'd rather chance it with Fatty Wynn myself."

"It's a case of Scylla and Charybdis," grinned Monty Lowther. "Linton is Scylla, and Fatty Wynn's Charybdis."

There was a chuckle, and Mr. Linton's attention was transferred for a moment to his class.

"Silence!" he thundered.

"Rats!"

Mr. Linton jumped almost clear of the floor as he heard that reply.

Who had spoken was not to be ascertained. The voice seemed to come from the back of the class.

The Shell fellows, almost dazed themselves, turned in their seats, craning their necks to look for the speaker.

There was a silence that could be felt in the Form-room.

Never in the history of St. Jim's had a Form-master been thus answered in his own Form-room, and it took away the breath of both master and pupils.

Mr. Linton found his voice at last.

He advanced towards the palpitating class, quite forgetful of Billy Bunter.

"What?" he stuttered. "Who—who spoke? I order that boy to stand out at once—immediately!"

There was no reply.

"Who spoke?" thundered Mr. Linton.

Silence.

"Was it you, Gore?"

George Gore jumped.

"I? Certainly not, sir!"

"It sounded like your voice!"

"It wasn't, sir. My hat! I—I never spoke! Did I speak, Skimmy?" exclaimed Gore, in great alarm.

Skimpole, who was seated beside Gore, shook his head.

"I assure you, sir, that Gore did not utter that extremely disrespectful remark," said Skimmy, in his solemn way.

"I demand to know the name of the boy who answered me!" exclaimed Mr. Linton. "If he does not come forward I shall punish the whole class. The boy must be known to several others at least."

There was dead silence.

"Very well," said Mr. Linton, compressing his lips. "The whole class will be detained for one hour after lessons."

He turned back to look for Bunter. But the Owl of Greyfriars was gone. The last of the Fourth had gone into their Form-room, and Bunter had ventured out into the corridor at last.

That afternoon was not a happy one for the Shell. Mr. Linton's temper was acidulated, his tongue bitter, and the weight of his wrath fell heavily upon the unfortunate Shell. And the suffering juniors, while feeling inclined to "scrag" their Form-master, were feeling still more keen to "scrag" the disrespectful youth who had answered "Rats!" and caused all the trouble. But who that disrespectful youth was remained a mystery.

CHAPTER 3.
A Terrible Temptation!

BILLY BUNTER rolled into the Fourth Form-room several minutes late. The Fourth were all in their places, and Mr. Lathom was at his desk, and he gave Bunter a reproving blink.

"Bunter, you are late!" said the master of the Fourth severely.

"Sorry, sir!" said Bunter meekly. "Mr. Linton was speaking to me, sir. I—I didn't like to interrupt him."

"Oh, in that case I excuse you, Bunter," said Mr. Lathom unsuspiciously. "You may go to your place."

Bunter's place, as it happened, was next to Fatty Wynn of the New House. He intended to find some other place, but he found that the juniors had not left him any other. Next to Fatty there was plenty of room; but the Fourth-Formers had spread themselves out to take up all other available space. Grinning looks were turned upon the fat junior as he stood blinking round him. It was evident that the whole Form had entered into that little joke.

"Why do you not sit down, Bunter?" called out Mr. Lathom

"I—I'm just going to, sir," stammered Bunter.

"Well, do so at once."

"I—I say, D'Arcy, make room for a chap," whispered Bunter.

"Your place is vacant, deah boy," answered Arthur Augustus, with a smile.

"I'd rather sit beside you."

"I would wathah not, Buntah, thank you all the same."

"Bunter!"

"Ye-e-es, sir?"

"Sit down at once!"

"Oh, dear! Yes, sir! I say, Mulvaney——"

"Go and eat coke, intirely," answered Mulvaney minor cheerily.

"I say, Blake——"

"Rats!"

"Digby, old chap——"

"If you old chap me, I'll biff you," answered Dig.

"Move up a bit, Roylance, old fellow——"

"Bow-wow!"

"I say, Julian, be a pal——"

"No fear!"

"Cardew! I say, Cardew——"

"Rats!"

"Bless my soul!" exclaimed Mr. Lathom, peering in great astonishment at Bunter. "What does this mean, Bunter? Are you aware, sir, that you are delaying the lesson? Do you desire me to administer chastisement, Bunter?"

The unhappy Owl made a dive for his seat.

He plumped down beside Fatty Wynn, palpitating. The Falstaff of the New House gave him a ferocious look.

"You fat villain," he whispered, "I'm coming out with you after lessons! I'll get hold of your neck—see? You wait a bit!"

"I—I say, Wynn, old chap——"

"Br-r-r-r!"

"You—you see, dear old fellow——" murmured Bunter.

"None of your soft sawder," answered Fatty Wynn. "And don't you dare to lay your fat paws on my jam-tart, that's all!"

"Silence in class!" rapped out Mr. Lathom.

The lesson proceeded; but Billy Bunter was not bestowing much attention upon Mr. Lathom. Fatty Wynn's warning words had caused him to blink under the desk; and there, within easy reach of his fat fingers, lay a juicy jam-tart, simply luscious to Bunter's greedy eyes.

Fatty Wynn had apparently provided against a possible "sinking" in his plump inside before tea-time. The jam-tart was large, it was flaky, it was thick with jam, and it looked very tempting. Billy Bunter felt an almost irresistible impulse to slide his fat hand along the ledge under the desk and capture it.

But he resisted the temptation.

He tried to turn attention elsewhere; he even listened to Mr. Lathom for some minutes.

Vengeance was still hovering over him for the "scoffing" of the aniseed-balls that morning. If the jam-tart followed the aniseed-balls there really was no telling what Fatty Wynn might do.

But as the afternoon wore on Bunter debated that matter in his mind, thus losing the advantage of the valuable instruction he might have derived from Mr. Lathom by paying a little attention to the Form-master.

Form-masters and form-work weighed little in Bunter's estimation in comparison with a fat, juicy jam-tart.

He was getting hungry; in fact, he had got. He generally was hungry; and the sight of tuck made him feel as if he had been three weeks in an open boat at sea.

He was no longer sorry that he had been forced to sit beside Fatty Wynn. He had felonious designs upon that jam-tart, and now he was only waiting for a favourable opportunity. He had argued the pros and cons of the case, and settled the point. If Fatty Wynn was going to "pitch into him" for bagging the aniseed-balls there was no help for it, and he might as well bag the jam-tart also, on the principle of being in for a penny in for a pound. As there was certain trouble in any case, why not bag the jam-tart and make it worth while?

That was unanswerable logic to Bunter's fat mind. And, utterly regardless of the valuable information Mr. Lathom was just then imparting with regard to the coal-fields of Great Britain, Billy Bunter watched for an opportunity.

Curious to relate, Fatty Wynn seemed to have forgotten the tart. He was listening to Mr. Lathom with rapt attention, as if he was specially desirous of knowing all about the coal-fields of Great Britain above and beyond any other subject in the universe. His head was turned from Bunter, and he seemed to have forgotten the tart, and Bunter, too, in his intense interest in the subject of coal-fields.

Bunter's fat hand slid under the desk, it slid along, and he trembled. If Fatty Wynn had looked round he would have withdrawn that filching paw hastily. But Fatty did not look round. He was listening to Mr. Lathom as if pearls of wisdom were falling from his lips.

The Owl's fat fingers touched the tart at last, and he drew it along slowly and cautiously in front of him. It was safe under his desk at last, and still Fatty Wynn seemed unaware.

Bunter's heart was beating fast now.

The jam-tart was his, but eating it was another matter. He could not sit in full view of Mr. Lathom, and bolt a jam-tart under his eyes. But great minds rise to all emergencies, and Bunter's rose. What was easier than dropping a pen, stooping under the desk to pick it up, and shoving the jam-tart into his mouth under cover of the desk?

Nothing was easier. It would not take more than a few seconds to bolt the tart, and he would rise like a giant refreshed with wine.

Clatter!

A pen and a pencil rolled on the floor by Bunter's feet. He moved off the form, and slipped down to grope for them. Even then Fatty Wynn did not look at him, but a fat grin might have been seen stealing over his visage.

Bunter, stooping under his desk, was not bothering about the pen and the pencil. His fat grasp was on the tart, and in an instant it was jammed into his eager mouth.

His teeth crunched into it ecstatically, and the next moment there was a fiendish yell, that woke every echo in the Form-room.

"Yaroooh! Groogh! Yoooooh! Gugggggggg!"

CHAPTER 4.
Hot Stuff!

"GUG-GUG-GUGGGG! Yooop! Groooch!"

Billy Bunter leaped up from the floor, howling and spluttering as if his senses had suddenly left him.

He knocked his head on the desk as he rose, and howled again.

Mr. Lathom spun towards him, staring. The Fourth-Formers all turned to stare. Bunter was spluttering, sputtering, snorting, gasping, and clutching at his mouth with frantic hands.

"Groogh! Oh, I'm burnt! Yoop! Help! Fire! Yow-ow-ow!"

"Bunter!" roared Mr. Lathom.

"Yarooooop!"

"Boy!"

"I'm burnt! Yooop! Mustard! Yaroooh!"

"Ha, ha, ha!"

"Is the boy mad?" gasped Mr. Lathom. "Bunter! Be silent! I command you to cease this commotion at once!"

"Yurrrrrggghh!"

"Bunter!"

"Gug-gug-gug-guggggg!"

"Bless my soul! Bunter, come out before the class at once! What is the matter with you? Is it a fit? Are you subject to fits? Blake, are you aware whether Bunter is subject to fits?"

"Ha, ha! I—I mean, no sir! I—I think not."

"Bunter! Come here at once! Bless my soul, the boy is foaming at the mouth! Goodness gracious!"

"Yurrrggggh! Mustard!" shrieked Bunter. "I'm burnt! Yah! You fat rotter! You did it on purpose! Yarooh! Ow-ow!"

"Mustard!" repeated Mr. Lathom dazedly. "Has the boy been eating mustard—in class, too? Bunter, what does this mean?"

"Grooogh! I'll pulverise him!" shrieked Bunter. "He did it on purpose, and he knew I was after that tart all the time! That's why he wasn't looking! Yow-ow!"

"Ha, ha, ha!"

"Silence! What does the boy mean? Bunter, if you are not out of your senses —— Why, bless my soul, stop him!" shrieked Mr. Lathom

Billy Bunter, beside himself with fury, turned upon Fatty Wynn and smote him hip and thigh. He was aware by that time that the jam-tart had been brought into the Form-room for his especial benefit—Fatty Wynn having previously concealed a thick slab of mustard under the jam!

Bunter had crunched that slab of mustard in his mouth, and the effect almost lifted the roof off his mouth.

Water was streaming from his eyes, and his fat face was like unto a newly-boiled beetroot in hue.

Fatty Wynn jumped up as he found himself attacked, and returned the assault with interest. Mr. Lathom waved his arms in great excitement, and shouted to the juniors to drag the infuriated Owl off. He was convinced that it was a fit by this time.

Blake and Roylance and Levison seized Bunter, and yanked him away from Fatty Wynn. The Owl was spun out before the class, still yelling.

"Be gentle with him!" gasped Mr. Lathom. "The unhappy boy is not responsible for his actions."

"Ha, ha, ha!" roared the Fourth.

"Silence! How dare you laugh!" thundered Mr. Lathom. "This is not a laughing matter. The unfortunate boy is out of his senses! Calm yourself, Bunter! Pray strive to calm yourself."

"Yaroooh!"

"My poor boy! Pray——"

"Gug-gug-guggg! Leggo! Yow-ow-ow!"

"Do not let him go, Blake! Hold him, Herries! Lay him gently on the floor, that will be best! Bless my soul! I am quite unacquainted with the treatment of fits! Lay him down gently—very gently."

Crack!

"Yaroop!" yelled Bunter, as his head came into contact with the Form room floor. "Ow! Yow! My napper! Yoooop!"

"Water! Someone fetch water!"

"Don't you chuck any water over me!" howled Bunter. "I ain't in a fit! Yarooh! If you don't take your knuckles out of my neck, Herries, I'll bung you in the eye!"

"Ha, ha, ha!"

"Herries, be careful——"

"'Tain't a fit!" shrieked Bunter. "I don't have fits! Yarooh! It was the mustard. It was that fat villain. Ow!"

"The poor boy's mind is wandering," said Mr. Lathom, with deep compassion. "There can be no mustard here. Calm yourself, Bunter."

"It was in the jam-tart!" raved Bunter.

"The what? There is no jam-tart here, Bunter. Pray—pray strive to collect your senses."

"Yarooh! Leggo my neck, Blake, you beast! I'll spifflicate you! Yoop! Take that, Herries, you rotter!"

"Oh!" roared Herries, as Bunter, getting a foot free, lunged at his waistcoat. Herries sat down quite suddenly.

"Bai Jove! Poor old Hewwies!" ejaculated Arthur Augustus. "Weally, Buntah——"

"Lemme go!"

Billy Bunter struggled to his feet, and jammed his spectacles on his little fat nose. He was snorting like a grampus, in a state of breathless wrath. Mr. Lathom blinked at him.

"Bunter! Is it possible that you are not in a fit?"

"Of course I'm not!" howled Bunter.

"Then what is the matter with you? You may leave him alone, boys. He does not, I think, require restraint."

"Go hon!" murmured Blake.

"What did you say, Blake?"

"'Hem! N-n-nothing, sir."

"You may go back to your places. Now, Bunter," said the master of the Fourth sternly, "tell me what this ridiculous scene means?"

"Wow! It was the mustard! My mouth's burnt off!" gasped Bunter. "I'm going to be ill! I think very likely I shall die! Wow! If I do, I hope they'll hang Fatty Wynn! Yow-ow!"

"You have been eating mustard?" ejaculated Mr. Lathom.

"It was in the tart," gasped Bunter.

"What utter nonsense! Tarts are not made with mustard—at least, I have never heard of such a thing. In any case, what were you doing with a tart in the Form-room, Bunter—if there is such a thing as a mustard tart, which I do not believe for one moment?"

There was a gasp of merriment from the Fourth at the idea of a mustard-tart. Billy Bunter pointed an accusing fat finger at Wynn.

"It was that fat rotter——" he began.

"Bunter! How dare you use such expressions!"

"I—I mean it was him who——"

"You should say it was 'he,' Bunter," interrupted Mr. Lathom.

"It was he—him—he, I mean—he who put the mustard in the tart, and nearly blew my head off!" gasped Bunter.

"Wynn! Can you explain this?"

"Yes, sir," said David Llewellyn Wynn cheerfully. "I put a tart with mustard in it under my desk, sir."

"You brought a tart here to eat in the Form-room, Wynn!" exclaimed Mr. Lathom severely.

"No fear! I—I mean, no, sir. I don't like mustard-tarts. It was to punish Bunter for stealing the tart. I knew he'd bag it, and I hoped it would be a lesson to him, sir."

"Bless my soul!" Mr. Lathom understood at last. "Wynn, you have no right to play such childish tricks in the Form-room. I shall cane you, Wynn. As for you, Bunter, you have been deservedly punished for your greediness. I am ashamed of you!"

"Ow!"

"Wynn, come here, and hold out your hand!"

Swish, swish!

Fatty Wynn looked a little green as he went back to his seat with his fat hands tucked under his arms. But he comforted himself with the reflection that it was worth it. Bunter was likely to think twice, if not three times, before he bagged tuck from under Fatty's desk again.

"Bunter," said Mr. Lathom severely, "you will stand in the corner till lessons are over. I am sorry to punish you like a little boy, Bunter, but if you act like one you must be treated like one. Stand in the corner!"

SOUNDING BUNTER'S HEART!

Billy Bunter rolled into the corner of the Form-room, the Fourth-Formers grinning at him as he went. Mr. Lathom's frowning glance restored them to gravity. But as the lesson proceeded the juniors glanced every now and then at the Owl and smiled. Billy Bunter's fat features were incessantly contorted as he stood in the corner. He was still feeling the effects of the mustard.

CHAPTER 5.
Very Mysterious!

"OH dear!"

That ejaculation came involuntarily from William George Bunter, about a quarter of an hour later, and Mr. Lathom looked round severely.

Billy Bunter was not sensitive, and he was rather glad, at first, to be standing in the corner instead of doing the work of the Form in his place. But his fat little legs were soon tired. They had a good deal of weight to support.

He shifted from one leg to the other, and back again, and grunted and mumbled, and finally ejaculated "Oh dear!"

"Kindly be silent, Bunter!" snapped Mr. Lathom.

"I'm tired, sir!"

"If you speak again I shall cane you!"

"Oh!"

Billy Bunter stood silent, shifting his legs again. His little round eyes were glittering behind his spectacles now. He was feeling very injured. His mouth was still smarting with mustard; and the juniors, instead of being properly sympathetic, evidently only looked on the matter as a joke. And he—the injured party—was set to stand in the corner! It was no wonder that the Owl of Greyfriars felt wrathful, and that he bethought him of his ventriloquial gift—which had earned him more kicks than halfpence, so to speak, at Greyfriars, but was, naturally, not known to the St. Jim's fellows. Some of them had heard of Billy Bunter's ventriloquism, certainly, when at Greyfriars on visits; but Bunter of the Fourth was supposed to be Wally Bunter, and Wally did not share his cousin's queer gift. Billy Bunter felt that it would be quite safe.

Mysterious voices in the Greyfriars studies were generally followed by fellows throwing things at Bunter; but at St. Jim's circumstances were quite different. No one was likely to suspect the supposed Wally.

Bunter cleared his throat with his fat little grunt, and prepared for business—clearing for action, as it were.

Mr. Lathom was devoting his attention just then to Baggy Trimble, who was discovered with bullseyes in his mouth. The Form-master was giving Trimble a severe lecture, to which Baggy listened with downcast eyes, fervently hoping that the little gentleman would not think of making him turn out his pockets. In the midst of Mr. Lathom's lecture a voice proceeded from the back of the class.

"Give us a rest, old nut!"

Mr. Lathom broke off suddenly. He could scarcely believe his ears.

"Mellish!" he thundered.

Percy Mellish stared.

"Yes, sir?" he stammered.

"How dare you interrupt me, and with such a remark, Mellish!"

"I didn't, sir! I never spoke!"

"It was your voice, Mellish!"

"Not at all! Someone behind me, I think, sir!" gasped Mellish.

"There is no one behind you, as you are in the back row, Mellish! It was you who spoke!"

"It—it wasn't! I swear it wasn't, sir! I never opened my lips! I——"

"You are on the w'ong twack, Lathom, old top!"

"Gussy!" gasped Blake, in amazement and alarm.

"D'Arcy!" roared Mr. Lathom.

"Yaas, sir?" said Arthur Augustus innocently, looking up in surprise.

"How dare you!"

"Bai Jove! I do not quite follow you, sir! Have I done anythin'?" asked the swell of St. Jim's.

"You spoke! You addressed me as—as—as old top!" shouted Mr. Lathom, justly incensed at being addressed as an old top.

"I, sir? Certainly not! I should wegard it as diswespectful to addwess a gentleman of your yeahs, sir, as an old top!" said Arthur Augustus warmly.

"I heard you, D'Arcy!"

"I assuah you, sir, that you are labahin' undah a misappwension. I heard the wemark made, but I certainly did not make it."

"I repeat, D'Arcy, that I know your voice perfectly well, and that you made the remark. Step out here!"

"Don't go!" came a voice from somewhere.

Mr. Lathom spun round.

"Bless my soul! This is more than impertinence—it is actual rebellion! Who spoke to D'Arcy?"

"Find out!"

"Wha-a-a-at?"

Mr. Lathom looked quite dazed—and so did the juniors. All the fellows were looking round in search of the speaker.

"What—what—what does this mean?" spluttered Mr. Lathom. "Boy! Step out at once! I shall chastise you most condignly!"

Apparently the speaker was not attracted by the prospect of condign chastisement. At all events, he did not step out. Mr. Lathom was almost purple by this time.

"If the boy does not immediately step out I shall punish the whole Form!" thundered Mr. Lathom.

"What rot!"

"Wynn! It was you who spoke!"

"Not at all, sir!" said Fatty Wynn in alarm. "Never opened my lips, sir!"

"It was your voice!"

"It wasn't, sir!"

Figgins and Kerr were staring blankly at their fat chum. They, as well as Mr. Lathom, were certainly under the impression that it was Fatty Wynn's voice that had spoken.

"Don't tell me untruths, Wynn! Step out here!"

"Go and eat coke!"

"WYNN!"

"I—I didn't speak, sir!" howled the unfortunate Fatty. "Not a word, sir! It was somebody else!"

"Nonsense! Will you come out here, or must I come and fetch you, Wynn?" shouted the Form-master.

Fatty Wynn reluctantly left his place, as Mr. Lathom grabbed a cane from his desk. In the corner, Billy Bunter grinned serenely. The affair of the mustard-tart was about to be avenged.

"Swish, swish!

"Now, Wynn, let that be a warning to you——"

"I never spoke, sir!" said Fatty Wynn, rubbing his hands ruefully. "I assure you, sir, I wouldn't speak to you like that! It was caddish, and I wouldn't do it!"

"Nonsense! Go to your place!"

"Wotten! This is vewy unjust!"

"D'Arcy!"

"If you are about to say that I made that wemark, sir, I assuah you that you are mistaken!"

"Hold out your hand, D'Arcy!"

"I will do as you wequest, sir, but I pwotest!" said Arthur Augustus firmly. "I certainly did not say anythin'!"

"It wasn't D'Arcy, sir!" gasped Blake. "I was looking at him, and he never moved his lips, sir!"

"I know D'Arcy's voice, Blake!"

"Rats!"

"Blake! How dare you!" shrieked Mr. Lathom.

"I didn't say rats!" exclaimed Blake. "I didn't! It—it—it's somebody playing tricks, or else the blessed place is haunted!"

"Yaas, wathah, it is a twick of some sort!" exclaimed Arthur Augustus. "Some wottah is hidden heah playin' twicks!"

"Oh, you're a silly ass, D'Arcy!"

"Weally, Hewwies——"

"Well?" said Herries, staring.

"Hewwies, I wegard that wemark——"

"What do you mean, fathead? I never spoke."

"Silence!" exclaimed Mr. Lathom, in bewilderment. "Really, it does seem that there is trickery of some sort! Surely there cannot be some extraneous person concealed in the Form-room!"

"Bow-wow!"

"Who—who—who was that?"

"Find out!"

Mr. Lathom was blinking blankly at his class. The voice came from somewhere, but where, was a mystery. He certainly could not put his finger on any of the juniors as the speaker.

"This — this — this is most extraordinary!" he exclaimed at last. "There is certainly someone—somehow——"

"I told you it wasn't me, sir!" said Fatty Wynn, with great dignity.

"I—I believe you, Wynn. I—I am sorry I punished you!" gasped Mr. Lathom. "But—but really, where—where is the person who is speaking? It is most extraordinary! Someone must be concealed here!"

Mr. Lathom glanced helplessly round the Form-room. There really was not any likely place where any person, extraneous or otherwise, could be concealed. He gave a jump as a voice came from the door.

"Ta-ta, old nut! I'm off!"

"Bless my soul! It is someone in the passage!" exclaimed Mr. Lathom. "Someone has called through the keyhole!"

"Keep your wool on!"

Mr. Lathom rushed to the door and threw it open. He rushed into the corridor, his cane ready for action. But the corridor was empty! If the owner of the mysterious voice had turned the corner he had certainly been very swift—at all events, he was not there.

Puzzled and perplexed, Mr. Lathom came back into the Form-room. In his corner Billy Bunter smiled, and winked at the ceiling. Fortunately, the Greyfriars ventriloquist stopped at that point, and the mysterious voice was heard no more in the Fourth Form-room. But there was much perplexity and great wrath in the Form, and William George Bunter felt that the ache in his fat little legs was avenged.

CHAPTER 6.
Bunter Takes the Cake!

"VEWY wemarkable!"

That was Arthur Augustus D'Arcy's opinion, delivered when the Fourth were dismissed from lessons.

The juniors gathered in groups in the corridor discussing the curious happenings of the afternoon. Mr. Lathom had gone to his study quite as perplexed as his pupils.

"Wemarkable!" went on Arthur Augustus, holding forth to a group on the subject. "There was some feahful wottah playin' twicks in the cowwidah, you know—speakin' thwough the keyhole all the time!"

"Blessed if I see how he could!" said Blake.

"Mr. Lathom spotted him at last, Blake—or, wathah, his voice. He must have got away wathah quickly. But it was vewy odd that he was able to imitate Fatty's voice so vewy neahly——"

"What rot!" said Fatty Wynn. "Why, it was a sort of fat gurgle when Lathom thought it was me speaking!"

"Yaas, wathah—that's what I mean!"

"Why, you silly ass——"

"Weally, Wynn——"

"He got your voice all right, though, Gussy," said Blake. "I thought it was you."

"I suppose that is a joke, Blake?" said Arthur Augustus stiffly. "The voice Mr. Lathom took for mine was simply a squeak!"

"Exactly!"

"I wegard you as an ass, Blake!"

"Nobody seemed to know his own toot when he heard it," grinned Levison. "It's a jolly queer thing. I suppose it must have been somebody in the passage. But who was it?"

"That is wathah a mystewy."

"I say, you fellows——"

"Oh, Bunter knows, of course!" said Blake sarcastically. "Bunter knows everything, and a few over. Who was it, Bunter?"

"I say, perhaps the place is haunted!" said Billy Bunter, blinking at them with owl-like seriousness.

"Fathead!"

"Ass!"

"I say, you fellows, I've heard that there's a ghost at St. Jim's—the ghost of some old monk, or monkey, or something——"

"So there is!" agreed Blake. "He's never been seen or heard, but he belongs to the place. But the ghost of St. Jim's wouldn't haunt the Form-room and cheek a Form-master. Ghosts don't do that."

"Wathah not! You are wathah asinine, Buntah!"

"Oh, really, D'Arcy——"

"Bai Jove! The Shell are not out yet," said Arthur Augustus, glancing up the corridor. "Linton's just gone by. I wondah what they are stickin' in the Form-room for?"

"Detained, perhaps," remarked Blake. "Linton was looking ratty. Let's give 'em a look-in."

Study No. 6 walked along to the Shell-room and looked in. They found the whole Shell sitting dismally at their desks. Evidently it was a case of detention.

Tom Merry glanced at them lugubriously.

"Linton in a wax this afternoon?" asked Jack Blake, with much sympathy.

"Yes!" groaned the captain of the Shell. "We're detained for an hour, and we're on blighted mathematics! Improving our minds——"

"Not our tempers!" groaned Monty Lowther.

"Bai Jove! That is wathah hard lines, deah boys!"

"All through some thumping ass saying 'Rats!' to Linton!" said Talbot. "He couldn't be expected to take it smiling."

"Bai Jove! But it is wathah wuff to detain the whole Form because one fellow said 'Wats!' Who was it?"

"Nobody knows; he wouldn't own up!" growled Tom Merry.

Jack Blake gave a sniff.

"In the Fourth Form a fellow would have owned up at once, under the circs," he remarked.

"In the Fourth a fellow wouldn't have had the nerve to say 'Rats!' to a Form-master at all!" retorted Tom Merry.

"My hat!" exclaimed Blake suddenly. "Perhaps it was the same bounder who's been playing tricks in our Form-room? Somebody's been yowling in from the passage through the keyhole, and put Lathom in no end of a wax, and we can't find out who it was!"

"It wasn't through the keyhole here," said Tom. "It was some silly ass in the class, and we're going to find him out presently, and I'll scalp him!"

"I say, you fellows, I believe the place is haunted——"

"Rats!"

"What are you doing here?" came the deep voice of Mr Linton, from behind the group of juniors in the doorway.

"Bai Jove!"

Blake & Co. did not stop to explain what they were doing there; they bolted.

Mr. Linton frowned, and went into the Form-room, possibly suspecting that the detention task would not be thoroughly done unless he was present. Mathematics might have been changed for leapfrog in the absence of the Form-master.

The Fourth-Formers gathered in the Common-room to discuss the incident of the mysterious voice; but Billy Bunter did not accompany them. He had other fish to fry. When the discussion was over—without any result being reached—Blake & Co. went up to Study No. 6 to tea.

There was a startled movement in that celebrated apartment as they entered it. Billy Bunter spun round from the cupboard, and blinked at them over his big glasses.

"I—I say, you fellows——" he gasped.

"The cake!" roared Herries. "He's after the cake!"

"I—I haven't touched the cake, Herries!" gasped Bunter, dodging round the table. "There wasn't any cake there, in fact. And—and it's still there, old chap—safe and sound. Just look!"

"Keep him in the study while I look!" said George Herries grimly.

Herries strode to the cupboard, and Bunter cast a longing blink towards the door, where Blake and Digby and D'Arcy barred the exit.

"I—I say, you fellows, I—I've got a rather pressing engagement——"

"You should have kept it before coming here, old top!" grinned Dig. "Now you'll be late for it!"

"Yaas, wathah!"

"I—I say, Kildare's asked me to tea!" pleaded Bunter. "I—I can't be late to tea with the captain of the school, can I?"

"The cake's gone!" roared Herries. "Just a few crumbs left, that's all! That fat burglar has scoffed the cake!"

"I—I say, you fellows, I—I haven't, you know. Besides, it was only a measly small one, and hardly any plums in it——"

"Collar him!"

"Hold on!" said Blake, so gravely that his chums started, and looked at him. "Don't touch him, you fellows! Bunter, have you eaten the plum-cake?"

"Certainly not!"

"Then it's all right," said Blake, in a tone of great relief. "Thank goodness you haven't eaten it, Bunter. I don't know whether it would be exactly fatal——"

Bunter jumped.

"Fatal!" he spluttered. "Why should a plum-cake be fatal, you ass?"

"It's all right if you haven't eaten it," said Blake. "When a fellow puts rat-poison in a cake and leaves it for the mice, of course he doesn't count on a greedy bounder coming along and scoffing the cake without asking permission. But it's all right if you haven't eaten it. I was afraid you had."

"Rat-poison!" said Bunter faintly.

"All serene, if you haven't eaten it! You can get out, Bunter!"

"I—I say, how—how much rat-poison did you put into the cake, Blake?" gasped Bunter, his fat face white as chalk.

"Not more than half a pound, I know," said Blake, with an air of deep reflection.

"Half a pound!" shrieked the fat junior.

"Certainly not more!"

"Yow-ow!"

"What's the matter, Bunter?"

"Yarooooh! Help! Send for a doctor! Fire! Murder! I'm poisoned!" yelled Billy Bunter. "Help!"

"It's all right—if you haven't eaten the cake——"

"Help!"

"You said you hadn't——"

"Yarooh! Send for a doctor! I'm poisoned!"

CHAPTER 7.

The Medicine Man!

"BAI Jove! Poor old Buntah!"

"Yaroooh!"

"Pway beah up, Buntah! Pewwaps it may not be fatal—I sincerely twust not——"

"Help! Yooop!"

Billy Bunter collapsed into the study armchair, howling. Arthur Augustus D'Arcy turned to Blake.

"Blake, you must have been a fwightful ass to put wat-poison in the cake and leave it in the cupboard!"

"How was I to know Bunter would come along scoffing our cake?" demanded Jack Blake defensively. "A fellow can't foresee these things!"

"You weally might have foreseen it, considewin' that it is Buntah. Bai Jove, I might have eaten the cake myself!" exclaimed Arthur Augustus. "That would have been a gweat deal more sewious!"

"Yarooop! Help! Send for a doctor!"

"Hush——"

"Yah! I won't hush! I'm not going to be poisoned!" roared Bunter. "I'm suffering fearful agony! I'm dying! Send for a doctor! Yooop!"

"What on earth's the matter?" exclaimed Tom Merry, looking into the study from the passage. "You fellows killing a pig?"

"The pig's killing himself, to judge by the sound," said Lowther. "What's the matter with Bunter?"

"Yarooh! I'm poisoned!"

"Poisoned!" exclaimed Manners.

"Help!"

"He's eaten a cake," said Jack Blake, closing one eye at the Terrible Three. "He didn't know it was poisoned for the mice. I didn't put more than half a pound of the rat-poison in it—not so much, in fact—and I don't think it will be really fatal——"

"Yarooh! I'm dying!"

"It was fwightfully careless of Blake. I am suah the cowonah will blame him vewy severely at the inquest."

Billy Bunter burst into a terrific howl at the mention of an inquest. The Owl of Greyfriars dearly loved the limelight as a rule; but he had no desire whatever to be the chief figure in a coroner's inquest.

"Yarooh! Help! Where's that doctor? Send for a medical man! I'm dying! My—my feet are cold already! I'm in awful pain!"

Tom Merry came towards the suffering youth with a very grave expression on his face.

"Where do you feel the pain, Bunter?" he asked

"Here—there—everywhere!" gasped Bunter. "Awful agony, like red-hot pins and needles, and stabbing daggers, you know!"

"Tell me if I touch the spot. Is it there?"

"Yarooh! Leave off punching me, you beast!"

"Ha, ha, ha!"

"Bai Jove! I am weally surpwised at your laughin' at such a time, you fellows! Pway have some sympathy!"

A crowd of fellows were gathering round the doorway now. A whisper passed among them, and there was a general grin. Arthur Augustus D'Arcy caught the whisper, and he grinned, too. He realised that the matter was not so serious as Bunter supposed.

"Bai Jove!" murmured D'Arcy. "You spoofin' boundah, Blake——"

"Shush!"

"But it is weally too bad——"

"Yarooh! Have you sent for a doctor?" howled Bunter. "Tell him to get a stomach-pump, some of you!"

"I've got a bike-pump!" called in Levison. "Will that do?"

"Yah! Beast! I believe you're glad I'm expiring in fearful agony! Tell the doctor to come quick! Ow-wow-yow!"

"Hold on a minute or two, Bunter!" exclaimed Lowther. "I'm going! Don't die till I come back, old chap! Doctor in two ticks!"

Monty Lowther rushed from the study.

But he did not rush for a medical man. He rushed into his own study and dragged open the box in which were kept the "properties" of the Junior Dramatic Society.

With swift, skilled hands, Lowther dabbed grease-paint on his face, affixed thereto a black beard and moustache, and jammed a grey wig on his head, and a pair of glasses on his nose. He hurried on a frock-coat, somewhat crumpled, over his Etons, with a silk muffler to cover up his collar. Monty Lowther was quite a quick-change artist—and though his change was not very thorough it was certainly very rapid.

He came speeding back along the passage, and there was a gasp from the juniors at the sight of him.

"Why—what——" exclaimed Levison.

"The doctor!" howled Cardew.

"Ha, ha, ha!"

"Hush, my boys!" said Dr. Lowther, in a deep bass voice. "I hear there is someone ill—where is my patient——"

"This way, doctor!" shrieked Bunter from the study. "Have you got the stomach-pump? I'm dying!"

There was a gasp from Blake & Co. as the "doctor" came in. Tom Merry jerked Bunter's glasses from his fat little nose. Bunter was short-sighted, but even Bunter might have spotted the hurried make-up of the medical man. Without his glasses, however, all was safe.

All Bunter saw was a bearded man in a frock-coat bending over him.

"Help!" he moaned faintly. "Help! I'm dying! The poison's working through my system!"

"Stand back, boys!" said the medical man, in his deep voice. "Give him room! Bunter—ahem!—I think your name is Bunter——"

"Ow—yes—yow——"

"You have swallowed poison?"

"Yow-ow—yes!"

"An attempt at suicide, I presume?"

"Yoop! No! It was in the cake!" gasped Bunter. "I never dreamed that that silly ass had put rat-poison in the cake. I'm suffering fearfully! Awful shooting pains, like—like daggers and things! Ow!"

William George Bunter quite imagined by that time that he was suffering fearful pains.

"My poor, poor boy!" said the medical man soothingly "Calm yourself! Let me feel your pulse!"

"Yaroooh!"

"What is the matter now?"

"Yow! You're pinching my wrist! Leggo!"

"I must feel your pulse, Bunter. Bless my soul! Five hundred and sixty-nine—a very high temperature! Keep still while I use my stethoscope, my unfortunate boy!"

"Yow-ow!"

The medical man jammed the end of a fountain-pen into Bunter's waistcoat, the juniors looking on as gravely as they could.

Lowther listened attentively at the end of the fountain-pen with an expression of owl-like solemnity.

Bunter's round eyes were fixed in anguish upon his face, as if striving to read his doom there.

"Am I—am I very bad?" he gasped.

The medical man sighed.

"My poor, poor boy——"

"Yaroooh!"

"I find traces of fatty degeneration," said the medical man. "I am afraid you are accustomed to over-eating yourself, Bunter."

"Ow! Wow!"

"Have you made your will, Bunter?"

"Yarooooh!"

"Can't you save him, sir?" asked Tom Merry, with a break in his voice.

"I will try," said the medical man gravely. "I have every hope of saving his life. Has anyone a stomach-pump?"

"Ahem! Would a footer-pump do?"

"It would not do, I am afraid. However, there is another method. Raise him from the chair."

Four or five juniors raised Bunter from the chair. It needed the efforts of four or five. Bunter was not a featherweight.

"Lay him face down on the hearthrug," said the medical man. "Let him touch the floor with a slight bump."

Bump!

"Yaroooh!"

"Get the fire-shovel——"

"Here you are, sir!"

"Now strike him gently with the shovel—the flat of the shovel—while I count. This will counteract the effects of the poison. One!"

Whack!

"Yoooop!"

"Two!"

Whack!

"Yarooooh!"

"Be quiet, Bunter! This is for your own good!" said the medical man soothingly. "I think you should strike a little harder—I see no signs of improvement so far."

Whack!

"Yah! Oh! Beast!" howled the patient.

"Ha, ha, ha!"

"Patience, Master Bunter—we are curing you! This is a new thing in first aid—very suitable to your case. Do you not feel better?"

"Yow! No! Wow!"

"Strike a little harder——"

Whack!

"Help!"

"Are you feeling better, Master Bunter?"

"No!" howled Bunter. "Worse! Yaroooh! Lemme alone! Yooop!"

"We must keep up the treatment till you feel better, my poor boy. It is the only way. A little harder, please, Master Merry!"

WHACK!

"Yow-ow-ow-ow-woooop!" roared the patient. "Leave off! I'm better—much better! Yow-ow!"

"You are sure you are better, Master Bunter?"

"Yes, you beast! Ow!"

"Do you still feel any pain?"

"Only where that rotter's been whacking me!" wailed Bunter.

"Perhaps a little further treatment will relieve——"

"Yarooooh!"

Bunter struggled furiously in the grasp of his helpers, evidently determined to have no further treatment on those lines. As the fat junior reared up, his head came in contact with the medical man's chin, with a loud concussion. It was the medical man who roared this time.

"Yarooh! You fat idiot!"

"Ha, ha, ha!"

"Give him some more——"

"Yaroooh! Help! Murder! Fire!"

"Cave!" yelled Levison minor from the corridor.

"My hat! Here's Railton!"

The crowd in the doorway melted away like snow in the sunshine. But the juniors in the study could not melt away, unfortunately, and they stood breathless round Bunter, who was sitting on the hearthrug, roaring, as the School House master strode into No. 6.

CHAPTER 8.
Not Fatal!

MR. RAILTON looked at Tom Merry & Co., and Tom Merry & Co. looked at Mr. Railton. Monty Lowther made himself as small as possible behind the other fellows. He did not want to meet his Housemaster in his character of an amateur medical man.

"What does this mean?" exclaimed Mr. Railton. "What is all this uproar, Blake?"

"This—this uproar, sir?" stammered Blake.

"Yes. A most extraordinary din has been proceeding from this study," said Mr. Railton sternly. "Someone was calling for help."

"Yow-ow-ow! Ow!"

"Is anything the matter with Bunter?"

"Ahem! I—I think he thinks he's ill, sir," mumbled Tom Merry.

"I am ill!" howled Bunter. "I'm poisoned! I'm dying! Where's that doctor? Has he gone?"

"Bless my soul!" exclaimed Mr. Railton. "What do you mean, Bunter? How can you possibly be poisoned?"

"It was Blake! I hope he will be hanged!" howled Bunter. "Make that doctor come back! Where is he? I'm dying!"

"Have you given Bunter anything, Blake?"

"Not at all, sir."

"He put the poison in the cake!" yelled Bunter. "Where's that doctor?"

"There is no doctor here, Bunter——"

"He was here a minute ago."

"Is he wandering in his mind?" exclaimed the Housemaster. "Surely there is no doctor here—— Why—what—who—who is that?"

The Housemaster jumped as his eyes fell upon Dr. Montague Lowther. The other fellows had screened the medical man of the Shell as much as they could—but it was in vain.

"Who are you, sir?" thundered the Housemaster.

"Oh dear! I'm Lowther, sir!" gasped the humorist of the Shell.

"And what does that absurd make-up mean, Lowther?"

"Only a little joke on Bunter, sir," murmured Monty Lowther. "One of the characters in our plays, sir—Dr. Killemquick——"

"Absurd! Is it possible that that ridiculous boy supposed you to be a doctor?" exclaimed Mr. Railton. "You should not play these absurd jokes, Lowther. I presume that there is nothing the matter with Bunter?"

"Nothing at all, sir," said Tom.

"Yarooh! I'm poisoned——"

"Be quiet, Bunter, and explain to me why you fancy you are poisoned. You certainly do not look ill."

"I'm dying, sir!" moaned Bunter. "The cake was poisoned—I ate it, not knowing that Blake had put rat-poison in it——"

Mr. Railton started.

"Blake! Were you so utterly reckless as to put rat-poison in a cake and leave it where it could be taken——"

"Not at all, sir," said Blake hastily. "Never had any rat-poison in the study, that I know of."

"What!" yelled Bunter.

The fat junior jumped up. As he realised that it was a case of "spoof" his fearful agonies departed all of a sudden.

"He told me!" shrieked Bunter, shaking a fat, furious fist at Jack Blake. "He told me——"

"You told Bunter you had poisoned the cake?" exclaimed the Housemaster angrily.

"No, sir," said Blake meekly. "I told him I hadn't put more than half a pound of poison in it. And I hadn't, sir. I couldn't have, could I, when I hadn't put any at all?"

Mr. Railton stared at Blake's meek face.

"I am afraid, Blake, that you led Bunter to suppose——" He broke off. "Did you find the cake in this study, Bunter?"

"In the cupboard, sir, and Blake said——"

"Whose was the cake?"

"Ours!" grunted Herries.

"Did Bunter take it without permission?"

Silence.

"I think I understand," said Mr. Railton. "I am afraid you have been playing this absurd joke on Bunter because he took your cake and ate it. Is that it?"

"Ahem!"

"Beast!" gasped Bunter.

"You should not play such pranks—and you have caused a great deal of disturbance," said Mr. Railton. "You will take fifty lines each. As for you, Bunter, this should be a lesson to you to respect the property of others."

"I never touched the cake, sir!" gasped Bunter.

"What?"

"I wouldn't do such a thing, sir! I should disdain to touch a cake that didn't belong to me."

"Bai Jove!" murmured Arthur Augustus.

"Bless my soul! If you did not eat the cake, Bunter, how was it that you fancied you were poisoned?" asked the Housemaster.

"Oh! Ah—ahem——"

"Answer me, Bunter!"

Mr. Railton simply blinked at the Owl of Greyfriars.

"I hope you believe me, sir!" said Bunter, with a great deal of dignity.

"Believe you!" gasped Mr. Railton. "No, I certainly do not believe you, Bunter! I have never heard such an abominable young liar! You will follow me to my study, Bunter."

"Wha-a-at for, sir?"

"I am going to cane you."

"B-b-but I'm the injured party, sir," gasped Bunter. "I—I've been treated ungratefully for performing an act of friendship——"

"Follow me!" thundered the Housemaster.

And Billy Bunter jumped, and followed him.

"Bai Jove!" murmured Arthur Augustus. "That boundah Buntah weally does take the cake, you know!"

"The dear boy's sorry he took that one by this time!" grinned Blake.

There was no doubt about that! Billy

THE CONFLICT IN THE CLASS-ROOM!

But Billy Bunter couldn't. For once even the Owl of Greyfriars was not ready with a "whopper." No "whopper" that he could think of on the spur of the moment would meet the case. He blinked helplessly at the Housemaster.

"You did eat the cake, Bunter!" exclaimed Mr. Railton sternly.

"I—I—I——"

"Did you or not?"

"I—I may have tasted it, sir," gasped Bunter. "Now I come to think of it, I certainly did taste it. I—I only wanted to see whether it was—was digestible, sir. Some cakes ain't, sir, and—and I was afraid these chaps might get indigestion, so——"

"Bai Jove!"

"It was really kindness on my part, sir," said Bunter, growing more confident. "I'm always doing these kind actions, and never getting any gratitude."

"Bless my soul!"

Bunter came along about five minutes later rubbing his fat hands. He paused to blink into Study No. 6.

"Yah!" was his elegant remark.

"Weally, Buntah——"

"Yah! I despise you! Yah!"

With that Parthian shot Bunter rolled on. There was a loud chortle in the Study as he went. The fact that W. G. Bunter despised them did not have the effect of dashing the spirits of Study No. 6.

CHAPTER 9.

Tea in No. 2!

"I'LL make 'em sit up!"

Bunter of the Fourth made that remark in his own study, No. 2 in the Fourth. His study-mates, Mellish and Trimble, were at tea. Bunter wasn't at tea. Bunter had had tea in Hall; for what that was worth—not much to Bunter, who was equal to half a dozen teas in Hall. But there was no tea in the study for the Owl of the Fourth, for funds were low—as they generally were with Bunter — and his study-mates were not the fellows to carry a passenger at tea-time—far from it.

Bunter reclined in the armchair, blinking morosely at his study-mates through his big spectacles, like a podgy Peri at the gates of Paradise. Mellish and Trimble had quite a good supply, and the amiable youths enjoyed it all the more owing to Bunter's hungry looks.

"Hallo! Whom are you going to make sit up?" asked Mellish, helping himself to pickles.

"Everybody!" said Bunter comprehensively. "I ain't having a good time at this school."

"Whose fault is that?" grinned Mellish. "You don't make yourself popular, old gun."

"I was jolly popular at Greyfriars——"

"Were you ever at Greyfriars?" exclaimed Mellish, in surprise.

"I—I—I mean, when I was there on a visit to my cousin in the Remove," stammered Bunter.

"You must have paid a jolly long visit to your Greyfriars cousin," said Percy Mellish, looking at him curiously. "You're always talking about that school."

"Better show than this," said Bunter. "Jolly good fellows there — and they liked me no end. You should have seen the way Wharton and Bob Cherry and the rest used to praise me. Always welcome in any study—fellows used to compete to get me to come in to tea."

"Jolly queer tastes they must have at Greyfriars—if that's true!"

"Which it isn't!" chuckled Baggy Trimble.

"The fellows nearly cried when I left!" said Bunter. "Bob Cherry simply couldn't bear up! My Form-master——"

"Your Form-master?"

"Yes; old Quelchy——"

"How the thump could he be your Form-master if you were a visitor at the school?"

"I—I—I mean, my cousin's Form-master, of course! You—you see, I—I stayed rather a long time. The Form-master, as I was saying, came and shook hands with me when I left—like a real pal. Old Lathom never treats me like that. The Form-masters here are beasts. This school ain't up to Greyfriars in any way. Why, even the lessons are on a lower scale—you learn the same stuff in the Fourth here that they have in the Remove at Greyfriars!"

"You mean the Forms are called by different names, you silly ass! The fellows are the same age."

"Everything's rotten here, in comparison," pursued Billy Bunter, who was plainly in a pessimistic mood. "Old Wingate, the captain of Greyfriars, was really chummy with me—used to call me Billy when——"

"Why the thump should he call you Billy when you're name's Walter?"

"I mean, he used to call me Bunty!" gasped the Owl. "Look at Kildare here! He called me a fat frog to-day!"

"Looks as if Kildare knows you better than Wingate does!"

"I'm getting fed up!" said Bunter. "I've a jolly good mind to go back to Greyfriars—I mean, to go to Greyfriars. Only—only——"

"Could you go to Greyfriars if you liked?" asked Mellish.

"Certainly I could!"

"My hat! I wish you would, old scout! I'll tell you what—go to Greyfriars, and stay there; and we'll all pass a vote of thanks!"

"Beast!" said Bunter. "If it wasn't for that cardsharper chap I owe money to, and some little debts, and—and some other things, I'd jolly well go! I'm not being treated here as I expected! I'm kept out of games, and I could play any fellow's head off here. D'Arcy is standoffish, though I was willing to be friendly with him. I'm stuck in this study, with two mean rotters who don't even ask a fellow if he's hungry at tea-time——"

"No good asking—we know!" grinned Mellish.

"I'll have some of those pickles, Mellish——"

"You jolly well won't!"

"No fear!" said Baggy Trimble emphatically.

"I call that mean!"

"Call it what you like, old chap—but you don't bag our tea!" chuckled Mellish. "Buy your own pickles, my son!"

"I've been disappointed about a postal-order——"

"The same one you were disappointed about last week?" asked Mellish.

"Or the one you were disappointed about the week before?" chuckled Trimble.

"Well, I'm going to make 'em sit up—and you, too!" said Bunter. "I can do it, too! I'm an awfully clever chap——"

"Never seen any signs of it! You turn poor old Lathom's hair grey in class!"

Bunter sniffed contemptuously.

"I don't mean class work—that rot! I could tell you something, if I chose!" said Bunter mysteriously.

"Lies, most likely!"

"Br-r-r-r!"

Billy Bunter relapsed into silence, and watched the feasters hungrily. He was feeling very dissatisfied. Certainly, there had been no realisation of the rosy dreams he had dreamed when he changed places with Wally Bunter and came to St. Jim's. It was his own fault, but Bunter found no comfort in that—even if he knew it.

Footsteps passed the door, and Bunter looked up quickly. It was a chance for the exercise of his weird powers as a ventriloquist—and Bunter's brain always worked actively when it was a question of grub.

"Come on, you chaps!" called a voice, apparently from the passage. "Ain't you coming, Baggy? Chance for you, Bunter!"

"What's on, Blake?" called back Mellish.

"Gussy's treat in the tuckshop—he's blowing a fiver!"

"I'm on!"

Mellish and Trimble jumped up at once. They had nearly finished tea, and the remnant was certainly not to be compared with a treat in the school shop stood by Arthur Augustus D'Arcy, if that youth was "blowing" a fiver!

"I'll go!" exclaimed Bunter. "You fellows stay here——"

"Catch us!" grinned Trimble. "Come on, Percy!"

And Mellish and Trimble ran out of the study, anxious not to be late at the festive spread in Dame Taggles' shop.

Billy Bunter grinned.

He lost no time when he was left alone. He picked up a bag, and crammed into it what was left of the eatables, and departed in hot haste—in the direction opposite to that taken by his study-mates.

Mellish and Trimble rushed downstairs, and sped across to the tuckshop.

They found that establishment empty. There was no feed going on, that was certain; and they were puzzled and disappointed.

"That beast Blake was pulling our leg!" growled Mellish. "Hallo, there's D'Arcy! Let's ask him!"

Arthur Augustus D'Arcy was sighted in the quad as the disappointed juniors came out of the tuckshop, and they bore down on him.

"Are you standing a feed?" demanded Mellish.

"Sowwy, dear boy—no!"

"Not blowing a fiver in the tuckshop?" exclaimed Trimble.

"I wegwet to state that I do not possess a fivah, Twimble; and if I did I should not blow it, as you expwess it!"

"Blake said so!" howled Mellish. "He called into our study——"

"Bai Jove! I weally fail to compwehend why Blake should have made such a statement, deah boys!"

Mellish and Trimble returned to the School House, and found Jack Blake in the hall talking to Roylance and Levison.

"Do you call that a joke?" demanded Mellish sourly.

"Eh?"

"I call it a lie, if you want to know!" snapped Mellish.

Blake stared at him.

"Are you talking to me?" he demanded.

"Yes, I am!"

"Will you explain what you're talking about, before I knock your silly head on the banisters?" inquired Blake politely.

"You called into our study that D'Arcy was standing a feed in the tuckshop——"

"I did?" ejaculated Blake.

"Yes; you did!"

"When?"

"Five or six minutes ago!"

"I've just come from the Common-room, where I've been for the last quarter of an hour," said Blake. "Somebody's been pulling your leg!"

"I suppose I know your voice?" sneered Mellish.

"I know I jolly well do!" said Trimble.

"You're mistaken!" said Blake gruffly. "I haven't been anywhere near your study."

"Rats!"

Blake's eyes gleamed.

"Don't you take my word?" he demanded.

"You're making a mistake, Mellish!" said Levison. "I was with Blake in the Common-room—so was Roylance."

"Oh, rot! I know Blake's voice!"

"Same here!" said Trimble. "No good telling me—— Yoooop!"

Jack Blake's temper was growing warm by that time. He made a grasp at the two, and seized their collars, and their heads came together with a sounding concussion.

Crack!

"Yaroooh!"

"Now do you take my word?" demanded Blake.

"Yow-ow-ow! Yes! Yah! Oh! Of course! Leggo! Oh, dear!"

Mellish and Trimble escaped up the staircase, rubbing their heads. They came back to Study No. 2 in a savage mood to finish their tea.

But their tea was already finished.

What they had left of it was gone—quite gone! And so was W. G. Bunter!

CHAPTER 10.
Haunted!

GEORGE ALFRED GRUNDY of the Shell rubbed his nose thoughtfully, and blinked at Wilkins and Gunn.

"It's awfully queer!" he said.

"Oh, I don't know about that!" said Wilkins. "A bit stubby, if you like; but I shouldn't call it awfully queer!"

"Stubby?" repeated Grundy.

"A bit pug!" said Wilkins. "But I've seen lots of noses worse!"

"Noses!" said Grundy, staring. "Who's talking about noses?"

"Eh? Didn't you remark that your nose was awfully queer?"

"You silly ass!" roared George Alfred. "No, I did not! I wasn't talking about my nose!"

"Oh! You were rubbing it, and you said—— So I thought——"

"Don't be such an ass, Wilkins! And if you give me too much of your funny back-chat, I'll make your nose awfully queer, and your eye, too!" said Grundy darkly. "I said it was awfully queer, and so it is! Blessed if I'm not beginning to think the place is haunted! You remember what happened in the Form-room the other day? Somebody said Rats!' to Linton, and we were detained. We never found out who it was. Then there was something of the sort in the Fourth Form-room, and I heard Mellish and Trimble talking about something of the kind. And now—— It's a corker!"

Grundy rubbed his nose again very thoughtfully, but Wilkins decided not to misunderstand this time.

"I was cuffing Bunter in the passage," went on Grundy.

"What for?"

"Oh, nothing special! I thought a cuff would do him good. He's rather a slithy cove, you know. I was cuffing him, and then I heard Railton call out to me from the stairs. Now, I know Railton's voice, don't I?"

"You ought to," agreed Gunn.

"Well, it was his toot. He called out to me to go to him at once, and I thought he was ratty. Hearing Bunter yell, he might have thought I was bullying him, or some such rot. However, I went. And he wasn't there!"

"He'd gone?"

"Well, you see, there wasn't anybody on the staircase at all," said Grundy. "Railton couldn't have got away in the time, unless he slid down the banisters. A Housemaster wouldn't do that would he?"

"Ye gods! I rather think not!"

"Besides, Railton couldn't very well, with his gammy arm. He's got a bad fin, you know, from when he was in the Army. Then how did it happen?" demanded Grundy. "Isn't it jolly queer? I'm beginning to think the place is really haunted. It's a mystery—it puzzles me."

Evidently Grundy considered that a mystery must be very deep indeed if it puzzled him.

"Perhaps you imagined it!" suggested Gunn, rather unfortunately.

Grundy gave him a freezing glare.

"Is that meant for a joke, Gunn?" he inquired.

"Nunno!"

"If you're serious, I can only say it shows you to be the silly ass I've always thought you, Gunn. I don't imagine I hear voices," said Grundy. "I heard Railton's toot right enough, and he wasn't there! It beats me! If the place isn't haunted, what does it mean?"

Gunn did not venture upon another suggestion.

"What do you think, Wilkins?"

"I think it's time we had tea."

"You silly ass——"

"I'm going to tea with Talbot," remarked Gunn. "Ta-ta!"

"I was thinking of giving Tom Merry a look-in," said Wilkins. And he followed Gunn from the study.

Grundy snorted.

He was very much perplexed by the mysterious happening that had happened, and he had expected his study-mates to enter deeply and seriously into the puzzling question. Perhaps his way of receiving suggestions was not encouraging to them. At all events, they left him o probe into the mystery on "his own," so to speak.

Grundy stirred the fire, and jammed the kettle on it. He was thus engaged when a fat face and pair of large spectacles glimmered in at the doorway.

"I say, you fellows—I mean, I say, Grundy——"

George Alfred looked round.

"Have you come back for another cuffing, Bunter?" he inquired.

"N-no."

"You'll get it, if you don't mizzle."

"I was going to ask you to tea," said Bunter, with dignity.

"I don't come to tea with fags."

"Well, I'll come to tea with you, old chap. It's all the same to me."

"It may be!" assented Gurndy. "But it isn't all the same to me, you fat bounder. I give you one second to clear."

"Oh, really, Grundy——"

George Alfred Grundy picked up the tongs, apparently to use either as a missile or as a weapon. Grundy was rather a heavy-handed youth, and he did not enjoy Bunter's society. Billy Bunter's eyes gleamed behind his glasses.

"One second!" said Grundy. "Now, I——"

"Oh, don't play the goat, Grundy!"

Grundy jumped.

It was the voice of George Wilkins, and it came—or seemed to come—from under the study table.

"Wilkins! What——"

"Oh, give your chin a rest, Grundy!"

"What?"

"You're always wagging your chin, old top. Dry up!"

Grundy's face was a study. He came towards the table with the tongs in his hand. The tongs were no longer intended for Bunter.

"You silly chump!" exclaimed Grundy. "You told me you were going to tea with Tom Merry, and you sneak into the study and hide under the table like a silly fag! Come out!"

"Sha'n't!"

"Come out!" roared Grundy. "I've got the tongs ready for you!"

There was a large cover over the table, and Grundy could not see under it. But he had no doubt that Wilkins was there! He knew Wilkins' voice—as well as he knew Mr. Railton's!

"Will you come out, Wilkins?"

"Not for you! Go and eat coke!"

"I'm going to wallop you!"

"You couldn't!"

"Couldn't I?" roared Grundy, in great wrath. "I'll jolly well show you! If you don't come out this minute I'll shove the tongs at you!"

"Rats!"

Grundy stopped, with a crimson face, and thrust the tongs under the table with a mighty thrust. If Wilkins of the Shell had been there, there was no doubt that Wilkins of the Shell would have been hurt. But as it happened the tongs met with no resistance at all, and that was so unexpected that Grundy pitched forward with the force of the thrust and his nose tapped against the edge of the table—hard!

"Yooooop!" gasped Grundy.

"He, he, he!"

"I'll give you something to cackle for in a minute, Bunter! Wait till I've finished with Wilkins! Now, Wilkins, you rotter——"

Grundy tore off the table-cover, and dropped on his knees, to make a frontal attack with the tongs on the junior under the table. But he did not make the attack. He remained petrified, glaring under the table as if mesmerised. For the space was empty. Wilkins was not there!

CHAPTER 11.

Trouble in Tom Merry's Study!

"OH!"

Grundy gasped.

The sight of the Kaiser sitting under his table could not have surprised Grundy more than the empty space, with no one at all sitting there!

He could scarcely believe his eyes.

"Oh!" he stuttered. "Ah! Oh!"

Grundy rose slowly to his feet, and backed away from the table with an expression almost of dread on his face. It was really a most unnerving experience.

"You—you heard him, Bunter?" he stammered.

The Owl nodded.

"Well, he—he's not there!"

"Extraordinary!" said Bunter. "How do you account for it, Grundy?"

"I can't account for it," said Grundy. "Unless the school is haunted, there's no accounting for it. And if I can't account for it you can bet that it's unaccountable!"

"He, he, he!"

"This isn't a laughing matter, Bunter!" roared Grundy, making a jump at the fat junior.

Billy Bunter made a jump at the same moment into the passage. He executed a strategic retreat into Tom Merry's study, farther along. There were seven juniors in that study—the Terrible Three, Blake & Co. from No. 6 in the Fourth. There had been a hamper from Miss Priscilla that day, and Tom Merry was whacking out his good luck.

Seven forefingers pointed to the door as Billy Bunter blinked in.

"Outside!" said Tom Merry.

"Room for one more?" pleaded Bunter.

Monty Lowther jumped up.

"I never finished doctoring Bunter yesterday," he said. "Get the shovel, Tommy, and we'll give him some more medical attentions."

"Yaas, wathah!"

"I say, you fellows——"

Billy Bunter was interrupted. Grundy came along the passage, shoved the fat junior unceremoniously aside, and strode into the study.

"Wilkins here?" he exclaimed.

"No," said Tom.

"He said he was coming here."

"He looked in, old top; but passed on, as we had a party," said Tom Merry. "I believe he's gone along to see Kangaroo, if you want him. Anything the matter?"

"Yes," said Grundy impressively. "I think now that Wilkins must have been playing a trick, somehow. He spoke to me from under my table, and when I looked for him he wasn't there."

"Eh?"

"Unless the dashed place is haunted, it's a trick of some sort!" said Grundy. "As Wilkins isn't here, I dare say he was around my study somewhere playing a trick, and I'm going to let Wilkins know that he can't play tricks on me. He's not hiding here I suppose?"

"No, ass!"

"Is he gone?" came a voice from behind the bookcase in the corner.

There was a general exclamation, and all eyes turned on the bookcase. Grundy uttered an exclamation.

"So he is here!"

"My hat! I—I suppose he is! That's his voice," said Tom Merry, in astonishment. "How the thump did he get behind that bookcase?"

"You didn't know he was there?" said Grundy sarcastically.

"No, fathead!"

"Well, I don't see how he could hide

behind your bookcase without your knowing it, that's all. He was asking you if I was gone, too!"

Tom Merry's lips opened for a sharp reply, but he closed them again. It was really very amazing. The bookcase was a big one, and it stood across a corner of the study, an arrangement which was supposed to save space. Behind it, of course, was a triangular space, between the bookcase and the corner of the room, in which a fellow could have stood; but he could only have reached it by climbing on top of the bookcase and dropping down behind. The bookcase was pretty well filled, and was too heavy for one fellow to move and replace, and certainly none of the tea-party had moved it.

Tom Merry & Co. stared at the bookcase blankly. There were several articles on top of it, such as foils and a hatbox and one or two other things, which did not seem to have been disturbed.

Grundy pushed back his cuffs, and came farther into the study. The fact that Wilkins had hidden himself like this was proof enough that he had, somehow, played that trick in Grundy's study—at least, it was proof good enough for George Alfred.

"I knew he was here," he said. "You can come out of that, Wilkins!"

"Look here, don't kick up a shindy in our study," said Manners. "Wilkins will keep."

"Yaas, wathah! Pway don't be a wuffian, Gwunday," said Arthur Augustus chidingly.

"I say, you fellows——"

"Oh, cut off, Bunter!"

"I'm going to have Wilkins out!" roared Grundy. "Do you think I'm going to be played tricks on? Why, he made me almost believe that the place was haunted. George Wilkins!"

"Oh, go away, Grundy!" came the well-known voice of Wilkins, and Tom Merry & Co. could only stare.

"How on earth did he get there, deah boys?" asked D'Arcy.

"Blessed if I know!" said Tom. "We were all here when he looked in and went along the passage."

"You think I'm going to believe that?" sneered Grundy.

"Please yourself!" growled Tom. "And go and eat coke!"

"I twust, Gwunday, that you are not wefusin' to accept Tom Mewwy's word!" exclaimed Arthur Augustus hotly. "If you are askin' for a feahful thwashin', Gwunday——"

Snort from Grundy.

"How did you get there, Wilkins?" he demanded.

"Tom Merry bunked me up over the bookcase."

"I didn't!" roared Tom.

"D'Arcy helped him."

"Bai Joe, that statement is an uttah fabwication!" exclaimed the swell of St. Jim's indignantly. "I was not even awah that you were in the studay at all, Wilkins."

"Likely story!" sneered Grundy.

Tom Merry jumped up.

"We'll have him out of that!" he exclaimed. "We'll jolly well see whether he'll repeat that when we can get at him. Come out, Wilkins, you rotter!"

"Sha'n't!"

"We'll soon have you out!" exclaimed Lowther. "Lend a hand with this bookcase, you fellows."

The tea-party were all on their feet now in great excitement. The only fellow who wasn't excited was Bunter of the Fourth, who was leaning against the doorpost with a fat grin on his face.

"Bai Jove! I wegard Wilkins with uttah contempt!" said Arthur Augustus. "He is actually beawin' false witness, you know. You fellows know I nevah helped bunk the wottah up."

"Help me with this blessed bookcase!" said Grundy, grasping the heavy article of furniture. "Now, then, careful!"

Many hands were laid upon the bookcase, and it swayed a little away from the wall. There was a roar as a pair of foils came tumbling down.

"Yarooh! What's that?" roared Grundy. "Who's chucking things at me? Ow, my napper!"

"Ha, ha, ha!"

"You cacklin' asses——"

"Weally, Gwunday—— Yawooooh!" yelled Arthur Augustus, as the bookcase swayed again, and a hatbox whizzed down and smote him on the head. "Yow-ow! Bai Jove!"

"My hat! Do you keep half your happy home on top of the bookcase?" exclaimed Blake, as he dodged a whizzing cricket-bat. "Look out!"

"Better take the things off the top first," grinned Digby.

Tom Merry mounted on a chair and cleared the rest of the articles off. Then the juniors grasped the bookcase again, and it swayed forward, catching a little in the rumpled carpet.

"Look out!" yelled Herries.

The glass doors flew open, and a shower of books came forth like a hailstorm. There was a crash as Grundy's elbow went through one glass panel, and a howl as Blake's head caught the edge of the other door. Some of the juniors jumped clear, and the others held on desperately as the bookcase rocked and swayed.

"Bai Jove!"

"Look out! Hold on!"

"It's going!"

"Oh, crikey!"

"Stand clear!" roared Lowther.

The juniors scrambled hastily out of the way as the bookcase lurched forward and fell. Showers of books, papers, inkpots, chess and draughts, and other articles, poured out and strewed the floor, and the top of the bookcase crashed on the tea-table, and the table danced. And there was a sound of smashing crockery.

"You clumsy asses!" gasped Grundy.

"You silly chump!" shrieked Tom Merry. "It was you who did it! What did you drag it forward for?"

"What a smash-up!" gasped Manners.

"That idiot Grundy——"

"That dangerous maniac Grundy——"

"Gweat Scott!" Arthur Augustus uttered a yell of amazement. "Where is Wilkins?"

In the excitement of the disaster the juniors had forgotten for a moment that they were removing the bookcase to get at Wilkins of the Shell. D'Arcy was the first to remember, and he looked in the corner for Wilkins. But the corner was empty. There was no trace of anybody there.

"Wilkins!" stuttered Grundy. "Where's Wilkins?"

"Great pip!"

"Bai Jove! He—he—he's not there!"

Tom Merry & Co. stared into the empty corner in blank amazement and consternation. George Wilkins was not there—that was certain.

"How—how—how did he get away?" stammered Grundy. "I—I say, was it Wilkins at all, or is the dashed place haunted?"

"I say, you fellows——"

"Oh, shut up, Bunter!"

"But I say, you fellows, Wilkins is coming along the passage!" chuckled Bunter.

"What?"

The fat junior grinned.

"He's just come out of Kangaroo's study," he said cheerfully. "He, he, he!"

"Wats!"

"He—he can't have. He was here!" stuttered Tom Merry.

"Bai Jove! If he was here, where is he now, Tom Mewwy? That is wathah a puzzle."

Grundy mopped his heated brow.

"It beats me!" he said. "It beats me hollow! And if a thing beats me hollow——"

"Look at our study!" groaned Manners. "Look at our bookcase!"

"He, he, he!"

"Hallo! You chaps breaking up the happy home?" asked a cheery voice at the door, and Wilkins of the Shell looked in in surprise. "What the merry dickens have you been up to?"

The juniors stared at Wilkins as if he had been a ghost. Indeed, they were half inclined to think that he was a ghost at that moment.

"W-W-W-Wilkins!" stuttered Grundy.

"Gweat Scott!"

"You there—here—— Oh, my hat!" babbled Blake.

Wilkins stared at them.

"Anything up?" he asked.

"How did you get out of this study?" roared Tom Merry.

"Eh? I haven't been in the study."

"You were behind the bookcase."

"Behind the bookcase!" repeated Wilkins in wonder. "I've been having tea in Kangaroo's study."

"Wha-a-at?"

"That's right," said Kangaroo of the Shell, looking in over Wilkins' shoulder. "Wilkins has had tea with us, you fellows. What about it?"

"He—he—he's been in your study?" babbled Tom Merry.

"Certainly!"

"Well, my hat!"

"Bai Jove! The place must weally be haunted!" said Arthur Augustus D'Arcy in an awed voice. "I must weally wemark that I fail to comprehend this. Bai Jove!"

"We—we—we heard somebody behind the bookcase. It—it—it was your voice, Wilkins!"

"Oh, don't be funny!"

"It was your voice!" roared Grundy.

Wilkins grinned.

"Well, I haven't lent anybody my voice that I know of, old top," he said. "If anybody's borrowed it without my permission I think it's cheeky. But I don't see how he could have, for I've been using it in Kangaroo's study—haven't I, Kangy?"

"All the time," assented Kangaroo, with a grin.

"Why, you ass——"

"But—but—but——" gasped Tom Merry, wondering whether he was awake or dreaming. "It—it's a trick of some sort. I—I——"

Tom Merry broke off. He was simply "beat," and so were the other fellows in the study. There was excited discussion as No. 10 in the Shell was put to rights. Billy Bunter did not join in the discussion, or in helping to put the study to right. The Owl of Greyfriars rolled away down the passage with a fat grin on his face.

He was feeling that he was scoring at last, and Tom Merry & Co. were not yet done with Bunter on the war-path. Billy Bunter was not enjoying his sojourn at St. Jim's as he had anticipated, and it looked as if the other fellows were not destined to enjoy it, either.

THE END.

(Don't miss next Wednesday's Great Story of Tom Merry & Co. at St. Jim's—"THE HAUNTED SCHOOL!"—by Martin Clifford.)

ROBIN HOOD'S RUSE! By Dick Brooke.

I.

MASTER PETER TUBB and his dancing bear, Barney, sat at the door of a hut, one of a number built around a little clearing in the heart of Sherwood Forest. During the week that had passed since Robin Hood and his merry men had rescued him from the clutches of the Sheriff of Nottingham, Peter and the bear had done little but eat, sleep, and grow fat, which suited them very well. Now they watched a broad-shouldered friar stirring a big pot slung above a fire in the middle of the glade, and felt happy.

Presently he tasted, and smacked his lips.

"It's near ready, Master Peter!" he cried. "And I'll warrant 'twill be to your liking, seeing I mixed it myself, and there be no prettier hand at a venison stew in all England."

"That be so, Father Tuck," replied Peter, "and Barney do know it, too. Look to 'un!"

Barney had risen on end and advanced towards the fire, whining softly as he always did when he was hungry.

"Nay, brother, stick not thy long nose in my pot! Be not greedy, or I will bestow upon thee a buffet. Nay, I will wrestle with thee, and put thee on thy back, an' thou comest nearer!" And, so saying, the friar turned back his wide sleeves, showing a pair of tremendous arms, and stood ready.

If ever bear smiled, Barney did. This was a game his masterhad taught him, and he accepted the invitation at once, throwing his forearms round Friar Tuck's shoulders with a grunt of pleasure. The friar gripped him and heaved. Barney shoved with all his weight, but neither gave way. Round and round they danced till, at the edge of the brook tinkling through the clearing, the friar's foot slipped, and the pair rolled, with a mighty splash, into the shallow water.

They scrambled out, dripping, and Barney stood up once again. But the friar shook his head, laughing.

"Nay, brother. Enough is as good as a feast; and I would rather wrestle wi' good venison stew than take another turn wi' thee now. Shake thy coat, and I will even change mine, and we'll to dinner."

Which, being done, he blew a whistle. A dozen men, who had spent the night on the watch by the forest paths, came yawning from the huts, and fell to with hearty good will. But scarcely was the first edge off their appetites when a sudden bugle-call rang down the glade, and a party, headed by Robin Hood himself, came in sight. In their midst, borne on a litter of boughs, was a lad of some fourteen or fifteen years, richly clothed, but sadly bedraggled with mud, his head bound up in blood-stained clouts. He seemed insensible, but revived when the litter was set down.

"Where am I?" he said in a faint voice. "Where is my horse?"

"You be safe, lad!" said Robin Hood, holding a horn of wine to his lips. "Drink, then talk. That is our rule in the greenwood. We found you lying like dead, and your horse with a broken neck beside you. Who might you be, and how came you to that pass?"

The wine seemed to put new life into the boy. He sat up.

"My thanks to you, good sir, whoever you may be!" said he. "My name is Richard Feveral, your friend—an' you need one—from this on. Yesterday I came to my manor of Walmering, which lies some way about the purlieus of this Sherwood, seeing it for the first time, because I am new come to England out of Normandy, where I have bided since my father fell a-fighting for England and her King. Now, this manor has since then lain in the hands of my father's cousin, Sir Ralph Petterley. Mayhap you know him, good sir?"

"I have heard tell of him," replied Robin drily.

"He seems in no very good repute hereabouts," went on the lad. "But he gave me welcome, and promised an account of his stewardship in a week from now. This morning he rode out with me to show me the boundaries, I on the beast you found me by. We had come to the forest's edge, and were halted, when from a covert stepped an ill-looking old fellow, with a red scar athwart his face, waving a lighted torch, at the which my horse took fright, bolting down the path into the forest, the bit in his teeth, so that I could not guide or rein him in, and presently ran full-tilt into a great oak. Then I wakened here. Prithee, good sir, have word sent by one of your fellows to my kinsman, who doubtless is seeking me even now."

"All in good season, young sir," quoth Robin. "Yet perchance there is more in this matter than may be seen at the first glance. Tell me, an' ye will, who is next of kin to you, to take your estate if you had left your life at yon tree's foot?"

"John Feveral, my natural uncle; but seeing that he hath long been attainted of treason, and cares not to venture within the realm, it would seem that the next is this same Sir Ralph."

"Ah, I thought as much!" Robin chuckled. "Come hither, John Ball! You know Sir Ralph Petterley?"

"Ay; and if ever I have him in arrow-shoot he will know me!" growled John. "Turned me from the house where my folks had bided time out o' mind, and took my cow and plenishing, because I was behind wi' the rent through the forest deer taking of my corn. He could ha' waited, but, seeing I would lick no man's boots, out I mun go!"

"And you know that black horse this young gentle was riding?"

"Sartain sure! That was Courtain. A good beast enough, but never could bide the sight of flames since the fire in the old stable when he were a colt."

"And know you an ill-looking man with a red-scarred face?"

"That would be Long Daniel, that hath done much dirty work for Sir Ralph."

"And here is somewhat we found fast to your horse's tail," went on Robin, holding up a bunch of thorns tied with whipcord. "There was a slip-noose thereto, as though it had been put on suddenly. Now, Master Feveral, ye have evidence. Doth it not all show that your good kinsman hath gone about to compass your death, the which would greatly enrich him?"

"That is a true word!" cried Feveral. "Here is ground for stern work. Come ye with me, good sir, and we will swear to this before a justice!"

"The law and we folks have nought to say to each other," said Robin, laughing. "Maybe ye have heard tell of Robin Hood? I am he, and these are my good followers."

The boy rose shakily to his feet.

"I have heard that ye take toll of the rich," said he. "Well, ye can take from me, and welcome, if ye will! I shall still owe ye thanks for your aid!" And, so saying, he proffered the heavy purse at his girdle.

Robin smiled.

"Nay, lad; you be our guest. Likewise you be in sad need of help, seeing you come among folks who are wolfish to you for their gain. Sit we to meat, and recover yourself at your leisure, while I think upon a way to be even with Sir Ralph, for the Manor House is strong, and hardly to be taken by my force. Hey? What is it, Master Peter?"

"If it please you," said Peter, "I have been a-listening. Now, it seems to me that this here Sir Ralph, knowing as there was bound to be a spill, most like knows by now how you have picked up this here gen'leman. 'Tis the way o' the wicked to think all folks is as bad as theirselves, so if I goes along to him, like as if I was from you, maybe we could turn an honest penny. Either he'd be willing to pay for his kinsman to be give to his loving hands, or wishful for us to finish the job for him. Anyways, I can spy the land. I can talk, having a lot o' practice at fairs. Let me go, cap'n!"

"All right!" said Robin. "Three of you go with him, but lie hid when he comes to the Manor House. An' you can get pence out yon man, Peter, a fair third shall be your portion. Get to it!"

II.

WALMERING MANOR stood some two miles beyond the forest's edge, a low, rambling house, surrounded by a high wall and a deep, water-filled moat, crossed by a drawbridge that was always kept raised. When Peter, leaving his companions hidden in the brushwood, advanced to the moat-side and shouted, a loud barking answered him, a face appeared at an arrow-slit in the low tower above the gate, and a harsh voice inquired his business.

"I come from the wild wood on the matter o' a black horse," said Peter. "A good beast, but dead. There is also a saddle, likewise something that was in it."

"Alive or dead?" asked the voice.

"Well," said Peter cheerfully, "'tis alive at this present, but there be allus time for t'other, which is what I come to see about."

At this the windlass in the tower began to creak, and with a groaning and screeching of unoiled bolts the narrow bridge descended.

"Come over!" said the voice.

Peter obeyed, found himself at a door, climbed a stair, and entered a little room, lit by narrow arrow-slits. A man, shrouded in a cloak, sat by the windlass, a dagger glinting in his hand.

"I give ye warning that if it's mischief you be after I will give you no mercy!" said he. "Now, what is this you babble of?"

"A horse, a thorn, a flaming torch, and a lad who is, mebbe, in some folks' way," replied Peter boldly. "We be no fools under the greenwood, and can put two and two together as well as most. We reckons either to tell the lad what we thinks and put him on the road to the King's justice, or bring him back to you. We ain't partic'lar about his health. What we thinks on is money most times, Sir Ralph."

The knight threw back the hood of his cloak and stood up.

"It seems ye know me, fellow! Well, no matter; I will be plain. This lad is dear to me for his father's sake, and I would not have his mind poisoned against me with wild tales such as the folks hereabouts take pleasure to tell of me. Is he much hurt? I searched long, but found only the horse, so feared the worst."

"He is hurt, but not so much as he might be," answered Peter. "But for fifty golden ducats we will bring him to the wood's edge over yonder in whatever case you choose."

"Fifty ducats! Yet, an' the lad be dying, 'tis worth it—to soothe his last moments, poor boy!" said Sir Ralph. "Fetch him to the little thicket by the pond at sundown to-morrow and the money is yours!"

"Done!" cried Peter. "We will bring him in a covered litter wi' all the care o' the world. Give ye good-even, Sir Knight!"

"A black beast he is!" said he, rejoining his comrades. "He would ha' us do the lad to death, or near it. Well, maybe we will find a lad that will have the laugh of him."

But, despite their entreaties, he would say no more.

On his return to camp he went straight to Robin Hood, and talked long with him before turning in for the night.

Next day, as dusk was coming on, a small band of foresters set down a litter covered with a canvas tilt in the midst of the little thicket by the pond where Sir Ralph had made tryst. A man who had been lurking there for near an hour thrust his scarred face cautiously from the covert.

"You have him?" he asked, in a whisper.

"Ah! O' course! What else do you reckon we'd be here for?" replied Peter. "But who be you, and where be your master and his money?"

"I be called Long Dan, and the money will be to hand when 'tis needed. But you sure didn't go for to think as the master would be fool enough to trust hisself to a gang o' runnagate knaves like you 'uns, did ye?" said Dan. "I be taking a bit of a chance myself belike, but needs must when the devil drives. Now, let's ha' a peep at the goods."

"He be mighty poorly," said Peter. "If you axes me, I'd say as he ain't got much chance, going on as he is." He grinned slyly.

Long Dan lifted the canvas and looked down on the face of Richard Feveral. He lay scarce breathing. His eyes were closed, and in the flickering light of a single torch looked as though he were near death.

"There's someone as we knows on will be pleased to see him looking that way, I reckon," said Dan. "I ain't; but that don't signify."

"It don't! So now for the ducats!" said Peter. "No tricks, now!"

"There ain't none intended!" growled Dan. And, burrowing under the bushes where he had waited, he drew out a leather bag. "This here's the money. Count it if you wants to."

"We ain't taking it on trust. Here, you look to it, good Sir Friar!" said Peter.

He slipped from the circle that closed around Dan, and Friar Tuck was at once lost in the gloom beyond the ring of torch-light.

Very slowly, often pausing to bite a coin or ring one upon a stone, the friar made the count.

"All told," said he at length. "Some be clipped and some sweated, I doubt. But we be not Jews, therefore we say nought more about them. And now, Master Daniel, seeing you ha' none wi' you, and ha' but one pair of hands, I will e'en take an end of yon litter to help, these others being uneasy of coming further this way. Together we can manage it."

"Thankee kindly!" said Dan. "'Tain't very far." And while the group of outlaws melted into the forest he laid hold of the front of the litter and lifted as Tuck bade him. "My bones!" he ejaculated. "It be terrible heavy! Who'd ha' thought as a lad would weigh that much?"

"'Tis the litter that weighs," explained Friar Tuck, "it being made o' green boughs. See that ye do not stumble, for 'twould be ill work hurting the boy after getting him this far."

"Oh, ay!" grunted Dan under his breath. "But he'll be hurted worse before he's better, I'm a-thinking!"

For a little there was silence; then, when they had left the shadow of the trees and come out upon the road close to the Manor House, something stirred ahead, and a voice challenged sharply.

"It be me, Sir Ralph, and one other—a good friar," replied Dan.

"Have ye got my kinsman?" asked the knight, stepping into sight. "Ay, I see ye have! Set him down. Good father, ye have my thanks. And good-night to ye! We can carry this to my house alone."

Tuck turned away, but his eyes never left the shadowy figure, for they caught the glint of something bright that slid from the knight's sleeve as he stooped over the litter.

"Hey, Richard, lad, is it well with ye?" cried Sir Ralph. "Speak! Or have those forest thieves done ye harm? Speak, lad!" And with that he thrust the long, slim dagger through the canvas.

Then an amazing thing happened. There was a grinding jar as of steel breaking upon steel, the canvas tilt was rent suddenly to a dozen pieces, and, instead of Richard Feveral, Barney, the bear, a chain-mail shirt grotesquely adorning the upper part of his body, rolled from the litter, and, with a fierce, growling roar, sprang at Sir Ralph.

Yes, Barney! Peter had kept him at hand in the wood, and, while Dan had watched the counting of the ducats, put him in Feveral's place, and bade him lie still. This the well-trained beast had done until the dagger broke upon the shirt which Peter, anticipating just such foul play, had girt upon him. Yes, he was a good bear, but the jar spoiled his temper for the moment.

"Witchcraft!" screamed Sir Ralph, and fled for the drawbridge, Barney hot on his heels. He reached it, set foot on it, and then, with a wild cry, plunged headlong into the black waters of the moat as Barney's flailing paw smote home.

"Bills and bows!" bellowed Friar Tuck, close behind the avenger. "Over, lad! I'm wi' ye!" And together they crossed the narrow bridge and stopped at the half-open gate. "Hold we this pass till the lads come!" he said. And from under his gown drew a heavy, knotted club.

Lights were flashing in the courtyard below. Half a score men snatched up weapons, and, bawling for their leader, dashed into the arch-way, to recoil as Tuck's club and Barney's paws beat down the foremost.

"Bring bows!" shouted one.

But before it could be done there was a clatter of hoofs, a rush of feet, and Richard Feveral, with Robin Hood by his side and half the Sherwood band at his back, swept the defenders clear into the yard.

"Down with your arms!" shouted Feveral. "Ye know me for your rightful lord! Know also that Sir Ralph went about to procure my death that he might inherit my lands! Now he hath paid for it, being drowned in this foul water here! Will ye serve me faithfully?"

"That we will!" they cried; and came forward to swear their obedience and loyalty.

It was later—so much later that the sun was warming the high tree-tops—when the Sherwood men straggled none too steadily back to their forest home, their pouches well lined with silver pennies from Feveral's store and their heads singing praises of his good wine. Peter and Friar Tuck marched on either side of Barney, each with a hand on his back—to steady him, of course.

"An' ye go on this way, ye may be a knight before ye die!" mumbled Tuck.

"M-m-mebbe!" stuttered Peter. "B-b-b-but I t-t-think B-Barney will be first!"

"Of what Order, think ye?" said Tuck sleepily.

"Of the Bath," replied Peter. "Who is f-fitter for the B-Bath than one wearing a b-bear skin?"

THE END.

Figgy's Rival.

"HE has lovely eyes!" said cousin Ethel dreamily.

It was on the occasion of one of cousin Ethel's numerous flying visits to Mrs. Holmes. Figgy's invitation to a study spread had been graciously accepted, and, after the meal, Figgins, Kerr, and Wynn were grouped round their honoured guest in front of a blazing fire. When cousin Ethel made that reflective remark Figgy's naturally long visage lengthened perceptibly.

"L-lovely eyes!" he muttered.

"Yes. And simply adorable hair!"

"A-a-adorable hair?" repeated poor Figgy, while Kerr and Fatty Wynn looked on in amazed silence.

But cousin Ethel did not appear to notice either Figgy's discomfiture or the others' amazement.

"That's the only word that describes it!" she said. "It's adorable! Yes, Tommy is a love!"

"Who—who is Tommy?" Figgins choked. "Surely, Ethel, I—I—you—you can't mean Tom M——"

No more could poor Figgy say. The lump in his throat simply would not let him. He was amazed, bewildered. He would never have credited this had it not come from cousin Ethel's own lips! He wondered vaguely whether he was dreaming.

Cousin Ethel gave him a sympathetic glance.

"Tommy is an angel!" she continued. "I love him! He carries himself so perfectly, too! His manner, his walk, his whole bearing——"

"Don't!" pleaded Figgy. "Who—who is Tommy? Tell me!"

Poor Figgins looked the picture of broken-hearted dejection. He stared straight into the fire, his chin in his cupped hands. He did not notice that cousin Ethel was looking at him in a way—well, a way in which she never looks at any of the rest of us!

"Then his tail!" she continued, ignoring Figgy's earnest entreaty.

Figgins looked up. Amazement was written all over his face.

"His—his t-tail?" he stuttered.

Cousin Ethel looked surprised.

"Yes, his tail!" she repeated.

"B-but fellows don't have t-tails!" stammered Figgy, forced to consider the awful possibility of cousin Ethel having taken leave of her senses.

"Boys! Who ever is talking about boys?" exclaimed cousin Ethel, in a tone which implied that she was not aware such creatures existed.

"Weren't you?" Figgy asked, hope gleaming in his eyes again.

"Of course not, you silly!"

"Then—then who on earth——"

Cousin Ethel laughed till the tears ran down her cheeks.

"Oh dear!" she sobbed, wiping her eyes with her handkerchief. "I am so sorry for taking you in! I am, really! I—I was talking about Mrs. Holmes' pet Persian!"

THE END.

A BALLAD OF TOWSER!

By MONTY LOWTHER.

Good old Towser! A toast to your name!
These verses are written to show
How deserving you are of your fame—
According to Herries, you know!

You're a wonderful bulldog, old chap,
And all of us worship you so.
You would eat out of anyone's lap—
According to Herries, you know!

You will make friends with everyone, too,
And even old Gussy (although—
Well, I can't say old Gussy likes *you*)—
According to Herries, you know!

Then your instinct's the talk of the town,
Though mean fellows say that you're slow.
(You can track down a kipper, I'll own)—
According to Herries, you know!

As a house-dog you'd really excel;
You'd soon bring a burglar to woe.
At the sight of your molars he'd yell—
According to Herries, you know!

Your dear master's command you obey,
And that of Tom Merry & Co.
(But you don't obey *me*, by the way)—
According to Herries, you know!

You're a champion pal in a fray;
You'd daunt e'en the hardiest foe.
You would keep a whole regiment at bay—
According to Herries, you know!

But I don't really mean to be hard.
We admit, dear old Towsy, though slow,
You may be, you are trusty on guard,
And determined and dogged, WE know.

Printed and published weekly by the Proprietors at The Fleetway House, Farringdon Street, London, E.C. 4, England. Subscription, 8s. 10d. per annum. Agents for Australasia: Gordon & Gotch, Melbourne, Sydney, Adelaide, Brisbane, and Wellington, N.Z. South Africa: The Central News Agency, Ltd., Cape Town and Johannesburg. Saturday, March 8th, 1919.

THE ST. JIM'S GALLERY.

No. 38.—Bernard Glyn.

THERE is quite a lot to tell about Bernard Glyn, the inventive genius from Lancashire. But it will not be necessary to tell it all. Reference to a few of his many inventions will serve our turn as well as a complete and detailed list of them. And, indeed, such a list would be impossible. Glyn is always at it. We have heard very little of him lately, but that does not mean that he has been idle. Some time before long, I dare say, we shall learn of something else that will astonish us.

Glyn is quite unlike the other St. Jim's inventor. His dodges work. Skimpole's never do.

There is another difference. Skimmy's inventions are for the benefit of humanity. Glyn's are usually for the amusement of St. Jim's.

I have no doubt that Skimmy reads Emerson, who told us to hitch our waggons to stars. What that means you may think out for yourselves; and if you cannot make sense of it you will not lose much. For it really is not very practical advice; and when Glyn is busy upon a mechanical dog or an automatic Arthur Augustus he never thinks of it, I am sure; whereas it might well be in Skimmy's mind all the time that he is inventing a flying-machine that will never fly, or a collapsible submarine that collapses at the wrong moment and never comes up again.

Glyn's talent is hereditary—to some extent, at least. His father was a famous engineer, who made pots of money. That is another way in which Glyn has the advantage of Skimmy. Money is always tight with the Shell genius, whereas the Fourth Form inventor has what Reilly might call "lashin's and lavin's of it." But if Skimmy had as much cash as his rival he would still be very far below him in practical ability.

Bernard Glyn's people live quite near St. Jim's—at Glyn House. Both his father and his sister Edith, the pretty girl with whom Ratty fell in love, and whom Kangaroo saved from peril when a horse ran away with her, are very hospitable folk, and there has been many a merry party at Glyn House. Do you remember the one to which Baggy Trimble went uninvited in borrowed plumage? That sticks in one's mind; but there have been plenty of others ungraced by the presence of the heir of the Trimbles.

But Glyn is not a day boy. Probably it is because he likes the full association with everything that goes on at school, which is so difficult for the fellow who goes home after classes, that Bernard himself elected to be a boarder.

There is a model railway in the grounds at Glyn House; and no doubt some of you will recall how Glyn took his friends at St. Jim's to see it, and how Gore and Mellish maliciously tried to upset the train when its owner and Tom Merry were whirling round at a high speed. The brakes were applied only just in time, and the train was pulled up a yard or so from the jagged fragment of wood that must have overturned it—with possible tragic results that the two young scoundrels had not sufficiently taken into account. The two took cover in the house itself. Mellish, the less guilty of them, escaped; but Gore was caught in Glyn's electric chair—his trespasser-catcher, as he called it. The chair was in his workshop, and when anyone sat in it a bell at once started ringing, and sooner or later the butler's attention was drawn. Also, when anyone sat in it the bottom collapsed, and the sitter was doubled up, legs and body much in the shape of a letter V. Skimmy, who was one of the party Glyn took along, had sat in it before Gore, and its mechanism had been explained to him and the rest.

Many other interesting things were on view in Glyn's workshop. Of course, there were aeroplane inventions. What inventor has not dabbled in that kind of thing? There was a burglar-stopper, in the shape of a bar with an electric current, easy to grip, but impossible to let go.

There was another armchair, but that was in Glyn's study at St. Jim's. When anyone sat in it the arms closed round him, and he could not get out. Skimmy sat in it, and Glyn wheeled him out of the room and left him in the passage. Herr Schneider sat in it, and the crusty Herr was not at all pleased. He could not get out until Glyn got the spring into working order—and Glyn did not get the spring working until the German master had mentioned that he was disposed to overlook the little matter of an electric-bell—not the official bell—which had caused him to dismiss his class ten minutes before time.

You have already been told how Glyn and Dane and Noble came to share a study. There was some squabbling before that was settled; but it has worked out all right in the long run, and the trio are the best of chums, almost as inseparable as the Terrible Three. No doubt Kangaroo and the Canadian junior grumble now and then at the mess Glyn's inventions make; no doubt they sometimes find themselves shut out of their own study when Glyn is specially busy; but they can stand that. After all, something does come out of all Glyn's labour, and something worth while, too.

The line machine was greatly worth while, for instance. What schoolboy would not welcome a machine that would make the getting of lines a matter of no importance at all? And that was how the things worked

out while Glyn's invention was in use. It was the machine that did them. But Gordon Gay got hold of it, as will fall to be told when one deals with that enterprising youth; and it was but a short time that Shell and Fourth revelled in the knowledge that lines were no longer hard lines for them.

Then there was Towser the Second, a very lifelike imitation of Herries' famous bulldog—lifelike enough to take in and frighten Knox of the Sixth, anyway. And there was the mechanical man. The mechanical man was over seven feet high. He walked with a jerky, heavy stride, and from his eyes came a terrible glare. The very shadow he cast was appalling. He was designed to scare the New House fellows; but he started by scaring Herries and Digby, who saw him in the dark, and he nearly scared the life out of Mellish. Mr. Selby was greatly alarmed, and even Kildare jumped when he saw the monstrosity. It was Mellish who sent the automaton into the room of the ill-tempered Third Form-master; and Mellish had to go and confess or to have the gloves on with Arthur Augustus. That was the alternative; but Mellish wangled out of it after his own crafty fashion. He confessed—that he had been pursued by the figure, and had run into Mr. Selby's room in sheer desperation. Which was a long way off being a full and true confession—as may easily be guessed.

Skimpole the Third was Kerr in disguise. But Skimpole the Second was another of Glyn's inventions. It was really a wonderful piece of work, and Glyn was naturally proud of it. It blinked its eyes and moved its mouth. It did not talk; but to those who know Skimmy well that might be regarded as a distinct improvement upon the original.

At the time when Glyn perfected his invention Skimmy was busy on a very special machine of his own—a weird arrangement of wheels and—er—other things (I am not an engineer) which was, somehow or other, to revolutionise domestic service by doing all the work that servants are kept to do. He showed it to Binks, the page—this was before the days of Toby—and Binks, perhaps too much impressed by its dread possibilities, perhaps merely clumsy, contrived to wreck it. Binks might have left that alone, if he really did it with intent, for Skimmy's inventions can be guaranteed not to throw anybody out of work by working on their own account. But the wrecking of the machine happened after the day when both Glyn and Skimpole, too absorbed to bother about classes, were absent from the Form-room, and Mr. Linton went in search of them. Glyn heard him coming, and slipped into the chest in which he usually kept the figure. The irate master took Skimpole the Second for the original Skimmy, and grew still more irate when to all he said the dumb figure returned no word. He started in with the cane, and the figure fell with a crash. Mr. Linton was greatly alarmed; he feared that he had done the harmless Skimmy some deadly injury. The heart of the figure did not beat, Glyn's genius stopping short at the provision of a heart. Mr. Linton rushed off to tell the Head. Skimmy, who had entered the Form-room the moment after the master left it, was able to prove an alibi; and it was well for him that he could, as the master naturally supposed a trick had been played upon him. And Glyn had to confess.

But that was not the end of Skimpole the Second. He was used to take in Herr Schneider, who had sentenced the real Skimpole to detention. The figure was substituted. The Herr found out the trick that had been played upon him, and went to fetch Dr. Holmes. Meanwhile, Skimmy himself came back, and the figure was thrust into the cupboard. The sequel was rather unpleasant for the genius of the Shell, into whom Herr Schneider thrust a pin in order to demonstrate to the Head that he could not feel—an error, as it turned out.

Then Glyn made the figure talk. It was done by means of phonograph records. Of course, it could not carry on a conversation; but that did not make it unlike Skimmy. When you come to think of it, Skimmy does not converse; he harangues, declaims, speechifies. The figure did that—all about determinism, and heredity, and environment, and so on.

And after that Kerr became Skimpole the Third. But what he did in that role, masquerading as the figure, not as the original, would take too long to tell here, and has not much to do with Glyn, anyway. In the event, when Kerr was bowled out, he was ransomed by Figgy's returning the automaton.

There was the patent bowling machine, too. It was in the form of a tripod, with the legs weighted down. From the top of it projected a disc, with a number of arms; there were a long spring, and a crank, and a handle, and a kind of feeder trough. It worked, though at first it hardly worked with the perfection Glyn had expected. It smashed some of the Form-room windows; it went wrong suddenly, and fairly rained balls upon Gussy at the wicket. But these things were due only to minor defects, which could be and were overcome; and the thing was obviously not only useful, but valuable. Bernard applied for a patent; but there was some wangling, and Levison—these were his bad days—got into heavy trouble for trying to steal the Shell fellow's invention.

Then there was the mechanical Gussy. That was really great value. Gussy came in while Glyn was at work on it, and was flattered when told that he could help—that, in fact, he was the only fellow who could. But it was only as a model that Glyn needed him; and when he touched the handle which worked the figure, and tumbled it off the table, Glyn tumbled him out of the door, and Arthur Augustus wanted to defer a proposed visit to the cinema till he had given Glyn the usual "feahful thwashin'," so much more often threatened than carried out.

Gussy, always patriotic, was especially so about this time. He would not go to the cinema after all, because American films were on exhibit. He tried to keep others from going, too. Glyn seized on the craze of the moment, and D'Arcy the Second spouted at length about the iniquity of going to see American films, and so failing to support properly British industries. It completely took in Kangaroo when tried upon him. Glyn had got Gussy to talk into the phonograph, of course.

But before that D'Arcy the Second had taken in Knox, very much in the same way as Skimpole the Second took in Mr. Linton. Knox knocked the figure over, and fancied that he had killed Gussy. He even offered Glyn five pounds to keep dark about it—to clear out and let someone else find the supposed corpse. All Knox's concern was for himself, and he thoroughly deserved the bad time through which Glyn made him go.

Towser was taken in. He bit the leg of D'Arcy the Second, but did not find it meaty. Herries, not yet in the secret, was quite alarmed—more for Towser's sake than for Gussy's, it is to be feared, however. But the real fun came when Gussy himself met his double, and got the automaton's head into chancery, and smashed the wax face beyond recognition, and was horrified by what he had done.

Glyn's inventions take up most of his spare time; and, though he is far from being a duffer at games, he has not the same keenness for them that his chum Kangaroo has. It was at Kangaroo's suggestion that Tom Merry made him skipper of the Shell Second Footer Eleven in the Sports Competition, and Glyn proved then that he could keep goal in fine style. But it is not likely that he will ever want to dispute honours with Fatty Wynn, or even with Herries.

The Editor's Chat.

For Next Wednesday:

"THE HAUNTED SCHOOL!"

By Martin Clifford.

It is not necessary to say much about next week's story to anyone who has read this week's, for it must be obvious that Billy Bunter has not finished his ventriloquial dodges, and that we are sure to hear more of them in this yarn.

Will Bunter be caught out? That is the question.

And it is a question which I am not going to answer here.

Are you telling all your chums about these great yarns? You should do so; it is greedy to keep anything so good to yourselves.

I really do not think that the GEM has ever had more humorous stories than these. To my mind Billy Bunter licks the much-vaunted Charlie Chaplin into a cocked hat.

THE "PENNY POPULAR."

Don't overlook the fact that there are tales of St. Jim's appearing regularly in this ripping paper, which has just been restarted after a period of suspension due to paper shortage. The reappearance has been a triumphant success—even a bigger success than we anticipated, and that is saying quite a lot.

Besides the St. Jim's story each week, there is another of Greyfriars, a school about which all GEM readers know something, and one of Rookwood, which is also more or less familiar to them.

But if you really mean to get the paper you must order in advance, you know. The price, by the way, is at present three-halfpence. War conditions have not yet disappeared, and war prices have not yet come down.

THE "MAGNET" SERIAL.

Do you remember Johnny Goggs' visit to St. Jim's, told of in the GEM eighteen months or so ago? That popular character is now at Rylcombe Grammar School, and the serial which has just started in the "Magnet"—

"Goggs, Grammarian"—

tells of his doings there; of how he made the Grammar School fellows believe him as simple as he looks; of how he made friends and enemies there; and so on. Before long Tom Merry and many other of your favourite figures will be appearing upon the scene, too. You should read this story.

NOTICES.

Correspondence, etc., Wanted by—

J. Sitenhof, 24, Lytton Road, Leytonstone, E. 11—with readers, 14-16, interested in forming a theatrical party.

Miss Rita Lee, 17, Lewisham High Road, New Cross, S.E. 14—with readers in the United Kingdom.

F. George, 28, Mount Pleasant, Southville, Bristol—with readers anywhere interested in stamps and back numbers.

Miss Rose Bagnall, 162, Green Lane, Walsall, Staffs—with girl reader, about 14, living in Australia, India, or Africa.

R. A. Matthews, The Bothy, R.H.S. Gardens, Ripley, Surrey—with readers interested in postcards and stamps. He can put correspondents in touch with exchange and educational clubs.

C. B. McMenamin, P.O. Box 120, Montreal, Quebec, Canada—with readers, 14-16, in the British Empire.

A. Walker, 20, Hustlers Row, Meanwood Leeds, wants members—12-14—for Junior Sports and Hobby Club.

J. W. Spencer, 5, Dogford Road, Rayton, near Oldham, Lancs, wants to hear from readers for the Mersey Correspondence Club. Members required, aged 16 or thereabouts. The M.C.C. is a serious collectors' club.

Miss N. Brown, 61, Scarborough Street, West Hartlepool—with girl readers, 18 and upwards.

F. McCarthy, 32, Surrey Grove, Walworth, S.E. 17, wants readers for amateur magazine and correspondence club. Magazine, 3d.

Charles E. Boyd, 113, Cemetery Road, Doncaster—with readers, 13-15, in India or Australia.

Eric W. Hutton, 52, Stapleton Road, Bristol, offers to write stories for amateur magazines.

Alick Morton Eglantine, Rathmines Road, Dublin, wants members for the United League; circulars hectographed for clubs and small magazines. Stamped addressed envelope for catalogue.

Back numbers wanted by—

M. Ridley, 94, Wessex Flats, Wedmore Street, Upper Holloway, London, N. 19—any numbers of GEM, "Magnet," and "Penny Popular" before 1916. 2d. each offered; 3d. double numbers.

Edward MacPherson, P.O. Box 311, Port Elizabeth, South Africa—"Boys' Friend" Library, Nos. 7, 11, 14, 15, 24, 32, 33, 41. Six shillings offered. Write first.

James O'Leary, 94, Cockburn Street, Dingle, Liverpool—"Magnets" and GEMS of or before Christmas, 1912. 2d. each. Write first.

Alfred J. Sharing, 32, West Terrace, North Ormesby, Middlesbrough, Yorks—GEMS and "Magnets," 1-400. Any condition. Write first.

Miss Annie Parker, 94, Livingstone Road, Hove, Sussex.—GEMS, 483, 484, 485. Double price offered.

Max Nochimovitz, P.O. Box 126, Oudtshoorn, Cape Province, South Africa—"Schoolboys Never Shall Be Slaves," "The Honour of a Jew." 3d. offered for each.

Sam Joseph, P.O. Box 159, Oudtshoorn, Cape Province, South Africa—"After Lights Out," "The Boy Without a Name." 8d. offered. "Bob Cherry's Barring-Out," 3d; "Schoolboys Never Shall Be Slaves," 4d.

Leonard Jacobson, P.O. Box 30, Oudtshoorn, Cape Province, South Africa—"School and Sport," 1s. offered; "Greyfriars v. St. Jim's," "The Sports of the School," "Bunter the Prize-Winner," "The Greyfriars Cricketers," 3d. each with postage.

F. Entwistle, 34, Cranbrook Street, Bethnal Green, E. 2—"Magnets," 238-280; GEMS, 50-200.

Gordon F. Anderson, 5, Seymour Street, Observatory Road, near Cape Town, South Africa—GEM, "A Sailor's Son" and following four numbers; also "Magnet," same numbers. Write first.

A. Harris, 8, Townshend Road, Richmond, Surrey—GEMS, 518, 519, 521, 522, 524, 525, 526, 528, 530, 532, 535.

Cedric F. F. Rickard, 172A, Hollingdean Terrace, Ditchling Road, Brighton—"Rivals and Chums," "School and Sport," "After Lights Out," "A Stolen Holiday"; "Magnet," 197. 3d. for Libraries; 1½d. others.

Nigel Van Biene, 9, Station Road, Finsbury Park, N.—"Nelson Lee Library," 1-50; 1s. for No. 1. Write first.

L. Turner, 49, Western Road, Wolverton, Bucks—GEM and "Magnet" Christmas Numbers before 1916. 2d. each. Write first.

Arthur Johnson, c/o Spring Valley Mills, Farsley, near Leeds—"Magnet," 504, "The Greyfriars Barring-Out," 3d. and postage.

F. S. Beney, 38, Nelson Road, Hastings—"Magnets," 179, 190, 149, 148, 160, 363, 373, 388, 392, 239, 243, 267, 278, 167, 171, 283, 264, 240.

Harold Ashton, 148, Admiral Street, Dingle, Liverpool—GEMS, 466, 467, 468, 470, 471, 473, 474, 476, 480, 485, 490, 497. Double price. Write first.

Miss Helen Florence, 31, Nightingale Road, Wood Green, N. 22—GEMS, 511, 488, 471, 475; also tales of Levison before 452; and Cardew and Vernon-Smith tales. Write first.

E. J. Blundell, 19, Kingston Road, Longfleet, Poole—any "Magnets" before 540. 1½d. offered. Write first.

George Lowrey, 33, Craven Road, Woodhouse Street, Leeds—"Magnets," 397, 399, 387. 2d. each offered.

PEACE!

By Ernest Levison.

When the Armistice was signed and the thrilling news was read,
Tom Merry called his liegemen bold, and to them all he said:
"To celebrate this day we'll have a dormitory spread!

The dorm that night was crowded, but we all squeezed in at last.
The candle-ends were lighted, and the door was bolted fast.
And everyone was thankful that the cloud of war had passed.

There were good things there in plenty, and at least four kinds of jam,
And New House mixed with School House, like the lion with the lamb.
And every fellow ate his fill—as much as he could cram!

('Tain't true! I didn't have half enough!—Bagley Trimble.)

Then Merry rose and made a speech; the proper thing to do.
"I think," he said, "that all of you will quite endorse my view,
That as between the Houses *we* are cock House of the two!"

"Rats!" came a score of voices, and "Hurrah!" Above the din,
"Rag him!" "Scrag him!" "Bump him!" came from Figgins, Kerr, and Wynn.
Then Figgy rapped a sharp command to all his men: "Pile in!"

The Shell dorm must have sounded like a barnyard full of geese,
When Mr. Railton forced the door and caused the fight to cease.
"We're sorry, sir!" said Tom. "We met to celebrate the PEACE!"

The GEM 1½d

No. 579. Vol. XIII. March 15th, 1919.

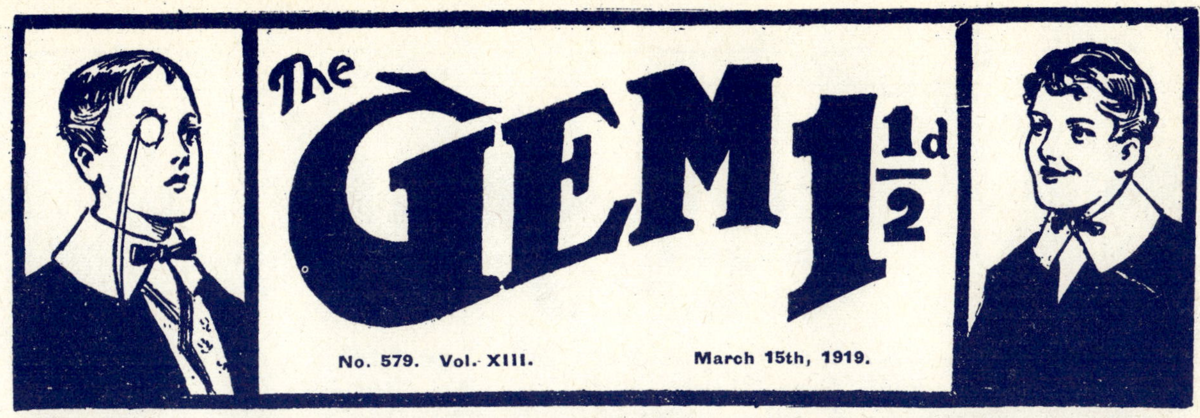

THE HAUNTED SCHOOL!

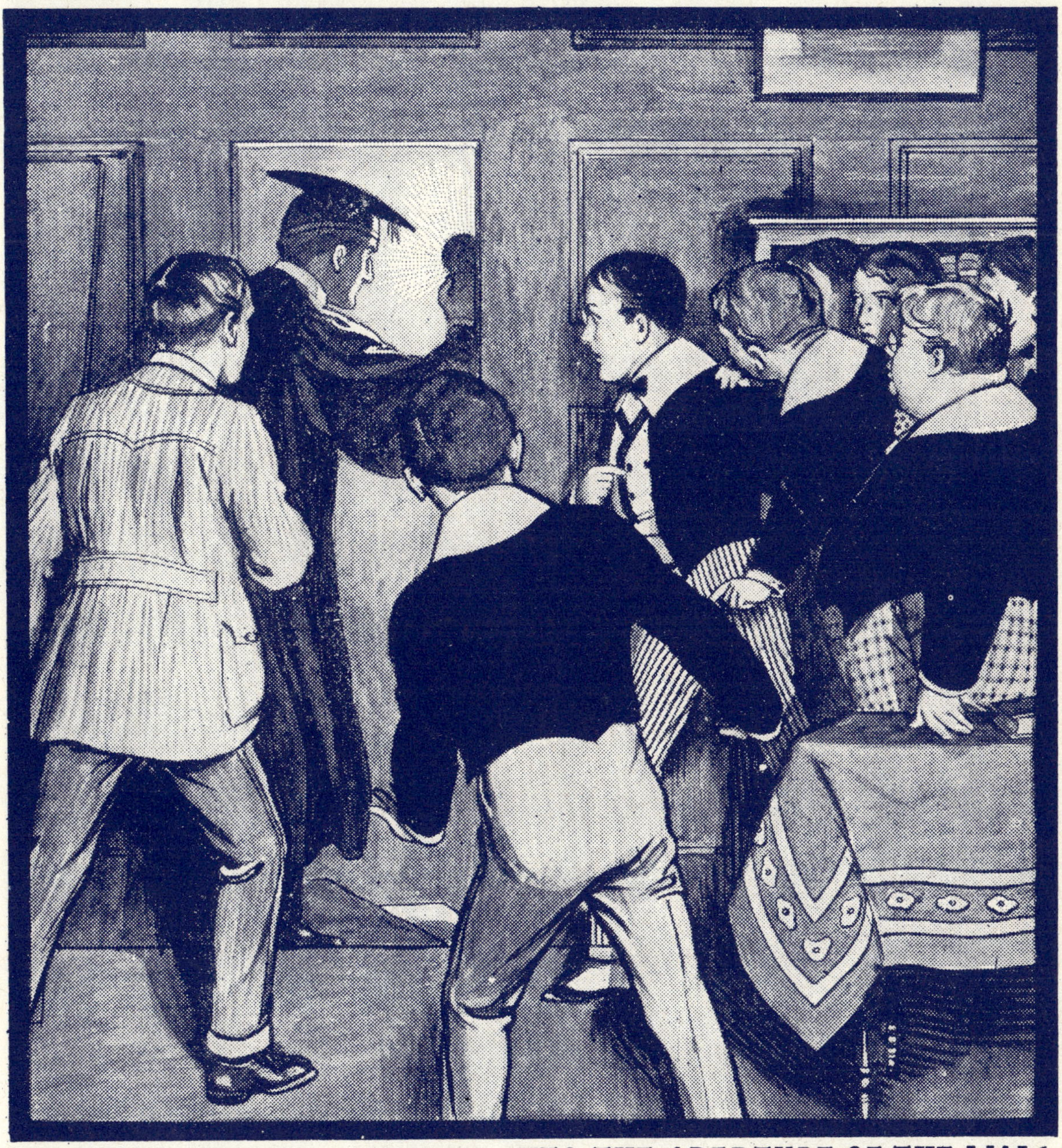

THE HOUSE-MASTER ADVANCED INTO THE APERTURE OF THE WALL!

(A Thrilling Scene in the Magnificent Long, Complete School Story contained in this Number.)

THE HAUNTED SCHOOL.

A Magnificent, Long, Complete Story of Tom Merry & Co. at St. Jim's.

By MARTIN CLIFFORD.

CHAPTER 1.
Fed Up With Bunter!

"BUNTER!"

"Are you there, Bunter?"

Quite a little crowd of juniors had gathered round the doorway of Study No. 2 in the Fourth Form passage in the School House.

Tom Merry had hurled open the door, and the juniors looked into the study, but all was dark within.

From the darkness came no sound.

If W. G. Bunter, of the Fourth Form, was there, he was following the celebrated example of Brer Fox, and "lying low."

"Bunter!" roared Jack Blake.

Silence.

"Bai Jove! The boundah has sneaked off, you know," remarked Arthur Augustus D'Arcy. "You ought to have kept an eye on him, Tom Mewwy."

"Oh, he's there right enough!" answered Tom Merry.

"I can hear a sound like a grampus grunting," said Monty Lowther. "There can't be a grampus in a St. Jim's study, so it must be Bunter."

"Are you there, Bunter?" hooted Manners.

"Nunno!" came a gasp from the dark study.

"What?"

"I—I'm not here, you know——"

"Ha, ha, ha!"

"Light the gas, somebody," said Tom Merry.

"Oh dear!" came another gasp.

Herries struck a match. There was a sound of movement in the study, and then silence again. George Herries ignited the gas, and the juniors looked round for Bunter.

He was not to be seen, however. Save for the new-comers, Study No. 2 seemed to be untenanted.

"Bai Jove! Where is the fat boundah?" asked D'Arcy. "I pwesume he has not disappeahed up the chimney?"

From under the study table there came a sound of stertorous breathing. The juniors chuckled as they heard it.

"Are you under the table, Bunter?" demanded Monty Lowther.

"Ow! No!"

"Herries, old scout, dig under the table with your foot—you've got the biggest feet at St. Jim's——"

"I haven't got the fattest head, anyway!" grunted Herries, with a glare at the humorous Lowther, apparently implying that Montague Lowther possessed that distinction.

"Ordah, deah boys! We have come here to wag Buntah, not to wag one anothah," said D'Arcy. "Buntah, you fat wottah, come out fwom undah the table. I know you are there—I can heah you gwuntin'."

"I'll try the poker——" began Tom Merry.

There was a hurried movement under the table, and Bunter rolled out into view without waiting for Tom Merry to try the poker.

He scrambled up, pink and breathless, and blinked at the St. Jim's juniors through his big spectacles.

"I—I say, you fellows——" he stammered.

"Lock the door, somebody!" commanded Tom Merry.

"I—I say, you know——"

Digby locked the door. Bunter of the Fourth backed away to the window, blinking at the juniors in great alarm. There was quite a representative gathering of the Lower School present. The Terrible Three of the Shell, Blake & Co. from Study No. 6, Figgins & Co. from the New House, and Levison, Cardew, Clive, and Julian.

Study No. 2 was crowded—not to say swarming—and there certainly seemed enough present to see justice done on the Owl of the Fourth. As he blinked at the crowd of juniors, Billy Bunter wished from the bottom of his heart that he had stayed at Greyfriars, and never tried his luck at St. Jim's.

"I—I say, you fellows——" he murmured.

Tom Merry held up his hand.

"Bunter!"

"Ye-es, old chap?"

"Don't 'old chap' me!" said the captain of the Shell sternly. "I suppose you know what we've come for?"

Bunter grinned feebly.

"Ye-es. You—you called on me because you're all my old pals, of course. I—I'm jolly glad to see you!"

"Eh?"

"W-w-won't you sit down?" gasped Bunter.

"Bai Jove!"

"We've called on you," said Tom Merry sternly, "to make an example of you."

"I—I say, it's n-n-no good making an example of me, you know!" gasped Bunter. "S-s-suppose you make an example of somebody else—D'Arcy, for instance. Then I could benefit by the example, couldn't I?"

"Gweat Scott!"

"That's not a bad idea," said Monty Lowther thoughtfully. "Does Gussy agree——"

"I certainly do not agwee, Lowthah. I wegard the suggestion as uttahly widiculous!"

"You are going to have justice, Bunter," went on Tom Merry.

"Oh dear! I—I'd rather not, if you don't mind!"

"Ha, ha, ha!"

"To come to business," continued the captain of the Shell, unheeding. "The School is getting fed up with you, Bunter. When we first met you we thought you were a decent chap, not at all like your precious cousin, Billy Bunter of Greyfriars. We were deceived in you. Why, what are you grinning at, you fat image?"

"I—I—I wasn't!"

"We gave you a welcome to the school," resumed Tom Merry. "You had every chance. And what have you done, Walter Bunter?"

"Everybody!" said Lowther.

"You've turned out a worm of the first water," said Tom. "You're not only exactly like your cousin Billy to look at, but you're exactly like him in every other way. We thought you were quite different; but it turns out that you're the same kind of fat worm over again."

"Oh, really, you know——"

"In fact, if we didn't know you were Walter Bunter, we should think that you were Billy Bunter himself, who'd got here somehow from Greyfriars," said Tom Merry sternly.

"Yaas, wathah!"

Bunter jumped.

He wondered for a moment what the juniors would have thought if they could have guessed how near Tom Merry's remark was to the exact facts.

"Oh, really——" murmured the Owl.

"We've often heard from the Greyfriars fellows about your cousin Billy's little games," went on Tom. "And we've thought to ourselves that if Billy Bunter was at St. Jim's, we'd—— What are you grinning at again?"

"N-n-nothing."

"We'd jolly well cure him!" said Tom. "Well, you've turned out exactly like Billy, and we're going to cure you—see? That's what we've come here for. You have been found guilty on many counts——"

"Don't recite the indictment," remarked Figgins. "We can't stay here all night."

"He's bagged grub," said Fatty Wynn, with a glare at the hapless Bunter. "He's bagged other fellows' grub in both Houses."

"He tells whoppahs!" said Arthur Augustus, with a sad shake of the head.

"His sins are as numberless as the sands on the giddy seashore," said Monty Lowther solemnly.

"I—I say, you fellows——"

"And we're all fed up," said Tom Merry. "No fellow's grub is safe when you are around, Bunter. There's a tin of pilchards missing from my study now."

"I—I haven't seen it, old chap. P-p-perhaps Blake had it."

"What?" roared Jack Blake.

"I—I mean Levison. It would be just like Levison——"

"Why, you fat rotter——" began Ernest Levison hotly.

"There's a cake missing from Study No. 6!" said Digby.

"I didn't know you had a cake!" gasped Bunter. "I never touched it. Besides, it was only a measly little cake——"

"Enough!" said the captain of the Shell. "You are going to be made an example of, Bunter!"

"Ow!"

"Yaas, wathah! A howwible example."

"I—I say, you fellows, I—I'd prefer the whole matter to drop," said Bunter, blinking at them.

"Bai Jove!"

"The matter isn't going to drop just yet," said Tom. "You're going to drop first—hard! This committee, representing the Lower School, has decided to take drastic measures. First, you are going to be bumped——"

"Ow!"

"Then you are going to have six with the fire-shovel——"

"Yow!"

"And then——"

Tom Merry was interrupted. A sharp, stern voice came from the direction of the locked door.

"What does this mean? Why is this door locked?"

"Bai Jove!" ejaculated Arthur Augustus. "Wailton!"

CHAPTER 2.
An Unexpected Visit!

"MR. RAILTON!"

"Oh dear!"

There was sudden silence in the study.

Tom Merry & Co. had gathered there to execute long-delayed and richly-deserved justice on the Owl of the Fourth. But they realised that their Housemaster would probably not see eye to eye with them in the matter. The sound of Mr. Railton's voice at the door was rather disconcerting.

Billy Bunter grinned. The interruption had come very fortunately for the fat junior

The voice went on sternly:

"Merry! Blake! Levison! All of you to follow me to my study at once. I will not allow this persecution of a new boy! At once! Do you hear?"

"Yes, sir!" gasped Tom Merry.

"Oh, cwikey!"

Dismay had fallen upon the administrators of justice. They looked at one another.

"Rotten!" mumbled Blake. "How on earth did Railton know we were here?"

"Wailton is undah a misappwehension," said Arthur Augustus. "He appeahs to wegard our pwoceedin's as persecution. I shall certainly explain the mattah to Mr. Wailton."

"Well, we'd better go" yawned Cardew. "Housemasters don't like to be kept waitin'. They're an unreasonable lot."

Blake was already unlocking the door.

The juniors had not heard the Housemaster walk away, and they expected to see him in the passage when they emerged. To their surprise, the passage was empty.

"Bai Jove! Wailton must have walked off vewy quietly!" said Arthur Augustus, scanning the passage through his eyeglass. "He is not heah."

"He, he, he!"

"What are you cacklin' at, Buntah?"

"Never mind Bunter," grunted Blake. "Let's get along and see Railton. May as well get it over. Oh dear!"

In a disconcerted crowd the juniors made their way to the staircase, leaving William George Bunter—supposed at St. Jim's to be Walter Gilbert Bunter—grinning in his study. Had they known that the supposed Wally Bunter was in reality the one and only Billy Bunter, they might have remembered that Billy Bunter of Greyfriars was a ventriloquist—but they did not know it, and they did not suspect.

"Hallo! You fellows look jolly cheerful!" Grundy of the Shell was on the landing, talking to Wilkins and Gunn, and he grinned at the downcast faces of the Co. "What's the row?"

"It is a slight misundahstandin' on the part of Mr. Wailton, Gwunday. It will be set wight, howevah. I shall put the mattah to him as one gentleman to anothah——"

"You jolly well won't!" growled Blake. "You'll keep your chin quiet, Gussy, and not get us a licking all round."

"Weally, Blake——"

"Oh, come on!"

"I shall insist upon explainin'——"

"Br-r-r-r!"

"I do not wegard that as an intelligible wemark, Blake."

And Arthur Augustus D'Arcy followed his chums, with his noble nose in the air.

In a disconsolate crowd Tom Merry & Co. arrived at the door of Mr. Railton's study. Tom Merry tapped on the door.

"Come in!"

The juniors marched in.

Mr. Railton was seated by the fire, chatting with Mr. Lathom, the master of the Fourth, who sat in an armchair on the opposite side. Both the masters glanced at the crowd of juniors in surprise, looking more and more surprised as more and more fellows came in. By the time they were all in the study the space between the door and the table was pretty well filled.

The School House master rose to his feet, frowning a little.

"What does this mean?" he demanded.

"We—we've come, sir," said Tom Merry.

"I can see that you have come, Merry," said the Housemaster tartly. "But why, pray, have you invaded my study in this manner?"

"We—we——" stammered Tom, quite astonished by this reception.

"You told us to come, sir," said Levison.

"I certainly told you nothing of the kind. What do you mean?"

"But—but you——" stammered Levison.

"I certainly have no recollection of telling so many juniors to come here," said Mr. Railton. "What have you come for?"

The juniors looked at one another.

"Pway allow me to explain, Mr. Wailton," said Arthur Augustus D'Arcy.

"I am waiting for you to explain," said Mr. Railton sharply.

"The fact is—— Yawooh!"

"D'Arcy!"

"Ow! Pway excuse me, sir. Some sillay ass twod on my foot. The fact is, sir—pway stop pokin' me in wibs, Blake—the fact is, sir, you are undah a complete misappwehension."

"What?"

"So fah fwom persecutin' Buntah, sir——"

"Bunter!"

"Yaas, sir. We certainly were not persecutin' him, but were only goin' to impwess upon his mind that it was wotten bad form to bag anothah chap's grub, sir."

"Is this impertinence, D'Arcy?"

"Bai Jove! Not at all, sir! I should wegard it as vewy bad taste to be impertinent to a Housemastah."

"What your dealings with Bunter may have been I do not know, and I do not see the necessity for mentioning the matter. I have asked you why you have crowded into my study in this manner."

"We could scarcely wefuse your wequest, sir."

"My request?"

"Certainly, sir. We came here because you told us, owin' to your misappwehension of what was happenin' in Buntah's studay."

"I had no knowledge of anything that may have been happening in Bunter's study, and I certainly did not tell you to come here."

"Wha-a-at?"

"I presume," said Mr. Railton sternly, "that this is what the juniors, I believe, call a rag. Your Housemaster, my boys, is not a proper subject for jesting. I shall——"

"Oh, no, sir!" gasped Tom Merry. "You told us——"

"When did I tell you?"

"Five minutes ago——"

"That is enough, Merry. I have not been out of this study during the last twenty minutes. "Mr. Railton picked up his cane. "You must not play these foolish pranks on me. Hold out your hand!"

Tom Merry simply blinked at him.

"But, sir—but——" he stuttered.

"I am waiting, Merry!"

"I pwotest, sir!" exclaimed Arthur Augustus hotly. "You have no wight, sir, to wegard this visit as a wag. You certainly told us to come here."

"D'Arcy!"

"Evewy fellow heah heard your voice, sir, when we were in Buntah's studay," said the swell of St. Jim's firmly. "Pewwaps you have forgotten, sir."

Mr. Railton lowered the cane. The astonishment in the juniors' faces was too genuine to be mistaken; and he realised that it was not a "rag."

"Let us have this clear," said the Housemaster. "It appears that you have been deceived. You say you heard me——"

"Vewy distinctly, sir."

"Where were you?"

"In Buntah's studay, sir."

"And you fancy that I spoke to you——"

"We certainly heard your voice from the passage, sir."

"Oh!" exclaimed Mr. Railton. "Was the door closed?"

"Yaas."

"I accept your statement that you supposed you heard my voice. You certainly did not hear it, however, as I was not there. Some one, apparently, has deceived you by imitating my voice."

"Bai Jove!"

"Oh!" ejaculated Tom Merry.

"It is very odd," said Mr. Railton, looking sharply at the juniors. "I should not have supposed it was possible for a boy to imitate my voice so exactly as to deceive you. That, apparently, is what has happened—if you are telling the truth."

"I twust, sir, that you do not think of doubtin' our word," said Arthur Augustus, with a great deal of dignity.

"I do not doubt your word, D'Arcy; but it is very odd indeed. However, as you are here you may as well explain what you were doing in Bunter's study."

"Ahem!"

"Well?"

"We—we were goin' to make wathah an example of Buntah, sir, as a warnin' not to bag othah fellows' grub," stammered D'Arcy.

"In what way, D'Arcy?"

"Ahem! Bumpin' him, sir—ahem!—and——"

"What else?"

"And—and whackin' him, sir, with a fire-shovel on his bags, sir."

"Is that all?"

"And waggin' him genewally, sir—— Yooop! If you persist in tweadin' on my feet, Lowthah——"

"I think I understand," said Mr. Railton. "You will take fifty lines each for ragging Bunter, as you call it. And I forbid you to enter his study again for any such purpose. Now you may go."

"Undah the circs, sir——"

"You may go, D'Arcy."

"Yaas, sir; but considewin'—— Pway don't dwag my arm in that way, Blake! Weally, Hewwies—— Dig, you ass——"

Arthur Augustus was got out of the study in rather a flustered state, and Tom Merry drew the door shut.

"You uttah asses!" exclaimed the swell of St. Jim's. "I was goin' to explain to Wailton at length——"

"Life's too short, dear boy," answered Blake, "and fifty lines each are enough, without having 'em doubled for your cheek. Kim on!"

"I think I had bettah go in again and explain to Wailton——"

"I think you had better not, old top," answered Blake cheerfully. "Take his other ear, Dig."

And Arthur Augustus was led up the staircase loudly expostulating.

CHAPTER 3.

A Deep Mystery!

TOM MERRY'S brows were wrinkled in thought. In the upper passage the juniors gathered in a rather excited crowd. The incident had puzzled them, and it exasperated them, too. Fifty lines each had rewarded them for the visit to the Housemaster's study, and they wanted to know who it was that had sent them there.

"There's some beast in the House playing tricks," said Tom Merry. "This isn't the first time it's happened. You remember somebody saying 'Rats' to Linton in the Form-room, and we never could find out where it came from."

"And somethin' of the sort occurred in the Fourth," said Arthur Augustus. "Some fellow was cheekin' Lathom through the keyhole, and he imitated othah fellows' voices."

"And then that affair in our study the other night," said Manners. "We thought Wilkins was behind the bookcase——"

"And he wasn't," remarked Lowther.

"He certainly wasn't. Now, we want to know who's playing these tricks," said Tom Merry. "There seems to be a fellow about with a gift for imitating voices. It's a gift that's going to get him into trouble."

"Yaas, wathah!"

"Let's ask Grundy," said Blake. "Grundy was at the end of the passage when we were called out of the study. He ought to have seen whoever it was."

"Good!"

The juniors looked for George Alfred Grundy of the Shell, and found him in his study with Wilkins and Gunn.

"Licked?" asked George Alfred cheerily, as the crowd of faces appeared in his doorway.

"Did you want us licked?" demanded Clive.

"The fact is, kid, I don't think you Fourth Form fags get lickings enough," replied Grundy. "If I were Housemaster I should warm you. I think you need it. That's my candid opinion."

"Weally, Gwunday——"

"And that's why you imitated Railton's toot and sent us to his study!" exclaimed Herries hotly.

"Eh? What?"

"Did you?" demanded Tom Merry.

"Eh? No. Why should I?"

"Well, somebody did," said the captain of the Shell. "We thought Railton called to us through the door, and it turns out he didn't. You were in the passage when we came out. Did you see who was outside the door of No. 2?"

"Nobody was."

"What?"

"I never noticed specially, of course; but I'm certain that nobody was in the passage at all till you came out," answered Grundy.

"That's rot, of course."

"What do you fellows say?" asked Manners, addressing Wilkins and Gunn. "You were there."

"Didn't see," answered Wilkins. "I had my back to the passage. Same with Gunny, I think."

And Gunn nodded assent.

"I hadn't," said Grundy, "and I know the passage was empty."

"How could it be empty when somebody called to us through the door of No. 2?" demanded Tom Merry.

"Don't ask me. Perhaps you imagined it."

"Fathead!"

"I wegard that suggestion as uttahly asinine, Gwunday."

"Did you notice whether Grundy came along to No. 2 a minute or two before we came out, Wilkins?" asked Tom.

"No, he didn't."

"Sure of that?"

"Quite."

And Gunn nodded assent again.

Tom Merry was staggered. Unless Grundy & Co. were disregarding the truth in the most reckless way, the trickster could not have been none of them. Yet if the passage had been empty, as Grundy averred, where had the mysterious voice come from?

"Blessed if it doesn't look as if the place was haunted!" said Blake soberly.

"Bai Jove, it is weally vewy extraordinaway! I do not undahstand it at all."

"There's something going on," said Grundy. "Look at what happened in this study the other day. I heard Wilkins speak. I thought he was under the table, and he wasn't! It beats me. Unless the blessed place is haunted, I can't account for it!"

There was evidently nothing to be learned in Grundy's study, and Tom Merry & Co. departed, with a lingering doubt as to whether George Alfred had been sticking to the truth.

"What about Buntah?" asked Arthur Augustus. "We were going to wag Buntah, and we haven't wagged him."

"Oh, bother Bunter!" answered Tom Merry. "Bunter will keep."

And the juniors dispersed, all of them puzzled and perplexed and a little worried.

That the School House of St. Jim's was haunted was really impossible; and yet, if it was not haunted, the mysterious happenings of late were not to be accounted for.

It might be supposed that there was some fellow in the House who had the trick of imitating voices, though it was a rare gift; but it could not be surmised how he remained invisible when he was playing his tricks.

With that queer problem in their minds Tom Merry & Co. had no attention to waste upon Bunter of the Fourth.

Figgins & Co. returned in a thoughtful mood to the New House. When they arrived in their study they found a fat junior ensconced in the armchair.

"Bunter!" ejaculated Fatty Wynn wrathfully.

The fat junior blinked at them amicably.

"I say, you fellows, no larks, you know! I've come over here to see you in a friendly way."

"We'll roll you downstairs in a friendly way," remarked Kerr.

"I say, it's jolly suspicious of you to keep your cupboard locked up," said Bunter. "Just as if you suspected fellows were after your grub."

"So you've been at the cupboard?" demanded Figgins.

"Nunno! I—I never even noticed whether it was locked or not," said Bunter hastily. "I say, you fellows, no larks! If you chuck that cushion at me, Fatty Wynn, I'll—I'll——"

"Well, what will you do?" asked Fatty Wynn grimly.

"I—I'll overlook it if you mean it as a joke." Bunter dodged the cushion. "He, he, he! But, I say, you fellows, I've got a suggestion to make. Some fellows have been grousing because of a few tarts and a cake or two, and so on. Mean, I call it. Well, I'm going to stand a big spread, and ask all the fellows, especially you chaps, to set the matter right."

"Oh!" said Fatty Wynn, laying down the stump he had picked up. "That's rather decent of you, Bunter. It's up to you, too."

"Just what I think, old chap. Now, tomorrow's a half-holiday. Can you fellows make it convenient to come?"

Fatty Wynn glanced at his chums.

"I don't see being down on Bunter if he wants to do the decent thing, you fellows," he remarked. "We might go."

"It will be rather a decent spread," said Bunter. "I'm giving it in the Hobby Club room. A study wouldn't be big enough for all the guests."

"What? Are you spending a fortune on it?" asked Figgins.

"I think about four quid will cover it," answered Bunter carelessly. "My idea is to make it a really decent thing, you know, so that fellows will feel it's worth their while. Cakes and buns and tarts, you know——"

"Good!" said Fatty Wynn, his eyes glistening.

"Several pots of jam, and meringues and——"

"Good!"

"Cold beef and ham to begin with," added Bunter.

"Nothing like laying a solid foundation," agreed Fatty Wynn. "That's a jolly good idea, Bunter."

"I thought you'd like the idea. If I have a couple of cold fowls, I suppose you could carve, Wynn?"

"Pleased to," said Fatty Wynn, beaming.

"Then it's a go. We'll discuss the details over tea if you like," said Bunter.

"Hold on a minute!" remarked Kerr grimly. "Before you bag a tea in this study, Bunter, we'll be a bit more precise. You've got the tin to stand this whacking spread to-morrow?"

"Oh, that's all right!"

"Let's see it," said Fatty Wynn suspiciously.

"Ahem! The—the fact is, I—I haven't got it at present," said Bunter cautiously, "but I'm expecting a postal-order——"

"What?" roared Figgins & Co.

"By the first post in the morning—from a titled relation of mine, you know," said Bunter, "and—— Yarooooh!"

Bunter did not finish. Three pairs of hands were laid upon him, and he went through the doorway like a sack of coal. There was a terrific concussion as he landed in the passage, and a still more terrific yell.

"Gimme the poker, quick!" howled Fatty Wynn.

Hurried footsteps rang along the passage. The poker was not needed. William George Bunter was gone.

CHAPTER 4.
A Surprise in Study No. 6!

"I'VE been treated badly since I came to St. Jim's!"

Billy Bunter made that statement in Study No. 6. Arthur Augustus D'Arcy was there. Blake and Herries and Digby had strolled out when Bunter strolled in. That was one of Bunter's grievances. Fellows seemed to have fallen into a regular habit of strolling away when the Owl came along.

Arthur Augustus lingered, constrained by politeness. Even Bunter was entitled to some politeness, D'Arcy thought. Blake & Co. did not seem to see it.

"Have you, weally, Buntah?" asked Arthur Augustus, with a glance at the doorway.

Bunter nodded impressively.

"I haven't been treated as I expected," he said. "I should never have come to St. Jim's at all, only all you fellows were so jolly friendly when I met you at Greyfriars. Now, are you friendly now? I ask you the question."

"Ahem! You see, deah boy——"

"Well?" said Bunter loftily.

"You see, you are such a howwid boundah, Buntah!" explained Arthur Augustus. "That accounts for it, you know."

Bunter snorted.

"I was offered a chance in the footer team," he said. "How many matches have I played in?"

"You play so wottenly, you know, and you nevah turn up to pwactice."

"I don't need so much practice as some chaps. Some fellows," said Bunter, "are born footballers. I'm one of them."

"Bai Jove!"

"Do I ever get a hearing in the Junior Debating Society?" demanded Bunter warmly.

"You talk such feahful piffle, you know."

"Have I been offered a part in any of the plays?" continued Bunter. "Never once, though I can act better than any other fellow at St. Jim's. That beast Lowther said they'd give me the part of Fat Jack when they played 'Fat Jack of the Bonehouse.' That's all."

"Ha, ha!"

"Blessed if I see anything to cackle at. I wasn't treated like this at Greyfriars. You should have seen the way Wibley used to chase me about, begging me to play Hamlet or Julius Cæsar——"

"Bai Jove! Did you stay a vewy long time at Gweyfwiahs, Buntah?" asked Arthur Augustus, in surprise.

"I—I—I mean—yes—no—exactly——" stammered the Owl of Greyfriars, realising that he had nearly given himself away once more. "What I mean is—— Ahem! Um!"

"I weally do not quite see what you mean, Buntah. Your wemarks are not vewy lucid."

"You've really let me down, D'Arcy," said Bunter, changing the subject. "I relied on your friendship when I came here."

"I am vewy sowwy, Buntah. But you must admit that I stood you as long as I weally could, you know."

"I'm afraid I rather despise you, you know," said Bunter, shaking his head solemnly. "This isn't quite up to my standard, D'Arcy."

"Bai Jove!" said Arthur Augustus, almost overcome. "Weally, Buntah, I——"

"But I'm going to give you a chance," said Bunter generously. "I don't want to be hard on you."

"Weally——"

"I'm willing to let bygones be bygones, and start afresh," said Bunter. "I'm willing—perfectly willing—to admit you to my friendship, D'Arcy."

"Oh!"

"Same with Blake and Digby," said Bunter, in the same vein of generosity. "Not Herries; he's got no money to speak of—I—I mean, I don't approve of him——"

"Buntah, do you see that dooah?"

Bunter blinked round at the door.

"Yes. Do you want it closed?" he asked.

"Yaas, with you on the othah side!" said Arthur Augustus warmly. "I wegard you as an offensive person, Buntah. I decline to have anythin' whatevah to do with you."

"Very well," said Bunter loftily. "Then I shall make you sit up, and all the rest, too. I'm going to punish you!"

Arthur Augustus smiled.

"Are you goin' to give us a feahful thwashin' all wound, deah boy?" he inquired.

"Worse than that! I'll jolly well turn your hair grey before I'm done with you!" said Bunter darkly. "I'll make you sit up! Wait and see!"

And Bunter rolled to the door.

"Bai Jove!" murmured Arthur Augustus D'Arcy. "I weally begin to think that that fat boundah is a little wocky in the cwumpet. I weally fail to see how he can make anybody sit up, exceptin' by baggin' his gwub. Bai Jove! What are you stawin' at, Buntah?"

Bunter had paused and turned, and he was blinking in a peculiarly fixed manner at the study wall near the bookcase. That wall was of old oak panels, part of the ancient building of St. Jim's before the studies were added.

It was well known in the school that an ancient secret passage existed behind the old wall, and the panel that gave access to it had been screwed up by order of the Head to prevent reckless juniors exploring the dark recesses. Arthur Augustus followed Bunter's gaze, but he could see nothing to attract special attention on the panelled wall.

Bunter blinked at him suddenly.

"Did you hear it?" he breathed.

"What are you alludin' to, Buntah?"

"Listen!"

Arthur Augustus jumped.

From the panelled wall came a faint, expiring voice.

"Let me out! Oh dear! I'm suffocating in here! Let me out!"

"Gweat Scott! Who—who is there?" gasped Arthur Augustus, staring blankly at the wall.

"I'm Grundy! Help!"

Arthur Augustus jumped. From the panelled wall came a faint, expiring voice. "Let me out! Oh dear! I'm suffocating in here! Let me out!"

"Oh deah!"

"Help!"

There was the sound of a faint groan, and then silence. Arthur Augustus, in horror, stared at the wall, rooted to the floor.

CHAPTER 5.
Only a False Alarm!

"GWUNDAY!" gasped Arthur Augustus at last.

Bunter blinked at him.

"How did he get there, D'Arcy?" he asked. "I know there's a secret passage—Trimble told me. But—but——"

"The uttah duffah must have got into it somehow, and lost his way!" said Arthur Augustus, aghast. He ran to the wall, and tapped on it. "Gwunday!"

Groan!

"Are you injahed, Gwunday?"

"I've fallen, and I think my leg's broken."

"Oh deah!"

"Help!"

"Beah up, deah boy—beah up! I will get help at once!" gasped D'Arcy.

He ran to the door of the study. Wilkins and Gunn were coming down the passage towards the stairs, and D'Arcy shouted to them.

"Come here—quick!"

"Can't, old top!" answered Wilkins. "We're off to Rylcombe to meet Grundy; we promised to meet him at the bunshop after he's done his shopping."

"Gwunday is not at Wylcombe, Wilkins——"

"He jolly well is!" said Gunn.

"He is heah, Gunn."

"Eh? We saw him start for Rylcombe," said Gunn. "Bunter saw him, too, for that matter—didn't you, tubby?"

"He must have come back, though," said Bunter, blinking at Gunn. "He's been playing tricks."

"My dear porpoise, if Grundy cuffed you, I dare say you deserved it," said Wilkins. "Perhaps he's a bit too free with his cuffs; but you can do with a lot."

"Help!"

Wilkins jumped.

"Hallo! That sounds like Grundy's toot. Where is he?"

"He is in the secwet passage, Wilkins, behind the wall of my studay! He says he has bwoken his leg."

"Eh? How could he get there? The panel's screwed up."

"There's another entrance from the vaults," said Gunn. "Has Grundy been down in the vaults? The thumping ass told us to meet him in Rylcombe."

"Help!"

Wilkins and Gunn, in great astonishment, came into the study. Arthur Augustus ran along the passage to call the Terrible Three. They received the startling news with amazement, and hurried to Study No. 6.

Trimble caught the news, and in a few minutes it was spreading through the School House.

Juniors came from near and far to crowd into Study No. 6 and round the doorway; there was quite a cram in the passage. Excited voices were heard on all sides.

"The thumping ass!" Jack Blake exclaimed, with more wrath than sympathy. "What has he been poking into the secret passage for? It's against Head's orders!"

"I wathah think the mystewy is explained now, Blake."

"Eh? What mystery?"

"Those mystewious voices, you know—it was Gwunday playin' twicks fwom behind the walls, you know," said D'Arcy, with conviction. "That is what the boundah is in the secwet passage for."

"My hat!"

"Looks like it, and no mistake," said Tom Merry. "That would explain! But he's got to be helped! We can get these screws out, I suppose?"

"Help!" came in faint tones.

"Better smash it in," exclaimed Bunter. "Here, give me room!"

Bunter picked up the poker and swung it back. There was a fiendish yell from Gore of the Shell.

"Yarooh! Keep that maniac away——Yoooop!"

"I wish you wouldn't put your head in the way, Gore. Give me room, you fellows, and I'll soon smash——"

Blake gripped the Owl just in time.

"You won't, you fat idiot!" he exclaimed. "You're not going to wreck this study. Get back!"

"Oh, really, Blake——"

"Out of the way, fathead! The screwdriver—quick!"

Tom Merry and Blake started to work with screwdrivers.

But the screws in the oak panel were many, and they were well driven in. There was a long task ahead of the rescuers. Behind the two juniors wielding the screwdrivers the study swarmed with a buzzing throng. The passage outside was crammed.

Kildare of the Sixth came pushing his way through the crowd.

"What's all this about?" exclaimed the St. Jim's captain. "Is the study on fire? Why—what—you young rascals! What are you taking out those screws for?"

"It's all wight, Kildare——"

"Stop it at once!" rapped out Kildare angrily.

"Gwunday is there, Kildare!"

"Nonsense!"

"It's true, Kildare!" gasped Tom Merry. "The silly ass has got into the old passages somehow, and he's calling for help. He says he's broken his leg."

"My hat!" said Kildare. He rapped on the panelled wall. "Are you there, Grundy?"

"Help!" came faintly to his ears.

"Are you hurt?"

"My leg—broken! Ow!"

"Good heavens!" muttered Kildare. "The utter young idiot! Here, give me that screwdriver, Merry! Some of you go and call Mr. Railton here."

Kildare set to work. Levison hurried away for the Housemaster, and soon returned with him. The swarming crowd made way for Mr. Railton, as he arrived at Study No. 6.

Five or six screws were out by this time, but there were many more to come. Mr. Railton's face was very grave, and it was plain that only his concern for the hapless junior behind the wall prevented him from being very angry indeed.

He looked on in silence while Kildare and Blake laboured at the hard screws, Herries soon taking Blake's place, to give him a rest. Bunter touched the Housemaster's sleeve, and Mr. Railton looked down at him.

"Shall I telephone for an ambulance, sir?" asked Bunter.

"Certainly not!"

"Grundy will have to go to the hospital, sir, won't he?"

Mr. Railton made a gesture, and the officious Owl backed away. The School House master tapped on the panels while the screwdrivers were still hard at work.

"Can you hear me, Grundy?" he called out.

"Yes!" came in faint tones.

"Are you really hurt?"

"My neck's broken, sir——"

"What?"

"I mean my arm, sir."

"Levison, did you not tell me that Grundy stated that he had broken his leg?"

"That's what I understood, sir," answered Levison of the Fourth.

"He certainly said so!" exclaimed Arthur Augustus.

"His statements appear to conflict with one another," said Mr. Railton, knitting his brows. "I doubt whether Grundy is injured at all. He would certainly know whether it was his arm or his leg that was broken. This appears to me to be a foolish prank on Grundy's part. However, proceed with opening the panel."

The screwdrivers proceeded.

The panel was released at last, and Kildare slid it open. A dark aperture was disclosed, where a huge block of stone was missing from the thick wall. Mr. Railton stared into the opening.

"Grundy!"

There was no reply; neither was any sign to be seen of George Alfred Grundy. Mr. Railton called again, angrily, but only the echo of his voice answered him. The juniors looked at one another blankly. They did not know in the least what to make of it.

"Get me a light!" said Mr. Railton abruptly.

Blake hastily lighted a bike-lantern.

Mr. Railton took it, and advanced into the aperture in the wall. There were steps in the passage within, and the Housemaster disappeared from sight. The juniors waited, breathless.

"Gwunday is gone!" said Arthur Augustus, in a hushed voice. "His leg cannot possibly be bwoken, aftah all. He has been pullin' our leg!"

"It's a lark, I suppose," said George Wilkins dazedly. "Grundy's been spoofing us. But fancy pulling a Housemaster's leg! Why, Railton will boil him in oil for this!"

"Serve him jolly well right!" growled Manners. "He must be off his rocker to play such an idiotic trick!"

"Is he off his rocker?" said Wilkins dubiously. "I've often thought there was something rather queer about Grundy. Look at the way he plays football, for instance."

"He will get a feahful thwashin' for this! I must say that it serves him wight!"

"Yes, rather!"

"Here comes Railton!" murmured Blake.

Mr. Railton emerged from the secret passage. His brow was as black as midnight.

"Have you found him, sir?" ventured Wilkins.

"No, Wilkins, I have not found him. Grundy must be deliberately hiding away in the passages," said Mr. Railton. "He cannot, therefore, be injured. The whole affair is an extraordinary prank, for which Grundy will pay the penalty when he is found!"

It was evident that the Housemaster was intensely angry and exasperated, which was not surprising. Kildare was looking very grim. Such a prank was really unpardonable, and it was quite certain that the vials of wrath would be poured out on Grundy when he turned up.

"Blake, you may close up that panel, and refasten it——"

"But, Grundy, sir——"

"He may leave the secret passage, Blake, where he entered it. There is no need for the panel to remain open. Kindly put in all the screws; I will examine it presently."

"Yes, sir."

Mr. Railton left the study. He looked back to speak to Wilkins.

"Tell Grundy to come to my study immediately you see him again, Wilkins."

The Housemaster strode away, followed by Kildare.

The juniors remained, in a buzz of excited discussion. The general opinion, freely expressed, was that George Alfred Grundy was "off his rocker."

Only on that hypothesis could his extraordinary conduct be accounted for. The reckoning that awaited him when he turned up was a heavy one.

Blake and his chums set to work screwing up the panel once more. It was a long and weary task. They offered the other fellows to give them a turn with the screwdrivers, but most of the fellows found that they had other engagements, and the crowd dispersed.

Tom Merry and Manners and Lowther kindly did a screw apiece, and then gracefully retired. Talbot did a couple, and Clive did one. The rest remained for Study No. 6 to negotiate.

And as they ground away with the screwdrivers, with aching palms, Blake & Co. made remarks about Grundy that would have made George Alfred's hair rise on his head if he could have heard them.

Bunter grinned into the study when they were nearly finished.

"I say, you fellows, enjoying yourselves?" he asked.

"Pitch something at that fat beast!" said Blake, in a sulphurous voice.

"He, he, he!"

Billy Bunter retreated before anything could be pitched. He rolled cheerfully into his own study, where Mellish and Trimble were having tea.

"Lots of hard work going on in No. 6," he remarked. "He, he, he! They don't seem to be enjoying it! Slackers, you know! He, he, he!"

"I should think they'd scalp Grundy!" remarked Mellish.

"I hope they will!" assented Bunter. "Grundy's a beast; always pitching into a chap! I told him I'd make him sit up! He, he, he!"

"Well, you haven't made him sit up!"

"Eh? Oh no, of course not!" said Bunter hastily.

In Study No. 6 the last screws were replaced, and Blake & Co. sat down, breathing hard, to a well-earned tea—rather late. Their feelings towards George Alfred Grundy were such as could not be expressed in words. Arthur Augustus D'Arcy tenderly rubbed a blister on his palm.

"Genewally speakin'," he remarked, "I am sowwy when a chap gets a lickin'. But I shall not sympathise with Gwunday if Wailton faihly skins him for this sillay twick!"

And Blake & Co. agreed.

CHAPTER 6.
A Little Surprise for Grundy!

"BY gad, it's Grundy!"

Racke and Crooke of the Shell were near the gates, chatting, when a burly figure came striding in. Racke and Crooke stared at him blankly. They had been talking about Grundy, and wondering where he was; but assuredly they had not expected to see him come in at the school gates.

Grundy was frowning; apparently not at all in a good temper. He noted the surprised stare of Racke and his chum, and stopped to return it.

"Well, do you take me for a ghost?" he demanded.

"Jolly nearly, I think!" gasped Racke. "Where on earth have you come from?"

"From Rylcombe, of course."

"Oh, draw it mild!" said Crooke.

"What—what do you mean?"

"What beats me is how you got out of gates," said Aubrey Racke. "How on earth did you manage it without being seen?"

"Eh? I walked out, of course!" said the astonished Grundy. "Nothing surprising in my being out of gates, is there?"

"Well, a little bit surprising," answered Racke. "Everybody's been looking for you since you played that trick in Study No. 6 an hour ago."

"Dreaming?" asked Grundy pleasantly. "I've been in Rylcombe the last two hours."

"Oh!" ejaculated Racke. "Is that the yarn you're going to spin to Railton?"

"Blessed if I see why Railton should want to know where I've been! I shall tell him if he asks me, of course."

"You'll tell him you've been in the village all the time?"

"Of course."

"Well, I don't want to shove advice at you, Grundy," said Racke. "But I'd try to think of a better one than that if I were you."

"That one won't wash!" said Crooke, shaking his head.

Grundy blinked at them.

"I don't know what you're driving at," he said. "But if you're hinting that I'm not telling you the truth——"

"The truth!" grinned Racke. "Oh, gad!"

"Yes, the truth!" hooted Grundy. "You silly ass, supposing I were a lying worm like you, why should I tell whoppers about where I've been? I suppose you don't think I've been to the Green Man, in your style?"

"No, I don't. I know where you've been—hiding behind the wall in Study No. 6, and pulling Railton's leg!"

"Are you potty?" asked Grundy, in wonder. "I've been waiting at the bunshop in Rylcombe for Wilkins and Gunn, and I'm jolly well going to give them a talking-to for not turning up!"

"Pile it on!" chuckled Crooke.

"Don't you believe me?" roared Grundy.

"Ha, ha! Not likely!"

"Here, hands off!" yelled Aubrey Racke, as the exasperated Grundy made a jump at them.

Grundy did not heed. He collared Racke and Crooke, and brought their heads together with a sounding crack. Then he strode on across the quad, leaving the two black sheep of the Shell roaring.

As he came striding into the School House there was a howl.

"Here's Grundy!"

"Here's the silly ass!"

"You're wanted, Grundy!"

George Alfred stared round at the juniors in amazement. Racke and Crooke had astonished him; but he was still more astonished now. Wilkins and Gunn came quickly towards him.

"How did you get out?" asked Gunn.

"Out!" repeated Grundy.

"Yes; some of the fellows are watching the vaults staircase," said Gunn. "They haven't seen you pass!"

"The vaults! I've not been in the vaults, you ass!"

"How did you get into the secret passage, then?" asked Wilkins.

"What secret passage?"

"Eh?"

"He doesn't know!" grinned Kerruish. "Ha, ha!"

"Where ignorance is bliss, 'tis folly to be wise!" said Cardew of the Fourth. "Are you goin' to keep that up to Railton, Grundy?"

"I say, you fellows, it's rather too thick, isn't it?" chuckled Bunter.

Grundy wondered for a moment or two whether he was dreaming, and would wake up presently in bed.

"Are you all potty?" he gasped. "I've been at Rylcombe——"

"Oh!"

"I've been waiting at the bunshop for you two slackers!" roared Grundy, with a glare at Wilkins and Gunn. "I want to know why you never came? Keeping a chap hanging about an hour!"

"What was the good of coming when you weren't there?" demanded Wilkins.

"I was there!" howled Grundy.

"You couldn't have been there and here, too, old top. You'd better go to Railton's study now; he wants you."

"What on earth does Railton want me for?"

"You don't know!" grinned Levison.

"No; how should I?"

"Oh, my hat!"

Darrel of the Sixth came along, and tapped Grundy on the shoulder.

"Go to Mr. Railton at once," he said.

"What for, Darrel?"

"I dare say he'll tell you!" answered the prefect drily.

"But—I say—— Darrell ——"

"Cut off!"

"Well, my hat!" stuttered Grundy, as he started for the Housemaster's study in blank bewilderment. "I believe everybody's gone potty."

He tapped at Mr. Railton's door, and entered, and found the School House master with a stern brow. Mr. Railton picked up his cane.

"Grundy," he said, fixing his eyes on the dismayed junior, "doubtless you will be punished with the greatest severity——"

"Wha-a-at for, sir?"

"For the unexampled impertinence you have been guilty of!" exclaimed the Housemaster. "I am very strongly inclined to report you to the Head for a flogging!"

Grundy staggered.

"A—a fuf-fuf-flogging!" he stuttered. "What have I done? Everybody seems to be down on me all of a sudden. I'd like to know what I've done!"

"You know perfectly well what you have done, Grundy. You have caused a disturbance and uproar in the House, and wasted my time——"

"I—I—I have, sir?" babbled Grundy. "Not at all, sir! How could I, when I've been out of gates?"

"Grundy! Do you dare to tell me that you have been out of gates, when I heard your voice distinctly in a junior study?"

"Mum-mum-my voice, sir!" said Grundy dazedly. "You couldn't have, sir; I had my voice with me, of course. When was it, sir?"

"An hour ago."

"I was in Rylcombe, sir——"

"Grundy!"

"I—I was, sir—I was at the bunshop, waiting for those two asses, Wilkins and Gunn! It's the truth, sir! They saw me start—so did Bunter—they'll tell you so, sir——"

"Then you returned, Grundy, to play this trick——"

"What trick?" howled Grundy. "How could I play any trick when I was at the bunshop in Rylcombe? I don't even know what's happened."

Mr. Railton looked at him fixedly. Grundy's bewilderment was so evidently genuine that it made an impression upon the Housemaster, angry as he was. The Shell fellow was in a perspiration with excitement and dismay.

"Grundy, someone has entered the secret passage which opens out of the vaults—forbidden precincts for juniors—and has played a trick, alarming the whole House. I certainly thought it was your voice that spoke from behind the panel in Study No. 6. Do you deny it?"

"Oh, my hat! Yes, sir, of course. I've been out of gates."

"I could not credit your denial, Grundy; but I recall, from a previous incident, that there is someone in this House who appears to possess the trick of imitating voices," said Mr. Railton. "Whoever it was, gave your name when spoken to."

"Oh, what a beast!" gasped Grundy.

"If you were at the bunshop, as you declare, you must have been seen there, Grundy?"

"Oh, yes, sir; I was talking to Miss Bunn most of the time!"

"Then you can have no objection to my telephoning to the shop and asking for confirmation of your statement?"

"None at all, sir," said Grundy, at once. "Ring up Mr. Bunn, and he'll jolly well tell you I've been kicking my heels in his place for an hour or more. I was waiting for Wilkins and Gunn, and they never came, and——"

"Wait!" said Mr. Railton.

He turned to the telephone. Grundy watched him, in quite a dazed state, while he was telephoning. A few minutes were enough to satisfy Mr. Railton. From the other end of the wire full confirmation of Grundy's statement came from Mr. Bunn.

Mr. Railton put up the receiver.

"I am very glad to say, Grundy, that Mr. Bunn bears out your statement," he said. "I am very glad indeed that this explanation came before your punishment was administered, my boy. I have been deceived. I am sorry, Grundy."

"Oh, that's all right, sir!" said Grundy, quite cheerful now. "It was some awful cad playing a trick, sir."

"Ahem! I shall make further investigation into the matter," said the Housemaster. "You may go, Grundy."

And George Alfred went.

CHAPTER 7.

The Mystery Deepens!

"LICKED?"

That question was asked by about twenty voices at once as Grundy of the Shell came down the passage. The news of Grundy's return had spread, and a crowd had gathered to see him after his interview with the Housemaster.

They expected to see him almost doubled up. But Grundy was looking quite cheery, and he carried his head high.

"Licked!" he answered. "Certainly not! Railton was very civil. He's not a bad sort, only a bit dense at times."

"Civil!" ejaculated Tom Merry.

"Certainly. After ringing up the bunshop, and finding that I was there, he was satisfied. Of course, he ought to have taken my word without asking for proof. But Housemasters will be Housemasters, you know. As I said, he's a bit dense sometimes. And now," said Grundy, "I want to know who's been playing tricks, and using my name and imitating my voice?"

One member of the crowd sidled away hastily and vanished; and the name of him was W. G. Bunter. But the other fellows blinked at Grundy.

"Would—would you mind saying that over again, Grundy?" gasped Tom Merry blankly.

Grundy said it over again.

"Bai Jove! Do you weally mean to say that it wasn't you all the time?" shouted Arthur Augustus D'Arcy.

"Of course it wasn't, ass!"

"Too thin!" said Levison.

"If you want a thick ear, Levison——"

"Let's ask Railton," said Blake. "Any objection to that, Grundy?"

"You can ask Railton if you like; but if you can't take my word, Blake, I'll have the gloves on with you——"

"Never mind the gloves at present," said Jack Blake. "If it was you busting up our study with your silly tricks you're going to get the ragging of your life. I'll ask Railton."

And Blake went to the Housemaster's study, the other fellows waiting very curiously for his return. He came back in a few minutes.

"All serene," he said. "Mr. Railton says it's proved that Grundy was at the bunshop in Rylcombe all the time. It—it wasn't Grundy."

"Bai Jove!"

"Then who was it?" howled Wilkins.

"I can tell you who it was," said Grundy. "It was the same chap who played a trick before—imitating Railton's voice, and sending you chaps to his study to get lines. You thought it was me then. You're all rather dense. Now, it was that chap, whoever he was—and I want to know who it was. I'm going to scalp him!"

"First catch your hare!" remarked Cardew.

"Bai Jove! This is vewy wemarkable, deah boys! I will not give you a feahful thwashin' aftah all, Gwunday."

Snort, from George Alfred.

"I'll take all the thrashings you can give me, and stand on my head all the time!" he snapped.

"Weally, Gwunday——"

"Let's go and finish tea," said Blake. "It wasn't Grundy; but we've got to find out who it was, somehow."

And the juniors dispersed, greatly perplexed.

Bunter of the Fourth met the Terrible Three as they were going to their study. Grundy's return had interrupted tea.

"I say, you fellows," began Bunter, blinking at them. "This is a jolly mysterious thing, isn't it?"

Tom Merry nodded.

"Looks as if the place is haunted, doesn't it?" asked Bunter.

"Well, it isn't."

"Some of the fellows think so," said Bunter. "Trimble says a light ought to be kept on in the dorm to-night."

"Trimble's an ass!"

"I think Grundy ought to be ragged," went on Bunter, following the chums of the Shell into their study. "You fellows ought to do it. Playing tricks like that, you know. He, he, he! He cuffed me, too—hard!"

"It wasn't Grundy played the trick."

"Oh, that's all rot, you know! Who else could it have been? I'll tell you what, Tom Merry. You could lick Grundy. I'll hold your jacket for you, if you like."

"Thanks; I won't trouble you."

"If you're funky of Grundy, Tom Merry——"

The captain of the Shell made a movement towards Bunter, and the Owl of the Fourth jumped into the passage.

"Oh, really, Merry—— I was going to say——"

"Cut off!" growled Tom.

"Aren't you going to lick, Grundy?"

"No!" snapped Tom. "For goodness' sake, Bunter, mizzle. You're too numerous, and you've got too much chin. Wriggle away!"

"I'm sorry to see you showing the white feather like this, Tom Merry," said Bunter, shaking his head.

"What!" roared Tom.

"You should get up a little pluck," said Bunter reprovingly. "Be a man, you know, like me!"

"Slay him!" murmured Lowther.

Tom Merry made a stride at the fat junior, and took him by the collar. His patience was exhausted.

"You fat idiot!" he said, shaking Bunter hard. "You silly chump! You porpoise——"

"Yaroooh!"

Shake, shake, shake!

"Yow-ow! Stoppit!" howled Bunter. "If you make my specs fall off—— Ow!"

Shake, shake!

"If they get bub-bub-broken—yaroooh!—you'll have to pip-pip-pay for them! Yooop!"

"Sit down!" said Tom.

Bunter sat down—hard, and roared. Tom Merry closed the study door on him. The next minute a howl came through the keyhole.

"Yah! Beasts!"

The Terrible Three grinned, and sat down to tea.

"Beasts! Yah!" continued the dulcet tones at the keyhole. "I've a jolly good mind to come in and lick you, Tom Merry!"

"Do!" said Tom.

"Yah! You come out here!" roared Bunter. "I'll mop up the passage with you!"

"All right!"

Tom Merry stepped to the door and looked out. He was just in time to see a fat figure vanishing round the corner. Billy Bunter had not stayed to mop up the passage with him.

Tom chuckled, and returned to the tea-table. The Terrible Three discussed the mysterious happenings in the School House over tea. The same discussion was going on all through the House. It was interrupted in No. 10, however, by a voice at the keyhole.

"You there, Tom Merry?"

Tom looked round towards the door.

"I'm here, Kangy. Trot in!"

"Confound your cheek, Tom Merry!"

"Wha-a-at!" stuttered Tom, astounded by that address from Kangaroo of the Shell, the cheery Cornstalk, with whom he was on the best of terms.

"You've been bullying Bunter! Don't ask me into your study. I won't come. But next time I see you I'll jolly well pull your nose! And I'm going to my study now, if you want to find me, you worm!"

Tom Merry sat petrified.

"Is—is—is he mad?" he gasped. "Kangaroo!"

There was no reply. Tom Merry rose to his feet with a glitter in his blue eyes.

"I think Kangaroo must be off his dot," he said. "But off it or on it, he's not going to talk to me like that! I'll go and see him."

And Tom Merry left his tea for the second time, and his chums followed him to Harry Noble's study, up the passage. Kangaroo and his study-mates—Glyn and Dane—were there, discussing the subject that was uppermost in all minds just them. They looked surprised at Tom Merry's frowning face as he strode in.

"Well, I've come!" said Tom.

"Anything up?" asked Bernard Glyn.

"Yes. I want to know what Noble means by insulting me through the keyhole of my study," said Tom Merry hotly. "You can say it over again here, Noble, and then put up your hands!"

Kangaroo looked at him.

"Nobody has to ask me twice to put up my hands, old scout," he answered calmly; "but let's know what the row's about first."

"You know well enough!" exclaimed Manners angrily.

"All I know is that Tom seems to have come here looking for trouble," said Kangaroo. "I'm ready to oblige him."

And he pushed back his cuffs. Clifton Dane interposed, and pushed the Cornstalk back into his chair.

"Don't be an ass, Kangy!" he said. "Tom's made some mistake. Let's hear what he's grousing about."

"I'm not grousing," said Tom. "I shook Bunter because he cheeked me, and if Noble thinks I was bullying him he——"

"My dear man, I don't think anything about it at all, as I didn't even know you'd shaken the fat treasure, and don't care twopence whether you did or not!" said Kangaroo.

"You said——"

"What do you mean?" broke in Lowther. "Only two minutes ago you were howling at Tom through our keyhole."

"You're dreaming, old man. Where was I two minutes ago, Glyn?"

"Sitting here, for the last quarter of an hour," said Glyn. "Is this some new joke of yours, Lowther? It's a bit deeper than the jokes in your Comic Column, then. They want some seeing; but this beats me hollow."

Tom Merry uttered an exclamation.

"Then—then it wasn't you, Kangaroo, old chap? I savvy, and I'm sorry! It was your voice!"

"Did you fellows notice my voice leaving the study for a stroll down the passage on its own?" asked the Cornstalk, appealing to his study-mates.

"Ha, ha! No."

"It was that beast again, of course," said Tom. "It was your voice right enough, Kangy. I thought it was you speaking. Of course, it was that sneaking, tricky cad who put on Grundy's voice this afternoon. We've been taken in again!"

"Oh!" exclaimed Kangaroo. "My dear man, next time you hear my voice at a keyhole, ask me whether I was there with it before you come along breathing fire and slaughter. Are you going to fight me?"

"No," said Tom, laughing.

"Thanks! I'd rather not, if it's all the same to you," said the Cornstalk, laughing, too. "But, I say, this is getting thick. That practical joker has got to be found."

The Terrible Three returned to their study. Tea was finished at last, without further interruption.

In the Common-room that evening there was only one topic—the unknown practical joker who had so weird a gift of imitating voices. Trimble of the Fourth declared that the House was haunted, Bunter supporting that view.

But the general belief was that it was a practical joker, and everybody wanted to know who it was. And the things that were promised that practical joker when he should be found out were enough to make him tremble in anticipation.

Discussion did not seem to let any light in upon the mysterious matter. As Talbot of the Shell remarked thoughtfully, it looked as if some malicious fellow had set out with the deliberate intention of making everybody thoroughly uncomfortable and disturbed, and was succeeding in his object!

That was, in fact, the exact truth, and the Greyfriars' ventriloquist had not finished yet.

"You are a young ass, Twimble! There are no such things as ghosts," said Arthur Augustus severely.

"Isn't there a ghost of St. Jim's?" asked Bunter. "I've heard of a ghost belonging to the school—an old monk who was murdered——"

"D-d-don't talk of it!" howled Trimble.

"Pooh! You're a funk, Trimble," said Bunter loftily. "I'm not afraid of ghosts. Keep your pecker up, and try to be brave, like me!"

"I shouldn't wonder if there's a ghost," remarked Mellish, with the pleasant idea of playing on Baggy's fears. "Hark! Was that a sound under your bed, Trimble?"

"Yaroooh!"

"Ha, ha, ha!"

"Anybody hear a groan?" chuckled Roylance.

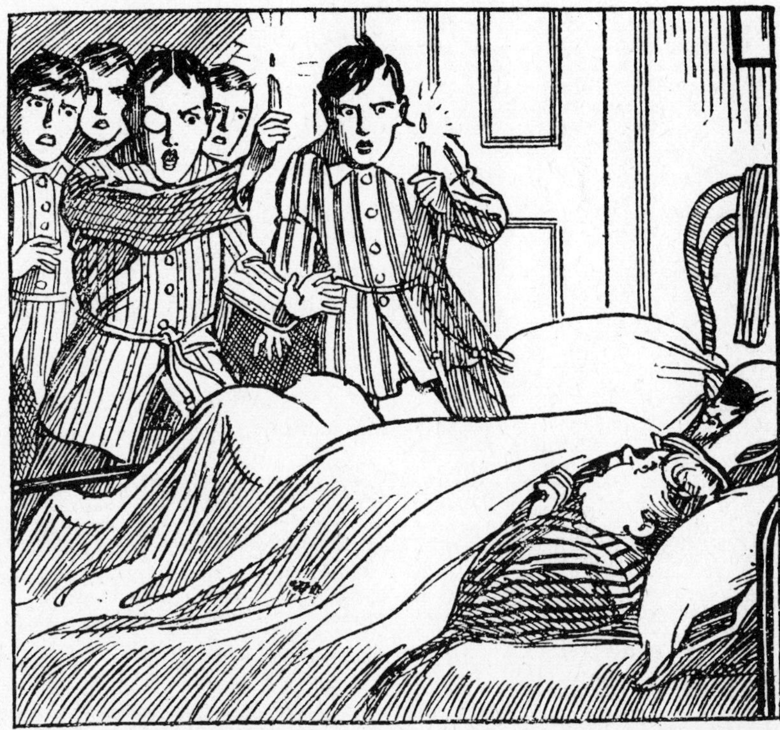

Jack Blake spun round. He fancied the weird sound came from behind him. But nothing was to be seen save the dancing shadows from the candle-light. From under Baggy Trimble's bedclothes came a series of ear-splitting yells. "Help! Ghosts! Spooks! Help! Yarooh! Help!"

CHAPTER 8.
Haunted!

"K-K-K-KILDARE!" stammered Baggy Trimble, in the Fourth Form dormitory that night, as the captain of St. Jim's was about to turn the light out. "I—I say, Kildare!"

Kildare looked at him.

"Well, Trimble?"

"C-c-can we have the light left on?" pleaded Baggy. "The—the blessed House is haunted, you know. There may be a —a ghost——"

"You young ass!" answered the Sixth-Former. "Good-night, kids!"

"Good-night, Kildare!"

Kildare turned out the light, and left the dormitory. There was a splutter from Baggy Trimble as the door closed after him.

"I—I think we ought to have a light, you know. I—I shall be dreaming of ghosts."

"I—I say, d-d-don't!" gasped Trimble. "I'm not nervous, of course——"

"Ha, ha!"

"But—but d-d-don't!"

"Bai Jove! You weally sound as if you were nervous," chuckled Arthur Augustus D'Arcy. "Buck up, deah boy; you won't heah any ghosts gwoanin' heah. Besides, suppose a ghost has a taste for gwoanin'—it won't hurt you."

Groan!

"G-g-gweat Scott! What's that?"

"Yow-ow!" came from Trimble.

Several of the juniors sat up in bed. A deep and horrid groan had come from somewhere in the darkness.

"Don't play tricks like that!" exclaimed Blake. "It sounds creepy."

Groan!

"Who was that?" exclaimed Herries.

Groan!

"I—I say, get a light!" moaned Baggy Trimble. "It's the g-g-ghost!"

"Shut up, you ass!"

"Help!"

"You cwass ass, Twimble, dwy up! There are no such things as ghosts. One of the fellows is pullin' your leg!"

Groan!

Silence fell on the Fourth-Formers as they listened to the repetition of the creepy, uncanny sound. The darkness of the dormitory added to its unearthly effect.

"Look here, the chap who's doing that had better stop!" exclaimed Blake angrily. "Enough's as good as a feast."

"I say, you fellows," came from Bunter, "I—I think it's a ghost."

"Fathead!"

Groan!

"That's you, D'Arcy, you howling ass!" exclaimed Cardew.

"Weally, Cardew, it is nothin' of the sort!"

"It came from your direction!"

"Wats!"

Groan!

"Gussy, you ass——" began Blake.

"I have alweady said, Blake, that I am not playing this widiculous twick!" said the swell of St. Jim's sternly.

"Then there's somebody close by your bed doing it." Blake jumped up. "We'll jolly well see who's out of bed, and nail him!"

Blake struck a match, and held it up. Arthur Augustus was sitting up in bed, but there was no one near him. As the match flickered there was a dismal groan close at hand.

"Under Gussy's bed!" exclaimed Digby.

"Yaas, wathah!"

"We'll give him a lesson!" said Blake. "Get a candle, Dig. I'll keep a match alight so that I can see if he dodges out."

"Right-ho!"

A candle was soon lighted, and Blake held it up and glanced over the beds. To his surprise, every one of them had an occupant. If there was anyone under D'Arcy's bed it was not a member of the dormitory.

"Some silly ass from another dorm!" exclaimed Levison. "Lowther, very likely—he's funny ass enough."

Groan!

"I'll jolly soon see!" growled Blake. "I'm fed up with this!"

He stooped, and cast the candle-light under D'Arcy's bed. Then he rose rather quickly to his feet, his face startled.

"Who is it, deah boy?"

"There's—there's nobody there!" stammered Blake.

"What!"

Half a dozen juniors were out of bed now, and two or three candles were lighted. Some of the fellows were looking rather scared. Trimble had buried his head under his bedclothes.

"Bai Jove! There is weally no one there!" exclaimed Arthur Augustus. "But I distinctly heard somebody gwoanin'. What—— Oh, cwumbs!"

Groan!

"I say, you fellows, that's under my bed!" exclaimed Bunter.

"Look under all the beds!" exclaimed Blake, in great perspiration. "There's some silly ass here playing tricks! Have him out!"

There was a rapid and angry search. But there was nobody to be found under the beds, and the juniors looked at one another in scared perplexity. And as a hush fell on them a deep groan resounded from somewhere.

"Oh, cwikey!" murmured Arthur Augustus. "This is weally gettin' unnervin'. Of course, it isn't a ghost!"

But Arthur Augustus's tone was not quite so assured now.

Groan!

Jack Blake spun round with a jump. He fancied the weird sound came from behind him. But nothing was to be seen save the dancing shadows from the candles. From under Baggy Trimble's bedclothes came a series of ear-splitting yells.

"Help! Ghosts! Spooks! Help! Yarooh! Help!"

"Shut up!" roared Blake. "Do you want to wake the whole House?"

"Yah! Help! Oh! Help!" yelled Trimble, unheeding.

Groan!

"I say, you fellows, isn't it awful!" exclaimed Bunter. "Is that something just behind you, D'Arcy?"

Arthur Augustus spun round like a top.

"Ow! You utter ass, Buntah, there is nothin' heah!"

"There's something just near you, Blake——"

"You thumping ass, be quiet!" gasped Blake. "It's only a shadow!"

"It's a ghost!" howled Trimble. "Help! Yocooop! Help! Ghosts! Help!"

The dormitory door opened, and a lamp gleamed in. Mr. Railton, with a black brow, strode into the dormitory.

CHAPTER 9.
Under Suspicion!

MR. RAILTON held up the lamp, and looked sternly at the crowd of juniors in pyjamas. And they looked at him. From under Trimble's bedclothes still came the yells of affright.

"Help! Yooop! Help!"

"What does this mean?" demanded Mr. Railton sternly.

"Yow-ow-woop! Help!"

"Silence!" thundered Mr. Railton.

But Baggy Trimble's head was muffled with blankets, and he was making too much noise himself to hear or heed the Housemaster's voice. He went on yelling.

"What is the matter with Trimble?" exclaimed the Housemaster.

"He—he thinks there's a ghost!" stammered Blake.

"What utter nonsense!"

"Help! Yooop! Ghosts! Yarooooh!"

Mr. Railton strode to Trimble's bed, and grasped the huddled blankets and jerked them back.

"Trimble!"

"Yaroooh!"

"Trimble! Boy!"

"Keep off!" yelled Trimble. "Yah! D-d-don't touch me! Help!"

"You stupid boy!" thundered Mr. Railton. "Do you not know me—your Housemaster?"

"Oh!" gasped Trimble, blinking at him. "I—I thought you were the ghost, sir. Oh dear! Oh dear! Ow!"

"Be quiet at once. Blake, tell me what this means. Has someone been frightening this foolish boy?"

"I—I wasn't frightened, sir," stuttered Trimble, much comforted by the light and the presence of the Housemaster. "Not at all. I——"

"Silence! Answer me, Blake! What has happened here?"

"We heard groans, sir," said Blake. "I—I suppose it was somebody playing a trick. There isn't anybody in the dormitory excepting us, but——"

"Groans!" repeated Mr. Railton. "That is very extraordinary! It must have been some boy present playing a trick."

"We couldn't spot him if it was, sir. And—and the sound came from under the beds, and when we looked there wasn't anybody there."

"Come, come!" said Mr. Railton. "You have allowed your imagination to run away with you. What you state is not possible, Blake."

"Unless it's a ghost, sir," said Billy Bunter.

"Do not be so absurd, Bunter!" Mr. Railton looked round. "Someone here has been playing a foolish trick. I command him to admit the fact at once."

There was no answer.

Mr. Railton's frown deepened.

"It is clearly the same person who has played tricks before," he said. "This occurrence proves that it is a member of the Fourth Form—of the School House portion of the Form. The boy who played the trick downstairs to-day is undoubtedly the same person, and here present, I think."

"Oh!" ejaculated Bunter.

The Greyfriars ventriloquist realised that it behoved him to tread warily now. The field of search was being narrowed down.

"Yaas, wathah, sir," said D'Arcy. "I nevah thought of that—but it's quite cleah. It cannot me Gwunday, as he is in the Shell dorm."

"I give the boy concerned another chance to speak up," said the Housemaster. "If it is left to me to discover him his punishment will be very severe!"

Silence.

"Very well," said Mr. Railton, compressing his lips, "I shall look into the matter. For the present, you may all go back to bed."

"I—I say, sir, can we have a light?" gasped Trimble.

"This is ridiculous, Trimble!" said the Housemaster sternly.

"Ye-e-es, sir, but—but can we have a light?"

"You should display more courage, Trimble."

"Oh, yes, sir, certainly; b-b-but can we have a light?"

Mr. Railton made an impatient gesture.

"I will leave a small light burning," he said. "Really, I am ashamed of you, Trimble. Go to bed at once, all of you!"

The Fourth-Formers turned in, and Mr. Railton, leaving a subdued light burning, quitted the dormitory, with a very dark frown on his face.

"I say, you fellows, shall we turn out the light?" asked Bunter.

"Let it alone!" howled Baggy Trimble. "You fat rotter, if you——"

"Oh, leave it alone!" said Blake.

"I say, you fellows, you're a blessed lot of funks!" went on Bunter cheerily.

"What?"

"Look at me! I'm not frightened," said the fat junior. "I'm the only chap here who wasn't."

"Perhaps it was you playing the trick!" grunted Herries.

"Bai Jove!"

Bunter jumped. He had been looking for a little cheap glory; not for suspicion that he was the mysterious japer. Herries' remark was too near the facts to please Bunter.

"Oh, really you fellows!" he stammered. "I like that! My belief is that it was Herries all the time."

"What!" roared Herries.

"I—I meant it was D'Arcy——"

"Bai Jove! Do you want me to come and give you a feahful thwashin', you fat boundah?" exclaimed the swell of St. Jim's indignantly.

"I—I—I mean, it—it was Tom Merry," stammered Bunter. "Now I come to think of it, it was Tom Merry—I'm sure of it. He shook me to-day——"

"You silly ass, what's that got to do with a groaning ghost?" snapped Blake.

"I—I mean, he's rather a beast, you know. I shouldn't wonder if he was hidden in the dorm all the time, laughing in his sleeve——"

"Fathead!"

"We've looked everywhere," remarked Levison. "But somebody must have been in the dorm——"

"It was one of our crowd," answered Blake. "We've only got to find out which one. And nothing of the kind happened before Bunter came to St. Jim's, either."

Billy Bunter quaked.

"I—I say, you fellows——" he stammered.

"Bai Jove! That is vewy twue, Blake," said D'Arcy. "It weally begins to look——"

"Oh, really, D'Arcy! I—I'm sure it was Tom Merry—now I come to think of it, I recognised his voice——"

"There wasn't any voice, Buntah—only a gwoan."

"I—I mean I recognised his groan——"

"Ha, ha, ha!"

"You uttah ass, Buntah! I weally cannot help suspectin'——"

"Gussy, old man, you're a silly ass!" came a voice from the shadows; and there was a howl from the juniors as Tom Merry's voice was recognised. "Good-night, kids! I'm tired of pulling your leg!"

Blake jumped up in bed.

There was only a dim light in the dormitory, and, such as it was, it did not reveal the presence of any intruder.

"Tom Merry!" howled Blake. "Why, you cheeky rotter——"

"Where are you, you feahful boundah?" shouted Arthur Augustus. "Bai Jove! We will sewag you for this, Tom Mewwy!"

"Ha, ha, ha!"

The laugh seemed to die away in the distance, and there was silence. The juniors stared round them in the shadows in utter amazement. Even Baggy Trimble was reassured now.

"Where is the rotter?" exclaimed Blake. "Tom Merry! You sneaking Shell-fish, where are you?"

"He's gone!" said Bunter. "I—I think I heard a door close—a sort of click. I say, you fellows, do you think there's a secret passage here somewhere—like the one in Study No. 6?"

"I didn't hear it," said Blake.

"Bai Jove! A secwet passage would account for it," said D'Arcy. "A secwet passage we don't know about——"

"Then how would Tom Merry know about it?" asked Julian.

"Bai Jove! I weally don't know! But I fail to see how Tom Mewwy can have got heah otherwise; the door has not been opened."

Blake settled his head on his pillow again.

"However he did it, he did it," he remarked; "and we'll jolly well talk to him in the morning. We'll teach the Shell bounders not to play giddy pranks in our dorm!"

"Yaas, wathah!"

The Fourth Form got to sleep at last; and Tom Merry, in the Shell dorm, slept the sleep of unsuspicious innocence, never even dreaming of the vials of wrath that were to be poured out upon his head in the morning.

CHAPTER 10.

A Little Too Previous!

TOM MERRY came out of the School House in the fresh morning while the rising-bell was still ringing, and Manners and Lowther followed him out. The Terrible Three were down early, as they often were. It was a sharp, clear morning, and the open air was very tempting for a run before breakfast.

The chums of the Shell were trotting cheerily round the quadrangle when Blake & Co. emerged from the House with some more of the Fourth. Jack Blake spotted the Terrible Three at once.

"There they are!" he said. "I dare say Manners and Lowther are in the game; but it's Tommy we've got to deal with. We've got to give him a tip about keeping chaps awake at night playing ghost. Some of you fellows collar Manners and Lowther and nail them, while we give Thomas the time of his life!"

"Yaas, wathah!"

Nine or ten juniors started to meet the Terrible Three. The Shell fellows came trotting on unsuspiciously, and gave a yell in chorus as they were suddenly collared.

"Hallo! What's this game?" exclaimed Tom Merry.

"Our turn!" grinned Blake. "Down him! Here, sit on him, Bunter!"

The Terrible Three, surprised and wrathful, struggled, but the odds were too heavy. Levison, Clive, and Cardew handled Manners—Monty Lowther was collared and held by Julian, Roylance, and Herries. Blake and Digby and D'Arcy levelled Tom Merry with the grass, and held him there—and Billy Bunter rolled up cheerily at Blake's call and sat on him. There was no resistance from the captain of the Shell after that. Bunter's weight was no joke.

"Gerroooh! Gerroff!" gasped Tom.

Bunter grinned, and settled down comfortably on Tom's shoulders, fairly flattening him.

"You shook me yesterday, you beast!" he remarked.

"Ow!" gasped Tom. "Gerroff!"

"Sit on him, Bunter!"

"I'm sitting on him—I'll jolly well squash him!" said the Owl, with a fat chuckle. "Playing tricks in the dorm, and frightening everybody but me—I'll show him!"

"Wow! Draggimoff!" wailed Tom Merry.

"Ha, ha, ha!"

Tom Merry's face was in the grass, and Bunter laid a fat hand on the back of his head and jammed it down hard. There was a gurgle of anguish from the captain of the Shell.

"Here, chuck that, Bunter!" said Blake sharply.

"Grooogh! Draggimoff!"

"Not yet, deah boy!" grinned Arthur Augustus. "You are goin' to have a lickin', deah boy. Did you bwing that stump, Blake?"

"Here it is! Steady, Tom! Don't kick, or you may get it in the wrong place!"

"Go it!"

Whack, whack, whack!

Blake laid on the stump—not hard, but sufficiently so to make the Shell captain yell. Manners and Lowther struggled to go to their leader's aid, but they struggled in vain. The Fourth-Formers roared with laughter.

"Stoppit!" howled Tom Merry. "Are you all potty? Stoppit! By Jove, I'll lick the lot of you! Ow!"

Whack, whack!

"Oh, you rotters! I'll—I'll——"

"This is for your own good," explained Blake. "Suppose Railton had caught you in our dorm last night playing ghost. You'd have got worse than this."

Whack!

"Yarooh! You silly ass, I wasn't in your dorm last night!" howled Tom Merry. "What do you mean, you frabjous chump?"

"Dwaw it mild, Tom Mewwy! You know vewy well you were playin' ghost in our dorm, and fwightenin' Twimble."

"I wasn't!" shrieked Tom. "I was in bed last night, you chumps!"

"Bai Jove! Is that honest Injun, Tom Mewwy?"

"Ow! Yes, you ass! Wow!"

"Oh!" exclaimed Blake. He stopped the operations of the stump. "This is jolly queer. If it wasn't you, Tom Merry, who was it?"

"How should I know, you thumping ass?" groaned the captain of the Shell. "How could I know, when I was in bed, asleep?"

"Roll off, Bunter."

"Oh, rot!" said Bunter. "Give him some more. He shook me yesterday——"

"I'll shake you to-day if you don't roll off," said Blake; and he poked the stump at Bunter's podgy ribs. "Now then——"

"Yooop!"

Billy Bunter rolled off, and Tom Merry sat up, draggled and breathless. Blake's followers released Manners and Lowther, who were in a state of towering wrath.

"You silly chumps!" roared Lowther. "Wade in and mop them up!"

"Hold on," said Blake. "There seems to have been a mistake. If Tom Merry wasn't in our dorm last night, he must have lent his voice to somebody who was."

"Yaas, wathah!"

Tom Merry gasped for breath.

"You frabjous jabberwocks!" he panted. "Couldn't you ask me the question first?"

"Well, you see, we were sure——"

"We were quite suah, Tom Mewwy. Howevah, if you deny the circumstance, we accept your statement," said Arthur Augustus gracefully. "You can wegard that stumpin' as withdrawn."

"Ha, ha, ha!"

"Ow! It doesn't feel withdrawn!" gasped Tom Merry. "I've a jolly good mind to knock all your silly heads together!" He scrambled to his feet. "Now, tell me what's happened, you asses, as you ought to have done at first?"

Blake explained.

"Fathead!" said Tom. "You ought to have known it wasn't I. How could I get in and out of the dorm without being seen?"

"Blessed if I know! But it was your voice."

"And it was Grundy's voice in your study, and Kangaroo's voice I heard at my door, and Railton's voice we heard another time!" growled Tom Merry. "That blessed trickster knows how to imitate voices. You ought to have thought of that."

"Perhaps we ought," admitted Blake. "But—but it was so exactly like your toot. The chap must be rather clever to be able to do it."

"Clever enough, I suppose," said Tom.

"Bai Jove! I was thinkin' of suspectin' Buntah, but that wathah knocks it on the head," remarked Arthur Augustus.

"Ha, ha, ha!"

"Hallo! There's brekker-bell."

Billy Bunter was rolling away to the School House; but, for once, it was not only a meal-time that drew him there. The conversation was taking a turn that the Owl of Greyfriars did not like.

"Bunter!" repeated Tom Merry, as the juniors started for the House. "How could Bunter play such a trick? He hasn't brains enough."

"I should certainly not wegard him as a bwainy chap," agreed Arthur Augustus. "But he was not fwightened last night—and he isn't vewy bwave, you know—and nothin' of the sort evah happened befoah Buntah came. And, weflectin' on the mattah, I wemembah that Buntah has always been somewhah about when these things are happenin'."

"The fat idiot couldn't do it," said Manners.

"Well, no, he certainly couldn't do anythin' that wequiahed bwains," said Arthur Augustus. "But Wailton said last night it must be somebody in our dorm, and I think he was wight. But who was it, then? If it was somebody; it—it must have been somebody, you know."

"Not really!" exclaimed Monty Lowther. "Did you work that out in your head, Gussy? This is what comes of belonging to the old nobility!"

"Weally, Lowthah——"

"Won't he make 'em sit up in the House of Lords some day, with a brain like that!" exclaimed Lowther enthusiastically. "They'll make him Lord High Warden of the Royal Inkpot at least."

"I wegard you as an ass, Lowthah! I do not believe there is such an office in existence as Lord High Warden of the Woyal Inkpot."

"Go hon!" murmured Lowther.

The juniors went in to breakfast, Tom Merry kindly allowing the affair of the stumping to drop. The mystery of the Fourth Form dormitory remained a mystery; but at the breakfast-table many glances were turned upon Bunter.

Billy Bunter did not notice it, however. His attention was devoted wholly and solely to his breakfast.

CHAPTER 11.

Sheer Neck!

"TWOUBLE for somebody!" murmured Arthur Augustus D'Arcy.

The Fourth were in their Form-room, and Mr. Lathom was about to take his class, when the School House master entered with a knitted brow. Mr. Railton spoke a few words in a low tone to the Form master, and then turned to the class amid a deep silence.

The juniors all looked as meek and mild as possible. It was plain from the Housemaster's look that there was "trouble" for somebody.

"My boys," said Mr. Railton in his deep voice, "you are all aware that a number of very extraordinary pranks have been played in this House lately. General disturbance has been the result. It is my duty to discover the culprit, and administer adequate punishment."

Billy Bunter kept his eyes fixed on his desk. He was anxious not to meet the Housemaster's glance at that moment.

"From what happened last night," continued Mr. Railton, "it is clear that the perpetrator of these absurd and troublesome practical jokes is a member of this Form, and a School House boy. Which boy it is I cannot say; but he is certainly here present, and hears me speak."

Bunter was sedulously studying an inkstain on his desk. He felt the Housemaster's keen glance on the class, and did not dare to look up.

"I call upon that boy to stand forward!" said Mr. Railton. "He will certainly be caned very severely. But if he does not admit his identity, and it is left to me to discover him, he will be sent to the Head to be flogged. I shall wait one minute for the boy to come forward."

The Housemaster stood silent, and waited; and the Fourth Form were silent, too. The New House members of the Form looked unconcerned enough, but the rest were somewhat excited. The big hand of the Form-room clock travelled round the space of sixty seconds, and there was no reply from the Form.

"Very well," said Mr. Railton, when the minute had elapsed. "I have given the boy an opportunity, and he has chosen to let it pass. The closest investigation will take place, and I have not the slightest doubt that the offender will be discovered. A flogging will follow. That is all."

The School House master quitted the Form-room, and there was a buzz among the juniors. Billy Bunter was looking a little pale now.

Lessons began with Mr. Lathom; but the Fourth were thinking quite as much about Mr. Railton's investigations as about Mr. Lathom's instructions. Billy Bunter was thinking a great deal more about them.

The Owl of Greyfriars was decidedly uneasy.

The matter had been narrowed down, and already suspicion in the Form had turned upon him. It was natural that it should turn upon a new fellow, before whose arrival nothing of the kind had occurred. In fact, it was only Bunter's well-known obtuseness that prevented the juniors from deciding that he was the offender. That such a complete ass as Bunter could worry the whole House, as the unknown trickster had done, did not seem probable to them.

But suspicion was on him, and might grow—in fact, would grow. And if the same suspicion occurred to the Housemaster——

Bunter quaked inwardly.

He had been determined to make the School House fellows "sit up," as he expressed it, for their supposed shortcomings towards him; and, as usual, he had overdone it.

And if he was found out——

"Bunter, you are not listening to me!" came Mr. Lathom's severe voice. "I have twice told you to construe, Bunter."

"Oh dear!" gasped Bunter.

He blundered through his construe a little more hopelessly than usual, but he hardly heard the admonitions that followed.

Billy Bunter was very glad when the Fourth Form was dismissed that morning.

His painful reflections in the Form-room had earned him severe reprimands from Mr. Lathom, but they had helped him to make up his mind. He realised that his little game was played out, and his chief object was to escape the punishment he had richly earned.

"I say, you fellows," said Bunter, as he came on the Terrible Three in the corridor. "I—I say, Tom, old chap——"

"Br-r-r-r!" said Tom Merry.

"You know Railton better than I do," said Bunter. "He's a man of his word, isn't he?"

"Of course he is, fathead!" answered Tom.

"If he made a chap a promise he'd keep it, wouldn't he?" said Bunter, blinking anxiously at the captain of the Shell.

"Yes, ass!"

"That's all right, then," said Bunter. And he rolled away to the Housemastermaster's study, Tom Merry & Co. looking after him in surprise.

Mr. Railton had just come in from the Sixth Form-room, and he glanced at the fat junior in the doorway.

"If—if you please, sir," began Bunter, venturing gingerly into the study. "I—I want to speak to you, sir."

"Well?"

"I—I can give you the name of the fellow who's been playing tricks, sir," said Bunter, blinking at him.

Mr. Railton frowned. Above all things, he detested tale-bearing. But he was in rather a difficult position. After what he had said in the Form-room he could scarcely refuse to listen to Bunter.

"Indeed! You are aware of his identity, Bunter?" he asked curtly.

"Yes, sir. I—I feel it my duty to tell you, sir."

Mr. Railton raised his hand.

"One moment, Bunter. I have not asked any boy to give me information, nor desired any boy to do so."

"I—I think I ought to tell you, sir," said Bunter. "The fact is, sir, the—the chap would like to own up, and get it over, only he's nervous. I—I knew who it was all along, and I know he'd like you to be told."

"In that case, Bunter, you may proceed."

"I—I suppose I sha'n't be punished, sir, if I tell you the chap's name?"

"There is no reason why you should be punished, Bunter."

"I—I knew about the chap doing it, sir——"

"You were not called upon to betray him, however," said the Housemaster. "I do not blame you for keeping the secret, though your Form-fellow was acting very foolishly and wrongly."

"Then—then I sha'n't be punished, sir, if I tell you?"

"Certainly not!"

"Thank you, sir!" said Bunter meekly. "But—but the other fellows, sir, may—may think I oughtn't to have told you; they—they don't understand how the matter stands. I—I don't want to be ragged, sir."

"Come, come!" said the Housemaster impatiently. "You are wasting my time, Bunter. If you have anything to tell me, tell me at once!"

"Yes, sir, certainly; but—but would you mind speaking to Tom Merry—he's in the corridor, sir—and telling him there's to be no ragging?"

Mr. Railton stepped to the door.

"Merry! Come here, please! You others may come also."

"Yes, sir," said Tom.

The Terrible Three came along to the Housemaster's door, and Study No. 6 and some other fellows came with them. Bunter blinked at them as they crowded round the doorway.

"Merry, and all of you," said Mr. Railton, "Bunter has come here to tell me the name of the reckless boy who has been plunging the House into uproar lately by a series of foolish tricks. He thinks exception may be taken to this by the others——"

"Sneak!" came a voice from somewhere.

"Silence!" exclaimed Mr. Railton. "Bunter assures me that the offender is anxious for the truth to be told, but shrinks from confessing. He is not, therefore, guilty of tale-bearing, and I forbid you, under any circumstances whatever, to punish Bunter in any way. I require your promise, Merry, as head boy in the Lower School, that there shall be no ragging."

Tom Merry hesitated.

"I say, Merry, it's all right," said Bunter. "The chap doesn't mind my giving him away—he's glad to get it over."

"I promise, sir," said Tom Merry quietly.

"Very good, Merry!" The Housemaster turned to Bunter. "Now, Bunter, you may give me the boy's name."

"You've promised that I shan't be punished, sir?"

"That is understood. Now, what is the name?"

"Bunter, sir."

"What?"

"Bunter!"

There was a gasp from the juniors in the corridor. Mr. Railton stared blankly at the Owl of the Fourth.

"Bunter!" he repeated. "There is no other boy at this school of that name but yourself."

"Yes, sir! I'm the chap!" said Bunter.

"What?" gasped Mr. Railton.

"I'm the chap, sir," said Bunter. "It—it was really only a joke on the fellows, sir."

"Bai Jove!"

"You see, sir," continued the Owl, blinking cheerfully at the astounded Housemaster, "I'm a jolly clever ventriloquist, like—like my cousin Billy at Greyfriars. That's how I did it. I can make my voice come from anywhere, sir. Shall I make the Head's voice come from the wastepaper-basket, sir, just to show you?"

"Certainly not!" stuttered Mr. Railton.

"I could, sir. I can imitate anybody's voice—especially a grunt like Grundy's, or a silly chirrup like D'Arcy's, or a snort like Herries'——"

"Bunter!" thundered the Housemaster. "I have already suspected that there was ventriloquism employed in these foolish tricks, and I had been making inquiries. Bunter! You confess——"

"Yes, sir."

Mr. Railton caught up the cane.

"Very well! I shall now administer a——"

"I—I say, sir, you promised——" howled Bunter.

"What?"

"You promised that I shouldn't be punished, sir, if I told you the name."

Mr. Railton stared speechlessly at the Owl.

"I asked Tom Merry first," said Bunter, in an injured tone. "He told me you were a man of your word, sir."

"Oh, my hat!" murmured Tom Merry, almost overcome.

"Gweat Scott! Of all the feahful cheek——"

"Bunter! I—I gave you that assurance under a misapprehension!" exclaimed the Housemaster. "You led me to believe you were going to name some other boy in the Fourth Form."

"I never said so, sir."

"You—you certainly did not say so. But—but, Bunter, you impertinent young rascal, do you imagine for one moment that you will escape your just punishment by this trickery?" exclaimed Mr. Railton.

"Certainly, sir! You promised!"

Tom Merry & Co. stood breathless. Mr. Railton's face was a study for some moments. But at last he lowered the cane.

He was fairly caught, and he realised it. He was caught—but a Housemaster's word could not possibly be broken.

"Bunter," said Mr. Railton, at last, breathing hard through his nose, "you may go. If there is any recurrence of these ventriloquial tricks you will be flogged. Go!"

"Thank you, sir!" said Bunter cheerfully.

And he rolled out of the study with a fat grin on his face, leaving Mr. Railton looking, as Cardew expressed it, absolutely stumped.

In the passage Tom Merry & Co. surrounded the Owl. Their looks were grim, but Billy Bunter grinned at them confidently.

"You've spoofed Railton," said Tom Merry. "But you can't spoof us. You're going to have the ragging of your life, Bunter!"

"I hope you're not going to break your word, Merry," said Bunter loftily. "Railton will be down on you, too, if you do!"

"Mum-mum-my word!"

"Certainly! Railton said there was to be no ragging; and you promised for all the fellows. I despise a chap who breaks his word," said Bunter. "I couldn't do it myself. I'm too honourable!"

"Well!" said Tom Merry, with a gasp. "Well! I—I suppose the fat beast has got us! Well! You—you—you can clear off, Bunter!"

Billy Bunter winked at the exasperated juniors, and rolled away, grinning. And as he rolled off an unmelodious cachinnation floated back to the exasperated juniors:

"He, he, he!"

THE END.

(Don't miss next Wednesday's Great Story of Tom Merry & Co. at St. Jim's—"THE RIVAL ENTERTAINERS!"—by Martin Clifford.)

COKER THE COMICAL! By Dick Russell.

I.

"BLOW Dr. Johnson!"

Horace James Coker uttered that disconcerting remark with startling suddenness.

Potter and Greene raised their heads from the impots they were engaged upon, and looked across at each other dismally.

After that they looked up, and found Coker glowering down upon them.

"Do get on with your impot!" implored Potter. "The footer begins in half an hour. We must get these dashed lines in to Prout before then!"

"I said blow Dr. Johnson!" repeated Coker firmly. "And I mean blow Dr. Johnson!"

"Two-thirty, Cokey, old man!" hinted Greene, pointing at the clock on the mantelpiece. "The match begins at three, you know!"

Coker glanced absently at the clock, and seemed inclined to resume his seat.

But he straightened up again like a Jack-in-the-box.

"What's Dr. Johnson got to do with it, anyway?" he demanded warmly. "Tell me that!"

That was precisely what Potter and Greene wanted to know. Or, to be a trifle more correct, that was precisely what they didn't want to know. The venerable Dr. Johnson didn't interest them in the slightest.

Wearily they shook their heads.

"Dry up, old chap?"

"The match, you know!"

"Talk about it after tea, old son!"

All of which soft pursuasions had utterly no effect upon the talkative Coker.

Not that they were anxious to escort the lordly one on to the field of leathery battle. Their side would stand a much better chance of winning without him.

But Latin poetry requires a deal of translating with a voice like Coker's booming in the vicinity. The thing was to still it.

"I'll tell you what!" exclaimed Coker, waxing hotter. "It's—it's traitorous, and unfeeling! That's what it is, every bit!"

"Well, what could you expect but lines?" murmured Potter patiently. "Prouty asked you what Dr. Johnson was, and you said a builder in Courtfield. Did you think it was funny, you ass?"

"I was thinking at the time of a building contractor in Courtfield!" grunted Coker. "How was I to know he meant Johnson out of the—the Stone Age?"

"And we were lined for cackling!" put in Greene dolefully. "As if you weren't made to be cackled at, Coker! But do let us finish, like a good chap! Save Dr. Johnson till to-morrow!"

"Blow Dr. Johnson! Do you, or don't you, know that there's a serious shortage of houses?"

"That's all very well——"

"Do you, or don't you, know that the streets are swarming with houseless people?" demanded Coker dramatically, but with some exaggeration "Go into Friardale or Courtfield this afternoon and look at the swarms of people walking through the streets, all without homes to cover them!"

"You thumping ass!" shouted Potter exasperatedly. "Do you think people carry their homes about like umbrellas?"

"Ahem! It's this demobilisation muddle that's holding things back!" said Coker, frowning at Potter. "I suppose they've made such a mess of it that the builders can't get out of the Army. Now, listen to this!"

Coker produced an old and dirty newspaper and laid it on the table.

"Grooh!" gasped Potter, starting back in his seat. "What a whiff!"

Greene fanned himself with his impot.

Coker frowned blackly.

"Don't be a pair of asses! I found this

behind the scuttle. Bloater been wrapped in it, or something. But that's immaterial, so listen!"

"Get it out, quick!" said Potter faintly. "And then throw it on the fire!"

"It's just a few lines from a reader of the paper, printed in the column reserved for letters. 'Sir,—The alarming want of houses, occasioned by the unfortunate ending of the war, must be remedied. Houses must be built. Every square inch of ground in the country must be used for this purpose. Are we pro-Germans? No. Where are our builders? What——'"

Potter and Greene rose rebelliously.

"Look here, Coker!" exclaimed the former. "If you think we're going to listen to that all the afternoon——"

"There's no need to read it all——"

"Good!"

"But it goes on to say that a certain stretch of waste ground in Courtfield could be used for building on," said Coker, wrinkling his brows. "At present it's used as a brickfield, or something like that. I saw it the other day. Bricks are scattered, some in piles. And—would you believe it?"

Coker paused momentously, then went on: "There's actually a big, wooden advertisement there, saying, 'Johnson, Building Contractor.' When houses are wanted so urgently, you know! My hat!"

Potter and Greene each winked an eye farthest from Coker. For the advertisement practically showed that 'Johnson was engaged building houses on that identical piece of ground.

"Now, I've looked up a few books on building matters," went on Coker thoughtfully. "Mind you, I don't say I could rig up a house as well as Johnson and his hirelings——"

"Not really?"

"You know I couldn't," said Coker suspiciously. "Don't try to be funny, Potter! Your face carries you far enough in that direction!"

"Twenty-five to three!" put in Greene irrelevantly.

"Blessed if your eyes ain't glued to the clock, Greeney!" said Coker peevishly. "I was saying, I couldn't do the job like Johnson's men, but I'll tell you what I could do!"

"You could dry up!" suggested Potter.

"I could make a beginning!" said Coker triumphantly.

"Make a whatter?"

"I mean, I could shame the bounders! Make them see that they're unpatriotic, slacking rotters! I could begin erecting a house, and if, of course, it shapes all right, as I rather expect it will, I'll finish it off!"

"Great Scott!"

"Holy Moses!"

"Then I'll bring along Mr. Johnson to see what a raw hand has done, guided purely by the spirit of patriotism. And if that doesn't make him set to work at once, building houses, and getting tenants for them—well, he must have a hide like a crocodile!"

"You—you think you could build a house?" said Potter faintly.

"On a brickfield?" said Greene, with equal faintness.

"No doubt of it!" said Coker promptly. "With your help this afternoon——"

"Oh!" Potter and Greene became grim in an instant.

"So that's what's behind this tosh about building!" said Potter coldly. "You want us to go piling bricks, do you?"

"Ahem! You may as well, you know, now that it's too late for the footer."

Potter spun round, and glanced anxiously at the clock.

"Ass!" he said, with a gasp of relief. "Twenty to three. A good twenty minutes yet."

"As a matter of fact," said Coker, rather awkwardly, "that clock's half an hour slow!"

"What! That clock gains!" exclaimed Potter. "It should be fast!"

Coker nodded.

"You're right, Potter; it gains," he said lamely. "So I put it back half an hour."

II.

Potter and Greene stared at their study-mate speechlessly.

Now that Coker's voice was quiet, some of the voices from the playing-fields were faintly audible. Some of them were:

"On the ball, Bland!"

"Shoot, man!"

"Goal! Hurrah!"

The match had begun without Potter and Greene.

"You purposely put back the clock," said Potter deliberately at last, "in order to make us miss the match! You—you imbecile!"

"It's only a practice, you know!" said Coker pleasantly. "Take it good-humouredly, old man!"

"G-g-good-humouredly!"

"Do you know, I guessed you would prefer a measly game of footer to my patriotic idea! I thought so!"

"You th-thought so!" stuttered Potter. "Oh, my hat, you th-thought so!"

"Oh," said Coker airily, "I know human nature, you know! I know a good many things, you know!"

"Yes!" said Greene, breathing hard. "But you don't know how near you are to being thrown out of the window, you frabjous ass!"

"Oh, come!" said Coker easily. "'Tain't like you to turn nasty, Greeney! Take a trot with me along to Courtfield, old scouts! When you get into the air you'll admit that it was rather a good idea of mine to turn the clock back. Ha, ha, ha!"

Potter and Greene looked at each other stonily. Coker looked beamingly out of the window, evidently to see how the weather was for building.

Suddenly Potter's grim visage broke into a grin, and he winked. Almost simultaneously Greene did likewise.

They had come to a tacit and mutual understanding.

"Well, Coker," said Potter, "if you really want our help in this potty business——"

"We'll give it," finished Greene.

Coker beamed as he turned from the window.

"I knew you'd take to it!" he said enthusiastically. "It's a jolly good idea of mine, even though I say so."

"Let's finish off these lines," grunted Potter.

And they got to work at last.

Potter and Greene exchanged many glances during the course of it. But Coker saw nothing of them. His face was wreathed in smiles as his pen straggled over the paper.

The two quickly finished, and laid down their pens. It was now a matter of waiting for Coker; and that somewhat lengthy period of waiting they spent gazing ominously at his beaming countenance.

"Finished!" he said cheerily, at length. "You chaps nearly done?"

"Nearly?" said Potter sarcastically.

"Oh, you have! Be getting on your coats, you know; I've one or two things to take with me."

Wherewith Coker opened the table drawer, and drew forth something that looked like a huge sheet of linen, folded.

"Oh, good!" said Potter, with awakening interest. "Rather a good idea of yours, Coker!"

Horace beamed at once.

"Glad you're seeing reason, Potter," he said amiably. "Even though we've never tried our hands at building before——"

"I mean, it's a good idea to have refreshments whilst we're at it."

"Refreshments?" repeated Coker. "Who said anything about refreshments?"

"Well, that tablecloth," said Potter argumentatively. "You're not going to lay bricks on it, I suppose?"

"Tablecloth!" snorted Coker, with great disparagement. "This is the plan."

"Eh? The what?"

"The design of the construction. Do you think you build houses as you pile bricks? You know nothing about the bizney, Potter!"

"What's the bag for?" asked Greene. For Coker had collared a small hand-bag, and, with his two chums, was making for the door.

"Measuring instruments," said Coker firmly. "Accuracy is going to be my motto. And as for the tools, I'm going to borrow them from Johnson."

"The builder whose bricks we're going to use?" exclaimed Potter.

"Just so!" chuckled Coker. "I'll pay him for the loan of them, of course. But it will pile on the agony, by Jove! If he's a patriotic man it—it should bring tears to his eyes—tears of repentance for his negligence."

"He'll be affected, no doubt," murmured Potter.

They made for the gates now, and Potter and Greene cast regretful glances at the playing-fields, where jerseyed figures were to be seen in miniature, and in rapid movement.

On the road to Courtfield Coker waxed quite voluble on the subject of building.

"And now that we've got the light in the evenings," he finished brilliantly, "we'll be able to put in all our spare time at our 'house'!"

"We'll see about that," said Potter shortly, "later."

"In the dim by-and-by!" added Greene, sotto voce.

Coker indicated the spare stretch of ground when they arrived at it. It was indeed quite a decent site for building, and houses would have been erected on it long ago but for the war.

"Lots of bricks lying about, you see," remarked Coker critically. "Some of 'em in piles, too, as I thought."

Potter and Greene saw that, and understood, which Coker did not. Anybody but Coker would have seen that the bricks had been placed carefully in position by the practised hands of builders.

"Johnson's office is quite near here—his address is on the signboard there," said Coker, pointing. "If he doesn't happen to be in his office, we'll bone the tools from the yard at the back. Still, someone's sure to be there, and the sight of a few John Bradburys will do the trick."

A short walk brought them to Johnson's office, which was remarkably dilapidated and ill-erected, bearing no great testimony to his prowess as a builder. But perhaps he hadn't built it himself.

Mr. Johnson was in his office, poring over accounts.

"Good-morning!" said Coker affably.

He was met with a discouraging stare.

"Well?"

"You are Mr. Johnson?"

"I'm Johnson, right enough! What do you want?"

For answer Coker drew forth his pocket-book, and displayed its contents. There was a visible softening of Mr. Johnson's expression.

"Hoh! You've called to pay an account, my lad?"

"Ahem! Not at all! I want you to do me a favour, Mr. Johnson—a little favour, but I'll pay well for it. All I want is the loan of a few of your building implements."

Mr. Johnson waved him off.

"My dear lad, I can't do that! That's a ridiculous thing to ask me!"

"Not so ridiculous! There's a deal of profit attached to what we've got to do," said Coker impressively, "and a lot—in fact, the whole—of that profit will go to you. We're not out to make money; it's just a little service for the country. Should we damage the tools I'll pay for them willingly. You can have my address—Coker, Greyfriars School. There's money in this, mind you, and it will go into your pocket. Honour bright!"

Coker was quite serious in saying this. He really believed that he could rig up a really valuable house, and that it would be a good thing for Mr. Johnson, who would have had nothing to pay out of the profits for labour.

Mr. Johnson looked thoughtful. All his implements were lying idle, for the simple reason that all his men were out on strike. But for that fact they would have been working on that piece of waste ground, and Coker would scarcely have made his blunder.

So Mr. Johnson naturally considered that this was a good chance for putting his instruments to a remunerative use, especially as he had securities against damage.

Coker and he quickly came to an understanding, during the course of which paper money changed hands.

Laden with various utensils, not to mention mortar, Coker & Co. returned to the brickfield.

Coker opened the bag he had brought from Greyfriars. And then, his face intent as if by making abstruse calculations, he made a number of mystical measurements.

Potter and Greene yawned repeatedly until these were finished.

"The cellar must go by the board," said Coker thoughtfully. "That can be dug afterwards by old Johnson's labourers. And—er—we'll rig up the scaffolding when we get more advanced, you know, and—er—

Printed and published every Wednesday by the Proprietors, the Amalgamated Press, Limited, The Fleetway House, Farringdon Street, London, E.C. 4. Advertisement offices: The Fleetway House, Farringdon Street, London, E.C. 4. Subscription rates: Inland and abroad (except South Africa and Australasia), 8s. 10d. per annum, 4s. 5d. for six months. Sole agents for South Africa: The Central News Agency, Ltd. Sole agents for Australia and New Zealand: Messrs. Gordon & Gotch, Ltd.; and for Canada: The Imperial News Co., Ltd.—Saturday, March 15th, 1919. N after I've had another look at the book. Ahem!"

His two helpers grinned. Coker was just beginning to realise that he was at a loss.

However, he removed his coat in quite a workmanlike manner.

"Better take off yours, you two!" he urged.

"No fear!"

Coker grunted. The three armed themselves with trowels, and looked about for bricks.

"Those piled straight are by far the best," said Coker critically. "They've been put that way purposely, I can see. They haven't been dumped down anyhow from a cart!"

"Wonderful!" murmured Potter.

Coker tugged at one of the bricks, but it refused to budge. The simple reason was that it was mortared down.

"Hallo!" he said suspiciously. "Someone's been monkeying here. Pass me a chisel, Potter, and a heavy hammer!"

Potter obligingly passed the chisel and heavy hammer.

Coker got to work.

Bang, bang, bang!

The brick gave way against that onslaught, and toppled off.

Coker looked at his chums dubiously. They were as serious as owls.

"Think the weather fixed them together like this, Potter? Anyway, they're the best bricks of the lot, and I'll loosen the whole dashed pile!"

And Coker set to work with a will, and the bricks were soon being rapidly dislodged.

But to return to Mr. Johnson.

Now, the truth was that Mr. Johnson was a patriotic man. He was also not unduly prejudiced against making a little money when the chance presented itself. And he found that both happy traits of character could be made use of by building houses for the Government.

His men had been engaged on one of these Government contracts before they struck, and the brickfield was the site. So, after finishing with his ledgers, Mr. Johnson thought he would stroll there to see how things had progressed.

When he reached the brickfield, and saw who were engaged there, and, worse than all, saw to what use his implements were being put, he simply stood and gaped.

He couldn't believe his eyes.

Potter and Greene could quite believe their eyes when they observed Mr. Johnson. They had been expecting something like this by way of a climax, and had kept wary eyes upon all four sides of the open field.

The amiable Coker kept eyes upon nothing but his work of destruction.

"Phew! They're stuck faster towards the bottom!" he gasped, without looking up. "Blessed if I'll be beaten, though!"

Bang, bang, bang!

Potter and Greene retreated to a strategical point which placed Coker between themselves and the fast-becoming-irate Mr. Johnson.

Coker looked up at last, and started violently. For he found the red face of Mr. Johnson glowering at him.

A torrent of abuse was coming from his lips, but the hammering had up to now deadened the sound.

"You young whelp!" he raved. "Scoundrel! So this is what you wanted the implements for! You—you—you——"

"My dear man," said Coker pacifically, "don't get excited."

"Excited! I——"

"If you'd given me time to finish you'd have been pleased, I can tell you!"

"Pleased!" Mr. Johnson glared, and was speechless.

"Now, let me talk to you straight, man to man," said Coker, laying down the tools. "Personally, I don't believe you're unpatriotic, Mr. Johnson. I think it's pure negligence on your part. But, I put it to you. Don't you think that when fellows have been four years in the trenches, fighting for you, they're worth at least a decent house to come back to?"

Mr. Johnson made a gurgling noise in his throat. Coker put it down to repentance, and went on:

"Here you are, a builder—a builder, moreover, with a patch of ground at his disposal. Isn't it your duty to get permission from the Government to build respectable houses upon it? Think, man!"

Mr. Johnson found his voice at last.

"You—you interfering fool! I'm already working against a contract from the Government——"

"Oh!"

"And—and that's the beginning of the job that you've just broken down, you—you——"

Mr. Johnson broke down again.

"Oh, my only hat!" gasped Coker, in dismay. "I—I say, I'm awfully sorry, Mr. Johnson——"

"You imbecile!"

"But still, you know, it didn't seem to be much of a beginning—— Ow!"

Mr. Johnson's podgy fist had shot forward, and thumped him upon the nose.

"My hat! Go easy, you know! I say——"

Coker fled precipitately, leaving Mr. Johnson roaring like a bull, and dancing like a dervish.

"Queer old file, that chap!" commented Coker, joining Potter and Greene. "Never known a chap fly into a rage so suddenly! He—— Yaroooh!"

A heavy brickbat caught him squarely between the shoulder-blades. Another whizzed over his head. And Potter and Greene had to jump wildly to escape similar missiles.

"Scat!" jerked Potter tersely, digging his elbows into his ribs. "Nothing else for it!"

Coker seemed inclined to favour "peace by negotiation," but a glance at Mr. Johnson changed his mind.

The three Fifth-Formers vanished at top speed, and left Mr. Johnson shying brickbats apparently at nothing.

THE END.

THE ST. JIM'S GALLERY.

No. 39 :
CLIFTON DANE.

Two of the trio of chums in Study No. 11 have already been dealt with—Noble some time since, Glyn as lately as last week. Now we come to Clifton Dane, the Canadian member of the firm of Cornstalk & Co.

The Terrible Three were sent to Rylcombe Station to meet Dane. Kildare sent them, having had a hint from the Head that someone should go. But the four chums of Study No. 6 and Figgins & Co. also went. No one sent them. The notion of going was entirely their own. Since the new fellow was booked for the Shell, Tom Merry and his chums regarded the action of the Fourth-Formers as mere butting-in and gross cheek. But the two parties joined forces when they found a crowd of village lads piling in on one fellow.

That fellow turned out to be Dane. He was dusty and dishevelled, and when Tom Merry helped him to his feet he was very angry.

He got over that, though, and his appearance and manner made a favourable impression on Tom and the rest. He was very dark, somewhat after the gipsy fashion. They soon found out the cause of this. He admitted that he was not wholly English; in fact, he was what is called a half-breed, a term which is apt to be used more contemptuously than it should be, for there have been many fine men of mixed Indian and white blood in North America. Dane was no more ashamed of his mother, a chief's daughter of the great Huron nation, than of his father, an Englishman and an old St. Jim's boy. He was proud of them both—a little homesick at the thought of the many hundreds of miles of sea between him and them in far-off Canada. He was very ready to resent any slight upon his birth. No such slight was likely to come from any decent fellow; and Dane had taken to Tom Merry and the rest, though at first he had the mistaken notion that Arthur Augustus was a mere fop.

But there were then, as there are now, fellows at St. Jim's who could not be classed as decent; and in those days George Gore was one of the worst of them. Gore and Mellish, in the shadow of the porter's lodge, had heard the new boy tell Tom Merry that he was not quite English; and as Dane crossed the hall, after his interview with the Head, Gore started in to behave after his own base nature.

Gore had his face covered with a handkerchief, and he held Mellish by the hand. Mellish was in it, though he did not feel quite as safe about it as Gore did. And Gore was soon to find that the half-Indian boy was a dangerous person to meddle with.

Dane had told Tom Merry, touched by the kindness of his greeting, that he liked him, and they had shaken hands on that. Because of this Gore held Mellish by the hand, and sobbed out:

"O-o-oh! I—I like you! O-oh! But—but I'm not quite English, you know. I am a nig-nig!"

Dane leaped at him like a cat, and Gore crashed against the wall. He made no real attempt at fight; he was too frightened for that. When Dane had finished with him Mellish had discreetly disappeared.

It was rather unfortunate that Dane should have been put into the study shared by Gore and Skimpole—at least, both Dane and Gore thought it unfortunate. Skimmy did not mind. He always has hopes that a new boy may be found to take some interest in his own special abstruse subjects; and, though always disappointed, he goes on hoping. Dane was one of his many disappointments; the Canadian junior had never heard of Professor Balmycrumpet, and did not care a row of pins for what Skimmy called the social questions of the day.

Among Dane's belongings were an album and a pocketful of tame snakes—queer pets, and hardly likely to be approved of by those in authority, but quite harmless. Several people got frights from those reptiles. Taggles was one of the victims. Kerr was another. Kerr has plenty of pluck; but even the pluckiest fellow may be a bit alarmed at finding a wriggling snake in his pocket in class. But Arthur Augustus had the worst fright of all. He fairly jumped on to the table when he found the floor of No. 6 all alive, as it seemed to him, with wriggling, squirming bodies. But he was only frightened, not hurt.

Gore had pretended that he wanted to bury

the hatchet when Dane came into his study. But that was only in order to wait his chance to get his own back. He took a particularly low way of revenge.

He found in Dane's album a portrait of the new boy's mother. He thought of flinging the book into the fire; but he dared not do that. So he plastered the opening in which the portrait was with paste, and believed that he had ruined it in a way which might be made out as accidental.

Lowther was the photographic enthusiast among the Terrible Three in those days; but he did not stick to the game as Manners did later. At that time, however, he was very keen indeed; and he offered to enlarge some of Dane's photos for him.

But when Dane fetched his album the damage done was revealed. It was a cruel trick—perhaps Gore had hardly realised how cruel it was. The new boy took it hard; but he promised Tom Merry that he would not attempt anything rash by way of revenge.

And he did nothing rash—in fact, his way of getting even was well thought out. First he made sure that Gore was the criminal, though of that there could have been little doubt from the first. Then he trapped Gore, overcame him, partly by main strength, partly by some power in his eyes that his enemy felt without understanding, tied him up, and dealt with him effectively. He had procured a number of tubes of some stuff of the seccotine kind. He smeared Gore all over with this, and stuck to him any number of pieces of paper with "Cad!" written upon them. Gore stormed and threatened; but he had to hold up on that when he was told that he would get the stuff in his mouth if he did not. After the business had been properly completed Gore was taken along the passage and thrust into the study of the Terrible Three. Dane said that he just wanted some friends of his to see what sort of rotter Gore really was, and that after that he might go and turn himself into a show, with a twopenny admission fee, if he liked.

Undoubtedly the power which Gore felt when Clifton Dane fastened his dark, gleaming eyes upon him was that of hypnotism. But it was not till some little time later that it was discovered that Dane was a hypnotist. It came out through the influence he wielded over a curious little animal Manners had—a cavy, which bit. The creature, not unlike a guinea-pig in appearance, and, indeed, really a species of guinea-pig, showed viciousness with others, but was at once subdued by Dane It ran up his arms and nestled on his shoulder—and did not bite his ear, as Manners had expected it to. Tom Merry said that Dane must be a mesmerist—which is, of course, the same thing as a hypnotist. Tom did not believe in hypnotism. Lowther did, and showed some alarm lest Dane should put the influence on him. Tom said it was all rot; Dane said he was sure it was nothing of the kind. He admitted, when pressed, that he had tried his hand at the game with some success. They wanted him to try it on Mr. Ratcliff; but Dane preferred to start with Arthur Augustus, whose wrath was less to be dreaded than that of the crusty New House master.

But Skimmy was the first victim—a willing victim. What will not Skimmy do in the cause of science? He did not believe that Dane could mesmerise him; he felt sure that his powerful will would offer an effective resistance to any such attempt. But he went off like a lamb, and did strange things before Mr. Lathom. Gussy was as confident as Skimmy that he could not be overcome; but he was overcome just as easily, and that turned out badly for Mellish. D'Arcy had lately lost a ring. Under the hypnotic influence he remembered where he had left it—in the bath-room, where Mellish was at the time. And Mellish, who has rather a loose way with unconsidered trifles upon which he may chance, had to give up the ring, and was tied up in a tablecloth and deposited in the quad by way of some slight punishment for what at best was a mean trick, though he averred that he had no intention of keeping the thing.

Fatty Wynn also came under the influence. Dane's magnetic gaze compelled him to hand down his plate of sausages to Towser. Fatty has no ill-will towards Towser, one feels sure; but his affection for that rather surly old fellow certainly does not extend to self-sacrifice in the matter of anything of such importance as sausages. He made that very clear when he knew what he had done His plump cheeks quivered with indignation when he was told of it. But he still would not believe that he had been mesmerised.

Perhaps the influence was still upon Fatty when he went to the bath-room and got into a hot bath and fell asleep there with the tap on, and caused a miniature flood, and missed Gussy's spread. But something—something considerable—was saved for him.

Glyn joined Kangaroo in No. 11 before Dane did, but only just before. The story of how Kangaroo got rid of the dandy Smythers has already been told. Noble suggested to Glyn that two in a study would be better than three; but it was not with Noble that Glyn sided when the tug-of-war came.

Kangaroo said that Mr. Railton had no objection to the two staying in their old quarters, and he made it plain that he was so very far from having an objection to that course that he would very much prefer it. But they could not see it his way; they were not keen on their old quarters, and they had no notion of giving way to the somewhat autocratic Cornstalk.

He told them that they were asking to be chucked out. They said they were. He did his best to chuck them out. But the pair were much too hefty for him. He found himself lying on the floor with the pair of them on top of him.

And he capitulated. From that time on the three have got on thoroughly well together.

Dane has shown his ability in the scouting line, and he is quite good at games, though not in the very first rank of the St. Jim's juniors either at cricket or footer. His batting is of the hit-or-miss type, with more strength than science; but his fielding leaves little to be desired. He is a capable half-back, though possibly better at taking the man than the ball. But it is as skater and runner that he comes nearest the top. He has had far more skating practice than most of the St. Jim's juniors; and some of you will remember how, when he and Noble and Koumi Rao spent Christmas at Greyfriars, he distinguished himself on the ice of the Priory pool. His Indian ancestry accounts in part for his running form. It is at long distances that he is best; there the tirelessness of the Huron sinew tells.

A good fellow, Dane, and a nice fellow, too!

The Editor's Chat.

For Next Wednesday:

"THE RIVAL ENTERTAINERS!"

By Martin Clifford.

Next Wednesday's grand, long, complete story of St. Jim's is of the humorous order, and chiefly concerns the rival efforts of the Shell and the Fourth to bring off a Grand Victory Concert. Tom Merry & Co. and Jack Blake & Co. are equally determined to run the show; and many amusing scenes—in which Bunter is conspicuous—are enacted before the Victory Concert duly takes place. Whether the Shell eventually succeed in outwitting the Fourth, or vice versa, is a question which must be left unsolved until the story is in my readers' hands. That Martin Clifford's fine yarn will afford them the keenest enjoyment is assured in advance.

A SHORT WAY WITH THE GROUSERS!

A Manchester Girl Reader Speaks Her Mind.

I am quoting this week a letter which is typical of many I have lately received on the same subject—namely, the grievances of the disgruntled ones.

"Manchester.

"Dear Editor,—I noticed your remarks concerning those amiable mud-slingers who express dissatisfaction with the GEM.

"I, for one, don't sympathise with them. I have been a reader for four years of all the companion papers, and there is scarcely a story which I have not thoroughly enjoyed. My friends are all keen readers, and they would like to get within hitting distance of the grumblers.

"The adventures—and misadventures!—of Bunter particularly amuse us, and waiting for the next issue is—well, torture!

"You can tell the grumblers that they will get short shrift in Manchester, should they disclose their identity—but that, of course, they would refrain from doing, for very sound reasons!

"Wishing your papers the best of luck,—Yours sincerely,

"A LOYAL GIRL READER."

In thanking my girl chum for her assurance of loyalty, I would point out that the grumblers—who are in a very small minority, and who are chiefly out for notoriety—are merely banging their heads against a brick wall in their endeavours to dislodge the companion papers from the impregnable position they hold in the esteem of the boys and girls of this country.

As I have said many times before, I am always open to receive criticism; but when that criticism degenerates into mere mud-slinging, the slingers deserve no consideration whatever. Should the quantity of mud greatly increase, however, it may be necessary to recall our Fighting Editor, who, although he has been four years with the Colours, is still spoiling for a scrap!

— —

THE "PENNY POP"!

Letters continue to pour in expressing delight and satisfaction at the reappearance of the "Penny Popular." The stories of that powerful trio of schools, St. Jim's, Greyfriars, and Rookwood, are proving an immense attraction.

Those who have not renewed their acquaintance with the "Penny Pop" in its new form should make a point of placing an order at once with their newsagent for Friday's issue.

Your Editor

NOTICES.

Correspondence, etc., Wanted by—

N. Prideaux, 76, Brynland Avenue, Bishopston, Bristol, wants more members for World-Wide Correspondence Club. Foreign and Colonial readers specially invited. Stamped envelope.

W. J. Summers, 201, Worcester Road, Bootle, near Liverpool—with a reader in the district interested in journalism.

H. Bradwell, Valley House, Great Longstone, near Bakewell, Derbyshire—with readers anywhere.

F. Anderson, 34, Henry Street, Woolwich, S.E. 18—with readers anywhere, especially those interested in engineering.

Miss G. Cooper, 12, Culmore Road, Balham, S.W. 12, wishes for more members for her GEM and "Magnet" Club.

A. E. Williams, 23, Prescot Road, Fairfield, Liverpool, wants members for F. A. Magazine and Correspondence Club. Stamped envelope.

Back numbers wanted by—

J. Arbott, 49, Waterworks Road, Trowbridge, Wilts—"Rival Ventriloquists," "Harry Wharton & Co.'s Pantomime," "Special Constable Coker," "Billy Bunter's Postal-Order." 2d. each and postage.

Frank Sykes, 153, Greg Street, South Reddish, Stockport—"Down on His Luck," "Ashamed of His Father," "Bob Cherry in Search of His Father," "The Toff." 5d. each offered.

R. Moseley, Stag's Head, Market Drayton, Salop—"For D'Arcy's Sake," "Under Bunter's Thumb." 2d. each offered.

S. Hodges, 81, Beacon Street, Springfields, Wolverhampton — wants complete set of "Greyfriars Herald." Clean. 2d. a copy offered.

Edward Langdon, the Clarendon Dairy, Clarendon Place, the Hoe, Plymouth—"Magnet" Christmas Numbers 1912, 13, 14; also GEM Christmas Number, 1913. 4d. each offered. Write first.

Miss E. Withers, Cheswerdyne, Newbridge Street, Whitmore Reans, Wolverhampton—GEM Christmas Number, 1916, "In the Seats of the Mighty." 3d. offered if clean. Write first.

M. Doyle, 25½, Rose Street, Darlington, Sydney, Australia—"For Another's Sake," "A Hero of Wales," and "The Honour of a Jew."

J. O. Cox, 106, Ritchie Street, Invercargill, New Zealand—"Magnets" and GEMS, 1-300. 1½d each offered.

The GEM 1½d

No. 585. Vol. XIII. April 26th, 1919.

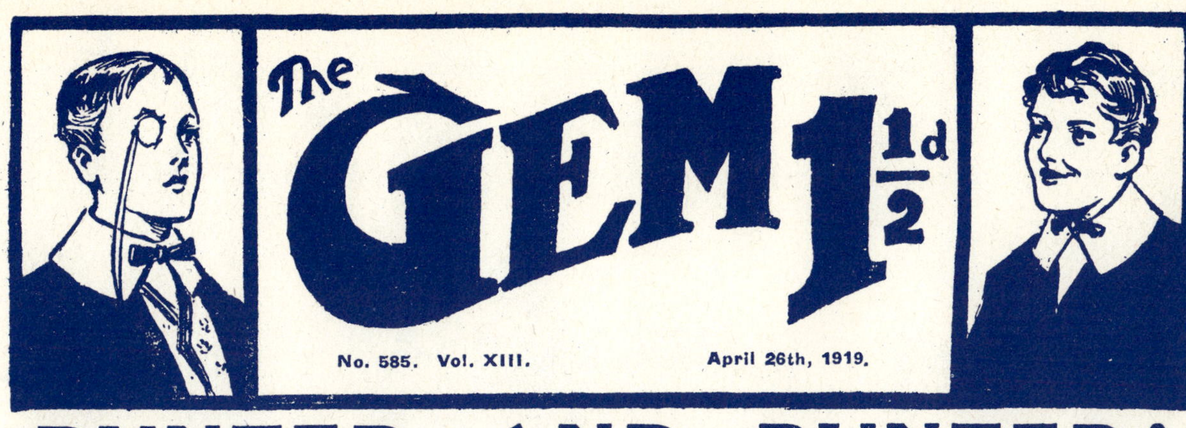

BUNTER—AND BUNTER!

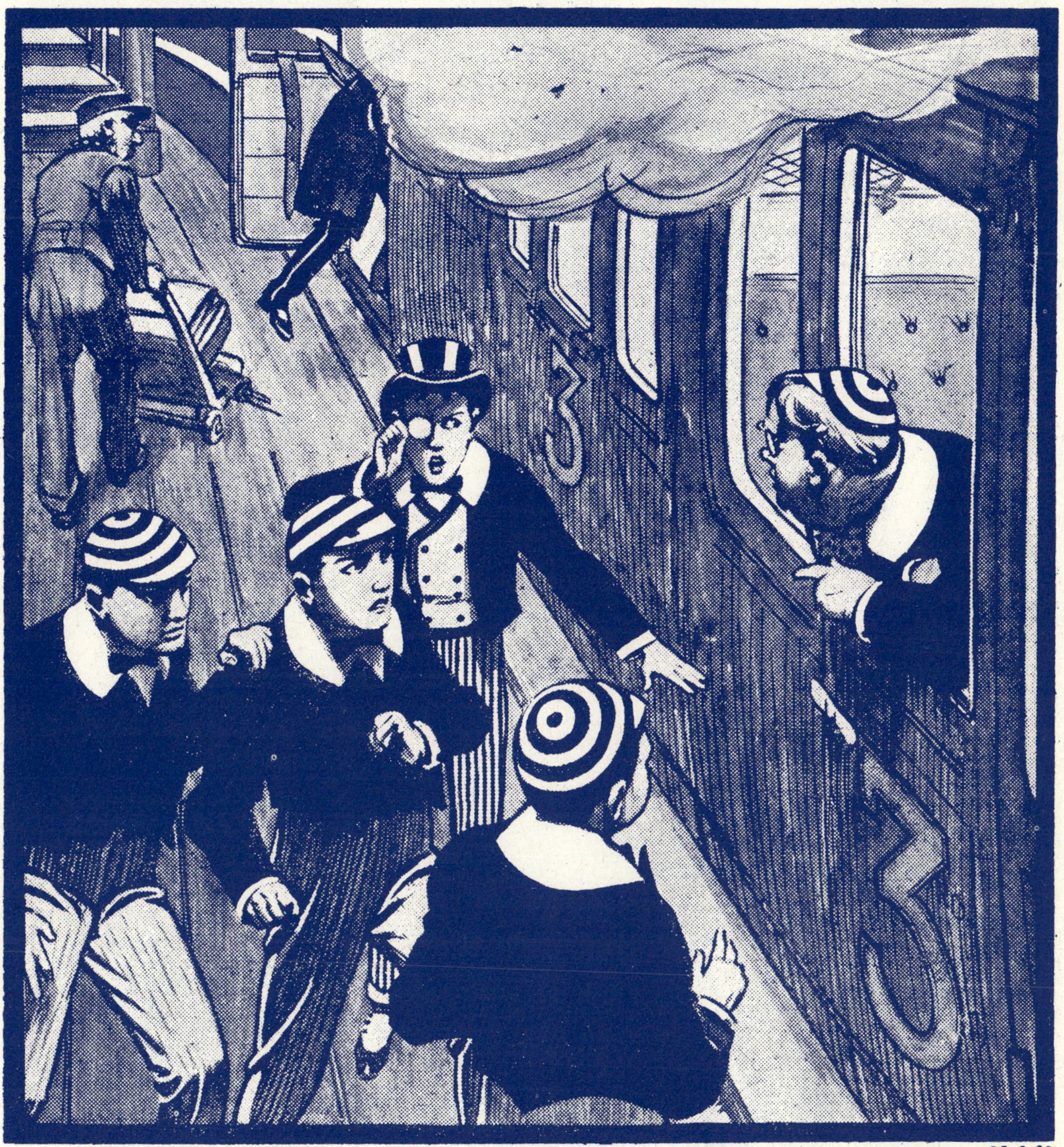

BILLY BUNTER'S FAREWELL TO ST. JIM'S. 26-4-19

(An Amazing Scene in the Grand, Long, Complete School Tale in this Issue.)

Bunter—and Bunter!

A Magnificent, New, Long, Complete School Story of TOM MERRY & CO. at St. Jim's.

By MARTIN CLIFFORD.

CHAPTER 1.
Bunter Takes the Cake !

"GRUNDY'S going it!" said Tom Merry, with a laugh.

The Terrible Three were coming along the Shell passage from the stairs when a loud and wrathful voice was heard from Study No. 3.

It was the voice of George Alfred Grundy of the Shell.

"I'll scalp him! I'll pulverise him! I'll burst him! My cake! My sultana-cake! I'll spificate him!"

Monty Lowther chuckled.

"Now, if I were a betting chap," he remarked, "I'd lay you two to one that Bunter's had Grundy's cake."

"No takers!" grinned Manners. "It's a cert!"

"I'll squash him!" came Grundy's powerful voice. "The fat bounder! The pilfering worm! My cake—my sultana-cake!"

The Terrible Three paused at the study doorway and looked in.

George Alfred Grundy was brandishing a pair of very large fists, his rugged face pink with wrath. He looked as if he were about to commit assault and battery upon his study-mates, Wilkins and Gunn. But he wasn't. The object of Grundy's wrath was, fortunately, not present.

"Easy, old scout!" said Tom Merry. "Your dulcet tones can be heard a mile off, Grundy."

"I'll squash him!" roared Grundy

"Put on the soft pedal," urged Manners. "You'll have Railton coming up to inquire soon."

"I'll burst him!"

"It's really too bad," said Wilkins. "Here we come in hungry after cricket, and somebody's pinched the cake. I suppose it was Bunter."

"Suppose!" roared Grundy. "Of course it was Bunter! No supposing about it. I'll spificate him!"

"Well, a chap naturally thinks of Bunter when a cake is missing," remarked Tom Merry. "But all Sussex doesn't want to hear about it, Grundy."

"Rats! Where is he? Where's Bunter?"

"Not in my waistcoat-pocket. If he's got your cake, I don't suppose you'll find him in a hurry," said Tom Merry, laughing.

"I'm going to find him. I'm going to pulverise him! I'll make him howl! I'll make him cringe! He's always raiding fellows' grub!" howled Grundy. "Come and help me look for him, you asses, and don't stand there blinking!"

That polite injunction was addressed to Grundy's study-mates.

Tom Merry & Co. went on to their own quarters, smiling. Grundy's cake had arrived by post that day—a terrific cake, from his affectionate Uncle Grundy—a cake that proved that the piping times of peace had really returned at last. A good many fellows had heard of that cake; and evidently Bunter of the Fourth had heard of it, and put his knowledge to account.

Grundy grabbed up a cricket-stump, and strode out of the study. Wilkins and Gunn did not follow, however. They wanted their tea; and, though the cake was missing, there were other things. They left George Alfred to look for Bunter, while they looked after their tea.

Grundy strode down the passage, stump in hand, with wrath in his brow. The destructive wrath of Achilles, so eloquently sung by Homer, was a mere joke to the wrath of George Alfred Grundy. If Bunter was discovered, it certainly meant a new recruit in the ranks of the noble army of martyrs, whether Bunter had the cake or not.

Arthur Augustus D'Arcy of the Fourth Form was glancing out of the doorway of Study No. 6 when Grundy came striding by. Grundy caught him by the shoulder.

"Seen him?" he demanded.

"Bai Jove!"

"Seen Bunter?"

"Pway welease my shouldah, Gwunday," said Arthur Augustus calmly. "You are sewiously incommodin' me by gwabbin' me in that wuff mannah."

"Have you seen Bunter?" roared Grundy.

"I wefuse to weply, Gwunday, until you have weleased my shouldah. Pewwaps you are not awah," added Arthur Augustus crushingly, "that you are wumplin' my jacket!"

Grundy looked very much disposed to begin operations with the cricket-stump. However, he restrained his wrath, and released Arthur Augustus' shoulder. The swell of St. Jim's carefully smoothed out his jacket.

"You have wumpled it," he said severely.

"Have you seen Bunter?" asked Grundy, breathing hard. "The fat beast is in your Form. Have you seen him?"

"Yaas, wathah!"

"Good! Where is he?"

"I weally do not know, Gwunday!"

"You ass! If you've seen him you know where he is, don't you?" howled Grundy.

"I wefuse to be called an ass, Gwunday!"

"You—you—you—— Where's Bunter?" gasped George Alfred. "You said you'd seen him."

"Yaas; but it is quite a considewable time since I have seen him, Gwunday. I do not wemembah seein' him since lessons."

"Fathead!" howled Grundy.

And he strode on. Arthur Augustus D'Arcy jammed his celebrated monocle into his eye, and gazed after the excited Shell fellow with strong disapproval in his gaze.

"Bai Jove!" he remarked. "Gwunday's mannahs seem to be gwowin' worse and worse. I weally wegard him as little bettah than a wuffian! Gwunday!"

Grundy looked back, perhaps expecting some information with regard to Bunter.

"Well?" he snapped.

"Gwunday, I feel bound to say that I wegard you as little bettah than a wuffian!"

"You—you—you silly idiot!"

"Bai Jove!"

Grundy tramped on to No. 2, the study which Bunter of the Fourth shared with Mellish and Trimble. There was little chance of finding Bunter so easily, if he really had the cake; but Grundy was beginning at the beginning, and he meant to leave no stone unturned.

The door of No. 2 flew open with a crash as Grundy's heavy boot was jammed upon it. Mellish and Trimble jumped up in surprise.

"What the thump——" began Mellish.

"Look here——" howled Trimble.

Grundy strode in.

"Is Bunter here?" he roared.

"Can't you see he isn't?" snorted Mellish.

Grundy glared round the study. Certainly, the fat junior was not visible there.

"Where is he?"

"Blessed if I know, or care!"

"He's got my cake!"

"Bother your cake!"

"My big cake—my big sultana-cake—the one my Uncle Grundy sent me today!"

"Bless your Uncle Grundy!"

"And I dare say you two are hand-in-glove with him!" roared Grundy. "I dare say you're sharing the loot with him. It would be like you! I'll teach you to raid my study!"

Whack, whack!

"Why, you ass," howled Mellish frantically, dodging the stump, "you dangerous maniac—yarooh!—I don't know anything about your silly cake! Oh crikey!"

"Keep off!" yelled Trimble. "I haven't seen—I don't know—I didn't—I wasn't —— Yooop!"

Whack, whack!

"Yow-ow! Help!"

Grundy strode out of the study, leaving Mellish and Trimble roaring. He had to search further for Bunter of the Fourth; but his visit to Bunter's study had given him a little solace to go on with, as it were.

CHAPTER 2.

The Way of the Transgressor!

"ANYTHING for tea?" asked Tom Merry.

"Lots of bread."

"Oh!"

"And a cold kipper——"

"H'm!"

"And bloater-paste. I rather wish Bunter would drop in to tea, and bring Grundy's cake with him!" remarked Monty Lowther.

"Hallo! I believe he's been here!" exclaimed Manners.

He pointed to the carpet. Strewn upon the carpet were crumbs—many crumbs—and a few sultanas. Somebody had had a cake there, that was clear.

"My hat!" exclaimed Tom Merry in great indignation. "The fat bounder brought it here to devour, like a blessed dog taking a bone to his kennel! I wish we'd caught him!"

"Especially before he'd finished the cake!" said Monty Lowther. "What rotten luck! Now it's cold kipper and bloater-paste!"

The Terrible Three sat down to tea. It was a frugal tea; but they were prepared to do it justice after an hour or so on the playing-fields.

"Manners, old chap, do you want all the floor?" inquired Lowther.

Manners stared at him.

"All the floor?" he repeated.

"Yes, if you don't, give a fellow room to put his feet under the table!"

"Ass!" said Manners politely. "My feet are on this side."

"Then it's your hoofs, Tommy!" said Lowther. "What are you spreading your hoofs all over the study for? Have you taken to wearing boots as big as Grundy's?"

"My feet are under my chair," answered Tom.

Lowther looked puzzled.

"Monty, old man, don't be a funny ass!" exclaimed Manners.

"Eh?"

"Stop bumping me on the knees, you duffer! You nearly made me spill my tea!" exclaimed Manners warmly.

"Bother your silly knees! I'm a yard or two from your idiotic knees! Blow your knees!"

"Why, there you go again!" roared Manners. "Look here, Monty, it isn't a joke to jam your boots on a fellow's bags!"

"I'm not!" howled Lowther.

"If it's you, Tom——"

"I'm not touching you, you ass! Why, who's bumping on me?" exclaimed Tom Merry. "My hat! There's something under the table! Has that silly ass Herries let his bulldog loose in the House?"

"Oh crumbs!"

Three juniors jumped up as suddenly as if they had been moved by an electric shock. If Herries' bulldog was under the table, it was not a safe pastime to stir him up with their feet.

"Towser!" gasped Lowther.

"Towser! Come out, you beast!"

There was no motion under the table, and no sound. The cover hid what was underneath it, and Lowther stretched out his hand to the cover, and drew it back again quickly.

"I'll shift him!" he said. "There's a golf-club here—I'll shove it under the table, and——"

"Yaroooh!"

A sudden howl came from under the table, and it certainly was not the voice of Towser, the bulldog.

"Bunter!" howled Tom Merry.

"Oh, my hat! Bunter! He's under the table! Come out, you fat rascal!" roared Monty Lowther.

"Ow! Keep that club away, you beast! I'm not here!"

"What?"

"I—I mean, I—I'm coming out!"

The cover was lifted, and a fat face and a large pair of spectacles glimmered out. Bunter of the Fourth blinked hastily round the study.

"That beast Grundy isn't here?" he gasped.

"No! Come out, you porpoise!"

Bunter rolled out from under the table. A large chunk of cake was grasped in his fat hand. Apparently it was all that remained of the big sultana-cake that had arrived that day from Uncle Grundy.

"The fat rotter!" exclaimed Manners. "He was here all the time! He dodged under the table when he heard us coming."

"I—I thought it was Grundy!" gasped Bunter, blinking at them. "That—that rotter Grundy might be after my cake, you know!"

"Grundy's cake, you mean!"

"I mean, my cake! It—it came to-day from—from one of my titled relations!" gasped Bunter. "It would be just like Grundy to say that it was his cake. He's untruthful!"

Tom Merry threw open the door.

"Travel!" he said curtly.

"I—I say, you fellows——"

"Cut!"

"You—you might look out and see if Grundy's in sight! The awful beast is after my cake——"

Tom Merry laughed, and glanced into the passage.

"All clear!" he answered.

"I say, you fellows, I'll stay to tea, if you like! I'll let you have some of my cake——"

"Hold him while I get the poker!" said Lowther.

"Ow!"

Bunter did not wait to be held. He bolted. Tom Merry slammed the door after him. Bunter paused in the passage, to yell "Beast!" through the keyhole, and then hurriedly retired. But his luck was out. As he headed for the staircase Grundy came up from below, after a fruitless search in the lower passages.

Grundy jumped as he saw Bunter—with the remains of the cake still in his fat hand.

"Now, you rotter!" he roared.

"I—I say, Grundy—— Yaroooh!"

Bunter dodged wildly. The fragments of the cake were strewn on the floor as the fat junior performed unaccustomed gymnastic exercises, frantically dodging the stump.

"Yoop! Help! Fire! Murder!" roared Bunter.

Whack, whack!

"Help! Yaroooh!"

"What's this row about?" exclaimed a sharp voice, as Kildare of the Sixth came up the stairs. "Grundy! Stop that at once——"

"He's pinched my cake!" howled Grundy.

"Stop it! Bunter, you're wanted!"

"I—I say, Kildare, I haven't pinched his cake! It—it was sent to me by—by —by one of my relations—my titled relations——"

"Cheese it!" said the St. Jim's captain. "Come downstairs at once, Bunter! You've been asked for on Mr. Railton's telephone."

"Oh! All right!" gasped Bunter.

The fat junior had never been so glad to see Kildare. The destructive wrath of George Alfred Grundy had been stopped in full career, as it were. Grundy shook the stump after Bunter as the latter went down the staircase with the Sixth-Former. The licking was unavoidably postponed.

But it was only postponed, and Bunter was not feeling happy as he accompanied the prefect downstairs. The Owl of Greyfriars was not finding his life at St. Jim's a path of roses.

CHAPTER 3.

A Peck of Troubles.

MR. RAILTON signed to Bunter to enter as the fat junior appeared in the doorway of his study. There were traces of cake all over Bunter—his mouth, his hands, and his fat waistcoat. Mr. Railton's glance expressed disapproval, but he made no remark on that.

"You are wanted on the telephone, Bunter," he said. "Mr. Penman has asked to be allowed to speak to you, and I have consented. Kindly take the receiver at once! It is a trunk-call from Canterbury."

"Oh dear!" gasped Bunter.

"Lose no time, Bunter!"

The fat junior blinked at the House-master and at the telephone, of which the receiver was off the hooks. He did not seem in a hurry to answer that trunk-call from Canterbury.

"I—I say, sir——" he gasped.

"Well, Bunter?" said Mr. Railton sharply.

"D-d-did you say Mr. Penman, sir?"

"Yes; your former employer," said the Housemaster. "Go to the telephone at once!"

"I—I think there's some mistake, sir. I—I don't think he can want to speak to me!"

"Bunter!"

"P-p-perhaps he's got the wrong number, sir!"

"Go to the telephone at once!" exclaimed Mr. Railton, in a voice that made the fat junior jump.

"Oh! Yes, sir!" gasped Bunter.

He rolled to the telephone, and the House-master quitted the study, to leave him to talk undisturbed to the gentleman at Canterbury.

Bunter took up the receiver, and put it to his fat ear in a very gingerly manner.

For reasons quite unknown to Mr. Railton, or to anyone else at St. Jim's, the fat junior was extremely reluctant to hold any communication with Mr. Penman.

Mr. Penman, the kind-hearted merchant of Canterbury, had sent Wally Bunter to St. Jim's, his old school, thus rewarding his junior clerk for the courage he had shown in preventing a burglary at the office. He was not in the least aware that Wally, who had made friends with Harry Wharton & Co. of Greyfriars, had changed places with his cousin and double, Billy Bunter of the Greyfriars Remove—Wally going to Greyfriars in Billy's place, and Billy Bunter starting a new career at St. Jim's.

Under those unusual circumstances the

less Bunter saw of Mr. Penman of Canterbury the better he liked it.

Almost a stranger at St. Jim's, he had easily passed himself there as his cousin Wally; but he was aware that a keen business man who knew Wally well was not likely to be easily deceived if they met.

Even with the length of the telephone wire between them, Billy Bunter did not look forward with pleasure to a talk with the Canterbury gentleman.

He hesitated, half-disposed to put up the receiver and cut off the interlocutor. But he reflected that in that case the obnoxious gentleman would only ring up again.

"Hallo!" he grunted into the transmitter ungraciously.

"Hallo! Is that you, Bunter?"

"Oh yes!"

"I have requested Mr. Railton to allow me to speak to you, Bunter. He has kindly consented."

"Oh, bother!"

"Eh?"

"N-n-nothing!"

"I have a very important communication to make to you, Bunter. I am coming down to see you, as it is a half-holiday on Wednesday."

"Oh dear!"

"What did you say, Bunter?"

"N-nothing!"

"For reasons that I will explain at length when I see you, Bunter, I have made a change in my plans regarding you."

"Oh!"

"You must not think, my boy," went on the kindly voice on the telephone, "that I am displeased with you, or disappointed in you in any way. I have not forgotten that you saved me from a very heavy loss on the occasion of the burglary in my office."

Billy Bunter grinned over the receiver. It was his cousin Wally who had done that creditable action; but Mr. Penman believed that he was speaking to Walter Gilbert Bunter. Probably he had never heard of William George.

"My intention," pursued Mr. Penman, little dreaming of whom he was addressing, "was to send you to my old school, Bunter, to prepare you for taking up, at a later date, a position of some importance. This was partly a reward for the great service you rendered me, and partly because I had a high opinion of your character, and was desirous of helping you to advance."

Billy Bunter grunted.

Why Mr. Penman, or anybody else, should think so highly of Wally Bunter was a mystery to him. So far as he could see, Wally was his "blessed poor relation"—merely that, and nothing more!

"Did you speak, Bunter?"

"Nunno!"

"If I have made a change in my plans, my boy, you must not think that you will lose thereby; you will, in fact, be a considerable gainer. But I shall not make this alteration without your consent. I will see you, and we can discuss the matter freely."

"Oh crumbs!"

"What—what did you say?"

Bunter jammed the receiver back on the hooks. He had had enough of Mr. Penman. He rose from the chair perspiring.

"The silly old ass!" he murmured. "He's been down to see me once, and I got Wally to come over from Greyfriars in time. What does he want to see me again for? I'm blessed if I want to see him! I'm jolly well not going to, either."

"Have you finished your talk with Mr. Penman, Bunter?"

The fat junior started. It was Mr. Railton's voice in the doorway.

"Ye-es, sir," he stammered. "He—he—he's coming here to-morrow, sir."

"Very well!"

Bunter hastily quitted the study, glad to get away from the Housemaster's keen eyes.

He blinked hastily round him as he went down the passage. Fortunately, Grundy was not in sight.

His fat face was glum in expression as he rolled on.

The Owl of Greyfriars had anticipated a glorious time when came to St. Jim's. Wally Bunter had met Tom Merry & Co., and made an agreeable impression upon them, especially upon Arthur Augustus D'Arcy. Billy Bunter had arrived at St. Jim's with Wally's blushing honours thick upon him, as it were. For a time Wally's good reputation had stood him in good stead.

But that had worn off. The juniors still supposed that he was Wally—but they concluded that they had been mistaken in Wally, and that he was Billy Bunter's counterpart in other things as well as looks.

Arthur Augustus, who was destined to be a sort of bank from which Billy Bunter was to draw unlimited loans, had been tired out—and the other fellows had been tired out much sooner. Much to his wrath and disappointment, Billy Bunter found, after a few weeks, that St. Jim's was much the same as Greyfriars, so far as he was concerned; and he might as well have remained in his old school for any benefit he obtained by the change.

It was his own fault; but that was no comfort to him, even if he had been aware of it.

In fact, when he had once worn out Wally's welcome, he found that the change was for the worse—for he had the imposture to keep up, and nothing to gain thereby.

He had agreed with Wally to keep up the change of places for the whole term; but an agreement mattered little to William George Bunter when it turned to his disadvantage.

He had pondered on the matter of late, and almost made up his mind to change back—irrespective of Wally Bunter's views in the matter.

The news that Mr. Penman was coming down on the morrow quite decided him. Somehow, he had to avoid meeting that gentleman.

"Bunter!"

The voice of Mr. Lathom, the master of the Fourth, interrupted Billy Bunter's dismal reflections.

"Yes, sir?" he stammered.

"I gave you a hundred lines in class this afternoon, Bunter, for gross carelessness and idleness," said the Fourth Form master severely.

"Oh, sir!"

"Have you done those lines?"

"Nunno, sir!"

"I told you to do them immediately after lessons, I think, Bunter."

"I—I haven't had time, sir."

"They are doubled, Bunter! Bring them to me by six o'clock, or I shall double them again!"

And Mr. Lathom, with a portentous shake of the head, walked on. Billy Bunter cast a ferocious blink after him.

"Beast!" he murmured.

He rolled out into the quadrangle dismally. His mind was quite made up; but there was a lion in the path, so to speak. Bunter was in his usual impecunious state, and the railway fare to Greyfriars was a considerable sum. If he was to "bolt" from St. Jim's and return to his old school it was necessary to raise the wind first.

Billy Bunter had considerable and unusual powers as a borrower. As Orpheus, with his lute, drew iron tears down Pluto's cheek, so Billy Bunter had often drawn reluctant loans from the most unlikely quarters. But there was a limit to all things. There were so many little loans outstanding now that it was difficult to think of a single person who was likely to "shell out," howsoever eloquently the fat junior pitched his tale.

"Bunter!"

"Oh dear! What do you want, Racke?"

Racke of the Shell stopped the fat junior in the quad, with a very unpleasant expression.

"You owe me money!" he said.

"Do I?" grunted Bunter. "Well, I owe other fellows money, too. I'm going to settle up all round shortly."

"What with?" sneered Racke.

"I'm expecting a postal-order——"

"Oh, dry up! You spoofed me into believing that you had a rich grandfather in Australia," snarled Racke. "I let you play banker on your I O U's. I've got a stack of them. What are they worth?"

Bunter grinned. He conjectured that the I O U's were worth their weight in wastepaper; but he did not tell Aubrey Racke so.

"So you think it's a laughing matter, do you?" growled Racke.

"Nunno! I——"

"I know you can't settle," continued the sportsman of the Shell. "But you can pay something! And you're going to!"

"When I get my postal-order——"

"Never mind your postal-order! You're going to hand me half your allowance every week," said Racke.

"I'm jolly well not!" howled Bunter. "You can't claim the money, and you know you can't! You'd get flogged if the Head knew you played banker in your study!"

"I can't claim it," assented Racke, with a dark look. "But I can take it out of your fat hide if you don't square. See?"

"Oh, really, Racke——"

"I'm beginning now," continued Racke. "Every time I see you I'm going to shake you—like this——"

"Yaroooh!"

"And kick you, like this——"

"Yooop!"

"Till you square. See?"

"Help!"

Aubrey Racke walked on, and left Bunter sitting in the quad, gasping.

It really looked as if the way of the transgressor was hard!

CHAPTER 4.

Bunter Has a Brain-Wave!

BILLY BUNTER wore a dismal expression in class the next day.

He was not enjoying life.

Much of his leisure time of late had been spent in dodging Grundy of the Shell. He had also had to display considerable dexterity in dodging Aubrey Racke.

With such worries on his mind, he considered that he was not at all to blame for having left Mr. Lathom's lines undone. His Form-master took quite a different view, and the lines, already doubled, were re-doubled. Billy Bunter had the happy prospect of spending his next half-holiday writing out verses from P. Virgilius Maro—a great poet, but quite unappreciated by William George Bunter.

No wonder the Owl of Greyfriars had made up his fat mind to "bolt" at the earliest opportunity, and return to his native lair, so to speak. The fellows at Greyfriars were beasts, doubtless, but the fellows at St. Jim's were equally beasts, and there was nothing to choose between them. Bunter had taken the decisive step, the previous evening, of writing to his cousin at Greyfriars to arrange a meeting at Friardale, near the school. At that meeting it was his firm intention to change places once more with the unfortunate Wally, whether Walter Gilbert liked it or not. And, in order to make sure that Wally would keep the appointment, Bunter had mentioned that if he didn't find him under the big oak in Friardale Wood he would come on to Greyfriars.

So it was certain that Wally Bunter would be there. The problem was, how was Billy Bunter to get there? The railway fare, or, rather, the lack of it, still stood as a lion in the path.

That morning Bunter's mind was occupied with the financial problem, and he had no time to waste on lessons. Financial problems were not supposed to be thought out in the Form-room, and Mr. Lathom woke Bunter up several times with the pointer.

The fat junior was rubbing his podgy hands dismally when the Fourth were dismissed. The Terrible Three of the Shell came on him in the passage, and they stopped, sympathetically.

"Had it bad?" asked Tom Merry.

"Yow-ow! Yes. Lathom's a beast!"

"Wants you to work?" asked Monty Lowther, with deep sympathy. "Just like these Form-masters!"

"Oh, don't be a funny ass!" groaned Bunter. "I can tell you I'm fed up with it. I'm not going to stand it any more!"

"Going to give Lathom a licking?" asked Manners.

"You wait and see!" said Bunter darkly. "I'm going to chuck up the whole game. I'm fed up! Wally can look out for himself."

"Wally?" ejaculated the Terrible Three together.

"I—I mean——"

"Well, what do you mean?"

"I—I——"

"Look out, Bunter!" yelled Jack Blake down the corridor. "Here comes Grundy!"

"Ha, ha, ha!"

"Oh crumbs!"

Billy Bunter disappeared into the quadrangle at a very creditable speed, considering the weight he had to carry.

He was not seen again till dinner, and then he came in a minute late—to keep clear of Grundy and Racke. This dodging existence was telling on Bunter, and his fat face wore a worried look. It really was a dog's life.

After dinner he was out just before Grundy, and he vanished again. It was the first time on record that Bunter was quickest to leave the dinner-table.

In the interval before classes began that afternoon George Alfred Grundy might have been seen—and in point of fact was seen—hunting up and down the quad and round the passages with wrath in his brow and a big stick in his hand. The fate of Uncle Grundy's sultana-cake had not yet been forgotten by the great Grundy. Apparently it would not be forgotten until Bunter of the Fourth had paid the penalty.

"Bai Jove!" Arthur Augustus D'Arcy remarked as the time for lessons drew near. "I wondah where Buntah is? There goes that sillay ass Gwunday lookin' for him!"

A good many of the juniors were interested in the question. But Bunter did not turn up before lessons. The Fourth went to their Form-room without him—and they found him there! The unhappy Owl of Greyfriars had taken refuge under the master's desk in the Form-room, and he did not come out till many footsteps told him that the Form was gathering, and that all danger from Grundy was over for the present.

There was a chortle as Bunter emerged from under Mr. Lathom's desk.

But Bunter did not join in it. He failed to see anything comic in this painful situation of affairs.

"I say, you fellows!" he gasped. "I say——"

"Look out!" yelled Julian. "Here he comes!"

Dick Julian was alluding to Mr. Lathom, who was whisking along the corridor, but Bunter supposed he was speaking of Grundy—as perhaps Julian expected. The fat junior dived under the Form-master's desk again.

"Ha, ha, ha!" roared Herries. "Come out of that, you fat duffer!"

"Keep him off!"

"Ha, ha, ha!"

"Bless my soul!" said Mr. Lathom, as he entered the Form-room. "You seem very hilarious this afternoon, my boys! Pray keep quiet in the Form-room. This is not a place for uproarious merriment."

The Fourth-Formers suppressed their uproarious merriment as well as they could, and went to their places. Billy Bunter peered out from his hiding-place, and popped back as he saw Mr. Lathom.

"Bai Jove!" murmured Arthur Augustus D'Arcy. "That uttah ass——"

"Silence in the class, please! One boy does not seem to be here," said Mr. Lathom, blinking over the juniors. "Bunter is not present."

Silence.

"Why has not Bunter come in to lessons? Blake, do you know where Bunter is?"

"Ahem!"

"Kindly answer me, Blake."

"I—I think he—he—he's not far away, sir," stammered Blake.

"Bunter is the most unpunctual boy in the Form!" said Mr. Lathom crossly as he went to his desk. "Why—what—bless my soul! Bunter!"

"Oh dear!"

"You utterly absurd boy! What are you doing under my desk?" thundered Mr. Lathom.

"Oh crumbs! I—I—I——"

"What absurd trick is this, Bunter?"

"I—I dropped something, sir!" gasped Bunter, crawling out, gasping. "I—I dropped a—a—a sovereign, sir——"

"Have you found it?"

"Nunno—yes—exactly! I mean——"

"You are a foolish boy, Bunter!"

"Yes, sir! Thank you, sir!" gasped Bunter.

"Go to your place at once!"

Billy Bunter went to his place, thankful that Mr. Lathom did not pick up his cane. The Form-master's frown reduced the grinning class to order, and lessons began.

If Bunter had been absent-minded and inattentive that morning, he was doubly so in the afternoon. Somehow, after

"Bunter is the most unpunctual boy in the Form!" said Mr. Lathom crossly, as he went to his desk. "Why!—What!—Bless my soul!—BUNTER!" (See Chapter 4.)

lessons that day, he was resolved to make a "break" for Greyfriars, and say a long farewell to St. Jim's. Somehow, he had to think out the transport problem. It was certain that he couldn't walk to Greyfriars, and equally certain that he couldn't travel by railway without paying his fare. The burning question was, what was going to be done—or perhaps it would be more correct to say, who was going to be done?

The geological strata of Great Britain were not likely to interest Bunter at such a time, and Mr. Lathom's voice was simply a worrying drone to his fat ears. Mr. Lathom could not be expected to sympathise with that point of view. Bunter was the recipient of some personal observations which ought to have made his ears burn—but didn't! His fat knuckles burned a little, however, when the pointer came into play.

But he hardly minded the pointer, for once; his fat brain had not worked without avail, and a little scheme had been hatched there. He blinked reproachfully at Mr. Lathom.

"You are the stupidest boy in the class, Bunter!" rapped out the Form-master. "But that is no reason why you should be the idlest!"

"I'm sorry, sir! I—I'm worried!" said Bunter.

"Nonsense!"

"I'm in fearful trouble, sir!"

"Indeed!" said Mr. Lathom, his manner altering. "If that is correct, Bunter, I am sorry! What is your trouble?"

"Bai Jove!" murmured Arthur Augustus D'Arcy to Digby. "Is the fat duffah goin' to tell Lathom about Gwunday?"

The Fourth listened breathlessly for Bunter's explanation. They were surprised by his next words.

"It's my cousin, sir—my cousin at Greyfriars——"

"I was not aware you had a cousin at Greyfriars, Bunter. Is anything the matter with him?"

"He's ill, sir."

"Indeed! I am sorry to hear that, Bunter!" Mr. Lathom was quite kindly now. "Do you mean to say that you have been so very inattentive in class because you are troubled by your cousin's illness?"

"Yes, sir. I—I'm a very tender-hearted chap."

"Very well, Bunter; you need take no further part in the lessons this afternoon," said Mr. Lathom.

Bunter's fat face brightened.

All was grist that came to his mill; and an opportunity of slacking during lessons was not to be despised. He sat in fat contentment till the Fourth were dismissed.

When the juniors went out, he joined Blake & Co. in the corridor—after a cautious blink round to ascertain that the Shell were not out yet.

"I say, you fellows——"

"I am sowwy your cousin is ill, Buntah!" said Arthur Augustus D'Arcy kindly.

Bunter's face assumed a sorrowful length.

"Yes, isn't it rotten?" he said. "And—and I can't go and see him! That's what I wanted to speak to you chaps for. I—I'd cut over to Greyfriars and see him if I could raise the railway fare. But—but I've been disappointed about a postal-order."

"Jolly long way to Greyfriars, to see a chap," said Blake.

"He's my cousin!" said Bunter, with dignity. "We were brought up together—ahem!—we played together as little children."

"Very pathetic!" grunted Herries.

"Oh, really, Herries——"

"I don't believe a word of it!" said Herries. George Herries was almost painfully candid at times. "You spun Lathom that yarn to get off lessons! You're a fat spoofer!"

"Bai Jove! Hewwies, old chap——"

"I think you're unfeeling, Herries!" said Bunter. "When my poor cousin is tossing in delirium——"

"Not much good going to see him if he's delirious!"

"I—I mean he's suffering the awful pangs of influenza——"

"My hat! If he's got influenza, you're jolly well not going to see him!" exclaimed Digby. "We don't want the 'flu here, you ass! The Head wouldn't let you go!"

"I—I don't mean influenza. I—I mean smallpox!"

"That's still more dangerous!" grinned Blake. "We don't want it here. You will have to bear up under this sorrow, Bunter."

"If you don't believe me, Blake——"

"Well, which am I to believe?" asked Blake. "The delirium, the influenza, or the smallpox? I don't mind which; but give it a name!"

"Ha, ha, ha!"

"The—the fact is, I don't know what he's ill of, but I know he's awfully ill—expiring, perhaps. My tender heart——"

"Tender rats!" grunted Herries.

"I call that brutal, Herries. I think you fellows might lend me the railway fare to Friardale, as we're in the same Form. I'll settle up out of my very next postal-order——"

"Weally, Buntah——"

"How do you know he's ill?" asked Blake suddenly.

"He wrote——"

"Trot out the letter, then; seeing is believing!"

"I mean he telephoned——"

"Got out of a sick-bed to get a trunk-call?" yelled Herries.

"He—he got another chap to telephone, I mean."

"That's an easier one," agreed Herries. "Why don't you think of a good lie to begin with, instead of trotting it out after a bad one?"

"Ha, ha, ha!"

"Chaps in the Fourth get a lot of trunk-calls on the telephone—I don't think!" grinned Digby. "Have you had a 'phone put up in your study, Bunter?"

Bunter blinked at Dig more in sorrow than in anger.

"It was on Railton's telephone," he said.

"Gammon!"

"You can ask Mr. Railton, if you like!"

"Ha, ha! I'm likely to ask the House-master that question!" chuckled Dig. "Why don't you say the Head?"

"You can ask Kildare, then—Kildare came to call me to answer the telephone yesterday," said Bunter calmly.

"Rats!"

"Oh, really, you fellows——"

"Bai Jove!" said Arthur Augustus. "We could ask Kildare, you chaps! There he is, in the quad, with Dawwel. He will tell us! And if we find that Buntah is lyin', as usual, we will give him a feahful thwashin'!"

"Done!" said Bunter, at once.

"Oh! You agree to that?" exclaimed Blake.

"Certainly—being a truthful chap——"

"Bow-wow! I'll speak to Kildare. Mind that he doesn't bunk, you fellows."

"Yaas, wathah!"

But Bunter showed no desire to "bunk." He knew what Kildare's answer to the question would be. The St. Jim's captain knew that he had been called to answer a trunk-call on Mr. Railton's telephone; but he knew nothing more. Jack Blake stepped out into the quad, while his comrades gathered round the Owl of Greyfriars.

"I say, Kildare——" began Blake.

"Hallo?" said the prefect, looking round.

"Did Bunter of our Form have a call on Mr. Railton's telephone yesterday?"

"Yes."

"Oh!" ejaculated Blake. "Was it a trunk-call, Kildare?"

"I believe so."

"Was it—was it from Greyfriars?"

"I don't know. Cut off!"

Jack Blake rejoined his chums, his face expressive of the great astonishment he felt.

"Bunter's told the truth!" he said, in a gasping voice.

And from his three chums came exclamations of amazement at that unexpected and startling information.

"Great Scott!"

CHAPTER 5.

All Clear at Last!

"HALLO! What's this game?" asked the cheery voice of George Figgins of the Fourth Form.

Figgins & Co. of the New House were coming along from the Form-room. They stopped, as they saw the chums of Study No. 6 gathered round Bunter, with blank astonishment in their faces.

"Bunter been prigging your rations?" asked Fatty Wynn, with a look of deep disfavour at the Owl of Greyfriars.

"He's told the truth!" said Blake.

"Yaas, wathah!"

"Hold me, somebody!" gasped Figgins.

"Bunter has?" yelled Kerr.

"Oh, fan me!" murmured Fatty Wynn.

Billy Bunter glared at the merry Fourth-Formers in great wrath. They seemed to think that this was the first time he had ever told the truth; and it wasn't. He had not done it often, perhaps; still, he had done it.

"Look here, you silly asses——" he began.

"He said he'd had a trunk-call on Railton's 'phone," said Blake—"and he had! It turns out that he really had! What do you think of that?"

"Extraordinary!" said Figgins & Co., with one voice.

"Yaas, wathah!"

"I say, you fellows, this is very unfeeling, considering that my poor cousin is lying——"

"If he's your cousin, he would naturally be lying," remarked Kerr.

"Lying on a sick bed, I mean," howled Bunter.

"Dash it all, he might stop lying at such a time as that!"

"Ha, ha, ha!"

"Suffering fearful agonies," said Bunter pathetically, "and here I want to run over to Greyfriars and see him, and I'm stuck for want of a quid or so. He's asking for me."

"Jolly queer taste, I must say!"

"Begging to see me, with tears in his eyes," said Bunter. "Wharton was crying on the telephone when he told me. I heard him sob."

"Bai Jove!"

"It's breaking my heart, you know," said Bunter. "I'm a very tender-hearted chap. I—I feel this as much as missing a meal—I do, really."

"Ha, ha, ha!"

"Blessed if I see anything to cackle at! If you'd heard Bob Cherry break down, in telling me on the 'phone——"

"It was Wharton a minute ago," said Kerr.

"I—I mean—that is—— It—it was Wharton first, and then Cherry—Wharton was so cut up he couldn't finish."

"Oh!"

"I'd be willing to travel third-class to Friardale to see poor old—ahem!—my poor old cousin. If you fellows——"

"Bai Jove! If Buntah is tellin' the twuth, it is wathah hard cheese!" said Arthur Augustus. "We weally ought to lend him the tin, if he wants to go and see a sick welation."

"Only he's spoofing," said Blake. "He wants the tin to blue on tuck."

"Yaas, I suppose that is more pwob."

"It's a dead cert!" grinned Figgins. "I think we know Bunter by this time."

Billy Bunter gave a snort. His bad reputation was rising up to smite him once more, as it often did.

And, as a matter of fact, he really had no designs on the tuckshop this time. He really did want the money to pay his fare to Greyfriars—though it was not to see a sick relation.

"I say, you fellows——" he began desperately.

"N. G.!" said Blake. "You really seem to have had a call on Railton's 'phone yesterday; but we don't know that it was from Greyfriars. I dare say it wasn't."

"I've told you——"

"What you've told us, my pippin, doesn't make any difference, one way or the other. If you want to know, I'd as soon take a Hun's word as yours!"

"But I say——"

"'Nuff said!"

"You can come to Wayland and see me off if you like!" gasped Bunter.

"What?"

"Come with me and take my ticket, if you don't trust me," said Bunter. "I can't say fairer than that."

"Bai Jove!"

Bunter had succeeded in making an impression at last. Kerr eyed him very keenly.

"If your cousin at Greyfriars is ill, and you want to see him on that account, we'll pass round the hat like a shot," he said; "but you're such an awful spoofer, Bunter. If you give one of us a walk to Wayland for nothing——"

"I really want to go!" protested Bunter, almost tearfully. It was really hard not to be believed, when he was telling the truth for once.

"Have you got leave to go?"

"No; I'm going on my own. I mightn't get leave."

"You'll be jolly late back——"

"That's all right," said Bunter, suppressing a grin. He had no intention of coming back, if the juniors had only known it. Indeed, if they had known all the facts it was quite possible that they would have raised Bunter's railway fare with a great deal of pleasure—to Greyfriars, or to anywhere else, on condition that he did not come back!

"I mean, you'll get a licking, Bunter," said Kerr.

"I don't care!"

"My hat!"

"Weally, deah boys, I believe that Buntah is statin' the facts for once," said Arthur Augustus D'Arcy. "Buntah, I will come to Wayland with you, if you like, and purchase your railway ticket."

"Thanks, old chap!" said Bunter. "Come on!"

"He really seems to mean business," said Jack Blake, in wonder.

"I'm ready," said Bunter. "I've only got to get my cap—I'll run up to my study for a minute——"

"I will meet you at the door in a few minutes, Buntah."

"Right-ho!"

Billy Bunter ran for the staircase. He was anxious to get off—before he met Grundy or Racke again, and before Mr. Lathom made any further reference to the over-due lines. The Fourth-Formers looked at one another.

Jack Blake expressed his feelings in a prolonged whistle.

"He's really going, then," he said. "Blessed if I catch on! He will get into a row for going without leave—he can't be back much before bed-time."

"It is wathah decent of him, Blake."

"Ye-es—if it's genuine."

"I am goin' to take his ticket."

"More likely he's depending on spoofing Gussy," said Kerr. "I think I'll go, too."

"Weally, Kerr——"

"And I, too!" said Figgins grimly. "And if he takes us to Wayland, we'll see that he gets into the express, if we have to bundle him in neck and crop."

"Hear, hear!"

"Good egg!" said Blake. "I'll come!"

And when Bunter of the Fourth came down to the door he found four juniors ready to accompany him to Wayland—and, to the surprise of all four, he did not seem to mind.

"You fellows ready?" he asked.

"We're ready!"

"Right—I'll be after you in a minute."

Bunter ran down the passage, to the door of Mr. Lathom's study. He did not enter that study. He stopped, and put his mouth to the keyhole, and yelled:

"Beast!"

"Bless my soul!" came Mr. Lathom's surprised voice from within. "That is Bunter's voice—— Bunter, you impertinent young rascal——"

The study door opened. But Bunter was gone; he was scuttling away as fast as his fat little legs would carry him, and had already turned the corner. In a few seconds he had joined Blake & Co. in the quad, and they were going down to the gates.

CHAPTER 6.

Bunter's Farewells!

GRUNDY of the Shell was strolling near the school gates with Wilkins and Gunn. He gave a growl, a good deal like Herries' bulldog Towser, as he saw Bunter, and started towards him.

"Hold on, Grundy!" said Figgins. "Hands off, fathead!"

"Yaas, wathah!"

"I'm going to lick that fat rotter!" roared Grundy. "He's had my cake, and I haven't licked him yet."

"I say, you fellows——"

"Pway stand back, Gwunday! Buntah is goin' to catch a twain——"

"He's going to catch a hiding, and he's going to catch it from me!" growled Grundy.

Bunter dodged behind Jack Blake.

"I say, you fellows, keep him off! I've no time to thrash Grundy now——"

"To—to thrash me!" gasped Grundy.

"Yes, you rotter!" said Bunter, blinking at him round Blake. "You're a bully, Grundy, and a rotter, and a worm, and a beast, and I'm going to lick you when I come back. You wait for me in the gym!"

"Why, I — I — I'll——" stuttered Grundy.

"Pway wetiah, Gwunday. You have heard Buntah's challenge," said D'Arcy. "It is up to you to wait for him in the gym."

And the juniors walked on, keeping Bunter in their midst, and forming a sort of guard round him. George Alfred Grundy blinked after them.

"Did you—did you hear him, you fellows?" he gasped, addressing Wilkins and Gunn.

"I heard him," grinned Wilkins. "It's up to you, Grundy."

"Do you think that fat rooster can stand up to me, for a minute?" roared Grundy.

"Well, he's undertaken to do it," remarked Gunn.

"I'll—I'll—I'll wait in the gym," gasped Grundy, "and when he doesn't turn up, I'll go and look for him, and squash him! I'll burst him!"

Billy Bunter rolled out of gates with the juniors, with a fat grin of satisfaction on his face. As he was not coming back to St. Jim's at all it was quite safe to slang the great Grundy, and he had found it agreeable. Outside the gates, Racke of the Shell was lounging with Crooke and Scrope, and he scowled at Bunter.

The Owl of Greyfriars halted. This was another chance for him to say a polite farewell.

"Hold on a minute, you fellows, I want to speak to Racke!" he said. "Racke, you sneaking, gambling rotter——"

"Eh? What?" ejaculated the astonished Aubrey.

"You say I owe you money, and you're going to pitch into me till I pay up!" said Bunter, blinking at him. "I've no time to thrash you now, Racke—I've got to catch a train. I'll thrash you in the gym this evening, if you've got pluck enough to come there and meet me."

"Wha-a-at?"

"You're a sneaking, card-sharping rotter!" said Bunter, wagging a fat and accusing forefinger at him. "I despise you, Racke! I believe you had cards up your sleeve in your study that time—you would, you know. That's why I'm not going to pay you! You're a sneaking worm, Racke! I despise you! Yah!"

With that elegant apostrophe Billy Bunter rolled on, leaving Racke rooted to the ground, and his companions grinning.

Blake & Co. glanced very curiously at Bunter as they walked on down the lane. Bunter seemed to be hurling reckless defiances about on all sides, regardless of the consequences. It really was not like Bunter to issue these challenges to meetings in the gym—it was more like him to dodge such a challenge if addressed to himself. The juniors were puzzled.

"That's two fights you've got on hand for this evening, Bunter," said Kerr.

"Nothing to me," said Bunter airily. "I'm a tip-top fighting-man, you know."

"Oh, my hat!"

They walked on, and turned into the wood, a short cut to Wayland. Almost at every step the juniors expected Bunter to "begin," as Blake called it. But he did not begin. He made no request for the railway fare to be handed to him—he did not tell the juniors that he wouldn't trouble them to come on to Wayland with him—in fact, he only seemed in a hurry to get to the station. And after a quick walk they reached the market town, and Kerr announced that they had ten minutes to catch the express.

"Time for a snack in the buffet!" said Bunter.

"I am goin' to get your ticket now, Buntah!" said Arthur Augustus D'Arcy, turning his eyeglass upon the fat junior, perhaps with a lingering doubt.

"Good. Get first class."

"Ahem!"

"I'm accustomed to travelling first. Of course, I shall settle up the amount later, D'Arcy—when my postal-order comes."

"Get third!" growled Blake. "What's the good of throwing money away?"

"I am afwaid it will not wun to first class, Buntah. The fare is wathah expensive. I should twavel third."

"You might!" grunted Bunter. "All right for you, I dare say. It's a bit different for me. I'm accustomed to the decencies of life."

"Oh, bai Jove!"

"Well, if you're going to get third, I suppose you can lend me a few bob for a snack before I start?" said Bunter, discontentedly.

"Y-a-a-as."

"We'll see to the snack," said Figgins. "You get the ticket, Gussy. We'll whack it out afterwards."

Arthur Augustus went to the booking-office. Bunter made no effort to detain him, and did not even ask for the money to take the ticket himself. The juniors had to be convinced at last; Bunter was really going to Greyfriars.

The swell of St. Jim's rejoined the party in the buffet, where Bunter was taking a snack; though, if appearances were to be relied upon, he was laying in provisions for at least seven lean years. He had not finished when the express came thundering in, but he had to stop.

"I'll take some of these cakes with me," he said. "You can settle, Blake. I'll square for the lot together. And a few oranges, and some buns."

"Get a move on."

"One of these pies, too, I think. Yaroooh! Leggo my collar!"

"Do you want to lose the train, fat-head?"

Kerr rushed the fat junior out of the buffet by the collar. It looked for a moment as if Bunter did want to lose the train, and suspicion revived. But only for a moment. The fat junior hopped into the train, and secured a corner seat and drew the door shut.

"Landed at last!" grinned Figgins.

"Yaas, wathah!"

Bunter's fat face looked from the window above the four juniors. He grinned down at them.

"All serene!" he said. "I say, you fellows, you might lend me a few bob to get a snack at Friardale?"

Arthur Augustus silently passed up his remaining small change to Bunter. The fat junior grunted as he blinked at it, and slipped it carelessly into his pocket.

"Off!" said Blake, as the guard waved his flag. "He's really going! Blessed if I quite believed it, till now."

Bunter leaned from the window.

"I say, you fellows——"

"Good-bye, Buntah!"

"I've got something to say to you fellows," said Bunter, as the train began to stir. "I've wanted to say it for a long time. You're a silly ass, Jack Blake!"

"What?"

"You're a long-legged scarecrow, Figgins!"

"Wha-a-at?"

"You're a skinny Scotchman, Kerr!"

"You fat, cheeky rotter——"

"Bai Jove! Weally, Buntah——"

"And you're a rotten, lazy, fat-headed, mean bounder, D'Arcy!"

"Gweat Scott!"

The train was moving now. Bunter waved a fat hand from the receding window, his fat features wrinkled into a scornful sneer.

"That's my opinion of you!" he shouted. "Tell Tom Merry, from me, that he's a lout, and tell Lowther he's a worm, and tell Manners——"

But the remainder of Bunter's farewell address was lost on the wind as the express rushed out of the station. The fat junior sank down in his seat with a grin on his face. He had had quite a happy parting with his schoolfellows of St. Jim's.

On the platform, Jack Blake and his comrades looked at one another in deep silence.

"Bai Jove!" said Arthur Augustus at last.

And they started for home.

CHAPTER 7.
Waiting for Bunter!

THAT evening quite a number of fellows in the School House at St. Jim's were waiting impatiently for Bunter's return.

If the Owl of Greyfriars had been the most attractive and charming fellow possible his return could not have been more eagerly awaited.

The fellows wanted to tell him what they thought of him; and it was only too probable that they would proceed from words to actions.

Even the kind-hearted Arthur Augustus was wrathy.

The juniors who had seen Bunter off at Wayland gave the Owl's kind message to the Terrible Three, and rather enjoyed the looks of Tom Merry as it was delivered.

"The fat worm!" exclaimed Tom indignantly. "What did he mean by it?"

"He slanged us all round," said Blake. "He waited till the train was moving, so that we couldn't get at him, and then slanged us high and low. He called Gussy——"

Arthur Augustus interrupted.

"Pway do not wepeat Buntah's oppwobwious wemarks, Blake. They are weally offensive to my eahs."

"He called us all names," said Blake. "Figgins and Kerr are going to scalp him. So am I. I'm going to squash him! Even Gussy is going to give him a hiding."

"I am certainly goin' to give him a feahful thwashin'. I wegard it as bein' up to me, though I shall be sowwy to soil my hands on the boundah!"

"And he called me——" said Tom Merry, with a deep breath.

"And told us to tell you," said Blake. "And Lowther——"

"I'll worm him!" said Monty Lowther.

"There was something for Manners, but we didn't catch it."

"I dare say it's no loss!" growled Manners. "I'll thump him, all the same, the cheeky, fat rotter!"

"Grundy and Racke are waiting for him, too," said Tom Merry, laughing.

"Bunter has booked himself for a high old time when he comes home."

"But what does he mean by it?" asked Blake, in perplexity. "He must know that he's going to get the ragging of his life."

"Yaas, wathah!"

Tom Merry shook his head.

"I give it up," he said. "Bunter can't mean to fight anybody, if he can help it; and he's booked himself for a whole series of thumping lickings. I suppose he's coming back, isn't he?"

"Why, he must be! He's not leaving St. Jim's that I know of."

"It looks as if he was going for good, and took the chance of slanging us before he went. But we should have heard something of it if he was leaving the school; so it can't be that. I give it up. The fact is, Bunter is rather a puzzle in a good many ways," remarked Tom Merry. "When we first met him we all liked him—he didn't seem anything like that cousin Billy of his, excepting in looks. Since he came here, though, he's seemed simply Billy Bunter over again, so far as I remember that fat bounder. Blessed if it didn't really look as if the two fat bounders got mixed up somehow, and the wrong one turned up here."

"Yaas, wathah!"

"We were mistaken in him," said Manners. "But he didn't leave us long in the mistake. He opened our eyes soon enough."

"Lathom has been inquiring for him," said Lowther. "He seems to have cheeked Lathom just before he went out, from what I hear. Old Lathom is wrathy as anything. The silly ass seems to have gone out of his way to arrange a hot reception for himself when he comes home."

"He'll get it, anyway," said Tom.

That much was certain. There was trouble, serious trouble, waiting for Bunter of the Fourth when he turned up again at St. Jim's. And as the evening wore on the fellows were very eager for his arrival.

But he did not arrive.

Lowther looked out trains in a timetable, and announced that Bunter could hardly be home before bed-time. He missed evening call-over, and Mr. Railton frowned, and marked him absent. After calling-over, Figgins of the New House gave Tom Merry a look-in.

"That fat slug crawled in yet?" asked Figgins.

Tom Merry smiled. He recognised W. G. Bunter by that description.

"Not yet," he answered.

"He'll get into a row with the Housemaster," said Figgins.

"As well as with us," said Tom.

"Well, Kerr and I are going to skin him," said Figgins. "But we'll leave it over till the morning. You chaps can have him to yourselves this evening, if you like."

"Thanks!" said Tom, laughing. "We shall keep him busy."

And Figgins went back to the New House, and allowed the sun to go down on his wrath.

Trimble and Mellish did their prep in Study No 2 without their fat study-mate. Evidently there was to be no prep for Bunter that evening. And Grundy looked in the gym for him in vain.

As bed-time drew near there was much speculation in the School House as to what had become of Bunter.

It was almost unprecedented for a fellow to stay out till nine o'clock without special permission; but Bunter was staying out. Soon after nine Jack Blake was sent for to Mr. Lathom's study.

"Has Bunter come in yet, Blake?" the Form-master asked.

"I think not, sir."

"It is extraordinary!" said Mr. Lathom. "Do you know where he is gone, Blake?"

"I—I think he's gone to Greyfriars, sir, to visit a sick relation," said Blake.

"Bless my soul! He told me that his cousin was ill at that school. But he had no right to take such a long journey without leave. Tell him to report to me the moment he comes in, Blake."

"Yes, sir."

Blake retired, leaving Mr. Lathom with a deep frown upon his usually kind face. Bunter's parting benediction through the keyhole was still echoing in Mr. Lathom's indignant ears. It was the first time any member of his Form had ventured to "slang" Mr. Lathom. It was really an almost incredible happening, and the Form-master almost suspected that Bunter was not quite in his right senses.

Blake returned to the Common-room, where quite a number of fellows were getting anxious about Bunter. They were anxious lest he should not turn up by bed-time.

"Bed in ten minutes," remarked Manners, as the clock indicated twenty past nine "The fat bounder is sticking it out."

There was a deep growl from Grundy.

"He knows what he's going to get," said George Alfred. "He's staying out on purpose."

"He will get something from the Housemaster if he stays out after bed-time," remarked Levison of the Fourth.

There was keen interest in the subject as the big hand of the clock moved round. When it indicated the half hour, Kildare of the Sixth looked into the junior Common-room.

"Has Bunter come in?" he asked, addressing nobody in particular.

"Not yet, Kildare."

"The young rascal! Get off to the dorm," said Kildare.

"We shall have to leave him over till to-morrow," murmured Monty Lowther regretfully.

"We sha'n't, though," said Jack Blake. "He's in our dorm. I'm going to stay awake for dear old Bunter!"

"Yaas, wathah!"

The juniors went to their dormitories. The Shell had to give up Bunter for that night; but the Fourth still expected to see him. And Blake and D'Arcy did not intend to be asleep when he came in. They had something to say to Bunter—and something to do!

CHAPTER 8.
Wally Arrives!

TING—TING-A-LING!

Taggles, the porter, growled.

"That there Bunter! Blow him!" said Taggles.

Taggles was aware that Bunter was out of bounds, and when the bell rang in his lodge he guessed who was the applicant for admission. Taggles did not hurry himself. The bell rang again twice before the old gentleman lumbered out to open the gates.

Through the bars of the gate a fat figure was visible in the gloom outside. A fat face looked through at Taggles, and there was a glimmer of spectacles, set very low down on a fat little nose.

"Ho!" said Taggles. "You, Master Bunter?"

"Little me!" answered a cheery voice.

"Nice goings on, I don't think!" said Taggles, with a grunt.

The fat junior smiled.

To all outward appearance that fat fellow was the Bunter who had quitted St. Jim's that afternoon. But he was only so in outward appearance. Taggles did not see any difference; but the difference was great.

For the Bunter at the gates was not the Bunter who had said such affectionate farewells to Blake & Co. at Wayland.

That Bunter was already in bed in the Remove dormitory at Greyfriars; back at his old school, and safe from the wrath he had roused at St. Jim's.

This was quite another Bunter; Walter Gilbert Bunter, the protege of Mr. Penman of Canterbury; the youth who had been destined for St. Jim's by his late employer, and who had changed places with Billy Bunter, and gone to Greyfriars instead.

The Bunters had changed back.

Wally Bunter, certainly, was not keen on changing back. He liked Greyfriars, and had been getting on well there, having succeeded at last in living down the reputation Billy had left for him.

But he had no choice in the matter.

Billy Bunter had insisted; and, as Billy was determined to get back to Greyfriars, there was nothing for Wally to do but to "clear." And, having solaced himself by bumping the unreliable Owl, hard, he had cleared.

His annoyance had faded away on the journey. He was a cheerful fellow, and disposed to make the best of things. It was necessary for him to be at St. Jim's on the morrow, in any case, when Mr. Penman was coming down to see him. He had visited the school before on a similar occasion. Now he had to stay; and though he would have preferred to remain at Greyfriars, he was cheerfully prepared to make the best of it.

Bunter had landed him into a row by this sudden change of plans. He was arriving late at St. Jim's—and he had to arrive as Bunter, without any explanation, of course, as to the change of identity. He expected a caning, and it was a comfort to reflect that he had bumped Bunter hard in the wood at Friardale. But in spite of the caning he knew loomed ahead, and the possibility that other things loomed ahead which he did not yet know of, his fat face was cheerful enough as he watched Taggles unlock the gate.

"Which you're to report yourself at once to Mr. Railton, in his study," said Taggles, with a grunt, as the fat junior rolled in.

"Right-ho!" said Wally Bunter. "Good-night, old scout!"

Grunt!

Wally Bunter cheerfully started for the School House. It was fortunate that, on his previous visit to St. Jim's, he had learned his way about the school. He looked portentously grave as he presented himself in Mr. Railton's study. He found Mr. Lathom there with the Housemaster. Both the gentlemen looked portentously grave as he presented himself.

What excuse to give for his supposed conduct Wally Bunter did not know. He had to trust to luck. He wondered, too, whether the two masters would discern any difference between him and the Bunter they were expecting. He was relieved to see that there was no doubt or suspicion in their faces.

"So you have returned, Bunter!" said Mr. Railton, in a deep, stern voice.

"I—I've come in, sir," said Wally meekly.

"It is now a quarter to ten."

"Is it, sir?"

"A quarter of an hour past your bed-time, Bunter. You have ventured to absent yourself until this unheard-of hour."

"I—I'm sorry, sir."

"Where have you been?"

"I've just come from Greyfriars, sir."

"You had no right to make such a journey without permission, as you know very well," said the School House master. "However, as Mr. Lathom informs me that your relative at that school is sick, I will excuse you on that point."

"Oh, my hat!" murmured Wally.

Grundy found himself gazing up at the branches overhead, and the blue sky beyond, in a dazed state. "Qweat Scott! Qwunday's down!" gasped Arthur Augustus D'Arcy. (See Chapter 11.)

"What did you say, Bunter?"

"I—I—n-n-nothing, sir!"

"You will be punished, Bunter, for staying out after bed-time. I shall cane you."

Wally was silent.

"But even that is not the most serious matter I have to refer to," said Mr. Railton, his voice growing sterner. "Immediately before you left, this afternoon, Bunter, you dared to insult Mr. Lathom."

"Oh, sir!" gasped Wally, in dismay.

"You shouted a disrespectful and opprobious expression through the keyhole of Mr. Lathom's study, Bunter."

"Oh!"

"A most disrespectful expression," said Mr. Lathom. "You had the insolence and temerity, Bunter, to apply the name 'beast' to your Form-master."

"Oh, no, sir! Not at all!" gasped Wally.

"I heard you!" said Mr. Lathom sternly. "I recognised your voice, Bunter, though you were gone before I could open my door."

Wally breathed hard. His chief regret, at that moment, was that he was not within punching distance of Billy Bunter's nose. He was glad, however, that Mr. Lathom had not actually seen Billy Bunter on the occasion. If Billy had been seen, certainly Wally's denial would not have been of much use.

"Have you anything to say, Bunter?" asked Mr. Railton, taking up his cane.

"I—I—oh, yes, sir!" gasped Wally. "Certainly, sir! There's a—a mistake. I never called through Mr. Lathom's keyhole, sir. I wouldn't do such a thing!"

"Mr. Lathom knew your voice, Bunter."

"Most certainly," nodded the Fourth Form master.

"I—I—I assure you, sir, it wasn't my voice," said Wally earnestly. "I should think such a thing caddish, sir. I haven't been near your study door, sir. I certainly never called you names. It—it must have been some other fellow with a voice like mine, sir."

Mr. Lathom looked at him very keenly over his glasses. There was an earnest and truthful ring in the junior's voice.

"That is absurd, Bunter!" said Mr. Railton.

"I assure you, sir, I'm speaking the truth. I—I don't mind a licking, sir, but I—I want Mr. Lathom to believe I wouldn't have done such a caddish thing!"

"Bless my soul!" said Mr. Lathom. "I certainly never expected to hear you deny your action, Bunter. I was quite certain that it was your voice."

"It was not, sir, on my word of honour!"

Mr. Lathom coughed.

"Well, well," he said. "You certainly appear to be speaking the truth, Bunter, and it is barely possible that a mistake may have been made. Mr. Railton——"

"The matter rests with you, Mr. Lathom, of course," said the Housemaster.

"In that case I should prefer to say no more about it," said the Fourth Form-master. "Although I felt sure at the time that it was Bunter's voice, there is a possibility of injustice being done."

"Very well. Bunter. Mr. Lathom prefers to give you the benefit of the doubt," said the School House master.

"Thank you very much, sir!" said Wally gratefully.

The new arrival had had one narrow escape. But his troubles were not over. He had to "face the music" for his late return—or, rather, his late arrival—and Mr. Railton felt it his duty to lay the cane on soundly.

Wally Bunter's fat palms were tingling when he was dismissed to his dormitory. In the corridor he rubbed his hands, and then sparred in the air with his fat fists clenched, as if he saw the podgy features of his cousin Billy before him.

Having thus relieved his feelings, Billy Bunter's double made his way to the Fourth Form dormitory.

CHAPTER 9.

In a Hornets' Nest.

"HEAH he comes!" murmured Arthur Augustus D'Arcy.

Jack Blake sat up in bed.

The dormitory door opened quietly, and a fat figure came in, and turned on the light.

"So you've come back, you fat rotter!" said Blake grimly.

Wally Bunter looked at him, and nodded.

"Hallo, Blake!" he said cheerily.

"I'll 'hallo, Blake' you!" answered Jack Blake. "Wait a minute, you fat worm, and I'll come to you!"

"My hat! What's the matter?"

"Weally, Buntah, you know vewy well what is the mattah. Pway don't get out of bed, Blake. I am goin' to thwash Buntah first."

"My turn first," answered Blake.

"Wats! He applied more oppwobious expwessions to me than to you, Blake," said Arthur Augustus warmly. "I claim the wight of givin' him a feahful thwashin' first."

"Oh, my hat!" murmured Wally.

Billy Bunter had evidently left a hornets' nest for him to walk into. It reminded him of his earlier experiences at Greyfriars.

Kildare looked into the dormitory. He had come to see the light out after the late arrival.

"Now, then, what are you getting up for, Blake?" he demanded. "Get back to bed at once!"

"I—I was going to speak to Bunter."

"Turn in!"

"Oh, all right!"

Blake turned in, and Arthur Augustus changed his mind about getting up. The head prefect of the School House was not to be argued with.

"Get to bed, Bunter," said Kildare. "Mind, Blake, no ragging in this dormitory to-night, or I shall come back. If I come back there will be trouble."

Wally Bunter grinned as he turned in. Kildare, with a warning look at Blake, turned out the light and left the dormitory.

Blake sat up again.

"Bunter!"

"Hallo, old trump?" said Wally.

"I can't lick you to-night——"

"You couldn't lick me any time."

"What?"

"Getting deaf in your old age?" asked Wally cheerily. "You couldn't lick me any time. Got it now?"

Jack Blake breathed hard.

"You fat worm, you know Kildare will come back if there's a row here," he said. "I'm going to burst you in the morning!"

"Yaas, wathah!"

"Sufficient for the evening is the evil thereof!" yawned Wally. "I'm sleepy. Put off your merry eloquence till the morning, old scout!"

And Wally laid his head on the pillow and closed his eyes, and was fast asleep a minute later.

"My word!" came a murmur from Cardew's bed. "Bunter's grown a big neck since this afternoon. Where is he gettin' all this nerve from?"

"The feahfully cheekay wottah——"

"I'll give him something to cure all that in the morning!" growled Blake.

And as thrashings were "off" for that night, Blake settled down to sleep.

If it had been the Owl of Greyfriars in Bunter's bed sleep would probably not have visited his eyes for some time, considering the alarming prospect before him in the morning; but Wally Bunter was untroubled by the prospect, alarming as it was, and he slept like a top.

His eyes did not open till the rising-bell was clanging out over St. Jim's. Then he sat up in bed, rubbed his eyes, and yawned.

The spring sunshine was glimmering in at the high windows cheerily. For a moment Wally expected to find himself in the familiar surroundings of the Remove dormitory at Greyfriars.

The strange faces round him recalled him to himself at once, however.

Greyfriars was a thing of the past. He was a St. Jim's fellow now, as he had been supposed to be all along.

Many glances turned towards him, and they could not be called friendly. Jack Blake, in particular, was looking very grim, and Arthur Augustus's face seemed to have lost its benign expression.

"There's the fat toad!" remarked Trimble.

Wally looked round.

"Hallo, old barrel!" he remarked. "Are you calling me names?"

"Get up, you fat slacker!" grunted Herries.

Wally turned promptly out of bed. He grinned as he dressed himself that morning. There was something rather entertaining, in a way, in his novel and peculiar position at St. Jim's.

Billy Bunter had always been the last out of the dormitory. Wally was one of the first. And some of the juniors had remarked, with surprise, that he had washed all over, instead of indulging in what Herries termed a "cat-lick"—such as Billy Bunter had always considered sufficient to begin the day on. And there was an unaccustomed springiness in the step of the fat junior as he went down and walked out into the quadrangle. It might have been noticed, too, that he wore his glasses so low on his nose that he did not use them, and yet he seemed to see better than ever.

The chums of Study No. 6 followed him into the quadrangle, and cornered him under the elms. They surrounded him as they came up, to cut off his escape; but, to their surprise, he showed no desire to dodge. He greeted them with an affable grin.

"Top of the morning, old tops!" he remarked. "You're looking quite merry and bright. Nice morning—what?"

"Weally, Buntah——"

"I don't know what this game is, Bunter," said Jack Blake. "If you think you're going to squirm out of a licking you're making a big mistake!"

"Yaas, wathah!"

There was a roar in the distance. Grundy had come out with Wilkins and Gunn.

"There he is!"

And Grundy of the Shell came speeding up.

At the same time the Terrible Three came out of the School House, and they also bore down on Bunter. And from the direction of the New House Figgins & Co. were sprinting towards the same spot.

It was quite a reception.

CHAPTER 10.

A Surprise for St. Jim's!

WALLY BUNTER did not look alarmed.

He looked puzzled.

"Is this a game?" he asked.

"A wathah sewious game for you, you fat boundah!" answered Arthur Augustus D'Arcy sternly.

"What's the matter with you, Gussy?"

"I wefuse to allow you to call me

Gussy, Buntah. I wegard you as a wogue and a wapscallion!"

"My hat!"

"Lemme get at him!" roared Grundy of the Shell. "Can't you get out of the way, Tom Merry?"

"Captain of the Form takes precedence," explained Tom. "Stand back a bit, Grundy."

"Look here——"

"Yaas, wathah! I'm going to thwash him first, Gwundy!"

"You can leave him to me!" exclaimed Aubrey Racke, arriving on the scene and pushing forward. "I owe him a licking for——"

"Gentlemen, chaps, and fellows," said Wally Bunter gravely. "Let us have this in order. It seems that you've all got up early to thrash me——"

"Yaas, wathah!"

"You can't all do it at once. You will simply have to take it in turns," said Wally, with a coolness that astounded the St. Jim's juniors. "Fair play's a jewel, you know. One at a time, gentlemen—one at a time!"

"You cheeky ass!" exclaimed Monty Lowther, "It's not a fight—you couldn't fight a bunny-rabbit. It's a ragging!"

"I've never tried fighting a bunny-rabbit, but I can fight a silly ass, old bean. And you can take your turn with the other asses!"

"Bai Jove!"

"What's come over him?" said Figgins.

The juniors stared at Bunter quite blankly. Instead of showing the least sign of alarm, he appeared to regard the matter as a huge joke. And really there was no joke in nine fellows competing for the privilege of thrashing him first—with the rest to follow in their turn.

"Is this sheer neck, or is he off his dot?" said Manners.

Wally Bunter raised a fat hand.

"Order, gentlemen! One at a time! I appear to have trodden on your honourable corns, or you think I have, which comes to the same thing. I don't know what I've done——"

"Why, you fat rotter——"

"You bagged my cake!" roared Grundy. "My big sultana-cake from my Uncle Grundy!"

"Did I? My hat!"

"You called us all names at Wayland Station yesterday!" roared Figgins.

"Oh!"

"You sent us insulting messages!" exclaimed Tom Merry.

"Oh, the beast!" gasped Wally.

He was thinking of his excellent cousin, William George Bunter; but naturally the St. Jim's juniors could not guess that.

"Bai Jove! He's beginnin' again!" exclaimed Arthur Augustus. "If you are alludin' to me as a beast, Buntah, I hurl back the expwession in your teeth! I wegard you——"

"Collar him!"

"Bump him!"

"Hands off!" roared Wally. "Look here——"

"Give him the frog's march, to begin with," said Kerr.

"Good! Collar him!"

"Let me get at him with my boot!" shouted Racke.

"Fair play!" yelled the unfortunate Wally, as the juniors closed on him, "I'll fight the lot of you, one after another! Fair play!"

"Rats! Spoof!"

"Hold on, though," said Tom Merry. "If that fat bounder means business, he's entitled to fair play! We'll let him fight it out, on condition that he begins on the spot."

"Yaas, wathah!"

"He's only spoofing!" exclaimed Blake, impatiently. "He wants to wriggle off!"

"I'm jolly well going to kick him," said Racke. "He asked me to meet him in the gym. He never came. I'm going to kick him!"

"Shut up, Racke!"

"Gentlemen," said Wally Bunter, "be calm—calmness, I beg. Racke—this chap is Racke——"

"Eh? Don't you know my name now?" jeered Racke. "What game are you playing now, you podgy spoofer?"

"You want to kick me, I understand?" said Wally. "I appear to have failed to keep an appointment with you in the gym. I'll keep it now. Put up your hands, and these chaps can stand round and see fair play."

"Bai Jove!"

"I'm not going to wait for Racke!" roared Grundy. "Me first!"

Wally looked at him.

"You're a bit hefty for me," he remarked cheerfully. "I'd rather have the gloves on when I tackle you, old trump."

"Tackle me? You couldn't tackle one side of me!" hooted Grundy. "I'm going to whop you!"

"Shut up, Grundy!"

"Yaas, wathah! If Buntah pwefers to begin with Wacke, Buntah has a wight to please himself. It is poss that he may lick Wacke, as Wacke is a wathah weeday and smokay boundah."

"You silly idiot!" snarled Racke.

"Weally, Wacke——"

"Let him begin with me," growled Aubrey. "I'll alter his podgy nose for him. Get behind the trees, where we can't be spotted—he thinks some of the masters may see us, and come out."

"Behind the trees, with pleasure," said Wally.

He moved off, and Jack Blake promptly caught him by the arm. He was prepared for dodging.

"You don't bunk just yet, my fat pippin," said Blake.

"I don't want to bunk, fathead!"

"Well, we'll see that you don't!"

The whole party moved on to a more secluded spot. Other fellows were gathering on the scene now from both Houses, and there was quite an army round Wally Bunter.

He was the cynosure of all eyes. The amazing coolness and pluck he was displaying simply astounded the juniors. It did not seem at all like the Bunter they knew, though it occurred to Tom Merry that it was quite like the Wally Bunter they had known earlier.

The ring was too thick for Bunter to have the slightest chance of fleeing from the wrath to come. But the amazing thing was that he plainly did not want to flee.

Racke was a little uneasy, as well as amazed. He was prepared to reap a little cheap glory by thrashing a fat and not very courageous fellow like Bunter of the Fourth. But the unexpected display of cool courage on Bunter's part made him feel less sure of an easy success.

But he was taller and older than Bunter, and really the fat junior did not look like having much chance. Anyhow, it was too late for the festive Aubrey to back out now.

"Ready, old infant?" asked Wally Bunter carelessly. He had measured the black sheep of St. Jim's with a keen eye, and he did not anticipate much difficulty with Racke.

"I'm ready, you fat rotter!"

"Who's going to keep time?"

"No need to keep time. You won't stand up for one round, and you know you won't, you fat worm!"

"You keep time, Talbot," said Tom Merry.

Talbot of the Shell nodded, and took out his watch. At the call of time Aubrey Racke rushed to the assault, and all eyes in the interested ring were on Bunter of the Fourth. The juniors expected to see him run, or at least to collapse under the attack.

Instead of which he stood up to Racke's rush with cool steadiness, and met the black sheep of the Shell with left and right. Aubrey Racke's heavy blows went nowhere, as his hands were rapped away, and Wally's right came into his eye, followed up by the left on his nose. And Aubrey Racke, with a howl of anguish, went to the ground with a crash.

CHAPTER 11.

Amazing!

"BAI Jove!"

"Oh, crumbs!"

"My only hat!"

There was a buzz of astonishment as Racke went down in a heap.

The fat junior had handled him as easily as a baby, and he stood grinning down at the collapsed Aubrey.

Arthur Augustus took off his eyeglass, polished it, and stuck it back in his eye, as if to make sure that he was seeing aright. He scarcely believed the evidence of his celebrated monocle.

Racke sat up dazedly. His sharp nose was streaming red.

"Ow, ow, ow, wow!" mumbled Aubrey.

"I'm waiting!" remarked Wally Bunter politely.

"Yow-ow-ow!"

"My only hat!" said Grundy. "Are we dreaming? I don't think Racke wants any more. Do you want any more, Racke?"

"Yow-ow-ow!"

It was pretty clear that Aubrey Racke did not want any more. He picked himself up, and limped away with his handkerchief to his nose. The crowd made room for him to pass.

Wally Bunter grinned at the staring faces round him.

"Next man in!" he said.

"This must be a giddy dream," said Tom Merry. "Racke isn't much of a fighting-man, but—but—but—well, my hat!"

Grundy of the Shell shoved forward.

"I'm your man, Bunter!"

"Weally Gwunday——"

"Oh, let him come on!" said Wally.

"I wefuse to allow him to come on. My turn comes first. Stand back, Gwunday!"

"Rats!"

But three or four pairs of hands dragged the obstreperous Grundy back. Arthur Augustus slipped his eyeglass into his pocket, and faced the fat junior.

"I am weady, Buntah!"

Wally Bunter put his hands into his pockets.

"I'm not going to fight you, Gussy!" he answered.

"And why not, pway?" demanded Arthur Augustus warmly.

"I don't want to."

"You have no choice in the mattah, Buntah, aftah the oppwobwious epithets you applied to me——"

"I didn't!"

"What?"

"I—I mean, I withdraw them," said Wally desperately. "Any old thing! I—I'll apologise if you like."

"If you apologise, Buntah, I feel bound to allow the mattah to dwop," said Arthur Augustus, after some consideration.

"Right-ho, old son! Let it drop."

"Cold feet!" came a chuckle from somewhere.

Wally looked round.

"If the chap who said cold feet will stand forward, I'll give a lesson in manners," he remarked. "I'm not going to fight Gussy or Tom Merry, but I'll fight anybody else here present."

"And why not me?" demanded Tom Merry.

"Because I rather like you, old top," answered Wally affably. "I should be sorry to spoil your good looks."

"You cheeky ass!" roared Tom.

"Same to you, and many of them. Let Grundy come forward. I'll oblige Grundy, if there's time before breakfast."

Grundy did not need asking twice. He rushed forward.

The next moment a battle royal was in progress.

The fat junior had to give ground, so heavy was the attack. But it was noted that none of Grundy's heavy drives reached his cool, fat face. His guard was always there, and the juniors, in utter amazement, had to realise that Bunter of the Fourth was as good a boxer as any fellow in the Lower School at St. Jim's. Grundy piled in with terrific vehemence, but he exhausted himself on a defence that seemed nearly impregnable; and when he paused at last for breath, Wally Bunter piled in, in his turn, with such suddenness that George Alfred was on his back before he knew what was happening.

Grundy found himself gazing up at the branches overhead, and the blue sky beyond, in a dazed state.

"Gweat Scott! Gwunday's down!" gasped Arthur Augustus.

"Bunter—Bunter's knocked down Grundy!" stuttered Figgins.

"Hallo! There goes the bell!"

It was the breakfast-bell, and at that sound Wally Bunter started for the School House.

"I'll see you again, Grundy, old top, if you like!" he called back.

Grundy did not answer. He was too dazed. Wilkins and Gunn picked him up, and George Alfred blinked at them like a fellow in a dream. Tom Merry joined Bunter as the latter rolled into the School House, giving the fat junior a keen glance.

"Where's your specs, Bunter?" he asked suddenly.

"Eh? In my pocket."

"Don't you need them?"

"Ahem! I've had a sudden recovery. I sha'n't wear specs any more," said Wally, with a chuckle. "Congratulate me, old fellow."

And he went in.

Tom Merry shook his head.

He simply could not understand Bunter that morning.

The fat junior found himself the centre of all glances at the breakfast-table.

Bunter had surprised the St. Jim's fellows before, but never so much as now.

He turned up cheerful and smiling for morning lessons, in the Fourth Form-room. Then there was another surprise.

Billy Bunter had become quite famous in the Fourth for the number of things he did not know, or could not understand. But Bunter—this Bunter—was easily up to the work of the Fourth. Indeed, he was ahead of a good many fellows there. Mr. Lathom, surprised and pleased, gave Bunter approving glances, and even words of commendation.

After dinner that day Wally Bunter went up to Study No. 2 in the Fourth Form passage. He was aware that that had been cousin Billy's study. As his old employer—Mr. Penman—was coming that afternoon, the fat junior proceeded to make the study very tidy, in case his visitor should come that way. Monty Lowther found him thus engaged.

"What on earth are you up to, Bunter?" ejaculated Lowther, as he saw the fat junior with a duster in his hand.

"Tidying up! I'm expecting a visitor."

"You haven't much time for tidying. There are several fellows waiting to slaughter you, including myself!"

Wally shook his head.

"No more scraps till my visitor's been," he said. "I can't show Mr. Penman a black eye or a red nose. I'm at anybody's service after six. Up to six I shall take the poker to anybody who bothers me!"

"Will you?" roared a voice in the passage, as George Alfred Grundy glared in over Lowther's shoulder.

"Just so."

"Let's see you do it!" grinned Grundy, and he pushed Lowther aside and rushed into the study.

Grundy did not really want to see Wally do it, as a matter of fact; but he did see Wally do it, all the same. The fat junior whipped up the poker, which he had thoughtfully placed between the bars of the grate. Grundy retreated with a loud yell as the glowing end came near his nose.

"Yaroooh! Keep off!" he roared.

"Travel!"

"I—I—I'll——"

"Better get out!" advised Wally. "Otherwise you might get a tap—like that!"

"Yow-ow-wooop!"

George Alfred fled.

Monty Lowther walked away with a smile. Tom Merry & Co. agreed that Bunter should not pay his dire penalties until after his distinguished visitor had come and gone; that was only considerate. The fact was that the Co. no longer nourished much wrath against Bunter. Pluck will tell; and the fat junior's undoubted pluck that morning, while it amazed the juniors, had raised him very much in their estimation.

So Wally Bunter was left in repose; and when Mr. Penman of Canterbury arrived, the fat junior greeted him with a cheery and smiling face.

CHAPTER 12.

Arthur Augustus Finds His Old Pal!

"ME first!" said Grundy.

"Wats!"

The dusk was gathering over St. Jim's. Play was over on Little Side, and fellows were coming in from the river. Near the gates of the school a group of juniors had gathered—the Terrible Three, Figgins & Co., Study No. 6, Grundy, and a few others. They were waiting for Bunter.

Bunter's visitor had stayed quite a long time, and most of the time he had been in Study No. 2 with Bunter, engaged in discussion.

When Mr. Penman left, Bunter walked to the station with him; and some of the juniors noticed that his fat face was very grave.

They were waiting for him now to come back, after seeing his visitor off at Rylcombe.

"It's my turn first!" persisted Grundy. "I've started, you know!"

"Wubbish!"

"The fact is, Grundy," said Tom Merry, "I don't think there's any need to rag Bunter. Somehow, he doesn't seem such a worm as he was. I think he might be let off."

"Yaas, wathah!"

"I was thinking the same," said Kerr, with a nod. And Figgins nodded, too; and there was a general nodding.

"He's knocked me down," said Grundy, but his tone was somewhat mollified. "Who'd have thought he'd have the pluck to try it? I owe him a thrashing. Still, I must say I think better of him than I did. But——"

"Heah he comes!"

Wally Bunter came in at the gates, the expression on his fat face still very serious. He smiled slightly as he saw the group of juniors.

"Waiting for my scalp?" he asked.

"No," said Tom. "We've decided to look over your being such a worm, Bunter. You don't seem such a worm to-day, somehow."

"Ha, ha, ha!" roared Wally.

"Bai Jove! What are you cacklin' at, Buntah?"

"Ahem! Never mind. You fellows may as well bury the hatchet," said Wally. "I'm leaving St. Jim's in a few days."

"Leaving?"

"Yes."

"Bai Jove! I should like to say I am sowwy, Buntah, but—but weally, you——"

"Only, it wouldn't be true!" grinned Wally. "All right, old bean. I'm glad to be able to make you happy like this. It's a pleasure to confer pleasure, you know!"

"Well, if you're going, I won't lick you!" said Grundy.

"Thank you for nothing, old hoss! You couldn't, anyway!"

"I'm jolly well——"

"No, you won't!" said Tom Merry. "Shut up, Grundy!"

And Wally Bunter passed in peace.

The fat junior seemed in a thoughtful mood that evening, though he was quite cheery. If he was leaving St. Jim's, it did not seem to weigh upon his spirits very much. As a matter of fact, the change in Mr. Penman's plans had not been much of a shock to him, as it might have been if he had been still at Greyfriars. Arthur Augustus D'Arcy, remembering the friendship he had once had for Wally Bunter, joined him in the Common-room that evening, where the fat junior sat looking reflectively into the fire.

"So you are goin', Buntah?" he remarked.

Wally looked up.

"Yes—on Saturday."

"I twust there is nothin' w'ong?"

"Nothing at all," answered Wally. "I'll tell you, if you like."

"I should be honahed by your confidence, Buntah!" said the swell of St. Jim's graciously.

"Mr. Penman's changed his plans—not without my agreeing, of course. His son is going to take charge of a branch of the business they're opening in Paris, and I'm to go with him. My French is A 1, you know."

"Bai Jove! Is it?" gasped Arthur Augustus. "I—I didn't know——"

Wally chuckled.

"You wouldn't know, under the circs," he said; "but it is. It's a big opening for me—no end of chances—and better than the post Mr. Penman had in his eye for me. Of course, I've accepted. It's the chance of a lifetime, and jolly good of the governor to give it to me. I mean to work jolly hard, and show that I'm worth what they're giving me."

"That is a vewy pwopah wesolution, Buntah. I—I twust you will be able to stick to it."

And Wally chuckled again. There was no doubt that he would stick to his resolution, whatever might have been the case with Billy Bunter.

The next morning there was a letter in the rack for Bunter. He opened it rather eagerly, as he saw that it was addressed in the hand of Harry Wharton of the Greyfriars Remove.

"Oh, my only sainted aunt!" he ejaculated, as he glanced over the letter.

"The game's given away! Well, it doesn't matter now!"

His eye lingered on a paragraph in the letter:

"We know all about it now, and Billy Bunter has owned up. Snoop seems to have known it all along. You bounder, I never heard of such a trick! But you're forgiven, and we shall be jolly glad to see you next time you can come along to Greyfriars—in your own name this time."

"Good old Wharton!" murmured Wally Bunter. "I must drop in and see them before I leave England. And—and I'm glad it's out! I can explain to the fellows here now, and not leave them thinking that that fat bounder was me!"

And after lessons that day Bunter of the Fourth dropped in at Study No. 6, where he found Blake & Co. and the Terrible Three at tea.

Seven forefingers pointed to the door, and seven voices pronounced in unison one expressive word:

"Cut!"

Wally Bunter did not cut. He grinned, and came into the study, and closed the door after him.

"I've got something to tell you fellows," he said calmly. "It's rather a secret—at least, the masters are not to know. I believe you don't think me such a worm as you did up to yesterday——"

"Well, that's true," said Tom Merry. "You seem to have changed, somehow. But what are you driving at?"

"I'm changed a lot," chuckled Wally—"lock, stock, and barrel! You see, I'm not the same person!"

"What?"

"Bai Jove!"

Tom Merry fairly blinked at the fat junior as he went on to explain the little game that had been played. Arthur Augustus' eyeglass seemed glued upon Wally Bunter, and his mouth was wide open—the first time it had ever been seen thus—so astonished was he.

"So, you see," Wally wound up, as the juniors gasped, "I'm me, and the other chap was my cousin Billy. He busted our agreement, and made me come here in a hurry. But it doesn't matter, as it turns out, as I'm leaving on Saturday. The Greyfriars chaps know now—so you may as well know. That's all!"

And he turned to the door.

Arthur Augustus D'Arcy jumped up and caught him by a fat arm.

"Pway wemain heah, Buntah——"

"I didn't come in to tea," grinned Wally. "I'm not Billy, you know."

"You're going to stay, all the same," said Jack Blake. "I really think we ought to have guesed how it was."

"Yaas, wathah! I don't want to tell you fellows that I told you so," said Arthur Augustus, turning his eyeglass severely upon his chums. "But I must remark that I said fwom the first that Wally Buntah was a splendid chap. He saved me fwom havin' my clobbah wuined on one occasion. I must say I am surpwised at you fellows!"

"Why, you fathead," howled Lowther, "you never guessed——"

"Pway don't argue, Lowthah! You are always arguin'. Pway make woom for my fwiend Buntah to sit down, Dig. Heah you are, Wally, old chap!"

And, for once, Bunter of the Fourth was an honoured guest in Study No. 6; but it was a different Bunter, and that made all the difference.

. . . .

Wally Bunter's time was passed most agreeably during the remainder of his stay at St. Jim's; and when he left quite a little army of juniors marched to the station with him to see him off. Tom Merry & Co. were quite sorry to see him go; and it was likely to be a long time before they forgot Bunter—and Bunter!

THE END.

(Don't miss next Wednesday's Great Story of Tom Merry & Co. at St. Jim's—"RATTY JUNIOR!"—by Martin Clifford.)

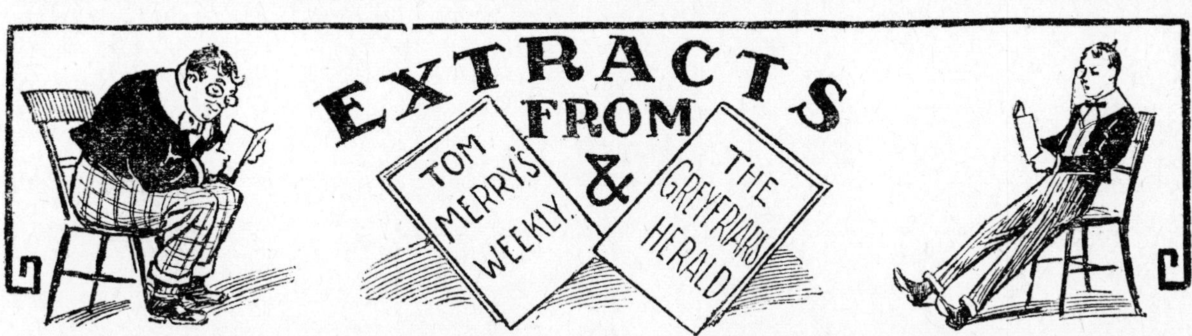

THE SLAUGHTER OF THE INNOCENTS!

An Easter Comedy at Greyfriars School. Related by S. Q. I. FIELD.

I.

EASTER, like Christmas, comes but once a year, and Harry Wharton, the President of the Remove Amateur Dramatic Society, had decided that when the first peace-time Easter came round he would hold a performance of "Hamlet"—a performance which would make the bones of Billy Shakespeare fairly rattle!

Wharton made no secret of his plans.

He pinned the following announcement on the notice-board for all the school to see:

"NOTICE!

"A full-dress rehearsal of 'HAMLET' will be held in the Common-room on Wednesday evening, at eight sharp, and the actual performance will take place in the Public Hall, Courtfield, on the following Saturday.

"Admission free!

"The principal members of the cast will be as follows:

Hamlet, Prince of Denmark ...	H. Wharton.
Claudius, King of Denmark ...	H. Vernon-Smith.
Gertrode, Queen of Denmark	W. Wibley.
Horatio, Friend to Hamlet ...	R. Cherry.
Polonius	J. Bull.
Ghost	P. Todd.
Laertes	M. Linley.
Ophelia	F. Nugent.
Bernardo	T. Brown.
Francisco	R. Rake.
Chief Grave-digger	H. J. R. Singh,

"There will be the usual collection of courtiers and other silly asses, and they are requested to keep as far away from the stage as possible.

"Greyfriars fellows are invited to roll up in their thousands!

"(Signed) HARRY WHARTON,
"President, Remove Amateur Dramatic Society."

The majority of the fellows needed no second bidding. The idea of Johnny Bull playing Polonius, and being slain behind the arras, was in itself a super-attraction; and Peter Todd as Ghost, to say nothing of Inky playing the part of Chief Grave-digger, would be sights to see and wonder at.

Long before eight o'clock on the fateful evening the Common-room was packed; and when the curtain went up there was a babel of applause:

"On the ball, there!"

"Don't trip over the battlements!"

"Ha, ha, ha!"

The opening went with a swing—until the ghost appeared.

Peter Todd tripped across the stage at a very unghostlike pace, and became hopelessly entangled in his robes.

"What do you think you're doing, fathead?" hissed Wharton.

"Me? I—I'm the ghost of your murdered father!"

"Shurrup, you ass! You've got it all wrong!"

"Me lord," said Bob Cherry, turning to Hamlet, "this is the same spook that Brown and Rake—I mean, Bernardo and Francisco—saw when we were keeping watch last night!"

"You burbling jabberwock!" muttered Wharton fiercely. "Those aren't Shakespeare's words!"

"Sorry! I was forgetting."

"Well, don't keep butting in, for goodness' sake! Half the audience are in hysterics already!"

Thus admonished, the wretched Horatio slunk to the back of the stage, and was no more seen.

Meanwhile, Peter Todd sorted himself out, and the players settled down once more.

Johnny Bull, in a flowing beard, was a great success. He gave Laertes—alias Mark Linley—his blessing, and bundled him off to France; and everything went swimmingly.

When the time came for Hamlet to despatch Polonius to his happy hunting-ground, however, he did it with such unnecessary violence that Johnny Bull roared with anguish for quite a long time after his death.

Inky proved an admirable Grave-digger.

He wielded the spade with great vigour, scattering dirt over everybody on the stage, and keeping the audience in roars of laughter.

But the greatest scene of all—the duel between Hamlet and Laertes—was the audience's chief delight.

All the time the duel was in progress there were weird noises going on underneath the platform; but in the excitement of seeing several people poisoned, and several more slain with the sword, nobody took much notice.

The stage was littered with players in recumbent attitudes, either dead or in the act of dying; and Hamlet himself was preparing to chuck in his mit.

He turned wearily to Horatio.

"'Absent thee from felicity awhile,
And in this harsh world draw thy breath
in pain
To tell my story.'"

Bang!

Something in the nature of an earthquake followed.

The entire platform suddenly collapsed, and king, queen, prince, and courtiers went toppling down to destruction.

Clouds of dust arose, and wild shrieks from the unfortunate players.

Then the curtain was hastily rung down, and the members of the audience hugged each other in the last stage of hysterics.

II.

"WE'VE been let down horribly!" said Wharton.

"In more senses than one!" groaned Bob Cherry.

As soon as they had recovered from the terrific collapse which had crowned the rehearsal, the performers set to work to try and discover who had caused the calamity.

They found that the wooden supports underneath the platform had been sawn through while the play was in progress.

But there was not a sign or a shadow of the practical jokers.

"Who is responsible for this rotten trick?" exclaimed Wharton.

"Coker, of course!" growled Johnny Bull. "Every time we get up a play Coker tries to muck it up. I've noticed that he's been cackling like a hyena for the last day or two!"

"My hat! Come to think of it, I've noticed the same thing!" said Bob Cherry. "Coker's at the bottom of this bizney right enough!"

Wharton nodded.

"There's only one thing to be done," he said. "We must go along and slaughter the bounders!"

"In full force!" said Nugent. "We'll smash their study, and their chivvies into the bargain! They make my blood boil!"

So the Remove players massed themselves together, and marched away to Coker's study in the Fifth Form passage.

Coker, Potter, and Greene were there; and they sprang to their feet in astonishment as the invaders trooped in.

"What the thump——" began Coker.

"Explain yourself, you cad!" said Harry Wharton warmly. "What do you mean by it?"

"You cheeky young ass!" snorted Coker. "Have you suddenly gone potty?"

"You won't wriggle out of it by pretending you're innocent!" said Nugent. "We guessed you'd deny it, as a matter of fact. Come on, you fellows! Sock it into 'em!"

"Why, you—you——" spluttered Coker.

"Pile in!" said Wharton. "We won't stand on ceremony!"

The Removites stood on a good many other things, though. They swept the mantelpiece clear, and trampled vases and pictures underfoot. They wrenched the chairs asunder; they hurled the table at the bookcase, with disastrous results to both; and by the time they had finished the study was in a state of absolute chaos.

Coker & Co. put up a desperate defence, of course; but they were hopelessly outnumbered.

"Now," said Wharton, catching up a cricket-stump, "hold these beauties down, some of you, while I wallop 'em!"

The "walloping" was carried through with great thoroughness, and Bob Cherry likened the performance to the beating of carpets.

Coker had his dose first, then Potter, and lastly Greene; and all three of them got it hot. Their yells of rage and pain were sufficient to awaken the celebrated Seven Sleepers.

Somewhat consoled by having let off steam to this extent, the avengers dispersed.

The Famous Five went along to Study No. 1.

On the table was a note, in the unmistakable handwriting of Temple of the Fourth.

It ran as follows:

"You must give us best over what happened this evening. We scored off you a treat! THE FOURTH."

The Famous Five stared at each other blankly.

"Oh, help!" gasped Bob Cherry. "It was Temple & Co. all the time!"

"And we've been and slaughtered Coker!"

"Oh dear!"

"Oh crumbs!"

"We were on the wrong track!"

"We've properly put our foot in it—or, rather, both feet!" said Harry Wharton. "For once in a way the innocent have suffered for the guilty. Coker & Co. got it in the neck for something they know nothing about!"

"However, we needn't reproach ourselves," said Nugent. "They've done dozens of things for which they've never been bowled out, so they only got their just deserts."

"All the same, I think it's up to us to apologise," said Wharton. "Poor old Coker! Ha, ha, ha!"

Coker accepted the apology with very ill grace. And the three Fifth-Formers showed a strange reluctance to sit down for several days afterwards!

* * * * * * *

In due course the real performance of "Hamlet" took place in Courtfield before a packed house.

Bob Cherry had mastered his part by this time, and he made no further lapse into very modern English.

Peter Todd, too, was careful not to trip over his robes; and the duel scene in the last act was got through without mishap.

The Greyfriars fellows were there to a man, and there was no further attempt on the part of Temple & Co. to wreck the performance. The Fourth-Formers had certainly spoilt the rehearsal, but they drew the line at spoiling the actual show.

The play was a stunning success from start to finish.

The Remove had intended to wreak vengeance on Temple & Co.; but they were so delighted at the complete success of the performance that they agreed to Bob Cherry's suggestion to bury the hatchet.

And when the amateur actors trooped back to Greyfriars in the cool of the evening they told themselves that Easter had turned up trumps after all.

Coker & Co. thought otherwise. But what they said about it would make the printing-machine go on strike!

THE END.

TUBBY & LANKY, THE TERRIBLE TWINS.

Drawn by JACK BLAKE of St. Jim's.

CASH ON DELIVERY

Some Interesting Correspondence.

[EDITOR'S NOTE.—The following interesting correspondence has been excavated from the ruins of Study No. 7 after a raid on that apartment by the Famous Five. We are publishing it herewith, as it gives one a good insight into the life and character of William George Bunter.]

I.

"FROM Master W. G. Bunter to the Boneshaker Bicycle Co., Ltd., London.

"Deer Sirs,—I have seen your advertissmeant in the 'Weekly Welsher,' offering a number of your famus Boneshaker bikes for sail.

"I am grately in need of a bike. The other feloes at this skool are an awfully mean lot, and they won't lend me theirs, becaws they say that my grate wate smashes the saddel in.

"Pleese send me won of your bikes (katalog price ten kwid), and address it to:

W. G. BUNTER, ESQ.,
Friardale Station,
Kent,

to be called for.

"I will let you have the money on reseat of my next remittans from my tytled rellations.

"Hopeing you are kwite well, as it leeves me at pressant,

"Yours trewly,
"W. G. BUNTER."

Printed and published every Wednesday by the Proprietors, the Amalgamated Press, Limited, The Fleetway House, Farringdon Street, London, E.C. 4. Advertisement offices: The Fleetway House, Farringdon Street, London, E.C. 4. Subscription rates: Inland and abroad (except South Africa and Australasia), 8s. 10d. per annum, 4s. 5d. for six months. Sole agents for South Africa: The Central News Agency, Ltd. Sole agents for Australia and New Zealand: Messrs. Gordon & Gotch, Ltd.; and for Canada: The Imperial News Co., Ltd.—Saturday, April 26th, 1919. N

II.

"From the Boneshaker Bicycle Co., Ltd., to the Headmaster, Greyfriars School.

"Dear Sir,—We are in receipt of a letter from W. G. Bunter, one of your pupils, who contemplates the purchase of one of our celebrated machines, value ten pounds.

"Before executing this order we should be glad if you would kindly inform us whether Master Bunter is in a position to pay for the bicycle.

"Might we take this opportunity of drawing your attention to our wonderful self-starting, three-speed, umpteen-horse-power, eighteen-carat bicycles, stamped in every link, jewelled in every movement?

"You are doubtless advanced in years, but this would not prevent your skimming along the roads like a swallow.

"DON'T DELAY! ORDER TO-DAY!

"We remain, dear sir,

"Your obedient servants,

"THE BONESHAKER BICYCLE CO.,

"per pro A. BEESTLY-CROCK,

"Manager."

III.

"From the Headmaster, Greyfriars School, to the Boneshaker Bicycle Co., Ltd., London.

"Sirs,—In reply to your communication, I regret to state that I do not consider Master Bunter sufficiently sound, either financially or physically, to receive one of your bicycles.

"With regard to your suggestion that I should avail myself of one of your machines, let me at once state that I decline to do so. I heard of a gentleman at Courtfield who was once misguided enough to purchase a bicycle from you and experiment upon it. They buried him in the local cemetery.

"Not only are your machines unsound, unstable, and unreliable, but they place the rider in a position of grave peril. I have no wish to be cut off untimely from a world which, although it harbours knaves and rogues, is well worth remaining in.

"Yours truly,

"HERBERT H. LOCKE."

IV.

"From Master W. G. Bunter, Greyfriars School, to the Boneshaker Bicycle Co., Ltd., London.

"Deer Sirs,—I am very indiggnant to find, after waiting pashuntly for menny days, that you have not yet sent the bike.

"Every day I have been to the station, but there has been no sine or shaddo of a bike. Is it never kumming?

"If it's the money that's trubbling you, I give you my word of onner that I will pay you the ten kwids as soon as my postal-order arives.

"Pleese shake a legg!

"Yours trewly,

"W. G. BUNTER.

"P.S.—Buck up with the bike!

"P.P.S.—Send it by passinger trane.

"P.P.PS.—Don't forget to send it 'karridge pade.'"

V.

"From the Boneshaker Bicycle Co., Ltd., London, to Master W G. Bunter, Greyfriars School.

"Sir,—We have had your letter translated, and, in reply, beg to state that it is impossible for us to despatch you the bicycle on account of your alleged impecuniosity.

"You will kindly refrain from troubling us again on this subject.

"Yours truly,

"THE BONESHAKER BICYCLE CO.,

"per pro. A. S. WINDLER,

"Assistant-Manager."

VI.

(Postcard.)

"From Master W. G. Bunter, Greyfriars School, to the Boneshaker Bicycle Co., Ltd., London.

"Yah! Beests!! Frawds!!! Spoofers!!!!

"GO AND EAT COKE!

"W. G. BUNTER."

The Editor's Chat.

The Companion Papers are:

THE MAGNET. Every Monday. **THE BOYS' FRIEND.** Every Monday. **THE GEM.** Every Wed. **THE PENNY POPULAR.** Every Friday. **CHUCKLES.** Every Friday.

YOUR EDITOR IS ALWAYS GLAD TO HEAR FROM HIS READERS.

EASTER GREETINGS TO ALL!

On the occasion of this, the first peace-time Easter, let me convey to all my chums—boys and girls; yes, and the old folks, too!—my sincere good wishes for a merry time. With the loyal aid of Mr. Martin Clifford, I have done my utmost to make this week's issue of the GEM Library contribute to the delights of Bank Holiday. Our space for reading-matter is still very restricted, but I have endeavoured to make this Easter Number as bright and enjoyable as possible.

EXIT BILLY BUNTER!

Billy Bunter has now left St. Jim's, and the school is the richer for his loss.

For next Wednesday we have:

"RATTY JUNIOR!"
By Martin Clifford.

Mr. Martin Clifford's renown as a humorous writer will extend yet further through the medium of this magnificent long complete story of the chums of St. Jim's.

Mr. Ratcliff, the sour, ill-tempered master of the New House, is expecting his nephew Bartholomew to arrive at the school, and he sends Figgins & Co. to meet the new boy. Figgins & Co., in turn, send Gussy; and the swell of St. Jim's puts his foot in it—in fact, both feet! Anyway,

"RATTY JUNIOR!"

has a most painful and surprising reception; and, as a result, Figgins & Co. get it "in the neck" for not having carried out Mr. Ratcliff's instructions in the first instance.

This is a refreshing story, brimful of fun and comedy, and the boy or girl who misses it is missing a real good thing!

THROUGH FIRE AND FLAME!
Coolness and Pluck at a Big Public School.

Some of the more critical of my readers are inclined to scoff at the idea of a big school being threatened with destruction by fire. They are apt to regard such incidents as far-fetched and impossible.

Before me is a letter from G. R. K., of Winchester, who writes:

"I am greatly enjoying your serial in the 'Magnet' entitled 'Goggs, Grammarian,' but I must say that the author shows a lamentable ignorance if he imagines his readers will swallow the absurd statement that Franklingham School was destroyed by fire. In some of your stories this 'fire, flame, and fury' business is carried to excess. I am at a big public school myself, and I know for a fact that such fires seldom or never happen."

Since writing this letter my Winchester chum will probably have seen the account of the great fire which recently occurred at Wellington College, and he will modify his views.

The fire in question was a gigantic blaze, and could be seen for many miles around. The coolness of the boys, and the plucky part played by one of the masters, were the outstanding features. The newspaper reports do not enlarge upon these two facts; and one does not wonder why. Coolness and pluck in a crisis are just what we may expect from British schoolboys, and from men who are responsible for their education.

The fire started in the wing in which the Orange, Blucher, Anglesey, and Beresford dormitories are situated. The Orange and Blucher dormitories, on the top floor, were burnt out; and the others, on the floor beneath, as well as some of the class-rooms on the ground-floor, were damaged by water.

About seventy boys who slept in the Orange and Blucher dormitories lost most of their personal belongings. The fire was detected by a porter, who saw smoke coming from the dormitories. He ran to the top of the water-tower and rang the alarm-bell. He was in danger of being overpowered by the smoke, but Mr. Whitehead, an assistant-master, dashed into the burning wing and assisted him down.

For an hour or two the fate of the college was in the balance. The school fire-brigade got to work promptly, but was unable to make much headway against the flames, which burst from the dormitory windows and through the roof, and could be seen for many miles around. Motor fire-engines arrived from Wokingham, Reading, Camberley, Guildford, Aldershot, and Broadmoor, and saved the situation.

The boys took the affair very calmly. One said, "Never mind about our things being burnt so long as we get a day off to-morrow!" His comrade straightway wagered him six doughnuts that lessons would carry on as usual—and he won!

The headmaster said that all the boys whose bed-rooms had been destroyed would be accommodated in the sanatorium, the class-rooms, or the masters' Houses.

"No one was hurt," he added, "and the usual evening service was held. Classes will be as usual to-morrow."

The parents of many of the boys were staying for the week-end at an hotel close by. They were at luncheon when they heard the fire-bell, and, rushing out, went to find if their sons were safe.

Fortunately, they were; and the great fire of Wellington is by this time only a memory.

SHOULD FATTY WYNN SPEAK IN WELSH?

Some of my Welsh chums seem to think he should, anyway. This is what one of them says:

"The boys of Talysarn, North Wales, would be extremely obliged, Mr. Editor, if you would persuade Mr. Martin Clifford to make Fatty Wynn speak in his native tongue.

"I am a Welsh boy, and if I can help I will do so with pleasure.

"ydwyf,
"yn gywir ac.
"yn ffyddlon,
"TREVOR WYNN OWEN."

I am afraid my English and Scottish readers would not take kindly to this idea at all; so Fatty Wynn must continue to talk in an intelligible manner. Why, if he started spouting in Welsh, the result would be worse than Grundy's spelling!

EVERYBODY'S HAPPY!

At least, they seem to be, if my postbag is any criterion. Not since happy pre-war days have I received such a budget of cheery letters.

Allan H., of Sheerness, bursts forth as follows:

"Dear Editor,—To-day is Wednesday, and the sun is shining, and the blue sky is out, and so I feel all merry and bright!"

Perhaps the fact that the GEM is out as well has something to do with it. Anyway, Allan H. feels so bucked with life that he sends me a crowd of drawings, which he assures me he did alone and unaided. One of them shows Wells and Beckett scrapping in the ring; another shows Arthur Augustus D'Arcy in one of his elegant attitudes; but the masterpiece of them all is a fearful and wonderful picture entitled "Emile Cottin's Attempt on the French Premier's Life." I am glad my chum explains what the subject is. Had he not done so I should have thought it was a bomb-raid on Cologne!

(Continued on page 16.)

However, Allan H. is probably very young, and as time goes on his work will improve. In fact, he may one day become the GEM Library's special artist. Who knows?

THERE'S A GREAT TIME COMING, BOYS!

Superstitious people will say that Friday is an unlucky day; but if they buy the "Penny Popular" week by week, and read the splendid stories of school-life contained therein, they will change their minds.

The circulation of the merry little "Pop" has already reached heights which make one's head turn dizzy; but it will soar yet higher in the near future because of a new and altogether unprecedented feature which will shortly be introduced. I may not at present divulge what this new feature is; but all my chums should make a point of buying the "Penny Pop" each week and endeavouring to solve the great secret themselves!

Weekly papers for boys continue to wax and wane, but

THE "PENNY POP" IS STILL ON TOP!

NOTICES.

Correspondence, etc., Wanted by—

G. Britton, 4, Rossiter's Lane, St. George, Bristol—with readers interested in geology.

Ernest Gundry, Unley, 24, Donald Street, North Brunswick, Melbourne, Victoria, Australia—with readers, about 17, in British Isles.

Chas. Findlay, 15, Glebe Street, Hobart, Tasmania—with readers in China, India, West Indies, West Africa, and Canada, interested in stamp-collecting.

James Eccles, 11, James Street, Preston, Lancs—with readers anywhere, especially those interested in amateur magazines. He would like to hear from Albert E. Thompson, South Wales.

H. Lambert, 141, Berners Street, Leicester, wants 100 members over 14 for GEM and "Magnet" League. Magazine monthly. Stamped addressed envelope.

Miss Lucy Wilkinson, 30, Alexander Street, Nelson, Lancs—with girl readers anywhere, 15-16.

T. Doyle, 38, Henry Street, Newport, Mon—with readers anywhere.

Miss Eileen Lawford, 1, Milton Street, West Hartlepool—with girl readers, 17 or over.

Charles H. Smith, 16, Chapel Street, Port Elizabeth, South Africa—with readers anywhere.

Victor G. Vivash, Waverley Road, East Caulfield, Melbourne, Victoria, Australia—with readers in Africa and England interested in photography.

Norman Stockton, Paraparap, Darwin, Northern Territory, Australia—with readers in United Kingdom, Canada, and the States.

Miss Joyce E. Warr, 63, Linda Crescent, Glenferrie, Victoria, Australia, wants members, 11-12, outside Victoria, for Girls' Own Correspondence Club.

G. Hollingworth, 1, Hardwick Terrace, Norton Road, Stockton-on-Tees, wants advertisements for amateur magazine. Stamped addressed envelope.

A. O., 23, Lillie Mansions, Lillie Road, Fulham, S.W. 6, wants hectograph jelly in good condition. State price. Envelope, please.

J. Howell, 236, Smithdown Lane, Edge Hill, Liverpool, wants members for correspondence club and amateur magazine. Addressed, stamped envelope.

Miss Hilda Opie, 24, Coventry Street, Upper Stoke, Coventry—with girl readers, 17, in Winnipeg.

Miss Nellie Mahoney, 87, George Street, Redfern, Sydney, New South Wales, Australia—with girl readers in British Islands or America.

A. Howden, 116, Rose Street, So. Lane, Edinburgh—with readers, 16-17, overseas, preferably North and South America.

Jack Kendall, 6, Thackray Street, Highroad Well, Halifax, Yorks, would like to contribute to amateur magazines, sports and athletics. Specimen copies asked for.

M. G. Clay, Manor Farm, Over Hadden, near Bakewell, Derbyshire—with readers anywhere.

Percy Rossiter, 23, White Road, Vicarage Lane, Stratford, E. 15, wants members for serious amateur theatricals.

Miss Maude Cook, 2, Essex Grove, Forest Road, Walthamstow, Essex—with readers anywhere.

Miss Agnes Rhynas, 47, St. Mary Road, Hoe Street, Walthamstow, Essex—with readers overseas.

Ned Sullivan, 66, Pasquier Road, Forest Road, Walthamstow, E.—with readers anywhere.

F. Wirtz, 12, Tavistock Place, Bloomsbury, W.C. 1, wants members for correspondence club and magazine—not on pass-round system.

John McGrau, 20, Carr Street, Stockton-on-Tees, wants readers for the "Universal Amateur Magazine." Post free, 3½d.

Miss L. Betts, The Beehive Inn, Henry Street, Chatham—with readers, 14-16, in America or Australia.

C. Morland, c/o Mrs. Kramer, 729H, Vandiventer Avenue, St. Louis, Montana, U.S.A., wants members for International Correspondence Club.

Jimmy King—13 years—32, Barnsbury Street, Barnsbury, N.—with readers of his own age, about the GEM and "Magnet" stories.

Arthur Griffiths, 5, Evans Street, Newport, Mon—with readers anywhere.

M. G. Hall, 54, Burley Lodge Road, Leeds, wants members for club, 10 miles of Leeds. Stamped addressed envelope.

C. A. Sherlaw, 3, Argyle Terrace, Porterfield, Inverness—with readers anywhere.

T. Ffrench, 6, Castlewood Avenue, Rathmines, Dublin, wants members for the Irish Amateur Press Association.

J. Howell, 236, Smithdown Lane, Edge Hill, Liverpool, wants members for correspondence club and amateur magazine.

F. C. Mulan, 164, Replingham Road, London, S.W. 18—with readers anywhere, 15½.

Amateur writers wanted for the International Amateur Press Club. Three magazines free monthly.—Joseph Parks, 38, Garnet Street, Saltburn-by-the-Sea, Yorks.

Jack Cully, 20, Villiers Street, Murton S.O., Durham, will contribute stories to amateur magazines.

S. Jackson, Police Station, Kemble, Gloucestershire—with readers anywhere.

Alfred E. C. Waugh, 3, Station Terrace, Haydon Bridge, Northumberland—with readers, 11-13, anywhere.

W. Duncan, 25, Beechfield Street, Cheetham Hill, Manchester, wants members for Stamp Exchange. Overseas readers especially invited; magazine, competitions, and prizes.

H. Swindells, 10, Vernon Street, Buxton Road, Macclesfield, offers advice to readers about amateur magazines.

Percy Gritten, 354, Beresford Avenue, Runnymede, West Toronto, Canada—with readers anywhere interested in postcards.

Miss Dorothy Davies, 15, Queen's Road, Chester, Ladies' Branch, Junior Arts Club, would like to hear of new members. Headquarters, E. Acott, 57, White Lion Street, Angel, Islington, London, N. 1.

B. Porter, 4, Percy Street, Fleetwood, Lancs—with readers abroad, 13-16, interested in stamps and photography.

Miss Winifred Lax, 1, Throston Street, West Hartlepool—with readers, 17 and over, anywhere.

Miss Ethel Cattermole, 3, Suggitt Street, West Hartlepool, Durham, with readers anywhere.

Frederick W. Archer, 53, Victoria Avenue, Tottenham, London, N. 17—with readers in stamp-collecting.

Miss Dorothy Barnes, 304, Burley Road, Leeds—with readers anywhere, 13-14.

Miss Curly Gibson, c/o 4, Cedar Road, Tottenham, London, N. 17—with readers in South Africa, 17 and over.

Miss Nance Carver, 85, Chester Road, West Hartlepool—with girl readers anywhere.

Hugh Stewart, 11, Burnbank Terrace, Lenzie, Dumbarton—with readers anywhere.

J. W. Penn, 125, Dartmouth Park Hill, Highgate, London, N. 19—with readers in foreign countries interested in stamps.

W. McNally, Glenview, Glenluce, Wigtownshire, Scotland, wants readers for amateur magazine. Copy, 2d., post free.

H. Ward, 28, Wansbeck Gardens, West Hartlepool, wants contributors for magazine—photograph exchange, etc.

W. McL. Sigston, 62, Enbridge Street, Salford, and A. B. Green, 32, Robertson Street, Weaste, Manchester, want members for their correspondence club. Stamped, addressed envelope.

Ronald Else, 7, Stolewood Terrace, Smedley Street, West Matlock, Derbyshire—with readers anywhere.

G. Mogridge, 35, Argyle Street, Swansea, South Wales—with readers anywhere.

W. Summerell, 38, Belle Vue Road, Bell Hill, St. George, Bristol—with a French boy. Would like to hear from Wm. Bezodis.

U. Carey, 1, Carpenters Yard, Tredegar, Mon., wants foreign coins (not French). Write, stating price.

C. M. Cowie, 46, King Edward's Road, Swansea—with readers anywhere, 16-18.

Thomas Reddan, 24, Irvine Street, Port Elizabeth, South Africa—with readers overseas.

C. D. Lea, c/o Brameld & Smith, 4, Cannon Street, Manchester—with a French reader.

Miss W. is anxious to have an answer from George.

Miss Joyce E. Bell, 12, Frank Street, Roker, Sunderland—with girl readers in the Colonies, aged 13.

N. J. Leaf, 66, Kenilworth Road, Handsworth, Birmingham, wants members for Junior Stamp Exchange Club.

Miss Marjorie Baugh, 50, Victoria Street, Clifton, Bristol—with girl readers interested in the cinema. All letters answered.

Football.

Boys wanted in Lewisham district to form a football club for next season, 15-16.—L. Williams, Blessington Road, Lee, S.E. 13.

Hugh Stewart, 11, Burnbank Terrace, Lenzie, by Glasgow, wants football fixtures in Glasgow district; ages 14-18.

Cricket.

ST. JAMES', CARDIFF—17—12 miles, home and away.—H. W. Tutcher, 16, Hendy Street, Roath Park, Cardiff.

H. A. H. (YOUR EDITOR.)

GRAND EASTER NUMBER!

THE RETURN OF THE NATIVE!

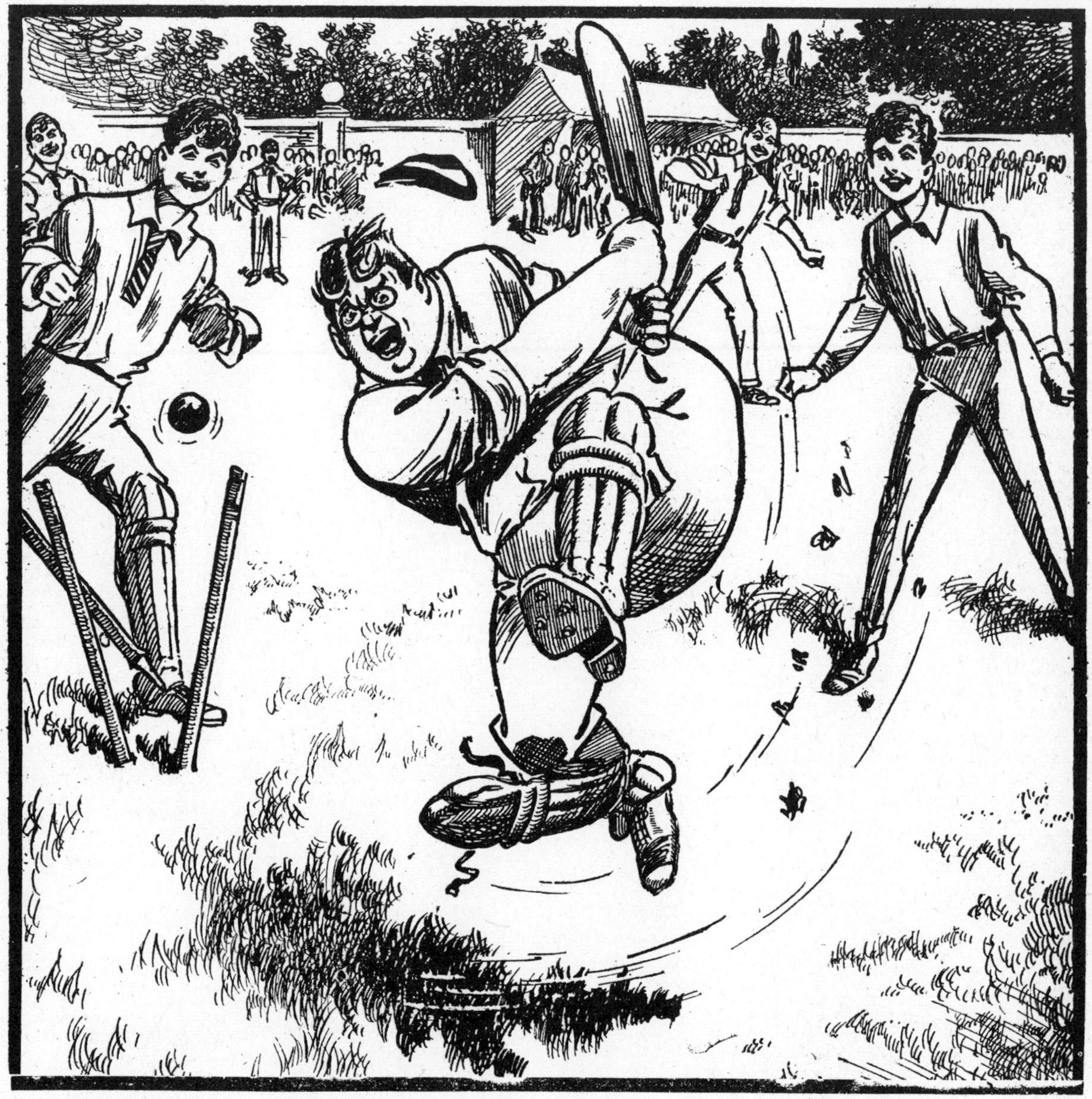

BILLY BUNTER—THE HOPE OF HIS SIDE!

(A Screamingly Funny Scene in the Long, Complete School Tale contained in this Number.) 26-4-19

The Return of the Native!

A Magnificent Long, Complete Story of
HARRY WHARTON & CO. AT GREYFRIARS SCHOOL.

BY FRANK RICHARDS.

THE FIRST CHAPTER.
Bunter's Appointment!

"BUNTER!"

Bunter of the Remove was making for the gates when Harry Wharton called out rather sharply.

Bunter did not seem to hear.

He rolled on towards the gates, quickening his pace a little.

"Bunter!" shouted Wharton.

Still the fat junior did not turn his head. It seemed that Bunter of the Remove was suddenly afflicted with deafness.

"Bunter!" roared the captain of the Remove.

And then, as the fat junior did not heed, Wharton rushed in pursuit. He overtook Bunter in the gateway, and caught him by a fat shoulder.

Bunter had to stop then.

He spun round on Wharton's sudden grip, and stood blinking at the captain of the Remove over his big glasses with a red face and a guilty expression.

"Didn't you hear me?" demanded Wharton.

"H'm—ahem——"

"Where are you off to?"

"I—I—I'm going out!" stammered the fat junior.

"You're jolly well not!" exclaimed Wharton warmly. "You're coming along to cricket practice!"

"You—you see——"

"Blessed if I ever heard of such cheek!" exclaimed Wharton. "Haven't I put your name down for the Remove Eleven for the first match of the season?"

"It's jolly good of you! But——"

"And here you are mooching off and dodging practice, and pretending not to hear me when I yell after you!" exclaimed Wharton indignantly. "What do you mean by it, you fat bounder?"

Bunters fat face became redder.

He evidently found it difficult to explain.

"Dont' you want to play against Redclyffe to-morrow?" demanded Harry.

"Oh yes! Yes, rather!"

"And do you think you're such a topping cricketer that you don't need any practice?"

"Nunno."

"Then come along!" said Wharton gruffly.

"I—I've got to go," stammered Bunter. "The—the fact is, I—I've got to meet a chap——"

"Bother the chap!"

"It's my cousin!" blurted out the fat junior.

"Oh!" Wharton looked a little more amiable. "Your cousin Wally, do you mean—your cousin at St. Jim's?"

The fat junior grinned.

"My cousin at St. Jim's," he assented. "He—he's come over to see me. I got his letter this morning, saying he would come to-day."

"Well, he'll come here, I suppose? Are you meeting him at the station?"

"Nunno."

"We'll be jolly glad to see him," said Harry. "We all like the chap. You've grown a good deal more like him, Bunty, since the time he was here on a visit."

"Oh!"

"I don't mean to look at. You were as like as two peas to look at any time," said Harry. "I mean in your ways. F'rinstance, if anybody had told me last term that I should be playing Billy Bunter in the Remove Eleven I should have thought he was off his dot."

"W-w-would you?"

"Oh, yes, rather! But you've turned out a good man, both at footer and cricket," said Wharton. "It seems like a giddy miracle; but it is so, and there's no denying it."

Bunter of the Remove grinned again.

He was wondering whether the Greyfriars fellows would ever guess that he was Wally Bunter, and not Billy Bunter at all, and that the two fat cousins had taken advantage of their remarkable resemblance to change schools.

It was such an unheard-of scheme that it was not surprising that no one "tumbled" to it, though the change in the supposed Billy was always causing surprise in the Greyfriars Remove.

"Well, if Wally's coming here we'll be glad to see him," continued Wharton. "Is he staying the night?"

"I—I hope not——"

"What?"

"I—I mean, I think not."

"If you've got to go and meet him, bring him along as soon as you can," said Wharton. "You simply must put in some practice to-day, Bunter. How long will you be?"

"I—I don't know."

"What rot! Think a minute!"

"The—the fact is——" stammered the unhappy impostor.

"Well, what is the fact? What are you stammering about?"

"The—the fact—the fact is——"

"Well?"

"The—the fact is——"

"Is that a game?" asked Wharton. "Are you wound up, or are you understudying a parrot?"

"The—the fact is, my cousin isn't coming to Greyfriars," stammered Wally. "I hope he's going straight back to St. Jim's—I mean, I think he is—that is to say, I—I'm just meeting him in the village for a—a—a jaw, that's all."

"I don't see why he can't come on to the school," said Wharton, in surprise. "He knows he's always welcome."

"Ye-es; but—but there's reasons——"

"Oh, all right! It's his bizney, I suppose. Get back in time for some practice at the nets if you can."

"I—I will."

"Hallo, hallo, hallo!" came the stentorian tones of Bob Cherry. "Are you coming, Wharton? We're waiting for you!"

"I'm coming."

Harry Wharton joined his chums, and Wally Bunter, in great relief at escaping further questioning, rolled out of the gates. The role he was playing at Greyfriars weighed upon him a little sometimes.

"Bunter going out?" asked Johnny Bull, as the Famous Five walked down to Little Side.

"Yes; it seems that his cousin is coming over from St. Jim's."

"Good! We'll be glad to see him!" said Frank Nugent heartily.

"The gladfulness will be terrific!"

"He's not coming here. Billy's meeting him in the village. Blessed if I quite understand Bunter," said Harry. "He doesn't seem to waste much affection on his relations. He's always dodging his minor in the Second Form. And the other day he was no end worried because his sister Bessie was coming here to see him. Now he seems quite bothered because his cousin's coming to see him from St. Jim's, and he won't bring him here. And his cousin Wally is a really splendid chap!"

"One of the best!" said Bob Cherry. "I think he has a good influence on our merry Bunter, too. Billy's no end improved since the time Wally stayed here on a visit."

"No doubt about that!" agreed Wharton. "Well, here we are!"

And the Bunters were dismissed from the minds of the Famous Five of the Remove, as they devoted their attention to the great game of cricket.

THE SECOND CHAPTER.
Rather Sudden!

WALLY BUNTER'S fat brow was contracted in a deep frown as he rolled away down the lane towards Friardale.

The fat junior was worried.

He had been so keen to come to Greyfriars, among the fellows he had learned to like, that he had fallen in cheerfully with Billy Bunter's hare-brained scheme of changing places. It had been easy enough, though difficulties had cropped up at times.

So far, only Snoop of the Remove had found out the secret, and he was friendly with Wally Bunter, and was keeping dark what he had discovered—and, indeed, had helped Wally to avoid a meeting with Billy's sister Bessie, which would have been perilous for the spoofer.

No one else had a suspicion—not even Sammy Bunter of the Second Form, partly owing to Wally's sedulous care in avoiding his attractive society.

But, glad as Wally was to be at Greyfriars, there were worries attached to the role he was playing. Billy Bunter was a very unreliable personage. The agreement had been that they should change places for the whole term; but of late Billy Bunter had written rather frequently letters full of complaints about St. Jim's. Apparently he had not found his new school so delightful a place as he had anticipated.

And now this sudden visit looked as if Billy was tired of the change, and wanted to change back. Which was not gratifying to Wally, who had succeeded at last in living down Billy's unenviable reputation, and was getting on famously in the Remove.

Wally turned off the road before entering the village, and walked into the woods, where the trees were glimmering with the green of spring. He stopped under a big oak, and looked about him.

"Late, of course!" he grunted.

Billy Bunter could always be depended upon to be late.

Wally paced to and fro under the oak, with his hands in his pockets, and the frown deepening on his face. He was thinking of the cricket-ground at Greyfriars, where he was wanted, and where he wanted to be.

It was just like William George Bunter to keep him hanging about like this, he reflected wrathfully.

He had been under the big oak about half an hour when a fat figure came through the trees.

The new-comer was so exactly like Wally Bunter to look at that at the first glance it would have been difficult to tell one from the other.

At the second glance, however, it would have been noted that Wally Bunter looked much fresher and more fit than his cousin. Fat as he was, he was fit as a fiddle, which Billy Bunter certainly was not.

There was a smear of jam about the new arrival's mouth, and a shiny look on his podgy face, and Wally Bunter could guess the cause of his delay in keeping the appointment.

"Hallo, Wally!" said Billy Bunter as he came up. "You're here!"

"I've been waiting for you half an hour!" growled Wally.

"Good! I was afraid you might keep me waiting," said Billy Bunter. "It's all right, then."

"Did you lose your train?"

"No. I shouldn't be here now if I had."

"I suppose you stopped to guzzle at Uncle Clegg's as you came by?" grunted Wally.

"I certainly stopped there for a snack," said Bunter, with dignity. "I was hungry after my journey. I don't like your tone, Wally!"

"Lump it, then!" grunted Wally.

"Look here——"

"Oh, not so much chin-wag!" said Wally. "What are you here for? That's what I want to know!"

"If you're not going to be civil——"

"Cut that out! I want to know what you're here for! I've got to get back to Greyfriars as quickly as I can!"

Billy Bunter grinned.

"You're not going back to Greyfriars!" he answered.

"What?"

Wally stared at his cousin.

"I've hooked it!" explained Billy.

"You've cleared off from St. Jim's?"

"Yes."

"Why, you—you—you silly ass!" gasped Wally. "What have you done that for?"

"I didn't find St. Jim's as I expected," said Bunter. "The fellows are not really up to my style. D'Arcy and Tom Merry and Figgins—all that lot. I've found them a lot of rotters."

"They've found you a rotter, you mean!"

"Look here, Wally!" roared Bunter. "Once and for all, I don't want any cheek from a poor relation!"

"Oh, dry up!"

Billy Bunter blinked in great wrath at his cousin through his big spectacles.

"You cheeky sweep!" he exclaimed. "Is this your gratitude?"

"Gratitude for what?" snapped Wally.

"For all that I've done for you!" said Billy Bunter warmly. "Didn't I let you take my place at Greyfriars——

"Because you'd got into trouble with a bookmaker, and wanted to shift it on to my shoulders!" said Wally hotly. "I found that out afterwards, when the man began pestering me for money. And nearly every chap in the Remove makes out that I owe him money——"

Bunter chuckled.

"Have you paid them?" he asked.

"I had to. They supposed I was you, but I couldn't act like you!" growled Wally. "I've had to square up no end of accounts you'd run up, and it's made a pretty hole in my pocket-money!"

"Good! That will see me clear!" said Bunter, with satisfaction.

"Eh?"

"Of course, I shall settle with you later," said Bunter loftily. "I hope you don't imagine for one moment that I shall remain in debt to a poor relation?"

"I jolly well do!" snorted Wally. "You know you won't pay me a cent!"

"If you take that tone, Wally, I decline to discuss the matter further. In my circle I'm accustomed to good breeding. An office chap like you wouldn't understand that, of course!"

"You—you fat Hun——"

Billy Bunter waved a fat hand at his incensed cousin.

"That's enough!" he said. "I'm going!"

"Where are you going?"

"To Greyfriars."

"And what am I going to do?" shrieked Wally.

"Anything you like!"

And with that William George Bunter walked away, with his fat little nose high in the air.

THE THIRD CHAPTER.

Billy Bunter Means Business!

"MY hat!"

Wally Bunter stared blankly after the Owl of the Remove for a moment or two. He was taken quite aback.

He had had his doubts about Billy, and it had been borne in on his mind that the peculiar arrangement would have to come to an end. But he had not expected this suddenness. Even Billy Bunter might have shown a little more consideration than this.

He stood rooted to the ground as William George walked loftily away. But only for a few moments. Then he rushed in pursuit of the Owl of the Remove, and grasped him by the shoulders.

Bump!

Billy Bunter sat down in the grass with a loud roar.

"Yarooooh!"

"Now, you fat rotter!" panted Wally.

"Yooop!"

"Gerrup!"

"Yow-ow-ow!"

"I've a jolly good mind to give you the biggest hiding you ever had in your life!" roared Wally. "What do you mean by going back on me like this? We arranged till the end of the term for——"

"Yow-ow-ow!"

"You can't go to Greyfriars to-day!"

"Yah! I'm going! Bother you! You're a low cad, Wally! Yow-ow! I despise you! Ow! Wow!"

Billy Bunter scrambled to his feet, glaring at Wally with a glare that bade fair to crack his spectacles. He shook his fat fist under his cousin's nose.

"Do you know what I've a jolly good mind to do?" he demanded. "I've a jolly good mind to give you a licking, only——"

"Go ahead!"

"Only you ain't worth a fellow soiling his hands on!" snorted Bunter.

"Jolly lucky for you!" said Wally. "Now then, don't try to roll off yet, you barrel, or I'll stop you again. We've got to have this out. Why have you bolted from St. Jim's?"

"Fed up with the place."

"Oh, I know—I know! You've borrowed all the money D'Arcy will lend you, and he's put the stopper on; you've made everybody fed up with you; and now you want to land me into it same as you did at Greyfriars!" exclaimed Wally, greatly incensed. "If I go to St. Jim's now, I shall find that I've got a reputation as juicy as the one you left for me at Greyfriars. Why can't you learn to play the game, you fat spoofer? I was an ass ever to listen to your rot!"

"I did it entirely for your sake, of course!" said Bunter.

"Rats!"

"I don't expect gratitude," continued Billy Bunter, "I'm always doing these kind actions, and never getting any gratitude. But there's such a thing as common decency, Wally. You might thank a chap."

"Oh, you—you——"

"You were going to St. Jim's—you, a bounder, who's worked for his living!" said Bunter warmly. "You'd have been a rank outsider, of course—and I gave you an easy start by letting you get into Greyfriars in my name. You passed there as a gentleman——"

"I passed there as you!"

"That's what I mean. And I actually allowed myself to be supposed a fellow who had worked, and who was sent to a public school by the kindness of his employer. That was a come-down—for me! Me—a fellow who had soiled his hands with work!" said Billy Bunter disdainfully.

"You seem to have soiled them with a good many other things, and your neck, too!"

"Once for all, I don't want any of your low cheek, Wally!" roared Billy Bunter. "Keep your low manners for your low circle. I'm fed up with St. Jim's, and I'm going back to Greyfriars. There may have been some mention of keeping it up for the whole term. I won't say there wasn't. But you ought to be thankful for what you've had. You can go to St. Jim's. You've been there before, and you know your way about. Besides, there's another reason. Old Penman——"

"My old governor?" said Wally.

"Yes, your dashed old governor, as you call him——"

"I don't call him my dashed old governor; I speak of him respectfully, and you'd better do so if you don't want your nose pulled! Mr. Penman is the kindest of men."

"Oh, bother him, anyway! He telephoned to-day."

"Is he coming down to the school?"

"Yes."

"Oh!" said Wally.

"He came before, and we dodged him," said Bunter. "But this time he'll see you there, and you'll stay there. It's quite simple. He said on the telephone that it was very important, and there had been a change in his plans. He had news for me—I mean for you—which he thought would please me—you, you know. I don't know what he was driving at. I don't care, either. I got tired of his talk, and rang off."

"You cheeky idiot!"

"Well, I couldn't be bothered—it was nearly tea-time, too. Besides, I dare say he thought they cut him off at the exchange. Anyway, I don't see that it matters."

"When is he going to St. Jim's?"

"To-morrow afternoon."

"Oh, crikey! I'm booked to play in the Redclyffe match at Greyfriars to-morrow afternoon."

"They've put you in the Remove Eleven?" exclaimed Bunter, in astonishment.

"Yes."

"That's all right, then! I'll play," said Billy Bunter. "It will come to the same thing."

"You howling ass, you can't play cricket!"

"Look here, Wally——"

"Look here, Billy——"

"Time I got on to Greyfriars. Good-bye!"

Wally caught the Owl of the Remove by the arm.

"Billy! You can't play this rotten trick on me. Go back to St. Jim's, and keep it up as we agreed, to the end of the term."

"Can't be done! Besides, there's Penman to-morrow."

"We could work that, as we did when he came before——"

"I'm fed up with the place," said Bunter peevishly. "I'm going back to Greyfriars. I've done enough for you, Wally. If you can't be grateful, you might at least show some sense of obligation. Anyhow, it's settled."

Wally set his lips.

"You won't go back to St. Jim's?"

"No, I won't!"

"Do you call this playing the game?"

"I'm not going to argue with you, Wally. Besides, there's no time. I've got to get in to tea. I only had a snack at Uncle Clegg's—a few sausage-rolls, and a ham pie, and some tarts. I'm hungry."

"Did you get leave to come here from St. Jim's?"

"Oh, no; I just bunked after lessons!"

"But—but if I go, I shall get in late—bed-time, I think—I shall get into a thumping row."

"Blessed if I thought about that. You can spin them some yarn—railway strike, or something."

"You mean I can tell them thumping lies, as you would in my place?" growled Wally. "Well, lies don't come so easy to me."

"I've said I don't want any of your low cheek, Wally. This discussion had better cease," said Billy Bunter. "I want my tea. Oh, there's one other thing!"

"What's that?"

"I'm rather short of money. Can you lend me a quid?"

Wally Bunter did not answer that question. It seemed rather too much for him. Instead of speaking, he took Billy Bunter by the collar.

"Hallo! Wharrar you at?" howled Bunter.

Wally did not explain; he left Billy to guess; and really, it was easy to guess what Wally was at. He spun the fat junior round, and applied his boot to the Owl's plump person with great energy.

Biff, biff, biff!

"Yarooooh! Help! Fire! Murder!" roared Bunter. "Yarooh! Leggo! Oh, my hat!"

Biff!

Then Wally released the Owl of Greyfriars, and without another word walked away.

His career at Greyfriars had been suddenly cut short, and he had to face a fresh set of troubles and difficulties the cheery Billy had prepared for him; but he had found some little solace in that final scene.

There was no solace in it for Billy Bunter. He sat in the grass and roared.

— —

THE FOURTH CHAPTER.
The Return of the Native!

"I SAY, you fellows——"

"Hallo, hallo, hallo! Too late for practice!" exclaimed Bob Cherry.

"Slacker!" grunted Johnny Bull.

"Oh, really, Bull——"

"Why didn't you bring Wally to see us?" demanded Nugent.

Billy Bunter grinned.

The Owl of the Remove had arrived at his old school, and rolled in at the gates as the dusk was beginning to gather. Harry Wharton & Co. were chatting near the doorway of the School House when the fat junior joined them.

Billy Bunter looked a little uncertain at first. He could not help wondering whether the chums of the Remove would observe any difference between the Bunter who had gone out and the Bunter who had come in.

"We'd all have been glad to see Wally," went on Bob Cherry, little guessing how much he had seen of Wally the past few weeks. "You ought to have brought him along, Bunter."

"Oh, really, Cherry——"

"Perhaps there wasn't time," remarked Harry Wharton. "Wally Bunter must be pretty late in getting back to St. Jim's, anyway."

"That's it," said the fat junior. "He had to start back at once—the next train, you know. I'm going to pack up his things for him and send them on."

"Eh?"

"His things!" repeated Wharton. "What on earth things did he bring to Friardale with him?"

"Oh!" gasped Bunter.

He lacked Wally's ready wit, and he was so taken aback by his own blunder that he could only stammer. He blinked at the Famous Five, who stared at him in utter astonishment.

"I — I — I mean——" stammered Bunter.

"Well, what do you mean?"

"Lemme see. I—I mean that—that he's been buying some things in the village, and—and I'm going to see them sent off!" gasped Bunter. He did not mean to explain that he had been referring to the things Wally had left about Study No. 7 in the Rmove.

"So he's come donkeys' miles to a little village to do shopping?" asked Frank Nugent, mystified.

"That's it!" gasped Bunter. "Just right! You've got it exactly, Nugent."

"Well, my hat!"

"The hatfulness is terrific!" remarked Hurree Jamset Ram Singh. "Although the esteemed Bunter has latefully cultivated the straight and narrow path of truthfulness, in the manner of the excellent and absurd George Washington, it really seems to me that he is now wandering from the facts."

"Oh, really, Inky——"

"Where's your cap?" asked Bob Cherry suddenly.

"My—my cap?"

"Yes, your cap."

"On my head, of course!"

"That isn't a Greyfriars cap."

"Oh my hat!" ejaculated Bunter.

"Not your hat—your cap!" grinned Bob. "Have you lost it?"

"Ye-e-es, exactly! You see, I meant to change with my cousin, but he cut up rusty, and I forgot——"

"What?"

"I—I mean——"

"What on earth do you mean?" exclaimed the astounded Bob. "Your cousin wears a St. Jim's cap, doesn't he?"

"Eh? No—oh, yes—of—of course! I—I mean—I—I didn't want to come here in a St. Jim's cap, so I put this on, and then I forgot—that is to say, I—I didn't put this on——"

"Eh?"

"I—I mean—I—my cap blew off!" gasped Bunter. "There was a fearful wind in the lane."

"There's been hardly a breath of wind since you went out."

"That—that's what I meant to say. I—I meant that a—a motor-car dashed past me, and the wind from it blew my cap off, and—and it fell into the river; so I bought this cap. See?"

The famous Five simply blinked at Bunter.

That the Owl of the Remove was departing from the straight line of veracity they could, of course, see easily. Why he should be lying it was not so easy to see.

But one thing was borne in upon their minds. Bunter was more like his old self now than he had been for weeks.

If the fat junior had lost his cap, and had bought a cheap cap in the village, there was nothing to lie about so far as the chums of the Remove could see.

Yet Bunter was plainly lying.

"Are you sure it wasn't a herd of wild elephants that passed you?" asked Bob Cherry.

"Oh, really, you know——"

"Didn't one of them hook your cap off with his trunk?"

"No!" roared Bunter.

"What are you telling whoppers for, anyway?"

"I decline to answer such a question as that, Cherry. I say, you fellows, is Toddy in the study?"

"I believe so," said Wharton.

"I hope he hasn't had tea yet," said Bunter anxiously. "I'm simply famished after my journey."

"What journey?"

Bunter jumped. He was putting his foot into it again.

"D-d-did I say journey?" he stammered.

"You did, you fat duffer!"

"I—I meant—that is, I haven't had a journey. Don't you fellows get the idea into your heads that I've just come from St. Jim's. I haven't."

"Wha-a-at?"

"When I say journey," proceeded Bunter cautiously, "I mean the walk home from Friardale. That's what I really meant."

"Is he off his rocker?" asked Bob Cherry, addressing space.

"Oh, really, Cherry——"

"He must be wandering in his mind,

I should think," said Harry Wharton, in wonder. "Blessed if he doesn't talk as if he'd been drinking! What's happened to you since you went out, Bunty?"

"N-n-nothing!"

"You're different, somehow," said the captain of the Remove, looking at the fat junior more closely. "Blessed if I quite understand; but there's some change in you. You seem all of a sudden to have become just like you were a few weeks ago, before your cousin came on a visit here."

"He, he, he!"

"Same old cackle, too!" exclaimed Bob Cherry, in surprise. "I haven't heard you give that alarm-clock cackle for weeks. Now you've suddenly turned it on again, along with the whoppers."

"I—I say, you fellows, I think I'll go and see Toddy!" exclaimed Bunter hastily. "I suppose I shall find him just the same—what?"

"He's not likely to have changed much in two hours," answered Wharton.

Bunter jumped again.

"Nunno! Of—of course not! I—I'll go up!"

And the Owl of the Remove rolled into the School House, and hurried up to the Remove passage. Harry Wharton & Co. looked at one another very oddly.

"Blessed if I quite catch on to this!" said Wharton slowly. "What's the matter with him?"

"He doesn't seem the same chap," said Bob. "It's extraordinary. I can't put my finger on any special thing, but it's there. He seems to be a different chap since he went out a couple of hours ago. It's just as if he suddenly turned into the old Bunter again."

"That's it—and it's a pity."

"The improvement was terrific," remarked the Nabob of Bhanipur. "Now it is gone from our gaze like the beautiful dreamfulness."

And the Famous Five strolled into the School House in a very puzzled mood. It really seemed as if Bunter would never leave off surprising them in one way or another.

THE FIFTH CHAPTER.
Welcome Home!

PETER TODD glanced up from the grate as Billy Bunter entered No. 7—his old study in the Remove passage. Peter nodded affably. Since Wally Bunter had been at Greyfriars in his cousin's name, Peter had grown quite to like his fat study-mate. He felt that he had never quite done Bunter justice, and though he was puzzled he had grown very friendly.

"Hallo, old scout!" he said genially. "You're in time. You oughtn't to have cut cricket, though."

"Couldn't be helped," said Bunter. "You see, I had to get off in such a hurry. They'd have stopped me if they'd known I was coming here——"

"What?"

"I—I mean—I—I mean, what is there for tea, Toddy?"

"Who'd have stopped you?"

"Nobody. What I meant to say was nobody would have stopped me. I say, Toddy. I'm awfully hungry! What is there for tea?"

"Well, there's lots of toast," said Peter, with a very curious look at the fat junior. "There's bloater-paste, too. Haven't you brought in anything?"

"Nunno!"

"Oh, all right! We'll make this do," said Toddy. "Dutton's gone to tea with Smithy and Redwing, as it happens."

"How's old Smithy? Same old Bounder, I suppose?"

Peter stared.

"I suppose so," he answered. "I don't see why he should have changed since you saw him in the Form-room."

"Oh—ah—yes! Quite so!" stammered Bunter. "By the way, Toddy, I owed you fifteen bob when I left——"

"When you left?"

"I—I mean, when I didn't leave——"

"Eh?"

"That is, when—when—some time ago—in fact, I owed you fifteen bob, didn't I?"

"You did," said Peter Todd, "and anybody could have knocked me down with a feather when you settled up."

"I settled up?"

"Have you forgotten you did?"

"Yes—no—of course I settled up! I always settle up, don't I?" said Billy Bunter. "What I was going to say is, that now I've settled up I hope you won't be mean about making a chap a small loan occasionally when he's hard up."

"I'll lend you some tin if you're hard up," answered Peter, "at once. Since you've turned honest, I don't mind."

"It's simply a question of waiting till this evening, Mrs. Mimble, till my postal-order comes!" Billy Bunter was saying, when Harry Wharton entered and clapped him on the shoulder. "Ow!" howled Bunter. "You beast, Bolsover——" *(See Chapter 10.)*

"The fact is, I'm expecting a postal-order——"

"What?" howled Peter.

"A postal-order, from a titled relation of mine——"

Billy Bunter stopped. The expression on Peter's face was so extraordinary. It was quite a long time since anything had been heard at Greyfriars of Billy Bunter's celebrated postal-order, which was always expected and which never arrived. His titled relations, too, had been unmentioned for a similar length of time. Now they had revived together—quite suddenly.

"You—you—you're expecting a postal-order?" stuttered Peter Todd.

"Yes. Haven't I said so?"

"From a—a—a titled relation?"

"Yes."

"Well, my only hat!"

"Blessed if I see anything to be surprised at in that, Peter Todd. Don't I often get postal-orders from my wealthy connections?"

"My only hat!" repeated Toddy. "He's started that again—postal orders, titled relations, whoppers, and all! What's come over you, Bunter? Have you got tired of turning over a new leaf?"

"Oh, rats!" said Bunter peevishly. "The point is, will you lend me ten shillings, and have it back out of my postal-order?"

Peter Todd shook his head.

"No," he said deliberately, "I won't, Bunty! If you've started the postal-order and the titled relations again, I've got strong doubts whether I should ever see my ten bob any more. If you're short of tin, you'd better send a wire to your wealthy connections. They may dub up—perhaps!"

"Look here, you silly ass——" roared Bunter.

Peter Todd dished up the toast, and opened the bloater-paste. Billy Bunter surveyed the frugal tea-table with a snort of disgust.

"So that's all there is for tea!" he snapped.

"That's all, old nut! You can add to it anything you like, though!" said Peter liberally.

"I happen to be short of money."

"Gammon!"

"Oh, really, Toddy——"

"You had plenty of tin to-day, and you said you were going to stand something for tea. You're getting like your old self again, Billy!"

"I want something better than this for tea! I can tell you, I'm not accustomed to this sort of grub. At St. Jim's we——" Bunter paused in time.

"Well, what about St. Jim's?"

"N-n-nothing!"

Billy Bunter sat down to tea. Such as it was, he was forced to be content with it—though he did not look contented. He helped himself to all the bloater-paste, Peter watching that performance with a sort of mesmerised stare. He made no remark on it, however. This reversion to type, so to speak, on the part of his fat study-mate took Peter Todd by surprise. It required getting used to.

Bunter travelled through the toast at a great speed, too. When the table was bare, he rose with a dissatisfied grunt.

"Call that a tea!" he said.

"You seem to have taken a fancy to most of it!" said Peter tartly.

"I'm jolly nearly famished, after a thumping long journey—I—I mean, after walking to Friardale. I could get a snack in the tuckshop, only I happen to be short of tin. Now, look here, Toddy! This really isn't the welcome home I expected——"

"The what?"

"I—I mean, I really think you might lend me ten bob, old chap. My postal-order will be here to-morrow morning—or the afternoon, at latest——"

"Bow-wow!"

"Dash it all! I'm half sorry I came back!" growled Bunter.

"Eh? Were you thinking of putting up in Friardale for the night?"

"Eh? No! Oh, no! I mean—— Look here, Peter! If you'll lend me ten bob, I'll let you come home with me next holidays to Bunter Court."

"Oh, my hat!"

"You'll meet a lot of titled people there, and it will give you an insight into high life," said Bunter, blinking at him. "That's rather a catch for a skinny solicitor's son like you, Peter!"

"Great Scott!" said Peter dazedly.

Bunter's charming old manners were coming back with a vengeance. It really seemed to Peter Todd as if he had had a different fellow entirely in the study for the past few weeks.

"I've been friendly with you," went on Bunter. "Nothing of the snob about me, I hope. You're not much class, Peter, as you know; but I've always taken you up, and been genial. The least you can do is to make me a small loan when I'm short of cash. Now, I put it to you."

"Is this a new and mysterious kind of joke?" asked Peter Todd.

"Eh? I'm not joking!"

Peter Todd rose to his feet.

"I used to keep a stump in the study for you, Bunter," he said. "Since you turned over a new leaf I haven't used it."

"Look here——"

"I wondered how long your giddy reform would last," pursued Peter. "It's lasted longer than I should have expected. But you seem to have got fed up on being decent. You're your own self again, Bunter—more than ever, I think. As you're the old Bunter once more, I shall have to use the old methods. You see that?"

"I—I say——" stammered Bunter, as Peter Todd picked up a cricket-stump from the corner of the study.

"Where will you have it?" asked Toddy.

"I—I say, you beast——"

"Say where!"

Instead of saying where he would have it, Billy Bunter made a jump for the doorway.

Peter Todd made a jump for Bunter at the same time, and he reached Bunter before Bunter reached the door.

Whack, whack!

"Yaroooh!" roared Bunter, as the stump smote him rearward. "Yow-ow! Beast! Oh, crikey! You rotter! Ow!"

Whack!

The stump landed again as Billy Bunter bolted through the doorway. Then he escaped into the passage.

"Come back and have some more!" roared Peter Todd, brandishing the stump.

"Yarooooh!"

Bunter was travelling—not towards Study No. 7. Peter Todd grinned, and slammed the door.

A minute later a wrathful voice was howling through the keyhole:

"Beast!"

Then Bunter's receding footsteps died away rapidly.

——

THE SIXTH CHAPTER.
Not So Popular!

"HALLO, hallo, hallo! Trot in, my fat tulip!"

Harry Wharton & Co. were at tea in Study No. 1 when a fat face looked in at the doorway.

Billy Bunter blinked in rather cautiously.

When he looked into a study at tea-time he was not unaccustomed to hearing emphatic objurgations, or even to receiving flying missiles in the shape of a cushion or a book.

But the cordial looks of the Famous Five showed that there were neither objurgations nor missiles to be looked for now, and Bunter was surprised. He grinned, however, as he remembered that the juniors supposed him to be the Bunter they had known during the last few weeks.

"I say, you fellows——" he began.

"Come in!" said Harry Wharton. "Had your tea?"

Bunter sniffed.

"What Toddy calls a tea," he answered. "I believe Toddy's growing meaner than ever!"

"Oh, don't talk out of your hat!" said Wharton, rather sharply. "Toddy's all right!"

"Fancy offering toast and bloater-paste to a fellow he's not seen for—for—for "—Bunter stammered—"for two hours!" he concluded, rather lamely.

"Well, two hours isn't a long time!" said Harry, laughing. "But if you haven't had tea, old kid, pile in! Lots!"

"The lotfulness is terrific, my esteemed Bunter!"

"Well, as you're so pressing, I will," said Bunter. "The fact is, I shouldn't object to digging in this study again. You know, I used to share this study with you and Nugent, Wharton. I'll tell you what—I'll come back, if you like!"

"Ahem! We won't rob Toddy of your company, old scout!"

"The fact is," said Bunter, with his mouth full of ham, "I can't stand Toddy. I'm not a snob, I hope, but I really feel that I ought to draw the line at chumming with a skinny solicitor's son. Hardly up to my social standing, you know!"

A sudden silence fell upon the Famous Five. They looked at Bunter, but they did not speak.

The difference they had already noticed in him seemed to be growing more pronounced. Bunter of the Remove had astonished them by improving in a very remarkable way. He seemed bent now on astonishing them by a reverse process.

"I say, you fellows, this ham is good!" said Bunter. "You don't mind if I finish it, do you? Are those hard-boiled eggs, Nugent? Pass them this way, will you? I hope you fellows have finished?"

Without waiting to be informed whether the fellows had finished, Billy Bunter rolled all the eggs upon his plate. He polished them off in great style. Then he began on the cake.

"Help yourself, old scout!" said Wharton hospitably.

"Well, I will, if you don't mind!" said Bunter. And he transferred the cake to his plate. "This will save time. No good fooling around with slicing. I say, you fellows, this is rather a good cake. I wonder you didn't try it!"

Bunter had not given them much chance of trying it, but the Famous Five made no remark.

Sidney James Snoop glanced into the study while Bunter was busy with the cake. He gave Bunter a very cordial smile.

"I was going to ask you to tea, Bunty," he remarked. "Too late, it seems!"

"Not at all!" answered Bunter, rising to his feet with his mouth full of cake. "I'll come, with pleasure!"

"Oh, my hat!" murmured Bob Cherry involuntarily.

"Just wait a minute, Snoopey," said Bunter. "I think I'll have a go at the biscuits; they look rather nice."

"Do!" gasped Wharton.

Bunter did. The biscuits disappeared in record time. Evidently Bunter did not believe in wasting anything.

"Now I'll get along, you fellows," he remarked, blinking at the five. "Sorry I can't stay longer. I'll give you a look in another time, you know. You can rely on me for the Redclyffe match to-morrow, Wharton."

"I've got your name down," said Harry.

"That's right! I'll beat Redclyffe for you, old chap."

"Well, we're going to help a little."

"Yes, of course; I shall expect the team to back me up," said Bunter, with a nod. "I make only one condition—that I open the innings. You see, you want to open the innings with your best batsman—it encourages the others."

"I am going to open the innings myself, with Smithy!" answered Harry Wharton curtly.

Bunter blinked at him.

"That won't do!" he said.

"Won't it?"

"Not at all," said the fat junior decidedly. "I shall insist—I feel that I must insist upon opening the innings. You've got one great drawback as cricket captain, Wharton!"

"Have I?" said Harry, breathing hard.

"Yes. You don't mind my mentioning, do you? Candid friend, you know——"

"Oh, don't mind me!" said the captain of the Remove sarcastically.

"Right—I won't! Your drawback is conceit," said Bunter. "You're a bit swelled-headed about what you can do on the pitch, you know."

"What-a-at?"

"As a matter of absolute fact, you're not a patch on me when it comes to cricket, you know."

"My hat!"

"My play," said Bunter, "is what a chap can really call play. It brings the runs, you know. What's wanted is runs. Well, I'm the man for runs. Of course, as cricket captain, you can swank around opening the innings, if you like. But my opinion is that you ought to stand back and leave a better man to do it. For the sake of the team, you know. I'm coming, Snoopey!"

And Billy Bunter rolled out of the study after Snoop, leaving Harry Wharton absolutely speechless. Deep silence reigned in Study No. 1 as the Owl of the Remove departed. He had taken away the breath of the Famous Five.

Sidney James Snoop had a rather peculiar expression on his face as he led the way to his study.

He had been quite chummy with Wally Bunter, whose little secret he knew; it was his observation of Wally's sterling good qualities that had first surprised him, and then made him suspect the truth. Except in outward appearance, Wally was quite unlike his cousin Billy; but the fat junior who had been talking "out of his hat" in Study No. 1 seemed to Snoop more like Billy than Wally. And he was puzzled.

Bunter gave him a fat wink as they entered No. 11. Skinner and Stott were downstairs, and they had the study to themselves.

"That's the way to talk to him!" remarked Bunter.

"Is it?" stammered Snoop.

"Yes, rather! Wharton wants taking down a peg or two at times. There's a little too much of His Majestic Magnificence about him, you know!"

"Oh!"

"Now, what is his play compared with mine?" said Bunter.

"Your play is good," said Snoop. "But, dash it all, it's not up to Wharton's, old fellow!"

"Fat lot you know about cricket," answered Bunter. "I could play Wharton's head off!"

"Hardly, I think," said Snoop, with a smile.

"Look here, I came here to tea, not to hear you display your ignorance of cricket!" said Bunter loftily. "What do you know about the game—you, a chap who mooches around making bets on gee-gees, and never touches a bat if he could help it?"

Snoop flushed.

"I've given all that up, Bunter," he said, in a low voice.

"Gammon!"

"Why, you know I have!" exclaimed Snoop sharply.

Bunter closed one eye.

"My dear man, keep that for those who aren't quite so fly as I am," he replied. "I know what it's worth."

"I don't understand you," said Snoop, after a pause. "It was you who helped me to get out of the rotten way I was in, Bunter. I thought you believed in me."

"He, he, he!"

"If you don't——" began Snoop, with a deep breath.

Bunter waved a fat hand.

"I'm fly!" he remarked. "My dear chap, you'd have to get up very early in the morning to pull the wool over my eyes! He, he, he!"

"You don't believe me, then?"

"He, he! No fear!"

Sidney James Snoop compressed his lips.

"You've done me some good turns, Bunter," he began, after a pause.

"Of course! I'm always doing fellows good turns," said Bunter, with a nod. "That's my sort. I don't think anybody could fairly deny that I'm the most generous fellow at Greyfriars."

"My hat!"

"Only, I'm wide," said Bunter, with a wink. "Very wide! You can't take me in, you know. No good spinning me yarns. He, he, he!"

"Let's have tea," said Snoop abruptly.

"Certainly; I'm quite ready."

There was a nice tea in Study No. 11, and Bunter did it full justice. Snoop's face was not very bright as he entertained his visitor. He was puzzled, and he was curiously troubled. Bunter was there, looking the same as ever—but it seemed to Snoop that he had lost his friend.

THE SEVENTH CHAPTER.
Remuneration Required!

HARRY WHARTON & CO. glanced rather curiously at Bunter when the Owl of the Remove came into the Common-room that evening.

Bunter had puzzled them a good deal of late; and now he puzzled them more than ever.

The remarkable improvement that had taken place in the fat junior was surprising enough; but that he should have slipped back into his old self in a single day was still more surprising.

Billy Bunter was aware that he was the object of more than usual interest, and he found it rather entertaining.

He was rather pleased to be back at Greyfriars.

Cousin Wally had more than kept his place warm for him. He had lived down Bunter's reputation for him, and made him almost popular. Fellows were civil to Bunter, in fact, quite friendly; his remarks were listened to without derisive grins—which was a pleasant change from former days. How long it would take the Owl of the Remove to spoil the good effect Wally had produced was another matter.

Bunter, as he stretched his fat toes to the fire, wondered how cousin Wally was getting on at St. Jim's now. Grundy of the Shell had promised Bunter a licking that evening; and the Owl wondered cheerfully whether the unfortunate Wally was getting it. If he got it, he deserved it for his cheek, Billy Bunter reflected. Wally had not been so respectful as a poor relation ought to be to so great a person as William George Bunter.

Billy Bunter kept his ears open that evening. He was very curious about what had happened at Greyfriars during his absence.

He was considerably surprised to learn how cousin Wally had won golden opinions from all sorts of people. Why fellows should think so much of his poor relation, when they had thought so little of William George himself, was a puzzle to the fat junior. But evidently they did.

Billy Bunter learned, for the first time, how Wally had rescued Frank Nugent from the frozen river, and how he had played a great part in a football match at Highcliffe. The affair of fishing Nugent out of the river had naturally made some impression on the juniors, and it was not forgotten—least of all by Nugent himself. Some allusion to it caused Bunter to prick up his fat ears, and he listened with avidity. He found that he was supposed to be not only a great footballer and a good cricketer, but a hero into the bargain.

The bare idea made him swell with importance.

The fat Owl had no scruple whatever about bagging another fellow's credit; and perhaps, as Wally had been using his name, he felt that he was entitled to bask in all the glory reaped under that name.

Later in the evening, when Wharton and Nugent went to their study to bake chestnuts, Billy Bunter followed them. He had not ventured to ask open questions as to the affair of the river, for fear of giving himself away; but he had a more or less clear idea of what had happened, and it was his idea to turn it to account.

"I say, you fellows——" he began, as he blinked into the study.

"Come in, fatty," said Nugent.

"Thanks, I will."

"Any more valuable opinions to hand out on the subject of cricket?" asked the captain of the Remove sarcastically.

"I could tell you a thumping lot you don't know, if you come to that!" answered Bunter. "But you'll see what real cricket's like when I play Redclyffe tomorrow."

"I hope so. If I hadn't seen you at practice I should have some jolly strong doubts, from the way you talk," said Harry. "Well, what are you giggling at? Have I said anything funny in that?"

"Oh, no—nunno! Of—of course, you've seen me at practice lots of times," grinned Bunter. "Naturally. But I didn't come here to talk about cricket."

"There's the chestnuts. Help yourself."

"Well, I will, as you're so pressing!" said Bunter. "But I didn't come here for chestnuts. The fact is, my postal-order hasn't come."

"The one you were expecting last term?"

"Oh, really, Wharton——"

"Or the one you were expecting when we were both fags in the Third?" chuckled Frank Nugent.

Billy Bunter gave Nugent a lofty blink.

"I'm surprised at you, Nugent!" he said.

"Go hon!"

"Considering all I've done for you, I think you might be a bit more civil. I don't expect gratitude, but——"

Frank Nugent stared at him.

"What do you mean, tubby?" he asked.

"I dare say you've forgotten how I plunged into the river and brought you out at the risk of my life."

"Eh?"

"I don't want to brag," said Bunter. "That's not my nature. But it was heroic. I can't say less than that. It isn't every fellow who'd have done it, I can tell you."

"Well, my hat!" stuttered Nugent.

Harry Wharton fixed his eyes on the Owl of the Remove. He was more astonished than words could express.

On the occasion when Wally Bunter had rescued Nugent the Removites had expected the fat junior to "spread" himself, but he hadn't done it. That wasn't Wally's way. In fact, the praise he had received had seemed rather to irritate him than otherwise, and he had shown a keen desire to hear the last of the affair. And now—after a lapse of weeks—here was Bunter bragging of what he had done in the most unpleasant way! It was the old Billy Bunter, with a vengeance.

Bunter did not seem to understand the strained silence in the study. He helped himself to chestnuts, and rattled on, with his mouth full.

"Where would you be now, Nugent, but for my bravery?"

"At the bottom of the river, very likely," said Frank Nugent quietly.

Billy Bunter nodded.

"That's it! Mind, I'm not bragging of what I did. Anything of that kind comes naturally to a fellow who's as brave as a lion. But there it is. I did it, and you ought to be grateful."

"I hope I am," said Frank, still more quietly.

"Well, I hope so," assented Bunter. "You certainly ought to be. What are you scowling at me for, Wharton?"

"I did not mean to scowl," said Harry mildly. "I think I ought to speak seriously to you, Bunter. For some weeks now you've surprised us all by being a really decent chap. We've got used to it, and most of the fellows have come to like you, and respect you, too. Some queer change seems to have come over you to-day, and you've suddenly become as mean and unpleasant as you ever were in the old days. I can't understand it."

"What rot!"

"If it's a joke of yours, you'd better chuck it. It's not funny, and it's not pleasant," said Wharton. "But if it's only that you're fed up with being decent, I suggest to you to keep it up till you like it. You did a splendid thing when you went into the water for Nugent, and you didn't spoil it by bragging. Now you've started all of a sudden. What's come over you?"

"I'm not surprised that you're jealous of me, Wharton——"

"What?" roared Wharton.

"You don't like me getting the limelight. I understand perfectly. But it's mean, and you should keep that kind of meanness in check!"

"Why, you—you——"

"I'm speaking to you candidly, as a friend, you know," said Bunter, blinking at him. "But to come back to business. My postal-order hasn't come, and I'm rather short of money. I was going to ask Nugent to lend me a pound."

"I haven't a pound," said Frank.

"Well, make it ten bob," said Bunter carelessly.

Frank Nugent looked at him oddly as he felt in his pockets. If Bunter was asking for his pocket-money, because he had pulled him out of the river, Bunter could have it—and a deep scorn along with it, which was not likely to trouble him much, however.

Nugent found nine-and-six in various coins in his pockets, and handed that sum over to Billy Bunter without a word.

Bunter's eyes glistened behind his big glasses as he received it. Wally's stay at Greyfriars was turning out an unexpectedly paying proposition for William George.

"Thanks!" he said carelessly. "Will you have this back out of my postal-order in the morning?"

"It doesn't matter."

"Well, let it stand over till next week, then, shall we?" said Bunter.

"Oh, yes!"

"Right-ho!"

And, the chestnuts being all gone, Billy Bunter rolled out of the study the richer by nine shillings and sixpence.

Wharton and Nugent looked at one another.

"Well!" said Frank, with a deep breath.

"Well!" said Harry.

And they said no more. There was nothing they could say that was equal to the occasion.

THE EIGHTH CHAPTER.
Wally's Warning!

"HALLO, hallo, hallo!" Bob Cherry's powerful voice was heard in the Remove passage. "Wharton! Where are you, Wharton?"

"Here!"

"You're wanted!"

Bob Cherry looked into Study No. 1.

"Quelchy wants you," he said. "I believe it's a telephone call. Quelchy looked a bit of a gorgon!"

"A telephone call!" repeated Wharton. "I can't be wanted on the telephone. My uncle wouldn't ring me up this time of the evening, anyway. Besides, he's not home yet from Cologne."

"May have turned up unexpectedly," said Bob. "Quelchy's telephone was buzzing. Anyway, he wants you in a hurry. Cut, my son!"

Harry Wharton hurried downstairs in a state of surprise. He found Mr. Quelch at his study door, with a severe expression on his face.

"Wharton, were you expecting a telephone call on my instrument?" he asked.

Wharton was glad to be able to reply in the negative. The Remove-master's expression did not indicate that he was keen to lend his telephone to fellows in his Form.

"No, sir!"

"Well, you have been asked for, from Wayland."

"Wayland!" repeated Wharton in astonishment. "That's the town near St. Jim's. It's a trunk call from there."

"Yes, and for that reason I have told the person that I will call you. It is a St. Jim's boy who desires to speak to you."

"Oh! Thank you sir!"

"This is a very extraordinary proceeding, Wharton, and although you may take this call, you must tell the person that such a thing must not occur again."

"Oh, certainly, sir!"

Mr. Quelch stepped out of the study, and Wharton went to the telephone. He was quite as surprised as the Form-master. It was incredible that Tom Merry or D'Arcy should have rung him up on the Form-master's telephone without asking permission, but he could not imagine who else it could be. He sat down to the instrument and took up the receiver.

"Hallo!"

"Hallo! Is that Wharton?"

"Yes. Who's speaking?"

"Wally Bunter!"

"My only hat!" ejaculated Wharton.

"Surprised you—what?"

"Well, rather!"

Wharton was more than surprised. He believed that he had not seen Wally Bunter since the latter had visited Billy at Greyfriars. This sudden and unexpected communication astonished him.

"I'm sorry," went on the fat voice on the telephone. "I'm afraid Mr. Quelch was rather waxy. But I told him it was important. I hope he won't rag you."

"That's all right; only it mustn't happen again."

"I understand."

"But what——"

"It's really important, Wharton. I couldn't let you go on without a warning. I can't tell you the whole story, because it's a promise. I can't let it out. But I can't let you go ahead without giving you a tip. It's about your cricket match to-morrow."

"We're playing Redclyffe to-morrow," said Harry, utterly mystified.

"Yes, that's it."

"I didn't know you were so well posted about our fixtures."

There was a chuckle on the telephone, which mystified the captain of the Remove still more. Wally Bunter's voice went on again.

"You're playing my cousin in your team?"

"Yes."

"Well, don't!"

"Eh?"

"That's the tip I want to give you. Don't play Billy Bunter against Redclyffe, or he will let you down."

"My hat!"

"He can't play cricket, you know."

"Oh!" said Harry, thinking he understood at last. "Billy met you in Friardale to-day, and I suppose he told you about the Redclyffe match, and that he was down to play? No wonder you're surprised. But Billy has improved wonderfully since you were here that time, Wally."

"Ha, ha!"

"Eh? Are you laughing? What do you mean?"

"N-n-nothing! But Billy hasn't improved—he's a bigger duffer than ever."

"Not at all," answered Harry. "I know it must surprise you, Wally, considering what a duffer he always was at games; but it's the fact. He helped us win a footer match soon after your visit here. Now he's turning out wonderfully well at cricket."

"He's not. You see—ahem!—I can't very well explain, but he's as big a duffer at cricket as he ever was."

"My dear chap," said Wharton, a little impatiently, "you haven't seen him for nearly a term, and you don't know. I've seen him every day."

"You haven't—I—I mean——"

"But I have," said Harry. "He's in my Form, you know. I know a chap's form at cricket, and Billy is as good as I've got in the Eleven. He bowls very nearly as well as Inky, and bats as well as Squiff. He's a good man in the field, too—quite good all round. You'll be surprised when you see him again. I know it's odd, but it's a fact."

"It isn't! You see——"

"Well?"

"I—I can't tell you the facts, because I promised Billy that the whole thing should be kept dark. But you simply mustn't play him!"

"I must, you know. His name's in the list on the board."

"He will let you down in the match."

"Bosh!" said Harry, a little nettled. Wally Bunter's remarks seemed a rather strong reflection upon his capacity as cricket captain. Wharton knew a good man when he saw one. And he was quite satisfied with what he had seen of Bunter at cricket practice. That it was another Bunter he was not aware, and Wally could not tell him.

"Wharton, old man, I wish you'd take my tip," went on Wally's voice earnestly. "I could prove what I say, only I'm bound by a promise. I suppose Billy hasn't told you anything?"

"What had he to tell me?"

"H'm! Does he intend to play in the match to-morrow?"

"Yes."

"I mean, has he said so since he saw me in Friardale this afternoon?"

"Yes."

"The fat rotter!"

"Look here, Wally, I don't see what

you're driving at. I suppose you mean this good-naturedly, but you're quite offside. Billy Bunter has turned out a good man at games, and we're making use of him."

"It may cost you the match if you do. I wish I could spin you the whole yarn, but it's a promise, as I said. But for your own sake, Wharton, don't play Billy Bunter in the Redclyffe match to-morrow. You'll be sorry if you do."

"It's all right," said Harry. "I wish you could come over and see the match."

"I wish I could come over; but Mr. Penman is coming down to-morrow. If I could come over I'd keep the fat rascal from spoofing you, somehow."

"What the——"

"Don't play him—take my tip, and don't! You——"

There was sudden silence.

Wharton listened, and spoke again. But he was cut off.

He put the receiver back on the hooks, and rose from the stool.

In great amazement he quitted Mr. Quelch's study. His chums met him at the corner of the passage, naturally curious to know what it was all about. They fairly blinked when Wharton explained.

"Is the fellow potty?" said Johnny Bull. "He must have gone out of bounds to go to Wayland, and get a trunk call from there. And all to tell you not to play his cousin in a cricket match to-morrow."

"Blessed if I understand it," said Harry, in perplexity. "I suppose Billy told him about it to-day; and from what he remembers of Billy. I suppose it seemed to him that I must be cracked to put the Owl into a good match. But—but really, it's not very complimentary to me. He oughtn't to conclude that I don't know a fellow's form at cricket."

"He means well," said Nugent.

"I've no doubt he does; but"—Wharton reddened a little—"he seems to take me for a silly ass, and it's a check! All that trouble and bother to tell me not to play a man I've selected on his merits. I must say, it's cheek!"

"It won't make any difference?"

"Of course not," said Harry. "Fancy the idea of shifting a man out of the Eleven because a fellow who hasn't seen him for months rings me up and tells me he's no good—when I know he is. I really think Wally Bunter must be going off his rocker!"

Wally's well-meant warning had been futile, as he probably feared it would be. He had done his best; but Billy Bunter was booked to play for the Remove on the morrow. When he had done so, there was no doubt that Wharton would wish that he had paid heed to Wally's warning.

— —

THE NINTH CHAPTER.
Nice Boy!

BILLY BUNTER turned up in the Remove Form-room the following morning, as usual—or, rather, as had been usual for Wally for the past few weeks. He was looking quite jaunty and smiling. Fortune was favouring the Owl of the Remove. He was booked to play in the first match of the season that afternoon; not one of the important fixtures, certainly, but a good match, and that was a distinction. Not for one moment did Bunter think of giving up the place that had been awarded to Wally. In the depths of his ineffable conceit he firmly believed himself to be a better cricketer than Wally Bunter, or, indeed, than any fellow in the Remove. Hitherto he had been kept in the background by jealousy of his great powers. Now he was going to have a chance to show all Greyfriars what he could do.

That was how Billy Bunter looked at it. That was his point of view, and he was quite satisfied with it.

He had other sources of satisfaction. At St. Jim's he had looked upon D'Arcy of the Fourth as a sort of horn of plenty; but the cornucopia had dried up at last. Frank Nugent was destined to take its place. Having saved Nugent's life—or, at least, being supposed to have saved it—Bunter felt that he was entitled to look upon Nugent as a gold-mine, which was to pay continual dividends, as it were. There was, so Bunter argued, such a thing as gratitude, and Nugent could hardly refuse a small loan now and then to the fellow who had saved his life.

The unfortunate Nugent's pocket-money was ear-marked in advance for whole terms, in Bunter's fat mind. Unless the victim discovered that he was being imposed upon, how could he refuse Bunter's requests, or demands? Doubtless he would be driven to resistance in the long run; but Bunter never thought of the long run. The present was enough for him. And he meant to be very careful not to let Nugent, or anyone else, discover the real facts.

Wally had promised, and Wally's promise was sacred. Billy had also promised, for that matter, and his promise was not exactly sacred; but it was to his interest to keep it.

Altogether, Billy Bunter felt that he had reason to be satisfied with himself and things in general, and he was glad that he had bolted from St. Jim's, and turned up at his old school.

But the fat smile faded from his face during the morning.

He found Mr. Quelch even more of a Tartar than he remembered him of old.

Wally had been a credit to the Remove; he had worked industriously in the Form-room and the study, and he had fifth place in the class, only Wharton, Mark Linley, Vernon-Smith, and Tom Redwing being above him. The Remove-master had learned to expect attention, industry, and keenness from Bunter. And that morning he was perplexed, puzzled, and, finally, very angry in dealing with the old, original Bunter.

Bunter was worried, too.

Quelchy seemed to expect him to know a lot of things he did not know, and to expect him to remember all kinds of things he never did remember, and had no intention of trying to remember.

Bunter did not believe in work, in class or out. So long as he scraped through without a licking he was content.

As dunce of the class he had been treated with a certain leniency; but since Wally had shown what he could do, more was naturally expected of him.

When Lord Mauleverer blundered in his construe, Bunter was told to take the book and show him how to do better; and the exhibition Bunter gave of his knowledge made the Removites open their eyes.

Lord Mauleverer did not benefit much by Bunter's assistance.

Towards the end of morning lessons Mr. Quelch called to Bunter. His brow

"You're Billy Bunter!" said Snoop. "You changed back with your cousin yesterday. That's clear enough now!" Bunter jumped. (*See Chapter* **11.**)

were knitted, and his eyes looked like gimlets.

"Bunter," he said, in a voice that made the fat junior quake, "for a considerable time past you have been one of my best pupils."

"Yes, sir," stammered Bunter. "I—I hope so, sir."

"I have considered you a clever boy, Bunter."

"Ye-es, sir. I—I'm considered rather clever at home. My sister Bessie thinks me an awfully clever chap."

"This morning, Bunter, you have displayed nothing but stupidity."

"Oh, sir!"

"As you have proved of late that you are not so stupid as I once supposed, I cannot believe that it is genuine stupidity you have displayed this morning."

"Oh!"

"And I warn you, Bunter, not to try my patience any further. I can make allowances for stupidity, but not for deliberate idleness and carelessness. Take warning, Bunter!"

"Oh, sir! Yes, sir! Certainly, sir! stuttered Bunter.

And the Owl of the Remove sat in dismay after Mr. Quelch's warning. If he had to live up to cousin Wally's scholarly reputation his return to Greyfriars was not likely to be all happiness.

He escaped the cane that morning; but it was very probable that he would not escape it the next day. Perhaps fortunately, Bunter took very short views; and the possible happenings of the next day did not worry him, once he was out of the Form-room.

Bob Cherry tapped him on the shoulder in the passage.

"What's the game, Fatty?" he asked.

"Game?" repeated Bunter.

"Yes. What were you playing the goat for in the Form-room? Quelchy is rather a tough customer to joke with."

"I wasn't joking with the old donkey!" growled Bunter.

"Do you mean to say that you're as big an idiot as you made out in class?" asked Bob.

"Oh, really, Cherry——"

"You got Quelchy's rag out, Bunter," said Sidney James Snoop, looking very curiously at the Owl. "He knew you were spoofing."

"I wasn't spoofing!" howled Bunter.

"You could construe better than that if you liked."

"Oh, I could do a lot of things if I liked!" said Bunter loftily. "I don't choose to waste my valuable time grinding Latin. What's the good of it? I'm going to be a stockbroker when I grow up, and a stockbroker doesn't have any Latin customers."

"His customers ain't Latin!" remarked Vernon-Smith. "They're sometimes let in! And you'll be equal to that!"

"Ha, ha, ha!"

"The fact is, I think this classical stuff is all rot!" said Billy Bunter. "I didn't come to Greyfriars to work like a nigger in a plantation. Besides, I'm going to give a lot of time to games this season, and I simply sha'n't be able to mug up classics. Rot, anyway! Talk about Virgil! I could write a better shipwreck scene than the one Quelchy is always harping on. As for Cæsar, it's rot—sheer rot! I jolly well wish the Gauls had done him in before he wrote his dashed piffle about them!"

And, having aired those valuable opinions, Billy Bunter rolled away, quite satisfied with himself. He caught Frank Nugent as the latter was going out into the quad.

"I say, Franky——"

Nugent quickened his pace, but slackened down again.

"Well?" he said.

"My postal-order hasn't come."

"You don't say so!" answered Frank sarcastically.

"But I do, old chap! And, you see, it leaves me rather in a hole. Can you lend me half-a-crown?"

Nugent did not speak.

"Dumb?" asked Bunter.

"You cleared me out yesterday, Bunter," said Frank Nugent at last. "I'm stony till the end of the week."

"I could do with two bob."

"I haven't two bob."

"Can't you borrow it off Wharton?"

"Eh?"

"Wharton would lend it to you, old chap!"

"If you want Wharton's money, you'd better ask him for it!" said Frank Nugent curtly.

"I don't think he'd make me a loan; anyway, I don't choose to ask him," said Bunter loftily. "I'm not the fellow to ask favours of anybody, I hope! If you don't choose to lend me money after I've saved your life——"

"I—I'll speak to Wharton."

"Go ahead, old fellow!" said Bunter encouragingly.

Frank Nugent joined his chum in the quad, and came back in a couple of minutes. He placed two shillings in Bunter's fat hand without speaking.

"Couldn't make it half-a-crown?" growled Bunter.

Nugent walked away without replying. Billy Bunter looked at the two shillings in his fat hand, and looked after Nugent, and then at the two shillings again. Then he ejaculated:

"Beast!"

And, having thus expressed his sense of obligation, Billy Bunter rolled away to the tuckshop, where the two shillings speedily disappeared into Mrs. Nimble's till.

THE TENTH CHAPTER.
The Redclyffe Match!

"WHERE'S Bunter?"

Harry Wharton was asking that question some time after dinner. The Remove fellows were beginning to gather on Little Side, and Billy Bunter was wanted.

"Anybody seen Bunter?"

"Look in the tuckshop!" grinned Hazeldene.

Wharton laughed, and went into Mrs. Mimble's little shop. It was not very long since dinner, but Bunter apparently had an aching void, which led him to the good lady's establishment. He was arguing with Mrs. Mimble over the counter.

"It's simply a question of waiting till this evening, Mrs. Mimble, till my postal-order comes!" the fat junior was explaining, when Wharton entered and clapped him on the shoulder.

"Ow!" howled Bunter, spinning round. "You beast, Bolsover——"

"You fat duffer!" answered Wharton.

"Oh, it's you, Harry, old chap!"

"Anything wrong with your blinkers?" demanded Wharton in surprise. "I thought you'd got over your short sight."

"What rot!"

"You seemed to, for the last few weeks."

"The fact is, I—I was joking!" stammered Bunter. "I knew it was you all the time! He, he, he! One of my little jokes!"

"I don't see the joke."

"You wouldn't; you haven't much brains, you know, Wharton! I say, can you lend me a couple of bob?"

"No!" said Wharton curtly.

"I must have a snack before we play Redclyffe!" said Bunter. "Otherwise I shall have to ask you to scratch my name!"

"All right!" said Wharton cheerfully. "Smithy's been bothering me no end to give his pal Redwing a chance, and he's a good man. You mean it?"

"Eh? Nunno!" said Bunter hurriedly. "Not at all! Only a—a—a joke."

"You seem to be full of jokes this afternoon, Bunter!"

"But the fact is, old chap, I simply must have a snack," said Bunter, blinking at the captain of the Remove. "Quelchy wouldn't let me have more than three helpings at dinner. Anybody would think it was still war-time, the way that old beak watches a chap eat. And I've had nothing since but a jam-tart and a slice of cake and a few apples. I'm going to play a tremendous game this afternoon; and I must have a few tarts to keep my strength up."

"Tarts won't do you any good just before a match."

"The very thing, my dear chap. You have some, too," said Bunter generously. "I'll stand them. Lend me two bob—say three——"

"I can stand myself tarts if I want them. No good lending you the money to stand them."

"I should square out of my postal-order, of course. That's understood," said Bunter, with dignity. "I think it's rather ungrateful of you to refuse me a small loan."

"Ungrateful!" repeated Wharton.

"Certainly. Considering that I have risked my life to save your pal from being run over by a motor-car——"

"What?"

"I—I mean, to save him from being drowned in a runaway river—that is to say, in a river—you might squeeze out half-a-crown."

"You're squeezing enough out of Nugent on the strength of that," said Wharton drily. "Come on Bunter; you're wanted on Little Side."

"I can't come till I've had a snack."

"Stay here, then," said Wharton gruffly. "I'll give your place to Tom Redwing. Blessed if I don't think I'd better, anyway!"

"Hold on! I'm coming!"

Bunter hurried out of the tuckshop after the captain of the Remove. He did not mean to lose his place in the Remove Eleven that afternoon if he could help it.

Wharton was growing very restive.

Somehow—he hardly knew how—his faith in Bunter as a cricketer was declining. He was resolved not to attach any importance to Wally Bunter's mysterious warning of the previous evening; but perhaps it lingered in his mind, all the same. Bunter seemed to have fallen back all of a sudden into his old manners and customs, which coincided strangely with Wally's warning.

Yet it seemed absurd to suppose that the fat junior could possibly have lost the skill he had seemed to acquire on the cricket-field. However like he was now to his old self, he could hardly have lapsed into his former obtuse clumsiness at games.

Still, Wharton was less satisfied than before with his selection of Bunter as a member of the Eleven, and he would not have been sorry if the fat junior had resigned his place in the team. That, however, was not at all likely to happen.

Billy Bunter rolled off to change for the match, and he reappeared on Little Side looking as if he were just about to burst out of his flannels. He came on the field with an important strut, his bat tucked under one fat arm.

"I say, you fellows, when are Redclyffe coming?" he inquired.

"Any minute," answered Wharton.

"Like their cheek to keep me waiting!"

"You!" ejaculated Bob Cherry.

"Yes, me!" answered the Owl of the Remove loftily.

"Are you captain and team all rolled into one, by any chance?" inquired Bob. "Or are you a fat, conceited duffer?"

"I'm sorry to see this jealousy in you as well as Wharton, Cherry. That's a great drawback in cricket," remarked Bunter sagely. "It leads to such a lot of jealousy."

Bob Cherry breathed hard.

"Dear old Bunter!" said Peter Todd affectionately. "We thought he had changed; as if a leopard could change his spots, and a giddy Ethiopian his skin! It's the dear old Bunter we always knew."

"Oh, really, Toddy——"

"Here come Redclyffe," said Vernon-Smith.

Fane of Redclyffe and his merry men had arrived. Some of them glanced rather curiously at Bunter, finding that ample youth in the Remove Eleven. Bunter ran Harry Wharton down after he had tossed for innings with the Redclyffe skipper.

"We bat first?" asked Bunter.

"Yes."

"It's a single innings match?" pursued the Owl of the Remove.

"You know it is—or you ought to know."

"Then a lot depends on the opening. Now, I'm going to speak to you quite plainly, Wharton——"

"You needn't trouble."

"I feel it's my duty to state my opinion," said Bunter firmly, "as a prominent member of the team——"

"Cut it short!"

"I think I ought to open the innings. You can take the bowler's end, if you like; I don't mind. But—— I wish you wouldn't walk away while I'm talking to you, Wharton!" roared Bunter.

But Wharton did walk away.

The captain of the Remove opened the innings, with Vernon-Smith at the other end. Billy Bunter expressed his feelings with a loud snort.

"Conceited ass!" he remarked to the fellow standing near him, who happened to be Frank Nugent.

"Oh, shut up!" was Frank's answer.

Bunter turned to Bolsover major for sympathy. Bolsover was looking on, giving laborious explanations of the game to the French junior, Dupont, which was rather good-natured of Bolsover.

"Just like Wharton to shove in like this, isn't it?" said Bunter. "You won't catch him putting his best man on to begin—no fear!"

Bolsover major stared at him.

"You silly chump!" he answered.

"Oh, really, Bolsover——"

"Dry up!"

And Billy Bunter sniffed, and dried up at last.

THE ELEVENTH CHAPTER.
Bunter in All His Glory!

"MAN in!"

"Bunter!"

"Where's that fat bounder?"

The Remove were five down for fifty when Bunter's name was called. But the Owl of the Remove was not to be seen.

Harry Wharton knitted his brows.

"You go in next, Frank," he said. "And some of you cut off to the tuckshop and roll that fat rotter here. Yank him along by the ears if necessary."

Nugent went to the wickets, and a few minutes later Billy Bunter reappeared on the field, escorted by Bob Cherry and Squiff, who had a grip on his fat arms. There was a smear of jam on the Owl's fat face, which looked as if he had raised a loan somewhere on the cricket-field.

"Why can't you stay where you're wanted, you duffer?" exclaimed Wharton.

"I might have guessed you'd soon be out," assented Bunter. "How many runs did you make—two, or three?"

"You're to go in next."

"Oh, I'm ready! The others won't be wanted."

"Oh, won't they?" demanded Bob Cherry.

"I shall knock up all the runs we need. I suppose we're going to give Redclyffe a look-in before dark. I advise Wharton to declare at a hundred."

"We haven't got the hundred yet, ass!"

"That's all right, when I get to work."

"Blessed is he that bloweth his own trumpet!" remarked Squiff.

"I don't think much of their bowling," said Bunter, blinking at the field. "Their fielding's rather poor, too. Look at that! Nugent's got a two. I should have caught him out if I'd been at short-slip."

"Short-slip never had an earthly, you duffer."

"I should have done it."

"Fathead!" was Squiff's reply to that.

Sidney James Snoop was among the onlookers near the pavilion, and he was listening to Bunter's remarks with a very odd expression on his face. What had come over Wally Bunter was a mystery to Snoop, and a strange and curious suspicion was beginning to take root in his mind. He, and only he, had known that Wally had taken Billy Bunter's place at Greyfriars, and he had come to know Wally better than the other fellows. And the startling thought came into his mind, as he listened to Bunter, that the cousins had, without his knowledge, changed back.

That really seemed the only way of accounting for Bunter's present manners and customs; but it was such a startling thought that Snoop dismissed it from his mind at first.

"Hallo, hallo, hallo! There goes Franky!"

Nugent was out for four runs.

"Man in, Bunter!"

"Oh, I'm ready! Where's my bat?"

"There it is, under your silly nose, Owl!"

"If Fane knows anything, he'll tell 'em to field deep," said Bunter, as he started. "They'll need to. You fellows can look out for some hard hitting. I'm going to surprise you!"

And Bunter rolled out to the wicket.

All eyes were upon him as he stood up to receive the rest of the over from Fane of Redclyffe.

Harry Wharton knitted his brows as he watched. Bunter had adopted an exaggerated straddle, which was not much like Wally's style. More than ever the fat junior seemed his old, clumsy, inept self.

Fane grinned along the pitch. He did not think it would take him long to get this batsman out.

He was right.

The ball came along, and Billy Bunter swiped at it—a mighty swipe. If the willow had met the leather the ball would probably have travelled somewhere. But it didn't! It missed by about a yard. The ball knocked out the middle stump, and the bat, meeting with no resistance, swept round, and Billy Bunter swept round after it. The fat junior spun a nearly complete circle, tangled his fat little legs, and sat down.

"Yow! Ow!"

"Ha, ha, ha!"

There was a roar of laughter all round the field. Harry Wharton did not laugh. His face was a study.

"Bravo, Bunter! Do that again!" howled Bolsover major.

"Ha, ha, ha!"

"Zat is somezing I have not seen before!" exclaimed Dupont. "Zat is some more cricket I have yet to learn. What you call him, Bolsover?"

"Ha, ha, ha!"

"How's that?" Fane was shrieking.

"Out!" gasped the umpire, almost overcome.

"Yaroooh!"

"You're out, Bunter!"

"Yow-ow! Where's my specs? Oh, my hat! I fell over something!"

"Ha, ha, ha!"

Billy Bunter scrambled up, set his glasses straight on his fat little nose, and blinked round at a howling field.

"I say, you fellows, I'm not out——"

"Out!"

"But I say——"

"Come off, you fat idiot!" roared Bob Cherry. "Prod him with your bat, Marky, and get a move on him!"

Mark Linley was coming out to the wicket. Billy Bunter, with a snort of indignation, rolled back to the pavilion.

"What price ducks' eggs?" howled Sammy Bunter, of the Second from the crowd.

"Cheap to-day!" grinned Squiff.

"The cheapfulness is terrific!"

Harry Wharton clapped Bunter on the shoulder.

"What do you mean by it?" he demanded.

"What do you mean?" snorted

Bunter. "I'm not out! The umpire's a silly ass! You're another!"

"Oh, my hat!"

"I fell over something——"

"Your own silly hoofs, you ass!" shrieked Bob Cherry.

"My only hat!" exclaimed Sidney James Snoop. "That's not Wally! I knew it!"

"Wally?" repeated Bob Cherry, looking at him. "What do you mean, Snoop? Who supposed it was Wally?"

"I did! I—I mean——" stammered Snoop.

"Bravo, Marky! Well hit!"

Mark Linley was doing well at the wickets. The attention of the juniors was turned to the game again, and Bunter was left to puff and pant unheeded.

Greyfriars were all down at last for seventy-five—the hundred promised by W. G. Bunter had not materialised. The duck's egg scored by the Owl of the Remove was rather serious for his side. Wharton had looked for at least twenty from him. He was puzzled and exasperated. Any batsman might have had bad luck—but Bunter's was not bad luck—it was sheer incompetence. It was plain to everyone on the field—excepting Bunter—that he could not play cricket, and it was hard to understand.

Snoop understood, however.

He had no further doubts. The two Bunters had changed back during that meeting at Friardale the previous day. That explained everything. Sidney James was sure of it at last.

He debated in his mind whether to explain to Wharton before the Redclyffe innings began. He had undertaken to keep Wally's secret; but now that Wally Bunter had gone from Greyfriars—as he evidently was—Snoop did not see any reason why the secret should be kept. It was too late to keep Bunter from losing a wicket for his side; but the obtuse Owl might be prevented from doing any further damage.

He decided to speak to Bunter first. He cornered the Owl of the Remove near the pavilion.

"I've found you out, you fat spoofer!" he said in a low voice.

Bunter blinked at him.

"Eh, what?" he exclaimed peevishly.

"You're not Wally!" said Snoop.

Bunter stared. As he was not aware that Snoop knew Wally's secret, the remark naturally astonished him.

"Potty?" he asked. "Who said I was Wally?"

"You're Billy Bunter!" said Snoop. "You changed back with your cousin yesterday. That's clear enough now!"

Bunter jumped.

"D-d-did you know?" he stuttered. "Did that silly ass Wally tell you? Oh, my hat!"

"You ought to have resigned the place in the team!" exclaimed Snoop. "It was given to Wally, not to you!"

"Oh really, Snoop——"

"If I'd known earlier I'd have told Wharton, in time to save that wicket," said Sidney James. "Wally oughtn't to have left Wharton in the lurch like this, with a silly idiot to play for him!"

"Look here——"

"He ought to have given Wharton the tip, somehow——"

"He couldn't!" grinned Bunter. "We promised each other to keep it dark, you see. How did you find it out? I don't believe Wally told you!"

"I found it out, and he had to own up! But I was going to keep it dark. Now he's gone it doesn't matter. I shall speak to Wharton."

"I—I say, don't do anything of the kind!" exclaimed Bunter in alarm. "Why, he will very likely push me out of the team. And I'm going to bowl for the Remove, you know, and take no end of wickets!"

"You silly chump!"

"If I'm dropped out it means losing the match for Greyfriars!" said Billy Bunter impressively. "Mind that!"

"Ass!" answered Snoop.

He turned away. Bunter's statement that he was to bowl for the Remove finally decided him. Wally had proved a first-class bowler, and, in spite of Bunter's exhibition at the wicket, he was certain to be given a chance with the ball. And that meant runs for Redclyffe—even one over, from Bunter, might be worth a dozen runs to them. Snoop felt that it was his duty to stop that.

It was not so easy to explain to Wharton, however. He was talking with Fane, before the visitors' innings started, and Snoop could not broach the matter in the presence of the Redclyffe fellows. It was not till the Remove players were going into the field that Sidney James had a chance to speak.

He caught Wharton by the arm and stopped him, and Harry looked at him with impatient inquiry.

"What do you want, Snoop? Let go!"

"You're playing Bunter——"

"Do let me go!"

"Don't let him bowl!"

"What do you mean? He can't bat to-day, somehow, but he's a good bowler," said Harry "Let go my arm, Snoop! I've got to go."

"He's not Wally—I mean—it's Billy Bunter!" stammered Snoop. "It was Wally you picked for the team—and now——"

Wharton stared at him.

"I don't understand you, Snoop," he said tartly. "Let go, I tell you!"

"But I tell you——"

Wharton jerked his arm away, and went into the field. He had not made head or tail of what Snoop was trying to say, and he really wondered for a moment whether Sidney James was quite right in his senses. Only for a moment, however; the next he had forgotten Snoop's existence.

Snoop shrugged his shoulders as he fell back into the crowd. He had done his best, but it had come to nothing. Billy Bunter was destined to exhibit to an astonished world his wonderful powers as a bowler.

Hurree Jamset Ram Singh took the first over, and Squiff relieved him. Billy Bunter blinked with indignant inquiry at his skipper. While the field crossed after an over, he found an opportunity of speaking to Wharton.

"Has Snoop been spinning you a yarn?" he demanded.

"Eh, what? He said something—some rot. What about it?"

"It's all rot!" said Bunter. "Don't you believe him! Wally's been at St. Jim's all the time, you know!"

"Eh?"

"As for me," said Bunter impressively, "I haven't been a mile from Greyfriars."

"What on earth are you talking about?"

"Snoop was simply talking out of his hat. Now, what I want to know is, why don't you put me on to bowl?"

"Next, after Inky's been on again," said Harry.

"Oh, all right!"

Hurree Jamset Ram Singh's next over cost Redclyffe a wicket. Fane was at the batting end when Bunter was put on to bowl.

The first ball made the Greyfriars fellows stare, and the Redcliffians smile. It was such a ball as a clumsy fag in the Second Form might have sent down to another fag. Fane grinned as he knocked it away for two.

The next ball gave him four, and the next another four. The Redcliffians grinned at one another.

Harry Wharton called to Bunter as he returned the ball to him.

"Play up, Bunter!"

"Oh, don't you worry!" answered the Owl of the Remove. "I know how to bowl, Wharton. Precious little you could teach me!"

"You're giving them runs," said Harry, compressing his lips.

"Rot! Your fielding's jolly bad!"

"Bunter, you—you——"

"I'm giving you easy catches, if you knew how to take them. You're all so jolly clumsy!"

"Oh!"

"The fact is, Wharton," said Bunter, blinking at his captain severely, "I expect better backing than this if my bowling's to be of any use. I might as well have a field of tin soldiers. Put some life into it!"

And Bunter went to his work, leaving his skipper speechless.

Fane carelessly knocked the next ball away to the boundary. A couple of twos finished the over.

"My hat!" murmured Harry Wharton in utter dismay.

He was not surprised to see the general grin on the Redclyffian visage. Bowling like this was enough to make anybody grin.

Bunter, much to his wrath and indignation, was not given the ball any more, so far as bowling went. But the Redclyffe batsmen showed a remarkable unanimity in knocking the leather into Bunter's territory whenever they could, so he had great chances in the field. Unfortunately, he did not improve any of those chances. With that involuntary support from the Greyfriars field the Redclyffe innings looked very prosperous.

But fortune favoured the Remove in spite of Bunter. The hat-trick by Hurree Jamset Ram Singh put a different complexion on matters, and it was repeated by Tom Brown, of New Zealand.

And so it came about that Redclyffe were all down at last for a run under the number they wanted to tie, and the Greyfriars Remove remained winners by a narrow margin.

"Just done it!" said Billy Bunter, as he rolled off the field. "You've stuck it out till nearly dark, and just done it! If I'd had the bowling——"

"It wouldn't have lasted so long, certainly," grinned Bob Cherry. "They'd have licked us pretty early!"

Snort!

"I want to have a word with you presently, Bunter," said Harry Wharton quietly.

"Oh, rats!" answered Bunter. "The fact is, Wharton, you can't play cricket, and you don't even know enough to play a good man when you've got one. That's your chief drawback—conceit and fatheadedness! So now you know!"

And Bunter rolled off.

THE TWELFTH CHAPTER.
Light at Last!

"YOU fat villain!"

"I say, you fellows——"

"You spoofing Hun!"

"Eh?"

"Bump him!"

"Squash him!"

Billy Bunter jumped up in alarm.

He was in Study No. 7, enjoying his tea. He had come in before the other fellows, and made a handsome collection of tuck from several studies. Now he was enjoying his plunder; but his enjoyment was interrupted by the sudden entrance of five wrathful juniors.

Bunter blinked at the Famous Five in alarm, and backed round the study table.

"I—I say, wharrer marrer?" he stammered. "If you're going to make a fuss about these saveloys, Bob Cherry, well——"

"You fat rotter!"

"Besides, I never took them from your study, they came by post; a present from one of my titled relations. As for this cake, Nugent——"

"You spoofing rascal!" roared Nugent.

"If you're going to grudge a cake to the fellow who risked his life to pull you out of the river, Nugent——"

"You didn't!" howled Nugent.

"Oh, really, you know——"

"It was your cousin Wally!" exclaimed Wharton. "You spoofer, we've had it all from Snoop!"

Bunter's jaw dropped.

"Sn-o-o-oop?" he stammered.

"Yes, Snoop!" growled Johnny Bull. "It seems that Snoop's known it for a long time. You changed places with your cousin Wally because he wanted to come to Greyfriars, and you wanted to go to St. Jim's——"

"Oh, really, Bull——"

"We were asses not to guess, knowing the two fat bounders to be so much alike," said Harry Wharton. "Still, who'd ever have thought of such a game of spoof?"

"Blessed if I should," said Bob.

"That's why Wally telephoned from St. Jim's last night, and warned me not to play that fat idiot," continued Wharton. "I understand now. I wish I'd taken his tip!"

"I—I say, you fellows——" stuttered Bunter.

"Well, what have you got to say?" demanded the captain of the Remove. "You shoved yourself into the Eleven, knowing it was your bounder of a cousin I'd given the place to——"

"N-n-not at all, I—I haven't been to St. Jim's——"

"What?"

"I've been here all the time, you know!"

"Why, you owned up to Snoop!" exclaimed Nugent.

"Not at all—Snoop's dreaming. Besides, he's untruthful. I've often been shocked at Snoop for his untruthfulness. If there's anything I really despise in a fellow, it's untruthfulness!"

"Oh, fan me, somebody!" gasped Bob Cherry.

"I haven't been anywhere near St. Jim's," continued Bunter cheerfully. "Not at all. I didn't bolt yesterday because old Lathom had given me a lot of lines, and Grundy of the Shell was going to lick me over a measly cake he'd lost from his study. Rotten measly cake, too—not at all like the cakes I get from home. Just like Grundy!"

"Oh, crumbs!"

"As for changing places with Wally, I don't even know what you mean. Besides, it was Wally's idea from the very beginning."

"It's no good talking to him," said Harry Wharton. "We shall have to keep this dark, you fellows, now we know. The Head would be no end waxy if he knew. But that spoofing rotter——"

"I really don't see why you're calling me names, Wharton. I rely upon you to keep it dark, of course. The Head would be wild, and he might pitch into me. Besides, it isn't true!"

"You jolly nearly lost us the Redclyffe match!" roared Bob Cherry.

"You mean you nearly lost it by your rotten play, I suppose. I don't want to brag, but I must say that I was about the only good cricketer on the field," said Bunter warmly. "I'm not a fellow to blow my own trumpet, I hope, but I must say that!"

"Collar him!" gasped Bob.

"Here, I say—hands off—I say, Nugent, you beast, after I saved your life—— Yarooooh! Help! Murder! Fire!"

Bump, bump, bump!

"Yooop! Help! Fire!" roared Billy Bunter. "I say, you fellows,, it was only a joke, you know! Simply a joke! He, he, he! Yoooop!"

Bump!

The Famous Five left Billy Bunter sitting on his study carpet. The way of the transgressor had proved hard once more!

(Don't miss "FOES OF THE REMOVE!"—next Monday's grand complete story of Harry Wharton & Co., by FRANK RICHARDS.)

Goggs, Grammarian

By Richard Randolph

SYNOPSIS.

Johnny Goggs—in company with Blount, Trickett, and Waters—come to Rylcombe Grammar School from Franklingham, which has been burnt down.

Goggs is a ventriloquist, a ju-jitsu expert, and an all-round sportsman, though he behaves like a simpleton.

Gordon Gay & Co. are discussing a plan of campaign with Goggs, in Gay's study, and Carker listens at the keyhole. He leaves a sixpenny-piece on the floor, as an excuse if he is discovered. Goggs comes out of the study and coolly appropriates the coin.

(Now read on.)

Phelim O'Haggarty.

THEY passed on their opposite ways, Carker scowling, Goggs smiling.

"Now, I wonder," said Goggs, to himself, "whether our dear friend Carker was indulging his curiosity at that door? I have gathered that he has pleasant little habits of that kind, and I have heard of such tricks as this to avert suspicion. We must keep an eye or two upon Carker!"

He went on to his own study, and returned to the rest in a minute or so with something hidden under his jacket.

"Will you all be so very kind as to offer me a view of your backs?" he asked.

"Eh?" said Lane and Harry Wootton together.

"He means that he wants you all to turn away from him for a minute," explained Bags.

"Then why in the world doesn't he say so?" growled Wootton minor.

"I was under the impression that my speech was perfectly clear, and impossible to be misunderstood by anyone of even infantile intelligence," Goggs said, rather sadly. "In the near future I hope to fit myself for my company by a prolonged course of reading in the nursery play-book direction. At present I see that I must submit to being interpreted by my dear friend Bagshaw."

"You'll submit to something a heap worse than that if you don't stop that rot!" growled Frank Monk.

"I think not, my dear—er—Nuts; I really think not! Will you please all turn round, close your eyes, and—er—hold your tongues? To make it perfectly clear what I mean, I may add that you are not necessarily expected to use your fingers for that purpose, though their use is not barred if it will be of any real assistance to you."

They turned round. Goggs whipped from under his jacket a red wig and a pair of glasses of the pince-nez type. Off came his big spectacles. The glasses were thrust into place. The red wig covered his smooth hair. The very expression of his face changed wonderfully.

"Shure, an' yez may now turrn round!" he said.

They turned, and gasped in surprise.

For to their eyes it was no longer Johnny Goggs who stood there, but someone quite unlike him. Possibly it was the manner of speech he had adopted that led them all—with the exception of Mont Blanc, whose views on the nationalities of the United Kingdom were as hazy as those of most people from the Continent are—to see in him a typical Irish boy.

"Allow me to inthrojuice to yez Phelim O'Hoggarty, from Ballynakillemall, a gintleman quite unknown to anny spalpeen at St. Jim's," said Goggs, in the richest of brogues.

"My hat!"

"Hanged if he isn't a fair knock-out!"

"That's the style! That does it!"

"You're licked, Gordon! You never did anything up to that mark!"

"It's jolly good," admitted Gay frankly. "But can he keep it up?"

"Bedad an' begorra an' bejabers, an' pwhy for would I not?" inquired Goggs.

"You're overdoing the thing," said Gay critically.

"I am adapting my impersonation of the part to the undeveloped minds with which I have to deal at present," replied Goggs, in his natural voice and his usual manner.

"Oh, come along!" said Carboy. "There isn't a giddy chap at St. Jim's keen enough to spot Goggles under that disguise! And yet it's nothing but a wig and a different pair of glasses! My hat!"

"I do not think it will serve any useful purpose for me to wear that, my dear Carbuncle," said Goggs gravely.

"Wear what, chump?"

"Your hat. It would not differ sufficiently from my own to help in the disguise. And it might be overdoing the part to wear the typical hat of the stage Hibernian—I really forget whether they call it a caubeen or a shillelagh."

"Ass! I didn't mean——"

Goggs shook his head sadly.

"I fear we shall never understand one another, Boil. There are centuries of progress and culture between your status and mine. By a great effort I may now and then get down to the level of your intelligence; but it is too much to hope that you should ever rise to the level of mine!"

"Well, I'm jiggered! Oh, look here, you fellows, does the silly, swanking ass mean all that?" demanded Carboy of Goggs' old chums.

"I suppose so," answered Bags.

"It's true enough, isn't it?" added Tricks.

"You really are a frightfully stupid, backward sort of chap compared to our Goggsbird, Carboy," chimed in Wagtail, shaking his head.

"Look here, I'm not going——"

"You are, Carboy, and you're going now!" broke in Gay. "If we waste any more time the dinner-bell will have gone before we're back. Quick march! Come along, Goggles, you blessed superman!"

"What? In these—er—trousers?" asked Goggs.

"What have your bags—— Oh, I see! No, take the giddy wig off till we're clear of the school. We don't want anyone here to spot Phelim."

Plots and Counterplots.

GOGGS drew Bags aside as the party passed into the corridor.

"Mind staying behind?" he asked.

The directness of his speech made it plain to Bags at once that this was no idle question.

"Not a bit, if you want me to," he answered.

"Might keep Wagtail, too. Carker wants watching."

"Carker?" said Bags, in surprise.

He hardly knew the junior named. If Snipe had been mentioned he would not have been surprised.

"Yes. I am not certain, but I suspect him of having found out more than suits our book. If you see him with Larking & Co., you may be sure I'm right."

"You're probably right anyway, old top—you generally are. Cut off! I'll collar Wagtail!"

It was not exactly with a good grace that Waters consented to stay behind; but he did consent.

The nine passed out of gates. A hundred yards or so down the road, with no one in sight, Goggs became Phelim O'Hoggarty, from Ballynakillemall, simply by substituting pince-nez for spectacles and donning the red wig.

"There's a risk in it," said Gay. "But none of our fellows seem to be about; and we can't have the Saints spotting Goggles."

They went on towards the barn. But they were still some little distance from it when three St. Jim's juniors came into sight.

"Cardew, Clive, and Levison," said Frank Monk. "Just as well you're ready for them, Goggles!"

"Rather!" agreed Gay. "Two of them are among the keenest chaps of the whole crowd at spotting anything. You may take Clive in, though he isn't a duffer; but Cardew and Levison need some spoofing."

"Sure, an' they shall be afther havin' all they nade," said Goggs.

"That's the style, Goggles!" said Jack Wootton.

"O'Hoggarty, av yez plase, Masther Wooden," replied Goggs solemnly.

"Hallo!" said Clive, as the three drew up to the nine. "Were you coming along to our show? The trouble's supposed to be over now, you know, though I must say you fellows did your little best to start it again at once."

"Yaas," drawled Cardew. "You succeeded in rousin' the ire of the dear Tommy to the highest pitch. He's really quite a good-tempered chap, is Tommy; but he came back breathin' fire an' slaughter against some of you."

"It was rather thick, you know," said Levison. "Poor old Tommy toddling along with nothing but peace and good will in his tender heart, and then some of you ruffians springing on him from behind and lowering his proud crest in the dust before he had time to say 'knife.' Ha, ha, ha!"

"Beastly thick, I call it!" remarked Clive, evidently in earnest.

"Positively sinful," observed Cardew, obviously not at all in earnest.

"He'll get over it," said Gordon Gay. "It was a—well, you might say it was a kind of mistake."

"We couldn't help it," added Jack Wootton.

"Sounds alarmin'," said Cardew, shrugging his shoulders. "Especially as at the moment you have odds of three to one. I do hope you are not often taken that way."

"Oh, we're not going to pile in on you, if that's what you're getting at!" said Gay.

"That is precisely what I am gettin' at, old gun! I admit candidly that I seldom have any but selfish thoughts. I may experience slight movements of sympathy towards Tommy for his misfortunes, y'know; but really to hurt my feelin's you would have to do likewise to me. An', as I'm not very vigorous to-day, I trust that I may be spared that shock to my delicate constitution."

"Hanged if I shouldn't like to jump on him!" grunted Harry Wootton in the ear of Carboy.

"So should I! That fellow always riles me. He's as long-winded as Goggles, and he is so beastly cool and cheeky."

"I perceive new faces," remarked Cardew. "An' I remember now that our dear Tommy an' the other warriors mentioned new boys as among their opponents of yesterday. Are these two of the doughty champions?"

He looked full at Goggs and Tricks as he spoke.

"Trickett was in it—O'Hoggarty wasn't," answered Gay.

"Shure, an' I don't foight," said Goggs.

"Ah! Sinn Fein, I presume?" returned Cardew.

"Faith, an' ye do presume!"

"Introduce us, Gay!" said Levison.

The ceremony of introduction was briefly put through. Cardew showed a disposition to linger which did not at all suit the Grammarians. He appeared to be interested in Phelim O'Hoggarty, the supposed Irish junior who announced himself a non-combatant.

"It wasn't us you were coming along to see, I take it, Cardew?" said Frank Monk pointedly.

"No, dear boy; though the sight of your cheerful an' ingenuous faces is always a pleasure to me, I assure you. As a matter of fact, I am about to look up my dear old pal Lacy. The separation from Algernon, playmate of my early days, has tried me severely; an' at the first available opportunity I naturally fly to his friendly embrace."

"Rats!" snapped Jack Wootton.

Everyone there knew that Cardew was saying the thing which was not, and some of them suspected him of designs quite unconnected with Lacy.

It was true that he and Algernon Lacy had been schoolfellows at Wodehouse in the past. But there was no love lost between them. Cardew held Lacy in contempt and dislike, and Lacy hated Cardew.

All this mattered little to Gordon Gay & Co. Lacy was no chum of theirs, and Cardew was not among the St. Jim's fellows whom most of them liked best; though between Gordon Gay and him there was a bond.

"Ah, but you don't know the depth of my feelin's, Wootton!" said Cardew. "I pine—I yearn—to look again upon the classic countenance of Algy! Come on, dear boys; let us fly to Algy! We are not really wanted here!"

That was true. Yet the Grammarians looked doubtfully after the St. Jim's chums as they passed on their way towards the Grammar School.

"I don't half like it!" admitted Gay.

"Those three are up to something," said Monk. "Cardew's deep as the Atlantic, and Levison's as wily as a Red Indian, and Clive's hefty enough, though he's not as dodgy as they are."

"Tom Merry wouldn't come along again to-day," Wootton major said, stroking the back of his head thoughtfully. "And neither would Blake and that crowd. But these are just the chaps they'd send to spy out the land."

"And we've something hanging on it," remarked his brother. "You challenged them, you know, Gordon!"

"I know. Well, I don't really see what they could do, and, as Goggs is with us, they can't find out a lot."

"They might happen on something by chance, though," said Lane.

"Ze dear Goggs—he might be mention by somevon," Mont Blanc added.

"Well, we've got to risk that. Kim on, you cripples!"

There was less risk than they fancied. The three were not really going to the Grammar School at all. But a risk—just that which had been guarded against—had already been run; and it had not left Cardew unsuspicious.

"Levison, dear boy," said Cardew, "what do you make of that freak O'Hagan?"

"O'Hoggarty," Clive corrected him.

"I was just thinking about the bounder," answered Ernest Levison. "I don't know what to make of him. There was something about his face that I seemed to know, and yet—no, he isn't quite like anyone else I ever saw. And his voice was strange to me, anyway."

"H'm! I'll freely admit that I can't place O'Hea——"

"O'Hoggarty," said Clive again.

"What a pedantically correct individual you are, Sidney dear! What does it matter? O'Hea, O'Hagan, or O'Hoggarty—it's all one. I don't a bit believe any of the names belongs to him!"

"Hanged if I can make out what you're driving at, Cardew!" said Clive, looking completely puzzled.

"My dear infant, you're not expected to! Don't get thinkin'—it will only make its poor, dear ickle head ache. What do you think, Levison, old bean?"

"Levison's allowed to think, then?" snorted Clive.

"Levison can't be kept out of it," answered Cardew gravely.

"Well, if Gay hadn't been there I should have thought it was Gay in disguise," said Levison slowly.

"Ass! He'd have been there all the same if he had been in disguise!" Clive put in.

But they took no notice of Clive.

"Good, Sherlock—good!" chirruped Cardew. "But it couldn't have been Gay, an' I can't think of any of the rest capable of doin' it in style like that."

Printed and published every Monday by the Proprietors, the Amalgamated Press, Limited, The Fleetway House, Farringdon Street, London, E.C. 4. Advertisement offices: The Fleetway House, Farringdon Street, London, E.C. 4. Subscription rates: Inland and abroad (except in South Africa and Australasia), 8s. 10d. per annum, 4s. 5d. for six months. Sole agents for South Africa: The Central News Agency, Ltd. Sole agents for Australia and New Zealand: Messrs. Gordon & Gotch, Ltd.; and for Canada: The Imperial News Co., Ltd.—Saturday, April 26th, 1919. D

"Must be one of the new fellows," said Levison. "There are three or four of them, I've heard!"

"But why should a new chap disguise himself?" asked Cardew.

"Was he disguised?" inquired Clive.

"I don't know, dashed if I do! The only thing I'm certain of is that there's somethin' fishy about it somewhere, by gad! But where it is, an' what it is—well, that's beyond me at present."

The three passed the Grammar School and held on their way to the house farther up the road to which they were bound. It was on their return journey that they saw Bags and Wagtail hurry out of the Grammar School gates with their bikes.

The two just glanced at the trio of St. Jim's juniors—not uninterested in them, it seemed, but in too big a hurry to do more than glance.

"Two more of the new chums!" observed Clive.

"He's comin' on, Levison," said Cardew. "That was a deduction. They wore Grammar School caps; Sidney has not seen them before—ergo, they are new fellows. No flaw in it, either. Good, dear boy, good—dashed good, by gad!"

"Oh, shut up, ass!" growled Clive.

"Larking, Carpenter, and Snipe ahead!" remarked Levison. "It's a rummy bizney; but it really looks to me as though the two new chaps were chasing those three."

"Queer taste!" yawned Cardew. "From the little I have been privileged to see of Larkin', Carpenter, an' Snipe, I would prefer to chase myself in the other direction. Snipe's a positively putrid cad! Larkin's not an agreeable person. An' even Carpenter's very so-so!"

"I don't fancy they are chasing them with any notion of falling on their necks and kissing them!" said Levison, with one of his sardonic grins.

"If you ask me," Clive said, "all this has something to do with Gay and that crowd, and that red-headed Irish bounder."

"Thinkin' again, Sidney—thinkin' again!" protested Cardew. "What a dashed crop of headaches you are raisin' for yourself!"

"I'll bet Clive's right, though!" said Levison.

And, of course, Clive was right.

A Mix-up!

Bags and Wagtail had done their best to carry out Goggs' instructions. They had kept a watch on Carker as long as it was possible. But Carker had tumbled to the fact that he was being watched, and had managed to slip away.

It was by the merest chance that they came upon him again—in close conference with Larking & Co.

The conference broke up directly they approached. Larking, Carpenter, and Snipe lounged off in one direction, hands in pockets, Carker went in another.

He had told them what was in the wind, and he had no intention of sharing any enterprise they might undertake in consequence of his information. That was not Carker's way. Whenever he could contrive it he got his grudges paid by deputy.

It was rather a risky enterprise that Larking and Carpenter meditated. They were very sore over their defeat of the night before, and both were ready to take risks.

Snipe, though also sore, was by no means so ready. Danger did not appeal to Snipe; he hated getting hurt. And he saw that none of them was likely to come through an attempt at interference with Gordon Gay & Co. without damage.

But he had to go. Larking and Carpenter gave him no choice in the matter.

They only waited until they thought Blount and Waters were out of the way, and then they fetched out their bikes and made for the gates.

But Wagtail, posted at a window, saw; and it was not a long start that the three got. Bags and Wagtail rode hard.

"Can we catch them up before they get to the barn, Bags?" panted Wagtail.

"May catch them—may get there in time to warn the fellows of their coming. My word! Hear Snipe blowing?"

Snipe was puffing hard, and would have fallen behind but for the determination of his companions to keep him with them. But Wagtail was also blowing a bit, and it became more and more evident that he and Bags would not arrive together in time to give an effective warning.

"I'm going on!" said Bags.

(Continued on page 16.)

The Editor's Chat.

The Companion Papers are:

THE MAGNET. Every Monday. **THE GEM.** Every Wed. **THE BOYS' FRIEND.** Every Monday. **CHUCKLES.** Every Friday. **THE PENNY POPULAR.** Every Friday.

YOUR EDITOR IS ALWAYS GLAD TO HEAR FROM HIS READERS.

YOUR EDITOR'S EASTER GREETING.

By the time this issue of the MAGNET Library is in my readers' hands Easter will be upon us.

In many respects Easter is a festival grander than Christmas. It brings with it the first flush of spring; and one's thoughts turn instinctively to holidays and cycling-tours and picnics.

No Bank Holiday is ever dull if spent in the right way. Certainly no Bank Holiday can be dull when the MAGNET Library figures on the list of attractions.

This week's story will, I feel confident, bring mirth and delight into the hearts of thousands; for wherever those magic words "By Frank Richards" appear, they bring in their train a heritage of happy laughter.

The first peace-time Easter has dawned; and, although all is not well with the world, and there are critical times ahead, we are living under much happier conditions than was the case last Easter.

I hope that my thousands of Magnetite chums will give themselves up to the enjoyment of a real good time—a time of sheer happiness and content.

Let every bell ring out!

There is peace and joy in our fair land to-day. Other troubles may come; but the nightmare of war is over, and we may look to the future with radiant faces, resolved to meet all its changes and chances in the same spirit which has animated the British nation during four years of crisis and upheaval.

For Next Monday:

"FOES OF THE REMOVE!"

By Frank Richards.

Napoleon Dupont, the French junior of the Remove, is the central figure in next week's grand long complete story of school-life.

Bolsover major, who, in spite of his bullying ways, has hitherto been on the best of terms with the French boy, breaks out at last, and the vials of his wrath descend upon the head of Dupont.

After a glove-fight in the gym between the two study-mates, Bolsover major considers the incident closed; but he is too premature! Napoleon Dupont broods on the treatment he has received, and, in order to defend his honour, he takes a step which is altogether without precedent in the history of Greyfriars. So grave a view do the authorities take of Dupont's action that his expulsion from the school seems more than probable; but the French junior takes Time by the forelock, and, without waiting for the sentence, disappears from the school, thus causing a temporary lull in the campaign between the

"FOES OF THE REMOVE!"

This story combines drama and humour with a fine study of character, and must surely rank with Frank Richards' best.

THE MAN WHO STAYED AT HOME!

No Easter Holiday for Frank Richards!

Shortly before going to press with this number I wrote to Mr. Frank Richards, urging him to take a much-needed holiday at Eastertide.

Few men have worked so untiringly, under adverse conditions, during the past few years, as the author of the famous MAGNET stories.

Some readers there are who imagine that Mr. Frank Richards is a machine, from which stories emerge with the regularity of clockwork. So far from this, Mr. Richards is a man, with all a man's worries and responsibilities; and many of his stories during the war were written under circumstances of great difficulty and danger. He once wrote a story telling how the Zeppelins came to Greyfriars. Not many people who read that story would imagine that during its composition the "Zepps" were raining down bombs in the vicinity of the author's house; yet such was the case.

And so, realising that Mr. Frank Richards stood greatly in need of a holiday, I wrote and urged him to take one. And this is his reply:

"My dear Ed,—It was very considerate of you to suggest sea-breezes, and all that sort of thing, for the undersigned; but I cannot throw down the pen at present for obvious reasons.

"I am sending you a MAGNET story herewith, and this puts me ahead with my work, so far as the MAGNET is concerned; but I am busy on a big scheme in connection with the 'Penny Popular'—a scheme which I want to tackle while it is red-hot, so to speak.

"My Easter 'holidays' will therefore be spent in my 'den,' and I will postpone the rest and change you kindly suggest until after the completion of my task.

"With kindest regards,

"Yours ever,

"FRANK RICHARDS."

It is useless to argue with such a determined person as Mr. Frank Richards. For the benefit of those who admire and look forward to his fine stories of school-life, I am allowing him to go ahead with his big scheme without let or hindrance.

When the summer is well advanced, and I ask Mr. Richards to take his long-deferred holiday, he will probably turn round and tell me that he is writing a long "Boys' Friend Library" story dealing with the adventures of Harry Wharton & Co., and that he will postpone his holiday until the following Christmas.

Such is the tireless spirit of the man who to-day stands second to none as a writer of stories for boys and girls. Mr. Richards is foolish, perhaps; but his is a splendid folly. I regard him as a brick; and I can already hear the unanimous chorus of my thousands of loyal reader-chums:

"Hear, hear!"

NOTICES.

Cricket.—Matches Wanted.

ST. JAMES' CARDIFF—17—12 miles—home and away.—H. W. Tutcher, 16, Hendy Street, Roath Park, Cardiff.

WANDLESIDE C.C.—16-17—5 miles.—A. O. Burroughs, 2, Stanley Terrace, Beddington Corner, Mitcham Junction, Surrey.

Back Numbers Wanted.

Emmett Francis Cross, 77, Waller Street, Ottawa, Ontario, Canada—all stories dealing with Talbot; also Christmas Numbers of the Companion Papers for 1912-13-14.

A. B. Lowrey, Glenwood, Watford Road, Croxley Green, Herts—"Bob Cherry's Barring-Out," "Heroes of Highcliffe," "The Toff"; "Penny Populars," 50-53; "Schoolboy Outcast," "Bunter the Blade," "The Schoolboy Earl." 1s. 6d. offered. Write first.

F. E. W. Sproat, 14, Rock Park, Rock Ferry, Cheshire—"Gem," "Stolen Holiday"; MAGNETS, "House on the Heath," "Schoolboys Never Shall Be Slaves," "Shunned by the Form," "Fall of the Fifth." 4d. each offered. Write first.

D. White, 82, Lowfield Street, Dartford, Kent—"Penny Popular," No. 1; good condition. 6d. offered. Write first.

Charles Rees, 15, Highfield Road, Rock Ferry, Birkenhead—"Bob Cherry's Barring-Out," "Bunter the Blade," "Rival Ventriloquists." 1d. each offered. Write first.

Miss M. Ridley, 94, Wessex Flats, Wedmore Street, Upper Holloway, N. 19—any numbers "Gem" and MAGNET; also "Penny Popular" before 1916. 2d. each offered. Christmas Numbers, 3d.

Miss G. M. Higgins, 37, Salisbury Street, Blandford, Dorset—MAGNET containing "A Very Gallant Gentleman."

H. A. H. (YOUR EDITOR.)

And he shot ahead.

As he drew near to the three in front Larking looked round.

"Here's that bounder Blount coming!" he said. "Spread across the road, and don't let him pass!"

Carpenter and Snipe obeyed, though it was not without a tremor on Snipe's part.

Larking was in the middle. Snipe would have preferred that place. But he had what might be considered the place of honour—that on the right, where the rider behind them was likeliest to attempt passing.

Bags tried another dodge. He put on speed as he drew near, and cut in between Larking and Snipe. Their purpose in spreading out had been so evident that he did not waste any words upon them at the outset.

But Larking thwarted him. He twisted the front wheel of his machine round to the right, and closed in on Snipe. Bags had to use his back-pedal brake in a hurry to avoid a collision.

"Are you going to let me pass, confound you?" snapped Bags.

"Do you want to pass?" inquired Larking mockingly.

Bags hung back for a moment, then tried to dash in on the other side of Larking.

But Carpenter and Larking combined to spoil him there, and he only just saved himself from a fall.

All this had somewhat slowed progress and Wagtail had caught up. But the arrival of Wagtail only complicated matters.

Bags made his third attempt on the right, where Snipe was. Riding in bumping fashion over the rough, grassy edge of the road, he very nearly got past, for Snipe's courage failed him when it came to risking a fall in stopping him.

But if Snipe could not summon up resolution to act, Larking had enough and to spare.

Bags felt his front wheel bump down into a drainage channel. At that moment Larking closed in on Snipe, and, leaning sideways, gave him his shoulder.

"Yowwwwp! You silly idiot" hooted Snipe as he reeled over towards Bags.

Bags did his best to push clear. But he had almost lost his balance before Snipe touched him, and when Snipe fell all over him he had no chance whatever.

He clattered down, with one leg pinned under his bike. Snipe, with a wild howl of rage, tumbled upon him; and next moment Wagtail, riding too hard to stop himself in time, sprawled on top of Snipe!

"Yoooop! Gerrup!" howled Bags.

"Owwwwwwww!" wailed Snipe.

"You silly coots!" roared Wagtail.

"Come on, Carp!" said Larking.

And the two hurried on.

"By gad, though, that was pretty fairly thick, Lark!" said Carpenter doubtfully.

He looked back over his shoulder. The three were struggling up, and bestowing kind words upon one another as they rose. It was plain that their machines had all taken damage, and it seemed unlikely that any of the riders had failed to take some damage also.

"Nobody actually done in, is there?" inquired Larking, not looking round.

"No; but——"

"Oh, don't be squeamish! Something had to be done. And, after all, what did I do? Merely fell against Snipey, who is a pal of mine. I didn't touch Blount or Waters. It might have been the most complete accident."

"But it wasn't!"

"Will you swear to that, Carp? I don't see how you could. Why, I jolly nearly tumbled myself!"

"Well, it's done now," replied Carpenter half sulkily. "And here we are at the barn. What's your programme?"

"You'll see that in a minutes or two. Are you game to follow my lead?"

"Yes!" Carpenter said recklessly.

But he did not like the look on his chum's face. Larking, with all his faults, was no coward. And at this moment he seemed ready for and desperate deed.

Carpenter reflected that they would be heavily outnumbered, however; and Larking would hardly have the opportunity to do anything really serious.

But it was just the realisation of the fact that the odds were so heavily against him that made Larking feel so desperate. What he meant to do had nothing tragic about it. Indeed, done in a different spirit, it would have been a mere joke, and would have been taken as such. As things were, however, Gordon Gay & Co. were hardly likely to see it in that way. And they were quite certain to take vengeance for it.

In the cover of the hedge Larking and Carpenter waited.

From inside the barn sounded voices. Goggs was making up Gordon Gay as Granny.

Down the road Bags and Wagtail and Snipe sorted themselves out, and Cardew and Clive and Levison drew near to them.

"You pimply-faced maniac!" fumed Bags, his usually serene temper very badly ruffled.

"It wasn't my fault, you cheeky idiot!" howled Snipe. "Didn't you see Larking push me over?"

"Why didn't you give way and let me pass, then?" yelled Bags.

"Yes, why didn't you do that?" snorted Wagtail. "That's what we want to know."

Bags turned in wrath upon his chum.

"You—you ought never to be trusted on a bike again!" he roared. "A perambulator's nearer your giddy mark! What did you go piling yourself up on top of me and this rotter for?"

"I couldn't draw aside," burbled Snipe. "Larking was in the way; you could see that! I was trying when——"

"A perambulator, eh?" shouted Wagtail, red as a peony and almost foaming at the mouth. "Put your fists up, Blount! I'm not jolly well going to stand that sort of thing, even from you!"

Snipe grinned maliciously. Nothing could have suited his book better than a fight between those two.

But Bags did not put up his fists. He knew himself Wagtail's master in the art of self-defence, and perhaps that "even you" helped to keep him from extremities. Wagtail was, in the opinion of his chums, a bit of an ass in many ways; he was swanky without much excuse for it, though not so swanky as he had been before the advent of Goggs. But he did put up with a good deal from all three of them; and Bags knew that it must be galling to him now and then to feel that his was always the fourth place in the brotherhood of four.

"Hallo!" drawled the cool voice of Ralph Reckness Cardew. "Trouble in the merry family—what?"

Blount and Waters and Snipe all swung round. They had been too busily occupied in slinging compliments at one another to note the approach of the three juniors from the rival school.

"Mind your own business!" snorted Wagtail.

"Oh, don't get ratty!" said Clive. "Look here, can we help?"

"If you contemplate makin' a start in a career as a bicycle repairer, old top," drawled Cardew, "don't fancy that I'm goin' into partnership with you."

"They do want a little attention," said Levison, grinning in a manner that was very different from Clive's, for the South African junior's had sympathy in it.

"Well, that's not your funeral!" snapped Bags.

"Better leave them to it, dear boys," said Cardew. "When people have the camelious hump it's no use bein' kind an' polite to them, y'know. May I venture to inquire how the smash happened?"

"You can inquire what you jolly well like, but I'm not going to answer you!" replied Wagtail hotly.

"Hallo! What, more trouble? Another bit of a mix-up?" said Cardew, looking along the road.

It certainly looked like that, and it certainly sounded like that.

Out of the field in which the barn stood poured a wild and whirling crowd. Somewhere in its centre were Larking and Carpenter, catching it hot. On its circumference appeared what looked like an elderly lady in a distinctly disreputable state.

Her hat was at the back of her head. Her hair hung down at the back of her neck, not in mane or pigtail, but dressed for the usual position on top of her head. Her skirt was slit right up. Her blouse hung in tatters.

If she really had been an elderly lady it would have been indeed a shocking spectacle. But, though the make-up might disguise his face, there was no possible mistake about the voice of Gordon Gay, raised high in anger, and proceeding from the mouth of the seeming female.

(Another grand long instalment of this magnificent school serial will appear in next Monday's issue. Order early.)